BRANDON SANDERSON

THE
WAY OF
KINGS

PART ONE

Book One of
THE STORMLIGHT ARCHIVE

Copyright © Dragonsteel Entertainment, LLC 2010
Interior illustrations copyright © Isaac Stewart,
Ben McSweeney and Greg Call

The right of Brandon Sanderson to be identified as the author
of this work has been asserted by him in accordance with the
Copyright, Designs and Patents Act 1988.

First published in Great Britain in 2010 by
Gollancz
An imprint of the Orion Publishing Group
Orion House, 5 Upper St Martin's Lane, London WC2H 9EA
An Hachette UK Company

This edition published in Great Britain in 2011 by Gollancz

20

A CIP catalogue record for this book is available
from the British Library.

ISBN 978 0 575 09736 0

Typeset by Input Data Services Ltd, Bridgewater, Somerset

Printed in Great Britain by Clays Ltd, St Ives plc

The Orion Publishing Group's policy is to use papers that are natural,
renewable and recyclable products and made from wood grown in sustainable
forests. The logging and manufacturing processes are expected to conform to
the environmental regulations of the country of origin.

www.brandonsanderson.com
www.orionbooks.co.uk

For Emily,
Who is too patient
Too kindly
And too wonderful
For words.
But I try anyway.

ACKNOWLEDGMENTS

I finished the first draft of *The Way of Kings* in 2003, but I started working on pieces of the book back in the late '90s. Threads of this novel go back even further in my brain. No book of mine has spent longer simmering; I've spent more than a decade building this novel. And so it should be no surprise that a lot of people have helped me with it. It's going to be impossible to mention them all; my memory simply isn't that good. However, there are some major players that I would like to thank most deeply.

First comes my wife, Emily, to whom this book is dedicated. She gave greatly of herself to see the novel come to pass. That included not only reading and giving advice on the manuscript, but giving up her husband during long stretches of writing time. If you readers get a chance to meet her, some thanks might be in order. (She likes chocolate.)

As always, my excellent editor and agent – Moshe Feder and Joshua Bilmes – worked quite hard on this novel. Moshe, by special note, doesn't get paid more when his authors turn in 400k-word monstrosities. But he edited the novel without a word of complaint; his help was invaluable in turning it into the novel you now hold. He also got F. Paul Wilson to check over the medical scenes, to their great benefit.

Special thanks also go to Harriet McDougal, one of the greatest editors of our time, who gave us a read and line edit on this novel out of the goodness of her heart. Wheel of Time fans will know her as the person who discovered, edited, and then married Robert Jordan. She doesn't do much editing these days outside of the Wheel of Time, and so I feel very honored and humbled to have her input and help here. Alan Romanczuk, working with her, should also be thanked for facilitating this edit.

At Tor Books, Paul Stevens has been a huge help. He's been our in-house liaison for my books, and he's done an amazing job. Moshe and I are lucky to have his aid. Likewise, Irene Gallo – the art director – has been wonderfully helpful and patient in dealing with an intrusive author who wanted to do some crazy things with the artwork in his book. Many thanks to Irene, Justin Golenbock, Greg Collins, Karl Gold, Nathan Weaver, Heather Saunders, Meryl Gross, and the entire team at Tor Books. Dot Lin, who was my publicist up until this book's release (and who is now working to put a few extra letters after her name), was a wonderful help not just in publicity, but in giving me advice and a cheering section over in New York. Thank you all.

And speaking of artwork, you may notice that the interior art for this book is far more extensive than what you normally find in an epic fantasy. This is due to the extraordinary efforts of Greg Call, Isaac Stewart, and Ben McSweeney. They worked hard, drafting artwork numerous times to get things right. Ben's work on Shallan's sketchbook pages is simply beautiful, a melding of my best imaginings and his artistic interpretations. Isaac, who also did the interior artwork for the Mistborn novels, went far above and beyond what should reasonably have been expected of him. Late nights and demanding deadlines were the norm for this novel. He is to be commended. (The chapter icons, maps, colored endpages, and Navani notebook pages came from him, if you are wondering.)

As always, my writing group has been an amazing help. The members of it are joined by a few alpha and beta readers. In no particular order, these are: Karen Ahlstrom, Geoff and Rachel Biesinger, Ethan Skarstedt, Nathan Hatfield, Dan Wells, Kaylynn ZoBell, Alan and Jeanette Layton, Janci Olds, Kristina Kugler, Steve Diamond, Brian Delambre, Jason Denzel, Mi'chelle Trammel, Josh Walker, Chris King, Austin and Adam Hussey, Brian T. Hill, and that Ben guy whose name I can't spell right. I'm sure I'm forgetting some of you. You are all wonderful people, and I'd give you Shardblades if I could.

Whew. This is turning into an epic acknowledgments. But there are still a few more people that need notice. The writing of these words is happening right around the one year anniversary of me hiring the Inevitable Peter Ahlstrom as my personal assistant, editorial aid, and extra brain. If you go through previous acknowledgments pages, you'll always find him there. He's been a dear friend of mine, and an advocate of my work, for years. I'm lucky to now have him working for me full time. He got up at three a.m. today to get the last proofread of the book done. When you next see him at a convention, buy him a block of cheese.

I would also be remiss if I didn't thank Tom Doherty for letting me get away with writing this book. It's because of Tom's belief in this project that we were able to get away with the novel being so long, and a personal call from Tom was what managed to get Michael Whelan to do the US cover. Tom has given me more here than I probably deserve; this novel (at the length it boasts, with the number of illustrations and artwork it contains) is the type that would make many publishers run away at full speed. This man is the reason Tor consistently releases such awesome books.

CONTENTS

ILLUSTRATIONS

ROSHAR

ENDLESS OCEAN

QUIL
ALM
KADRIX

Rall Elorim

RESHI

IRI

RIRA

Kurth

Kasitor

Reshi

Eila

BABATHARNAM

MARABETHIA

Panatham

The Purelake

SHINOVAR

YULAY

Fu Namir

DESH

AZIR

Aimian Sea

ALM

UEZIER

Azimir

The Valley

AIMIA

STEEN
LIAFOR
TASHIKK
EMUL
GREATER
HEXI

Sesemalex Dar

Icewater
TUKAR
MARAT

N

LEEWARD

STORMWARD

S

SOUTHERN DEPTHS

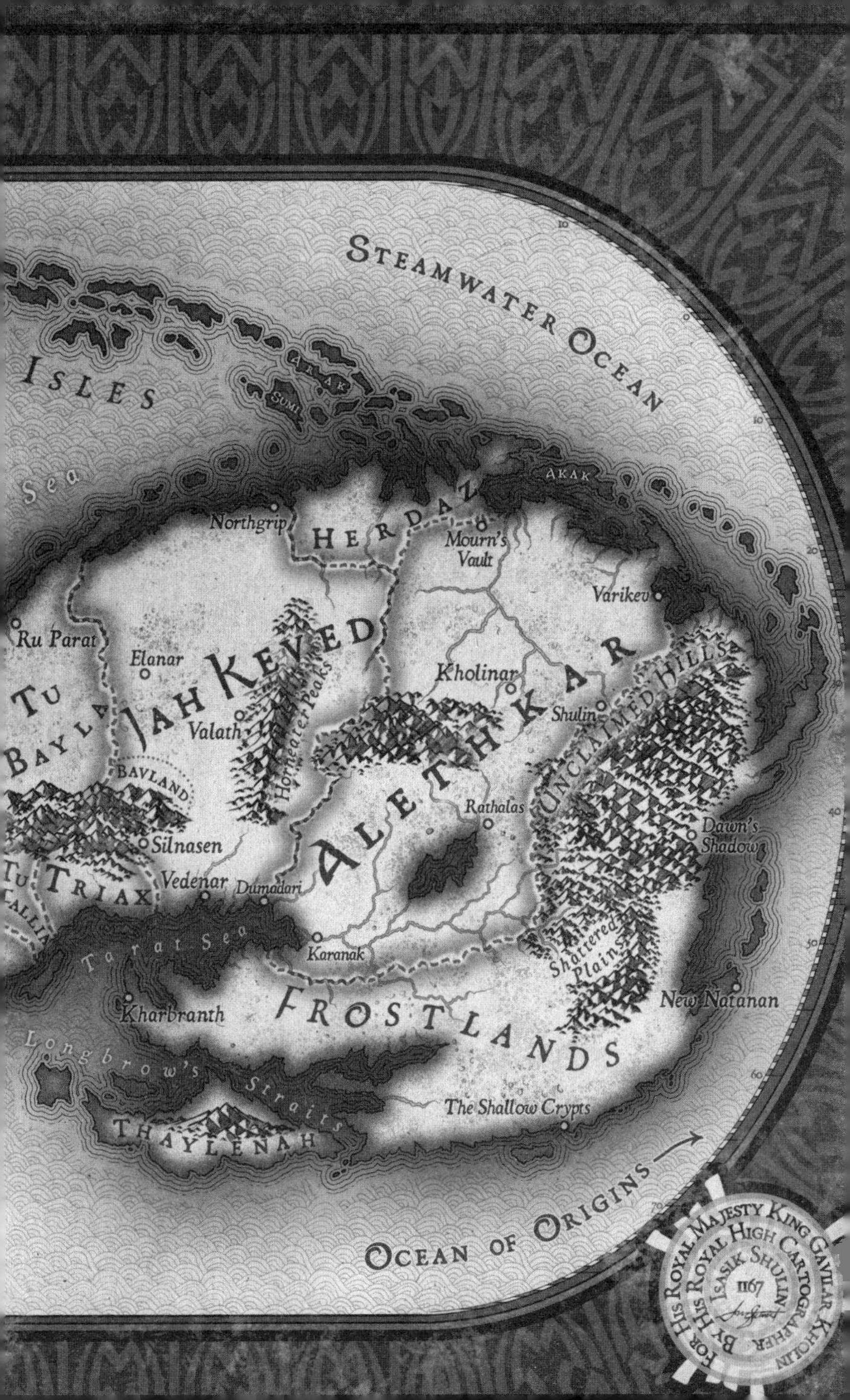

STEAMWATER OCEAN

ISLES

Sea

AIMAK

SOMI

AKAK

Northgrip

HERDAZ

Mourn's
Vault

Varikev

Ru Parat

Elanar

JAH KEVED

Kholinar

Shulin

Tu
Bayla

Valath

Hornwater Peaks

ALETHKAR

UNCLAIMED HILLS

BAVLAND

Rathalas

Dawn's
Shadow

Silnasen

TRIAX

Vedenar

Dumadari

Tu
Calli

Karanak

Tarat Sea

Shattered
Plains

Kharbranth

FROSTLANDS

New Natanan

Longbrow's

Straits

The Shallow Crypts

THAYLENAH

OCEAN OF ORIGINS

THE STORMLİGHT ARCHİVE

Kalak rounded a rocky stone ridge and stumbled to a stop before the body of a dying thunderclast. The enormous stone beast lay on its side, riblike protrusions from its chest broken and cracked. The monstrosity was vaguely skeletal in shape, with unnaturally long limbs that sprouted from granite shoulders. The eyes were deep red spots on the arrowhead face, as if created by a fire burning deep within the stone. They faded.

Even after all these centuries, seeing a thunderclast up close made Kalak shiver. The beast's hand was as long as a man was tall. He'd been killed by hands like those before, and it hadn't been pleasant.

Of course, dying rarely was.

He rounded the creature, picking his way more carefully across the battlefield. The plain was a place of misshapen rock and stone, natural pillars rising around him, bodies littering the ground. Few plants lived here.

The stone ridges and mounds bore numerous scars. Some were shattered, blasted-out sections where Surgebinders had fought. Less frequently, he passed cracked, oddly shaped hollows where thunderclasts had ripped themselves free of the stone to join the fray.

Many of the bodies around him were human; many were not. Blood mixed. Red. Orange. Violet. Though none of the bodies around him stirred, an indistinct haze of sounds hung in the air. Moans of pain, cries of grief. They did not seem like the sounds of victory. Smoke curled from the occasional patches of growth or heaps of burning corpses. Even some sections of rock smoldered. The Dustbringers had done their work well.

But I survived, Kalak thought, hand to breast as he hastened to the meeting place. *I actually survived this time.*

That was dangerous. When he died, he was sent back, no choice. When he survived the Desolation, he was supposed to go back as well. Back to that place that he dreaded. Back to that place of pain and fire. What if he just decided . . . not to go?

Perilous thoughts, perhaps traitorous thoughts. He hastened on his way.

The place of meeting was in the shadow of a large rock formation, a spire rising into the sky. As always, the ten of them had decided upon it before the battle. The survivors would make their way here. Oddly, only one of the others was waiting for him. Jezrien. Had the other eight all died? It was possible. The battle had been so furious this time, one of the worst. The enemy was growing increasingly tenacious.

But no. Kalak frowned as he stepped up to the base of the spire. Seven magnificent swords stood proudly here, driven point-first into the stone ground. Each was a masterly work of art, flowing in design, inscribed with glyphs and patterns. He recognized each one. If their masters had died, the Blades would have vanished.

These Blades were weapons of power beyond even Shardblades. These were unique. Precious. Jezrien stood outside the ring of swords, looking eastward.

'Jezrien?'

The figure in white and blue glanced toward him. Even after all these centuries, Jezrien looked young, like a man barely into his thirtieth year. His short black beard was neatly trimmed, though his once-fine clothing was scorched and stained with blood. He folded his arms behind his back as he turned to Kalak.

'What is this, Jezrien?' Kalak asked. "Where are the others?'

'Departed.' Jezrien's voice was calm, deep, regal. Though he hadn't worn a crown in centuries, his royal manner lingered. He always seemed to know what to do. 'You might call it a miracle. Only one of us died this time.'

'Talenel,' Kalak said. His was the only Blade unaccounted for.

'Yes. He died holding that passage by the northern waterway.'

Kalak nodded. Taln had a tendency to choose seemingly hopeless fights and win them. He also had a tendency to die in the process. He would be back now, in the place where they went between Desolations. The place of nightmares.

Kalak found himself shaking. When had he become so weak? 'Jezrien, I can't return this time.' Kalak whispered the words, stepping up and gripping the other man's arm. 'I *can't*.'

Kalak felt something within him break at the admission. How long had it been? Centuries, perhaps millennia, of torture. It was so hard to keep track. Those fires, those hooks, digging into his flesh anew each day.

Searing the skin off his arm, then burning the fat, then driving to the bone. He could smell it. Almighty, he could *smell* it!

'Leave your sword,' Jezrien said.

'What?'

Jezrien nodded to the ring of weapons. 'I was chosen to wait for you. We weren't certain if you had survived. A ... a decision has been made. It is time for the Oathpact to end.'

Kalak felt a sharp stab of horror. 'What will that do?'

'Ishar believes that so long as there is one of us still bound to the Oathpact, it may be enough. There is a chance we might end the cycle of Desolations.'

Kalak looked into the immortal king's eyes. Black smoke rose from a small patch to their left. Groans of the dying haunted them from behind. There, in Jezrien's eyes, Kalak saw anguish and grief. Perhaps even cowardice. This was a man hanging from a cliff by a thread.

Almighty above, Kalak thought. *You're broken too, aren't you?* They all were.

Kalak turned and walked to the side, where a low ridge overlooked part of the battlefield.

There were so many corpses, and among them walked the living. Men in primitive wraps, carrying spears topped by bronze heads. Juxtaposed between them were others in gleaming plate armor. One group walked past, four men in their ragged tanned skins or shoddy leather joining a powerful figure in beautiful silver plate, amazingly intricate. Such a contrast.

Jezrien stepped up beside him.

'They see us as divinities,' Kalak whispered. 'They rely upon us, Jezrien. We're all that they have.'

'They have the Radiants. That will be enough.'

Kalak shook his head. 'He will not remain bound by this. The enemy. He will find a way around it. You know he will.'

'Perhaps.' The king of Heralds offered no further explanation.

'And Taln?' Kalak asked. *The flesh burning. The fires. The pain over and over and over ...*

'Better that one man should suffer than ten,' Jezrien whispered. He seemed so cold. Like a shadow caused by heat and light falling on someone honorable and true, casting this black imitation behind.

3

Jezrien walked back to the ring of swords. His own Blade formed in his hands, appearing from mist, wet with condensation. 'It has been decided, Kalak. We will go our ways, and we will not seek out one another. Our Blades must be left. The Oathpact ends now.' He lifted his sword and rammed it into the stone with the other seven.

Jezrien hesitated, looking at the sword, then bowed his head and turned away. As if ashamed. 'We chose this burden willingly. Well, we can choose to drop it if we wish.'

'What do we tell the people, Jezrien?' Kalak asked. 'What will they say of this day?'

'It's simple,' Jezrien said, walking away. 'We tell them that they finally won. It's an easy enough lie. Who knows? Maybe it will turn out to be true.'

Kalak watched Jezrien depart across the burned landscape. Finally, he summoned his own Blade and slammed it into the stone beside the other eight. He turned and walked in the direction opposite from Jezrien.

And yet, he could not help glancing back at the ring of swords and the single open spot. The place where the tenth sword should have gone.

The one of them who was lost. The one they had abandoned.

Forgive us, Kalak thought, then left.

THE WAY OF KINGS

4,500 Years Later

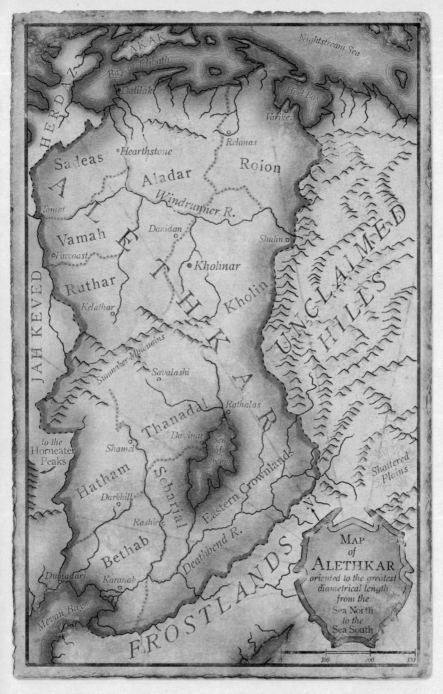

Map of Alethkar and surroundings, created by His Majesty Gavilar Kholin's royal surveyors, circa 1167.

PROLOGUE

TO KILL

'The love of men is a frigid thing, a mountain stream only three steps from the ice. We are his. Oh Stormfather ... we are his. It is but a thousand days, and the Everstorm comes.'

—Collected on the first day of the week Palah of the month Shash of the year 1171, thirty-one seconds before death. Subject was a darkeyed pregnant woman of middle years. The child did not survive.

Szeth-son-son-Vallano, Truthless of Shinovar, wore white on the day he was to kill a king. The white clothing was a Parshendi tradition, foreign to him. But he did as his masters required and did not ask for an explanation.

He sat in a large stone room, baked by enormous firepits that cast a garish light upon the revelers, causing beads of sweat to form on their skin as they danced, and drank, and yelled, and sang, and clapped. Some fell to the ground red-faced, the revelry too much for them, their stomachs proving to be inferior wineskins. They looked as if they were dead, at least until their friends carried them out of the feast hall to waiting beds.

Szeth did not sway to the drums, drink the sapphire wine, or stand to dance. He sat on a bench at the back, a still servant in white robes. Few at the treaty-signing celebration noticed him. He was just a servant, and Shin were easy to ignore. Most out here in the East

7

thought Szeth's kind were docile and harmless. They were generally right.

The drummers began a new rhythm. The beats shook Szeth like a quartet of thumping hearts, pumping waves of invisible blood through the room. Szeth's masters – who were dismissed as savages by those in more civilized kingdoms – sat at their own tables. They were men with skin of black marbled with red. Parshendi, they were named – cousins to the more docile servant peoples known as parshmen in most of the world. An oddity. They did not call themselves Parshendi; this was the Alethi name for them. It meant, roughly, 'parshmen who can think.' Neither side seemed to see that as an insult.

The Parshendi had brought the musicians. At first, the Alethi lighteyes had been hesitant. To them, drums were base instruments of the common, darkeyed people. But wine was the great assassin of both tradition and propriety, and now the Alethi elite danced with abandon.

Szeth stood and began to pick his way through the room. The revelry had lasted long; even the king had retired hours ago. But many still celebrated. As he walked, Szeth was forced to step around Dalinar Kholin – the king's own brother – who slumped drunken at a small table. The aging but powerfully built man kept waving away those who tried to encourage him to bed. Where was Jasnah, the king's daughter? Elhokar, the king's son and heir, sat at the high table, ruling the feast in his father's absence. He was in conversation with two men, a dark-skinned Azish man who had an odd patch of pale skin on his cheek and a thinner, Alethi-looking man who kept glancing over his shoulder.

The heir's feasting companions were unimportant. Szeth stayed far from the heir, skirting the sides of the room, passing the drummers. Musicspren zipped through the air around them, the tiny spirits taking the form of spinning translucent ribbons. As Szeth passed the drummers, they noted him. They would withdraw soon, along with all of the other Parshendi.

They did not seem offended. They did not seem angry. And yet they were going to break their treaty of only a few hours. It made no sense. But Szeth did not ask questions.

At the edge of the room, he passed rows of unwavering azure lights that bulged out where wall met floor. They held sapphires infused with Storm-light. Profane. How could the men of these lands use something

8

so sacred for mere illumination? Worse, the Alethi scholars were said to be close to creating new Shardblades. Szeth hoped that was just wishful boasting. For if it *did* happen, the world would be changed. Likely in a way that ended with people in all countries – from distant Thaylenah to towering Jah Keved – speaking Alethi to their children.

They were a grand people, these Alethi. Even drunk, there was a natural nobility to them. Tall and well made, the men dressed in dark silk coats that buttoned down the sides of the chest and were elaborately embroidered in silver or gold. Each one looked a general on the field.

The women were even more splendid They wore grand silk dresses tightly fitted, the bright colors a contrast to the dark tones favored by the men. The left sleeve of each dress was longer than the right one, covering the hand. Alethi had an odd sense of propriety.

Their pure black hair was pinned up atop their heads, either in intricate weavings of braids or in loose piles. It was often woven with gold ribbons or ornaments, along with gems that glowed with Stormlight. Beautiful. Profane, but beautiful.

Szeth left the feasting chamber behind. Just outside, he passed the doorway into the Beggars' Feast. It was an Alethi tradition, a room where some of the poorest men and women in the city were given a feast complementing that of the king and his guests. A man with a long grey and black beard slumped in the doorway, smiling foolishly – though whether from wine or a weak mind, Szeth could not tell.

'Have you seen me?' the man asked with slurred speech. He laughed, then began to speak in gibberish, reaching for a wineskin. So it was drink after all. Szeth brushed by, continuing past a line of statues depicting the Ten Heralds from ancient Vorin theology. Jezerezeh, Ishi, Kelek, Talenelat. He counted off each one, and realized there were only nine here. One was conspicuously missing. Why had Shalash's statue been removed? King Gavilar was said to be very devout in his Vorin worship. Too devout, by some people's standards.

The hallway here curved to the right, running around the perimeter of the domed palace. They were on the king's floor, two levels up, surrounded by rock walls, ceiling, and floor. That was profane. Stone was not to be trod upon. But what was he to do? He was Truthless. He did as his masters demanded.

Today, that included wearing white. Loose white trousers tied at the waist with a rope, and over them a filmy shirt with long sleeves, open at the front. White clothing for a killer was a tradition among the Parshendi. Although Szeth had not asked, his masters had explained why.

White to be bold. White to not blend into the night. White to give warning.

For if you were going to assassinate a man, he was entitled to see you coming.

Szeth turned right, taking the hallway directly toward the king's chambers. Torches burned on the walls, their light unsatisfying to him, a meal of thin broth after a long fast. Flamespren danced around them, like large insects made solely of congealed light. The torches were useless to him. He reached for his pouch and the spheres it contained, but then hesitated when he saw more of the blue lights ahead: a pair of Stormlight lamps hanging on the wall, brilliant sapphires glowing at their hearts. Szeth walked up to one of these holding out his hand to cup it around the glass-shrouded gemstone.

'You there!' a voice called in Alethi. There were two guards at the intersection. Double guard, for there were savages abroad in Kholinar this night. True, those savages were supposed to be allies now. But alliances could be shallow things indeed.

This one wouldn't last the hour.

Szeth looked as the two guards approached. They carried spears; they weren't lighteyes, and were therefore forbidden the sword. Their painted blue breastplates were ornate, however, as were their helms. They might be darkeyed, but they were high-ranking citizens with honored positions in the royal guard.

Stopping a few feet away, the guard at the front gestured with his spear. 'Go on, now. This is no place for you.' He had tan Alethi skin and a thin mustache that ran all the way around his mouth, becoming a beard at the bottom.

Szeth didn't move.

'Well?' the guard said. 'What are you waiting for?'

Szeth breathed in deeply, drawing forth the Stormlight. It streamed into him, siphoned from the twin sapphire lamps on the walls, sucked in as if by his deep inhalation. The Stormlight raged inside of him, and the hallway suddenly grew darker, falling into shade like a hilltop cut off from the sun by a transient cloud.

Szeth could feel the Light's warmth, its fury, like a tempest that had been injected directly into his veins. The power of it was invigorating but dangerous. It pushed him to act. To move. To strike.

Holding his breath, he clung to the Stormlight. He could still feel it leaking out. Stormlight could be held for only a short time, a few minutes at most. It leaked away, the human body too porous a container. He had heard that the Voidbringers could hold it in perfectly. But, then, did they even exist? His punishment declared that they didn't. His honor demanded that they did.

Afire with holy energy, Szeth turned to the guards. They could see that he was leaking Stormlight, wisps of it curling from his skin like luminescent smoke. The lead guard squinted, frowning. Szeth was sure the man had never seen anything like it before. As far as he knew, Szeth had killed every stonewalker who had ever seen what he could do.

'What . . . what are you?' The guard's voice had lost its certainty. 'Spirit or man?'

'What am I?' Szeth whispered, a bit of Light leaking from his lips as he looked past the man down the long hallway. 'I'm . . . sorry.'

Szeth blinked, Lashing himself to that distant point down the hallway. Stormlight raged from him in a flash, chilling his skin, and the ground immediately stopped pulling him downward Instead he was pulled toward that distant point – it was as if, to him, that direction had suddenly become *down*.

This was a Basic Lashing, first of his three kinds of Lashings. It gave him the ability to manipulate whatever force, spren, or god it was that held men to the ground. With this Lashing, he could bind people or objects to different surfaces or in different directions.

From Szeth's perspective, the hallway was now a deep shaft down which he was falling, and the two guards stood on one of the sides. They were shocked when Szeth's feet hit them, one for each face, throwing them over. Szeth shifted his view and Lashed himself to the floor. Light leaked from him. The floor of the hallway again became *down*, and he landed between the two guards, clothes crackling and dropping flakes of frost. He rose, beginning the process of summoning his Shardblade.

One of the guards fumbled for his spear. Szeth reached down, touching the soldier's shoulder while looking up. He focused on a point above him while willing the Light out of his body and into the guard, Lashing the poor man to the ceiling.

The guard yelped in shock as *up* became *down* for him. Light trailing from his form, he crashed into the ceiling and dropped his spear. It was not Lashed directly, and clattered back down to the floor near Szeth.

To kill. It was the greatest of sins. And yet here Szeth stood, Truthless, profanely walking on stones used for building. And it would not end. As Truthless, there was only one life he was forbidden to take.

And that was his own.

At the tenth beat of his heart, his Shardblade dropped into his waiting hand. It formed as if condensing from mist, water beading along the metal length. His Shardblade was long and thin, edged on both sides, smaller than most others. Szeth swept it out, carving a line in the stone floor and passing through the second guard's neck.

As always, the Shardblade killed oddly; though it cut easily through stone, steel, or anything inanimate, the metal fuzzed when it touched living skin. It traveled through the guard's neck without leaving a mark, but once it did, the man's eyes smoked and burned. They blackened, shriveling up in his head, and he slumped forward, dead. A Shardblade did not cut living flesh; it severed the soul itself.

Above, the first guard gasped. He'd managed to get to his feet, even though they were planted on the ceiling of the hallway. 'Shardbearer!' he shouted. 'A Shardbearer assaults the king's hall! To arms!'

Finally, Szeth thought. Szeth's use of Stormlight was unfamiliar to the guards, but they knew a Shardblade when they saw one.

Szeth bent down and picked up the spear that had fallen from above. As he did so he released the breath he'd been holding since drawing in the Stormlight. It sustained him while he held it, but those two lanterns hadn't contained much of it, so he would need to breathe again soon. The Light began to leak away more quickly, now that he wasn't holding his breath.

Szeth set the spear's butt against the stone floor, then looked upward. The guard above stopped shouting, eyes opening wide as the tails of his shirt began to slip downward, the earth below reasserting its dominance. The Light steaming off his body dwindled.

He looked down at Szeth. Down at the spear tip pointing directly at his heart. Violet fearspren crawled out of the stone ceiling around him.

The Light ran out. The guard fell.

He screamed as he hit, the spear impaling him through the chest. Szeth let the spear fall away, carried to the ground with a muffled thump by the body twitching on its end. Shardblade in hand, he turned down a side corridor, following the map he'd memorized. He ducked around a corner and flattened himself against the wall just as a troop of guards reached the dead men. The newcomers began shouting immediately, continuing the alarm.

His instructions were clear. Kill the king, but be seen doing it. Let the Alethi know he was coming and what he was doing. Why? Why did the Parshendi agree to this treaty, only to send an assassin the very night of its signing?

More gemstones glowed on the walls of the hallway here. King Gavilar liked lavish display, and he couldn't know that he was leaving sources of power for Szeth to use in his Lashings. The things Szeth did hadn't been seen for millennia. Histories from those times were all but nonexistent, and the legends were horribly inaccurate.

Szeth peeked back out into the corridor. One of the guards at the intersection saw him, pointing and yelling. Szeth made sure they got a good look, then ducked away. He took a deep breath as he ran, drawing in Storm-light from the lanterns. His body came alive with it, and his speed increased, his muscles bursting with energy. Light became a storm inside of him; his blood thundered in his ears. It was terrible and wonderful at the same time.

Two corridors down, one to the side. He threw open the door of a storage room, then hesitated a moment – just long enough for a guard to round the corner and see him – before dashing into the room. Preparing for a Full Lashing, he raised his arm and commanded the Stormlight to pool there, causing the skin to burst alight with radiance. Then he flung his hand out toward the doorframe, spraying white luminescence across it like paint. He slammed the door just as the guards arrived.

The Stormlight held the door in the frame with the strength of a hundred arms. A Full Lashing bound objects together, holding them fast until the Stormlight ran out. It took longer to create – and drained Stormlight far more quickly – than a Basic Lashing. The door handle shook and then the wood began to crack as the guards threw their weight against it, one man calling for an axe.

Szeth crossed the room in rapid strides, weaving around the shrouded furniture that had been stored here. It was of red cloth and deep expensive woods. He reached the far wall and – preparing himself for yet another blasphemy – he raised his Shardblade and slashed horizontally through the dark grey stone. The rock sliced easily; a Shardblade could cut any inanimate object. Two vertical slashes followed, then one across the bottom, cutting a large square block. He pressed his hand against it, willing Stormlight into the stone.

Behind him the room's door began to crack. He looked over his shoulder and focused on the shaking door, Lashing the block in that direction. Frost crystallized on his clothing – Lashing something so large required a great deal of Stormlight. The tempest within him stilled, like a storm reduced to a drizzle.

He stepped aside. The large stone block shuddered, sliding into the room. Normally, moving the block would have been impossible. Its own weight would have held it against the stones below. Yet now, that same weight pulled it free; for the block, the direction of the room's door was *down*. With a deep grinding sound, the block slid free of the wall and tumbled through the air, smashing furniture.

The soldiers finally broke through the door, staggering into the room just as the enormous block crashed into them.

Szeth turned his back on the terrible sound of the screams, the splintering of wood, the breaking of bones. He ducked and stepped through his new hole, entering the hallway outside.

He walked slowly, drawing Stormlight from the lamps he passed, siphoning it to him and stoking anew the tempest within. As the lamps dimmed, the corridor darkened. A thick wooden door stood at the end, and as he approached, small fearspren – shaped like globs of purple goo – began to wriggle from the masonry, pointing toward the doorway. They were drawn by the terror being felt on the other side.

Szeth pushed the door open, entering the last corridor leading to the king's chambers. Tall, red ceramic vases lined the pathway, and they were interspersed with nervous soldiers. They flanked a long, narrow rug. It was red, like a river of blood.

The spearmen in front didn't wait for him to get close. They broke into a trot, lifting their short throwing spears. Szeth slammed his hand to the side, pushing Stormlight into the doorframe, using the third and final type of Lashing, a Reverse Lashing. This one worked differently from the other two. It did not make the doorframe emit Stormlight; indeed, it seemed to pull nearby light *into* it, giving it a strange penumbra.

The spearmen threw, and Szeth stood still, hand on the doorframe. A Reverse Lashing required his constant touch, but took comparatively little Stormlight. During one, anything that approached him – particularly lighter objects – was instead pulled toward the Lashing itself.

The spears veered in the air, splitting around him and slamming into the wooden frame. As he felt them hit, Szeth leaped into the air and Lashed himself to the right wall, his feet hitting the stone with a slap.

He immediately reoriented his perspective. To his eyes, he wasn't standing on the wall, the soldiers were, the blood-red carpet streaming between them like a long tapestry. Szeth bolted down the hallway, striking with his Shardblade, shearing through the necks of two men who had thrown spears at him. Their eyes burned, and they collapsed.

The other guards in the hallway began to panic. Some tried to attack him, others yelled for more help, still others cringed away from him. The attackers had trouble – they were disoriented by the oddity of striking at someone who hung on the wall. Szeth cut down a few, then flipped into the air, tucking into a roll, and Lashed himself back to the floor.

He hit the ground in the midst of the soldiers. Completely surrounded, but holding a Shardblade.

According to legend, the Shardblades were first carried by the Knights Radiant uncounted ages ago. Gifts of their god, granted to allow them to fight horrors of rock and flame, dozens of feet tall, foes whose eyes burned with hatred. The Voidbringers. When your foe had skin as hard as stone itself, steel was useless. Something supernal was required.

Szeth rose from his crouch, loose white clothes rippling, jaw clenched against his sins. He struck out, his weapon flashing with reflected torch-light. Elegant, wide swings. Three of them, one after another. He could neither close his ears to the screams that followed nor avoid seeing the men fall. They dropped round him like toys knocked over by a child's careless kick. If the Blade touched a man's spine, he died, eyes burning. If it cut through the core of a limb, it killed that limb. One soldier stumbled away from Szeth, arm flopping uselessly on his shoulder. He would never be able to feel it or use it again.

Szeth lowered his Shardblade, standing among the cinder-eyed corpses.

Here, in Alethkar, men often spoke of the legends – of mankind's hard-won victory over the Voidbringers. But when weapons created to fight nightmares were turned against common soldiers, the lives of men became cheap things indeed.

Szeth turned and continued on his way, slippered feet falling on the soft red rug. The Shardblade, as always, glistened silver and clean. When one killed with a Blade, there was no blood. That seemed like a sign. The Shardblade was just a tool; it could not be blamed for the murders.

The door at the end of the hallway burst open. Szeth froze as a small group of soldiers rushed out, ushering a man in regal robes, his head ducked as if to avoid arrows. The soldiers wore deep blue, the color of the King's Guard, and the corpses didn't make them stop and gawk. They were prepared for what a Shardbearer could do. They opened a side door and shoved their ward through, several leveling spears at Szeth as they backed out.

Another figure stepped from the king's quarters; he wore glistening blue armor made of smoothly interlocking plates. Unlike common plate armor, however, this armor had no leather or mail visible at the joints – just smaller plates, fitting together with intricate precision. The armor was beautiful, the blue inlaid with golden bands around the edges of each piece of plate, the helm ornamented with three waves of small, hornlike wings.

Shardplate, the customary complement to a Shardblade. The newcomer carried a sword as well, an enormous Shardblade six feet long with a design along the blade like burning flames, a weapon of silvery metal that gleamed and almost seemed to glow. A weapon designed to slay dark gods, a larger counterpart to the one Szeth carried.

Szeth hesitated. He didn't recognize the armor; he had not been warned that he would be set at this task, and hadn't been given proper time to memorize the various suits of Plate or Blades owned by the Alethi. But a Shardbearer would have to be dealt with before he chased the king; he could not leave such a foe behind.

Besides, perhaps a Shardbearer could defeat him, kill him and end his miserable life. His Lashings wouldn't work directly on someone in Shard-plate, and the armor would enhance the man, strengthen him. Szeth's honor would not allow him to betray his mission or seek death. But if that death occurred, he *would* welcome it.

The Shardbearer struck, and Szeth Lashed himself to the side of the hallway, leaping with a twist and landing on the wall. He danced backward, Blade held at the ready. The Shardbearer fell into an aggressive posture, using one of the swordplay stances favored here in the East. He moved far more nimbly than one would expect for a man in such bulky armor. Shardplate was special, as ancient and magical as the Blades it complemented.

The Shardbearer struck. Szeth skipped to the side and Lashed himself to the ceiling as the Shardbearer's Blade sliced into the wall. Feeling a thrill at the contest, Szeth dashed forward and attacked downward with an overhand blow, trying to hit the Shardbearer's helm. The man ducked, going down on one knee, letting Szeth's Blade cleave empty air.

Szeth leaped backward as the Shardbearer swung upward with his Blade, slicing into the ceiling. Szeth didn't own a set of Plate himself, and didn't care to. His Lashings interfered with the gemstones that powered Shardplate, and he had to choose one or the other.

As the Shardbearer turned, Szeth sprinted forward across the ceiling. As expected, the Shardbearer swung again, and Szeth leaped to the side, rolling. He came up from his roll and flipped, Lashing himself to the floor again. He spun to land on the ground behind the Shardbearer. He slammed his Blade into his opponent's open back.

Unfortunately, there was one major advantage Plate offered: It could block a Shardblade. Szeth's weapon hit solidly, causing a web of glowing lines to spread out across the back of the armor, and Stormlight began to leak free from them. Shardplate didn't dent or bend like common metal. Szeth would have to hit the Shardbearer in the same location at least once more to break through.

Szeth danced out of range as the Shardbearer swung in anger, trying to cut at Szeth's knees. The tempest within Szeth gave him many advantages – including the ability to quickly recover from small wounds. But it would not restore limbs killed by a Shardblade.

He rounded the Shardbearer, then picked a moment and dashed forward. The Shardbearer swung again, but Szeth briefly Lashed himself to the ceiling for lift. He shot into the air, cresting over the swing, then immediately Lashed himself back to the floor. He struck as he landed, but the Shardbearer recovered quickly and executed a perfect followthrough stroke, coming within a finger of hitting Szeth.

The man was dangerously skilled with that Blade. Many Shardbearers depended too much on the power of their weapon and armor. This man was different.

Szeth jumped to the wall and struck at the Shardbearer with quick, terse attacks, like a snapping eel. The Shardbearer fended him off with wide, sweeping counters. His Blade's length kept Szeth at bay.

This is taking too long! Szeth thought. If the king slipped away into hiding, Szeth would fail in his mission no matter how many people he killed. He ducked in for another strike, but the Shardbearer forced him back. Each second this fight lasted was another for the king's escape.

It was time to be reckless. Szeth launched into the air, Lashing himself to the other end of the hallway and falling feet-first toward his adversary. The Shardbearer didn't hesitate to swing, but Szeth Lashed himself down at an angle, dropping immediately. The Shardblade swished through the air above him.

He landed in a crouch, using his momentum to throw himself forward, and swung at the Shardbearer's side, where the Plate had cracked. He hit with a powerful blow. That piece of the Plate shattered, bits of molten metal streaking away. The Shardbearer grunted, dropping to one knee, raising a hand to his side. Szeth raised a foot to the man's side and shoved him backward with a Stormlight-enhanced kick.

The heavy Shardbearer crashed into the door of the king's quarters, smashing it and falling partway into the room beyond. Szeth left him, ducking instead through the doorway to the right, following the way the king had gone. The hallway here had the same red carpet, and Stormlight lamps on the walls gave Szeth a chance to recharge the tempest within.

Energy blazed within him again, and he sped up. If he could get far enough ahead, he could deal with the king, then turn back to fight off the Shardbearer. It wouldn't be easy. A Full Lashing on a doorway wouldn't stop a Shardbearer, and that Plate would let the man run supernaturally fast. Szeth glanced over his shoulder.

The Shardbearer wasn't following. The man sat up in his armor, looking dazed. Szeth could just barely see him, sitting in the doorway, surrounded by broken bits of wood. Perhaps Szeth had wounded him more than he'd thought.

Or maybe . . .

Szeth froze. He thought of the ducked head of the man who'd been rushed out, face obscured. The Shardbearer *still* wasn't following. He was so skilled. It was said that few men could rival Gavilar Kholin's swordsmanship. Could it be?

Szeth turned and dashed back, trusting his instincts. As soon as the Shardbearer saw him, he climbed to his feet with alacrity. Szeth ran faster. What was the safest place for your king? In the hands of some guards, fleeing? Or protected in a suit of Shardplate, left behind, dismissed as a bodyguard?

Clever, Szeth thought as the formerly sluggish Shardbearer fell into another battle stance. Szeth attacked with renewed vigor, swinging his Blade in a flurry of strikes. The Shardbearer – the king – aggressively struck out with broad, sweeping blows. Szeth pulled away from one of these, feeling the wind of the weapon passing just inches before him. He timed his next move, then dashed forward, ducking underneath the king's follow-through.

The king, expecting another strike at his side, twisted with his arm held protectively to block the hole in his Plate. That gave Szeth the room to run past him and into the king's chambers.

The king spun around to follow, but Szeth ran through the lavishly furnished chamber, flinging out his hand, touching pieces of furniture he passed. He infused them with Stormlight, Lashing them to a point behind the king. The furniture tumbled as if the room had been turned on its side, couches, chairs, and tables dropping toward the surprised king. Gavilar made the mistake of chopping at them with his Shardblade. The weapon easily sheared through a large couch, but the pieces still crashed into him, making him stumble. A footstool hit him next, throwing him to the ground.

Gavilar rolled out of the way of the furniture and charged forward, Plate leaking streams of Light from the cracked sections. Szeth gathered himself, then leaped into the air, Lashing himself backward and to the right as the king arrived. He zipped out of the way of the king's blow, then Lashed himself forward with two Basic Lashings in a row. Stormlight flashed out of him, clothing freezing, as he was pulled toward the king at twice the speed of a normal fall.

The king's posture indicated surprise as Szeth lurched in midair, then spun toward him, swinging. He slammed his Blade into the king's helm, then immediately Lashed himself to the ceiling and fell upward, slamming into the stone roof above. He'd Lashed himself in too many directions too quickly, and his body had lost track, making it difficult to land gracefully. He stumbled back to his feet.

Below, the king stepped back, trying to get into position to swing up at Szeth. The man's helm was cracked, leaking Stormlight, and he stood protectively, defending the side with the broken plate. The king used a one-handed swing, reaching for the ceiling. Szeth immediately Lashed himself downward, judging that the king's attack would leave him unable to get his sword back in time.

Szeth underestimated his opponent. The king stepped into Szeth's attack, trusting his helm to absorb the blow. Just as Szeth hit the helm a second time – shattering it – Gavilar punched with his off hand, slamming his gauntleted fist into Szeth's face.

Blinding light flashed in Szeth's eyes, a counterpoint to the sudden agony that crashed across his face. Everything blurred, his vision fading.

Pain. So much *pain*!

He screamed, Stormlight leaving him in a rush, and he slammed back into something hard. The balcony doors. More pain broke out across his shoulders, as if someone had stabbed him with a hundred daggers, and he hit the ground and rolled to a stop, muscles trembling. The blow would have killed an ordinary man.

No time for pain. No time for pain. No time for pain!

He blinked, shaking his head, the world blurry and dark. Was he blind? No. It was dark outside. He was on the wooden balcony; the force of the blow had thrown him through the doors. Something was thumping. Heavy footfalls. The Shardbearer!

Szeth stumbled to his feet, vision swimming. Blood streamed from the side of his face, and Stormlight rose from his skin, blinding his left eye. The Light. It would heal him, if it could. His jaw felt unhinged. Broken? He'd dropped his Shardblade.

A lumbering shadow moved in front of him; the Shardbearer's armor had leaked enough Stormlight that the king was having trouble walking. But he was coming.

Szeth screamed, kneeling, infusing Stormlight into the wooden balcony, Lashing it downward. The air frosted around him. The tempest roared, traveling down his arms into the wood. He Lashed it downward, then did it again. He Lashed a fourth time as Gavilar stepped onto the balcony. It lurched under the extra weight. The wood cracked, straining.

The Shardbearer hesitated.

Szeth Lashed the balcony downward a fifth time. The balcony supports shattered and the entire structure broke free from the building. Szeth screamed through a broken jaw and used his final bit of Stormlight to Lash himself to the side of the building. He fell to the side, passing the shocked Shardbearer, then hit the wall and rolled.

The balcony dropped away, the king looking up with shock as he lost his footing. The fall was brief. In the moonlight, Szeth watched solemnly – vision still fuzzy, blinded in one eye – as the structure crashed to the stone ground below. The wall of the palace trembled, and the crash of broken wood echoed from the nearby buildings.

Still lying on the side of the wall, Szeth groaned, climbing to his feet. He felt weak; he'd used up his Stormlight too quickly, straining his body. He stumbled down the side of the building, approaching the wreckage, barely able to remain standing.

The king was still moving. Shardplate would protect a man from such a fall, but a large length of bloodied wood stuck up through Gavilar's side, piercing him where Szeth had broken the Plate earlier. Szeth knelt down, inspecting the man's pain-wracked face. Strong features, square chin, black beard flecked with white, striking pale green eyes. Gavilar Kholin.

'I ... expected you ... to come,' the king said between gasps.

Szeth reached underneath the front of the man's breastplate, tapping the straps there. They unfastened, and he pulled the front of the breastplate free, exposing the gemstones on its interior. Two had been cracked and burned out. Three still glowed. Numb, Szeth breathed in sharply, absorbing the Light.

The storm began to rage again. More Light rose from the side of his face, repairing his damaged skin and bones. The pain was still great; Stormlight healing was far from instantaneous. It would be hours before he recovered.

The king coughed. 'You can tell ... Thaidakar ... that he's too late. ...'

'I don't know who that is,' Szeth said, standing, his words slurring from his broken jaw. He held his hand to the side, resummoning his Shardblade.

The king frowned. 'Then who ...? Restares? Sadeas? I never thought ...'

'My masters are the Parshendi,' Szeth said. Ten heartbeats passed, and his Blade dropped into his hand, wet with condensation.

'The Parshendi? That makes no sense.' Gavilar coughed, hand quivering, reaching toward his chest and fumbling at a pocket. He pulled out a small crystalline sphere tied to a chain. 'You must take this. They must not get it.' He seemed dazed. 'Tell . . . tell my brother . . . he must find the most important words a man can say. . . .'

Gavilar fell still.

Szeth hesitated, then knelt down and took the sphere. It was odd, unlike any he'd seen before. Though it was completely dark, it seemed to glow somehow. With a light that was black.

The Parshendi? Gavilar had said. *That makes no sense.*

'Nothing makes sense anymore,' Szeth whispered, tucking the strange sphere away. 'It's all unraveling. I am sorry, King of the Alethi. I doubt that you care. Not anymore, at least.' He stood up. 'At least you won't have to watch the world ending with the rest of us.'

Beside the king's body, his Shardblade materialized from mist, clattering to the stones now that its master was dead. It was worth a fortune; kingdoms had fallen as men vied to possess a single Shardblade.

Shouts of alarm came from inside the palace. Szeth needed to go. But . . .

Tell my brother . . .

To Szeth's people, a dying request was sacred. He took the king's hand, dipping it in the man's own blood, then used it to scrawl on the wood, *Brother. You must find the most important words a man can say.*

With that, Szeth escaped into the night. He left the king's Shardblade; he had no use for it. The Blade Szeth already carried was curse enough.

ONE

Above Silence

KALADIN • SHALLAN

STORMBLESSED

'You've killed me. Bastards, you've killed me! While the sun is still hot. I die!'

—Collected on the fifth day of the week Chach of the month Betab of the year 1171, ten seconds before death. Subject was a darkeyed soldier thirty-one years of age. Sample is considered questionable.

FIVE YEARS LATER

'm going to die, aren't I?' Cenn asked.

The weathered veteran beside Cenn turned and inspected him. The veteran wore a full beard, cut short. At the sides, the black hairs were starting to give way to grey.

I'm going to die, Cenn thought, clutching his spear – the shaft slick with sweat. *I'm going to die. Oh, Stormfather. I'm going to die . . . .*

'How old are you, son?' the veteran asked. Cenn didn't remember the man's name. It was hard to recall anything while watching that other army form lines across the rocky battlefield. That lining up seemed so civil. Neat, organized. Shortspears in the front ranks, longspears and javelins next, archers at the sides. The darkeyed spearmen wore equipment like Cenn's: leather jerkin and knee-length skirt with a simple steel cap and a matching breastplate.

Many of the lighteyes had full suits of armor. They sat astride horses, their honor guards clustering around them with breastplates that gleamed burgundy and deep forest green. Were there Shardbearers among them? Brightlord Amaram wasn't a Shardbearer Were any of his men? What if Cenn had to fight one? Ordinary men didn't kill Shardbearers. It had happened so infrequently that each occurrence was now legendary.

It's really happening, he thought with mounting terror. This wasn't a drill in the camp. This wasn't training out in the fields, swinging sticks. This was *real*. Facing that fact – his heart pounding like a frightened animal in his chest, his legs unsteady–Cenn suddenly realized that he was a coward. He shouldn't have left the herds! He should never have—

'Son?' the veteran said, voice firm. 'How old are you?'

'Fifteen, sir.'

'And what's your name?'

'Cenn, sir.'

The mountainous, bearded man nodded. 'I'm Dallet.'

'Dallet,' Cenn repeated, still staring out at the other army. There were so many of them! Thousands. 'I'm going to die, aren't I?'

'*No.*' Dallet had a gruff voice, but somehow that was comforting. 'You're going to be just fine. Keep your head on straight. Stay with the squad.'

'But I've barely had three months' training!' He swore he could hear faint clangs from the enemy's armor or shields. 'I can barely hold this spear! Stormfather, I'm *dead*. I can't—'

'Son,' Dallet interrupted, soft but firm. He raised a hand and placed it on Cenn's shoulder. The rim of Dallet's large round shield reflected the light from where it hung on his back. 'You are *going* to be *fine*.'

'How can you know?' It came out as a plea.

'Because, lad. You're in Kaladin Stormblessed's squad.' The other soldiers nearby nodded in agreement.

Behind them, waves and waves of soldiers were lining up – thousands of them. Cenn was right at the front, with Kaladin's squad of about thirty other men. Why had Cenn been moved to a new squad at the last moment? It had something to do with camp politics.

Why was this squad at the very front, where casualties were bound to be the greatest? Small fearspren – like globs of purplish goo – began to climb up out of the ground and gather around his feet. In a moment of sheer panic, he nearly dropped his spear and scrambled away. Dallet's hand tightened on his shoulder. Looking up into Dallet's confident black eyes, Cenn hesitated.

'Did you piss before we formed ranks?' Dallet asked.

'I didn't have time to—'

'Go now.'

'*Here?*'

'If you don't, you'll end up with it running down your leg in battle, distracting you, maybe killing you. Do it.'

Embarrassed, Cenn handed Dallet his spear and relieved himself onto the stones. When he finished, he shot glances at those next to him. None of Kaladin's soldiers smirked. They stood steady, spears to their sides, shields on their backs.

The enemy army was almost finished. The field between the two forces was bare, flat slickrock, remarkably even and smooth, broken only by occasional rockbuds. It would have made a good pasture. The warm wind blew in Cenn's face, thick with the watery scents of last night's highstorm.

'Dallet!' a voice said.

A man walked up through the ranks, carrying a shortspear that had two leather knife sheaths strapped to the haft. The newcomer was a young man – perhaps four years older than Cenn's fifteen – but he was taller by several fingers than even Dallet. He wore the common leathers of a spearman, but under them was a pair of dark trousers. That wasn't supposed to be allowed.

His black Alethi hair was shoulder-length and wavy, his eyes a dark brown. He also had knots of white cord on the shoulders of his jerkin, marking him as a squadleader.

The thirty men around Cenn snapped to attention, raising their spears in salute. *This is Kaladin Stormblessed?* Cenn thought incredulously. *This youth?*

'Dallet, we're soon going to have a new recruit,' Kaladin said. He had a strong voice. 'I need you to . . .' He trailed off as he noticed Cenn.

'He found his way here just a few minutes ago, sir,' Dallet said with a smile. 'I've been gettin' him ready.'

'Well done,' Kaladin said. 'I paid good money to get that boy away from Gare. That man's so incompetent he might as well be fighting for the other side.'

What? Cenn thought. *Why would anyone pay to get me?*

'What do you think about the field?' Kaladin asked. Several of the other spearmen nearby raised hands to shade from the sun, scanning the rocks.

'That dip next to the two boulders on the far right?' Dallet asked.

Kaladin shook his head. 'Footing's too rough.'

'Aye. Perhaps it is. What about the short hill over there? Far enough to avoid the first fall, close enough to not get too far ahead.'

Kaladin nodded, though Cenn couldn't see what they were looking at. 'Looks good.'

'The rest of you louts hear that?' Dallet shouted.

The men raised their spears high.

'Keep an eye on the new boy, Dallet,' Kaladin said. 'He won't know the signs.'

'Of course,' Dallet said, smiling. Smiling! How could the man smile? The enemy army was blowing horns Did that mean they were ready? Even though Cenn had just relieved himself, he felt a trickle of urine run down his leg.

'Stay firm,' Kaladin said, then trotted down the front line to talk to the next squadleader over. Behind Cenn and the others, the dozens of ranks were still growing. The archers on the sides prepared to fire.

'Don't worry, son,' Dallet said. 'We'll be fine. Squadleader Kaladin is lucky.'

The soldier on the other side of Cenn nodded. He was a lanky, red-haired Veden, with darker tan skin than the Alethi. Why was he fighting in an Alethi army? 'That's right. Kaladin, he's stormblessed, right sure he is. We only lost ... what, one man last battle?'

'But someone *did* die,' Cenn said.

Dallet shrugged. 'People always die. Our squad loses the fewest. You'll see.'

Kaladin finished conferring with the other squadleader, then jogged back to his team. Though he carried a shortspear – meant to be wielded one-handed with a shield in the other hand – his was a hand longer than those held by the other men.

'At the ready, men!' Dallet called. Unlike the other squadleaders, Kaladin didn't fall into rank, but stood out in front of his squad.

The men around Cenn shuffled, excited. The sounds were repeated through the vast army, the stillness giving way before eagerness. Hundreds of feet shuffling, shields slapping, clasps clanking. Kaladin remained motionless, staring down the other army. 'Steady, men,' he said without turning.

Behind, a lighteyed officer passed on horseback. 'Be ready to fight! I want their blood, men. Fight and kill!'

'Steady,' Kaladin said again, after the man passed.

'Be ready to run,' Dallet said to Cenn.

'Run? But we've been trained to march in formation! To stay in our line!'

'Sure,' Dallet said. 'But most of the men don't have much more training than you. Those who can fight well end up getting sent to the Shattered Plains to battle the Parshendi. Kaladin's trying to get us into shape to go there, to fight for the king.' Dallet nodded down the line. 'Most of these here will break and charge; the lighteyes aren't good enough commanders to keep them in formation. So stay with us and run.'

'Should I have my shield out?' Around Kaladin's team, the other ranks were unhooking their shields. But Kaladin's squad left their shields on their backs.

Before Dallet could answer, a horn blew from behind.

'Go!' Dallet said

Cenn didn't have much choice. The entire army started moving in a clamor of marching boots. As Dallet had predicted, the steady march didn't last long. Some men began yelling, the roar taken up by others. Lighteyes called for them to go, run, fight. The line disintegrated.

As soon as that happened, Kaladin's squad broke into a dash, running out into the front at full speed. Cenn scrambled to keep up, panicked and terrified. The ground wasn't as smooth as it had seemed, and he nearly tripped on a hidden rockbud, vines withdrawn into its shell.

He righted himself and kept going, holding his spear in one hand, his shield clapping against his back. The distant army was in motion as well, their soldiers charging down the field. There was no semblance of a battle formation or a careful line. This wasn't anything like the training had claimed it would be.

Cenn didn't even know who the enemy was. A landlord was encroaching on Brightlord Amaram's territory – the land owned, ultimately, by Highprince Sadeas. It was a border skirmish, and Cenn thought it was with another Alethi princedom. Why were they fighting each other?

Perhaps the king would have put a stop to it, but he was on the Shattered Plains, seeking vengeance for the murder of King Gavilar five years before.

The enemy had a lot of archers. Cenn's panic climbed to a peak as the first wave of arrows flew into the air. He stumbled again, itching to take out his shield. But Dallet grabbed his arm and yanked him forward.

Hundreds of arrows split the sky, dimming the sun. They arced and fell, dropping like skyeels upon their prey. Amaram's soldiers raised shields. But not Kaladin's squad. No shields for them.

Cenn screamed.

And the arrows slammed into the middle ranks of Amaram's army, behind him. Cenn glanced over his shoulder, still running. The arrows fell *behind* him. Soldiers screamed, arrows broke against shields; only a few straggling arrows landed anywhere near the front ranks.

'Why?' he yelled at Dallet. 'How did you know?'

'They want the arrows to hit where the men are most crowded,' the large man replied. 'Where they'll have the greatest chance of finding a body.'

Several other groups in the van left their shields lowered, but most ran awkwardly with their shields angled up to the sky, worried about arrows that wouldn't hit them. That slowed them, and they risked getting trampled by the men behind who *were* getting hit. Cenn itched to raise his shield anyway; it felt so wrong to run without it.

The second volley hit, and men screamed in pain. Kaladin's squad barreled toward the enemy soldiers, some of whom were dying to arrows from Amaram's archers. Cenn could hear the enemy soldiers bellowing war cries, could make out individual faces. Suddenly Kaladin's squad pulled to a halt, forming a tight group. They'd reached the small incline that Kaladin and Dallet had chosen earlier.

Dallet grabbed Cenn and shoved him to the very center of the formation. Kaladin's men lowered spears, pulling out shields as the enemy bore down on them. The charging foe used no careful formation; they didn't keep the ranks of longspears in back and shortspears in front. They all just ran forward, yelling in a frenzy.

Cenn scrambled to get his shield unlatched from his back. Clashing spears rang in the air as squads engaged one another. A group of enemy spearmen rushed up to Kaladin's squad, perhaps coveting the higher ground. The three dozen attackers had some cohesion, though they weren't in as tight a formation as Kaladin's squad was.

The enemy seemed determined to make up for it in passion; they bellowed and screamed in fury, rushing Kaladin's line. Kaladin's team held rank, defending Cenn as if he were some lighteyes and they were his honor guard. The two forces met with a crash of metal on wood, shields slamming together. Cenn cringed back.

It was over in a few eyeblinks. The enemy squad pulled back, leaving two dead on the stone. Kaladin's team hadn't lost anyone. They held their bristling V formation, though one man stepped back and pulled out a bandage to wrap a thigh wound. The rest of the men closed in to fill the spot. The wounded man was hulking and thick-armed; he cursed, but the wound didn't look bad. He was on his feet in a moment, but didn't return to the place where he'd been. Instead, he moved down to one end of the V formation, a more protected spot.

The battlefield was chaos. The two armies mingled indistinguishably; sounds of clanging, crunching, and screaming churned in the air. Many of the squads broke apart, members rushing from one encounter to another. They moved like hunters, groups of three or four seeking lone individuals, then brutally falling on them.

Kaladin's team held its ground, engaging only enemy squads that got too close. Was this what a battle really was? Cenn's practice had trained him for long ranks of men, shoulder to shoulder. Not this frenzied intermixing, this brutal pandemonium. Why didn't more hold formation?

The real soldiers are all gone, Cenn thought. *Off fighting in a real battle at the Shattered Plains. No wonder Kaladin wants to get his squad there.*

Spears flashed on all sides; it was difficult to tell friend from foe, despite the emblems on breastplates and colored paint on shields. The battlefield broke down into hundreds of small groups, like a thousand different wars happening at the same time.

After the first few exchanges, Dallet took Cenn by the shoulder and placed him in the rank at the very bottom of the V pattern. Cenn, however was worthless. When Kaladin's team engaged enemy squads, all of his training fled him. It took everything he had to just remain there, holding his spear outward and trying to look threatening.

For the better part of an hour, Kaladin's squad held their small hill, working as a team, shoulder to shoulder. Kaladin often left his position at the front, rushing this way and that, banging his spear on his shield in a strange rhythm.

Those are signals, Cenn realized as Kaladin's squad moved from the V shape into a ring. With the screams of the dying and the thousands of men calling to others, it was nearly impossible to hear a single person's voice. But the sharp clang of the spear against the metal plate on Kaladin's shield was clear. Each time they changed formations, Dallet grabbed Cenn by the shoulder and steered him.

Kaladin's team didn't chase down stragglers. They remained on the defensive. And, while several of the men in Kaladin's team took wounds, none of them fell. Their squad was too intimidating for the smaller groups, and larger enemy units retreated after a few exchanges, seeking easier foes.

Eventually something changed. Kaladin turned, watching the tides of the battle with discerning brown eyes. He raised his spear and smacked his shield in a quick rhythm he hadn't used before. Dallet grabbed Cenn by the arm and pulled him away from the small hill. Why abandon it now?

Just then, the larger body of Amaram's force broke, the men scattering. Cenn hadn't realized how poorly the battle in this quarter had been going for his side. As Kaladin's team retreated, they passed many wounded and dying, and Cenn grew nauseated. Soldiers were sliced open, their insides spilling out.

He didn't have time for horror; the retreat quickly turned into a rout. Dallet cursed, and Kaladin beat his shield again. The squad changed direction, heading eastward. There, Cenn saw, a larger group of Amaram's soldiers was holding.

But the enemy had seen the ranks break, and that made them bold. They rushed forward in clusters, like wild axehounds hunting stray hogs. Before Kaladin's team was halfway across the field of dead and dying, a large group of enemy soldiers intercepted them. Kaladin reluctantly banged his shield; his squad slowed.

Cenn felt his heart begin to thump faster and faster. Nearby, a squad of Amaram's soldiers was consumed; men stumbled and fell, screaming, trying to get away. The enemies used their spears like skewers, killing men on the ground like cremlings.

Kaladin's men met the enemy in a crash of spears and shields. Bodies shoved on all sides and Cenn was spun about. In the jumble of friend and foe, dying and killing, Cenn grew overwhelmed. So many men running in so many directions!

He panicked, scrambling for safety. A group of soldiers nearby wore Alethi uniforms. Kaladin's squad. Cenn ran for them, but when some turned toward him, Cenn was terrified to realize he didn't recognize them. This *wasn't* Kaladin's squad, but a small group of unfamiliar soldiers holding an uneven, broken line. Wounded and terrified, they scattered as soon as an enemy squad got close.

Cenn froze, holding his spear in a sweaty hand. The enemy soldiers charged right for him. His instincts urged him to flee, yet he had seen so many men picked off one at a time. He had to stand! He had to face them! He couldn't run, he couldn't—

He yelled, stabbing his spear at the lead soldier. The man casually knocked the weapon aside with his shield, then drove his shortspear into Cenn's thigh. The pain was hot, so hot that the blood squirting out on his leg felt cold by comparison. Cenn gasped.

The soldier yanked the weapon free. Cenn stumbled backward, dropping his spear and shield. He fell to the rocky ground, splashing in someone else's blood. His foe raised a spear high, a looming silhouette against the stark blue sky, ready to ram it into Cenn's heart.

And then *he* was there.

Squadleader. Stormblessed. Kaladin's spear came as if out of nowhere, narrowly deflecting the blow that was to have killed Cenn. Kaladin set himself in front of Cenn, alone, facing down six spearmen. He didn't flinch. He *charged*.

It happened so quickly. Kaladin swept the feet from beneath the man who had stabbed Cenn. Even as that man fell, Kaladin reached up and flipped a knife from one of the sheaths tied about his spear. His hand snapped, knife flashing and hitting the thigh of a second foe. That man fell to one knee, screaming.

A third man froze, looking at his fallen allies. Kaladin shoved past a wounded enemy and slammed his spear into the gut of the third man. A fourth man fell with a knife to the eye. When had Kaladin grabbed that knife? He spun between the last two, his spear a blur, wielding it like a quarterstaff. For a moment, Cenn thought he could see something

33

surrounding the squadleader. A warping of the air, like the wind itself become visible.

I've lost a lot of blood. It's flowing out so quickly. . . .

Kaladin spun, knocking aside attacks, and the last two spearmen fell with gurgles that Cenn thought sounded surprised. Foes all down, Kaladin turned and knelt beside Cenn. The squadleader set aside his spear and whipped a white strip of cloth from his pocket, then efficiently wrapped it tight around Cenn's leg. Kaladin worked with the ease of one who had bound wounds dozens of times before.

'Kaladin, sir!' Cenn said, pointing at one of the soldiers Kaladin had wounded. The enemy man held his leg as he stumbled to his feet. In a second, however, mountainous Dallet was there, shoving the foe with his shield. Dallet didn't kill the wounded man, but let him stumble away, unarmed.

The rest of the squad arrived and formed a ring around Kaladin, Dallet, and Cenn. Kaladin stood up, raising his spear to his shoulder; Dallet handed him back his knives, retrieved from the fallen foes.

'Had me worried there, sir,' Dallet said. 'Running off like that.'

'I knew you'd follow,' Kaladin said. 'Raise the red banner. Cyn, Korater, you're going back with the boy. Dallet, hold here. Amaram's line is bulging in this direction. We should be safe soon.'

'And you, sir?' Dallet asked.

Kaladin looked across the field. A pocket had opened in the enemy forces, and a man rode there on a white horse, swinging about him with a wicked mace. He wore full plate armor, polished and gleaming silver.

'A Shardbearer,' Cenn said.

Dallet snorted. 'No, thank the Stormfather. Just a lighteyed officer. Shardbearers are far too valuable to waste on a minor border dispute.'

Kaladin watched the lighteyes with a seething hatred. It was the same hatred Cenn's father had shown when he'd spoken of chull rustlers, or the hatred Cenn's mother would display when someone mentioned Kusiri, who had run off with the cobbler's son.

'Sir?' Dallet said hesitantly.

'Subsquads Two and Three, pincer pattern,' Kaladin said, his voice hard. 'We're taking a brightlord off his throne.'

'You sure that's wise, sir? We've got wounded.'

34

Kaladin turned toward Dallet. 'That's one of Hallaw's officers. He might be the one.'

'You don't know that, sir.'

'Regardless, he's a battalionlord. If we kill an officer that high, we're all but guaranteed to be in the next group sent to the Shattered Plains. We're taking him.' His eyes grew distant. 'Imagine it, Dallet. Real soldiers. A warcamp with discipline and lighteyes with integrity. A place where our fighting will *mean* something.'

Dallet sighed, but nodded. Kaladin waved to a group of his soldiers; then they raced across the field. A smaller group of soldiers, including Dallet, waited behind with the wounded. One of those – a thin man with black Alethi hair speckled with a handful of blond hairs, marking some foreign blood – pulled a long red ribbon from his pocket and attached it to his spear. He held the spear aloft, letting the ribbon flap in the wind.

'It's a call for runners to carry our wounded off the field,' Dallet said to Cenn. 'We'll have you out of here soon. You were brave, standing against those six.'

'Fleeing seemed stupid,' Cenn said, trying to take his mind off his throbbing leg. 'With so many wounded on the field, how can we think that the runners'll come for us?'

'Squadleader Kaladin bribes them,' Dallet said. 'They usually only carry off lighteyes, but there are more runners than there are wounded lighteyes. The squadleader puts most of his pay into the bribes.'

'This squad *is* different,' Cenn said, feeling light-headed.

'Told you.'

'Not because of luck. Because of training.'

'That's part of it. Part of it is because we know if we get hurt, Kaladin will get us off the battlefield.' He paused, looking over his shoulder. As Kaladin had predicted, Amaram's line was surging back, recovering.

The mounted enemy lighteyes from before was energetically laying about with his mace. A group of his honor guard moved to one side, engaging Kaladin's subsquads. The lighteyes turned his horse. He wore an open-fronted helm that had sloping sides and a large set of plumes on the top. Cenn couldn't make out his eye color, but he knew it would be blue or green, maybe yellow or light grey. He was a brightlord, chosen at birth by the Heralds, marked for rule.

He impassively regarded those who fought nearby. Then one of Kaladin's knives took him in the right eye.

The brightlord screamed, falling back off the saddle as Kaladin somehow slipped through the lines and leaped upon him, spear raised.

'Aye, it's part training,' Dallet said, shaking his head. 'But it's mostly him. He fights like a storm, that one, and thinks twice as fast as other men. The way he moves sometimes . . .'

'He bound my leg,' Cenn said, realizing he was beginning to speak nonsense due to the blood loss. Why point out the bound leg? It was a simple thing.

Dallet just nodded. 'He knows a lot about wounds. He can read glyphs too. He's a strange man, for a lowly darkeyed spearman, our squadleader is.' He turned to Cenn. 'But you should save your strength, son. The squad-leader won't be pleased if we lose you, not after what he paid to get you.'

'Why?' Cenn asked. The battlefield was growing quieter, as if many of the dying men had already yelled themselves hoarse. Almost everyone around them was an ally, but Dallet still watched to make sure no enemy soldiers tried to strike at Kaladin's wounded.

'Why, Dallet?' Cenn repeated, feeling urgent. 'Why bring me into his squad? Why *me*?'

Dallet shook his head. 'It's just how he is. Hates the thought of young kids like you, barely trained, going to battle. Every now and again, he grabs one and brings him into his squad. A good half dozen of our men were once like you.' Dallet's eyes got a far-off look. 'I think you all remind him of someone.'

Cenn glanced at his leg. Painspren – like small orange hands with overly long fingers – were crawling around him, reacting to his agony. They began turning away, scurrying in other directions, seeking other wounded. His pain was fading, his leg – his whole body – feeling numb.

He leaned back, staring up at the sky. He could hear faint thunder. That was odd. The sky was cloudless.

Dallet cursed.

Cenn turned, shocked out of his stupor. Galloping directly toward them was a massive black horse bearing a rider in gleaming armor that seemed to radiate light. That armor was seamless – no chain underneath, just smaller plates, incredibly intricate. The figure wore an unornamented full helm, and the plate was gilded. He carried a massive sword in one hand, fully as long as a man was tall. It wasn't a simple, straight sword – it was curved, and the side that wasn't sharp was ridged, like flowing waves. Etchings covered its length.

It was beautiful. Like a work of art. Cenn had never seen a Shardbearer, but he knew immediately what this was. How could he ever have mistaken a simple armored lighteyes for one of *these* majestic creatures?

Hadn't Dallet claimed there would be no Shardbearers on this battlefield? Dallet scrambled to his feet, calling for the subsquad to form up. Cenn just sat where he was. He couldn't have stood, not with that leg wound.

He felt so light-headed. How much blood had he lost? He could barely think.

Either way, he couldn't fight. You didn't fight something like this. Sun gleamed against that plate armor. And that gorgeous, intricate, sinuous sword. It was like ... like the Almighty himself had taken form to walk the battlefield.

And why would you want to fight the Almighty?

Cenn closed his eyes.

2

HONOR IS DEAD

'Ten orders. We were loved, once. Why have you forsaken us, Almighty! Shard of my soul, where have you gone?'

—Collected on the second day of Kakash, year 1171, five seconds before death. Subject was a lighteyed woman in her third decade.

EIGHT MONTHS LATER

Kaladin's stomach growled as he reached through the bars and accepted the bowl of slop. He pulled the small bowl – more a cup – between the bars, sniffed it, then grimaced as the caged wagon began to roll again. The sludgy grey slop was made from over-cooked tallew grain, and this batch was flecked with crusted bits of yesterday's meal.

Revolting though it was, it was all he would get. He began to eat, legs hanging out between the bars, watching the scenery pass. The other slaves in his cage clutched their bowls protectively, afraid that someone might steal from them. One of them tried to steal Kaladin's food on the first day. He'd nearly broken the man's arm. Now everyone left him alone.

Suited him just fine.

He ate with his fingers, careless of the dirt. He'd stopped noticing dirt months ago. He hated that he felt some of that same paranoia that the others showed. How could he not, after eight months of beatings, deprivation, and brutality?

He fought down the paranoia. He *wouldn't* become like them. Even if he'd given up everything else – even if all had been taken from him, even if there was no longer hope of escape. This one thing he would retain. He was a slave. But he didn't need to think like one.

He finished the slop quickly. Nearby, one of the other slaves began to cough weakly. There were ten slaves in the wagon, all men, scragglybearded and dirty. It was one of three wagons in their caravan through the Unclaimed Hills.

The sun blazed reddish white on the horizon, like the hottest part of a smith's fire. It lit the framing clouds with a spray of color, paint thrown carelessly on a canvas. Covered in tall, monotonously green grass, the hills seemed endless. On a nearby mound, a small figure flitted around the plants, dancing like a fluttering insect. The figure was amorphous, vaguely translucent. Windspren were devious spirits who had a penchant for staying where they weren't wanted. He'd hoped that this one had gotten bored and left, but as Kaladin tried to toss his wooden bowl aside, he found that it stuck to his fingers.

The windspren laughed, zipping by, nothing more than a ribbon of light without form. He cursed, tugging on the bowl. Windspren often played pranks like that. He pried at the bowl, and it eventually came free. Grumbling, he tossed it to one of the other slaves. The man quickly began to lick at the remnants of the slop.

'Hey,' a voice whispered.

Kaladin looked to the side. A slave with dark skin and matted hair was crawling up to him, timid, as if expecting Kaladin to be angry. 'You're not like the others.' The slave's black eyes glanced upward, toward Kaladin's forehead, which bore three brands. The first two made a glyphpair, given to him eight months ago, on his last day in Amaram's army. The third was fresh, given to him by his most recent master. *Shash*, the last glyph read. Dangerous.

The slave had his hand hidden behind his rags. A knife? No, that was ridiculous. None of these slaves could have hidden a weapon; the leaves hidden in Kaladin's belt were as close as one could get. But old instincts could not be banished easily, so Kaladin watched that hand.

'I heard the guards talking,' the slave continued, shuffling a little closer.

He had a twitch that made him blink too frequently. 'You've tried to escape before, they said. You *have* escaped before.'

Kaladin made no reply.

'Look,' the slave said, moving his hand out from behind his rags and revealing his bowl of slop. It was half full. 'Take me with you next time,' he whispered. 'I'll give you this. Half my food from now until we get away. Please.' As he spoke, he attracted a few hungerspren. They looked like brown flies that flitted around the man's head, almost too small to see.

Kaladin turned away, looking out at the endless hills and their shifting, moving grasses. He rested one arm across the bars and placed his head against it, legs still hanging out.

'Well?' the slave asked.

'You're an idiot. If you gave me half your food, you'd be too weak to escape if I *were* to flee. Which I won't. It doesn't work.'

'But—'

'Ten times,' Kaladin whispered. 'Ten escape attempts in eight months, fleeing from five different masters. And how many of them worked?'

'Well ... I mean ... you're still here. ...'

Eight months. Eight months as a slave, eight months of slop and beatings. It might as well have been an eternity. He barely remembered the army anymore. 'You can't hide as a slave,' Kaladin said. 'Not with that brand on your forehead. Oh, I got away a few times. But they always found me. And then back I went.'

Once, men had called him lucky. Stormblessed. Those had been lies – if anything, Kaladin had *bad* luck. Soldiers were a superstitious sort, and though he'd initially resisted that way of thinking, it was growing harder and harder. Every person he had ever tried to protect had ended up dead. Time and time again. And now, here he was, in an even worse situation than where he'd begun. It was better not to resist. This was his lot, and he was resigned to it.

There was a certain power in that, a freedom. The freedom of not having to care.

The slave eventually realized Kaladin wasn't going to say anything further, and so he retreated, eating his slop. The wagons continued to roll, fields of green extending in all directions. The area around the rattling wagons was bare, however. When they approached, the grass pulled away, each individual stalk withdrawing into a pinprick hole in the stone. After the wagons moved on, the grass timidly poked back out and stretched its blades toward the air. And so, the cages moved along what appeared to be an open rock highway, cleared just for them.

This far into the Unclaimed Hills, the highstorms were incredibly powerful. The plants had learned to survive. That's what you had to do, learn to survive. Brace yourself, weather the storm.

Kaladin caught a whiff of another sweaty, unwashed body and heard the sound of shuffling feet. He looked suspiciously to the side, expecting that same slave to be back.

It was a different man this time, though. He had a long black beard stuck with bits of food and snarled with dirt. Kaladin kept his own beard shorter, allowing Tvlakv's mercenaries to hack it down periodically. Like Kaladin the slave wore the remains of a brown sack tied with a rag and he was darkeyed, of course – perhaps a deep dark green, though with darkeyes it was hard to tell. They all looked brown or black unless you caught them in the right light.

The newcomer cringed away, raising his hands. He had a rash on one hand, the skin just faintly discolored. He'd likely approached because he'd seen Kaladin respond to that other man. The slaves had been frightened of him since the first day, but they were also obviously curious.

Kaladin sighed and turned away. The slave hesitantly sat down. 'Mind if I ask how you became a slave, friend? Can't help wondering. We're all wondering.'

Judging by the accent and the dark hair, the man was Alethi, like Kaladin. Most of the slaves were. Kaladin didn't reply to the question.

'Me, I stole a herd of chull,' the man said. He had a raspy voice, like sheets of paper rubbing together. 'If I'd taken one chull, they might have just beaten me. But a whole herd. Seventeen head ... ' He chuckled to himself, admiring his own audacity.

In the far corner of the wagon, someone coughed again. They were a sorry lot, even for slaves. Weak, sickly, underfed. Some, like Kaladin, were repeat runaways – though Kaladin was the only one with a *shash* brand. They were the most worthless of a worthless caste, purchased at a steep discount. They were probably being taken for resale in a remote place where men were desperate for labor. There were plenty of small, independent cities along the coast of the Unclaimed Hills, places where Vorin rules governing the use of slaves were just a distant rumor.

Coming this way was dangerous. These lands were ruled by nobody, and by cutting across open land and staying away from established trade routes, Tvlakv could easily run afoul of unemployed mercenaries. Men who had no honor and no fear of slaughtering a slavemaster and his slaves in order to steal a few chulls and wagons.

Men who had no honor. Were there men who *had* honor?

No, Kaladin thought. *Honor died eight months ago.*

'So?' asked the scraggly-bearded man. 'What did you do to get made a slave?'

Kaladin raised his arm against the bars again. 'How did you get caught?'

'Odd thing, that,' the man said. Kaladin hadn't answered his question, but he *had* replied. That seemed enough. 'It was a woman, of course. Should have known she'd sell me.'

'Shouldn't have stolen chulls. Too slow. Horses would have been better.'

The man laughed riotously. 'Horses? What do you think me, a madman? If I'd been caught stealing *those*, I'd have been hanged. Chulls, at least, only earned me a slave's brand.'

Kaladin glanced to the side This man's forehead brand was older than Kaladin's, the skin around the scar faded to white. What was that glyph-pair? '*Sas morom*,' Kaladin said. It was the highlord's district where the man had originally been branded.

The man looked up with shock. 'Hey! You know glyphs?' Several of the slaves nearby stirred at this oddity. 'You must have an even better story than I thought, friend.'

Kaladin stared out over those grasses blowing in the mild breeze. Whenever the wind picked up, the more sensitive of the grass stalks shrank down into their burrows, leaving the landscape patchy, like the coat of a sickly horse. That windspren was still there, moving between patches of grass. How long had it been following him? At least a couple of months now. That was downright odd. Maybe it wasn't the same one. They were impossible to tell apart.

'Well?' the man prodded. 'Why are you here?'

'There are many reasons why I'm here,' Kaladin said. 'Failures. Crimes. Betrayals. Probably the same for most every one of us.'

Around him, several of the men grunted in agreement; one of those grunts then degenerated into a hacking cough. *Persistent coughing*, a part of Kaladin's mind thought, *accompanied by an excess of phlegm and fevered mumbling at night. Sounds like the grindings.*

'Well,' the talkative man said, 'perhaps I should ask a different question. Be more specific, that's what my mother always said. Say what you mean and ask for what you want. What's the story of you getting that first brand of yours?'

Kaladin sat, feeling the wagon thump and roll beneath him. 'I killed a lighteyes.'

His unnamed companion whistled again, this time even more appreciative than before. 'I'm surprised they let you live.'

'Killing the lighteyes isn't why I was made a slave,' Kaladin said. 'It's the one I *didn't* kill that's the problem.'

'How's that?'

Kaladin shook his head, then stopped answering the talkative man's questions. The man eventually wandered to the front of the wagon's cage and sat down, staring at his bare feet.

◆◆

Hours later, Kaladin still sat in his place, idly fingering the glyphs on his forehead. This was his life, day in and day out, riding in these cursed wagons.

His first brands had healed long ago, but the skin around the *shash* brand was red, irritated, and crusted with scabs. It throbbed, almost like a second heart. It hurt even worse than the burn had when he grabbed the heated handle of a cooking pot as a child.

Lessons drilled into Kaladin by his father whispered in the back of his brain, giving the proper way to care for a burn. Apply a salve to prevent infection, wash once daily. Those memories weren't a comfort; they were an annoyance. He didn't *have* fourleaf sap or lister's oil; he didn't even have water for the washing.

The parts of the wound that had scabbed over pulled at his skin, making his forehead feel tight. He could barely pass a few minutes without scrunching up his brow and irritating the wound. He'd grown accustomed to reaching up and wiping away the streaks of blood that trickled from the cracks; his right forearm was smeared with it. If he'd had a mirror, he could probably have spotted tiny red rotspren gathering around the wound.

The sun set in the west, but the wagons kept rolling. Violet Salas peeked over the horizon to the east, seeming hesitant at first, as if making sure the sun had vanished. It was a clear night, and the stars shivered high above. Taln's Scar – a swath of deep red stars that stood out vibrantly from the twinkling white ones – was high in the sky this season.

That slave who'd been coughing earlier was at it again. A ragged, wet cough. Once, Kaladin would have been quick to go help, but something within him had changed. So many people he'd tried to help were now dead. It seemed to him – irrationally – that the man would be better off without his interference. After failing Tien, then Dallet and his team, then ten successive groups of slaves, it was hard to find the will to try again.

Two hours past First Moon, Tvlakv finally called a halt. His two brutish mercenaries climbed from their places atop their wagons, then moved to build a small fire. Lanky Taran – the serving boy – tended the chulls. The large crustaceans were nearly as big as wagons themselves. They settled down, pulling into their shells for the night with clawfuls of grain. Soon they were nothing more than three lumps in the darkness, barely distinguishable from boulders. Finally, Tvlakv began checking on the slaves one at a time, giving each a ladle of water, making certain his investments were healthy. Or, at least, as healthy as could be expected for this poor lot.

Tvlakv started with the first wagon, and Kaladin – still sitting – pushed his fingers into his makeshift belt, checking on the leaves he'd hidden there. They crackled satisfactorily, the stiff, dried husks rough against his skin. He still wasn't certain what he was going to do with them. He'd grabbed them on a whim during one of the sessions when he'd been allowed out of the wagon to stretch his legs. He doubted anyone else in the caravan knew how to recognize blackbane – narrow leaves on a trefoil prong – so it hadn't been too much of a risk.

Absently, he took the leaves out and rubbed them between forefinger and palm. They had to dry before reaching their potency. Why did he carry them? Did he mean to give them to Tvlakv and get revenge? Or were they a contingency, to be retained in case things got too bad, too unbearable?

Surely I haven't fallen that far, he thought. It was just more likely his instinct of securing a weapon when he saw one, no matter how unusual.

The landscape was dark. Salas was the smallest and dimmest of the moons, and while her violet coloring had inspired countless poets, she didn't do much to help you see your hand in front of your face.

'Oh!' a soft, feminine voice said. 'What's that?'

A translucent figure – just a handspan tall – peeked up from over the edge of the floor near Kaladin. She climbed up and into the wagon, as if scaling some high plateau. The windspren had taken the shape of a young woman – larger spren could change shapes and sizes – with an angular face and long, flowing hair that faded into mist behind her head. She – Kaladin couldn't help but think of the windspren as a she – was formed of pale blues and whites and wore a simple, flowing white dress of a girlish cut that came down to midcalf. Like the hair, it faded to mist at the very bottom. Her feet, hands, and face were crisply distinct, and she had the hips and bust of a slender woman.

Kaladin frowned at the spirit. Spren were all around; you just ignored them most of the time. But this one was an oddity. The windspren walked upward, as if climbing an invisible staircase. She reached a height where she could stare at Kaladin's hand, so he closed his fingers around the black leaves. She walked around his fist in a circle. Although she glowed like an afterimage from looking at the sun, her form provided no real illumination.

She bent down, looking at his hand from different angles, like a child expecting to find a hidden piece of candy. 'What is it?' Her voice was like a whisper. 'You can show me. I won't tell anyone. Is it a treasure? Have you cut off a piece of the night's cloak and tucked it away? Is it the heart of a beetle, so tiny yet powerful?'

He said nothing, causing the spren to pout. She floated up, hovering though she had no wings, and looked him in the eyes. 'Kaladin, why must you ignore me?'

Kaladin started. 'What did you say?'

She smiled mischievously, then sprang away, her figure blurring into a long white ribbon of blue-white light. She shot between the bars – twisting and warping in the air, like a strip of cloth caught in the wind – and darted beneath the wagon.

'Storm you!' Kaladin said, leaping to his feet. 'Spirit! What did you say? Repeat that!' Spren didn't use people's names. Spren weren't intelligent. The larger ones – like windspren or riverspren – could mimic voices and expressions, but they didn't actually think. They didn't . . .

'Did any of you hear that?' Kaladin asked, turning to the cage's other occupants. The roof was just high enough to let Kaladin stand. The others were lying back, waiting to get their ladle of water. He got no response beyond a few mutters to be quiet and some coughs from the sick man in the corner. Even Kaladin's 'friend' from earlier ignored him. The man had fallen into a stupor, staring at his feet, wiggling his toes periodically.

Maybe they hadn't seen the spren. Many of the larger ones were invisible except to the person they were tormenting. Kaladin sat back down on the floor of the wagon, hanging his legs outside. The windspren *had* said his name, but undoubtedly she'd just repeated what she'd heard before. But . . . none of the men in the cage knew his name.

Maybe I'm going mad, Kaladin thought. *Seeing things that aren't there. Hearing voices.*

He took a deep breath, then opened his hand. His grip had cracked and broken the leaves. He'd need to tuck them away to prevent further—

'Those leaves look interesting,' said that same feminine voice. 'You like them a lot, don't you?'

Kaladin jumped, twisting to the side. The windspren stood in the air just beside his head, white dress rippling in a wind Kaladin couldn't feel.

'How do you know my name?' he demanded.

The windspren didn't answer. She walked on air over to the bars, then poked her head out, watching Tvlakv the slaver administer drinks to the last few slaves in the first wagon. She looked back at Kaladin. 'Why don't you fight? You did before. Now you've stopped.'

'Why do you care, spirit?'

She cocked her head. 'I don't know,' she said, as if surprised at herself. 'But I do. Isn't that odd?'

It was more than odd. What did he make of a spren that not only used his name, but seemed to *remember* things he had done weeks ago?

'People don't eat leaves, you know, Kaladin,' she said, folding translucent arms. Then she cocked her head. 'Or do you? I can't remember. You're so strange, stuffing some things into your mouths, leaking out other things when you don't think anyone is looking.'

'How do you know my name?' he whispered.

'How do *you* know it?'

'I know it because ... because it's mine. My parents told it to me. I don't know.'

'Well I don't either,' she said, nodding as if she'd just won some grand argument.

'Fine,' he said. 'But why are you *using* my name?'

'Because it's polite. And you are *im*polite.'

'Spren don't know what that means!'

'See, there,' she said, pointing at him. 'Impolite.'

Kaladin blinked. Well, he was far from where he'd grown up, walking foreign stone and eating foreign food. Perhaps the spren who lived here were different from those back home.

'So why don't you fight?' she asked, flitting down to rest on his legs, looking up at his face. She had no weight that he could feel.

'I can't fight,' he said softly.

'You did before.'

He closed his eyes and rested his head forward against the bars. 'I'm so tired.' He didn't mean the physical fatigue, though eight months eating leftovers had stolen much of the lean strength he'd cultivated while at war. He *felt* tired. Even when he got enough sleep. Even on those rare days when he wasn't hungry, cold, or stiff from a beating. So tired ...

'You have been tired before.'

'I've failed, spirit,' he replied, squeezing his eyes shut. 'Must you torment me so?'

They were all dead. Cenn and Dallet, and before that Tukks and the Takers. Before that, Tien. Before that, blood on his hands and the corpse of a young girl with pale skin.

Some of the slaves nearby muttered, likely thinking he was mad. Anyone could end up drawing a spren, but you learned early that talking to one was pointless. *Was* he mad? Perhaps he should wish for that – madness was an escape from the pain. Instead, it terrified him.

He opened his eyes. Tvlakv was finally waddling up to Kaladin's wagon with his bucket of water. The portly, brown-eyed man walked with a very faint limp; the result of a broken leg, perhaps. He was Thaylen, and all Thaylen men had the same stark white beards – regardless of their age or the color of the hair on their heads – and white eyebrows. Those eyebrows grew very long, and the Thaylen wore them pushed back over the ears.

That made him appear to have two white streaks in his otherwise black hair.

His clothing – striped trousers of black and red with a dark blue sweater that matched the color of his knit cap – had once been fine, but it was now growing ragged. Had he once been something other than a slaver? This life – the casual buying and selling of human flesh – seemed to have an effect on men. It wearied the soul, even if it did fill one's money pouch.

Tvlakv kept his distance from Kaladin, carrying his oil lantern over to inspect the coughing slave at the front of the cage. Tvlakv called to his mercenaries. Bluth – Kaladin didn't know why he'd bothered to learn their names – wandered over. Tvlakv spoke quietly pointing at the slave. Bluth nodded, slablike face shadowed in the lanternlight, and pulled the cudgel free from his belt.

The windspren took the form of a white ribbon, then zipped over toward the sick man. She spun and twisted a few times before landing on the floor, becoming a girl again. She leaned in to inspect the man. Like a curious child.

Kaladin turned away and closed his eyes, but he could still hear the coughing. Inside his mind, his father's voice responded. *To cure the grinding coughs*, said the careful, precise tone, *administer two handfuls of bloodivy, crushed to a powder, each day. If you don't have that, be certain to give the patient plenty of liquids, preferably with sugar stirred in. As long as the patient stays hydrated, he will most likely survive. The disease sounds far worse than it is.*

Most likely survive . . .

Those coughs continued. Someone unlatched the cage door. Would they know how to help the man? Such an easy solution. Give him water, and he would live.

It didn't matter. Best not to get involved.

Men dying on the battlefield. A youthful face, so familiar and dear, looking to Kaladin for salvation. A sword wound slicing open the side of a neck. A Shardbearer charging through Amaram's ranks.

Blood. Death. Failure. Pain.

And his father's voice. *Can you really leave him, son? Let him die when you could have helped?*

Storm it!

'Stop!' Kaladin yelled, standing.

The other slaves scrambled back. Bluth jumped up, slamming the cage door closed and holding up his cudgel. Tvlakv shied behind the mercenary, using him as cover.

Kaladin took a deep breath, closing his hand around the leaves and then raising the other to his head, wiping away a smear of blood. He crossed the small cage, bare feet thumping on the wood. Bluth glared as Kaladin knelt beside the sick man. The flickering light illuminated a long, drawn face and nearly bloodless lips. The man had coughed up phlegm; it was greenish and solid. Kaladin felt the man's neck for swelling, then checked his dark brown eyes.

'It's called the grinding coughs,' Kaladin said. 'He will live, if you give him an extra ladle of water every two hours for five days or so. You'll have to force it down his throat. Mix in sugar, if you have any.'

Bluth scratched at his ample chin, then glanced at the shorter slaver.

'Pull him out,' Tvlakv said.

The wounded slave awoke as Bluth unlocked the cage. The mercenary waved Kaladin back with his cudgel and Kaladin reluctantly withdrew. After putting away his cudgel, Bluth grabbed the slave under the arms and dragged him out, all the while trying to keep a nervous eye on Kaladin. Kaladin's last failed escape attempt had involved twenty armed slaves. His master should have executed him for that, but he had claimed Kaladin was 'intriguing' and branded him with *shash*, then sold him for a pittance.

There always seemed to be a reason Kaladin survived when those he'd tried to help died. Some men might have seen that as a blessing, but he saw it as an ironic kind of torment. He'd spent some time under his previous master speaking with a slave from the West, a Selay man who had spoken of the Old Magic from their legends and its ability to curse people. Could that be what was happening to Kaladin?

Don't be foolish, he told himself.

The cage door snapped back in place, locking. The cages were necessary – Tvlakv had to protect his fragile investment from the highstorms. The cages had wooden sides that could be pulled up and locked into place during the furious gales.

Bluth dragged the slave over to the fire, beside the unpacked water barrel. Kaladin felt himself relax. *There*, he told himself. *Perhaps you can still help. Perhaps there's a reason to care.*

Kaladin opened his hand and looked down at the crumbled black leaves in his palm. He didn't need these. Sneaking them into Tvlakv's drink would not only be difficult, but pointless. Did he really want the slaver dead? What would that accomplish?

A low crack rang in the air, followed by a second one, duller, like someone dropping a bag of grain. Kaladin snapped his head up, looking to where Bluth had deposited the sick slave. The mercenary raised his cudgel one more time, then snapped it down, the weapon making a cracking sound as it hit the slave's skull.

The slave hadn't uttered a cry of pain or protest. His corpse slumped over in the darkness; Bluth casually picked it up and slung it over his shoulder.

'No!' Kaladin yelled, leaping across the cage and slamming his hands against the bars.

Tvlakv stood warming himself by the fire.

'Storm you!' Kaladin screamed. 'He could have lived, you bastard!'

Tvlakv glanced at him. Then, leisurely, the slaver walked over, straightening his deep blue knit cap. 'He would have gotten you all sick, you see.' His voice was lightly accented, smashing words together, not giving the proper syllables emphasis. Thaylens always sounded to Kaladin like they were mumbling. 'I would not lose an entire wagon for one man.'

'He's past the spreading stage!' Kaladin said, slamming his hands against the bars again. 'If any of us were going to catch it, we'd have done so by now.'

'Hope that you don't. I think he was past saving.'

'I told you otherwise!'

'And I should believe you, deserter?' Tvlakv said, amused. 'A man with eyes that smolder and hate? You would kill me.' He shrugged. 'I care not. So long as you are strong when it is time for sales. You should bless me for saving you from that man's sickness.'

'I'll bless your cairn when I pile it up myself,' Kaladin replied.

Tvlakv smiled, walking back toward the fire. 'Keep that fury, deserter, and that strength. It will pay me well on our arrival.'

Not if you don't live that long, Kaladin thought. Tvlakv always warmed the last of the water from the bucket he used for the slaves. He'd make himself tea from it, hanging it over the fire. If Kaladin made sure he was watered last, then powdered the leaves and dropped them into the—

Kaladin froze, then looked down at his hands. In his haste, he'd forgotten that he'd been holding the blackbane. He'd dropped the flakes as he slammed his hands against the bars. Only a few bits stuck to his palms, not enough to be potent.

He spun to look backward; the floor of the cage was dirty and covered with grime. If the flakes had fallen there, there was no way to collect them. The wind gathered suddenly, blowing dust, crumbs, and dirt out of the wagon and into the night.

Even in this, Kaladin failed.

He sank down, his back to the bars, and bowed his head. Defeated. That cursed windspren kept darting around him, looking confused.

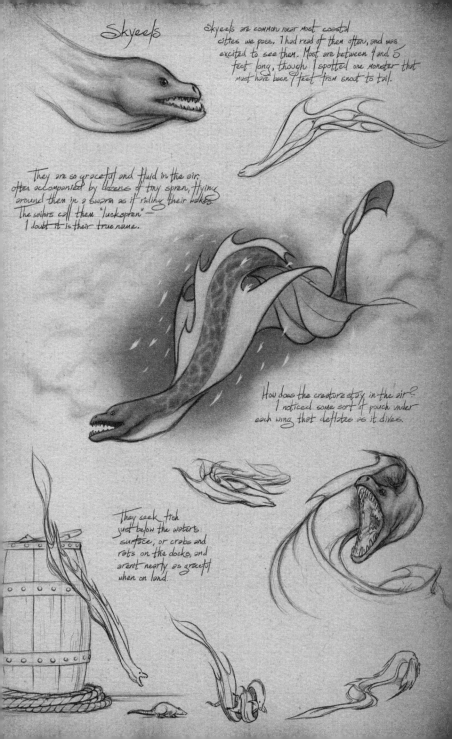

Skyeels

Skyeels are common near most coastal cities we pass. I had read of them often, and was excited to see them. Most are between 1 and 5 feet long, though I spotted one monster that must have been 9 feet from snout to tail.

They are so graceful and fluid in the air, often accompanied by dozens of tiny spren, flying around them in a swarm as if riding their wakes. The sailors call them "luckspren" — I doubt it is their true name.

How does the creature stay in the air? I noticed some sort of pouch under each wing that deflates as it dives.

They seek fish just below the water's surface, or crabs and rats on the docks, and aren't nearly as graceful when on land.

CITY OF BELLS

'A man stood on a cliffside and watched his homeland fall into dust. The waters surged beneath, so far beneath. And he heard a child crying. They were his own tears.'

—Collected on the 4th of Tanates, year 1171, thirty seconds before death. Subject was a cobbler of some renown.

Kharbranth, City of Bells, was not a place that Shallan had ever imagined she would visit. Though she'd often dreamed of traveling, she'd expected to spend her early life sequestered in her family's manor, only escaping through the books of her father's library. She'd expected to marry one of her father's allies, then spend the rest of her life sequestered in *his* manor.

But expectations were like fine pottery. The harder you held them, the more likely they were to crack.

She found herself breathless, clutching her leather-bound drawing pad to her chest as longshoremen pulled the ship into the dock. Kharbranth was enormous. Built up the side of a steep incline, the city was wedge-shaped, as if it were built into a wide crack, with the open side toward the ocean. The buildings were blocky, with square windows, and appeared to have been constructed of some kind of mud or daub. Crem, perhaps? They were painted bright colors, reds and oranges most often, but occasional blues and yellows too.

She could hear the bells already, tinkling in the wind, ringing with pure voices. She had to strain her neck to look up toward the city's loftiest rim; Kharbranth was like a mountain towering over her. How many people lived in a place like this? Thousands? Tens of thousands? She shivered again – daunted yet excited – then blinked pointedly, fixing the image of the city in her memory.

Sailors rushed about. The *Wind's Pleasure* was a narrow, single-masted vessel, barely large enough for her, the captain, his wife, and the half-dozen crew. It had seemed so small at first, but Captain Tozbek was a calm and cautious man, an excellent sailor, even if he was a pagan. He'd guided the ship with care along the coast, always finding a sheltered cove to ride out highstorms.

The captain oversaw the work as the men secured the mooring. Tozbek was a short man, even-shouldered with Shallan, and he wore his long white Thaylen eyebrows up in a curious spiked pattern. It was like he had two waving fans above his eyes, a foot long each. He wore a simple knit cap and a silver-buttoned black coat. She'd imagined him getting that scar on his jaw in a furious sea battle with pirates. The day before, she'd been disappointed to hear it had been caused by loose tackle during rough weather.

His wife, Ashlv, was already walking down the gangplank to register their vessel. The captain saw Shallan inspecting him, and so walked over. He was a business connection of her family's, long trusted by her father. That was good, since the plan she and her brothers had concocted had contained no place for her bringing along a lady-in-waiting or nurse.

That plan made Shallan nervous. Very, *very* nervous. She hated being duplicitous. But the financial state of her house ... They either needed a spectacular infusion of wealth or some other edge in local Veden house politics. Otherwise, they wouldn't last the year.

First things first, Shallan thought, forcing herself to be calm. *Find Jasnah Kholin. Assuming she hasn't moved off without you again.*

'I've sent a lad on your behalf, Brightness,' Tozbek said. 'If the princess is still here, we shall soon know.'

Shallan nodded gratefully, still clutching her drawing pad. Out in the city, there were people *everywhere*. Some wore familiar clothing – trousers and shirts that laced up the front for the men, skirts and colorful blouses for the women. Those could have been from her homeland, Jah Keved. But Kharbranth was a free city. A small, politically fragile city-state, it held little territory but had docks open to all ships that passed, and it asked no questions about nationality or status. People flowed to it.

That meant many of the people she saw were exotic. Those single-sheet wraps would mark a man or woman from Tashikk, far to the west. The long coats, enveloping down to the ankles, but open in the front like cloaks ... where were those from? She'd rarely seen so many parshmen as she noted working the docks carrying cargo on their backs. Like the parshmen her father had owned, these were stout and thick of limb, with their odd marbled skin – some parts pale or black, others a deep crimson. The mottled pattern was unique to each individual.

After chasing Jasnah Kholin from town to town for the better part of six months, Shallan was beginning to think she'd never catch the woman. Was the princess avoiding her? No, that didn't seem likely – Shallan just wasn't important enough to wait for. Brightness Jasnah Kholin was one of the most powerful women in the world. And one of the most infamous. She was the only member of a faithful royal house who was a professed heretic.

Shallan tried not to grow anxious. Most likely, they'd discover that Jasnah had moved on again. The *Wind's Pleasure* would dock for the night, and Shallan would negotiate a price with the captain – steeply discounted, because of her family's investments in Tozbek's shipping business – to take her to the next port.

Already, they were months past the time when Tozbek had expected to be rid of her. She'd never sensed resentment from him; his honor and loyalty kept him agreeing to her requests. However, his patience wouldn't last forever, and neither would her money. She'd already used over half the spheres she'd brought with her. He wouldn't abandon her in an unfamiliar city, of course, but he might regretfully insist on taking her back to Vedenar.

'Captain!' a sailor said, rushing up the gangplank. He wore only a vest and loose, baggy trousers, and had the darkly tanned skin of one who worked in the sun. 'No message, sir. Dock registrar says that Jasnah hasn't left yet.'

'Ha!' the captain said, turning to Shallan. 'The hunt is over!'

'Bless the Heralds,' Shallan said softly.

The captain smiled, flamboyant eyebrows looking like streaks of light coming from his eyes. 'It must be your beautiful face that brought us this favorable wind! The windspren themselves were entranced by you, Brightness Shallan, and led us here!'

Shallan blushed, considering a response that wasn't particularly proper.

'Ah!' the captain said, pointing at her. 'I can see you have a reply – I see it in your eyes, young miss! Spit it out. Words aren't meant to be kept inside, you see. They are free creatures, and if locked away will unsettle the stomach.'

'It's not polite,' Shallan protested.

Tozbek bellowed a laugh. 'Months of travel, and still you claim that! I keep telling you that we're sailors! We forgot how to be polite the moment we set first foot on a ship; we're far beyond redemption now.'

She smiled. She'd been trained by stern nurses and tutors to hold her tongue – unfortunately her brothers had been even more determined in encouraging her to do the opposite. She'd made a habit of entertaining them with witty comments when nobody else was near. She thought fondly of hours spent by the crackling greatroom hearth, the younger three of her four brothers huddled around her, listening as she made sport of their father's newest sycophant or a traveling ardent. She'd often fabricated silly versions of conversations to fill the mouths of people they could see, but not hear.

That had established in her what her nurses had referred to as an 'insolent streak.' And the sailors were even more appreciative of a witty comment than her brothers had been.

'Well,' Shallan said to the captain, blushing but still eager to speak, 'I was just thinking this: You say that my beauty coaxed the winds to deliver us to Kharbranth with haste. But wouldn't that imply that on other trips, my lack of beauty was to blame for us arriving late?'

'Well . . . er . . . '

'So in reality,' Shallan said, 'you're telling me I'm beautiful precisely one-sixth of the time.'

'Nonsense! Young miss, you're like a morning sunrise, you are!'

'Like a sunrise? By that you mean entirely too crimson' – she pulled at her long red hair – 'and prone to making men grouchy when they see me?'

He laughed, and several of the sailors nearby joined in. 'All right then,' Captain Tozbek said, 'you're like a flower.'

She grimaced. 'I'm allergic to flowers.'

He raised an eyebrow.

'No, really,' she admitted. 'I think they're quite captivating. But if you were to give me a bouquet, you'd soon find me in a fit so energetic that it would have you searching the walls for stray freckles I might have blown free with the force of my sneezes.'

'Well, be that true, I still say you're as *pretty* as a flower.'

'If I am, then young men my age must be afflicted with the same allergy – for they keep their distance from me noticeably.' She winced. 'Now, see, I told you this wasn't polite. Young women should not act in such an irritable way.'

'Ah, young miss,' the captain said, tipping his knit cap toward her. 'The lads and I will miss your clever tongue. I'm not sure what we'll do without you.'

'Sail, likely,' she said. 'And eat, and sing, and watch the waves. All the things you do now, only you shall have rather *more* time to accomplish all of it, as you won't be stumbling across a youthful girl as she sits on your deck sketching and mumbling to herself. But you have my thanks, Captain, for a trip that was wonderful – if somewhat exaggerated in length.'

He tipped his cap to her in acknowledgment

Shallan grinned – she hadn't expected being out on her own to be so liberating. Her brothers had worried that she'd be frightened. They saw her as timid because she didn't like to argue and remained quiet when large groups were talking. And perhaps she *was* timid – being away from Jah Keved was daunting. But it was also wonderful. She'd filled three sketchbooks with pictures of the creatures and people she'd seen, and while her worry over her house's finances was a perpetual cloud, it was balanced by the sheer delight of experience.

Tozbek began making dock arrangements for his ship. He was a good man. As for his praise of her supposed beauty, she took that for what it was. A kind, if overstated, mark of affection. She was pale-skinned in an era when Alethi tan was seen as the mark of true beauty, and though she had light blue eyes, her impure family line was manifest in her auburn-red hair. Not a single lock of proper black. Her freckles had faded as she reached young womanhood – Heralds be blessed – but there were still some visible, dusting her cheeks and nose.

'Young miss,' the captain said to her after conferring with his men, 'Your Brightness Jasnah, she'll undoubtedly be at the Conclave, you see.'

'Oh, where the Palanaeum is?'

'Yes, yes. And the king lives there too. It's the center of the city, so to speak. Except it's on the top.' He scratched his chin. 'Well, anyway, Brightness Jasnah Kholin is sister to a king; she will stay nowhere else, not in Kharbranth. Yalb here will show you the way. We can deliver your trunk later.'

'Many thanks, Captain,' she said. '*Shaylor mkabat nour.*' *The winds have brought us safely.* A phrase of thanks in the Thaylen language.

The captain smiled broadly. '*Mkai bade fortenthis!*'

She had no idea what that meant. Her Thaylen was quite good when she was reading, but hearing it spoken was something else entirely. She smiled at him, which seemed the proper response, for he laughed, gesturing to one of his sailors.

'We'll wait here in this dock for two days,' he told her. 'There is a high-storm coming tomorrow, you see, so we cannot leave. If the situation with the Brightness Jasnah does not proceed as hoped, we'll take you back to Jah Keved.'

'Thank you again.'

''Tis nothing, young miss,' he said. 'Nothing but what we'd be doing anyway. We can take on goods here and all. Besides, that's a right nice likeness of my wife you gave me for my cabin. Right nice.'

He strode over to Yalb, giving him instructions. Shallan waited, putting her drawing pad back into her leather portfolio. Yalb. The name was difficult for her Veden tongue to pronounce. Why were the Thaylens so fond of mashing letters together, without proper vowels?

Yalb waved for her. She moved to follow.

'Be careful with yourself, lass,' the captain warned as she passed. 'Even a safe city like Kharbranth hides dangers. Keep your wits about you.'

'I should think I'd prefer my wits inside my skull, Captain,' she replied, carefully stepping onto the gangplank. 'If I keep them "about me" instead, then someone has gotten entirely too close to my head with a cudgel.'

The captain laughed, waving her farewell as she made her way down the gangplank, holding the railing with her freehand. Like all Vorin women, she kept her left hand – her safehand – covered, exposing only her freehand. Common darkeyed women would wear a glove, but a woman of her rank was expected to show more modesty than that. In her case, she kept her safehand covered by the oversized cuff of her left sleeve, which was buttoned closed.

The dress was of a traditional Vorin cut, formfitting through the bust, shoulders, and waist, with a flowing skirt below. It was blue silk with chullshell buttons up the sides, and she carried her satchel by pressing it to her chest with her safehand while holding the railing with her freehand.

She stepped off the gangplank into the furious activity of the docks, messengers running this way and that, women in red coats tracking cargos on ledgers. Kharbranth was a Vorin kingdom, like Alethkar and like Shallan's own Jah Keved. They weren't pagans here, and writing was a feminine art; men learned only glyphs, leaving letters and reading to their wives and sisters.

She hadn't asked, but she was certain Captain Tozbek could read. She'd seen him holding books; it had made her uncomfortable. Reading was an unseemly trait in a man. At least, men who weren't ardents.

'You wanna ride?' Yalb asked her, his rural Thaylen dialect so thick she could barely make out the words.

'Yes, please.'

He nodded and rushed off, leaving her on the docks, surrounded by a group of parshmen who were laboriously moving wooden crates from one pier to another. Parshmen were thick-witted, but they made excellent workers. Never complaining, always doing as they were told. Her father had preferred them to ordinary slaves.

Were the Alethi really fighting *parshmen* out on the Shattered Plains? That seemed so odd to Shallan. Parshmen didn't fight. They were docile and practically mute. Of course, from what she'd heard, the ones out on the Shattered Plains – the Parshendi, they were called – were physically different from normal parshmen. Stronger, taller, keener of mind. Perhaps they weren't really parshmen at all, but distant relatives of some kind.

To her surprise, she could see signs of animal life all around the docks. A few skyeels undulated through the air, searching for rats or fish. Tiny crabs hid between cracks in the dock's boards and a cluster of haspers clung to the dock's thick logs. In a street inland of the docks, a prowling mink skulked in the shadows, watching for morsels that might be dropped.

She couldn't resist pulling open her portfolio and beginning a sketch of a pouncing skyeel. Wasn't it afraid of all the people? She held her sketch-pad with her safehand, hidden fingers wrapping around the top as she used a charcoal pencil to draw. Before she was finished, her guide returned with a man pulling a curious contraption with two large wheels and a canopy-covered seat. She hesitantly lowered her sketchpad. She'd expected a palanquin.

The man pulling the machine was short and dark-skinned, with a wide smile and full lips. He gestured for Shallan to sit, and she did so with the modest grace her nurses had drilled into her. The driver asked her a question in a clipped, terse-sounding language she didn't recognize.

'What was that?' she asked Yalb.

'He wants to know if you'd like to be pulled the long way or the short way.' Yalb scratched his head. 'I'm not right sure what the difference is.'

'I suspect one takes longer,' Shallan said.

'Oh, you *are* a clever one.' Yalb said something to the porter in that same clipped language, and the man responded.

'The long way gives a good view of the city,' Yalb said. 'The short way goes straight up to the Conclave. Not many good views, he says. I guess he noticed you were new to the city.'

'Do I stand out that much?' Shallan asked, flushing.

'Eh, no, of course not, Brightness.'

'And by that you mean that I'm as obvious as a wart on a queen's nose.'

Yalb laughed. 'Afraid so. But you can't go someplace a second time until you been there a first time, I reckon. Everyone has to stand out sometime, so you might as well do it in a pretty way like yourself!'

She'd had to get used to gentle flirtation from the sailors. They were never too forward, and she suspected the captain's wife had spoken to them sternly when she'd noticed how it made Shallan blush. Back at her father's manor, servants – even those who had been full citizens – had been afraid to step out of their places.

The porter was still waiting for an answer. 'The short way, please,' she told Yalb, though she longed to take the scenic path. She was finally in a *real* city and she took the direct route? But Brightness Jasnah had proven to be as elusive as a wild songling. Best to be quick.

The main roadway cut up the hillside in switchbacks, and so even the short way gave her time to see much of the city. It proved intoxicatingly rich with strange people, sights, and ringing bells. Shallan sat back and took it all in. Buildings were grouped by color, and that color seemed to indicate purpose. Shops selling the same items would be painted the same shades – violet for clothing, green for foods. Homes had their own pattern, though Shallan couldn't interpret it. The colors were soft, with a washed-out, subdued tonality.

Yalb walked alongside her cart, and the porter began to talk back toward her. Yalb translated, hands in the pockets of his vest. 'He says that the city is special because of the lait here.'

Shallan nodded. Many cities were built in laits – areas protected from the highstorms by nearby rock formations.

'Kharbranth is one of the most sheltered major cities in the world,' Yalb continued, translating, 'and the bells are a symbol of that. It's said they were first erected to warn that a highstorm was blowing, since the winds were so soft that people didn't always notice.' Yalb hesitated. 'He's just saying things because he wants a big tip, Brightness. I've heard that story, but I think it's blustering ridiculous. If the winds blew strong enough to move bells, then people'd notice. Besides, people didn't notice it was *raining* on their blustering heads?'

Shallan smiled. 'It's all right. He can continue.'

The porter chatted on in his clipped voice – what language *was* that, anyway? Shallan listened to Yalb's translation, drinking in the sights, sounds, and – unfortunately – scents. She'd grown up accustomed to the crisp smell of freshly dusted furniture and flatbread baking in the kitchens. Her ocean journey had taught her new scents, of brine and clean sea air.

There was nothing clean in what she smelled here. Each passing alleyway had its own unique array of revolting stenches. These alternated with the spicy scents of street vendors and their foods, and the juxta-position was even more nauseating. Fortunately, her porter moved into the central part of the roadway, and the stenches abated, though it did slow them as they had to contend with thicker traffic. She gawked at those they passed. Those men with gloved hands and faintly bluish skin were from Natanatan. But who were those tall, stately people dressed in robes of black? And the men with their beards bound in cords, making them rodlike?

The sounds put Shallan in mind of the competing choruses of wild songlings near her home, only multiplied in variety and volume. A hundred voices called to one another, mingling with doors slamming, wheels rolling on stone, occasional skyeels crying. The ever-present bells tinkled in the background, louder when the wind blew. They were displayed in the windows of shops, hung from rafters. Each lantern pole along the street had a bell hung under the lamp, and her cart had a small silvery one at the very tip of its canopy. When she was about halfway up the hillside, a rolling wave of loud clock bells rang the hour. The varied, unsynchronized chimes made a clangorous din

The crowds thinned as they reached the upper quarter of the city, and eventually her porter pulled her to a massive building at the very apex of the city. Painted white, it was carved from the rock face itself, rather than built of bricks or clay. The pillars out front grew seamlessly from the stone, and the back side of the building melded smoothly into the cliff. The outcroppings of roof had squat domes atop them, and were painted in metallic colors. Lighteyed women passed in and out, carrying scribing utensils and wearing dresses like Shallan's, their left hands properly cuffed. The men entering or leaving the building wore military-style Vorin coats and stifftrousers, buttons up the sides and ending in a stiff collar that wrapped the entire neck. Many carried swords at their waists, the belts wrapping around the knee-length coats.

The porter stopped and made a comment to Yalb. The sailor began arguing with him, hands on hips. Shallan smiled at his stern expression, and she blinked pointedly, affixing the scene in her memory for later sketching.

'He's offering to split the difference with me if I let him inflate the price of the trip,' Yalb said, shaking his head and offering a hand to help Shallan from the cart. She stepped down, looking at the porter, who shrugged, smiling like a child who had been caught sneaking sweets.

She clutched her satchel with her cuffed arm, searching through it with her freehand for her money pouch. 'How much should I actually give him?'

'Two clearchips should be more than enough. I'd have offered one. The thief wanted to ask for *five*.'

Before this trip, she'd never used money; she'd just admired the spheres for their beauty. Each one was composed of a glass bead a little larger than a person's thumbnail with a much smaller gemstone set at the center. The gemstones could absorb Stormlight, and that made the spheres glow. When she opened the money pouch, shards of ruby, emerald, diamond, and sapphire shone out on her face. She fished out three diamond chips, the smallest denomination. Emeralds were the most valuable, for they could be used by Soulcasters to create food.

The glass part of most spheres was the same size; the size of the gemstone at the center determined the denomination. The three chips, for instance, each had only a tiny splinter of diamond inside. Even that was enough to glow with Stormlight, far fainter than a lamp, but still visible. A mark – the medium denomination of sphere – was a little less bright than a candle, and it took five chips to make a mark.

She'd brought only infused spheres, as she'd heard that dun ones were considered suspect, and sometimes a moneylender would have to be brought in to judge the authenticity of the gemstone. She kept the most valuable spheres she had in her safepouch, of course, which was buttoned to the inside of her left sleeve.

She handed the three chips to Yalb, who cocked his head. She nodded at the porter, blushing, realizing that she'd reflexively used Yalb like a master-servant intermediary. Would he be offended?

He laughed and stood up stiffly, as if imitating a master-servant, paying the porter with a mock stern expression. The porter laughed, bowed to Shallan, then pulled his cart away.

'This is for you,' Shallan said, taking out a ruby mark and handing it to Yalb.

'Brightness, this is too much!'

'It's partially out of thanks,' she said, 'but is also to pay you to stay here and wait for a few hours, in case I return.'

'Wait a few hours for a firemark? That's wages for a week's sailing!'

'Then it should be enough to make certain you don't wander off.'

'I'll be right here!' Yalb said, giving her an elaborate bow that was surprisingly well-executed.

Shallan took a deep breath and strode up the steps toward the Conclave's imposing entrance. The carved rock really was remarkable – the artist in her wanted to linger and study it, but she didn't dare. Entering the large building was like being swallowed. The hallway inside was lined with Stormlight lamps that shone with white light. Diamond broams were probably set inside them; most buildings of fine construction used Storm-light to provide illumination. A broam – the highest denomination of sphere – glowed with about the same light as several candles.

Their light shone evenly and softly on the many attendants, scribes, and lighteyes moving through the hallway. The building appeared to be constructed as one broad, high, and long tunnel, burrowed into the rock. Grand chambers lined the sides, and subsidiary corridors branched off the central grand promenade. She felt far more comfortable than she had outdoors. This place – with its bustling servants, its lesser brightlords and brightladies – was familiar.

She raised her freehand in a sign of need, and sure enough, a master-servant in a crisp white shirt and black trousers hurried over to her. 'Brightness?' he asked, speaking her native Veden, likely because of the color of her hair.

'I seek Jasnah Kholin,' Shallan said. 'I have word that she is within these walls.'

The master-servant bowed crisply. Most master-servants prided themselves on their refined service – the very same air that Yalb had been mocking moments ago. 'I shall return, Brightness.' He would be of the second nahn, a darkeyed citizen of very high rank. In Vorin belief, one's Calling – the task to which one dedicated one's life – was of vital importance. Choosing a good profession and working hard at it was the best way to ensure good placement in the afterlife. The specific devotary that one visited for worship often had to do with the nature of one's chosen Calling.

Shallan folded her arms, waiting. She had thought long about her own Calling. The obvious choice was her art, and she did so love sketching. But it was more than just the drawing that attracted her – it was the *study*, the questions raised by observation. Why weren't the skyeels afraid of people? What did haspers feed on? Why did a rat population thrive in one area, but fail in another? So she'd chosen natural history instead.

She longed to be a true scholar, to receive real instruction, to spend time on deep research and study. Was that part of why she'd suggested this daring plan of seeking out Jasnah and becoming her ward? Perhaps. However, she needed to remain focused. Becoming Jasnah's ward – and therefore student – was only one step.

She considered this as she idly walked up to a pillar, using her freehand to feel the polished stone. Like much of Roshar – save for certain coastal regions – Kharbranth was built on raw, unbroken stone. The buildings outside had been set directly on the rock, and this one sliced into it. The pillar was granite, she guessed, though her geological knowledge was sketchy.

The floor was covered with long, burnt-orange rugs. The material was dense, designed to look rich but bear heavy traffic. The broad, rectangular hallway had an *old* feel to it. One book she'd read claimed that Kharbranth had been founded way back into the shadowdays, years before the Last Desolation. That would make it old indeed. Thousands of years old, created before the terrors of the Hierocracy, long before – even – the Recreance. Back when Voidbringers with bodies of stone were said to have stalked the land.

'Brightness?' a voice asked.

Shallan turned to find that the servant had returned.

'This way, Brightness.'

She nodded to the servant, and he led her quickly down the busy hallway. She went over how to present herself to Jasnah. The woman was a legend. Even Shallan – living in the remote estates of Jah Keved – had heard of the Alethi king's brilliant, heretic sister. Jasnah was only thirty-four years old, yet many felt she would already have obtained the cap of a master scholar if it weren't for her vocal denunciations of religion. Most specifically, she denounced the devotaries, the various religious congregations that proper Vorin people joined.

Improper quips would not serve Shallan well here. She would have to be proper. Wardship to a woman of great renown was the best way to be schooled in the feminine arts: music, painting, writing, logic, and science. It was much like how a young man would train in the honor guard of a brightlord he respected.

Shallan had originally written to Jasnah requesting a wardship in desperation; she hadn't actually expected the woman to reply in the affirmative. When she had – via a letter commanding Shallan to attend her in Dumadari in two weeks – Shallan had been shocked. She'd been chasing the woman ever since.

Jasnah was a heretic. Would she demand that Shallan renounce her faith? She doubted she could do such a thing. Vorin teachings regarding one's Glory and Calling had been one of her few refuges during the difficult days, when her father had been at his worst.

They turned into a narrower hallway, entering corridors increasingly far from the main cavern. Finally, the master-servant stopped at a corner and gestured for Shallan to continue. There were voices coming from the corridor to the right.

Shallan hesitated. Sometimes, she wondered how it had come to this. She was the quiet one, the timid one, the youngest of five siblings and the only girl. Sheltered, protected all her life. And now the hopes of her entire house rested on her shoulders.

Their father was dead. And it was vital that remain a secret.

She didn't like to think of that day – she all but blocked it from her mind, and trained herself to think of other things. But the effects of his loss could not be ignored. He had made many promises – some business deals, some bribes, some of the latter disguised as the former. House Davar owed great amounts of money to a great number of people, and without her father to keep them all appeased, the creditors would soon begin making demands.

There was nobody to turn to. Her family, mostly because of her father, was loathed even by its allies. Highprince Valam – the brightlord to whom her family gave fealty – was ailing, and no longer offered them the protection he once had. When it became known that her father was dead and her family bankrupt, that would be the end of House Davar. They'd be consumed and subjugated to another house.

They'd be worked to the bone as punishment – in fact, they might even face assassination by disgruntled creditors. Preventing that depended on Shallan, and the first step came with Jasnah Kholin.

Shallan took a deep breath, then strode around the corner.

'I'm dying, aren't I? Healer, why do you take my blood? Who is that beside you, with his head of lines? I can see a distant sun, dark and cold, shining in a black sky.'

—Collected on the 3rd of Jesnan, 1172, 11 seconds pre-death. Subject was a Reshi chull trainer. Sample is of particular note.

'Why don't you cry?' the windspren asked.

Kaladin sat with his back to the corner of the cage, looking down. The floor planks in front of him were splintered, as if someone had dug at them with nothing but his fingernails. The splintered section was stained dark where the dry grey wood had soaked up blood. A futile, delusional attempt at escape.

The wagon continued to roll. The same routine each day. Wake up sore and aching from a fitful night spent without mattress or blanket. One wagon at a time, the slaves were let out and hobbled with leg irons and given time to shuffle around and relieve themselves. Then they were packed away and given morning slop, and the wagons rolled until afternoon slop. More rolling. Evening slop, then a ladle of water before sleep.

Kaladin's *shash* brand was still cracked and bleeding. At least the cage's top gave shade from the sun.

The windspren shifted to mist, floating like a tiny cloud. She moved in close to Kaladin, the motion outlining her face at the front of the cloud, as if blowing back the fog and revealing something more substantial underneath. Vaporous, feminine, and angular. With such curious eyes. Like no other spren he'd seen.

'The others cry at night,' she said. 'But you don't.'

'Why cry?' he said, leaning his head back against the bars. 'What would it change?'

'I don't know. Why *do* men cry?'

He smiled, closing his eyes. 'Ask the Almighty why men cry, little spren. Not me.' His forehead dripped with sweat from the Eastern summer humidity, and it stung as it seeped into his wound. Hopefully, they'd have some weeks of spring again soon. Weather and seasons were unpredictable. You never knew how long they would go on, though typically each would last a few weeks.

The wagon rolled on. After a time, he felt sunlight on his face. He opened his eyes. The sun shone in through the upper side of the cage. Two or three hours past noon, then. What of afternoon slop? Kaladin stood, pulling himself up with one hand on the steel bars. He couldn't make out Tvlakv driving the wagon up ahead, only flat-faced Bluth behind. The mercenary had on a dirty shirt that laced up the front and wore a wide-brimmed hat against the sun, his spear and cudgel riding on the wagon bench beside him. He didn't carry a sword – not even Tvlakv did that, not near Alethi land.

The grass continued to part for the wagons, vanishing just in front, then creeping out after the wagons passed. The landscape here was dotted with strange shrubs that Kaladin didn't recognize. They had thick stalks and stems and spiny green needles. Whenever the wagons grew too close, the needles pulled into the stalks, leaving behind twisted, wormlike trunks with knotted branches. They dotted the hilly landscape, rising from the grass-covered rocks like diminutive sentries.

The wagons just kept on going, well past noon. *Why aren't we stopping for slop?*

The lead wagon finally pulled to a stop. The other two lurched to a halt behind it, the red-carapaced chulls fidgeted, their antennae waving back and forth. The box-shaped animals had bulging, stony shells and thick, trunklike red legs. From what Kaladin had heard, their claws could snap a man's arm. But chulls were docile, particularly domesticated ones, and he'd never known anyone in the army to get more than a halfhearted pinch from one.

Bluth and Tag climbed down from their wagons and walked up to meet Tvlakv. The slavemaster stood on his wagon's seat, shading his eyes against the white sunlight and holding a sheet of paper in his hand. An argument ensued. Tvlakv kept waving in the direction they had been going, then pointing at his sheet of paper.

'Lost, Tvlakv?' Kaladin called. 'Perhaps you should pray to the Almighty for guidance. I hear he has a fondness for slavers. Keeps a special room in Damnation just for you.'

To Kaladin's left, one of the slaves – the long-bearded man who had talked to him a few days back – sidled away, not wanting to stand close to a person who was provoking the slaver.

Tvlakv hesitated, then waved curtly to his mercenaries, silencing them. The portly man hopped down from his wagon and walked over to Kaladin. 'You,' he said. 'Deserter. Alethi armies travel these lands for their war. Do you know anything of the area?'

'Let me see the map,' Kaladin said. Tvlakv hesitated, then held it up for Kaladin.

Kaladin reached through the bars and snatched the paper. Then, without reading it, Kaladin ripped it in two. In seconds he'd shredded it into a hundred pieces in front of Tvlakv's horrified eyes.

Tvlakv called for the mercenaries, but by the time they arrived, Kaladin had a double handful of confetti to toss out at them. 'Happy Middlefest, you bastards,' Kaladin said as the flakes of paper fluttered around them. He turned and walked to the other side of the cage and sat down, facing them.

Tvlakv stood, speechless. Then, red-faced, he pointed at Kaladin and hissed something at the mercenaries. Bluth took a step toward the cage, but then thought better of it. He glanced at Tvlakv, then shrugged and walked away. Tvlakv turned to Tag, but the other mercenary just shook his head, saying something soft.

After a few minutes of stewing at the cowardly mercenaries, Tvlakv rounded the cage and approached where Kaladin was sitting. Surprisingly, when he spoke, his voice was calm. 'I see you are clever, deserter. You have made yourself invaluable. My other slaves, they aren't from this area, and I have never come this way. You can bargain. What is it you wish in exchange for leading us? I can promise you an extra meal each day, should you please me.'

'You want me to lead the caravan?'

'Instructions will be acceptable.'

'All right. First, find a cliff.'

'That, it will give you a vantage to see the area?'

'No,' Kaladin said. 'It will give me something to throw you off of.'

Tvlakv adjusted his cap in annoyance, brushing back one of his long white eyebrows. 'You hate me. That is good. Hatred will keep you strong, make you sell for much. But you will not find vengeance on me unless I have a chance to take you to market. I will not let you escape. But perhaps someone else would. You want to be sold, you see?'

'I don't want vengeance,' Kaladin said. The windspren came back – she'd darted off for a time to inspect one of the strange shrubs. She landed in the air and began walking around Tvlakv's face, inspecting him. He didn't seem to be able to see her.

Tvlakv frowned. 'No vengeance?'

'It doesn't work,' Kaladin said. 'I learned that lesson long ago.'

'Long ago? You cannot be older than eighteen years, deserter.'

It was a good guess. He was nineteen. Had it really only been four years since he'd joined Amaram's army? Kaladin felt as if he'd aged a dozen.

'You are young,' Tvlakv continued. 'You could escape this fate of yours. Men have been known to live beyond the slave's brand – you could pay off your slave price, you see? Or convince one of your masters to give you your freedom. You could become a free man again. It is not so unlikely.'

Kaladin snorted. 'I'll never be free of these brands, Tvlakv. You must know that I've tried – and failed – to escape ten times over. It's more than these glyphs on my head that makes your mercenaries wary.'

'Past failure does not prove that there is not chance in the future, yes?'

'I'm finished. I don't care.' He eyed the slaver. 'Besides, you don't actually believe what you're saying. I doubt a man like you would be able to sleep at night if he thought the slaves he sold would be free to seek him out one day.'

Tvlakv laughed. 'Perhaps, deserter. Perhaps you are right. Or perhaps I simply think that if you *were* to get free, you would hunt down the first man who sold you to slavery, you see? Highlord Amaram, was it not? His death would give me warning so I can run.'

How had he known? How had he heard about Amaram? *I'll find him*, Kaladin thought. *I'll gut him with my own hands. I'll twist his head right off his neck, I'll—*

'Yes,' Tvlakv said, studying Kaladin's face, 'so you were not so honest when you said you do not thirst for vengeance. I see.'

'How do you know about Amaram?' Kaladin said, scowling. 'I've changed hands a half-dozen times since then.'

'Men talk. Slavers more than most. We must be friends with one another, you see, for nobody else will stomach us.'

'Then you know that I didn't get this brand for deserting.'

'Ah, but it is what we must pretend, you see? Men guilty of high crimes, they do not sell so well. With that *shash* glyph on your head, it will be difficult enough to get a good price for you. If I cannot sell you, then you ... well, you will not wish for that status. So we will play a game together. I will say you are a deserter. And you will say nothing. It is an easy game, I think.'

'It's illegal.'

'We are not in Alethkar,' Tvlakv said, 'so there is no law. Besides, desertion was the official reason for your sale. Claim otherwise, and you will gain nothing but a reputation for dishonesty.'

'Nothing besides a headache for you.'

'But you just said you have no desire for vengeance against me '

'I could learn.'

Tvlakv laughed. 'Ah, if you have not learned that already, then you probably never will! Besides, did you not threaten to throw me off a cliff? I think you have learned already. But now, we *must* discuss how to proceed. My map has met with an untimely demise, you see.'

Kaladin hesitated, then sighed. 'I don't know,' he said honestly. 'I've never been this way either.'

Tvlakv frowned. He leaned closer to the cage, inspecting Kaladin, though he still kept his distance. After a moment, Tvlakv shook his head. 'I believe you, deserter. A pity. Well, I shall trust my memory. The map was poorly rendered anyway. I am almost glad you ripped it, for I was tempted to do the same myself. If I should happen across any portraits of my former wives, I shall see that they cross your path and take advantage of your unique talents.' He strolled away.

Kaladin watched him go, then cursed to himself.

'What was that for?' the windspren said, walking up to him, head cocked.

'I almost find myself liking him,' Kaladin said, pounding his head back against the cage.

'But ... after what he did ... '

Kaladin shrugged. 'I didn't say Tvlakv isn't a bastard. He's just a likable bastard.' He hesitated, then grimaced. 'Those are the worst kind. When you kill them, you end up feeling guilty for it.'

❖

The wagon leaked during highstorms. That wasn't surprising; Kaladin suspected that Tvlakv had been driven to slaving by ill fortune. He would rather be trading other goods, but something – lack of funds, a need to leave his previous environs with haste – had forced him to pick up this least reputable of careers.

Men like him couldn't afford luxury, or even quality. They could barely stay ahead of their debts. In this case, that meant wagons which leaked. The boarded sides were strong enough to withstand highstorm winds, but they weren't comfortable.

Tvlakv had almost missed getting ready for this highstorm. Apparently, the map Kaladin had torn up had also included a list of highstorm dates purchased from a roving stormwarden. The storms could be predicted mathematically; Kaladin's father had made a hobby of it. He'd been able to pick the right day eight times out of ten.

The boards rattled against the cage's bars as wind buffeted the vehicle, shaking it, making it lurch like a clumsy giant's plaything. The wood groaned and spurts of icy rainwater sprayed through cracks. Flashes of lightning leaked through as well, accompanied by thunder. That was the only light they got.

Occasionally, light would flash without the thunder. The slaves would groan in terror at this, thinking about the Stormfather, the shades of the Lost Radiants, or the Voidbringers – all of which were said to haunt the most violent highstorms. They huddled together on the far side of the wagon, sharing warmth. Kaladin left them to it, sitting alone with his back to the bars.

Kaladin didn't fear stories of things that walked the storms. In the army, he'd been forced to weather a highstorm or two beneath the lip of a protective stone overhang or other bit of impromptu shelter. Nobody liked to be out during a storm, but sometimes you couldn't avoid it. The things that walked the storms – perhaps even the Stormfather himself – weren't nearly so deadly as the rocks and branches cast up into the air. In fact, the storm's initial tempest of water and wind – the stormwall – was the most dangerous part. The longer one endured after that, the weaker the storm grew, until the trailing edge was nothing more than sprinkling rain.

No, he wasn't worried about Voidbringers looking for flesh to feast upon. He was worried that something would happen to Tvlakv. The slave-master waited out the storm in a cramped wooden enclosure built into the bottom of his wagon. That was ostensibly the safest place in the caravan, but an unlucky twist of fate – a tempest-thrown boulder, the collapse of the wagon – could leave him dead. In that case, Kaladin could see Bluth and Tag running off, leaving everyone in their cages, wooden sides locked up. The slaves would die a slow death by starvation and dehydration, baking under the sun in these boxes.

The storm continued to blow, shaking the wagon. Those winds felt like live things at times. And who was to say they weren't? Were windspren attracted *to* gusts of wind, or *were* they the gusts of wind? The souls of the force that now wanted so badly to destroy Kaladin's wagon?

That force – sentient or not – failed. The wagons were chained to nearby boulders with their wheels locked. The blasts of wind grew more lethargic. Lightning stopped flashing, and the maddening drumming of rain became a quiet tapping instead. Only once during their journey had a wagon toppled during a highstorm. Both it and the slaves inside had survived with a few dents and bruises.

The wooden side to Kaladin's right shook suddenly, then fell open as Bluth undid its clasps. The mercenary wore his leather coat against the wet, streams of water falling from the brim of his hat as he exposed the bars – and the occupants – to the rain. It was cold, though not as piercingly so as during the height of the storm. It sprayed across Kaladin and the huddled slaves. Tvlakv always ordered the wagons uncovered before the rain stopped; he said it was the only way to wash away the slaves' stink.

Bluth slid the wooden side into place beneath the wagon, then opened the other two sides. Only the wall at the front of the wagon – just behind the driver's seat – couldn't be brought down.

'Little early to be taking down the sides, Bluth,' Kaladin said. It wasn't quite the riddens yet – the period near the end of a highstorm when the rain sprinkled softly. This rain was still heavy, the wind still gusting on occasion.

'The master wants you plenty clean today.'

'Why?' Kaladin asked, rising, water streaming from his ragged brown clothing.

Bluth ignored him. *Perhaps we're nearing our destination*, Kaladin thought as he scanned the landscape.

Over the last few days, the hills had given way to uneven rock formations – places where weathering winds had left behind crumbling cliffs and jagged shapes. Grass grew up the rocky sides that saw the most sun, and other plants were plentiful in the shade. The time right after a highstorm was when the land was most alive. Rockbud polyps split and sent out their vines. Other kinds of vine crept from crevices, licking up water. Leaves unfolded from shrubs and trees. Cremlings of all kinds slithered through puddles, enjoying the banquet. Insects buzzed into the air; larger crustaceans – crabs and leggers – left their hiding places. The very rocks seemed to come to life.

Kaladin noted a half-dozen windspren flitting overhead, their translucent forms chasing after – or perhaps cruising along with – the highstorm's last gusts. Tiny lights rose around the plants. Lifespren. They looked like motes of glowing green dust or swarms of tiny translucent insects.

A legger – its hairlike spines lifted to the air to give warning of changes in the wind – climbed along the side of the cart, its long body lined with dozens of pairs of legs. That was familiar enough, but he'd never seen a legger with such a deep purple carapace. Where was Tvlakv taking the caravan? Those uncultivated hillsides were perfect for farming. You could spread stumpweight sap on them – mixed with lavis seeds – during seasons of weaker storms following the Weeping. In four months, you'd have polyps larger than a man's head growing all along the hill, ready to break open for the grain inside.

The chulls lumbered about, feasting on rockbuds, slugs, and smaller crustaceans that had appeared after the storm. Tag and Bluth quietly hitched the beasts to their harnesses as a grumpy-looking Tvlakv crawled out of his waterproof refuge. The slavemaster pulled on a cap and deep black cloak against the rain. He rarely came out until the storm had passed completely; he was *very* eager to get to their destination. Were they that close to the coast? That was one of the only places where they'd find cities in the Unclaimed Hills.

Within minutes, the wagons were rolling again across the uneven ground. Kaladin settled back as the sky cleared, the highstorm a smudge of blackness on the western horizon. The sun brought welcome warmth, and the slaves basked in the light, streams of water dripping from their clothing and running out the back of the rocking wagon.

Presently, a translucent ribbon of light zipped up to Kaladin. He was coming to take the windspren's presence for granted. She had gone out during the storm, but she'd come back. As always.

'I saw others of your kind,' Kaladin said idly.

'Others?' she asked, taking the form of a young woman. She began to step around him in the air, spinning occasionally, dancing to some unheard beat.

'Windspren,' Kaladin said. 'Chasing after the storm. Are you certain you don't want to go with them?'

She glanced westward, longingly. 'No,' she finally said, continuing her dance. 'I like it here.'

Kaladin shrugged. She'd ceased playing as many pranks as she once had, and so he'd stopped letting her presence annoy him.

'There are others near,' she said. 'Others like you.'

'Slaves?'

'I don't know. People. Not the ones here. Other ones.'

'Where?'

She turned a translucent white finger, pointing eastward. 'There. Many of them. Lots and lots.'

Kaladin stood up. He couldn't imagine that a spren had a good handle on how to measure distance and numbers. *Yes* ... Kaladin squinted, studying the horizon. *That's smoke. From chimneys?* He caught a gust of it on the wind; if not for the rain, he'd probably have smelled it sooner.

Should he care? It didn't matter where he was a slave; he'd still be a slave. He'd accepted this life. That was his way now. Don't care, don't bother.

Still, he watched with curiosity as his wagon climbed the side of a hill and gave the slaves inside a good vantage of what was ahead. It wasn't a city. It was something grander, something larger. An enormous army encampment.

'Great Father of Storms . . . ' Kaladin whispered.

Ten masses of troops bivouacked in familiar Alethi patterns – circular, by company rank, with camp followers on the outskirts, mercenaries in a ring just inside them, citizen soldiers near the middle, lighteyed officers at the very center. They were camped in a series of enormous craterlike rock formations, only the sides were more irregular, more jagged. Like broken eggshells.

Kaladin had left an army much like this eight months ago, though Amaram's force had been much smaller. This one covered miles of stone stretching far both north and south. A thousand banners bearing a thousand different family glyphpairs flapped proudly in the air. There were some tents – mainly on the outside of the armies – but most of the troops were housed in large stone barracks. That meant Soulcasters.

That encampment directly ahead of them flew a banner Kaladin had seen in books. Deep blue with white glyphs – *khokh* and *linil*, stylized and painted as a sword standing before a crown. House Kholin. The king's house.

Daunted, Kaladin looked beyond the armies. The landscape to the east was as he'd heard it described in a dozen different stories detailing the king's campaign against the Parshendi betrayers. It was an enormous riven plain of rock – so wide he couldn't see the other side – that was split and cut by sheer chasms, crevasses twenty or thirty feet wide. They were so deep that they disappeared into darkness and formed a jagged mosaic of uneven plateaus. Some large, others tiny. The expansive plain looked like a platter that had been broken, its pieces then reassembled with small gaps between the fragments.

'The Shattered Plains,' Kaladin whispered.

'What?' the windspren asked. 'What's wrong?'

Kaladin shook his head, bemused. 'I spent years trying to get to this place. It's what Tien wanted, in the end at least. To come here, fight in the king's army . . . '

And now Kaladin was here. Finally. *Accidentally.* He felt like laughing at the absurdity. *I should have realized*, he thought. *I should have known. We weren't ever heading toward the coast and its cities. We were heading here. To war.*

This place would be subject to Alethi law and rules. He'd expected that

Tvlakv would want to avoid such things. But here, he'd probably also find the best prices.

'The Shattered Plains?' one of the slaves said. 'Really?'

Others crowded around, peering out. In their sudden excitement, they seemed to forget their fear of Kaladin.

'It *is* the Shattered Plains!' another man said. 'That's the king's army!'

'Perhaps we'll find justice here,' another said.

'I hear the king's household servants live as well as the finest merchants,' said another. 'His slaves have to be better off too. We'll be in Vorin lands; we'll even make wages!'

That much was true. When worked, slaves had to be paid a small wage – half what a nonslave would be paid, which was already often less than a full citizen would make for the same work. But it was something, and Alethi law required it. Only ardents – who couldn't own anything anyway – didn't have to be paid. Well, them and parshmen. But parshmen were more animal than anything else.

A slave could apply his earnings to his slave debt and, after years of labor, earn his freedom. Theoretically. The others continued to chatter as the wagons rolled down the incline, but Kaladin withdrew to the back of the wagon. He suspected that the option to pay off a slave's price was a sham, intended to keep slaves docile. The debt was enormous, far more than a slave sold for, and virtually impossible to earn out.

Under previous masters, he'd demanded his wages be given to him. They had always found ways to cheat him – charging him for his housing, his food. That's how lighteyes were. Roshone, Amaram, Katarotam … Each lighteyes Kaladin had known, whether as a slave or a free man, had shown himself to be corrupt to the core, for all his outward poise and beauty. They were like rotting corpses clothed in beautiful silk.

The other slaves kept talking about the king's army, and about justice. *Justice?* Kaladin thought, resting back against the bars. *I'm not convinced there is such a thing as justice.* Still, he found himself wondering. That was the king's army – the armies of all ten highprinces – come to fulfill the Vengeance Pact.

If there was one thing he still let himself long for, it was the chance to hold a spear. To fight again, to try and find his way back to the man he had been. A man who had cared.

If he would find that anywhere, he'd find it here.

'I have seen the end, and have heard it named. The Night of Sorrows, the True Desolation. The Everstorm.'

—Collected on the 1st of Nanes, 1172, 15 seconds pre-death. Subject was a darkeyed youth of unknown origin.

Shallan had not expected Jasnah Kholin to be so beautiful.

It was a stately, mature beauty – as one might find in the portrait of some historical scholar. Shallan realized that she'd naively been expecting Jasnah to be an ugly spinster, like the stern matrons who had tutored her years ago. How else could one picture a heretic well into her mid-thirties and still unmarried?

Jasnah was nothing like that. She was tall and slender, with clear skin, narrow black eyebrows, and thick, deep onyx hair. She wore part of it up, wrapped around a small, scroll-shaped golden ornament with two long hairpins holding it in place. The rest tumbled down behind her neck in small, tight curls. Even twisted and curled as it was, it came down to Jasnah's shoulders – if left unbound, it would be as long as Shallan's hair, reaching past the middle of her back.

She had a squarish face and discriminating pale violet eyes. She was listening to a man dressed in robes of burnt orange and white, the Kharbranthian royal colors. Brightness Kholin was several fingers taller than the man – apparently, the Alethi reputation for height was no exaggeration. Jasnah glanced at Shallan, noting her, then returned to her conversation.

Stormfather! This woman *was* the sister of a king. Reserved, statuesque, dressed immaculately in blue and silver. Like Shallan's dress, Jasnah's buttoned up the sides and had a high collar, though Jasnah had a much fuller chest than Shallan. The skirts were loose below the waist, falling generously to the floor. Her sleeves were long and stately, and the left one was buttoned up to hide her safehand.

On her freehand was a distinctive piece of jewelry: two rings and a bracelet connected by several chains, holding a triangular group of gemstones across the back of the hand. A Soulcaster – the word was used for both the people who performed the process and the fabrial that made it possible.

Shallan edged into the room, trying to get a better look at the large, glowing gemstones. Her heart began to beat a little faster. The Soulcaster looked identical to the one she and her brothers had found in the inside pocket of her father's coat.

Jasnah and the man in robes began walking in Shallan's direction, still talking. How would Jasnah react, now that her ward had finally caught up to her? Would she be angry because of Shallan's tardiness? Shallan couldn't be blamed for that, but people often expect irrational things from their inferiors.

Like the grand cavern outside, this hallway was cut from the rock, but it was more richly furbished, with ornate hanging chandeliers made with Stormlit gemstones. Most were deep violet garnets, which were among the less valuable stones. Even so, the sheer number hanging there glistening with violet light would make the chandelier worth a small fortune. More than that, however, Shallan was impressed with the symmetry of the design and the beauty of the pattern of crystals hanging at the sides of the chandelier.

As Jasnah grew near, Shallan could hear some of what she was saying. '... realize that this action might prompt an unfavorable reaction from the devotaries?' the woman said, speaking in Alethi. It was very near to Shallan's native Veden, and she'd been taught to speak it well during her childhood.

'Yes, Brightness,' said the robed man. He was elderly, with a wispy white beard, and had pale grey eyes. His open, kindly face seemed very concerned, and he wore a squat, cylindrical hat that matched the orange and white of his robes. Rich robes. Was this some kind of royal steward, perhaps?

No. Those gemstones on his fingers, the way he carried himself, the way other lighteyed attendants deferred to him ... *Stormfather!* Shallan thought. *This has to be the king himself!* Not Jasnah's brother, Elhokar, but the king of Kharbranth. Taravangian.

Shallan hastily performed an appropriate curtsy, which Jasnah noted.

'The ardents have much sway here, Your Majesty,' Jasnah said with a smooth voice.

'As do I,' the king said. 'You needn't worry about me.'

'Very well,' Jasnah said. 'Your terms are agreeable. Lead me to the location, and I shall see what can be done. If you will excuse me as we walk, however, I have someone to attend to.' Jasnah made a curt motion toward Shallan, waving her to join them.

'Of course, Brightness,' the king said. He seemed to defer to Jasnah. Kharbranth was a very small kingdom – just a single city – while Alethkar was one of the world's most powerful. An Alethi princess might well outrank a Kharbranthian king in real terms, however protocol would have it.

Shallan hurried to catch up to Jasnah, who walked a little behind the king as he began to speak to his attendants. 'Brightness,' Shallan said. 'I am Shallan Davar, whom you asked to meet you. I deeply regret not being able to get to you in Dumadari.'

'The fault was not yours,' Jasnah said with a wave of the fingers. 'I didn't expect that you would make it in time. I wasn't certain where I would be going after Dumadari when I sent you that note, however.'

Jasnah wasn't angry; that was a good sign. Shallan felt some of her anxiety recede.

'I am impressed by your tenacity, child,' Jasnah continued. 'I honestly didn't expect you to follow me this far. After Kharbranth, I was going to forgo leaving you notes, as I'd presumed that you'd have given up. Most do so after the first few stops.'

Most? Then it was a *test* of some sort? And Shallan had passed?

'Yes indeed,' Jasnah continued, voice musing. 'Perhaps I will actually allow you to petition me for a place as my ward.'

Shallan almost stumbled in shock. *Petition* her? Wasn't that what she'd already done? 'Brightness,' Shallan said, 'I thought that ... Well, your letter ...'

Jasnah eyed her. 'I gave you leave to *meet* me, Miss Davar. I did not promise to take you on. The training and care of a ward is a distraction for which I have little tolerance or time at the present. But you have traveled far. I will entertain your request, though understand that my requirements are strict.'

Shallan covered a grimace.

'No tantrum,' Jasnah noted. 'That is a good sign.'

'Tantrum, Brightness? From a lighteyed woman?'

'You'd be surprised,' Jasnah said dryly. 'But attitude alone will not earn your place. Tell me, how extensive is your education?'

'Extensive in some areas,' Shallan said. Then she hesitantly added, 'Extensively lacking in others.'

'Very well,' Jasnah said. Ahead, the king seemed to be in a hurry, but he was old enough that even an urgent walk was still slow. 'Then we shall do an evaluation. Answer truthfully and do not exaggerate, as I will soon discover your lies. Feign no false modesty, either. I haven't the patience for a simperer.'

'Yes, Brightness.'

'We shall begin with music. How would you judge your skill?'

'I have a good ear, Brightness,' Shallan said honestly. 'I'm best with voice, though I have been trained on the zither and the pipes. I would be far from the best you'd heard, but I'd also be far from the worst. I know most historical ballads by heart.'

'Give me the refrain from "Lilting Adrene."'

'Here?'

'I'm not fond of repeating myself, child.'

Shallan blushed, but began to sing. It wasn't her finest performance, but her tone was pure and she didn't stumble over any of the words.

'Good,' Jasnah said as Shallan paused for a breath. 'Languages?'

Shallan fumbled for a moment, bringing her attention away from frantically trying to remember the next verse. Languages? 'I can speak your native Alethi, obviously,' Shallan said. 'I have a passable reading knowledge of Thaylen and good spoken Azish. I can make myself understood in Selay, but not read it.'

Jasnah made no comment either way. Shallan began to grow nervous.

'Writing?' Jasnah asked.

'I know all of the major, minor, and topical glyphs and can paint them calligraphically.'

'So can most children.'

'The glyphwards that I paint are regarded by those who know me as quite impressive.'

'Glyphwards?' Jasnah said. 'I had reason to believe you wanted to be a scholar, not a purveyor of superstitious nonsense.'

'I have kept a journal since I was a child,' Shallan continued, 'in order to practice my writing skills.'

'Congratulations,' Jasnah said. 'Should I need someone to write a treatise on their stuffed pony or give an account of an interesting pebble they discovered, I shall send for you. Is there nothing you can offer that shows you have true skill?'

Shallan blushed. 'With all due respect, Brightness, you have a letter from me yourself, and it was persuasive enough to make you grant me this audience.'

'A valid point,' Jasnah said, nodding. 'It took you long enough to make it. How is your training in logic and its related arts?'

'I am accomplished in basic mathematics,' Shallan said, still flustered, 'and I often helped with minor accounts for my father. I have read through the complete works of Tormas, Nashan, Niali the Just, and – of course – Nohadon.'

'Placini?'

Who? 'No.'

'Gabrathin, Yustara, Manaline, Syasikk, Shauka-daughter-Hasweth?'

Shallan cringed and shook her head again. That last name was obviously Shin. Did the Shin people even *have* logicmasters? Did Jasnah really expect her wards to have studied such obscure texts?

'I see,' Jasnah said. 'Well, what of history?'

History. Shallan shrank down even further. 'I . . . This is one of the areas where I'm obviously deficient, Brightness. My father was never able to find a suitable tutor for me. I read the history books he owned. . . .'

'Which were?'

'The entire set of Barlesha Lhan's *Topics*, mostly.'

Jasnah waved her freehand dismissively. 'Barely worth the time spent scribing them. A popular survey of historical events at best.'

'I apologize, Brightness.'

'This is an embarrassing hole. History is *the* most important of the literary subarts. One would think that your parents would have taken specific care in this area, if they'd hoped to submit you to study under a historian like myself.'

'My circumstances are unusual, Brightness.'

'Ignorance is hardly unusual, Miss Davar. The longer I live, the more I come to realize that it is the natural state of the human mind. There are many who will strive to defend its sanctity and then expect you to be impressed with their efforts.'

Shallan blushed again. She'd realized she had some deficiencies, but Jasnah had unreasonable expectations. She said nothing, continuing to walk beside the taller woman. How long was this hallway, anyway? She was so flustered she didn't even look at the paintings they passed. They turned a corner, walking deeper into the mountainside.

'Well, let us move on to science, then,' Jasnah said, tone displeased. 'What can you say of yourself there?'

'I have the reasonable foundation in the sciences you might expect of a young woman my age,' Shallan said, more stiffly than she would have liked.

'Which means?'

'I can speak with skill about geography, geology, physics, and chemistry. I've made particular study of biology and botany, as I was able to pursue them with a reasonable level of independence on my father's estates. But if you expect me to be able to solve Fabrisan's Conundrum with a wave of my hand, I suspect you shall be disappointed.'

'Have I not a right to make reasonable demands of my potential students, Miss Davar?'

'Reasonable? Your demands are about as *reasonable* as the ones made of the Ten Heralds on Proving Day! With all due respect, Brightness, you seem to want potential wards to be master scholars already. I may be able to find a pair of eighty-year-old ardents in the city who *might* fit your requirements. They could interview for the position, though they may have trouble hearing well enough to answer your questions.'

'I see,' Jasnah replied. 'And do you speak with such pique to your parents as well?'

Shallan winced. Her time spent with the sailors had loosened her tongue far too much. Had she traveled all this way only to offend Jasnah? She thought of her brothers, destitute, keeping up a tenuous facade back home. Would she have to return to them in defeat, having squandered this opportunity? 'I did not speak to them this way, Brightness. Nor should I to you. I apologize.'

'Well, at least you are humble enough to admit fault. Still, I am disappointed. How is it that your mother considered you ready for a wardship?'

'My mother passed away when I was just a child, Brightness.'

'And your father soon remarried. Malise Gevelmar, I believe.'

Shallan started at her knowledge. House Davar was ancient, but only of middling power and importance. The fact that Jasnah knew the name of Shallan's stepmother said a lot about her. 'My stepmother passed away recently. She didn't send me to be your ward. I took this initiative upon myself.'

'My condolences,' Jasnah said. 'Perhaps you should be with your father, seeing to his estates and comforting him, rather than wasting my time.'

The men walking ahead turned down another side passage. Jasnah and Shallan followed, entering a smaller corridor with an ornate red and yellow rug, mirrors hanging on the walls.

Shallan turned to Jasnah. 'My father has no need of me.' Well, that was true. 'But I have great need of you, as this interview itself has proven. If ignorance galls you so much, can you in good conscience pass up the opportunity to rid me of mine?'

'I've done so before, Miss Davar. You are the twelfth young woman to ask me for a wardship this year.'

Twelve? Shallan thought. *In one year?* And she'd assumed that women would stay away from Jasnah because of her antagonism toward the devotaries.

The group reached the end of the narrow hallway, turning a corner to find – to Shallan's surprise – a place where a large chunk of rock had fallen from the ceiling. A dozen or so attendants stood here, some looking anxious. What was going on?

Much of the rubble had evidently been cleared away, though the gouge in the ceiling gaped ominously. It didn't look out on the sky; they had been progressing downward, and were probably far underground. A massive stone, taller than a man, had fallen into a doorway on the left. There was no getting past it into the room beyond. Shallan thought she heard sounds on the other side. The king stepped up to the stone, speaking in a comforting voice. He pulled a handkerchief out of his pocket and wiped his aged brow.

'The dangers of living in a building cut directly into the rock,' Jasnah said, striding forward. 'When did this happen?' Apparently she hadn't been summoned to the city specifically for this purpose; the king was simply taking advantage of her presence.

'During the recent highstorm, Brightness,' the king said. He shook his head, making his drooping, thin white mustache tremble. 'The palace architects might be able to cut a way into the room, but it would take time, and the next highstorm is scheduled to hit in just a few days. Beyond that, breaking in might bring down more of the ceiling.'

'I thought Kharbranth was protected from the highstorms, Your Majesty,' Shallan said, causing Jasnah to shoot her a glance.

'The city is sheltered, young woman,' the king said. 'But the stone mountain behind us is buffeted quite strongly. Sometimes it causes avalanches on that side, and that can cause the entire mountainside to shake.' He glanced at the ceiling. 'Cave-ins are very rare, and we thought this area was quite safe, but ... '

'But it is rock,' Jasnah said, 'and there is no telling if a weak vein lurks just beyond the surface.' She inspected the monolith that had fallen from the ceiling. 'This will be difficult. I will probably lose a very valuable focal stone.'

'I—' the king began, wiping his brow again. 'If only we had a Shard-blade—'

Jasnah cut him off with a wave of the hand. 'I was not seeking to renegotiate our bargain, Your Majesty. Access to the Palanaeum is worth the cost. You will want to send someone for wet rags. Have the majority of the servants move down to the other end of the hallway. You may wish to wait there yourself.'

'I will stay here,' the king said, causing his attendants to object, including a large man wearing a black leather cuirass, probably his bodyguard. The king silenced them by raising his wrinkled hand. 'I will not hide like a coward when my granddaughter is trapped.'

No wonder he was so anxious. Jasnah didn't argue further, and Shallan could see from her eyes that it was of no consequence to her if the king risked his life. The same apparently went for Shallan, for Jasnah didn't order her away. Servants approached with wetted cloths and distributed them. Jasnah refused hers. The king and his bodyguard raised theirs to their faces, covering mouth and nose.

Shallan took hers. What was the point of it? A couple of servants passed some wet cloths through a space between the rock and the wall to those inside. Then all of the servants rushed away down the hallway.

Jasnah picked and prodded at the boulder. 'Miss Davar,' she said, 'what method would you use to ascertain the mass of this stone?'

Shallan blinked. 'Well, I suppose I'd ask His Majesty. His architects probably calculated it.'

Jasnah cocked her head. 'An elegant response. Did they do that, Your Majesty?'

'Yes, Brightness Kholin,' the king said. 'It's roughly fifteen thousand kavals.'

Jasnah eyed Shallan. 'A point in your favor, Miss Davar. A scholar knows not to waste time rediscovering information already known. It's a lesson I sometimes forget.'

Shallan felt herself swell at the words. She already had an inkling that Jasnah did not give such praise lightly. Did this mean that the woman was still considering her as a ward?

Jasnah held up her freehand, Soulcaster glistening against the skin. Shallan felt her heartbeat speed up. She'd never seen Soulcasting done in person. The ardents were very secretive in using their fabrials, and she hadn't even known that her father had one until they'd found it on him. Of course, his no longer worked. That was one of the main reasons she was here.

The gemstones set into Jasnah's Soulcaster were enormous, some of the largest that Shallan had ever seen, worth many spheres each. One was smoke-stone, a pure glassy black gemstone. The second was a diamond. The third was a ruby. All three were cut – a cut stone could hold more Stormlight – into glistening, many-faceted oval shapes.

Jasnah closed her eyes, pressing her hand against the fallen boulder. She raised her head, inhaling slowly. The stones on the back of her hand began to glow more fiercely, the smokestone in particular growing so bright it was difficult to look at.

Shallan held her breath. The only thing she dared do was blink, committing the scene to memory. For a long, extended moment, nothing happened.

And then, briefly, Shallan heard a sound. A low thrumming, like a distant group of voices, humming together a single, pure note.

Jasnah's hand *sank* into the rock.

The stone vanished

A burst of dense black smoke exploded into the hallway. Enough to blind Shallan; it seemed the output of a thousand fires, and smelled of burned wood. Shallan hastily raised the wet rag to her face, dropping to her knees. Oddly, her ears felt stopped up, as if she'd climbed down from a great height. She had to swallow to pop them.

She shut her eyes tightly as they began to water, and she held her breath. Her ears filled with a rushing sound.

It passed. She blinked open her eyes to find the king and his bodyguard huddled against the wall beside her. Smoke still pooled at the ceiling; the hallway smelled strongly of it. Jasnah stood, eyes still closed, oblivious of the smoke – though grime now dusted her face and clothing. It had left marks on the walls too.

Shallan had read of this, but she was still in awe. Jasnah had transformed the boulder into smoke, and since smoke was far less dense than stone, the change had pushed the smoke away in an explosive outburst.

It was true; Jasnah really *did* have a functioning Soulcaster. And a powerful one too. Nine out of ten Soulcasters were capable of a few limited transformations: creating water or grain from stone; forming bland, single-roomed rock buildings out of air or cloth. A greater one, like Jasnah's, could effectuate any transformation. Literally turn any substance into any other one. How it must grate on the ardents that such a powerful, holy relic was in the hands of someone outside the ardentia. And a heretic no less!

Shallan stumbled to her feet, leaving the cloth at her mouth, breathing humid but dust-free air. She swallowed, her ears popping again as the hall's pressure returned to normal. A moment later, the king rushed into the now-accessible room. A small girl – along with several nursemaids and other palace servants – sat on the other side, coughing. The king pulled the girl into his arms. She was too young to have a modesty sleeve.

Jasnah opened her eyes, blinking, as if momentarily confused by her location. She took a deep breath, and didn't cough. Indeed, she actually *smiled*, as if enjoying the scent of the smoke.

Jasnah turned to Shallan, focusing on her. 'You are still waiting for a response. I'm afraid you will not like what I say.'

'But you haven't finished your testing of me yet,' Shallan said, forcing herself to be bold. 'Surely you won't give judgment until you have.'

'I haven't finished?' Jasnah asked, frowning.

'You didn't ask me about all of the feminine arts. You left out painting and drawing.'

'I have never had much use for them.'

'But *they* are of the arts,' Shallan said, feeling desperate. This was where she was most accomplished! 'Many consider the visual arts the most refined of them all. I brought my portfolio. I would show you what I can do.'

Jasnah pursed her lips. 'The visual arts are frivolity. I have weighed the facts, child, and I cannot accept you. I'm sorry.'

Shallan's heart sank.

'Your Majesty,' Jasnah said to the king, 'I would like to go to the Palanaeum.'

'Now?' the king said, cradling his granddaughter. 'But we are going to have a feast—'

'I appreciate the offer,' Jasnah said, 'but I find myself with an abundance of everything *but* time.'

'Of course,' the king said. 'I will take you personally. Thank you for what you've done. When I heard that you had requested entrance . . .' He continued to babble at Jasnah, who followed him wordlessly down the hallway, leaving Shallan behind.

She clutched her satchel to her chest, lowering the cloth from her mouth. Six months of chasing, for this. She gripped the rag in frustration, squeezing sooty water between her fingers. She wanted to cry. That was what she probably would have done if she'd been that same child she had been six months ago.

But things had changed. *She* had changed. If she failed, House Davar would fall. Shallan felt her determination redouble, though she wasn't able to stop a few tears of frustration from squeezing out of the corners of her eyes. She was not going to give up until Jasnah was forced to truss her up in chains and have the authorities drag her away.

Her step surprisingly firm, she walked in the direction Jasnah had gone. Six months ago, she had explained a desperate plan to her brothers. She would apprentice herself to Jasnah Kholin, scholar, heretic. Not for the education. Not for the prestige. But in order to learn where she kept her Soulcaster.

And then Shallan would steal it.

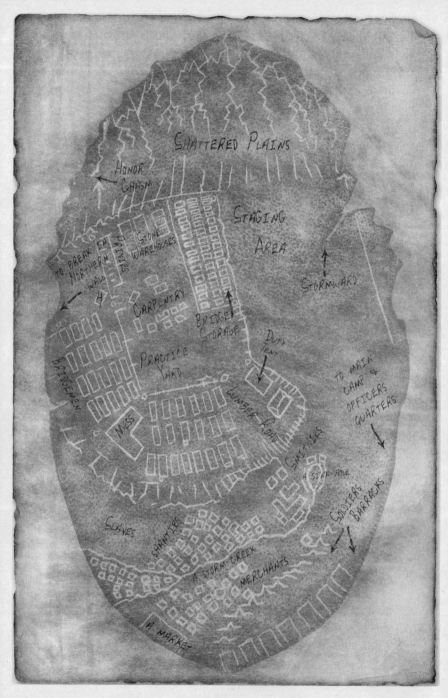

Charcoal rubbing of a map of Sadeas's warcamp as used by a common spearman. It was scratched on the back of a palm-sized cremling shell. Rubbing labeled in ink by an anonymous Alethi scholar, circa 1173.

6

BRIDGE FOUR

'I'm cold. Mother. I'm cold. Mother? Why can I still hear the rain? Will it stop?'

—Collected on Vevishes, 1172, 32 seconds pre-death. Subject was a light-eyed female child, approximately six years old.

Tvlakv released all of the slaves from their cages at once. This time, he didn't fear runaways or a slave rebellion – not with nothing but wilderness behind them and over a hundred thousand armed soldiers just ahead.

Kaladin stepped down from the wagon. They were inside one of the craterlike formations, its jagged stone wall rising just to the east. The ground had been cleared of plant life, and the rock was slick beneath his unshod feet. Pools of rainwater had gathered in depressions. The air was crisp and clean, and the sun strong overhead, though with this Eastern humidity, he always felt damp.

Around them spread the signs of an army long settled; this war had been going on since the old king's death, nearly six years ago. Everyone told stories of that night, the night when Parshendi tribesmen had murdered King Gavilar.

Squads of soldiers marched by, following directions indicated by painted circles at each intersection. The camp was packed with long stone bunkers, and there were more tents than Kaladin had discerned from above. Soulcasters couldn't be used to create every shelter. After the stink of the slave caravan, the place smelled good, brimming with familiar scents like treated leather and oiled weapons. However, many of the soldiers had a disorderly look. They weren't dirty, but they didn't seem particularly disciplined either. They roamed the camp in packs with coats undone. Some pointed and jeered at the slaves. This was the army of a highprince? The elite force that fought for Alethkar's honor? This was what Kaladin had aspired to join?

Bluth and Tag watched carefully as Kaladin lined up with the other slaves, but he didn't try anything. Now was not the time to provoke them—Kaladin had seen how mercenaries acted when around commissioned troops. Bluth and Tag played their part, walking with their chests out and hands on their weapons. They shoved a few of the slaves into place, ramming a cudgel into one man's belly and cursing him gruffly.

They stayed clear of Kaladin.

'The king's army,' said the slave next to him. It was the dark-skinned man who had talked to Kaladin about escaping. 'I thought we were meant for mine work. Why, this won't be so bad at all. We'll be cleaning latrines or maintaining roads.'

Odd, to look forward to latrine work or labor in the hot sun. Kaladin hoped for something else. Hoped. Yes, he'd discovered that he could still hope. A spear in his hands. An enemy to face. He could live like that.

Tvlakv spoke with an important-looking lighteyed woman. She wore her dark hair up in a complex weave, sparkling with infused amethysts, and her dress was a deep crimson. She looked much as Laral had, at the end. She was probably of the fourth or fifth dahn, wife and scribe to one of the camp's officers.

Tvlakv began to brag about his wares, but the woman raised a delicate hand. 'I can see what I am purchasing, slaver,' she said in a smooth, aristocratic accent. 'I will inspect them myself.'

She began to walk down the line, accompanied by several soldiers. Her dress was cut in the Alethi noble fashion – a solid swath of silk, tight and formfitting through the top with sleek skirts below. It buttoned up the sides of the torso from waist to neck, where it was topped by a small, gold-embroidered collar. The longer left cuff hid her safehand. Kaladin's mother had always just worn a glove, which seemed far more practical to him.

Judging by her face, she was not particularly impressed with what she saw. 'These men are half-starved and sickly,' she said, taking a thin rod from a young female attendant. She used it to lift the hair from one man's forehead, inspecting his brand. 'You are asking two emerald broams a head?'

Tvlakv began to sweat. 'Perhaps one and a half?'

'And what would I use them for? I wouldn't trust men this filthy near food, and we have parshmen to do most other work.'

'If Your Ladyship is not pleased, I could approach other high-princes . . . .'

'No' she said smacking the slave she'd been regarding as he shied away from her. 'One and a quarter. They can help cut timber for us in the northern forests . . . .' She trailed off as she noticed Kaladin. 'Here now. This is far better stock than the others.'

'I thought that you might like this one,' Tvlakv said, stepping up to her. 'He *is* quite—'

She raised the rod and silenced Tvlakv. She had a small sore on one lip. Some ground cussweed root could help with that.

'Remove your top, slave,' she commanded.

Kaladin stared her right in her blue eyes and felt an almost irresistible urge to spit at her. No. No, he couldn't afford that. Not when there was a chance. He pulled his arms out of the sacklike clothing, letting it fall to his waist, exposing his chest.

Despite eight months as a slave, he was far better muscled than the others. 'A large number of scars for one so young,' the noblewoman said thoughtfully. 'You are a military man?'

'Yes.' His windspren zipped up to the woman, inspecting her face.

'Mercenary?'

'Amaram's army,' Kaladin said. 'A citizen, second nahn.'

'*Once* a citizen,' Tvlakv put in quickly. 'He was—'

She silenced Tvlakv again with her rod, glaring at him. Then she used the rod to push aside Kaladin's hair and inspect his forehead.

'*Shash* glyph,' she said, clicking her tongue. Several of the soldiers nearby stepped closer, hands on their swords. 'Where I come from, slaves who deserve these are simply executed.'

'They are fortunate,' Kaladin said.

'And how did you end up here?'

'I killed someone,' Kaladin said, preparing his lies carefully. *Please*, he thought to the Heralds. *Please*. It had been a long time since he had prayed for anything.

The woman raised an eyebrow.

'I'm a murderer, Brightness,' Kaladin said. 'Got drunk, made some mistakes. But I can use a spear as well as any man. Put me in your bright-lord's army. Let me fight again.' It was a strange lie to make, but the woman would never let Kaladin fight if she thought he was a deserter. In this case, better to be known as an accidental murderer.

Please . . . he thought. To be a soldier again. It seemed, in one moment, the most glorious thing he could ever have wanted. How much better it would be to die on the battlefield than waste away emptying chamber pots.

To the side, Tvlakv stepped up beside the lighteyed woman. He glanced at Kaladin, then sighed. 'He's a deserter, Brightness. Don't listen to him.'

No! Kaladin felt a blazing burst of anger consume his hope. He raised hands toward Tvlakv. He'd strangle the rat, and—

Something cracked him across the back. He grunted, stumbling and falling to one knee. The noblewoman stepped back, raising her safehand to her breast in alarm. One of the army soldiers grabbed Kaladin and towed him back to his feet.

'Well,' she finally said. 'That is unfortunate.'

'I *can* fight,' Kaladin growled against the pain. 'Give me a spear. Let me—'

She raised her rod, cutting him off.

'Brightness,' Tvlakv said, not meeting Kaladin's eyes. 'I would not trust him with a weapon. It is true that he is a murderer, but he is also known to disobey and lead rebellions against his masters. I couldn't sell him to you as a bonded soldier. My conscience, it would not allow it.' He hesitated. 'The men in his wagon, he might have corrupted them all with talk of escape. My honor demands that I tell you this.'

Kaladin gritted his teeth. He was tempted to try to take down the soldier behind him, grab that spear and spend his last moments ramming it through Tvlakv's portly gut. Why? What did it matter to Tvlakv how Kaladin was treated by this army?

94

I should never have ripped up the map, Kaladin though. *Bitterness is repaid more often than kindness.* One of his father's sayings.

The woman nodded, moving on. 'Show me which ones,' she said. 'I'll still take them, because of your honesty. We need some new bridgemen.'

Tvlakv nodded eagerly. Before moving on, he paused and leaned in to Kaladin. 'I cannot trust that you will behave. The people in this army, they will blame a merchant for not revealing all he knew. I ... am sorry.' With that, the merchant scuttled away.

Kaladin growled in the back of his throat, and then pulled himself free of the soldiers, but remained in line. So be it. Cutting down trees, building bridges, fighting in the army. None of it mattered. He would just keep living. They'd taken his freedom, his family, his friends, and – most dear of all – his dreams. They could do nothing more to him.

After her inspection, the noblewoman took a writing board from her assistant and made a few quick notations on its paper. Tvlakv gave her a ledger detailing how much each slave had paid down on their slave debt. Kaladin caught a glimpse; it said that not a single one of the men had paid anything. Perhaps Tvlakv lied about the figures. Not unlikely.

Kaladin would probably just let all of his wages go to his debt this time. Let them squirm as they saw him actually call their bluff. What would they do if he got close to earning out his debt? He'd probably never find out – depending on what these bridgemen earned, it could take anything from ten to fifty years to get there.

The lighteyed woman assigned most of the slaves to forest duty. A halfdozen of the more spindly ones were sent to work the mess halls, despite what she'd said before. 'Those ten,' the noblewoman said, raising her rod to point at Kaladin and the others from his wagon. 'Take them to the bridge crews. Tell Lamaril and Gaz that the tall one is to be given special treatment.'

The soldiers laughed, and one began shoving Kaladin's group along the pathway. Kaladin endured it; these men had no reason to be gentle, and he wouldn't give them a reason to be rougher. If there was a group citizen soldiers hated more than mercenaries, it was deserters.

As he walked, he couldn't help noticing the banner flying above the camp. It bore the same symbol emblazoned on the soldiers' uniform coats: a yellow glyphpair in the shape of a tower and a hammer on a field of deep green. That was the banner of Highprince Sadeas, ultimate ruler of

Kaladin's own home district. Was it irony or fate that had landed Kaladin here?

Soldiers lounged idly, even those who appeared to be on duty, and the camp streets were littered with refuse. Camp followers were plentiful: whores, worker women, coopers, chandlers, and wranglers. There were even children running through the streets of what was half city, half warcamp.

There were also parshmen. Carrying water, working on trenches, lifting sacks. That surprised him. Weren't they fighting parshmen? Weren't they worried that these would rise up? Apparently not. The parshmen here worked with the same docility as the ones back in Hearthstone. Perhaps it made sense. Alethi had fought against Alethi back in his armies at home, so why shouldn't there be parshmen on both sides of this conflict?

The soldiers took Kaladin all the way around to the northeastern quarter of the camp, a hike that took some time. Though the Soulcast stone barracks each looked exactly the same, the rim of the camp was broken distinctively, like ragged mountains. Old habits made him memorize the route. Here, the towering circular wall had been worn away by countless high-storms, giving a clear view eastward. That open patch of ground would make a good staging area for an army to gather on before marching down the incline to the Shattered Plains themselves.

The northern edge of the field contained a subcamp filled with several dozen barracks, and at their center a lumberyard filled with carpenters. They were breaking down some of the stout trees Kaladin had seen on the plains outside: stripping off their stringy bark, sawing them into planks. Another group of carpenters assembled the planks into large contraptions.

'We're to be woodworkers?' Kaladin asked.

One of the soldiers laughed roughly. 'You're joining the bridge crews.' He pointed to where a group of sorry-looking men sat on the stones in the shade of a barrack, scooping food out of wooden bowls with their fingers. It looked depressingly similar to the slop that Tvlakv had fed them.

One of the soldiers shoved Kaladin forward again, and he stumbled down the shallow incline and crossed the grounds. The other nine slaves followed, herded by the soldiers. None of the men sitting around the barracks so much as glanced at them. They wore leather vests and simple trousers, some with dirty laced shirts, others bare-chested. The grim, sorry lot weren't much better than the slaves, though they did look to be in slightly better physical condition.

'New recruits, Gaz,' one of the soldiers called.

A man lounged in the shade a distance from the eating men. He turned, revealing a face that was so scarred his beard grew in patches. He was missing one eye – the other was brown – and didn't bother with an eye patch. White knots at his shoulders marked him as a sergeant, and he had the lean toughness Kaladin had learned to associate with someone who knew his way around a battlefield.

'These spindly things?' Gaz said, chewing on something as he walked over. 'They'll barely stop an arrow.'

The soldier beside Kaladin shrugged, shoving him forward once more for good measure. 'Brightness Hashal said to do something special with this one. The rest are up to you.' The soldier nodded to his companions, and they began to trot away.

Gaz looked the slaves over. He focused on Kaladin last.

'I have military training,' Kaladin said. 'In the army of Highlord Amaram.'

'I don't really care,' Gaz cut in, spitting something dark to the side.

Kaladin hesitated. 'When Amaram—'

'You keep mentioning that name,' Gaz snapped. 'Served under some unimportant landlord, did you? Expect me to be impressed?'

Kaladin sighed. He'd met this kind of man before, a lesser sergeant with no hope of advancement. His only pleasure in life came from his authority over those even sorrier than himself. Well, so be it.

'You have a slave's mark,' Gaz said, snorting. 'I doubt you ever held a spear. Either way, you'll have to condescend to join us now, Lordship.'

Kaladin's windspren flitted down and inspected Gaz, then closed one of her eyes, imitating him. For some reason, seeing her made Kaladin smile. Gaz misinterpreted the smile. The man scowled and stepped forward, pointing.

At that moment, a loud chorus of horns echoed through the camp. Carpenters glanced up, and the soldiers who had guided Kaladin dashed back toward the center of camp. The slaves behind Kaladin looked around anxiously.

'Stormfather!' Gaz cursed. 'Bridgemen! Up, up, you louts!' He began kicking at some of the men who were eating. They scattered their bowls, scrambling to their feet. They wore simple sandals instead of proper boots.

'You, Lordship,' Gaz said, pointing at Kaladin.

'I didn't say—'

'I don't care what in Damnation you said! You're in Bridge Four.' He pointed at a group of departing bridgemen. 'The rest of you, go wait over there. I'll divide you up later. Get moving, or I'll see you strung up by your heels.'

Kaladin shrugged and jogged after the group of bridgemen. It was one of many teams of such men pouring out of barracks or picking themselves up out of alleys. There seemed to be quite a lot of them. Around fifty barracks, with – perhaps – twenty or thirty men in each … that would make nearly as many bridgemen in this army as there had been soldiers in Amaram's entire force.

Kaladin's team crossed the grounds, weaving between boards and piles of sawdust, approaching a large wooden contraption. It had obviously weathered a few highstorms and some battles. The dents and holes scattered along its length looked like places where arrows had struck. The bridge in bridgeman, perhaps?

Yes, Kaladin thought. It was a wooden bridge, over thirty feet long, eight feet wide. It sloped down at the front and back, and had no railings. The wood was thick, with the largest boards for support through the center. There were some forty or fifty bridges lined up here. Perhaps one for each barrack, making one crew for each bridge? About twenty bridge crews were gathering at this point.

Gaz had found himself a wooden shield and a gleaming mace, but there were none for anyone else. He quickly inspected each team. He stopped beside Bridge Four and hesitated. 'Where's your bridgeleader?' he demanded.

'Dead,' one of the bridgemen said. 'Tossed himself down the Honor Chasm last night.'

Gaz cursed. 'Can't you keep a bridgeleader for even a week? Storm it! Line up; I'll run near you. Listen for my commands. We'll sort out another bridgeleader after we see who survives.' Gaz pointed at Kaladin. 'You're at the back, lordling. The rest of you, get moving! Storm you, I won't suffer another reprimand because of you fools! Move, move!'

The others were lifting. Kaladin had no choice but to go to the open slot at the tail of the bridge. He'd been a little low in his assessment; looked like about thirty-five to forty men per bridge. There was room for five men across – three under the bridge and one on each side – and eight deep, though this crew didn't have a man for each position.

He helped lift the bridge into the air. They were probably using a very light wood for the bridges, but the thing was still storms-cursed heavy. Kaladin grunted as he struggled with the weight, hoisting the bridge up high and then stepping underneath. Men dashed in to fill the middle slots down the length of the structure, and slowly they all set the bridge down on their shoulders. At least there were rods on the bottom to use as hand-holds.

The other men had pads on the shoulders of their vests to cushion the weight and adjust their height to fit the supports. Kaladin hadn't been given a vest, so the wooden supports dug directly into his skin. He couldn't see a thing; there was an indentation for his head, but wood cut off his view to all sides. The men at the edges had better views; he suspected those spots were more coveted.

The wood smelled of oil and sweat.

'Go!' Gaz said from outside, voice muffled.

Kaladin grunted as the crew broke into a jog. He couldn't see where he was going, and struggled to keep from tripping as the bridge crew marched down the eastern slope to the Shattered Plains. Soon, Kaladin was sweating and cursing under his breath, the wood rubbing and digging into the skin on his shoulders. He was already starting to bleed.

'Poor fool,' a voice said from the side.

Kaladin glanced to the right, but the wooden handholds obstructed his view. 'Are you . . . ' Kaladin puffed. 'Are you talking to me?'

'You shouldn't have insulted Gaz,' the man said. His voice sounded hollow. 'He sometimes lets new men run in an outside row. Sometimes.'

Kaladin tried to respond, but he was already gasping for breath. He'd thought himself in better shape than this, but he'd spent eight months being fed slop, being beaten, and waiting out highstorms in leaking cellars, muddy barns, or cages. He was hardly the same man anymore.

'Breathe in and out deeply,' said the muffled voice. 'Focus on the steps. Count them. It helps.'

Kaladin followed the advice. He could hear other bridge crews running nearby. Behind them came the familiar sounds of men marching and hoofbeats on the stone. They were being followed by an army.

Below, rockbuds and small shalebark ridges grew from the stone, tripping him. The landscape of the Shattered Plains appeared to be broken, uneven, and rent, covered with outcroppings and shelves of rock. That explained why they didn't use wheels on the bridges – porters were probably much faster over such rough terrain.

Soon, his feet were ragged and battered. Couldn't they have given him shoes? He set his jaw against the agony and kept on going. Just another job. He would continue, and he would survive.

A thumping sound. His feet fell on wood. A bridge, a permanent one, crossing a chasm between plateaus on the Shattered Plains. In seconds the bridge crew was across it, and his feet fell on stone again.

'Move, move!' Gaz bellowed. 'Storm you, keep going!'

They continued jogging as the army crossed the bridge behind them, hundreds of boots resounding on the wood. Before too long, blood ran down Kaladin's shoulders. His breathing was torturous, his side aching painfully. He could hear others gasping, the sounds carrying through the confined space beneath the bridge. So he wasn't the only one. Hopefully, they would arrive at their destination quickly.

He hoped in vain.

The next hour was torture. It was worse than any beating he'd suffered as a slave, worse than any wound on the battlefield. There seemed to be no end to the march. Kaladin vaguely remembered seeing the permanent bridges, back when he'd looked down on the plains from the slave cart. They connected the plateaus where the chasms were easiest to span, not where it would be most efficient for those traveling. That often meant detours north or south before they could continue eastward.

The bridgemen grumbled, cursed, groaned, then fell silent. They crossed bridge after bridge, plateau after plateau. Kaladin never got a good look at one of the chasms. He just kept running. And running. He couldn't feel his feet any longer. He kept running. He knew, somehow, that if he stopped, he'd be beaten. He felt as if his shoulders had been rubbed to the bone. He tried counting steps, but was too exhausted even for that.

But he didn't stop running.

Finally, mercifully, Gaz called for them to halt. Kaladin blinked, stumbling to a stop and nearly collapsing.

'Lift!' Gaz bellowed.

The men lifted, Kaladin's arms straining at the motion after so much time holding the bridge in one place.

'Drop!'

They stepped aside, the bridgemen underneath taking handholds at the sides. It was awkward and difficult, but these men had practice, apparently. They kept the bridge from toppling as they set it on the ground.

'Push!'

Kaladin stumbled back in confusion as the men pushed at their handholds on the side or back of the bridge. They were at the edge of a chasm lacking a permanent bridge. To the sides, the other bridge crews were pushing their own bridges forward.

Kaladin glanced over his shoulder. The army was two thousand men in forest green and pure white. Twelve hundred darkeyed spearmen, several hundred cavalry atop rare, precious horses. Behind them, a large group of heavy foot, lighteyed men in thick armor and carrying large maces and square steel shields.

It seemed that they'd intentionally chosen a point where the chasm was narrow and the first plateau was a little higher than the second. The bridge was twice as long as the chasm's width here. Gaz cursed at him, so Kaladin joined the others, shoving the bridge across the rough ground with a scraping sound. When the bridge thumped into place on the other side of the chasm, the bridge crew drew back to let the cavalry trot across.

He was too exhausted to watch. He collapsed to the stones and lay back, listening to sounds of foot soldiers tromping across the bridge. He rolled his head to the side. The other bridgemen had lain down as well. Gaz walked among the various crews, shaking his head, his shield on his back as he muttered about their worthlessness.

Kaladin longed to lie there, staring at the sky, oblivious of the world. His training, however, warned that might cause him to cramp up. That would make the return trip even worse. That training ... it belonged to another man, from another time. Almost from the shadowdays. But while Kaladin might not *be* him any longer, he could still *heed* him.

And so, with a groan, Kaladin forced himself to sit up and begin rubbing his muscles. Soldiers crossed the bridge four across, spears held high, shields forward. Gaz watched them with obvious envy, and Kaladin's windspren danced around the man's head. Despite his fatigue, Kaladin felt a moment of jealousy. Why was she bothering that blowhard instead of Kaladin?

After a few minutes, Gaz noticed Kaladin and scowled at him.

'He's wondering why you aren't lying down,' said a familiar voice. The man who had been running beside Kaladin lay on the ground a short distance away, staring up at the sky. He was older, with greying hair, and he had a long, leathery face to complement his kindly voice. He looked as exhausted as Kaladin felt.

Kaladin kept rubbing his legs, pointedly ignoring Gaz. Then he ripped off some portions of his sacklike clothing and bound his feet and shoulders. Fortunately, he was accustomed to walking barefoot as a slave, so the damage wasn't too bad.

As he finished, the last of the foot soldiers passed over the bridge. They were followed by several mounted lighteyes in gleaming armor. At their center rode a man in majestic, burnished red Shardplate. It was distinct from the one other Kaladin had seen – each suit was said to be an individual work of art – but it had the same *feel*. Ornate, interlocking, topped by a beautiful helm with an open visor.

The armor felt *alien* somehow. It had been crafted in another epoch, a time when gods had walked Roshar.

'Is that the king?' Kaladin asked.

The leathery bridgeman laughed tiredly. 'We could only wish.'

Kaladin turned toward him, frowning.

'If that were the king,' the bridgeman said, 'then that would mean we were in Brightlord Dalinar's army.'

The name was vaguely familiar to Kaladin. 'He's a highprince, right? The king's uncle?'

'Aye. The best of men, the most honorable Shardbearer in the king's army. They say he's never broken his word.'

Kaladin sniffed in disdain. Much the same had been said about Amaram.

'You should wish to be in Highprince Dalinar's force, lad,' the older man said. 'He doesn't use bridge crews. Not like these, at least.'

'All right, you cremlings!' Gaz bellowed. 'On your feet!'

The bridgemen groaned, stumbling upright. Kaladin sighed. The brief rest had been just enough to show how exhausted he was. 'I'll be glad to get back,' he muttered.

'Back?' the leathery bridgeman said.

'We aren't turning around?'

His friend chuckled wryly. 'Lad, we aren't *nearly* there yet. Be glad we aren't. Arriving is the worst part.'

And so the nightmare began its second phase. They crossed the bridge, pulled it over behind them, then lifted it up on sore shoulders once more. They jogged across the plateau. At the other side, they lowered the bridge again to span another chasm. The army crossed, then it was back to carrying the bridge again.

They repeated this a good dozen times. They did get to rest between carries, but Kaladin was so sore and overworked that the brief respites weren't enough. He barely caught his breath each time before being forced to pick up the bridge again.

They were expected to be quick about it. The bridgemen got to rest while the army crossed, but they had to make up the time by jogging across the plateaus – passing the ranks of soldiers – so that they could arrive at the next chasm before the army. At one point, his leathery-faced friend warned him that if they didn't have their bridge in place quickly enough, they'd be punished with whippings when they returned to camp.

Gaz gave orders, cursing the bridgemen, kicking them when they moved too slowly, never doing any real work. It did take long for Kaladin to nurture a seething hatred of the scrawny, scar-faced man. That was odd; he hadn't felt hatred for his other sergeants. It was their *job* to curse at the men and keep them motivated.

That wasn't what burned Kaladin. Gaz had sent him on this trip without sandals or a vest. Despite his bandages, Kaladin would bear scars from his work this day. He'd be so bruised and stiff in the morning that he'd be unable to walk.

What Gaz had done was the mark of a petty bully. He risked the mission by losing a carrier, all because of a hasty grudge.

Storming man, Kaladin thought, using his hatred of Gaz to sustain him through the ordeal. Several times after pushing the bridge into place, Kaladin collapsed, feeling sure he'd never be able to stand again. But when Gaz called for them to rise, Kaladin somehow struggled to his feet. It was either that or let Gaz win.

Why were they going through all of this? What was the point? Why were they running so much? They had to protect their bridge, the precious weight, the cargo. They had to hold up the sky and run, they had to . . .

He was growing delirious. Feet, running. One, two, one, two, one, two.

'Stop!'

He stopped.

'Lift!'

He raised his hands up.

'Drop!'

He stepped back, then lowered the bridge.

'Push!'

He pushed the bridge.

Die.

That last command was his own, added each time. He fell back to the stone, a rockbud hastily withdrawing its vines as he touched them. He closed his eyes, no longer able to care about cramps. He entered a trance, a kind of half sleep, for what seemed like one heartbeat.

'Rise!'

He stood, stumbling on bloody feet.

'Cross!'

He crossed, not bothering to look at the deadly drop on either side.

'Pull!'

He grabbed a handhold and pulled the bridge across the chasm after him.

'Switch!'

Kaladin stood up dumbly. He didn't understand that command; Gaz had never given it before. The troops were forming ranks, moving with that mixture of skittishness and forced relaxation that men often went through before a battle. A few anticipationspren – like red streamers, growing from the ground and whipping in the wind – began to sprout from the rock and wave among the soldiers.

A battle?

Gaz grabbed Kaladin's shoulder and shoved him to the front of the bridge. 'Newcomers get to go first at this part, Your Lordship.' The sergeant smiled wickedly.

Kaladin dumbly picked up the bridge with the others, raising it over his head. The handholds were the same here, but this front row had a notched opening before his face, allowing him to see out. All of the bridgemen had changed positions; the men who had been running in the front moved to the back, and those at the back – including Kaladin and the leathery-faced bridgeman – moved to the front.

Kaladin didn't ask the point of it. He didn't care. He liked the front, though; jogging was easier now that he could see ahead of him.

The landscape on the plateaus was that of rough stormlands; there were scattered patches of grass, but the stone here was too hard for their seeds to fully burrow into. Rockbuds were more common, growing like bubbles across the entire plateau, imitating rocks about the size of a man's head. Many of the buds were split, trailing out their vines like thick green tongues. A few were even in bloom.

After so many hours breathing in the stuffy confines beneath the bridge, running in the front was almost relaxing. Why had they given such a wonderful position to a newcomer?

'Talenelat'Elin, bearer of all agonies,' said the man to his right, voice horrified. 'It's going to be a bad one. They're already lined up! It's going to be a bad one!'

Kaladin blinked, focusing on the approaching chasm. On the other side of the rift stood a rank of men with marbled crimson and black skin. They were wearing a strange rusty orange armor that covered their forearms, chests, heads, and legs. It took his numbed mind a moment to understand.

The Parshendi.

They weren't like common parshman workers. They were far more muscular, far more *solid*. They had the bulky build of soldiers, and each one carried a weapon strapped to his back. Some wore dark red and black beards tied with bits of rock, while others were clean-shaven.

As Kaladin watched, the front row of Parshendi knelt down. They held shortbows, arrows nocked. Not longbows intended to launch arrows high and far. Short, recurve bows to fire straight and quick and strong. An excellent bow to use for killing a group of bridgemen before they could lay their bridge.

Arriving is the worst part . . . .

Now, finally, the *real* nightmare began.

Gaz hung back, bellowing at the bridge crews to keep going. Kaladin's instincts screamed at him to get out of the line of fire, but the momentum of the bridge forced him forward. Forced him down the throat of the beast itself, its teeth poised to snap closed.

Kaladin's exhaustion and pain fled. He was shocked alert. The bridges charged forward, the men beneath them screaming as they ran. Ran toward death.

The archers released.

The first wave killed Kaladin's leathery-faced friend, dropping him with three separate arrows. The man to Kaladin's left fell as well–Kaladin hadn't even seen his face. That man cried out as he dropped, not dead immediately, but the bridge crew trampled him. The bridge got noticeably heavier as men died.

The Parshendi calmly drew a second volley and launched. To the side, Kaladin barely noticed another of the bridge crews floundering. The Parshendi seemed to focus their fire on certain crews. That one got a full wave of arrows from dozens of archers, and the first three rows of bridge-men dropped and tripped those behind them. Their bridge lurched, skidding on the ground and making a sickening crunch as the mass of bodies fell over one another.

Arrows zipped past Kaladin, killing the other two men in the front line with him. Several other arrows smacked into the wood around him, one slicing open the skin of his cheek.

He screamed. In horror, in shock, in pain, in sheer bewilderment. Never before had he felt so powerless in a battle. He'd charged enemy fortifications, he'd run beneath waves of arrows, but he'd always felt a measure of control. He'd had his spear, he'd had his shield, he could fight back.

Not this time. The bridge crews were like hogs running to the slaughter.

A third volley flew, and another of the twenty bridge crews fell. Waves of arrows came from the Alethi side as well, falling and striking the Parshendi. Kaladin's bridge was almost to the chasm. He could see the black eyes of the Parshendi on the other side, could make out the features of their lean marbled faces. All around him, bridgemen were screaming in pain, arrows cutting them out from underneath their bridges. There was a crashing sound as another bridge dropped, its bridgemen slaughtered.

Behind, Gaz called out. 'Lift and down, you fools!'

The bridge crew lurched to a stop as the Parshendi launched another volley. Men behind Kaladin screamed. The Parshendi firing was interrupted by a return volley from the Alethi army. Though he was shocked senseless, Kaladin's reflexes knew what do to. Drop the bridge, get into position to push.

This exposed the bridgemen who had been safe in the back ranks. The Parshendi archers obviously knew this was coming; they prepared and launched one final volley. Arrows struck the bridge in a wave, dropping a half-dozen men, spraying blood across the dark wood. Fearspren – wiggling and violet – sprang up through the wood and wriggled in the air. The bridge lurched, growing much harder to push as they suddenly lost those men

Kaladin stumbled, hands slipping. He fell to his knees and pitched out, leaning over the chasm. He barely managed to catch himself.

He teetered, one hand dangling above the void, the other gripping the edge. His overextended mind wavered with vertigo as he stared down that sheer cliff, down into darkness. The height was beautiful; he'd always loved climbing high rock formations with Tien.

By reflex, he shoved himself back onto the plateau, scrambling backward. A group of foot soldiers, protected by shields, had taken up positions pushing the bridge. The army's archers exchanged arrows with the Parshendi as the soldiers pushed the bridge into place and heavy cavalry thundered across, smashing into the Parshendi. Four bridges had fallen, but sixteen had been placed in a row, allowing for an effective charge.

Kaladin tried to move, tried to crawl away from the bridge. But he just collapsed where he was, his body refusing to obey. He couldn't even roll over onto his stomach.

I should go . . . he thought in exhaustion. *See if that leathery-faced man is still alive . . . . Bind his wounds . . . . Save. . . .*

But he couldn't. He couldn't move. Couldn't think. To his shame, he just let himself close his eyes and gave himself over to unconsciousness.

❖

'Kaladin.'

He didn't want to open his eyes. To wake meant returning to that awful world of pain. A world where defenseless, exhausted men were made to charge lines of archers.

That world was the nightmare.

'Kaladin!' The feminine voice was soft, like a whisper, yet still urgent. 'They're going to leave you. Get up! You'll die!'

I can't . . . I can't go back. . . .

Let me go.

Something snapped against his face, a slight *slap* of energy with a sting to it. He cringed. It was nothing compared with his other pains, but somehow it was far more demanding. He raised a hand, swatting. The motion was enough to drive away the last vestiges of stupor.

He tried to open his eyes. One refused, blood from a cut on his cheek having run down and crusted around the eyelid. The sun had moved. Hours had passed. He groaned – sitting up, rubbing the dried blood from his eye. The ground near him was littered with bodies. The air smelled of blood and worse.

A pair of sorry bridgemen were shaking each man in turn, checking for life then pulling the vests and sandals off their bodies, shooing away the cremlings feeding on the bodies. The men would never have checked on Kaladin. He didn't have anything for them to take. They'd have left him with the corpses, stranded on the plateau.

Kaladin's windspren flitted through the air above him, moving anxiously. He rubbed his jaw where she'd struck him. Large spren like her could move small objects and give little pinches of energy. That made them all the more annoying.

This time, it had probably saved Kaladin's life. He groaned at all the places where he hurt. 'Do you have a name, spirit?' he asked, forcing himself to his battered feet.

On the plateau the army had crossed to, soldiers were picking through the corpses of the dead Parshendi, looking for something. Harvesting equipment, maybe? It appeared that Sadeas's force had won. At least, there didn't seem to be any Parshendi still alive. They'd either been killed or had fled.

The plateau they'd fought on seemed exactly like the others they'd crossed. The only thing that was different here was that there was a large lump of . . . something in the center of the plateau. It looked like an enormous rockbud, perhaps some kind of chrysalis or shell, a good twenty feet tall. One side had been hacked open, exposing slimy innards. He hadn't noticed it on the initial charge; the archers had demanded all of his attention.

'A name,' the windspren said, her voice distant. 'Yes. I *do* have a name.' She seemed surprised as she looked at Kaladin. 'Why do I have a name?'

'How should I know?' Kaladin said, forcing himself to move. His feet blazed with pain. He could barely limp.

The nearby bridgemen looked to him with surprise, but he ignored them, limping across the plateau until he found the corpse of a bridgeman who still had his vest and shoes. It was the leathery-faced man who had been so kind to him, dead with an arrow through the neck. Kaladin ignored those shocked eyes, staring blankly into the sky, and harvested the man's clothing – leather vest, leather sandals, lacing shirt stained red with blood. Kaladin felt disgusted with himself, but he wasn't going to count on Gaz giving him clothing.

Kaladin sat down and used the cleaner parts of the shirt to change his improvised bandages, then put on the vest and sandals, trying to keep from moving too much. A breeze now blew, carrying away the scents of blood and the sounds of soldiers calling to one another. The cavalry was already forming up, as if eager to return.

'A name,' the windspren said, walking through the air to stand beside his face. She was in the shape of a young woman, complete with flowing skirt and delicate feet. 'Sylphrena.'

'Sylphrena,' Kaladin repeated, tying on the sandals.

'Syl,' the spirit said. She cocked her head. 'That's amusing. It appears that I have a nickname.'

'Congratulations.' Kaladin stood up again, wobbling.

To the side, Gaz stood with hands on hips, shield tied to his back. 'You,' he said, pointing at Kaladin. He then gestured to the bridge.

'You've got to be kidding,' Kaladin said, looking as the remnants of the bridge crew – fewer than half of their previous number remained – gathered around the bridge.

'Either carry or stay behind,' Gaz said. He seemed angry about something.

I was supposed to die, Kaladin realized. *That's why he didn't care if I had a vest or sandals. I was at the front.* Kaladin was the only one on the first row who had lived.

Kaladin nearly sat down and let them leave him. But dying of thirst on a lonely plateau was not the way he'd choose to go. He stumbled over to the bridge.

'Don't worry,' said one of the other bridgemen. 'They'll let us go slow this time, take lots of breaks. And we'll have a few soldiers to help – takes at least twenty-five men to lift a bridge.'

Kaladin sighed, getting into place as some unfortunate soldiers joined them. Together, they heaved the bridge into the air. It was terribly heavy, but they managed it, somehow.

Kaladin walked, feeling numb. He'd thought that there was nothing more life could do to him, nothing worse than the slave's brand with a *shash*, nothing worse than losing all he had to the war, nothing more terrible than failing those he'd sworn to protect.

It appeared that he'd been wrong. There *had* been something more they could do to him. One final torment the world had reserved just for Kaladin.

And it was called Bridge Four.

7

ANYTHING REASONABLE

'*They are aflame. They burn. They bring the darkness when they come, and so all you can see is that their skin is aflame. Burn, burn, burn. ...*'

—Collected on Palahishev, 1172, 21 seconds pre-death. Subject was a baker's apprentice.

Shallan hurried down the hallway with its burnt-orange colorings, the ceiling and upper walls now stained by the passing of black smoke from Jasnah's Soulcasting. Hopefully, the paintings on the walls hadn't been ruined.

Ahead, a small group of parshmen arrived, bearing rags, buckets, and stepladders to use in wiping off the soot. They bowed to her as she passed, uttering no words. Parshmen could speak, but they rarely did so. Many seemed mute. As a child, she'd found the patterns of their marbled skin beautiful. That had been before her father forbade her to spend any time with the parshmen.

She turned her mind to her task. How was she going to convince Jasnah Kholin, one of the most powerful women in the world, to change her mind about taking Shallan as a ward? The woman was obviously stubborn; she had spent years resisting the devotaries' attempts at reconciliation.

She reentered the broad main cavern, with its lofty stone ceiling and bustling, well-dressed occupants. She felt daunted, but that brief glimpse of the Soulcaster seduced her. Her family, House Davar, had prospered in recent years, coming out of obscurity. This had primarily been because of her father's skill in politics – he had been hated by many but his ruthlessness had carried him far. So had the wealth lent by the discovery of several important new marble deposits on Davar lands.

Shallan had never known enough to be suspicious of that wealth's origins. Every time the family had exhausted one of its quarries, her father had gone out with his surveyor and discovered a new one. Only after interrogating the surveyor had Shallan and her brothers discovered the truth: Her father, using his forbidden Soulcaster, had been *creating* new deposits at a careful rate. Not enough to be suspicious. Just enough to give him the money he needed to further his political goals.

Nobody knew where he'd gotten the fabrial, which she now carried in her safepouch. It was unusable, damaged on the same disastrous evening that her father had died. *Don't think about that*, she told herself forcefully.

They'd had a jeweler repair the broken Soulcaster, but it no longer worked. Their house steward – one of her father's close confidants, an advisor named Luesh – had been trained to use the device, and he could no longer make it function.

Her father's debts and promises were outrageous. Their choices were limited. Her family had some time – perhaps as long as a year – before the missed payments became egregious, and before her father's absence became obvious. For once, her family's isolated, backcountry estates were an advantage, providing a reason that communications were being delayed. Her brothers were scrambling, writing letters in her father's name, making a few appearances and spreading rumors that Brightlord Davar was planning something big.

All to give her time to make good on her bold plan. Find Jasnah Kholin. Become her ward. Learn where she kept her Soulcaster. Then replace it with the nonfunctional one.

With the fabrial, they'd be able to make new quarries and restore their wealth. They'd be able to make food to feed their house soldiers. With enough wealth in hand to pay off debts and make bribes, they could announce their father's death and not suffer destruction.

Shallan hesitated in the main hallway, considering her next move. What she planned to do was very risky. She'd have to escape without implicating herself in the theft. Though she'd devoted much thought to that, she still didn't know how she'd manage it. But Jasnah was known to have many enemies. There had to be a way to pin the fabrial's 'breaking' on them instead.

That step would come later. For now, Shallan *had* to convince Jasnah to accept her as a ward. All other results were unacceptable.

Nervously, Shallan held her arms in the sign of need, covered safehand bent across her chest and touching the elbow of her freehand, which was raised with fingers outspread. A woman approached, wearing the well-starched white laced shirt and black skirt that were the universal sign of a master-servant.

The stout woman curtsied. 'Brightness?'

'The Palanaeum,' Shallan said.

The woman bowed and led Shallan farther into the depths of the long hallway. Most of the women here – servants included – wore their hair bound, and Shallan felt conspicuous with hers loose. The deep red color made her stand out even more.

Soon, the grand hallway began to slope down steeply. But when the half-hour arrived, she could still hear distant bells ring behind her. Perhaps that was why the people here liked them so much; even in the depths of the Conclave, one could hear the outside world.

The servant led Shallan to a pair of grand steel doors. The servant bowed and Shallan dismissed her with a nod.

Shallan couldn't help but admire the beauty of the doors; their exterior was carved in an intricate geometric pattern with circles and lines and glyphs. It was some kind of chart, half on each door. There was no time to study the details, unfortunately, and she passed them by.

Beyond the doors was a breathtakingly large room. The sides were of smooth rock and they stretched high; the dim illumination made it impossible to tell just how high, but she saw flickers of distant light. Set into the walls were dozens of small balconies, much like the private box seats of a theater. Soft light shone from many of these. The only sounds were turning pages and faint whispers. Shallan raised her safehand to her breast, feeling dwarfed by the magnificent chamber.

'Brightness?' a young male master-servant said, approaching. 'What do you need?'

'A new sense of perspective, apparently,' Shallan said absently. 'How . . .'

'This room is called the Veil,' the servant explained softly. 'That which comes before the Palanaeum itself. Both were here when the city was founded. Some think these chambers might have been cut by the Dawn-singers themselves.'

'Where are the books?'

'The Palanaeum proper is this way.' The servant gestured, leading her to a set of doors on the other side of the room. Through them, she entered a smaller chamber that was partitioned with walls of thick crystal. Shallan approached the nearest one, feeling it. The crystal's surface was rough like hewn rock.

'Soulcast?' she asked.

The servant nodded. Behind him, another servant passed leading an elderly ardent Like most ardents, the aged man had a shaved head and a long beard. His simple grey robes were tied with a brown sash. The servant led him around a corner, and Shallan could vaguely make out their shapes on the other side, shadows swimming through the crystal.

She took a step forward, but her servant cleared his throat. 'I will need your chit of admittance, Brightness.'

'How much does one cost?' Shallan asked hesitantly.

'A thousand sapphire broams.'

'So much?'

'The king's many hospitals require much upkeep,' the man said apolo-getically. 'The only things Kharbranth has to sell are fish, bells, and information. The first two are hardly unique to us. But the third ... well, the Palanaeum has the finest collection of tomes and scrolls on Roshar. More, even, than the Holy Enclave in Valath. At last count, there were over seven hundred thousand separate texts in our archive.'

Her father had owned exactly eighty-seven books. Shallan had read them all several times over. How much could be contained in *seven hundred thousand* books? The weight of that much information dazzled her. She found herself hungering to look through those hidden shelves. She could spend months just reading their titles.

But no. Perhaps once she'd made certain her brothers were safe – once her house's finances were restored – she could return. Perhaps.

She felt like she was starving, yet leaving a warm fruit pie uneaten. 'Where might I wait?' she asked. 'If someone I know is inside.'

'You may use one of the reading alcoves,' the servant said, relaxing. Perhaps he'd feared that she would make a scene. 'No chit is required to sit in one. There are parshman porters who will raise you to the higher levels, if that is what you wish.'

'Thank you,' Shallan said, turning her back on the Palanaeum. She felt like a child again, locked in her room, not allowed to run through the gardens because of her father's paranoid fears. 'Does Brightness Jasnah have an alcove yet?'

'I can ask,' the servant said, leading the way back into the Veil, with its distant, unseen ceiling. He hurried off to speak with some others, leaving Shallan standing beside the doorway to the Palanaeum.

She could run in. Sneak through—

No. Her brothers teased her for being too timid, but it was not timidity that held her back. There would undoubtedly be guards; bursting in would not only be futile, it would ruin any chance she had of changing Jasnah's mind.

Change Jasnah's mind, prove herself. Considering it made her sick. She *hated* confrontation. During her youth, she'd felt like a piece of delicate crystalware locked in a cabinet to be displayed but never touched. The only daughter, the last memory of Brightlord Davar's beloved wife. It still felt odd to her that *she* been the one to take charge after ... After the incident ... After ...

Memories attacked her. Nan Balat bruised, his coat torn. A long, silvery sword in her hand, sharp enough to cut stones as if they were water.

No, Shallan thought, her back to the stone wall, clutching her satchel. *No. Don't think of the past.*

She sought solace in drawing, raising fingers to her satchel and reaching for her paper and pencils. The servant came back before she had a chance to get them out, however. 'Brightness Jasnah Kholin has indeed asked that a reading alcove be set aside for her,' he said. 'You may wait there for her, if you wish it.'

'I do,' Shallan said. 'Thank you.'

The servant led her to a shadowed enclosure, inside of which four parshmen stood upon a sturdy wooden platform. The servant and Shallan stepped onto the platform, and the parshmen pulled ropes that were strung into a pulley above, raising the platform up the stone shaft. The only lights were broam spheres set at each corner of the lift's ceiling. Amethysts, which had a soft violet light.

She needed a plan. Jasnah Kholin did not seem the type to change her mind easily. Shallan would have to surprise her, impress her.

They reached a level about forty feet or so off the ground, and the servant waved for the porters to stop. Shallan followed the master-servant down a dark hallway to one of the small balconies that extended out over the Veil. It was round, like a turret, and had a waist-high stone rim with a wooden railing above that. Other occupied alcoves glowed with different colors from the spheres being used to light them; the darkness of the huge space made them seem to hover in the air.

This alcove had a long, curving stone desk joined directly into the rim of the balcony. There was a single chair and a gobletlike crystal bowl. Shallan nodded in thanks to the servant, who withdrew, then she pulled out a handful of spheres and dropped them into the bowl, lighting the alcove.

She sighed, sitting down in the chair and laying her satchel on the desk. She undid the laces on her satchel, busying herself as she tried to think of something – anything – that would persuade Jasnah.

First, she decided, *I need to clear my mind.*

From her satchel she removed a sheaf of thick drawing paper, a set of charcoal pencils of different widths, some brushes and steel pens, ink, and watercolors. Finally, she took out her smaller notebook, bound in codex form, which contained the nature sketches she'd done during her weeks aboard the *Wind's Pleasure*.

These were simple things really but worth more to her than a chest full of spheres. She took a sheet off the stack, then selected a fine-pointed charcoal pencil, rolling it between her fingers. She closed her eyes and fixed an image in her mind: Kharbranth as she'd memorized it in that moment soon after landing on the docks. Waves surging against the wooden posts, a salty scent to the air, men climbing rigging calling one another with excitement. And the city itself, rising up the hillside, homes stacked atop homes, not a speck of land wasted. Bells, distant, tinkling softly in the air.

She opened her eyes and began to draw. Her fingers moved on their own, sketching broad lines first. The cracklike valley the city was situated in. The port. Here, squares to be homes, there a slash to mark a switchback of the grand roadway that led up to the Conclave. Slowly, bit by bit, she added detail. Shadows as windows. Lines to fill out the roadways. Hints of people and carts to show the chaos of the thoroughfares.

She had read of how sculptors worked. Many would take a blank stone block and work it into a vague shape first. Then, they'd work it over again, carving more detail with each pass. It was the same for her in drawing. Broad lines first, then some details, then more, then down to the finest of lines. She had no formal training in pencils; she simply did what felt right.

The city took shape beneath her fingers. She coaxed it free, line by line, scratch by scratch. What would she do without this? Tension bled from her body, as if released from her fingertips into the pencil.

She lost track of time as she worked. Sometimes she felt like she was entering a trance, everything else fading. Her fingers almost seemed to draw of their own accord. It was so much easier to think while drawing.

Before too long, she had copied her Memory onto the page. She held up the sheet, satisfied, relaxed, her mind clear. The memorized image of Kharbranth was gone from her head; she'd released it into her sketch. There was a sense of relaxation to that too. As if her mind was put under tension holding Memories until they could be used.

She did Yalb next, standing shirtless in his vest and gesturing to the short porter who had pulled her up to the Conclave. She smiled as she worked, remembering Yalb's affable voice. He'd likely returned to the *Wind's Pleasure* by now. Had it been two hours? Probably.

She was always more excited by drawing animals and people than she was by drawing things. There was something energizing about putting a living creature onto the page. A city was lines and boxes, but a person was circles and curves. Could she get that smirk on Yalb's face right? Could she show his lazy contentedness, the way he would flirt with a woman far above his station? And the porter, with his thin fingers and sandaled feet, his long coat and baggy pants. His strange language, his keen eyes, his plan to increase his tip by offering not just a ride, but a tour.

When she drew, she didn't feel as if she worked with only charcoal and paper. In drawing a portrait, her medium was the soul itself. There were plants from which one could remove a tiny cutting – a leaf, or a bit of stem – then plant it and grow a duplicate. When she collected a Memory of a person, she was snipping free a bud of their soul, and she cultivated and grew it on the page. Charcoal for sinew, paper pulp for bone, ink for blood, the paper's texture for skin. She fell into a rhythm, a cadence, the scratching of her pencil like the sound of breathing from those she depicted.

Creationspren began to gather around her pad, looking at her work. Like other spren, they were said to always be around, but usually invisible. Sometimes you attracted them. Sometimes you didn't. With drawing, skill seemed to make a difference.

Creationspren were of medium size, as tall as one of her fingers, and they glowed with a faint silvery light. They transformed perpetually, taking new shapes. Usually the shapes were things they had seen recently. An urn, a person, a table, a wheel, a nail. Always of the same silvery color, always the same diminutive height. They imitated shapes exactly, but moved them in strange ways. A table would roll like a wheel, an urn would shatter and repair itself.

Her drawing gathered about a half-dozen of them, pulling them by her act of creation just as a bright fire would draw flamespren. She'd learned to ignore them. They weren't substantial – if she moved her arm through one, its figure would smear like scattered sand, then re-form. She never felt a thing when touching one.

Eventually, she held up the page, satisfied. It depicted Yalb and the porter in detail, with hints of the busy city behind. She'd gotten their eyes right. That was the most important. Each of the Ten Essences had an analogous part of the human body – blood for liquid, hair for wood, and so forth. The eyes were associated with crystal and glass. The windows into a person's mind and spirit.

She set the page aside. Some men collected trophies. Others collected weapons or shields. Many collected spheres.

Shallan collected people. People, and interesting creatures. Perhaps it was because she'd spent so much of her youth in a virtual prison. She'd developed the habit of memorizing faces, then drawing them later, after her father had discovered her sketching the gardeners. His daughter? Drawing pictures of darkeyes? He'd been furious with her – one of the infrequent times he'd directed his infamous temper at his daughter.

After that, she'd done drawings of people only when in private, instead using her open drawing times to sketch the insects, crustaceans, and plants of the manor gardens. Her father hadn't minded this – zoology and botany were proper feminine pursuits – and had encouraged her to choose natural history as her Calling.

She took out a third blank sheet. It seemed to beg her to fill it. A blank page was nothing but potential, pointless until it was used. Like a fully infused sphere cloistered inside a pouch, prevented from making its light useful.

Fill me.

The creationspren gathered around the page. They were still, as if curious, anticipatory. Shallan closed her eyes and imagined Jasnah Kholin, standing before the blocked door, the Soulcaster glowing on her hand. The hallway hushed, save for a child's sniffles. Attendants holding their breath. An anxious king. A still reverence.

Shallan opened her eyes and began to draw with vigor, intentionally losing herself. The less she was in the *now* and the more she was in the *then*, the better the sketch would be. The other two pictures had been warm-ups; this was the day's masterpiece. With the paper bound onto the board – safehand holding that – her freehand flew across the page, occasionally switching to other pencils. Soft charcoal for deep, thick blackness, like Jasnah's beautiful hair. Hard charcoal for light greys, like the powerful waves of light coming from the Soulcaster's gems.

For a few extended moments, Shallan was back in that hallway again, watching something that should not be: a heretic wielding one of the most sacred powers in all the world. The power of change itself, the power by which the Almighty had created Roshar. He had another name, allowed to pass only the lips of ardents. *Elithanathile.* He Who Transforms.

Shallan could smell the musty hallway. She could hear the child whimpering. She could feel her own heart beating in anticipation. The boulder would soon change. Sucking away the Stormlight in Jasnah's gemstone, it would give up its essence, becoming something new. Shallan's breath caught in her throat.

And then the memory faded, returning her to the quiet, dim alcove. The page now held a perfect rendition of the scene, worked in blacks and greys. The princess's proud figure regarded the fallen stone, demanding that it give way before her will. It *was* her. Shallan knew, with the intuitive certainty of an artist, that this was one of the finest pieces she had ever done. In a very small way, she had captured Jasnah Kholin, something the devotaries had never managed. That gave her a euphoric thrill. Even if this woman rejected Shallan again, one fact would not change. Jasnah Kholin had joined Shallan's collection.

Shallan wiped her fingers on her cleaning cloth, then lifted the paper. She noted absently that she'd attracted some two dozen creationspren now. She would have to lacquer the page with plytree sap to set the charcoal and protect it from smudges. She had some in her satchel. First she wanted to study the page and the figure it contained. Who *was* Jasnah Kholin? Not one to be cowed, certainly. She was a woman to the bone, master of the feminine arts, but not by any means delicate.

Such a woman would appreciate Shallan's determination. She *would* listen to another request for wardship, assuming it was presented properly.

Jasnah was also a rationalist, a woman with the audacity to deny the existence of the Almighty himself based on her own reasoning. Jasnah would appreciate strength, but only if it was shaped by logic.

Shallan nodded to herself, taking out a fourth sheet of paper and a fine-tipped brushpen, then shaking and opening her jar of ink. Jasnah had demanded proof of Shallan's logical and writing skills. Well, what better way to do that than to supplicate the woman with words?

Brightness Jasnah Kholin, Shallan wrote, painting the letters as neatly and beautifully as she could. She could have used a reed instead, but a brushpen was for works of art. She intended this page to be just that. *You have rejected my petition. I accept that. Yet, as anyone trained in formal inquiry knows, no supposition should be treated as axiomatic.* The actual argument usually read 'no supposition – save for the existence of the Almighty himself – should be held as axiomatic.' But this wording would appeal to Jasnah.

A scientist must be willing to change her theories if experiment disproves them. I hold to the hope that you treat decisions in a like manner: as preliminary results pending further information.

From our brief interaction, I can see that you appreciate tenacity. You complimented me on continuing to seek you out. Therefore, I presume that you will not find this letter a breach of good taste. Take it as proof of my ardor to be your ward, and not as disdain for your expressed decision.

Shallan raised the end of her brushpen to her lips as she considered her next step. The creationspren slowly faded away, vanishing. There were said to be logicspren – in the form of tiny stormclouds – who were attracted to great arguments, but Shallan had never seen them.

You expect proof of my worthiness, Shallan continued. *I wish I could demonstrate that my schooling is more complete than our interview revealed.*

Unfortunately, I haven't the grounds for such an argument. I have weaknesses in my understanding. That is plain and not subject to reasonable dispute.

But the lives of men and women are more than logical puzzles; the context of their experiences is invaluable in making good decisions. My study in logic does not rise to your standards, but even I know that the rationalists have a rule: One cannot apply logic as an absolute where human beings are concerned. We are not beings of thought only.

Therefore, the soul of my argument here is to give perspective on my ignorance. Not by way of excuse, but of explanation. You expressed displeasure that one such as I should be trained so inadequately. What of my stepmother? What of my tutors? Why was my education handled so poorly?

The facts are embarrassing. I have had few tutors and virtually no education. My stepmother tried, but she had no education herself. It is a carefully guarded secret, but many of the rural Veden houses ignore the proper training of their women.

I had three different tutors when I was very young, but each left after a few months, citing my father's temper or rudeness as her reason. I was left to my own devices in education. I have learned what I could through reading, filling in the gaps by taking advantage of my own curious nature. But I will not be capable of matching knowledge with someone who has been given the benefit of a formal – and expensive – education.

Why is this an argument that you should accept me? Because everything I have learned has come by way of great personal struggle. What others were handed, I had to hunt. I believe that because of this, my education – limited though it is – has extra worth and merit. I respect your decisions, but I do ask you to reconsider. Which would you rather have? A ward who is able to repeat the correct answers because an overpriced tutor drilled them into her, or a ward who had to struggle and fight for everything she has learned?

I assure you that one of those two will prize your teachings far more than the other.

She raised her brush. Her arguments seemed imperfect now that she considered them. She exposed her ignorance, then expected Jasnah to welcome her? Still, it seemed the right thing to do, for all the fact that this letter was a lie. A lie built of truths. She hadn't truly come to partake of Jasnah's knowledge. She had come as a thief.

That made her conscience itch, and she nearly reached out and crumpled the page. Steps in the hallway outside made her freeze. She leaped to her feet, spinning, safehand held to her breast. She fumbled for words to explain her presence to Jasnah Kholin.

Light and shadows flickered in the hallway, then a figure hesitantly looked into the alcove, a single white sphere cupped in one hand for light. It was *not* Jasnah. It was a man in his early twenties wearing simple grey robes. An ardent. Shallan relaxed.

The young man noticed her. His face was narrow, his blue eyes keen. His beard was trimmed short and square, his head shaved. When he spoke, his voice had a cultured tone. 'Ah, excuse me, Brightness. I thought this was the alcove of Jasnah Kholin.'

'It is,' Shallan said.

'Oh. You're waiting for her too?'

'Yes '

'Would you mind terribly if I waited with you?' He had a faint Herdazian accent.

'Of course not, Ardent.' She nodded her head in respect, then gathered up her things in haste, preparing the seat for him.

'I can't take your seat, Brightness! I'll fetch another for myself.'

She raised a hand in protest, but he had already retreated. He returned a few moments later, carrying a chair from another alcove. He was tall and lean, and – she decided with slight discomfort – rather handsome. Her father had owned only three ardents, all elderly men. They had traveled his lands and visited the villages, ministering to the people, helping them reach Points in their Glories and Callings. She had their faces in her collection of portraits.

The ardent set down his chair. He hesitated before sitting, glancing at the table. 'My, my,' he said in surprise.

For a moment, Shallan thought he was reading her letter, and she felt an irrational surge of panic. The ardent, however, was regarding the three drawings that lay at the head of the table, awaiting lacquer.

'You did these, Brightness?' he said.

'Yes, Ardent,' Shallan said, lowering her eyes.

'No need to be so formal!' the ardent said, leaning down and adjusting his spectacles as he studied her work. 'Please, I am Brother Kabsal, or just Kabsal. Really, it's fine. And you are?'

'Shallan Davar.'

'By Vedeledev's golden keys, Brightness!' Brother Kabsal said, seating himself. 'Did Jasnah Kholin teach you this skill with the pencil?'

'No, Ardent,' she said, still standing.

'Still so formal,' he said, smiling at her. 'Tell me, am I so intimidating as that?'

'I have been brought up to show respect to ardents.'

'Well, I myself find that respect is like manure. Use it where needed, and growth will flourish. Spread it on too thick, and things just start to smell.' His eyes twinkled.

Had an *ardent*–a servant of the Almighty – just spoken of *manure*? 'An ardent is a representative of the Almighty himself,' she said. 'To show you lack of respect would be to show it to the Almighty.'

'I see. And this is how you'd respond if the Almighty himself appeared to you here? All of this formality and bowing?'

She hesitated. 'Well, no.'

'Ah, and how *would* you react?'

'I suspect with screams of pain,' she said, letting her thought slip out too easily. 'As it is written that the Almighty's glory is such that any who look upon him would immediately be burned to ash.'

The ardent laughed at that. 'Wisely spoken indeed. Please, do sit, though.'

She did so, hesitant.

'You still appear conflicted,' he said, holding up her portrait of Jasnah. 'What must I do to put you at ease? Shall I step up onto this desk here and do a jig?'

She blinked in surprise.

'No objection?' Brother Kabsal said. 'Well, then ... ' He set down the portrait and began to climb up on his chair.

'No, please!' Shallan said, holding out her freehand.

'Are you certain?' he glanced at the desk appraisingly.

'Yes,' Shallan said, imagining the ardent teetering and making a misstep, then falling off the balcony and plunging dozens of feet to the ground below. 'Please, I promise not to respect you any longer!'

He chuckled, hopping down and seating himself. He leaned closer to her, as if conspiratorially. 'The table jig threat almost always works. I've only ever had to go through with it once, due to a lost bet against Brother Lhanin. The master ardent of our monastery nearly keeled over in shock.'

Shallan found herself smiling. 'You're an ardent; you're forbidden to have possessions. What did you bet?'

'Two deep breaths of a winter rose's fragrance,' said Brother Kabsal, 'and the sunlight's warmth on your skin.' He smiled. 'We can be rather creative at times. Years spent marinating in a monastery can do that to a man. Now, you were about to explain to me where you learned such skill with a pencil.'

'Practice,' Shallan said. 'I should suspect that is how everyone learns, eventually.'

'Wise words again. I am beginning to wonder which of us it the ardent. But surely you had a master to teach you.'

'Dandos the Oilsworn.'

'Ah, a true master of pencils if there ever was one. Now, not that I doubt your word, Brightness, but I'm rather intrigued how Dandos Heraldin could have trained you in arts, as – last I checked – he's suffering a rather terminal and perpetual ailment. Namely, that of being *dead*. For three hundred years.'

Shallan blushed. 'My father had a book of his instruction.'

'You learned this,' Kabsal said, lifting up her drawing of Jasnah, 'from a *book*.'

'Er . . . yes?'

He looked back at the picture. 'I need to read more.'

Shallan found herself laughing at the ardent's expression, and she took a Memory of him sitting there, admiration and perplexity blending on his face as he studied the picture, rubbing his bearded chin with one finger.

He smiled pleasantly, setting down the picture. 'You have lacquer?'

'I do,' she said, getting it out of her satchel. It was contained in a bulb sprayer of the type often used for perfume.

He accepted the small jar and twisted the clasp on the front, then gave the bottle a shake and tested the lacquer on the back of his hand. He nodded in satisfaction and reached for the drawing. 'A piece such as this should not be allowed to risk smudging.'

'I can lacquer it,' Shallan said. 'No need to trouble yourself.'

'It is no trouble; it's an honor. Besides, I am an ardent. We don't know what to do with ourselves when we aren't busying about, doing things others could do for themselves. It is best just to humor me.' He began to apply the lacquer, dusting the page with careful puffs.

She had trouble keeping herself from reaching to snatch the sketch away. Fortunately, his hands were careful, and the lacquer went on evenly. He'd obviously done this before.

'You are from Jah Keved, I presume?' he asked.

'From the hair?' she asked, raising a hand to her red locks. 'Or from the accent?'

'From the way you treat ardents. The Veden Church is by far the most traditional. I have visited your lovely country on two occasions; while your food sits well in my stomach, the amount of bowing and scraping you show ardents made me uncomfortable.'

'Perhaps you should have danced on a few tables.'

'I considered it,' he said, 'but my brother and sister ardents from your country would likely have dropped dead of embarrassment. I would hate to have that on my conscience. The Almighty is not kind toward those who kill his priests.'

'I should think that killing in general would be frowned upon,' she responded, still watching him apply the lacquer. It felt odd to let someone else work on her art.

'What does Brightness Jasnah think of your skill?' he asked as he worked.

'I don't think she cares,' Shallan said, grimacing and remembering her conversation with the woman. 'She doesn't seem terribly appreciative of the visual arts.'

'So I have heard. It's one of her few faults, unfortunately.'

'Another being that little matter of her heresy?'

'Indeed,' Kabsal said, smiling. 'I must admit, I stepped in here expecting indifference, not deference. How did you come to be part of her entourage?'

Shallan started, realizing for the first time that Brother Kabsal must have assumed her to be one of the Brightlady Kholin's attendants. Perhaps a ward.

'Bother,' she said to herself.

'Hum?'

'It appears I've inadvertently misled you, Brother Kabsal. I'm not associated with Brightness Jasnah. Not yet, anyway. I've been trying to get her to take me on as a ward.'

'Ah,' he said, finishing his lacquering.

'I'm sorry.'

'For what? You did nothing wrong.' He blew on the picture, then turned it for her to see. It was perfectly lacquered, without any smears. 'If you would do me a favor, child?' he said, setting the page aside.

'Anything.'

He raised an eyebrow at that.

'Anything reasonable,' she corrected.

'By whose reason?'

'Mine, I guess.'

'Pity,' he said, standing. 'Then I will limit myself. If you would kindly let Brightness Jasnah know that I called upon her?'

'She knows you?' What business had a Herdazian ardent with Jasnah, a confirmed atheist?

'Oh, I wouldn't say that,' he replied. 'I'd hope she's heard my name, though, since I've requested an audience with her several times.'

Shallan nodded, rising. 'You want to try to convert her, I presume?'

'She presents a unique challenge. I don't think I could live with myself if I didn't at least *try* to persuade her.'

'And we wouldn't want you to be unable to live with yourself,' Shallan noted, 'as the alternative harks back to your nasty habit of almost killing ardents.'

'Exactly. Anyway, I think a personal message from you might help where written requests have been ignored.'

'I ... doubt that.'

'Well, if she refuses, it only means that I'll be back.' He smiled. 'That would mean – hopefully – that we shall meet each other again. So I look forward to it.'

'I as well. And I'm sorry again about the misunderstanding.'

'Brightness! Please. Don't take responsibility for *my* assumptions.'

She smiled. 'I should hesitate to take responsibility for you in *any* manner or regard, Brother Kabsal. But I still feel bad.'

'It will pass,' he noted, blue eyes twinkling. 'But I'll do my best to make you feel well again. Is there anything you're fond of? Other than respecting ardents and drawing amazing pictures, that is?'

'Jam.'

He cocked his head.

'I like it,' she said, shrugging. 'You asked what I was fond of. Jam.'

'So it shall be.' He withdrew into the dark corridor, fishing in his robe pocket for his sphere to give him light. In moments, he was gone.

Why didn't he wait for Jasnah to return himself? Shallan shook her head, then lacquered her other two pictures. She had just finished letting them dry – packing them in her satchel – when she heard footsteps in the hallway again and recognized Jasnah's voice speaking.

Shallan hurriedly gathered her things, leaving the letter on the desk, then stepped up to the side of the alcove to wait. Jasnah Kholin entered a moment later, accompanied by a small group of servants.

She did not look pleased.

'Victory! We stand atop the mount! We scatter them before us! Their homes become our dens, their lands are now our farms! And they shall burn, as we once did, in a place that is hollow and forlorn.'

—Collected on Ishashan, 1172, 18 seconds pre-death. Subject was a light-eyed spinster of the eighth dahn.

S hallan's fears were confirmed as Jasnah looked straight at her, then lowered her safehand to her side in a mark of frustration. 'So you *are* here.'

Shallan cringed. 'The servants told you, then?'

'You didn't think that they would leave someone in my alcove and not warn me?' Behind Jasnah, a small group of parshmen hesitated in the hallway, each carrying an armload of books.

'Brightness Kholin,' Shallan said. 'I just—'

'I have wasted enough time on you already,' Jasnah said, eyes furious. 'You will withdraw, Miss Davar. And I will not see you again during my time here. Am I *understood*?'

Shallan's hopes crumbled. She shrank back. There was a gravity to Jasnah Kholin. One did not disobey her. One need only look into those eyes to understand.

'I'm sorry to have bothered you,' Shallan whispered, clutching her satchel and leaving with as much dignity as she could manage. She barely kept the tears of embarrassment and disappointment from her eyes as she hastened down the hallway, feeling like a complete fool.

She reached the porter's shaft, though they had already returned below after bringing up Jasnah. Shallan didn't pull the bell to summon them. Instead she placed her back to the wall and sank down to the floor, knees up against her chest, satchel in her lap. She wrapped her arms around her legs, freehand clasping her safehand through the fabric of her cuff, breathing quietly.

Angry people unsettled her. She couldn't help but think of her father in one of his tirades, couldn't help but hear screams, bellows, and whimpers. Was she weak because confrontation unsettled her so? She felt that she was.

Foolish, idiot girl, she thought, a few painspren crawling out of the wall near her head. *What made you think you could do this? You've only set foot off your family grounds a half-dozen times during your life. Idiot, idiot,* idiot!

She had persuaded her brothers to trust her, to put hope in her ridiculous plan. And now what had she done? Wasted six months during which their enemies circled closer.

'Brightness Davar?' asked a hesitant voice.

Shallan looked up, realizing she'd been so wrapped in her misery that she hadn't seen the servant approach. He was a younger man, wearing an all black uniform, no emblem on the breast. Not a master-servant, but perhaps one in training.

'Brightness Kholin would like to speak with you.' The young man gestured back down the hallway.

To berate me further? Shallan thought with a grimace. But a highlady like Jasnah got what she wanted. Shallan forced herself to stop shaking, then stood. At least she'd been able to keep the tears away; she hadn't ruined her makeup. She followed the servant back to the lit alcove, satchel clutched before her like a shield on the battlefield.

Jasnah Kholin sat in the chair Shallan had been using, stacks of books on the table. Jasnah was rubbing her forehead with her freehand. The Soul-caster rested against the back of her skin, the smokestone dark and cracked. Though Jasnah looked fatigued, she sat with perfect posture, her fine silk dress covering her feet, her safehand held across her lap.

Jasnah focused on Shallan, lowering her freehand. 'I should not have treated you with such anger, Miss Davar,' she said in a tired voice. 'You were simply showing persistence, a trait I normally encourage. Storms alight, I've oft been guilty of stubbornness myself. Sometimes we find it hardest to accept in others that which we cling to in ourselves. My only excuse can be that I have put myself under an unusual amount of strain lately.'

Shallan nodded in gratitude, though she felt terribly awkward.

Jasnah turned to look out of the balcony into the dark space of the Veil. 'I know what people say of me. I should hope that I am not as harsh as some say, though a woman could have far worse than a reputation for sternness. It can serve one well.'

Shallan had to forcibly keep herself from fidgeting. Should she withdraw?

Jasnah shook her head to herself, though Shallan could not guess what thoughts had caused the unconscious gesture. Finally, she turned back to Shallan and waved toward the large, gobletlike bowl on the desk. It held a dozen of Shallan's spheres.

Shallan raised her freehand to her lips in shock. She'd completely forgotten the money. She bowed to Jasnah in thanks, then hurriedly collected the spheres. 'Brightness, lest I forget, I should mention that an ardent – Brother Kabsal – came to see you while I waited here. He wished me to pass on his desire to speak with you.'

'Not surprising,' Jasnah said. 'You seem surprised about the spheres, Miss Davar. I assumed that you were waiting outside to recover them. Is that not why you were so close?'

'No, Brightness. I was just settling my nerves.'

'Ah.'

Shallan bit her lip. The princess appeared to have gotten past her initial tirade. Perhaps ... 'Brightness,' Shallan said, cringing at her brashness, 'what did you think of my letter?'

'Letter?'

'I ...' Shallan glanced at the desk. 'Beneath that stack of books, Brightness.'

A servant quickly moved aside the stack of books; the parshman must have set it on the paper without noticing. Jasnah picked up the letter, raising an eyebrow, and Shallan hurriedly undid her satchel and placed the spheres in her money pouch. Then she cursed herself for being so quick, as now she had nothing to do but stand and wait for Jasnah to finish reading.

'This is true?' Jasnah looking up from the paper. 'You are self-trained?'

'Yes, Brightness.'

'That is remarkable.'

'Thank you, Brightness.'

'And this letter was a clever maneuver. You correctly assumed that I would respond to a written plea. This shows me your skill with words, and the rhetoric of the letter gives proof that you can think logically and make a good argument.'

'Thank you, Brightness,' Shallan said, feeling another surge of hope, mixed with fatigue. Her emotions had been jerked back and forth like a rope being used for a tugging contest.

'You should have left the note for me, and withdrawn before I returned.'

'But then the note would have been lost beneath that stack of books.'

Jasnah raised an eyebrow at her, as if to show that she did not appreciate being corrected. 'Very well. The context of a person's life *is* important. Your circumstances do not excuse your lack of education in history and philosophy, but leniency is in order. I will allow you to petition me again at a later date, a privilege I have never given any aspiring ward. Once you have a sufficient groundwork in those two subjects, come to me again. If you have improved suitably, I will accept you.'

Shallan's emotions sank. Jasnah's offer *was* kindly, but it would take years of study to accomplish what she asked. House Davar would have fallen by then, her family's lands divided among its creditors, her brothers and herself stripped of title and perhaps enslaved.

'Thank you, Brightness,' Shallan said, bowing her head.

Jasnah nodded, as if considering the matter closed. Shallan withdrew, walking quietly down the hallway and pulling the cord to ring for the porters.

Jasnah had all but promised to accept her at a later date. For most, that would be a great victory. Being trained by Jasnah Kholin – thought by some to be the finest living scholar – would have ensured a bright future. Shallan would have married extremely well, likely to the son of a high-prince, and would have found new social circles open to her. Indeed, if Shallan had possessed the time to train under Jasnah, the sheer prestige of a Kholin affiliation might have been enough to save her house.

If only.

Eventually, Shallan made her way out of the Conclave; there were no gates on the front, just pillars set before the open maw. She was surprised to discover how dim it was outside. She trailed down the large steps, then took a smaller, more cultivated side path where she would be out of the way. Small shelves of ornamental shalebark had been grown along this walkway, and several species had let out fanlike tendrils to wave in the evening breeze. A few lazy lifespren – like specks of glowing green dust – flitted from one frond to the next.

Shallan leaned back against the stonelike plant, the tendrils pulling in and hiding. From this vantage, she could look down at Kharbranth, lights glowing beneath her like a cascade of fire streaming down the cliff face. The only other option for her and her brothers was to run. To abandon the family estates in Jah Keved and seek asylum. But where? Were there old allies her father *hadn't* alienated?

There was that matter of the strange collection of maps they'd found in his study. What did they mean? He'd rarely spoken of his plans to his children. Even her father's advisors knew very little. Helaran – her eldest brother – had known more, but he had vanished over a year ago, and her father had proclaimed him dead.

As always, thinking of her father made her feel ill, and the pain started to constrict her chest. She raised her freehand to her head, suddenly overwhelmed by the weight of House Davar's situation, her part in it, and the secret she now carried, hidden ten heartbeats away.

'Ho, young miss!' a voice called. She turned, shocked to see Yalb standing up on a rocky shelf a short distance from the Conclave entrance. A group of men in guard uniforms sat on the rock around him.

'Yalb?' she said, aghast. He should have returned to his ship hours ago. She hurried over to stand below the short stone outcropping. 'Why are you still here?'

'Oh,' he said, grinning, 'I found myself a game of kabers here with these fine, upstanding gentlemen of the city guard. Figured officers of the law were right unlikely to cheat me, so we entered into a friendly-type game while I waited.'

'But you didn't *need* to wait.'

'Didn't need to win eighty chips off these fellows neither,' Yalb said with a laugh. 'But I did both!'

The men sitting around him looked far less enthusiastic. Their uniforms were orange tabards tied about the middle with white sashes.

'Well, I suppose I should be leading you back to the ship, then,' Yalb said, reluctantly gathering up the spheres in the pile at his feet. They glowed with a variety of hues. Their light was small – each was only a chip – but it was impressive winnings.

Shallan stepped back as Yalb hopped off the rock shelf. His companions protested his departure, but he gestured to Shallan. 'You'd have me leave a lighteyed woman of her stature to walk back to the ship on her own? I figured you for men of honor!'

That quieted their protests.

Yalb chuckled to himself, bowing to Shallan and leading her away down the path. He had a twinkle to his eyes. 'Stormfather, but it's fun to win against lawmen. I'll have free drinks at the docks once this gets around.'

'You shouldn't gamble,' Shallan said. 'You shouldn't try to guess the future. I didn't give you that sphere so you could waste it on such practices.'

Yalb laughed. 'It ain't gambling if you know you're going to win, young miss.'

'You *cheated*?' she hissed, horrified. She glanced back at the guardsmen, who had settled down to continue their game, lit by the spheres on the stones before them.

'Not so loud!' Yalb said in a low voice. However, he seemed very pleased with himself. 'Cheating four guardsmen, now that's a trick. Hardly believe I managed it!'

'I'm disappointed in you. This is *not* proper behavior.'

'It is if you're a sailor, young miss.' He shrugged. 'It's what they right expected from me. Watched me like handlers of poisonous skyeels, they did. The game wasn't about the cards – it was about them trying to figure how I was cheating and me trying to figure how to keep them from hauling me off. I think I might not have managed to walk away with my skin if you hadn't arrived!' That didn't seem to worry him much.

The roadway down to the docks was not nearly as busy as it had been earlier, but there were still a surprisingly large number of people about. The street was lit by oil lanterns – spheres would just have ended up in someone's pouch – but many of the people about carried sphere lanterns, casting a rainbow of colored light on the roadway. The people were almost like spren, each a different hue, moving this way or that.

'So, young miss,' Yalb said, leading her carefully through the traffic. 'You really want to go back? I just said what I did so I could extract myself from that game there.'

'Yes, I do want to go back, please.'

'And your princess?'

Shallan grimaced. 'The meeting was . . . unproductive.'

'She didn't take you? What's wrong with her?'

'Chronic competence, I should guess. She's been so successful in life that she has unrealistic expectations of others.'

Yalb frowned, guiding Shallan around a group of revelers stumbling drunkenly up the roadway. Wasn't it a little early for that sort of thing? Yalb got a few steps ahead, turning and walking backward, looking at her. 'That doesn't make sense, young miss. What more could she want than you?'

'Much more, apparently.'

'But you're perfect! Pardon my forwardness.'

'You're walking backward.'

'Pardon my backwardness, then. You look good from any side, young miss, that you do.'

She found herself smiling. Tozbek's sailors had far too high an opinion of her.

'You'd make an ideal ward,' he continued. 'Genteel, pretty, refined and such. Don't much like your opinion on gambling, but that's to be expected. Wouldn't be right for a proper woman not to scold a fellow for gambling. It'd be like the sun refusing to rise or the sea turning white.'

'Or Jasnah Kholin smiling.'

'Exactly! Anyway, you're perfect.'

'It's kind of you to say so.'

'Well, it's true,' he said, putting hands on hips, stopping. 'So that's it? You're going to give up?'

She gave him a perplexed stare. He stood there on the busy roadway, lit from above by a lantern burning yellow-orange, hands on his hips, white Thaylen eyebrows drooping along the sides of his face, bare-chested under his open vest. That was a posture no citizen, no matter how high ranked, had ever taken at her father's mansion.

'I *did* try to persuade her,' Shallan said, blushing. 'I went to her a second time, and she rejected me again.'

'Two times, eh? In cards, you always got to try a third hand. It wins the most often.'

Shallan frowned. 'But that's not really true. The laws of probability and statistics—'

'Don't know much blustering math,' Yalb said, folding his arms. 'But I do know the Passions. You win when you need it most, you see.'

The Passions. Pagan superstition. Of course, Jasnah had referred to glyphwards as superstition too, so perhaps it all came down to perspective.

Try a third time . . . Shallan shivered to consider Jasnah's wrath if Shallan bothered her yet again. She'd surely withdraw the offer to come study with her in the future.

But Shallan would never get to take that offer. It was like a glass sphere with no gemstone at the center. Pretty, but worthless. Was it not better to take one last chance at getting the position she needed *now*?

It wouldn't work. Jasnah had made it quite clear that Shallan was not yet educated enough.

Not yet educated enough . . .

An idea sparked in Shallan's head. She raised her safehand to her breast, standing on that roadway, considering the audacity of it. She'd likely get herself thrown from the city at Jasnah's demand.

Yet if she returned home without trying every avenue, could she face her brothers? They depended on her. For once in her life, someone *needed* Shallan. That responsibility excited her. And terrified her.

'I need a book merchant,' she found herself saying, voice wavering slightly.

Yalb raised an eyebrow at her.

'Third hand wins the most. Do you think you can find me a book merchant who is open at this hour?'

'Kharbranth is a major port, young miss,' he said with a laugh. 'Stores stay open late. Just wait here.' He dashed off into the evening crowd, leaving her with an anxious protest on her lips.

She sighed, then seated herself in a demure posture on the stone base of a lantern pole. It should be safe. She saw other lighteyed women passing on the street, though they were often carried in palanquins or those small, hand-pulled vehicles. She even saw the occasional real carriage, though only the very wealthy could afford to keep horses.

A few minutes later, Yalb popped out of the crowd as if from nowhere and waved for her to follow. She rose and hurried to him.

'Should we get a porter?' she asked as he led her to a large side street that ran laterally across the city's hill. She stepped carefully; her skirt was long enough that she worried about tearing the hem on the stone. The strip at the bottom was designed to be easily replaced, but Shallan could hardly afford to waste spheres on such things.

'Nah,' Yalb said. 'It's right here.' He pointed along another cross street. This one had a row of shops climbing up the steep slope, each with a sign hanging out front bearing the glyphpair for *book*, and those glyphs were often styled into the shape of a book. Illiterate servants who might be sent to a shop had to be able to recognize them.

'Merchants of the same type like to clump together,' Yalb said, rubbing his chin. 'Seems dumb to me, but I guess merchants are like fish. Where you find one, you'll find others.'

'The same could be said of ideas,' Shallan said, counting. Six different shops. All were lit with Stormlight in the windows, cool and even.

'Third one on the left,' Yalb said, pointing. 'Merchant's name is Artmyrn. My sources say he's the best.' It was a Thaylen name. Likely Yalb had asked others from his homeland, and they had pointed him here.

She nodded to Yalb and they climbed up the steep stone street to the shop. Yalb didn't enter with her; she'd noticed that many men were uncomfortable around books and reading, even those who weren't Vorin.

She pushed through the door – stout wood set with two crystal panels – and stepped into a warm room, uncertain what to expect. She'd never gone into a store to purchase anything; she'd either sent servants, or the merchants had come to her.

The room inside looked very inviting, with large, comfortable easy chairs beside a hearth. Flamespren danced on burning logs there, and the floor was wood. Seamless wood; it had probably been Soulcast that way directly from the stone beneath. Lavish indeed.

A woman stood behind a counter at the back of the room. She wore an embroidered skirt and blouse, rather than the sleek, silk, one-piece havah that Shallan wore. She was darkeyed, but she was obviously affluent. In Vorin kingdoms, she'd likely be of the first or second nahn. Thaylens had their own system of ranks. At least they weren't completely pagan – they respected eye color, and the woman wore a glove on her safehand.

There weren't many books in the place. A few on the counter, one on a stand beside the chairs. A clock ticked on the wall, its underside hung with a dozen shimmering silver bells. This looked more like a person's home than a shop.

The woman slid a marker into her book smiling at Shallan. It was a smooth, eager smile. Almost predatory. 'Please, Brightness, sit,' she said, waving toward the chairs. The woman had curled her long, white Thaylen eyebrows so they hung down the sides of her face like locks from her bangs.

Shallan sat hesitantly as the woman rang a bell on the underside of the counter. Soon, a portly man waddled into the room wearing a vest that seemed ready to burst from the stress of holding in his girth. His hair was greying, and he kept his eyebrows combed back, over his ears.

'Ah,' he said, clapping ample hands, 'dear young woman. Are you in the market for a nice novel? Some leisure reading to pass the cruel hours while you are separated from a lost love? Or perhaps a book on geography, with details of exotic locations?' He had a slightly condescending tone and spoke in her native Veden.

'I— No, thank you. I need an extensive set of books on history and three on philosophy.' She thought back, trying to recall the names Jasnah had used. 'Something by Placini, Gabrathin, Yustara, Manaline, or Shauka-daughter-Hasweth.'

'Heavy reading for one so young,' the man said, nodding to the woman, who was probably his wife. She ducked into the back room. He'd use her for reading; even if he could read himself, he wouldn't want to offend customers by doing so in their presence. He would handle the money; commerce was a masculine art in most situations.

'Now, why is a young flower like yourself bothering herself with such topics?' the merchant said, easing himself down into the chair across from her. 'Can't I interest you in a nice romantic novel? They are my specialty, you see. Young women from across the city come to me, and I always carry the best.'

His tone set her on edge. It was galling enough to *know* she was a sheltered child. Was it really necessary to remind her of it? 'A romantic novel,' she said, holding her satchel close to her chest. 'Yes, perhaps that would be nice. Do you by chance have a copy of *Nearer the Flame*?'

The merchant blinked. *Nearer the Flame* was written from the viewpoint of a man who slowly descended into madness after watching his children starve.

'Are you certain you want something so, er, ambitious?' the man asked.

'Is ambition such an unseemly attribute in a young woman?'

'Well, no, I suppose not.' He smiled again – the thick, toothy smile of a merchant trying to put someone at ease. 'I can see you are a woman of discriminating taste.'

'I am,' Shallan said, voice firm though her heart fluttered. Was she destined to get into an argument with everyone she met? 'I *do* like my meals prepared very carefully, as my palate is quite delicate.'

'Pardon. I meant that you have discriminating taste *in books*.'

'I've never eaten one, actually.'

'Brightness, I believe you are having sport with me.'

'Not yet I'm not. I haven't even really begun.'

'I—'

'Now,' she said, 'you were right to compare the mind and the stomach.'

'But—'

'Too many of us,' she said, 'take great pains with what we ingest through our mouths, and far less with what we partake of through our ears and eyes. Wouldn't you say?'

He nodded, perhaps not trusting her to let him speak without interrupting. Shallan knew, somewhere in the back of her mind, that she was letting herself go too far – that she was tense and frustrated after her interactions with Jasnah.

She didn't care at the moment. 'Discriminating,' she said, testing the world. 'I'm not certain I agree with your choice of words. To discriminate is to maintain prejudice against. To be exclusive. Can a person afford to be exclusive with what they ingest? Whether we speak of food or of thoughts?'

'I think they must be,' the merchant said. 'Isn't that what you just said?'

'I said we should take thought for what we read or eat. Not that we should be exclusive. Tell me, what do you think would happen to a person who ate only sweets?'

'I know well,' the man said. 'I have a sister-in-law who periodically upsets her stomach by doing that.'

'See, she was *too* discriminating. The body needs many different foods to remain healthy. And the mind needs many different ideas to remain sharp. Wouldn't you agree? And so if I were to read only these silly romances you presume that my ambition can handle, my mind would grow sick as surely as your sister-in-law's stomach. Yes, I should think that the metaphor is a solid one. You are quite clever, Master Artmyrn.'

His smile returned.

'Of course,' she noted, not smiling back, 'being talked down to upsets both the mind *and* the stomach. So nice of you to give a poignant object lesson to accompany your brilliant metaphor. Do you treat all of your customers this way?'

'Brightness . . . I believe you stray into sarcasm.'

'Funny. I thought I'd run straight into it, screaming at the top of my lungs.'

He blushed and stood. 'I'll go help my wife.' He hurriedly withdrew.

She sat back, and realized she was annoyed at herself for letting her frustration boil out. It was just what her nurses had warned her about. A young woman had to mind her words. Her father's intemperate tongue had earned their house a regrettable reputation; would she add to it?

She calmed herself, enjoying the warmth and watching the dancing flamespren until the merchant and his wife returned, bearing several stacks of books. The merchant took his seat again, and his wife pulled over a stool, setting the tomes on the floor and then showing them one at a time as her husband spoke.

'For history, we have two choices,' the merchant said, condescension – and friendliness – gone. '*Times and Passage*, by Rencalt, is a single volume survey of Rosharan history since the Hierocracy.' His wife held up a red, cloth-bound volume. 'I told my wife that you would likely be insulted by such a shallow option, but she insisted.'

'Thank you,' Shallan said. 'I am not insulted, but I do require something more detailed.'

'Then perhaps *Eternathis* will serve you,' he said as his wife held up a blue-grey set of four volumes. 'It is a philosophical work which examines the same time period by focusing only on the interactions of the five Vorin kingdoms. As you can see, the treatment is exhaustive.'

The four volumes were thick. The *five* Vorin kingdoms? She'd thought there were four. Jah Keved, Alethkar, Kharbranth, and Natanatan. United by religion, they had been strong allies during the years following the Recreance. What was the fifth kingdom?

The volumes intrigued her. 'I will take them.'

'Excellent,' the merchant said, a bit of the gleam returning to his eye. 'Of the philosophical works you listed, we didn't have anything by Yustara. We have one each of works by Placini and Manaline; both are collections of excerpts from their most famous writings. I've had the Placini book read to me; it's quite good.'

Shallan nodded.

'As for Gabrathin,' he said, 'we have four different volumes. My, but he was a prolific one! Oh, and we have a single book by Shauka-daughter-Hasweth.' The wife held up a thin green volume. 'I have to admit, I've never had any of her work read to me. I didn't realize that there were any Shin philosophers of note.'

Shallan looked at the four books by Gabrathin. She had no idea which one she should take, so she avoided the question, pointing at the two collections he had mentioned first and the single volume by Shauka-daughter-Hasweth. A philosopher from distant Shin, where people lived in mud and worshipped rocks? The man who had killed Jasnah's father nearly six years before – prompting the war against the Parshendi in Natanatan – had been Shin. The Assassin in White, they called him.

'I will take those three,' Shallan said, 'along with the histories.'

'Excellent!' the merchant repeated. 'For buying so many, I will give you a fair discount. Let us say, ten emerald broams?'

Shallan nearly choked. An emerald broam was the largest denomination of sphere, worth a thousand diamond chips. Ten of them was more than her trip to Kharbranth had cost by several magnitudes!

She opened her satchel, looking in at her money pouch. She had around eight emerald broams left. She'd have to take fewer of the books, obviously, but which ones?

Suddenly, the door slammed open. Shallan jumped and was surprised to see Yalb standing there, holding his cap in his hands, nervous. He rushed to her chair, going down on one knee. She was too stunned to say anything. Why was he so worried?

'Brightness,' he said, bowing his head. 'My master bids you return. He's reconsidered his offer. Truly, we can take the price you offered.'

Shallan opened her mouth, but found herself stupefied.

Yalb glanced at the merchant. 'Brightness, don't buy from this man.

He's a liar and a cheat. My master will sell you much finer books at a better price.'

'Now, what's this?' Artmyrn said, standing. 'How dare you! Who is your master?'

'Barmest,' Yalb said defensively.

'That rat. He sends a boy into *my* shop trying to steal *my* customer? Outrageous!'

'She came to our shop first!' Yalb said.

Shallan finally recovered her wits. *Stormfather! He's quite the actor.* 'You had your chance,' she said to Yalb. 'Run along and tell your master that I refuse to be swindled. I will visit every bookshop in the city if that is what it takes to find someone reasonable.'

'Artmyrn isn't reasonable,' Yalb said, spitting to the side. The merchant's eyes opened wide with rage.

'We shall see,' Shallan said.

'Brightness,' Artmyrn said, red-faced. 'Surely you don't believe these allegations!'

'And how much were you going to charge her?' Yalb asked.

'Ten emerald broams,' Shallan said. 'For those seven books.'

Yalb laughed. 'And you didn't stand up and walk right out! You practically had my master's ears, and he offered you a better deal than that! Please, Brightness, return with me. We're ready to—'

'Ten was just an opening figure,' Artmyrn said. 'I didn't expect her to take them.' He looked at Shallan. 'Of course, *eight*. . . .'

Yalb laughed again. 'I'm sure we have those same books, Brightness. I'll bet my master gives them to you for two.'

Artmyrn grew more red-faced, muttering. 'Brightness, surely you wouldn't patronize someone so *crass* as to send a servant into someone else's shop to steal his customers!'

'Perhaps I would,' Shallan said. 'At least he didn't insult my intelligence.'

Artmyrn's wife glared at her husband, and the man grew even more red in the face. 'Two emerald, three sapphire. That is as low as I can go. If you want cheaper than that, then buy from that scoundrel Barmest. The books will probably be missing pages, though.'

Shallan hesitated, glancing at Yalb; he was caught up in his role, bowing and scraping. She caught his eyes, and he just kind of gave a shrug.

'I'll do it,' she said to Artmyrn, prompting a groan from Yalb. He slunk away with a curse from Artmyrn's wife. Shallan rose and counted out the spheres; the emerald broams she retrieved from her safepouch.

Soon, she walked from the shop bearing a heavy canvas bag. She walked down the steep street, and found Yalb lounging beside a lamppost. She smiled as he took the bag from her. 'How did you know what a fair price for a book was?' she asked.

'Fair price?' he said, slinging the bag over his shoulder. 'For a book? I've no idea. I just figured he'd be trying to take you for as much as he could. That's why I asked around for who his biggest rival was and came back to help get him to be more reasonable.'

'It was that obvious I'd let myself be swindled?' she asked with a blush, the two of them walking out of the side street.

Yalb chuckled. 'Just a little. Anyway, conning men like him is almost as much fun as cheating guards. You probably could have gotten him down further by actually leaving with me, then coming back later to give him another chance.'

'That sounds complicated.'

'Merchants is like mercenaries, my gammer always said. Only difference is that merchants will take your head off, then pretend to be your friend all the same.'

This from a man who had just spent the evening cheating a group of guards at cards. 'Well, you have my thanks, anyway.'

'Wasn't nothing. It was fun, though I can't believe you paid what you did. It's just a bunch of wood. I could find some driftwood and put some funny marks on it. Would you pay me pure spheres for that too?'

'I can't offer that,' she said, fishing in her satchel. She took out the picture she'd drawn of Yalb and the porter. 'But please, take this, with my thanks.'

Yalb took the picture and stepped up beneath a nearby lantern to get a look. He laughed, cocking his head, smiling broadly. 'Stormfather! Ain't that something? Looks like I'm seeing myself in a polished plate, it does. I can't take this, Brightness!'

'Please. I insist.' She did, however, blink her eyes, taking a Memory of him standing there, one hand on his chin as he studied the picture of himself. She'd redraw him later. After what he'd done for her, she dearly wanted him in her collection.

Yalb carefully tucked the picture between the pages of a book, then hefted the bag and continued. They stepped back onto the main roadway. Nomon – the middle moon – had begun to rise, bathing the city in pale blue light. Staying up this late had been a rare privilege for her in her father's house, but these city people around them barely seemed to notice the late hour. What a strange place this city was.

'Back to the ship now?' Yalb asked.

'No,' Shallan said, taking a deep breath. 'Back to the Conclave.'

He raised an eyebrow, but led her back. Once there, she bid Yalb farewell, reminding him to take his picture. He did so, wishing her luck before hastening from the Conclave, probably worried about meeting the guardsmen he'd cheated earlier.

Shallan had a servant carry her books, and made her way down the hallway back to the Veil. Just inside the ornate iron doors, she caught the attention of a master-servant.

'Yes, Brightness?' the man asked. Most of the alcoves were now dim, and patient servants were returning tomes to their safe place beyond the crystal walls.

Shaking off her fatigue, Shallan counted up the rows. There was still a light in Jasnah's alcove. 'I'd like to use the alcove there,' she said, pointing to the next balcony over.

'Do you have a chit of admittance?'

'I'm afraid not.'

'Then you'll have to rent the space if you wish to use it regularly. Two skymarks.'

Wincing at the price, Shallan dug out the proper spheres and paid. Her money pouches were looking depressingly flat. She let the parshman porters haul her up to the appropriate level, then she quietly walked to her alcove. There, she used all her remaining spheres to fill the oversized goblet lamp. To get enough light, she was forced to use spheres of all nine colors and all three sizes, so the illumination was patchy and varied.

Shallan peeked over the side of her alcove, out at the next balcony over. Jasnah sat studying, heedless of the hour, her goblet filled to the brim with pure diamond broams. They were best for light, but less useful in Soulcasting, so weren't as valuable.

Shallan ducked back around. There was a place at the very edge of the alcove's table where she could sit, hidden by the wall from Jasnah, so she sat there. Perhaps she should have chosen an alcove on another level, but she wanted to keep an eye on the woman. Hopefully Jasnah would spend weeks here studying. Enough time for Shallan to dedicate herself to some fierce cramming. Her ability to memorize pictures and scenes didn't work as well on text, but she could learn lists and facts at a rate that her tutors had found remarkable.

She settled herself in the chair, pulling out the books and arranging them. She rubbed her eyes. It was really quite late, but there wasn't time to waste. Jasnah had said that Shallan could make another petition when the gaps in her knowledge were filled. Well, Shallan intended to fill those gaps in record time, then present herself again. She'd do it when Jasnah was ready to leave Kharbranth.

It was a last, desperate hope, so frail that a strong gust of circumstance seemed likely to topple it. Taking a deep breath, Shallan opened the first of the history books.

'I'm never going to be rid of you, am I?' a soft, feminine voice asked.

Shallan jumped up, nearly knocking over her books as she spun toward the doorway. Jasnah Kholin stood there, deep blue dress embroidered in silver, its silken sheen reflecting the light of Shallan's spheres. The Soulcaster was covered by a fingerless black glove to block the bright gemstones.

'Brightness,' Shallan said, rising and curtsying in an awkward rush. 'I didn't mean to disturb you. I—'

Jasnah quieted her with a wave of the hand. She stepped aside as a parshman entered Shallan's alcove, carrying a chair. He placed it beside Shallan's desk, and Jasnah glided over and sat.

Shallan tried to judge Jasnah's mood, but the older woman's emotions were impossible to read. 'I honestly didn't want to disturb you.'

'I bribed the servants to tell me if you returned to the Veil,' Jasnah said idly, picking up one of Shallan's tomes, reading the title. 'I didn't want to be interrupted again.'

'I—' Shallan looked down, blushing furiously.

'Don't bother apologizing,' Jasnah said. She looked tired; more tired than Shallan felt. Jasnah picked through the books. 'A fine selection. You chose well.'

'It wasn't really much of a choice,' Shallan said. 'It was just about all the merchant had.'

'You intended to study their contents quickly, I assume?' Jasnah said musingly. 'Try to impress me one last time before I left Kharbranth?'

Shallan hesitated, then nodded.

'A clever ploy. I should have put a time restriction on your reapplication.' She looked at Shallan, glancing her over. 'You are very determined. That is good. And I know why you wish so desperately to be my ward.'

Shallan started. She *knew*?

'Your house has many enemies,' Jasnah continued, 'and your father is reclusive. It will be difficult for you to marry well without a tactically sound alliance.'

Shallan relaxed, though she tried to keep it from showing.

'Let me see your satchel,' Jasnah said.

Shallan frowned, resisting the urge to pull it close. 'Brightness?'

Jasnah held out her hand. 'You recall what I said about repeating myself?'

Reluctantly, Shallan handed it over. Jasnah carefully removed its contents, neatly lining up the brushes, pencils, pens, jar of lacquer, ink, and solvent. She placed the stacks of paper, the notebooks, and the finished pictures in a line. Then she got out Shallan's money pouches, noting their emptiness. She glanced at the goblet lamp, counting its contents. She raised an eyebrow.

Next, she began to look through Shallan's pictures. First the loose-leaf ones, where she lingered on Shallan's picture of Jasnah herself. Shallan watched the woman's face. Was she pleased? Surprised? Displeased at how much time Shallan spent sketching sailors and serving women?

Finally, Jasnah moved on to the sketchbook filled with drawings of plants and animals Shallan had observed during her trip. Jasnah spent the longest on this, reading through each notation. 'Why have you made these sketches?' Jasnah asked at the end.

'Why, Brightness? Well, because I wanted to.' She grimaced. Should she have said something profound instead?

Jasnah nodded slowly. Then she rose. 'I have rooms in the Conclave, granted to me by the king. Gather your things and go there. You look exhausted.'

'Brightness?' Shallan asked, rising, a thrill of excitement running through her.

Jasnah hesitated at the doorway. 'At first meeting, I took you for a rural opportunist, seeking only to ride my name to greater wealth.'

'You've changed your mind?'

'No,' Jasnah said, 'there is undoubtedly some of that in you. But we are each many different people, and you can tell much about a person by what they carry with them. If that notebook is any indication, you pursue scholarship in your free time for its own sake. That is encouraging. It is, perhaps, the best argument you could make on your own behalf.

'If I cannot be rid of you, then I might as well make use of you. Go and sleep. Tomorrow we will begin early, and you will divide your time between your education and helping me with my studies.'

With that, Jasnah withdrew.

Shallan sat, bemused, blinking tired eyes. She got out a sheet of paper and wrote a quick prayer of thanks, which she'd burn later. Then she hurriedly gathered up her books and went looking for a servant to send to the *Wind's Pleasure* for her trunk.

It had been a very, *very* long day. But she'd won. The first step had been completed.

Now her real task began.

Chulls

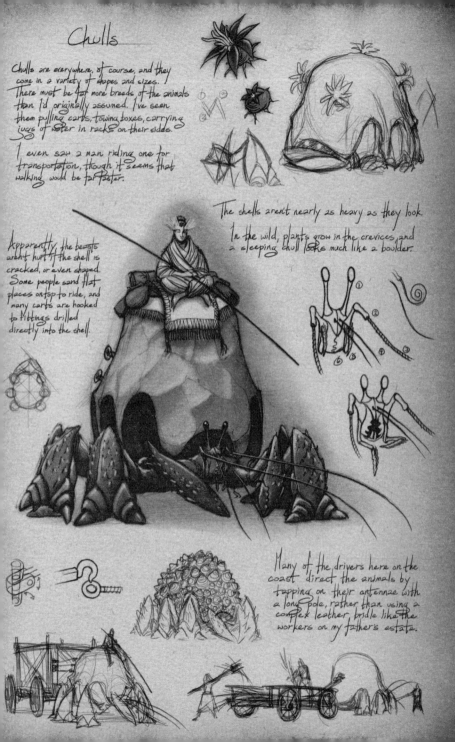

Chulls are everywhere, of course, and they come in a variety of shapes and sizes. There must be far more breeds of the animals than I'd originally assumed. I've seen them pulling carts, towing boxes, carrying jugs of water in racks on their sides.

I even saw a man riding one for transportation, though it seems that walking would be far faster.

Apparently, the beasts aren't hurt if the shell is cracked, or even shaped. Some people sand flat places on top to ride, and many carts are hooked to fittings drilled directly into the shell.

The shells aren't nearly as heavy as they look.

In the wild, plants grow in the crevices, and a sleeping chull looks much like a boulder.

Many of the drivers here on the coast direct the animals by tapping on their antennae with a long pole, rather than using a complex leather bridle like the workers on my father's estate.

9

DAMNATION

'Ten people, with Shardblades alight, standing before a wall of black and white and red.'

—Collected: Jesachev, 1173, 12 seconds pre-death. Subject: one of our own ardents, overheard during his last moments.

Kaladin had not been assigned to Bridge Four by chance. Out of all the bridge crews, Bridge Four had the highest casualty rate. That was particularly notable, considering that average bridge crews often lost one-third to one-half of their number on a single run.

Kaladin sat outside, back to the barrack wall, a sprinkle of rain falling on him. It wasn't a highstorm. Just an ordinary spring rain. Soft. A timid cousin to the great storms.

Syl sat on Kaladin's shoulder. Or hovered on it. Whatever. She didn't seem to have any weight. Kaladin sat slumped, chin against his chest, staring at a dip in the stone, which was slowly collecting rainwater.

He should have moved inside Bridge Four's barrack. It was cold and unfurnished, but it would keep off the rain. But he just ... couldn't care. How long had he been with Bridge Four now? Two weeks? Three? An eternity?

Of the twenty-five men who had survived his first bridge deployment, twenty-three were now dead. Two had been moved to other bridge crews because they'd done something to please Gaz, but they'd died there. Only one other man and Kaladin remained. Two out of nearly forty.

The bridge crew's numbers had been replenished with more unfortunates, and most of those had died too. They had been replaced. Many of those had died. Bridgeleader after bridgeleader had been chosen. It was supposed to be a favored position on a bridge crew, always getting to run in the best places. It didn't matter for Bridge Four.

Some bridge runs weren't as bad. If the Alethi arrived before the Parshendi, no bridgemen died. And if they arrived too late, sometimes another highprince was already there. Sadeas wouldn't help in that case; he'd take his army and go back to camp. Even in a bad run, the Parshendi would often choose to focus their arrows on certain crews, trying to bring them down one at a time. Sometimes, dozens of bridgemen would fall, but not a single one from Bridge Four.

That was rare. For some reason, Bridge Four always seemed to get targeted. Kaladin didn't bother to learn the names of his companions. None of the bridgemen did. What was the point? Learn a man's name, and one of you would be dead before the week was out. Odds were, you'd both be dead. Maybe he *should* learn names. Then he'd have someone to talk to in Damnation. They could reminisce about how terrible Bridge Four had been, and agree that eternal fires were much more pleasant.

He smirked dully, still staring at the rock in front of him. Gaz would come for them soon, send them to work. Scrubbing latrines, cleaning streets, mucking stables, gathering rocks. Something to keep their minds off their fate.

He still didn't know why they fought on those blustering plateaus. Something about those large chrysalises. They had gemstones at their hearts, apparently. But what did that have to do with the Vengeance Pact?

Another bridgeman – a youthful Veden with reddish-blond hair – lay nearby, staring up into the spitting sky. Rainwater pooled in the corners of his brown eyes, then ran down his face. He didn't blink.

They couldn't run. The warcamp might as well have been a prison. The bridgemen could go to the merchants and spend their meager earnings on cheap wine or whores, but they couldn't leave the warcamp. The perimeter was secure. Partially, this was to keep out soldiers from the other camps – there was always rivalry where armies met. But mostly it was so bridgemen and slaves could not flee.

Why? Why did this all have to be so horrible? None of it made *sense*. Why not let a few bridgemen run out in front of the bridges with shields to block arrows? He'd asked, and had been told that would slow them down too much. He'd asked again, and had been told he'd be strung up if he didn't shut his mouth.

The lighteyes acted as if this entire mess were some kind of grand game. If it was, the rules were hidden from bridgemen, just as pieces on a board had no inkling what the player's strategy might be.

'Kaladin?' Syl asked, floating down and landing on his leg, holding the girlish form with the long dress flowing into mist. 'Kaladin? You haven't spoken in days.'

He kept staring, slumped. There *was* a way out. Bridgemen could visit the chasm nearest the camp. There were rules forbidding it, but the sentries ignored them. It was seen as the one mercy that could be given the bridgemen.

Bridgemen who took that path never returned.

'Kaladin?' Syl said, voice soft, worried.

'My father used to say that there are two kinds of people in the world,' Kaladin whispered, voice raspy. 'He said there are those who take lives. And there are those who save lives.'

Syl frowned, cocking her head. This kind of conversation confused her; she wasn't good with abstractions.

'I used to think he was wrong. I thought there was a third group. People who killed in order to save.' He shook his head. 'I was a fool. There *is* a third group, a big one, but it isn't what I thought.'

'What group?' she said, sitting down on his knee, brow scrunched up.

'The people who exist to be saved or to be killed. The group in the middle. The ones who can't do anything but die or be protected. The victims. That's all I am.'

He looked up across the wet lumberyard. The carpenters had retreated, throwing tarps over untreated wood and bearing away tools that could rust. The bridgeman barracks ran around the west and north sides of the yard. Bridge Four's was set off a little from the others, as if bad luck were a disease that could be caught. Contagious by proximity, as Kaladin's father would say.

'We exist to be killed,' Kaladin said. He blinked, glancing at the other few members of Bridge Four sitting apathetically in the rain. 'If we're not dead already.'

⁘

'I hate seeing you like this,' Syl said, buzzing about Kaladin's head as his team of bridgemen dragged a log down into the lumberyard. The Parshendi often set fire to the outermost permanent bridges, so Highprince Sadeas's engineers and carpenters were always busy.

The old Kaladin might have wondered why the armies didn't work harder to defend the bridges. *There's something wrong here!* a voice inside him said. *You're missing part of the puzzle. They waste resources and bridgeman lives. They don't seem to care about pushing inward and assaulting the Parshendi. They just fight pitched battles on plateaus, then come back to the camps and celebrate. Why? WHY?*

He ignored that voice. It belonged to the man he had been.

'You used to be vibrant,' Syl said. 'So many looked up to you, Kaladin. Your squad of soldiers. The enemies you fought. The other slaves. Even some lighteyes.'

Lunch would come soon. Then he could sleep until their bridgeleader kicked him awake for afternoon duty.

'I used to watch you fight,' Syl said. 'I can barely remember it. My memories of then are fuzzy. Like looking at you through a rainstorm.'

Wait. That was odd. Syl hadn't started following him until after his fall from the army. And she'd acted just like an ordinary windspren back then. He hesitated, earning a curse and a lash on his back from a taskmaster's whip.

He started pulling again. Bridgemen who were laggard in work were whipped, and bridgemen who were laggard on runs were executed. The army was very serious about that. Refuse to charge the Parshendi, try to lag behind the other bridges, and you'd be beheaded. They reserved that fate for that specific crime, in fact.

There were lots of ways to get punished as a bridgeman. You could earn extra work detail, get whipped, have your pay docked. If you did something really bad, they'd string you up for the Stormfather's judgment, leaving you tied to a post or a wall to face a highstorm. But the only thing you could do to be executed directly was refuse to run at the Parshendi.

The message was clear. Charging with your bridge *might* get you killed, but refusing to do so *would* get you killed.

Kaladin and his crew lifted their log into a pile with others, then unhooked their dragging lines. They walked back toward the edge of the lumberyard, where more logs waited.

'Gaz!' a voice called. A tall, yellow-and-black-haired soldier stood at the edge of the bridge grounds, a group of miserable men huddled behind him. That was Laresh, one of the soldiers who worked the duty tent. He brought new bridgemen to replace those who'd been killed.

The day was bright, without a hint of clouds, and the sun was hot on Kaladin's back. Gaz hustled up to meet the new recruits, and Kaladin and the others happened to be walking in that direction to pick up a log.

'What a sorry lot,' Gaz said, looking over the recruits. 'Of course, if they weren't, they wouldn't be sent *here*.'

'That's the truth,' Laresh said. 'These ten at the front were caught smuggling. You know what to do.'

New bridgemen were constantly needed, but there were always enough bodies. Slaves were common, but so were thieves or other lawbreakers from among the camp followers. Never parshmen. They were too valuable, and besides, the Parshendi were some kind of cousins to the parshmen. Better not to give the parshman workers in camp the sight of their kind fighting.

Sometimes a soldier would be thrown into a bridge crew. That only happened if he'd done something extremely bad, like striking an officer. Acts that would earn a hanging in many armies meant being sent to the bridge crews here. Supposedly, if you survived a hundred bridge runs, you'd be released. It had happened once or twice, the stories said. It was probably just a myth, intended to give the bridgemen some tiny hope for survival.

Kaladin and the others walked past the newcomers, gazes down, and began hooking their ropes to the next log.

'Bridge Four needs some men,' Gaz said, rubbing his chin.

'Four always needs men,' Laresh said. 'Don't worry. I brought a special batch for it.' He nodded toward a second group of recruits, much more ragtag, walking up behind.

Kaladin slowly stood upright. One of the prisoners in that group was a boy of barely fourteen or fifteen. Short, spindly, with a round face. 'Tien?' he whispered, taking a step forward.

He stopped, shaking himself. Tien was dead. But this newcomer looked so familiar, with those frightened black eyes. It made Kaladin want to shelter the boy. Protect him.

But . . . he'd failed. Everyone he'd tried to protect – from Tien to Cenn – had ended up dead. What was the point?

He turned back to dragging the log.

'Kaladin,' Syl said, landing on the log, 'I'm going to leave.'

He blinked in shock. Syl. Leave? But . . . she was the last thing he had left. 'No,' he whispered. It came out as a croak.

'I'll try to come back,' she said. 'But I don't know what will happen when I leave you. Things are strange. I have odd memories. No, most of them aren't even memories. Instincts. One of those tells me that if I leave you, I might lose myself.'

'Then don't go,' he said, growing terrified.

'I have to,' she said, cringing. 'I can't watch this anymore. I'll try to return.' She looked sorrowful. 'Goodbye.' And with that, she zipped away into the air, adopting the form of a tiny group of tumbling, translucent leaves.

Kaladin watched her go, numb.

Then he turned back to hauling the log. What else could he do?

❖

The youth, the one that reminded him of Tien, died during the very next bridge run.

It was a bad one. The Parshendi were in position, waiting for Sadeas. Kaladin charged the chasm not even flinching as men were slaughtered around him. It wasn't bravery that drove him; it wasn't even a wish that those arrows would take him and end it all. He ran. That was what he did. Like a boulder rolled down a hill, or like rain fell from the sky. They didn't have a choice. Neither did he. He wasn't a man; he was a thing, and things just did what they did.

The bridgemen laid their bridges in a tight line. Four crews had fallen. Kaladin's own team had lost nearly enough to stop them.

Bridge placed, Kaladin turned away, the army charging across the wood to start the real battle. He stumbled back across the plateau. After a few moments, he found what he was looking for. The boy's body.

Kaladin stood, wind whipping at his hair, looking down at the corpse. It lay faceup in a small hollow in the stone. Kaladin remembered lying in a similar hollow, holding a similar corpse.

Another bridgeman had fallen nearby, bristling with arrows. It was the man who'd lived through Kaladin's first bridge run all those weeks back. His body slumped to the side, lying on a stone outcropping a foot or so above the corpse of the boy. Blood dripped from the tip of an arrow sticking out his back. It fell, one ruby drop at a time, splattering on the boy's open, lifeless eye. A little trail of red ran from the eye down the side of his face. Like crimson tears.

That night, Kaladin huddled in the barrack, listening to a highstorm buffet the wall. He curled against the cold stone. Thunder shattered the sky outside.

I can't keep going like this, he thought. *I'm dead inside, as sure as if I'd taken a spear through the neck.*

The storm continued its tirade. And for the first time in over eight months, Kaladin found himself crying.

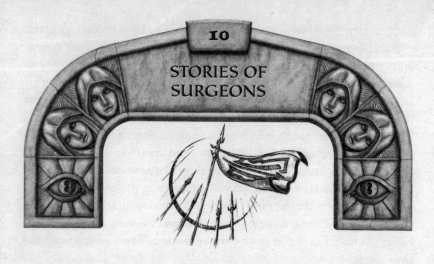

10

STORIES OF SURGEONS

NINE YEARS AGO

Kal stumbled into the surgery room, the open door letting in bright white sunlight. At ten years old, he was already showing signs that he would be tall and lanky. He'd always preferred Kal to his full name, Kaladin. The shorter name made him fit in better. Kaladin sounded like a lighteyes's name.

'I'm sorry, Father,' he said.

Kal's father, Lirin, carefully tightened the strap around the arm of the young woman who was tied onto the narrow operating table. Her eyes were closed; Kal had missed the administration of the drug. 'We will discuss your tardiness later,' Lirin said, securing the woman's other hand. 'Close the door.'

Kal cringed and closed the door. The windows were dark, shutters firmly in place, and so the only light was that of the Stormlight shining from a large globe filled with spheres. Each of those spheres was a broam, in total an incredible sum that was on permanent loan from Hearthstone's landlord. Lanterns flickered, but Stormlight was always true. That could save lives, Kal's father said.

Kal approached the table, anxious. The young woman, Sani, had sleek black hair, not tinged with even a single strand of brown or blond. She was fifteen, and her freehand was wrapped with a bloody, ragged bandage. Kal grimaced at the clumsy bandaging job – it looked like the cloth had been ripped from someone's shirt and tied in haste.

Sani's head rolled to the side, and she mumbled, drugged. She wore only a white cotton shift, her safehand exposed. Older boys in the town sniggered about the chances they'd had – or *claimed* to have had – at seeing girls in their shifts, but Kal didn't understand what the excitement was all about. He *was* worried about Sani, though. He always worried when someone was wounded.

Fortunately, the wound didn't look terrible. If it had been life-threatening, his father would have already begun working on it, using Kal's mother – Hesina – as an assistant.

Lirin walked to the side of the room and gathered up a few small, clear bottles. He was a short man, balding despite his relative youth. He wore his spectacles, which he called the most precious gift he'd ever been given. He rarely got them out except for surgery, as they were too valuable to risk just wearing about. What if they were scratched or broken? Hearth-stone was a large town, but its remote location in northern Alethkar would make replacing the spectacles difficult.

The room was kept neat, the shelves and table washed clean each morning, everything in its place. Lirin said you could tell a lot about a man from how he kept his workspace. Was it sloppy or orderly? Did he respect his tools or did he leave them casually about? The town's only fabrial clock sat here on the counter. The small device bore a single dial at the center and a glowing Smokestone at its heart; it had to be infused to keep the time. Nobody else in the town cared about minutes and hours as Lirin did.

Kal pulled over a stool to get a better vantage. Soon he wouldn't need the stool; he was growing taller by the day. He inspected Sani's hand. *She'll be all right*, he told himself, as his father had trained him. *A surgeon needs to be calm. Worry just wastes time.*

It was hard advice to follow.

'Hands,' Lirin said, not turning away from gathering his tools.

Kal sighed, hopping off his stool and hurrying over to the basin of warm, soapy water by the door. 'Why does it matter?' He wanted to be at work, helping Sani.

'Wisdom of the Heralds,' Lirin said absently, repeating a lecture he'd given many times before. 'Deathspren and rotspren hate water. It will keep them away.'

'Hammie says that's silly,' Kal said. 'He says deathspren are mighty good at killing folk, so why should they be afraid of a little water?'

'The Heralds were wise beyond our understanding.'

Kal grimaced. 'But they're *demons*, father. I heard it off that ardent who came teaching last spring.'

'That's the Radiants he spoke of,' Lirin said sharply. 'You're mixing them again.'

Kal sighed.

'The Heralds were sent to teach mankind,' Lirin said. 'They led us against the Voidbringers after we were cast from heaven. The Radiants were the orders of knights they founded.'

'Who were demons.'

'Who betrayed us,' Lirin said, 'once the Heralds left.' Lirin raised a finger. 'They were not demons, they were just men who had too much power and not enough sense. Either way, you are *always* to wash your hands. You can see the effect it has on rotspren with your own eyes, even if deathspren cannot be seen.'

Kal sighed again, but did as he was told. Lirin walked over to the table again, bearing a tray lined with knives and little glass bottles. His ways were odd – though Lirin made certain that his son didn't mix up the Heralds and the Lost Radiants, Kal had heard his father say that he thought the Voidbringers weren't real. Ridiculous. Who else could be blamed when things went missing in the night, or when a crop got infected with digger-worms?

The others in town thought Lirin spent too much time with books and sick people, and that made him strange. They were uncomfortable around him, and with Kal by association. Kal was only just beginning to realize how painful it could feel to be different.

Hands washed, he hopped back up onto the stool. He began to feel nervous again, hoping that nothing would go wrong. His father used a mirror to focus the spheres' light onto Sani's hand. Gingerly, he cut off the makeshift bandage with a surgeon's knife. The wound wasn't life-threatening, but the hand *was* pretty badly mangled. When his father had started training Kal two years before, sights like this had sickened him. Now he was used to torn flesh.

That was good. Kal figured this would be useful when he went to war someday, to fight for his highprince and the lighteyes.

Sani had three broken fingers and the skin on her hand was scraped and gouged, the wound cluttered with sticks and dirt. The third finger was the worst, shattered and twisted nastily, splinters of bone protruding through the skin. Kal felt its length, noting the fractured bones, the blackness on the skin. He carefully wiped away dried blood and dirt with a wet cloth, picking out rocks and sticks as his father cut thread for sewing.

'The third finger will have to go, won't it?' Kal said, tying a bandage around the base of the finger to keep it from bleeding.

His father nodded, a hint of a smile on his face. He'd hoped Kal would discern that. Lirin often said that a wise surgeon must know what to remove and what to save. If that third finger had been set properly at first ... but no, it was beyond recovery. Sewing it back together would mean leaving it to fester and die.

His father did the actual amputation. He had such careful, precise hands. Training as a surgeon took over ten years, and it would be some time yet before Lirin let Kal hold the knife. Instead, Kal wiped away blood, handed his father knives, and held the sinew to keep it from tangling as his father sewed. They repaired the hand so far as they could, working with deliberate speed.

Kal's father finished the final suture, obviously pleased at having been able to save four of the fingers. That wasn't how Sani's parents would see it. They'd be disappointed that their beautiful daughter would now have a disfigured hand. It almost always happened that way – terror at the initial wound, then anger at Lirin's inability to work wonders. Lirin said it was because the townsfolk had grown accustomed to having a surgeon. To them, the healing had become an expectation, rather than a privilege.

But Sani's parents were good people. They'd make a small donation, and Kal's family – his parents, him, and his younger brother Tien – would continue to be able to eat. Odd, how they survived because of others' misfortune. Maybe that was part of what made the townsfolk resent them.

Lirin finished by using a small heated rod to cauterize where he felt the stitches wouldn't be enough. Finally, he spread pungent lister's oil across the hand to prevent infection – the oil frightened away rotspren even better than soap and water. Kal wrapped on clean bandages, careful not to disturb the splints.

Lirin disposed of the finger, and Kal began to relax. She'd be all right.

'You still need to work on those nerves of yours, son,' Lirin said softly, washing blood from his hands.Kal looked down. 'It is good to care,' Lirin said. 'But caring – like anything else – can be a problem if it interferes with your ability to perform surgery.'

Caring too much can be a problem? Kal thought back at his father. *And what about being so selfless that you never charge for your work?* He didn't dare say the words.

Cleaning the room came next. It seemed like half of Kal's life was spent cleaning, but Lirin wouldn't let him go until they were done with it. At least he opened the shutters, letting sunlight stream in. Sani continued to doze; the winterwort would keep her unconscious for hours yet.

'So where were you?' Lirin asked, bottles of oil and alcohol clinking as he returned them to their places.

'With Jam.'

'Jam is two years your senior,' Lirin said. 'I doubt he has much fondness for spending his time with those much younger than he.'

'His father started training him in the quarterstaff,' Kal said in a rush. 'Tien and I went to see what he's learned.' Kal cringed, waiting for the lecture.

His father just continued, wiping down each of his surgeon's knives with alcohol, then oil, as the old traditions dictated. He didn't turn toward Kal.

'Jam's father was a soldier in Brightlord Amaram's army,' Kal said tentatively. Brightlord Amaram! The noble lighteyed general who watched over northern Alethkar. Kal wanted so much to see a *real* light-eyes, not stuffy old Wistiow. A soldier, like everyone talked about, like the stories were about.

'I know about Jam's father,' Lirin said. 'I've had to operate on that lame leg of his three times now. A gift of his glorious time as a soldier.'

'We *need* soldiers, father. You'd have our borders violated by the Thaylens?'

'Thaylenah is an island kingdom,' Lirin said calmly. 'They don't share a border with us.'

'Well, then, they could attack from the sea!'

'They're mostly tradesmen and merchants. Every one I've met has tried to swindle me, but that's hardly the same thing as invading.'

All the boys liked to tell stories about far-off places. It was hard to remember that Kal's father – the only man of second nahn in the town – had traveled all the way to Kharbranth during his youth.

'Well, we fight with *someone*,' Kal continued, moving to scrub the floor.

'Yes,' his father said after a pause. 'King Gavilar always finds people for us to fight. That much is true.'

'So we need soldiers, like I said.'

'We need surgeons more.' Lirin sighed audibly, turning away from his cabinet. 'Son, you nearly cry each time someone is brought to us; you grind your teeth anxiously during even simple procedures. What makes you think you could actually *hurt* someone?'

'I'll get stronger.'

'That's foolishness. Who's put these ideas in your head? *Why* would you want to learn to hit other boys with a stick?'

'For honor, Father,' Kal said. 'Who tells stories about *surgeons*, for the Heralds' sake!'

'The children of the men and women whose lives we save,' Lirin said evenly, meeting Kal's gaze. 'That's who tell stories of surgeons.'

Kal blushed and shrank back, then finally returned to his scrubbing.

'There are two kinds of people in this world, son,' his father said sternly. 'Those who save lives. And those who take lives.'

'And what of those who protect and defend? The ones who save lives *by* taking lives?'

His father snorted. 'That's like trying to stop a storm by blowing harder. Ridiculous. You can't protect by killing.'

Kal kept scrubbing.

Finally, his father sighed, walking over and kneeling down beside him, helping with the scrubbing. 'What are the properties of winterwort?'

'Bitter taste,' Kal said immediately, 'which makes it safer to keep, since people won't eat it by accident. Crush it to powder, mix it with oil, use one spoonful per ten brickweight of the person you're drugging. Induces a deep sleep for about five hours.'

'And how can you tell if someone has the fiddlepox?'

'Nervous energy,' Kal said, 'thirst, trouble sleeping, and swelling on the undersides of the arms.'

'You've got such a good mind, son,' Lirin said softly. 'It took me years to learn what you've done in months. I've been saving. I'd like to send you to Kharbranth when you turn sixteen, to train with real surgeons.'

Kal felt a spike of excitement. Kharbranth? That was in an entirely different kingdom! Kal's father had traveled there as a courier, but he hadn't trained there as a surgeon. He'd learned from old Vathe in Shorse-broon, the nearest town of any size.

'You have a gift from the Heralds themselves,' Lirin said, resting a hand on Kal's shoulder. 'You could be ten times the surgeon I am. Don't dream the small dreams of other men. Our grandfathers bought and worked us to the second nahn so that we could have full citizenship and the right of travel. Don't waste that on killing.'

Kal hesitated, but soon found himself nodding.

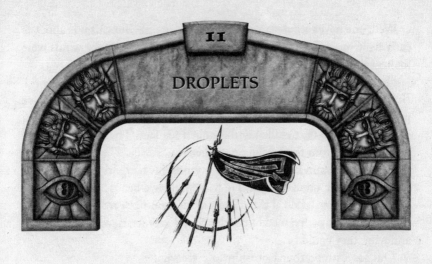

11

DROPLETS

'Three of sixteen ruled, but now the Broken One reigns.'

—Collected: Chachanan, 1173, 84 seconds pre-death. Subject: a cutpurse with the wasting sickness, of partial Iriali descent.

The highstorm eventually subsided. It was the dusk of the day the boy had died, the day Syl had left him. Kaladin slid on his sandals – the same ones he'd taken from the leathery-faced man on that first day – and stood up. He walked through the crowded barrack.

There were no beds, just one thin blanket per bridgeman. One had to choose whether to use it for cushioning or warmth. You could freeze or you could ache. Those were a bridgeman's options, though several of the bridgemen had found a third use for the blankets. They wrapped them around their heads, as if to block out sight, sound, and smell. To hide from the world.

The world would find them anyway. It was good at these kinds of games.

Rain fell in sheets outside, the wind still stiff. Flashes lit the western horizon, where the center of the storm flew onward. This was an hour or so before the riddens, and was as early as one would want to go out in a high-storm.

Well, one never *wanted* to go out in a highstorm. But this was about as early as it was *safe* to go out. The lightning had passed; the winds were manageable.

He passed through the dim lumberyard, hunched against the wind. Branches lay scattered about like bones in a whitespine's lair. Leaves were plastered by rainwater to the rough sides of barracks. Kaladin splashed through puddles that chilled and numbed his feet. That felt good; they were still sore from the bridge run earlier.

Waves of icy rain blew across him, wetting his hair, dripping down his face and into his scruffy beard. He hated having a beard, particularly the way the whiskers itched at the corners of his mouth. Beards were like axehound pups. Boys dreamed of the day they'd get one, never realizing how annoying they could be.

'Out for a stroll, Your Lordship?' a voice said.

Kaladin looked up to find Gaz huddled in a nearby hollow between two of the barracks. Why was he out in the rain?

Ah. Gaz had fastened a small metal basket on the leeward wall of one of the barracks, and a soft glowing light came from within. He left his spheres out in the storm, then had come out early to retrieve them.

It was a risk. Even a sheltered basket could get torn free. Some people believed that the shades of the Lost Radiants haunted the storms, stealing spheres. Perhaps that was true. But during his time in the army, Kaladin had known more than one man who had been wounded sneaking around during full storm, looking for spheres. No doubt the superstition was due to more worldly thieves.

There were safer ways to infuse spheres. Moneychangers would exchange dun spheres for infused ones, or you could pay them to infuse yours in one of their safely guarded nests.

'What are you doing?' Gaz demanded. The short, one-eyed man clutched the basket to his chest. 'I'll have you strung up if you've stolen anyone's spheres.'

Kaladin turned away from him.

'Storm you! I'll have you strung up anyway! Don't think you can run away; there are still sentries. You—'

'I'm going to the Honor Chasm,' Kaladin said quietly. His voice would barely be audible over the storm.

Gaz shut up. The Honor Chasm. He lowered his metal basket and made no further objections. There was a certain deference given to men who took that road.

Kaladin continued to cross the courtyard.

'Lordling,' Gaz called.

Kaladin turned.

'Leave the sandals and vest,' Gaz said. 'I don't want to have to send someone down to fetch them.'

Kaladin pulled the leather vest over his head and dropped it to the ground with a splash, then left the sandals in a puddle. That left him in a dirty shirt and stiff brown trousers, both taken off a dead man.

Kaladin walked through the storm to the east side of the lumberyard. A low thundering rumbled from the west. The pathway down to the Shattered Plains was familiar to him now. He'd run this way a dozen times with the bridge crews. There wasn't a battle every day – perhaps one in every two or three – and not every bridge crew had to go on every run. But many of the runs were so draining, so horrific, that they left the bridgemen stunned, almost unresponsive, for the days between.

Many bridgemen had trouble making decisions. The same happened to men who were shocked by battle. Kaladin felt those effects in himself. Even deciding to come to the chasm had been difficult.

But the bleeding eyes of that unnamed boy haunted him. He wouldn't make himself go through something like that again. He *couldn't*.

He reached the base of the slope, wind-driven rain pelting his face as if trying to shove him back toward the camp. He kept on, walking up to the nearest chasm. The Honor Chasm, the bridgemen called it, for it was the place where they could make the one decision left to them. The 'honorable' decision. Death.

They weren't natural, these chasms. This one started narrow, but as it ran toward the east, it grew wider – and deeper – incredibly quickly. At only ten feet long, the crack was already wide enough that it would be difficult to jump. A group of six rope ladders with wooden rungs hung here, affixed to spikes in the rock, used by bridgemen sent down to salvage from corpses that had fallen into the chasms during bridge runs.

Kaladin looked out over the plains. He couldn't see much through the darkness and rain. No, this place wasn't natural. The land had been broken. And now it broke the people who came to it. Kaladin walked past the ladders, a little farther along the edge of the chasm. Then he sat down, legs over the side, looking down as the rain fell around him, the droplets plunging into the dark depths.

To his sides, the more adventurous cremlings had already left their lairs, scuttling about, feeding on plants that lapped up the rainwater. Lirin had once explained that highstorm rains were rich with nutrients. Storm-wardens in Kholinar and Vedenar had proven that plants given storm water did better than those given lake or river water. Why was it that scientists were so excited to discover facts that farmers had known for generations and generations?

Kaladin watched the drops of water streaking down toward oblivion in the crevasse. Little suicidal jumpers. Thousands upon thousands of them. Millions upon millions. Who knew what awaited them in that darkness? You couldn't see it, couldn't know it, until you joined them. Leaping off into the void and letting the wind bear you down . . .

'You were right, Father,' Kaladin whispered. 'You can't stop a storm by blowing harder. You can't save men by killing others. We should all become surgeons. Every last one of us. . . .'

He was rambling. But, oddly, his mind felt clearer now than it had in weeks. Perhaps it was the clarity of perspective. Most men spent their entire lives wondering about the future. Well, his future was empty now. So he turned backward, thinking about his father, about Tien, about decisions.

Once, his life had seemed simple. That was before he'd lost his brother, before he'd been betrayed in Amaram's army. Would Kaladin go back to those innocent days, if he could? Would he prefer to pretend everything was simple?

No. He'd had no easy fall, like those drops. He'd earned his scars. He'd bounced off walls, bashed his face and hands. He'd killed innocent men by accident. He'd walked beside those with hearts like blackened coals, adoring them. He'd scrambled and climbed and fallen and stumbled.

And now here he was. At the end of it all. Understanding so much more, but somehow feeling no wiser. He climbed to his feet on the lip of that chasm, and could feel his father's disappointment looming over him, like the thunderheads above.

He put one foot out over the void.

'Kaladin!'

He froze at the soft but piercing voice. A translucent form bobbed in the air, approaching through the weakening rain. The figure lunged forward, then sank, then surged higher again, like it was bearing something heavy. Kaladin brought his foot back and held out his hand. Syl unceremoniously alighted upon it, shaped like a skyeel clutching something dark in its mouth.

She switched to the familiar form of a young woman, dress fluttering around her legs. She held in her hands a narrow, dark green leaf with a point divided in three. Blackbane.

'What is this?' Kaladin asked.

She looked exhausted. 'These things are heavy!' She lifted the leaf. 'I brought it for you!'

He took the leaf between two fingers. Blackbane. Poison. 'Why did you bring this to me?' he said harshly.

'I thought ...' Syl said, shying back. 'Well, you kept those other leaves so carefully. Then you lost them when you tried to help that man in the slave cages. I thought it would make you happy to have another one.'

Kaladin almost laughed. She had no concept of what she'd done, fetching him a leaf of one of Roshar's most deadly natural poisons because she'd wanted to make him happy. It was ridiculous. And sweet.

'Everything seemed to go wrong when you lost that leaf,' Syl said in a soft voice. 'Before that, you fought.'

'I failed.'

She cowered down, kneeling on his palm, misty skirt around her legs, drops of rainwater passing through her and rippling her form. 'You don't like it then? I flew so far ... I almost forgot myself. But I came back. I came *back*, Kaladin.'

'Why?' he pled. 'Why do you care?'

'Because I do,' she said, cocking her head. 'I watched you, you know. Back in that army. You'd always find the young, untrained men and protect them, even though it put you into danger. I can remember. Just barely, but I do.'

'I failed them. They're dead now.'

'They would have died more quickly without you. You made it so they

167

had a family in the army. I remember their gratitude. It's what drew me in the first place. You helped them.'

'No,' he said, clutching the blackbane in his fingers. 'Everything I touch withers and dies.' He teetered on the ledge. Thunder rumbled in the distance.

'Those men in the bridge crew,' Syl whispered. 'You could help them.'

'Too late.' He closed his eyes, thinking of the dead boy earlier in the day. 'It's too late. I've failed. They're dead. They're all going to die, and there's no way out.'

'What is one more try, then?' Her voice was soft, yet somehow stronger than the storm. 'What could it hurt?'

He paused.

'You can't fail this time, Kaladin. You've said it. They're all going to die anyway.'

He thought of Tien, and his dead eyes staring upward.

'I don't know what you mean most of the time when you speak,' she said. 'My mind is so cloudy. But it seems that if you're worried about hurting people, you shouldn't be afraid to help the bridgemen. What more could you do to them?'

'I . . .'

'One more try, Kaladin,' Syl whispered. 'Please.'

One more try. . . .

The men huddled in the barrack with barely a blanket to call their own. Frightened of the storm. Frightened of each other. Frightened of what the next day would bring.

One more try. . . .

He thought of himself, crying at the death of a boy he hadn't known. A boy he hadn't even tried to help.

One more try.

Kaladin opened his eyes. He was cold and wet, but he felt a tiny, warm candle flame of determination come alight inside him. He clenched his hand, crushing the blackbane leaf inside, then dropped it over the side of the chasm. He lowered the other hand, which had been holding Syl.

She zipped up into the air, anxious. 'Kaladin?'

He stalked away from the chasm, bare feet splashing in puddles and stepping heedlessly on rockbud vines. The incline he'd come down was covered with flat, slatelike plants that had opened like books to the rain, ruffled lacy red and green leaves connecting the two halves. Lifespren – little green blips of light, brighter than Syl but small as spores – danced among the plants, dodging raindrops.

Kaladin strode up, water streaming past him in tiny rivers. At the top, he returned to the bridge yard. It was still empty save for Gaz, who was tying a ripped tarp back into place.

Kaladin had crossed most of the distance to the man before Gaz noticed him. The wiry sergeant scowled. 'Too cowardly to go through with it, Your Lordship? Well, if you think I'm giving back—'

He cut off with a gagging noise as Kaladin lunged forward, grabbing Gaz by the neck. Gaz lifted an arm in surprise, but Kaladin batted it away and swept the man's legs out from under him, slamming him down to the rocky ground, throwing up a splash of water. Gaz's eye opened wide with shock and pain, and he began to strangle under the pressure of Kaladin's grip on his throat.

'The world just changed, Gaz,' Kaladin said, leaning in close. 'I died down at that chasm. Now you've got my vengeful spirit to deal with.'

Squirming, Gaz looked about frantically for help that wasn't there. Kaladin didn't have trouble holding him down. There was one thing about running bridges: If you survived long enough, it built up the muscles.

Kaladin let up slightly on Gaz's neck, allowing him a gasping breath. Then Kaladin leaned down further. 'We're going to start over new, you and I. Clean. And I want you to understand something from the start. I'm *already* dead. You can't hurt me. Understand?'

Gaz nodded slowly and Kaladin gave him another breath of frigid, humid air.

'Bridge Four is mine,' Kaladin said. 'You can assign us tasks, but I'm bridgeleader. The other one died today, so you have to pick a new leader anyway. Understand?'

Gaz nodded again.

'You learn quickly,' Kaladin said, letting the man breathe freely. He stepped back, and Gaz hesitantly got to his feet. There was hatred in his eyes, but it was veiled. He seemed worried about something – something more than Kaladin's threats.

'I want to stop paying down my slave debt,' Kaladin said. 'How much do bridgemen make?'

'Two clearmarks a day,' Gaz said, scowling at him and rubbing his neck.

So a slave would make half that. One diamond mark. A pittance, but Kaladin would need it. He'd also need to keep Gaz in line. 'I'll start taking my wages,' Kaladin said, 'but you get to keep one mark in five.'

Gaz started, glancing at him in the dim, overcast light.

'For your efforts,' Kaladin said.

'For what efforts?'

Kaladin stepped up to him. 'Your efforts in staying the *Damnation* out of my way. Understood?'

Gaz nodded again. Kaladin walked away. He hated to waste money on a bribe, but Gaz needed a consistent, repetitive reminder of why he should avoid getting Kaladin killed. One mark every five days wasn't much of a reminder – but for a man who was willing to risk going out in the middle of a highstorm to protect his spheres, it might be enough.

Kaladin walked back to Bridge Four's small barrack, pulling open the thick wooden door. The men huddled inside, just as he'd left them. But something had changed. Had they always looked that pathetic?

Yes. They had. Kaladin was the one who had changed, not they. He felt a strange dislocation, as if he'd allowed himself to forget – if only in part – the last nine months. He reached back across time, studying the man he had been. The man who'd still fought, and fought well.

He couldn't be that man again – he couldn't erase the scars – but he could *learn* from that man, as a new squadleader learned from the victorious generals of the past. Kaladin Stormblessed was dead, but Kaladin Bridgeman was of the same blood. A descendant with potential.

Kaladin walked to the first huddled figure. The man wasn't sleeping – who could sleep through a highstorm? The man cringed as Kaladin knelt beside him.

'What's your name?' Kaladin asked, Syl flitting down and studying the man's face. He wouldn't be able to see her.

The man was older, with drooping cheeks, brown eyes, and close-cropped, white-salted hair. His beard was short and he didn't have a slave mark.

'Your name?' Kaladin repeated firmly.

'Storm off,' the man said, rolling over.

Kaladin hesitated, then leaned in, speaking in a low voice. 'Look, friend. You can either tell me your name, or I'll keep pestering you. Continue refusing, and I'll tow you out into that storm and hang you over the chasm by one leg until you tell me.'

The man glanced back over his shoulder. Kaladin nodded slowly, holding the man's gaze.

'Teft,' the man finally said. 'My name's Teft.'

'That wasn't so hard,' Kaladin said, holding out his hand. 'I'm Kaladin. Your bridgeleader.'

The man hesitated, then took Kaladin's hand, wrinkling his brow in confusion. Kaladin vaguely remembered the man. He'd been in the crew for a while, a few weeks at least. Before that, he'd been on another bridge crew. One of the punishments for bridgemen who committed camp infractions was a transfer to Bridge Four.

'Get some rest,' Kaladin said, releasing Teft's hand. 'We're going to have a hard day tomorrow.'

'How do you know?' Teft asked, rubbing his bearded chin.

'Because we're bridgemen,' Kaladin said, standing. '*Every* day is hard.'

Teft hesitated, then smiled faintly. 'Kelek knows that's true.'

Kaladin left him, moving down the line of huddled figures. He visited each man, prodding or threatening until the man gave his name. They each resisted. It was as if their names were the last things they owned, and wouldn't be given up cheaply, though they seemed surprised – perhaps even encouraged – that someone cared to ask.

He clutched to these names, repeating each one in his head, holding them like precious gemstones. The names mattered. The men mattered. Perhaps Kaladin would die in the next bridge run, or perhaps he would break under the strain, and give Amaram one final victory. But as he settled down on the ground to plan, he felt that tiny warmth burning steadily within him.

It was the warmth of decisions made and purpose seized. It was responsibility.

Syl alighted on his leg as he sat, whispering the names of the men to himself. She looked encouraged. Bright. Happy. He didn't feel any of that. He felt grim, tired, and wet. But he wrapped himself in the responsibility he had taken, the responsibility for these men. He held to it like a climber clung to his last handhold as he dangled from a cliff side.

He *would* find a way to protect them.

THE END OF

Part One

INTERLUDES

◆

ISHIKK • NAN BALAT • SZETH

ISHIKK

I shikk splashed toward the meeting with the strange foreigners, whist-ling softly to himself, his pole with buckets on each end resting on his shoulders. He wore lake sandals on his submerged feet and a pair of knee-length breeches. No shirt. Nu Ralik forbid! A good Purelaker never covered his shoulders when the sun was shining. A man could get sick that way, not getting enough sunlight.

He whistled, but not because he was having a pleasant day. In point of fact, the day Nu Ralik had provided was close to horrible. Only five fish swam in Ishikk's buckets, and four were of the dullest, most common variety. The tides had been irregular, as if the Purelake itself was in a foul mood. Bad days were coming; sure as the sun and the tide, they were.

The Purelake extended in all directions, hundreds of miles wide, its glassy surface perfectly transparent. At its deepest, it was never more than six feet from shimmering surface to the bottom – and in most places, the warm, slow-moving water came up only to about midcalf. It was filled with tiny fish, colorful cremlings, and eel-like riverspren.

The Purelake was life itself. Once, this land had been claimed by a king. Sela Tales, the nation had been called, one of the Epoch Kingdoms. Well, they could name it what they wanted, but Nu Ralik knew that the boundaries of nature were far more important than the boundaries of nations. Ishikk was a Purelaker. First and foremost. By tide and sun he was.

He walked confidently through the water, though the footing could sometimes be precarious. The pleasantly warm water lapped at his legs just below the knees, and he made very few splashes. He knew to move slowly, careful not to put his weight down before he was sure he wasn't stepping on a spikemane or a sharp lip of rock.

Ahead, the village of Fu Abra broke the glassy perfection, a cluster of buildings perched on blocks beneath the water. Their domed roofs made them look like the rockbuds that sprouted from the ground, and they were the only things for miles around that broke the surface of the Purelake.

Other people walked about here, moving with the same slow gait. It was possible to run through the water, but there was rarely a reason. What could be so important that you had to go and make a splash and ruckus getting to it?

Ishikk shook his head at that. Only foreigners were so hasty. He nodded to Thaspic, a dark-skinned man who passed him pulling a small raft. It was stacked with a few piles of cloth; he'd probably taken them out for washing.

'Ho, Ishikk,' the scrawny man said. 'How's fishing?'

'Terrible,' he called. 'Vun Makak has blighted me right good today. And you?'

'Lost a shirt while washing,' Thaspic replied, his voice pleasant.

'Ah, that's the way of things. Are my foreigners here?'

'Sure are. Over at Maib's place.'

'Vun Makak send they don't eat her out of home,' Ishikk said, continuing on his way. 'Or infect her with their constant worries.'

'Sun and tides send it!' Thaspic said with a chuckle, continuing on.

Maib's house was near the center of the village. Ishikk wasn't sure what made her want to live inside the building. Most nights he did just fine sleeping on his raft. It never got cold in the Purelake, except during highstorms, and you could last through those right well, Nu Ralik send the way.

The Purelake drained into pits and holes when the storms came, and so you just shoved your raft into a crevice between two ridges of stone and huddled up next to it, using it to break the fury of the tempest. The storms weren't so bad out here as they were in the East, where they flung boulders and blew down buildings. Oh, he'd heard stories about that sort of life. Nu Ralik send he never had to go to such a terrible place.

Besides, it was probably cold there. Ishikk pitied those who had to live in the cold. Why didn't they just come to the Purelake?

Nu Ralik send that they don't, he thought, walking up to Maib's place. If everyone knew how nice the Purelake was, surely they'd all want to live here, and there wouldn't be a place to walk without stumbling over some foreigner!

He stepped up into the building, exposing his calves to the air. The floor was low enough that a few inches of water still covered it; Purelakers liked it that way. It was natural, though if the tide dropped, sometimes buildings would drain.

Minnows shot out around his toes. Common types, not worth anything. Maib stood inside, fixing a pot of fish soup, and she nodded to him. She was a stout woman and had been chasing Ishikk for years, trying to bait him to wed her on account of her fine cooking. He just might let her catch him someday.

His foreigners were in the corner, at a table only they would choose – the one that was raised up an extra bit, with footrests so that the outsiders wouldn't have to get their toes wet. *Nu Ralik, what fools!* he thought with amusement. *Inside out of the sun, wearing shirts against its warmth, feet out of the tide. No wonder their thoughts are so odd.*

He set his buckets down, nodding to Maib.

She eyed him. 'Good fishing?'

'Terrible.'

'Ah well, your soup is free today, Ishikk. To make up for Vun Makak's cursing.'

'Thanks much kindly,' he said, taking a steaming bowl from her. She smiled. Now he owed her. Enough bowls, and he'd be forced to wed her.

'There's a kolgril in the bucket for you,' he noted. 'Caught it early this morning.'

Her stout face grew uncertain. A kolgril was a *very* lucky fish. Cured aching joints for a good month after you ate it, and sometimes let you see when friends were going to visit by letting you read the shapes of the clouds. Maib had quite a fondness for them, on account of the finger aches Nu Ralik had sent her. One kolgril would be two weeks of soup, and would put *her* in debt to *him*.

'Vun Makak eye you,' she muttered in annoyance walking over to check. 'That's one all right. How am I ever going to catch you, man?'

'I'm a fisher, Maib,' he said, taking a slurp of his soup – the bowl was shaped for easy slurping. 'Hard to catch a fisher. You know that.' He chuckled to himself, walking up to his foreigners as she plucked out the kolgril.

There were three of them. Two were dark-skinned Makabaki, though they were the strangest Makabaki he'd ever seen. One was thick limbed where most of his kind were small and fine-boned, and he had a completely bald head. The other was taller, with short dark hair, lean muscles, and broad shoulders. In his head, Ishikk called them Grump and Blunt, on account of their personalities.

The third man had light tan skin, like an Alethi. He didn't seem quite right either, though. The eyes were the wrong shape, and his accent was certainly *not* Alethi. He spoke the Selay language worse than the other two, and usually stayed quiet. He seemed thoughtful, though. Ishikk called him Thinker.

Wonder how he earned that scar across his scalp, Ishikk thought. Life outside the Purelake was very dangerous. Lots of wars, particularly to the east.

'You are late, traveler,' said tall, stiff Blunt. He had the build and air of a soldier, though none of the three carried weapons.

Ishikk frowned, sitting and reluctantly pulling his feet out of the water. 'Isn't it warli-day?'

'The day is right, friend,' Grump said. 'But we were to meet at noon. Understand?' He generally did most of the talking.

'We're close to that,' Ishikk said. Honestly. Who paid attention to what *hour* it was? Foreigners. Always so busy.

Grump just shook his head as Maib brought them some soup. Her place was the closest thing the village had to an inn. She left Ishikk a soft cloth napkin and nice cup of sweet wine, trying to balance that fish as quickly as possible.

'Very well,' Grump said. 'Let us have your report, friend.'

'I've been by Fu Ralis, Fu Namir, Fu Albast, and Fu Moorin this month,' Ishikk said, taking a slurp of soup. 'Nobody has seen this man you search for.'

'You asked right questions?' Blunt said. 'You are certain?'

'Of course I'm certain,' Ishikk said. 'I have been doing this for ages now.'

'Five months,' Blunt corrected. 'And no results.'

Ishikk shrugged. 'You wish me to make up stories? Vun Makak would like me to do that.'

'No, no stories, friend,' Grump said. 'We want only the truth.'

'Well, I've given it to you.'

'You swear it by Nu Ralik, that god of yours?'

'Hush!' Ishikk said. 'Don't say his name. Are you idiots?'

Grump frowned. 'But he is your god. Understand? Is his name holy? Not to be spoken?'

Foreigners were so stupid. Of course Nu Ralik was their god, but you always *pretended* that he wasn't. Vun Makak – his younger, spiteful brother – had to be tricked into thinking you worshipped him, otherwise he'd get jealous. It was only safe to speak of these things in a holy grotto.

'I swear it by Vun Makak,' Ishikk said pointedly. 'May he watch over me and curse me as he pleases. I have looked diligently. No foreigner like this one you mention – with his white hair, clever tongue, and arrowlike face – has been seen.'

'He dyes his hair sometimes,' Grump said. 'And wears disguises.'

'I've asked, using the names you gave me,' Ishikk said. 'Nobody has seen him. Now, perhaps I could find you a *fish* that could locate him.' Ishikk rubbed his stubbly chin. 'I'll bet a stumpy cort could do it. Might take me a while to find one, though.'

The three looked at him. 'There may be something to these fish, you know,' Blunt said.

'Superstition,' Grump replied. 'You always look for superstition, Vao.'

Vao wasn't the man's real name; Ishikk was sure they used fake names. That was why he used his own names for them. If they were going to give him fake names, he'd give them fake names back.

'And you, Temoo?' Blunt snapped. 'We can't pontificate our way to—'

'Gentlemen,' Thinker said. He nodded to Ishikk, who was still slurping his soup. All three of them switched to another language and continued their argument.

Ishikk listened with half an ear, trying to determine what language it was. He never had been good with other kinds of languages. Why did he need them? Didn't help with fishing or selling fish.

He *had* searched for their man. He got around a lot, visited a lot of places around the Purelake. It was one of the reasons why he didn't want to be caught by Maib. He'd have to settle down, and that wasn't good for catching fish. Not the rare ones, at least.

He didn't bother wondering why they were looking for this Hoid, whoever he was. Foreigners were always looking for things they couldn't have. Ishikk sat back, dangling his toes in the water. That felt good. Eventually, they finished their argument. They gave him some more instructions, handed him a pouch of spheres, and stepped down into the water.

Like most foreigners, they wore thick boots that came all the way up to their knees. They splashed in the water as they walked to the entrance. Ishikk followed, waving to Maib and picking up his buckets. He'd be back later in the day for an evening meal.

Maybe I should *let her catch me*, he thought, stepping back out into the sunlight and sighing in relief. *Nu Ralik knows I'm getting old. Might be nice to relax.*

His foreigners splashed down into the Purelake. Grump was last. He seemed very dissatisfied. 'Where are you, Roamer? What a fool's quest this is.' Then, he added in his own tongue, *'Alavanta kamaloo kayana.'*

He splashed after his companions.

'Well, you've got the "fool" part right,' Ishikk said with a chuckle, turning his own direction and heading off to check on his traps.

I-2

NAN BALAT

Nan Balat liked killing things.

Not people. Never people. But animals, those he could kill. Particularly the little ones. He wasn't sure why it made him feel better; it simply did.

He sat on the porch of his mansion, pulling the legs off a small crab one at a time. There was a satisfying rip to each one – he pulled on it lightly at first, and the animal grew stiff. Then he pulled harder, and it started to squirm. The ligament resisted, then started ripping, followed by a quick pop. The crab squirmed some more, and Nan Balat held up the leg, pinching the beast with two fingers on his other hand.

He sighed in satisfaction. Ripping a leg free soothed him, made the aches in his body retreat. He tossed the leg over his shoulder and moved on to the next one.

He didn't like to talk about his habit. He didn't even speak of it to Eylita. It was just something he did. You had to keep your sanity somehow.

He finished with the legs, then stood up, leaning on his cane, looking out over the Davar gardens, which were made up of stonework walls covered with different kinds of vines. They were beautiful, though Shallan had been the only one who truly appreciated them. This area of Jah Keved – to the west and south of Alethkar, of higher elevation and broken by mountains such as the Horneater Peaks – had a profusion of vines. They grew on everything, covering the mansion, growing over the steps. Out in the wilds, they hung from trees, grew over rocky expanses, as ubiquitous as grass was in other areas of Roshar.

Balat walked to the edge of the porch. Some wild songlings began to sing in the distance, scraping their ridged shells. They each played a different beat and notes, though they couldn't really be called melodies. Melodies were things of humans, not animals. But each one *was* a song, and at times they seemed to sing back and forth to one another.

Balat walked down the steps one at a time, the vines shaking and pulling away before his feet fell. It had been nearly six months since Shallan's departure. This morning, they'd had word from her via spanreed that she'd succeeded in the first part of her plan, becoming Jasnah Kholin's ward. And so, his baby sister – who before this had never left their estates – was preparing to rob the most important woman in the world.

Walking down the steps was depressingly hard work for him. *Twenty-three years old*, he thought, *and already a cripple*. He still felt a constant, latent ache. The break had been bad, and the surgeon had nearly decided to cut off the entire leg. Perhaps he could be thankful that hadn't proven necessary, though he would always walk with a cane.

Scrak was playing with something in the sitting green, a place where cultivated grass was grown and kept free of vines. The large axehound rolled about, gnawing at the object, antennae pulled back flat against her skull.

'Scrak,' Balat said, hobbling forward, 'what have you got there, girl?'

The axehound looked up at her master, antennae cocking upward. The hound trumped with two echoing voices overlapping one another, then went back to playing.

Blasted creature, Balat thought fondly, *never would obey properly*. He'd been breeding axehounds since his youth, and had discovered – as had many before him – that the smarter an animal was, the more likely it was to disobey. Oh, Scrak was loyal, but she'd ignore you on the little things. Like a young child trying to prove her independence.

As he got closer, he saw that Scrak had managed to catch a songling. The fist-size creature was shaped like a peaked disc with four arms that reached out from the sides and scraped rhythms along the top. Four squat legs underneath normally held it to a rock wall, though Scrak had chewed those off. She had two of the arms off too, and had managed to crack the shell. Balat almost took it away to pull the other two arms off, but decided it was best to let Scrak have her fun.

Scrak set the songling down and looked up at Balat, her antennae rising inquisitively. She was sleek and lean, six legs extending before her as she sat on her haunches. Axehounds didn't have shells or skin; instead, their body was covered with some fusion of the two, smooth to the touch and more pliable than true carapace, but harder than skin and made of interlocking sections. The axehound's angular face seemed curious, her deep black eyes regarding Balat. She trumped softly.

Balat smiled, reaching down and scratching behind the axehound's ear holes. The animal leaned against him – she probably weighed as much as he did. The bigger axehounds came up to a man's waist, though Scrak was of a smaller, quicker breed.

The songling quivered and Scrak pounced on it eagerly, crunching at its shell with her strong outer mandibles.

'Am I a coward, Scrak?' Balat asked, sitting down on a bench. He set his cane aside and snatched a small crab that had been hiding on the side of the bench, its shell having turned white to match the stone.

He held up the squirming animal. The green's grass had been bred to be less timid, and it poked out of its holes only a few moments after he passed. Other exotic plants bloomed, poking out of shells or holes in the ground, and soon patches of red, orange, and blue waved in the wind around him. The area around the axehound remained bare, of course. Scrak was having far too much fun with her prey, and she kept even the cultivated plants hidden in their burrows.

'I couldn't have gone to chase Jasnah,' Balat said, starting to pull the crab's legs off. 'Only a woman could get close enough to her to steal the Soulcaster. We decided that. Besides, someone needs to stay back and care for the needs of the house.'

The excuses were hollow. He *did* feel like a coward. He pulled off a few more legs, but it was unsatisfying. The crab was too small, and the legs came off too easily.

'This plan probably won't even work,' he said, taking off the last of the legs. Odd, looking at a creature like this when it had no legs. The crab was still alive. Yet how could you know it? Without the legs to wiggle, the creature seemed as dead as a stone.

The arms, he thought, *we wave them about to make us seem alive. That's what they're good for*. He put his fingers between the halves of the crab's shell and began to pry them apart. This, at least, had a nice feeling of resistance to it.

They were a broken family. Years of suffering their father's brutal temper had driven Asha Jushu to vice and Tet Wikim to despair. Only Balat had escaped unscathed. Balat and Shallan. She'd been left alone, never touched. At times, Balat had hated her for that, but how could you truly hate someone like Shallan? Shy, quiet, delicate.

I should never have let her go, he thought. *There should have been another way.* She'd never manage on her own; she was probably terrified. It was a wonder she'd done as much as she had.

He tossed the pieces of crab over his shoulder. *If only Helaran had survived.* Their eldest brother – then known as Nan Helaran, as he'd been the first son – had stood up to their father repeatedly. Well, he was dead now, and so was their father. They'd left behind a family of cripples.

'Balat!' a voice cried. Wikim appeared on the porch. The younger man was past his recent bout of melancholy, it appeared.

'What?' Balat said, standing.

Wikim rushed down the steps, hurrying up to him, vines – then grass – pulling back before him. 'We have a problem.'

'How large a problem?'

'Pretty big, I'd say. Come on.'

THE GLORY OF IGNORANCE

Szeth-son-son-Vallano, Truthless of Shinovar, sat on the wooden tavern floor, lavis beer slowly soaking through his brown trousers. Grimy, worn, and fraying, his clothing was far different from the simple – yet elegant – whites he had worn over five years before when he'd assassinated the king of Alethkar.

Head bowed, hands in his lap, he carried no weapons. He hadn't summoned his Shardblade in years, and it felt equally long since he'd had a bath. He did not complain. If he looked like a wretch, people treated him as a wretch. One did not ask a wretch to assassinate people.

'So he'll do whatever you say?' asked one of the mine workers sitting at the table. The man's clothing was little better than Szeth's, covered with so much dirt and dust that it was difficult to tell grimy skin from grimy cloth. There were four of them, holding ceramic cups. The room smelled of mud and sweat. The ceiling was low, the windows – on the leeward side only – mere slots. The table was precariously held together with several leather straps, as the wood was cracked down the middle.

Took – Szeth's current master – set his cup down on the table's tilted side. It sagged under the weight of his arm. 'Yeah, he sure will. Hey, kurp, look at me.'

Szeth looked up. 'Kurp' meant child in the local Bay dialect. Szeth was accustomed to such pejorative labels. Though he was in his thirty-fifth year – and his seventh year since being named Truthless – his people's large, round eyes, shorter stature, and tendency toward baldness led Easterners to claim they looked like children.

'Stand up,' Took said.

Szeth did so.

'Jump up and down.'

Szeth complied.

'Pour Ton's beer on your head.'

Szeth reached for it.

'Hey!' Ton said, pulling the cup away. 'None of that, now! Oi ain't done with this yet!'

'If you were,' said Took, 'he couldn't right pour it on his head, could he?'

'Get 'im to do something else, Took,' Ton griped.

'All right.' Took pulled out his boot knife and tossed it to Szeth. 'Kurp, cut your arm up.'

'Took ... ' said one of the other men, a sniffly man named Amark. 'That ain't right, you know it.'

Took didn't rescind the order, so Szeth complied, taking the knife and cutting at the flesh of his arm. Blood seeped out around the dirty blade.

'Cut your throat,' Took said.

'Now, Took!' Amark said, standing. 'Oi won't—'

'Oh hush, you,' Took said. Several groups of men from other tables were watching now. 'You'll see. Kurp, cut your throat.'

'I am forbidden to take my own life,' Szeth said softly in the Bav language. 'As Truthless, it is the nature of my suffering to be forbidden the taste of death by my own hand.'

Amark settled back down, looking sheepish.

'Dustmother,' Ton said, 'he always talks like that?'

'Like what?' Took asked, taking a gulp from his mug.

'Smooth words, so soft and proper. Like a lighteyes.'

'Yeah,' Took said. 'He's like a slave, only better 'cuz he's a Shin. He don't run or talk back or anything. Don't have to pay him, neither. He's like a parshman, but smarter. Worth a right many spheres, Oi'd say.' He eyed the other men. 'Could take him to the mines with you to work, and collect his pay. He'd do things you don't wanna. Muck out the privy, whitewash the home. All kinds of useful stuff.'

'Well, how'd you come by him, then?' one of the other men asked, scratching his chin. Took was a transient worker, moving from town to town. Displaying Szeth was one of the ways he made quick friends.

'Oh, now, that's a story,' Took said. 'Oi was traveling in the mountains down south, you know, and Oi heard this weird howling noise. It wasn't just the wind, you know, and ...'

The tale was a complete fabrication; Szeth's previous master – a farmer in a nearby village – had traded Szeth to Took for a sack of seeds. The farmer had gotten him from a traveling merchant, who had gotten him from a cobbler who'd won him in an illegal game of chance. There had been dozens before him.

At first the darkeyed commoners enjoyed the novelty of owning him. Slaves were far too expensive for most, and parshmen were even more valuable. So having someone like Szeth to order around was quite the novelty. He cleaned floors, sawed wood, helped in the fields, and carried burdens. Some treated him well, some did not.

But they always got rid of him.

Perhaps they could sense the truth, that he was capable of so much more than they dared use him for. It was one thing to have a slave of your own. But when that slave talked like a lighteyes and knew more than you did? It made them uncomfortable.

Szeth tried to play the part, tried to make himself act less refined. It was very difficult for him. Perhaps impossible. What would these men say if they knew that the man who emptied their chamber pot was a Shard-bearer and a Surgebinder? A Windrunner, like the Radiants of old? The moment he summoned his Blade, his eyes would turn from dark green to pale – almost glowing – sapphire, a unique effect of his particular weapon.

Best that they never discovered. Szeth gloried in being wasted; each day he was made to clean or dig instead of kill was a victory. That evening five years ago still haunted him. Before then, he had been ordered to kill – but always in secret, silently. Never before had he been given such deliberately terrible instructions.

Kill, destroy, and cut your way to the king. Be seen doing it. Leave witnesses. Wounded but alive. ...

'... and *that* is when he swore to serve me my entire life,' Took finished. 'He's been with me ever since.'

The listening men turned to Szeth. 'It is true,' he said, as he'd been ordered earlier. 'Every word of it.'

Took smiled. Szeth didn't make him uncomfortable; he apparently considered it natural that Szeth obeyed him. Perhaps as a result he would remain Szeth's master longer than the others.

'Well,' Took said, 'Oi should be going. Need to get an early start tomorrow. More places to see, more unseen roads to dare ...'

He liked to think of himself as a seasoned traveler, though as far as Szeth could tell, he just moved around in a wide circle. There were many small mines – and therefore small villages – in this part of Bavland. Took had probably been to this same village years back, but the mines made for a lot of transient workers. It was unlikely he'd be remembered, unless someone had noted his terribly exaggerated stories.

Terrible or not, the other miners seemed to thirst for more. They urged him on, offering him another drink, and he modestly agreed.

Szeth sat quietly, legs folded, hands in his lap, blood trickling down his arm. Had the Parshendi known what they were consigning him to by tossing his Oathstone away as they fled Kholinar that night? Szeth had been required to recover it, then stand there beside the road, wondering if he would be discovered and executed – *hoping* he'd be discovered and executed – until a passing merchant had cared enough to inquire. By then, Szeth had stood only in a loincloth. His honor had forced him to discard the white clothing, as it would have made him easier to recognize. He had to preserve himself so that he could suffer.

After a short explanation that left out incriminating details, Szeth had found himself riding in the back of the merchant's cart. The merchant – a man named Avado – had been clever enough to realize that in the wake of the king's death, foreigners might be treated poorly. He'd made his way to Jah Keved, never knowing that he harbored Gavilar's murderer as his serving man.

The Alethi didn't search for him. They assumed that he, the infamous 'Assassin in White,' had retreated with the Parshendi. They probably expected to discover him in the middle of the Shattered Plains.

The miners eventually tired of Took's increasingly slurred stories. They bid him farewell, ignoring his broad hints that another cup of beer would prompt him to tell his greatest tale: that of the time when he'd seen the Nightwatcher herself and stolen a sphere that glowed black at night. That tale always discomforted Szeth, as it reminded him of the strange black sphere Gavilar had given him. He'd hidden that carefully in Jah Keved.

He didn't know what it was, but he didn't want to risk a master taking it from him.

When nobody offered Took another drink, he reluctantly stumbled from his chair and waved Szeth to follow him from the tavern. The street was dark outside. This town, Ironsway, had a proper town square, several hundred homes, and three different taverns. That made it practically a metropolis for Bavland – the small, mostly ignored stretch of land just north of the mountains near Silnasen. The area was technically part of Jah Keved, but even its highprince tended to stay away from it.

Szeth followed his master through the streets toward the poorer district. Took was too cheap to pay for a room in the nice, or even modest, areas of a town. Szeth looked over his shoulder, wishing that the Second Sister – known as Nomon to these Easterners – had risen to give a little more light.

Took stumbled drunkenly, then fell over in the street. Szeth sighed. It would not be the first night he carried his master home to his bed. He knelt to lift Took.

He froze. A warm liquid was pooling beneath his master's body. Only then did he notice the knife in Took's neck.

Szeth instantly came alert as a group of footpads slipped out of the alleyway. One raised a hand the knife in it reflecting starlight, preparing to throw at Szeth. He tensed. There were infused spheres he could draw upon in Took's pouch.

'Wait,' hissed one of the footpads.

The man with the knife paused. Another man came closer, inspecting Szeth. 'He's Shin. Won't hurt a cremling.'

Others pulled the corpse into the alleyway. The one with the knife raised his weapon again. 'He could still yell.'

'Then why hasn't he? Oi'm telling you, they're harmless. Almost like parshmen. We can sell him.'

'Maybe,' the second said. 'He's terrified. Look at 'im.'

'Come 'ere,' the first footpad said, waving Szeth forward.

He obeyed, walking into the alley, which was suddenly illuminated as the other footpads pulled open Took's pouch.

'Kelek,' one of them said, 'hardly worth the effort. A handful of chips and two marks, not a single broam in the lot.'

'Oi'm telling you,' the first man said. 'We can sell this fellow as a slave. People like Shin servants.'

'He's just a kid.'

'Nah. They all look like that. Hey, whacha got there?' The man plucked a twinkling, sphere-size chunk of rock from the hand of the man counting the spheres. It was fairly ordinary, a simple piece of rock with a few quartz crystals set into it and a rusty vein of iron on one side. 'What is this?'

'Worthless,' one of the men said.

'I am required to tell you,' Szeth said quietly, 'that you are holding my Oathstone. So long as you possess it, you are my master.'

'What's that?' one of the footpads said, standing.

The first one closed his hand around the stone, shooting a wary glance at the others. He looked back at Szeth. 'Your master? What does that mean exactly, in precise terms and all?'

'I must obey you,' Szeth said. 'In all things, though I will not follow an order to kill myself.' He also couldn't be ordered to give up his Blade, but there was no need to mention that at the moment.

'You'll obey me?' the footpad said. 'You mean, you'll do what Oi say?'

'Yes.'

'*Anything* Oi say?'

Szeth closed his eyes. 'Yes.'

'Well, ain't that something interestin',' the man said, musing. 'Something interestin' indeed. . . .'

TWO

The Illuminating Storms

DALINAR • KALADIN • ADOLIN

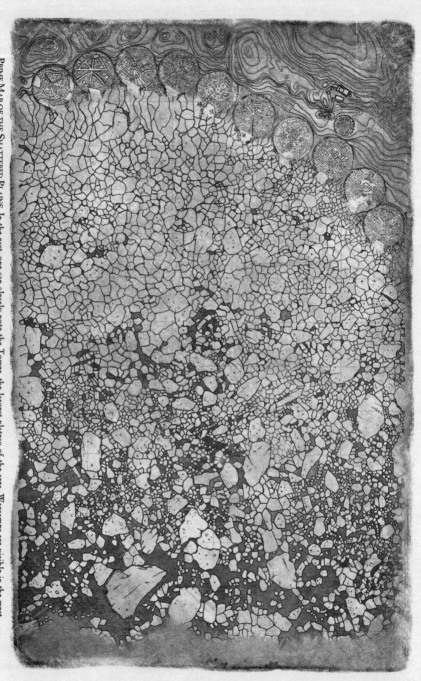

PRIME MAP OF THE SHATTERED PLAINS. In the east, one can clearly note the Tower, the largest plateau of the area. Warcamps are visible in the west. Glyphpairs and plateau numbers have been removed to preserve the clarity of this smaller reproduction of the original hanging in His Majesty Elhokar's Gallery of Maps.

UNITY

Old friend. I hope this missive finds you well. Though, as you are now essentially immortal. I would guess that wellness on your part is something of a given.

Today,' King Elhokar announced, riding beneath the bright open sky, 'is an excellent day to slay a god. Wouldn't you say?'

'Undoubtedly, Your Majesty.' Sadeas's reply was smooth, quick, and said with a knowing smile. 'One might say that gods, as a rule, should fear the Alethi nobility. Most of us at least.'

Adolin gripped his reins a little more tightly; it put him on edge every time Highprince Sadeas spoke.

'Do we have to ride up here at the front?' Renarin whispered.

'I want to listen,' Adolin replied softly.

He and his brother rode near the front of the column, near the king and his highprinces. Behind them extended a grand procession: a thousand soldiers in Kholin blue, dozens of servants, and even women in palanquins to scribe accounts of the hunt. Adolin glanced at them all as he reached for his canteen.

He was wearing his Shardplate, and so he had to be careful when grabbing it, lest he crush it. One's muscles reacted with increased speed, strength, and dexterity when wearing the armor, and it took practice to use it correctly. Adolin was still occasionally caught by surprise, though he'd held this suit – inherited from his mother's side of the family – since his sixteenth birthday. That was now seven years past.

He turned and took a long drink of lukewarm water. Sadeas rode to the king's left, and Dalinar – Adolin's father – was a solid figure riding at the king's right. The final highprince on the hunt was Vamah, who wasn't a Shardbearer.

The king was resplendent in his golden Shardplate – of course, Plate could make any man look regal. Even *Sadeas* looked impressive when wearing his red Plate, though his bulbous face and ruddy complexion weakened the effect. Sadeas and the king flaunted their Plate. And ... well, perhaps Adolin did too. He'd had his painted blue, a few ornamentations welded onto the helm and pauldrons to give an extra look of danger. How could you *not* show off when wearing something as grand as Shardplate?

Adolin took another drink, listening to the king talk about his excitement for the hunt. Only one Shardbearer in the procession – indeed, only one Shardbearer in the entirety of the ten armies – used no paint or ornamentations on his Plate. Dalinar Kholin. Adolin's father preferred to leave his armor its natural slate-grey color.

Dalinar rode beside the king, his face somber. He rode with his helm tied to his saddle, exposing a square face topped by short black hair that had gone white at the temples. Few women had ever called Dalinar Kholin handsome; his nose was the wrong shape, his features blocky rather than delicate. It was the face of a warrior.

He rode astride a massive black Ryshadium stallion, one of the largest horses that Adolin had ever seen – and while the king and Sadeas looked regal in their armor, somehow Dalinar managed to look like a soldier. To him, the Plate was not an ornament. It was a tool. He never seemed to be surprised by the strength or speed the armor lent him. It was as if, for Dalinar Kholin, wearing his Plate was his natural state – it was the times without that were abnormal. Perhaps that was one reason he'd earned the reputation of being one of the greatest warriors and generals who ever lived.

Adolin found himself wishing, passionately, that his father would do a little more these days to live up to that reputation.

He's thinking about the visions, Adolin thought, regarding his father's distant expression and troubled eyes. 'It happened again last night,' Adolin said softly to Renarin. 'During the highstorm.'

'I know,' Renarin said. His voice was measured, controlled. He always paused before he replied to a question, as if testing the words in his mind. Some women Adolin knew said Renarin's ways made them feel as if he were dissecting them with his mind. They'd shiver when they spoke of him, though Adolin had never found his younger brother the least bit discomforting.

'What do you think they mean?' Adolin asked, speaking quietly so only Renarin could hear. 'Father's ... episodes.'

'I don't know.'

'Renarin, we *can't* keep ignoring them. The soldiers are talking. Rumors are spreading through all ten armies!'

Dalinar Kholin was going mad. Whenever a highstorm came, he fell to the floor and began to shake. Then he began raving in gibberish. Often, he'd stand, blue eyes delusional and wild, swinging and flailing. Adolin had to restrain him lest he hurt himself or others.

'He sees things,' Adolin said. 'Or he thinks he does.'

Adolin's grandfather had suffered from delusions. When he'd grown old, he'd thought he was back at war. Was that what happened to Dalinar? Was he reliving youthful battles, days when he'd earned his renown? Or was it that terrible night he saw over and over, the night when his brother had been murdered by the Assassin in White? And why did he so often mention the Knights Radiant soon after his episodes?

It all made Adolin feel sick. Dalinar was the Blackthorn, a genius of the battlefield and a living legend. Together, he and his brother had reunited Alethkar's warring highprinces after centuries of strife. He had defeated countless challengers in duels, had won dozens of battles. The entire kingdom looked up to him. And now this.

What did you do, as a son, when the father you loved – the greatest man alive – started to lose his wits?

Sadeas was speaking about a recent victory. He'd won another gem-heart two days back, and the king – it appeared – hadn't heard of it. Adolin tensed at the boasts.

'We should move back,' Renarin said.

'We are of rank enough to be here,' Adolin said.

'I don't like how you get when you're around Sadeas.'

We have to keep an eye on the man, Renarin, Adolin thought. *He knows Father is weakening. He'll try to strike.* Adolin forced himself to smile, however. He tried to be relaxed and confident for Renarin. Generally, that wasn't difficult. He'd happily spend his entire life dueling, lounging, and courting the occasional pretty girl. Of late, however, life didn't seem content to let him enjoy its simple pleasures.

'. . . model of courage lately, Sadeas,' the king was saying. 'You've done very well in capturing gemhearts. You are to be commended.'

'Thank you, Your Majesty. Though the competition grows unexciting, as some people don't seem interested in participating. I guess even the best weapons eventually grow dull.'

Dalinar, who might once have responded to the veiled slur, said nothing. Adolin gritted his teeth. It was flat-out unconscionable for Sadeas to be taking shots at his father in his present state. Perhaps Adolin should offer the pompous bastard a challenge. You didn't duel highprinces – it just wasn't done, not unless you were ready to make a big storm of it. But maybe he was. Maybe—

'Adolin . . . ' Renarin said warningly.

Adolin looked to the side. He'd held out his hand, as if to summon his Blade. He picked up his reins with the hand instead. *Storming man*, he thought. *Leave my father alone.*

'Why don't we talk about the hunt?' Renarin said. As usual, the younger Kholin rode with a straight back and perfect posture, eyes hidden behind his spectacles, a model of propriety and solemnity. 'Aren't you excited?'

'Bah,' Adolin said. 'I never find hunts as interesting as everyone says they're going to be. I don't care how big the beast is – in the end, it's really just butchery.'

Now, dueling, *that* was exciting. The feel of the Shardblade in your hand, of facing someone crafty, skilled, and careful. Man against man, strength against strength, mind against mind. Hunting some dumb beast just couldn't compare to that.

'Maybe you should have invited Janala along,' Renarin said.

'She wouldn't have come,' Adolin said. 'Not after . . . well, you know. Rilla was very vocal yesterday. It was best to just leave.'

'You really should have been wiser in your treatment of her,' Renarin said, sounding disapproving.

Adolin mumbled a noncommittal reply. It wasn't *his* fault that his relationships often burned out quickly. Well, technically, this time it *was* his fault. But it wasn't usually. This was just an oddity.

The king began complaining about something. Renarin and Adolin had lagged behind, and Adolin couldn't hear what was being said.

'Let's ride up closer,' Adolin said, nudging his mount forward.

Renarin rolled his eyes, but followed.

❖

Unite them.

The words whispered in Dalinar's mind. He couldn't rid himself of them. They consumed him as he trotted Gallant across a rocky, boulder-strewn plateau on the Shattered Plains.

'Shouldn't we be there by now?' the king asked.

'We're still two or three plateaus away from the hunting site, Your Majesty,' Dalinar said, distracted. 'It will be another hour, perhaps, observing proper protocols. If we had vantage, we could probably see the pavilion to—'

'Vantage? Would that rock formation up ahead do?'

'I suppose,' Dalinar said, inspecting the towerlike length of rock. 'We could send scouts to check.'

'Scouts? Bah. I need a run, Uncle. I'll bet you five full broams that I can beat you to the top.' And with that, the king galloped away in a thunder of hooves, leaving behind a shocked group of lighteyes, attendants, and guards.

'Storm it!' Dalinar cursed, kicking his horse into motion. 'Adolin, you have command! Secure the next plateau, just in case.'

His son, who had been lagging behind, nodded sharply. Dalinar galloped after the king, a figure in golden armor and a long blue cape. Hoofbeats pounded the stone, rock formations whipping past. Ahead, the steep, spikelike spire of rock rose from the lip of the plateau. Such formations were common out here on the Shattered Plains.

Curse that boy. Dalinar still thought of Elhokar as a boy, though the king was in his twenty-seventh year. But sometimes he acted like a boy. Why couldn't he give more warning before leaping into one of these stunts?

Still, as Dalinar rode, he admitted to himself that it *did* feel good to charge freely, helm off, face to the wind. His pulse picked up as he got into the race, and he forgave its impetuous beginning. For the moment, Dalinar let himself forget his troubles and the words that had been echoing in his head.

The king wanted a race? Well, Dalinar would give him one.

He charged past the king. Elhokar's stallion was a good breed, but it could never match Gallant, who was a full Ryshadium, two hands taller and much stronger than an ordinary horse. The animals chose their own riders, and only a dozen men in all of the warcamps were so fortunate. Dalinar was one, Adolin another.

In seconds, Dalinar reached the formation's base. He threw himself from the saddle while Gallant was still moving. He hit hard, but the Shardplate absorbed the impact, stone crunching beneath his metal boots as he skidded to a stop. Men who hadn't ever worn Plate – particularly those who were accustomed to its inferior cousin, simple plate and mail – could never understand. Shardplate wasn't merely armor. It was so much more.

He ran to the bottom of the rock formation as Elhokar galloped up behind. Dalinar leaped – Plate-assisted legs propelling him up some eight feet – and grabbed a handhold in the stone. With a heave, he pulled himself up, the Plate lending him the strength of many men. The Thrill of contest began to rise within him. It wasn't nearly as keen as the Thrill of battle, but it was a worthy substitute.

Rock scraped below. Elhokar had begun to climb as well. Dalinar didn't look down. He kept his eyes fixed on the small natural platform at the top of the forty-foot-high formation. He groped with steel-covered fingers, finding another handhold. The gauntlets covered his hands, but the ancient armor somehow transferred sensation to his fingers. It was as if he were wearing thin leather gloves.

A scraping sound came from the right, accompanied by a voice cursing softly. Elhokar had taken a different path, hoping to pass Dalinar, but the king had found himself at a section without handholds above. His progress was stalled.

The king's golden Shardplate glittered as he glanced at Dalinar. Elhokar set his jaw and looked upward, then launched himself in a powerful leap toward an outcropping.

Fool boy, Dalinar thought, watching the king seem to hang in the air for a moment before he snatched the projecting rock and dangled. Then the king pulled himself up and continued to climb.

Dalinar moved furiously, stone grinding beneath his metal fingertips, chips falling free. The wind ruffled his cape. He heaved, strained, and pushed himself, managing to get just ahead of the king. The top was mere feet away. The Thrill sang at him. He reached for the goal, determined to win. He couldn't lose. He had to—

Unite them.

He hesitated, not quite certain why, and let his nephew get ahead.

Elhokar hauled himself to his feet atop the rock formation, then laughed in triumph. He turned toward Dalinar, holding out a hand. 'Stormwinds, Uncle, but you made a fine race of it! At the end there, I thought for sure you had me.'

The triumph and joy in Elhokar's face brought a smile to Dalinar's lips. The younger man needed victories these days. Even little ones would do him good. Gloryspren – like tiny golden translucent globes of light – began to pop into existence around him, attracted by his sense of accomplishment. Blessing himself for hesitating, Dalinar took the king's hand, letting Elhokar pull him up. There was just enough room on top of the natural tower for them both.

Breathing deeply, Dalinar slapped the king on the back with a clank of metal on metal. 'That *was* a fine contest, Your Majesty. And you played it very well.'

The king beamed. His golden Shardplate gleamed in the noonday sun; he had his faceplate up, revealing light yellow eyes, a strong nose, and a clean-shaven face that was almost too handsome, with its full lips, broad forehead, and firm chin. Gavilar had looked like that too, before he'd suffered a broken nose and that terrible scar on his chin.

Below them, the Cobalt Guard and some of Elhokar's attendants rode up, including Sadeas. His Plate gleamed red, though he wasn't a full Shardbearer – he had only the Plate, not the Blade.

Dalinar looked up. From this height, he could scan a large swath of the Shattered Plains, and he had an odd moment of familiarity. He felt as if he'd been atop this vantage point before, looking down at a broken landscape.

The moment was gone in a heartbeat.

'There,' Elhokar said, pointing with a golden, gauntleted hand. 'I can see our destination.'

Dalinar shaded his eyes, picking out a large cloth pavilion three plateaus away, flying the king's flag. Wide, permanent bridges led there; they were relatively close to the Alethi side of the Shattered Plains, on plateaus

Dalinar himself maintained. A fully grown chasmfiend living here was his to hunt, the wealth at its heart his privilege to claim.

'You were correct again, Uncle,' Elhokar said.

'I try to make a habit of it.'

'I can't blame you for that, I suppose. Though I can beat you at a race now and then.'

Dalinar smiled. 'I felt like a youth again, chasing after your father on some ridiculous challenge.'

Elhokar's lips tightened to a thin line, and the gloryspren faded away. Mentioning Gavilar soured him; he felt others compared him unfavorably to the old king. Unfortunately, he was often right.

Dalinar moved on quickly. 'We must have seemed of the ten fools, charging away like that. I do wish you'd given me more notice to prepare your honor guard. This *is* a war zone.'

'Bah. You worry too much, Uncle. The Parshendi haven't attacked this close to our side of the Plains in years.'

'Well, you seemed worried about your safety two nights ago.'

Elhokar sighed audibly. 'How many times must I explain this to you, Uncle? I can face enemy soldiers with Blade in hand. It's what they might send when we're not looking, when all is dark and quiet, that you should be trying to protect me from.'

Dalinar didn't reply. Elhokar's nervousness – paranoia, even – regarding assassination was strong. But who could blame him, considering what had happened to his father?

I'm sorry, brother, he thought, as he did every time he thought of the night when Gavilar had died. Alone, without his brother to protect him.

'I looked into the matter you asked me about,' Dalinar said, forcing away bad memories.

'You did? What did you discover?'

'Not much, I'm afraid. There were no traces of trespassers on your balcony, and none of the servants reported any strangers in the area.'

'There *was* someone watching me in the darkness that night.'

'If so, they haven't returned, Your Majesty. And they left no clues behind.'

Elhokar seemed dissatisfied, and the silence between them grew stark. Below, Adolin met with scouts and prepared for the troop crossing. Elhokar had protested at how many men Dalinar had brought. Most of them wouldn't be needed on the hunt – the Shardbearers, not the soldiers, would slay the beast. But Dalinar *would* see his nephew protected. Parshendi raids had grown less bold during the years of fighting – Alethi scribes guessed their numbers were three-quarters their prior strength, though it was difficult to judge – but the king's presence might be enough to entice them into a reckless attack.

The winds blew across Dalinar, returning with them that faint familiarity he'd felt a few minutes before. Standing atop a peak, looking out at desolation. A sense of an awful and amazing perspective.

That's it, he thought. *I did* stand atop a formation like this. It happened during—

During one of his visions. The very first one.

You must unite them, the strange, booming words had told him. *You must prepare. Build of your people a fortress of strength and peace, a wall to resist the winds. Cease squabbling and unite. The Everstorm comes.*

'Your Majesty,' Dalinar found himself saying. 'I . . . ' He trailed off as quickly as he began. What could he say? That he'd been seeing visions? That – in defiance of all doctrine and common sense – he thought those visions might be from the Almighty? That he thought they should withdraw from the battlefield and go back to Alethkar?

Pure foolishness.

'Uncle?' the king asked. 'What do you want?'

'Nothing. Come, let's get back to the others.'

⋄⋄

Adolin twisted one of his hogshide reins around his finger while he sat astride his horse, awaiting the next batch of scout reports. He'd managed to get his mind off his father and Sadeas, and was instead contemplating just how he was going to explain his falling out with Rilla in a way that would earn him some sympathy with Janala.

Janala loved ancient epic poems; could he phrase the falling out in dramatic terms? He smiled, thinking her luxurious black hair and sly smile. She'd been daring, teasing at him while he was known to be courting someone else. He could use that too. Maybe Renarin was right, perhaps he should have invited her on the hunt. The prospect of fighting a greatshell would have been far more interesting to him if someone beautiful and long-haired were watching. . . .

'New scout reports are in, Brightlord Adolin,' Tarilar said, jogging up.

Adolin turned his mind back to business. He'd taken up position with some members of the Cobalt Guard beside the base of the high rock formation where his father and the king were still conversing. Tarilar, scoutlord, was a gaunt-faced man with a thick chest and arms. From some angles, his head looked so relatively small on his body that it appeared to have been smashed.

'Proceed,' Adolin said.

'Advance runners have met with the lead huntmaster and have returned. There are no sightings of Parshendi on any nearby plateaus. Companies Eighteen and Twenty-one are in position, though there are still eight companies to go.'

Adolin nodded. 'Have Company Twenty-one send some outriders to watch from plateaus fourteen and sixteen. And two each on plateaus six and eight.'

'Six and eight? Behind us?'

'If I were going to ambush the party,' Adolin said, 'I'd round back this way and cut us off from fleeing. Do it.'

Tarilar saluted. 'Yes, Brightlord.' He hurried away to pass the orders.

'You really think that's necessary?' Renarin asked, riding up beside Adolin.

'No. But Father will want it done anyway. You know he will.'

There was motion up above. Adolin looked up just in time to see the king leap off the rock formation, cape streaming behind him as he fell some forty feet to the rock floor. Adolin's father stood at the lip above, and Adolin could imagine him cursing to himself at what he saw as a foolhardy move. Shardplate could withstand a fall that far, but it was high enough to be dangerous.

Elhokar landed with an audible crack, throwing up chips of stone and a large puff of Stormlight. He managed to stay upright. Adolin's father took a safer way down, descending to a lower ledge before jumping.

He seems to take the safer pathway more and more often lately, Adolin thought idly. *And he often seems to find reasons to give me command as well.* Thoughtful, Adolin trotted his horse out of the shadow of the rock formation. He needed to get a report from the rear guard – his father would want to hear it.

His path took him past a group of lighteyes from Sadeas's party. The king, Sadeas, and Vamah each had a collection of attendants, aides, and sycophants accompanying them. Looking at them riding in their comfortable silks, open-fronted jackets, and shade-covered palanquins made Adolin aware of his sweaty, bulky armor. Shardplate was wonderful and empowering, but beneath a hot sun, it could still leave a man wishing for something less confining.

But, of course, he couldn't have worn casual clothing like the others. Adolin was to be in uniform, even on a hunt. The Alethi War Codes commanded it. Never mind that nobody had followed those Codes in centuries. Or at least nobody but Dalinar Kholin – and, by extension, his sons.

Adolin passed a pair of lounging lighteyes, Vartian and Lomard, two of Sadeas's recent hangers-on. They were talking loudly enough that Adolin could hear. Probably on purpose. 'Chasing after the king again,' Vartian said, shaking his head. 'Like pet axehounds nipping at their master's heels.'

'Shameful,' Lomard said. 'How long has it been since Dalinar won a gemheart? The only time he can get one is when the king lets them hunt it without competition.'

Adolin set his jaw and rode on. His father's interpretation of the Codes wouldn't let Adolin challenge a man to a duel while he was on duty or in command. He chafed at the needless restrictions, but Dalinar had spoken as Adolin's commanding officer. That meant there was no room for argument. He'd have to find a way to duel the two idiot sycophants in another setting, put them in their places. Unfortunately, he couldn't duel everyone who spoke out against his father.

The biggest problem was, the things they said had some real truth to them. The Alethi princedoms were like kingdoms unto themselves, still mostly autonomous despite having accepted Gavilar as king. Elhokar had inherited the throne, and Dalinar, by right, had taken the Kholin Princedom as his own.

However, most of the highprinces gave only token nods to the paramount rule of the king. That left Elhokar without land that was specifically his own. He tended to act like a highprince of the Kholin Princedom, taking great interest in its day-to-day management. So, while Dalinar should have been a ruler unto himself, he instead bent to Elhokar's whims and dedicated his resources to protecting his nephew. That made him weak in the eyes of the others – nothing more than a glorified bodyguard.

Once, when Dalinar had been feared, men had not dared whisper about these things. But now? Dalinar went on fewer and fewer plateau assaults, and his forces lagged behind in capturing precious gemhearts. While the others fought and won, Dalinar and his sons spent their time in bureaucratic administration.

Adolin wanted to be out there fighting, killing Parshendi. What was the good of following the Codes of War when he rarely got to *go* to war? *It's the fault of those delusions.* Dalinar wasn't weak, and he certainly wasn't a coward, no matter what people said. He was just troubled.

The rearguard captains weren't formed up yet, so Adolin decided to give the king a report instead. He trotted up toward the king – joining Sadeas, who was doing the same. Not unexpectedly, Sadeas frowned at him. The highprince hated that Adolin had a Blade while Sadeas had none; he had coveted one for years now.

Adolin met the highprince's eyes, smiling. *Anytime you want to duel me for my Blade, Sadeas, go ahead and try.* What Adolin wouldn't do to get that eel of a man in the dueling ring.

When Dalinar and the king rode up, Adolin spoke quickly, before Sadeas could speak. 'Your Majesty, I have scout reports.'

The king sighed. 'More of nothing, I expect. Honestly, Uncle, must we have a report on every little detail of the army?'

'We are at war, Your Majesty,' Dalinar said.

Elhokar sighed sufferingly.

You're a strange man, cousin, Adolin thought. Elhokar saw murderers in every shadow, yet often dismissed the Parshendi threat. He'd go charging off like he had today, with no honor guard, and would leap off a forty-foottall rock formation. Yet he'd stay up nights, terrified of assassination.

'Give your report, son,' Dalinar said.

Adolin hesitated, now feeling foolish at the lack of substance to what he had to say. 'The scouts have seen no sign of the Parshendi. They've met with the huntmaster. Two companies have secured the next plateau, and the other eight will need some time to cross. We're close, though.'

'Yes, we saw from above,' Elhokar said. 'Perhaps a few of us could ride ahead. . . .'

'Your Majesty,' Dalinar said. 'The point of bringing my troops along would be somewhat undermined if you left them behind.'

Elhokar rolled his eyes. Dalinar did not yield, his expression as immobile as the rocks around them. Seeing him like that – firm, unyielding before a challenge – made Adolin smile with pride. Why couldn't he be like this *all* of the time? Why did he back down so often before insults or challenges?

'Very well,' the king said. 'We'll take a break and wait while the army crosses.'

The king's attendants responded immediately, men climbing off horses, women having their palanquin bearers set them down. Adolin moved off to get that rearguard report. By the time he returned, Elhokar was practically holding court. His servants had set up a small awning to give him shade, and others served wine. Chilled, using one of the new fabrials that could make things cold.

Adolin removed his helm and wiped his brow with his saddle rag, again wishing he could join the others and enjoy a little wine. Instead, he climbed down from his horse and went looking for his father. Dalinar stood outside the awning, gauntleted hands clasped behind his back, looking eastward, toward the Origin – the distant, the unseen place where highstorms began. Renarin stood at his side, looking out as well, as if trying to see what it was that his father found so interesting.

Adolin rested a hand on his brother's shoulder, and Renarin smiled at him. Adolin knew that his brother – now nineteen years old – felt out of place. Though he wore a side sword, he barely knew how to use it. His blood weakness made it difficult for him to spend any reasonable amount of time practicing.

'Father,' Adolin said. 'Maybe the king was right. Perhaps we should have moved on quickly. I'd rather have this entire hunt over with.'

Dalinar looked at him. 'When I was your age, I looked forward to a hunt like this. Taking down a greatshell was the highlight of a young man's year.'

Not this again, Adolin thought. Why was everyone so offended that he didn't find hunts exciting? 'It's just an oversized chull, Father.'

'These "oversized chulls" grow to fifty feet tall and are capable of crushing even a man in Shardplate.'

'Yes,' Adolin said, 'and so we'll bait it for hours while baking in the hot sun. If it decides to show up, we'll pelt it with arrows, only closing in once it's so weak it can barely resist as we hack it to death with Shardblades. Very honorable.'

'It's not a duel,' Dalinar said, 'it's a hunt. A grand tradition.'

Adolin raised an eyebrow at him.

'And yes,' Dalinar added. 'It can be tedious. But the king was insistent.'

'You're just still smarting over the problems with Rilla, Adolin,' Renarin said. 'You were eager a week ago. You really should have invited Janala.'

'Janala hates hunts. Thinks they're barbarous.'

Dalinar frowned. 'Janala? Who's Janala?'

'Daughter of Brightlord Lustow,' Adolin said.

'And you're courting her?'

'Not yet, but I've sure been trying.'

'What happened to that other girl? The short one, with the fondness for silver hair ribbons?'

'Deeli?' Adolin said. 'Father, I stopped courting her over two months back!'

'You did?'

'Yes.'

Dalinar rubbed his chin.

'There have been two between her and Janala, Father,' Adolin noted. 'You really need to pay more attention.'

'Almighty help any man who tries to keep track of your tangled courtships, son.'

'The most recent was Rilla,' Renarin said.

Dalinar frowned. 'And you two ...'

'Had some problems yesterday,' Adolin said. He coughed, determined to change the subject. 'Anyway, don't you find it odd that the king would insist on coming to hunt the chasmfiend himself?'

'Not particularly. It isn't often that a full-sized one makes its way out here, and the king rarely gets to go on plateau runs. This is a way for him to fight.'

'But he's so paranoid! Why does he now want to go and hunt, exposing himself on the Plains?'

Dalinar looked toward the king's awning. 'I know he seems odd, son. But the king is more complex a man than many give him credit for being. He worries that his subjects see him as a coward because of how much he fears assassins, and so he finds ways to prove his courage. Foolish ways, sometimes – but he's not the first man I've known who will face battle without fear, yet cower in terror about knives in the shadows. The hallmark of insecurity is bravado.

'The king is learning to lead. He needs this hunt. He needs to prove to himself, and to others, that he's still strong and worthy to command a kingdom at war. That's why I encouraged him. A successful hunt, under controlled circumstances, could bolster his reputation and his confidence.'

Adolin slowly closed his mouth, his father's words cutting down his complaints. Strange, how much the king's actions made sense when explained that way. Adolin looked up at his father. *How can the others whisper that he's a coward? Can't they see his wisdom?*

'Yes,' Dalinar said, eyes growing distant. 'Your cousin is a better man than many think him, and a stronger king. At least he could be. I just have to figure out how to persuade him to leave the Shattered Plains.'

Adolin started. '*What?*'

'I didn't understand at first,' Dalinar continued. 'Unite them. I'm supposed to unite them. But aren't they already united? We fight together here on the Shattered Plains. We have a common enemy in the Parshendi. I'm beginning to see that we're united only in name. The highprinces give lip service to Elhokar, but this war – this siege – is a game to them. A competition against one another.

'We can't unite them here. We need to return to Alethkar and stabilize our homeland, learn how to work together as one nation. The Shattered Plains divide us. The others worry too much about winning wealth and prestige.'

'Wealth and prestige are what being Alethi is *about*, Father!' Adolin said. Was he really hearing this? 'What of the Vengeance Pact? The highprinces vowed to seek retribution upon the Parshendi!'

'And we *have* sought it.' Dalinar looked to Adolin. 'I realize that it sounds terrible, son, but some things are more important than vengeance. I loved Gavilar. I miss him fiercely, and I hate the Parshendi for what they did. But Gavilar's life work was to unite Alethkar, and I'll go to Damnation before I let it break apart.'

'Father,' Adolin said, feeling pained, 'if there's something wrong here, it's that we're not trying hard enough. You think the highprinces are playing games? Well, show them the way it should be done! Instead of talking of retreat, we should be talking of advancing, striking at the Parshendi instead of besieging them.'

'Perhaps.'

'Either way, we cannot speak of withdrawing,' Adolin said. The men *already* talked of Dalinar losing his spine. What would they say if they got hold of this? 'You haven't brought this up with the king, have you?'

'Not yet. I haven't found the right way.'

'Please. Don't talk to him about it.'

'We shall see.' Dalinar turned back toward the Shattered Plains, his eyes growing distant again.

'Father . . .'

'You've made your point, son, and I've replied to it. Do not press the issue. Have you gotten the report from the rear guard?'

'Yes.'

'What of the vanguard?'

'I just checked with them and . . .' He trailed off. Blast. It had been long enough that it was probably time to move the king's party onward. The last of the army couldn't leave this plateau until the king was safely on the other side.

Adolin sighed and went off to collect the report. Before long, they were all across the chasm and riding over the next plateau. Renarin trotted up to Adolin and tried to engage him in conversation, but Adolin gave only halfhearted replies.

He was beginning to feel an odd longing. Most of the older men in the army – even those only a few years older than Adolin – had fought alongside his father during the glory days. Adolin found himself jealous of all of those men who had known his father and had seen him fight when he hadn't been so wrapped up in the Codes.

The changes in Dalinar had begun with the death of his brother. That terrible day was when everything had started to go wrong. The loss of Gavilar had nearly crushed Dalinar, and Adolin would *never* forgive the Parshendi for bringing his father such pain. Never. Men fought on the Plains for different reasons, but this was why Adolin had come. Perhaps if they beat the Parshendi, his father would go back to the man he had been. Perhaps those ghostly delusions that haunted him would vanish.

Ahead, Dalinar was speaking quietly with Sadeas. Both men wore frowns. They barely tolerated one another, though they had once been friends. That had also changed the night of Gavilar's death. What had happened between them?

The day wore on, and they eventually arrived at the hunt site – a pair of plateaus, one where the creature would be lured up to attack, and another one a safe distance away for those who would watch. Like most others, these plateaus had an uneven surface inhabited by hardy plants adapted to regular storm exposure. Rocky shelves, depressions, and uneven footing made fighting on them treacherous.

Adolin joined his father, who waited beside the final bridge as the king moved over onto the viewing plateau, followed by a company of soldiers. The attendants would be next.

'You're doing well with your command, son,' Dalinar said, nodding to a group of soldiers as they passed and saluted.

'They're good men, Father. They hardly need someone to command them during a march from plateau to plateau.'

'Yes,' Dalinar said. 'But you need experience leading, and they need to learn to see you as a commander.' Renarin trotted up to them on his horse; it was probably time to cross to the viewing plateau. Dalinar nodded for his sons to go first.

Adolin turned to go, but hesitated as he noticed something on the plateau behind them. A rider, moving quickly to catch up with the hunting party, coming from the direction of the warcamps.

'Father,' Adolin said, pointing.

Dalinar turned immediately, following the gesture. However, Adolin soon recognized the newcomer. Not a messenger, as he'd expected. 'Wit!' Adolin called, waving. The newcomer trotted up to them. Tall and thin, the King's Wit rode easily on a black gelding. He wore a stiff black coat and black trousers, a color matched by his deep onyx hair. Though he wore a long, thin sword tied to his waist, as far as Adolin knew, the man had never drawn it. A dueling foil rather than a military blade, it was mostly symbolic.

Wit nodded to them as he approached, wearing one of those keen smiles of his. He had blue eyes, but he wasn't really a lighteyes. Nor was he a dark-eyes. He was ... well, he was the King's Wit. That was a category all its own.

'Ah, young Prince Adolin!' Wit exclaimed. 'You actually managed to pry yourself away from the camp's young women long enough to join this hunt? I'm impressed.'

Adolin chuckled uncomfortably. 'Well, that's been a topic of some discussion lately. . . .'

Wit raised an eyebrow.

Adolin sighed. Wit would find out eventually anyway – it was virtually impossible to keep anything from the man. 'I made a lunch appointment with one woman yesterday, but I was . . . well, I was courting another. And she's the jealous type. So now neither will speak with me.'

'It's a constant source of amazement that you get yourself into such messes, Adolin. Each one is more exciting than the previous!'

'Er, yes. Exciting. That's *exactly* how it feels.'

Wit laughed again, though he maintained a sense of dignity in his posture. The King's Wit was not a silly court fool such as one might find in other kingdoms. He was a sword, a tool maintained by the king. Insulting others was beneath the dignity of the king, so just as one used gloves when forced to handle something vile, the king retained a Wit so he didn't have to debase himself to the level of rudeness or offensiveness.

This new Wit had been with them for some months, and there was something . . . different about him. He seemed to know things that he shouldn't, important things. Useful things.

Wit nodded to Dalinar. 'Your Lordship.'

'Wit,' Dalinar said stiffly.

'And young Prince Renarin!'

Renarin kept his eyes down.

'No greeting for me, Renarin?' Wit said, amused.

Renarin said nothing.

'He thinks you'll mock him if he speaks to you, Wit,' Adolin said. 'Earlier this morning, he told me he'd determined not to say anything around you.'

'Wonderful!' Wit exclaimed. 'Then I can say whatever I wish, and he'll not object?'

Renarin hesitated.

Wit leaned in to Adolin. 'Have I told you about the night Prince Renarin and I had two days back, walking the streets of the warcamp? We came across these two sisters, you see, blue eyed and—'

'That's a lie!' Renarin said, blushing.

'Very well,' Wit said without missing a beat, 'I'll confess there were actually *three* sisters, but Prince Renarin quite unfairly ended up with two of them, and I didn't wish to diminish my reputation by—'

'Wit.' Dalinar was stern as he cut in.

The black-clad man looked to him.

'Perhaps you should restrict your mockery to those who deserve it.'

'Brightlord Dalinar. I believe that was what I *was* doing.'

Dalinar's frown deepened. He never had liked Wit, and picking on Renarin was a sure way to raise his ire. Adolin could understand that, but Wit was almost always good-natured with Renarin.

Wit moved to leave, passing Dalinar as he did. Adolin could barely overhear what was said as Wit leaned over to whisper something. 'Those who "deserve" my mockery are those who can benefit from it, Brightlord Dalinar. That one is less fragile than you think him.' He winked, then turned his horse to move on over the bridge.

'Stormwinds, but I like that man,' Adolin said. 'Best Wit we've had in ages!'

'I find him unnerving,' Renarin said softly.

'That's half the fun!'

Dalinar said nothing. The three of them crossed the bridge, passing Wit, who had stopped to torment a group of officers – lighteyes of low enough rank that they needed to serve in the army and earn a wage. Several of them laughed while Wit poked fun at another.

The three of them joined the king, and were immediately approached by the day's huntmaster. Bashin was a short man with a sizable paunch; he wore rugged clothing with a leather overcoat and a wide-brimmed hat. He was a darkeyes of the first nahn, the highest and most prestigious rank a darkeyes could have, worthy even of marrying into a lighteyed family.

Bashin bowed to the king. 'Your Majesty! Wonderful timing! We've just tossed down the bait.'

'Excellent,' Elhokar said, climbing from the saddle. Adolin and Dalinar did likewise, Shardplate clinking softly, Dalinar untying his helm from the saddle. 'How long will it take?'

'Two or three hours is likely,' Bashin said, taking the reins of the king's horse. Grooms took the two Ryshadium. 'We've set up over there.'

Bashin pointed toward the hunting plateau, the smaller plateau where the actual fighting would take place away from the attendants and the bulk of the soldiers. A group of hunters led a lumbering chull around its perimeter, towing a rope draped over the side of the cliff. That rope would be dragging the bait.

'We're using hog carcasses,' Bashin explained. 'And we poured hog's blood over the sides. The chasmfiend has been spotted by patrols here a good dozen times. He's got his nest nearby, for certain – he's not here to pupate. He's too big for that, and he's remained in the area too long. So it should be a fine hunt! Once he arrives, we'll loose a group of wild hogs as distractions, and you can begin weakening him with arrows.'

They had brought grandbows: large steel bows with thick strings and such a high draw weight that only a Shardbearer could use them, to fire shafts as thick as three fingers. They were recent creations, devised by Alethi engineers through the use of fabrial science, and each required a small infused gemstone to maintain the strength of its pull without warping the metal. Adolin's aunt Navani – the widow of King Gavilar, mother of Elhokar and his sister Jasnah – had led the research to develop the bows. *It would be nice if she hadn't left*, Adolin thought idly. Navani was an interesting woman. Things were never boring around her.

Some had started calling the bows Shardbows, but Adolin didn't like the term. Shardblades and Shardplate were something special. Relics from another time, a time when the Radiants had walked Roshar. No amount of fabrial science had even approached re-creating them.

Bashin led the king and his highprinces toward a pavilion at the center of the viewing plateau. Adolin joined his father, intending to give a report on the crossing. About half of the soldiers were in place, but many of the attendants were still making their way across the large, permanent bridge onto the viewing plateau. The king's banner flapped above the pavilion, and a small refreshment station had been erected. A soldier at the back was setting up the rack of four grandbows. They were sleek and dangerous-looking, with thick black shafts in four quivers beside them.

'I think you'll have a fine day for the hunt,' Bashin said to Dalinar. 'Judging by reports, the beast is a big one. Larger than you've ever slain before, Brightlord.'

'Gavilar always wanted to slay one of these,' Dalinar said wistfully. 'He loved greatshell hunts, though he never got a chasmfiend. Odd that I've now killed so many.'

The chull pulling the bait bleated in the distance.

'You need to go for the legs on this one, Brightlords,' Bashin said. Pre-hunt advice was one of Bashin's responsibilities, and he took those seriously. 'Chasmfiends, well, you're used to attacking them in their chrysalises. Don't forget how mean they are when they're not pupating. With one this big, use a distraction and come in from ...' He trailed off, then groaned, cursing softly. 'Storms take that animal. I swear, the man who trained it must have been daft.'

He was looking across at the next plateau. Adolin followed his glance. The crablike chull that had been towing the bait was lumbering away from the chasm with a slow, yet determined gait. Its handlers were yelling, running after it.

'I'm sorry, Brightlord,' Bashin said. 'It's been doing this all day.'

The chull bleated in a gravelly voice. Something seemed wrong to Adolin.

'We can send for another one,' Elhokar said. 'It shouldn't take too long to—'

'Bashin?' Dalinar said, his voice suddenly alarmed. 'Shouldn't there be *bait* on the end of that beast's rope?'

The huntmaster froze. The rope the chull was towing was frayed at the end.

Something dark – something mind-numbingly enormous – rose out of the chasm on thick, chitinous legs. It climbed onto the plateau – not the small plateau where the hunt was supposed to take place, but the viewing plateau where Dalinar and Adolin stood. The plateau filled with attendants, unarmed guests, female scribes, and unprepared soldiers.

'Aw, Damnation,' Bashin said.

13

TEN HEARTBEATS

I realize that you are probably still angry. That is pleasant to know. Much as your perpetual health, I have come to rely upon your dissatisfaction with me. It is one of the cosmere's great constants, I should think.

Ten heartbeats.

One.

That was how long it took to summon a Shardblade. If Dalinar's heart was racing, the time was shorter. If he was relaxed, it took longer.

Two.

On the battlefield, the passing of those beats could stretch like an eternity. He pulled his helm on as he ran.

Three.

The chasmfiend slammed an arm down, smashing the bridge filled with attendants and soldiers. People screamed, plunging into the chasm. Dalinar dashed forward on Plate-enhanced legs, following the king.

Four.

The chasmfiend towered like a mountain of interlocking carapace the color of dark violet ink. Dalinar could see why the Parshendi called these things gods. It had a twisted, arrowhead-like face, with a mouth full of barbed mandibles. While it was vaguely crustacean, this was no bulky, placid chull. It had four wicked foreclaws set into broad shoulders, each claw the size of a horse, and a dozen smaller legs that clutched the side of the plateau.

Five.

Chitin made a grinding noise against stone as the creature finished pulling itself onto the plateau, snatching a cart-pulling chull with a swift claw.

Six.

'To arms, to arms!' Elhokar bellowed ahead of Dalinar. 'Archers, fire!'

Seven.

'Distract it from the unarmed!' Dalinar bellowed at his soldiers.

The creature cracked the chull's shell – platter-size fragments clattering to the plateau – then stuffed the beast into its maw and began looking down at the fleeing scribes and attendants. The chull stopped bleating as the monster crunched down.

Eight.

Dalinar leaped a rocky shelf and sailed five yards before slamming into the ground, throwing up chips of rock.

Nine.

The chasmfiend bellowed with an awful screeching sound. It trumpeted with four voices, overlapping one another.

Archers drew. Elhokar yelled orders just in front of Dalinar, his blue cape flapping.

Dalinar's hand tingled with anticipation.

Ten!

His Shardblade – Oathbringer – formed in his hand, coalescing from mist, appearing as the tenth beat of his heart thudded in his chest. Six feet long from tip to hilt, the Blade would have been unwieldy in the hands of any man not wearing Shardplate. To Dalinar, it felt perfect. He'd carried Oathbringer since his youth, Bonding to it when he was twenty Weepings old. It was long and slightly curved, a handspan wide, with wavelike serrations near the hilt. It curved at the tip like a fisherman's hook, and was wet with cold dew.

This sword was a part of him. He could sense energy racing along its blade, as if it were eager. A man never really knew life itself until he charged into battle with Plate and Blade.

'Make it *angry!*' Elhokar bellowed, his Shardblade – Sunraiser – springing from mist into his hand. It was long and thin with a large crossguard, and was etched up the sides with the ten fundamental glyphs. He didn't want the monster to escape; Dalinar could hear it in his voice. Dalinar was more worried about the soldiers and attendants; this hunt had already turned terribly wrong. Perhaps they should distract the monster long enough for everyone to escape, then pull back and let it dine on chulls and hogs.

The creature screamed its multivoiced wail again, slamming a claw down among the soldiers. Men screamed; bones splintered and bodies crumpled.

Archers loosed, aiming for the head. A hundred shafts zipped into the air, but only a few hit the soft muscle between plates of chitin. Behind them, Sadeas was calling for his grandbow. Dalinar couldn't wait for that – the creature was here, dangerous, killing his men. The bow would be too slow. This was a job for the Blade.

Adolin charged past, riding Sureblood. The lad had gone racing for his horse, rather than charging like Elhokar had. Dalinar himself had been forced to stay with the king. The other horses – even the warhorses – panicked, but Adolin's white Ryshadium stallion held steady. In a moment, Gallant was there, trotting beside Dalinar. Dalinar grabbed the reins and heaved himself into the air with Plate-enhanced legs, jumping up into the saddle. The force of his landing might have strained the back of an ordinary horse, but Gallant was made of stronger stone than that.

Elhokar closed his helm, the sides misting.

'Hold back, Your Majesty,' Dalinar called, riding past. 'Wait until Adolin and I weaken it.' Dalinar reached up, slamming down his own visor. The sides misted, locking it into place, and the sides of the helm became translucent to him. You still needed the eye slit – looking through the sides was like looking through dirty glass – but the translucence was one of the most wonderful parts of Shardplate.

Dalinar rode into the monster's shadow. Soldiers scrambled about, clutching spears. They hadn't been trained to fight thirty-foot-tall beasts, and it was a testament to their valor that they formed up anyway, trying to draw attention away from the archers and the fleeing attendants.

Arrows rained down, bouncing off the carapace and becoming more deadly to the troops below than they were to the chasmfiend. Dalinar raised his free arm to shade his eye slit as an arrow clanged off his helm.

Adolin fell back as the beast swung at a batch of archers, crushing them with one of its claws. 'I'll take left,' Adolin yelled, voice muffled by his helm.

Dalinar nodded, cutting to the right, galloping past a group of dazed soldiers and into sunlight again as the chasmfiend raised a foreclaw for another sweep. Dalinar raced under the limb, transferring Oathbringer to his left hand and holding the sword out to the side, slashing it through one of the chasmfiend's trunklike legs.

The Blade sheared the thick chitin with barely a tug of resistance. As always, it didn't cut living flesh, though it killed the leg as surely as if it had been cut free. The large limb slipped, falling numb and useless.

The monster roared with its deep, overlapping, trumpeting voices. On the other side, Dalinar could make out Adolin slicing at a leg.

The creature shook, turning toward Dalinar. The two legs that had been cut dragged lifelessly. The monster was long and narrow like a crayfish, and had a flattened tail. It walked on fourteen legs. How many could it lose before collapsing?

Dalinar rounded Gallant, meeting up with Adolin, whose blue Shard-plate was gleaming, cape streaming behind him. They switched sides as they turned in wide arcs, each heading for another leg.

'Meet your enemy, monster!' Elhokar bellowed.

Dalinar turned. The king had found his mount and had managed to get it under control. Vengeance wasn't a Ryshadium, but the animal was of the best Shin stock. Astride the animal, Elhokar charged, Blade held above his head.

Well, there was no forbidding him the fight. He should be all right in his Plate so long as he kept moving. 'The legs, Elhokar!' Dalinar shouted.

Elhokar ignored him, charging directly for the beast's chest. Dalinar cursed, heeling Gallant as the monster swung. Elhokar turned at the last moment, leaning low, ducking under the blow. The chasmfiend's claw hit stone with a cracking sound. It roared in anger at missing Elhokar, the sound echoing through the chasms.

The king veered toward Dalinar, riding past him in a rush. 'I'm distracting it, you fool. Keep attacking!'

'I have the Ryshadium!' Dalinar yelled back at him. 'I'll distract – I'm faster!'

Elhokar ignored him again. Dalinar sighed. Elhokar, characteristically, could not be contained. Arguing would only cost more time and more lives, so Dalinar did as he'd been told. He rounded to the side for another approach, Gallant's hooves beating against the stone ground. The king drew the monster's direct attention, and Dalinar was able to ride in and slam his Blade through another leg.

The beast emitted four overlapping screams and turned toward Dalinar. But as it did, Adolin rode past on the other side, cutting at another leg with a deft strike. The leg slumped, and arrows rained down as archers continued to fire.

The creature shook, confused by the attacks coming from every side. It was getting weak, and Dalinar raised his arm, gesturing. The command ordered the rest of the foot soldiers to retreat toward the pavilion. Orders given, he slipped in and killed another leg. That meant five down. Perhaps it was time to let the beast limp away; killing it now wasn't worth risking lives.

He called to the king, who rode – Blade held out to the side – a short distance away. The king glanced at him, but obviously didn't hear. As the chasmfiend loomed in the background, Elhokar wheeled Vengeance in a sharp right turn toward Dalinar.

There was a soft *snap*, and suddenly the king – and his saddle – went tumbling through the air. The horse's quick turn had caused the saddle girth to break. A man in Shardplate was heavy and put a great strain on both his mount and saddle.

Dalinar felt a spike of fear, and he reined in Gallant. Elhokar slammed to the ground, dropping his Shardblade. The weapon reverted to mist, vanishing. It was a protection from keeping a Blade from being taken by your enemies; they vanished unless you willed them to stay when releasing them.

'Elhokar!' Dalinar bellowed. The king rolled, cape wrapping around his body, then came to rest. He lay dazed for a moment; the armor was cracked on one shoulder, leaking Stormlight. The Plate would have cushioned the fall. He'd be all right.

Unless—

A claw loomed above the king.

Dalinar felt a moment of panic, turning Gallant to charge toward the king. He was going to be too slow! The beast would—

An enormous arrow slammed into the chasmfiend's head, cracking chitin. Purple gore spurted free, causing the beast to trump in agony. Dalinar twisted in the saddle.

Sadeas stood in his red Plate, taking another massive arrow from an attendant. He drew, launching the thick bolt into the chasmfiend's shoulder with a sharp crack.

Dalinar raised Oathbringer in salute. Sadeas acknowledged, raising his bow. They were not friends, and they did not like one another.

But they *would* protect the king. That was the bond that united them.

'Get to safety!' Dalinar yelled to the king as he charged past. Elhokar stumbled to his feet and nodded.

Dalinar moved in. He *had* to distract the beast long enough for Elhokar to get away. More of Sadeas's arrows flew true, but the monster started to ignore them. Its sluggishness vanished, and its bleats became angry, wild, crazed. It was growing truly enraged.

This was the most dangerous part; there would be no retreating now. It would follow them until it either killed them or was slain.

A claw smashed to the ground just beside Gallant, throwing chips of stone into the air. Dalinar hunkered low, careful to keep his Shardblade out, and he cut free another leg. Adolin had done the same on the other side. Seven legs down, half of them. How long before the beast dropped? Normally, at this stage, they had launched several dozen arrows into the animal. It was difficult to guess what one would do without that prior softening – beside that, he'd never fought one this large before.

He turned Gallant, trying to draw the creature's attention. Hopefully, Elhokar had—

'Are you a god!' Elhokar bellowed.

Dalinar groaned, looking over his shoulder. The king had *not* fled. He strode toward the beast, hand to the side.

'I defy you, creature!' Elhokar screamed. 'I claim your life! They will see their gods crushed, just as they will see their king dead at my feet! I *defy* you!'

Damnation's own fool! Dalinar thought, rounding Gallant.

Elhokar's Shardblade re-formed in his hands, and he charged toward the monster's chest, his cracked shoulder leaking Stormlight. He got close and swung at the beast's torso, cutting free a piece of chitin – like a person's hair or nails, it could be cut by a Blade. Then Elhokar slammed his weapon into the monster's breast, seeking its heart.

The beast roared and shook, knocking Elhokar free. The king barely kept hold of his Blade. The beast spun. That movement, unfortunately, brought its tail at Dalinar. He cursed, yanking Gallant in a tight turn, but the tail came too quickly. It slammed into Gallant, and in a heartbeat Dalinar found himself rolling, Oathbringer tumbling from his fingers and slicing a gash in the stone ground before puffing to mist.

'Father!' a distant voice yelled.

Dalinar came to rest on the stones, dizzy. He raised his head to see Gallant stumbling to his feet. Blessedly, the horse hadn't broken a leg, though the animal bled from scrapes and was favoring one leg.

'Away!' Dalinar said. The command word would send the horse to safety. Unlike Elhokar, *it* would obey.

Dalinar climbed to his feet, unsteady. A scraping sound came from his left, and Dalinar spun just in time for the chasmfiend's tail to take him in the chest, tossing him backward.

Again the world lurched, and metal hit stone in a cacophony as he slid.

No! he thought, getting a gauntleted hand beneath himself and heaving, using the momentum of his slide to throw himself upright. As the sky spun, something seemed to *right*, as if the Plate itself knew which way was up. He landed – still moving, feet grinding on stone.

He got his balance, then charged toward the king, beginning the process of summoning his Shardblade again. Ten heartbeats. An eternity.

The archers continued to fire, and more than a few of their shafts bristled from the chasmfiend's face. It ignored them, though Sadeas's larger arrows still seemed to distract it. Adolin had sheared through another leg, and the creature lumbered uncertainly, eight of its fourteen legs dragging uselessly.

'Father!'

Dalinar turned to see Renarin – dressed in a stiff blue Kholin uniform, with a long coat buttoning to the neck – riding across the rocky ground. 'Father, are you well? Can I help?'

'Fool boy!' Dalinar said, pointing. 'Go!'

'But—'

'You're unarmored and unarmed!' Dalinar bellowed. 'Get back before you get yourself killed!'

Renarin pulled his roan horse to a halt.

'GO!'

Renarin galloped away. Dalinar turned and ran toward Elhokar, Oathbringer misting into existence in his waiting hand. Elhokar continued to hack at the beast's lower torso, and sections of flesh blackened and died when the Shardblade struck. If he rammed the Shardblade in just right, he could stop the heart or lungs, but that would be difficult while the beast was upright.

Adolin – stalwart as always – had dismounted beside the king. He tried to stop the claws, striking at them as they fell. Unfortunately, there were four claws and only one of Adolin. Two swung at him at once, and though Adolin sliced a chunk out of one, he didn't see the other sweeping at his back.

Dalinar called out too late. Shardplate *snapped* as the claw tossed Adolin into the air. He arced and hit in a tumble. His Plate didn't shatter, thank the Heralds, but the breastplate and side cracked widely, leaking trails of white smoke.

Adolin rolled lethargically, hands moving. He was alive.

No time to think about him now. Elhokar was alone.

The beast struck, pounding the ground beside the king, knocking him off his feet. His blade vanished and Elhokar fell face-first on the stones.

Something changed inside of Dalinar. Reservations vanished. Other concerns became meaningless. His brother's son was in danger.

He had failed Gavilar, had lain drunk in his wine while his brother fought for his life. Dalinar should have been there to defend him. Only two things remained of his beloved brother, two things that Dalinar could protect in a hope to earn some form of redemption: Gavilar's kingdom and Gavilar's son.

Elhokar was alone and in danger.

Nothing else mattered.

❖

Adolin shook his head, dazed. He slammed his visor up, taking a gasp of fresh air to clear his mind.

Fighting. They were fighting. He could hear men screaming, rocks shaking, an enormous bleating sound. He smelled something moldy. Greatshell blood.

The chasmfiend! he thought. Before his mind was even clear, Adolin began summoning his Blade again and forced himself to his hands and knees.

The monster loomed a short distance away, a dark shadow upon the sky. Adolin had fallen near its right side. As his vision lost its fuzziness, he saw that the king was down, and his armor was cracked from the blow he'd taken earlier.

The chasmfiend raised a massive claw, preparing to slam it down. Adolin knew – suddenly – that disaster was upon them. The king would be killed on a simple hunt. The kingdom would shatter, the highprinces divided, the one tenuous link that kept them together cut away.

No! Adolin thought, stunned, still dazed, trying to stumble forward.

And then he saw his father.

Dalinar charged toward the king, moving with a speed and grace no man – not even one wearing Shardplate – should be able to manage. He leaped over a rock shelf, then ducked and skidded beneath a claw swinging for him. Other men thought they understood Shardblades and Shardplate, but Dalinar Kholin ... at times, he proved them all children.

Dalinar straightened and leaped – still moving forward – cresting by inches a second claw that smashed apart the rocky shelf behind him.

It was all just a moment. A breath. The third claw was falling toward the king, and Dalinar roared, leaping forward. He dropped his Blade – it hit the ground and puffed away – as he skidded beneath the falling claw. He raised his hands and—

And he caught it. He bent beneath the blow, going down on one knee, and the air rang with a resounding clang of carapace against armor.

But he *caught it.*

Stormfather! Adolin thought, watching his father stand over the king, bowed beneath the enormous weight of a monster many times his size. Shocked archers hesitated. Sadeas lowered his grandbow. Adolin's breath caught in his chest.

Dalinar held back the claw and matched its strength, a figure in dark, silvery metal that almost seemed to glow. The beast trumpeted above, and Dalinar bellowed back a powerful, defiant yell.

In that moment, Adolin knew he was seeing *him.* The Blackthorn, the very man he'd been wishing he could fight alongside. The Plate of Dalinar's gauntlets and shoulders began to crack, webs of light moving down the ancient metal. Adolin finally shook himself into motion. *I have to help!*

His Shardblade formed in his hand and he scrambled to the side and sheared through the leg nearest to him. There was a crack in the air. With so many legs down, the beast's other legs couldn't hold its weight, particularly when it was trying so hard to crush Dalinar. The remaining legs on its right side snapped with a sickening crunch, spraying out violet ichor, and the beast toppled to the side.

The ground shook, nearly knocking Adolin to his knees. Dalinar tossed aside the now-limp claw, Stormlight from the many cracks steaming above him. Nearby, the king picked himself up off the ground – it had been mere seconds since he'd fallen.

Elhokar stumbled to his feet, looking at the fallen beast. Then he turned to his uncle, the Blackthorn.

Dalinar nodded thankfully to Adolin, then gestured sharply toward what passed for the beast's neck. Elhokar nodded, then summoned his Blade and rammed it deeply into the monster's flesh. The creature's uniform green eyes blackened and shriveled, smoke twisting into the air.

Adolin walked up to join his father, watching as Elhokar plunged his Blade into the chasmfiend's chest. Now that the beast was dead, the Blade could cut its flesh. Violet ichor spurted out, and Elhokar dropped his sword and reached into the wound, questing with Plate-enhanced arms, grabbing something.

He ripped free the beast's gemheart – the enormous gemstone that grew within all chasmfiends. It was lumpy and uncut, but it was a pure emerald and as big as a man's head. It was the largest gemheart Adolin had ever seen, and even the small ones were worth a fortune.

Elhokar held aloft the grisly prize, golden gloryspren appearing around him, and the soldiers yelled in triumph.

14

PAYDAY

Let me first assure you that the element is quite safe. I have found a good home for it. I protect its safety like I protect my own skin, you might say.

The morning after his decision in the highstorm, Kaladin made certain to arise before the others. He threw off his blanket and strode through the room full of blanketed lumps. He didn't feel excited, but he *did* feel resolute. Determined to fight again.

He began that fight by throwing the door open to the sunlight. Groans and curses sounded behind him as the groggy bridgemen awoke. Kaladin turned toward them, hands on hips. Bridge Four currently had thirty-four members. That number fluctuated, but at least twenty-five were needed to carry the bridge. Anything below that, and the bridge would topple for certain. Sometimes, it did even with more members.

'Up and organize!' Kaladin shouted in his best squadleader's voice. He shocked himself with the authority in it.

The men blinked bleary eyes.

'That *means*,' Kaladin bellowed, 'out of the barrack and form ranks! You'll do it now, storm you, or I'll haul you out one by one myself!'

Syl fluttered down and landed on his shoulder, watching curiously. Some of the bridgemen sat up, staring at him, baffled. Others turned over in their blankets, putting their backs to him.

Kaladin took a deep breath. 'So be it.' He strode into the room and chose a lean Alethi named Moash. He was a strong man; Kaladin needed an example, and one of the skinnier men like Dunny or Narm wouldn't do. Plus, Moash was one of those who'd turned over to go back to sleep.

Kaladin grabbed Moash by one arm and heaved, pulling with all his strength. Moash stumbled to his feet. He was a younger man, perhaps near Kaladin's age, and had a hawkish face.

'Storm off!' Moash snapped, pulling his arm back.

Kaladin punched Moash right in the gut, where he knew it would wind him. Moash gasped in shock, doubling over, and Kaladin stepped forward to grab him by the legs, slinging Moash over his shoulder.

Kaladin almost toppled from the weight. Luckily, carrying bridges was harsh but effective strength training. Of course, few bridgemen survived long enough to benefit from it. It didn't help that there were unpredictable lulls between runs. That was part of the problem; the bridge crews spent most of their time staring at their feet or doing menial chores, then were expected to run for miles carrying a bridge.

He carted the shocked Moash outside and set him down on the stone. The rest of the camp was awake, woodworkers arriving at the lumberyard, soldiers jogging to their breakfast or training. The other bridge crews, of course, were still asleep. They were often allowed to sleep late, unless they were on morning bridge duty.

Kaladin left Moash and walked back into the low-ceilinged barrack. 'I'll do the same to each of you, if I have to.'

He didn't have to. The shocked bridgemen filed out into the light, blinking. Most stood bare-backed to the sunlight, wearing only knee-length trousers. Moash climbed to his feet, rubbing his stomach and glaring at Kaladin.

'Things are going to change in Bridge Four,' Kaladin said. 'For one thing, there will be no more sleeping in.'

'And what are we going to do instead?' Sigzil demanded. He had dark brown skin and black hair – that meant he was Makabaki, from southwestern Roshar. He was the only bridgeman without a beard, and judging by his smooth accent, he was probably Azish or Emuli. Foreigners were common in bridge crews – those who didn't fit in often made their way to the crem of an army.

'Excellent question,' Kaladin said. 'We are going to train. Each morning before our daily chores, we will run the bridge in practice to build up our endurance.'

More than one of the men's expressions grew dark at this.

'I know what you are thinking,' Kaladin said. 'Aren't our lives hard enough? Shouldn't we be able to relax during the brief times we have for it?'

'Yeah,' said Leyten, a tall, stout man with curly hair. 'That's right.'

'*No*,' Kaladin snapped. 'Bridge runs exhaust us because we spend most of our days lounging. Oh, I know we have chores – foraging in the chasms, cleaning latrines, scrubbing floors. But the soldiers don't expect us to work hard; they just want us busy. The work helps them ignore us.

'As your bridgeleader, my primary duty is to keep you alive. There's not much I can do about the Parshendi arrows, so I have to do something about *you*. I have to make you stronger, so that when you charge that last leg of a bridge run – arrows flying – you can run quickly.' He met the eyes of the men in the line, one at a time. 'I intend to see that Bridge Four never loses another man.'

The men stared at him incredulously. Finally, a hefty, thick-limbed man at the back bellowed out a laugh. He had tan skin, deep red hair, and was nearly seven feet tall, with large arms and a powerful torso. The Unkalaki – simply called Horneaters by most – were a group of people from the middle of Roshar, near Jah Keved. He'd given his name as 'Rock' the previous night.

'Crazy!' said the Horneater. 'Is crazy man who now thinks to lead us!' He laughed in a deep-bellied way. The others joined him, shaking their heads at Kaladin's speech. A few laughterspren – minnowlike silver spirits that darted through the air in circular patterns – began to zip about them.

'Hey Gaz,' Moash called, cupping his hand around his mouth.

The short, one-eyed sergeant was chatting with some soldiers nearby. 'What?' Gaz yelled back with a scowl.

'This one wants us to carry bridges about as practice,' Moash called back. 'Do we have to do what he says?'

'Bah,' Gaz said, waving a hand. 'Bridgeleaders only have authority in the field.'

Moash glanced back at Kaladin. 'Looks like you can storm off, friend. Unless you're going to beat us all into submission.'

They broke apart, some men wandering back into the barrack, some walking toward the mess halls. Kaladin was left standing alone on the stones.

'That didn't go so well,' Syl said from his shoulder.

'No. It didn't.'

'You look surprised.'

'No, just frustrated.' He glared at Gaz. The bridge sergeant turned away from him pointedly. 'In Amaram's army, I was given men who were inexperienced, but never ones who were blatantly insubordinate.'

'What's the difference?' Syl asked. Such an innocent question. The answer should have been obvious, but she cocked her head in confusion.

'The men in Amaram's army knew they had worse places they could go. You could punish them. These bridgemen know they've reached the bottom.' With a sigh, he let some of his tension bleed away. 'I'm lucky I got them out of the barrack.'

'So what do you do now?'

'I don't know.' Kaladin glanced to the side, where Gaz still stood chatting with the soldiers. 'Actually, yes I do.'

Gaz caught sight of Kaladin approaching and displayed a look of urgent, wide-eyed horror. He broke off his conversation and hastily rushed around the side of a stack of logs.

'Syl,' Kaladin said, 'could you follow him for me?'

She smiled, then became a faint line of white, shooting through the air and leaving a trail that vanished slowly. Kaladin stopped where Gaz had been standing.

Syl zipped back a short time later and reassumed her girlish form. 'He's hiding between those two barracks.' She pointed. 'He's crouched there, watching to see if you follow.'

With a smile, Kaladin took the long way around the barracks. In the alleyway, he found a figure crouching in the shadows, watching in the other direction. Kaladin crept forward, then grabbed Gaz's shoulder. Gaz let out a yelp, spinning, swinging. Kaladin caught the fist easily.

Gaz looked up at Kaladin with horror. 'I wasn't going to lie! Storm you, you *don't* have authority anywhere other than on the field. If you hurt me again, I'll have you—'

'Calm yourself, Gaz,' Kaladin said, releasing the man. 'I'm not going to hurt you. Not yet, at least.'

The shorter man backed away, rubbing his shoulder and glaring at Kaladin.

'Today's third pass,' Kaladin said. 'Payday.'

'You get your pay in an hour like everyone else.'

'No. You have it now; I saw you talking to the courier there.' He held out his hand.

Gaz grumbled, but pulled out a pouch and counted spheres. Tiny, tentative white lights shone at their centers. Diamond marks, each worth five diamond chips. A single chip would buy a loaf of bread.

Gaz counted out four marks, though there were five days to a week. He handed them to Kaladin, but Kaladin left his hand open, palm forward. 'The other one, Gaz.'

'You said—'

'*Now.*'

Gaz jumped, then pulled out a sphere. 'You have a strange way of keeping your word, lordling. You promised me . . .'

He trailed off as Kaladin took the sphere he'd just been given and handed it back.

Gaz frowned.

'Don't forget where this comes from, Gaz. I'll keep to my word, but you aren't keeping part of my pay. I'm *giving* it to you. Understand?'

Gaz looked confused, though he did snatch the sphere from Kaladin's hand.

'The money stops coming if something happens to me,' Kaladin said, tucking the other four spheres into his pocket. Then he stepped forward. Kaladin was a tall man, and he loomed over the much shorter Gaz. 'Remember our bargain. Stay out of my way.'

Gaz refused to be intimidated. He spat to the side, the dark spittle clinging to the rock wall, oozing slowly. 'I ain't going to lie for you. If you think one cremstained mark a week will—'

'I expect only what I said. What is Bridge Four's camp duty today?'

'Evening meal. Scrubbing and cleaning.'

'And bridge duty?'

'Afternoon shift.'

That meant the morning would be open. The crew would like that; they could spend payday losing their spheres on gambling or whores, perhaps forgetting for a short time the miserable lives they lived. They'd have to be back for afternoon duty, waiting in the lumberyard in case there was a bridge run. After evening meal, they'd go scrub pots.

Another wasted day. Kaladin turned to walk back to the lumberyard.

'You aren't going to change anything,' Gaz called after him. 'Those men are bridgemen for a reason.'

Kaladin kept walking, Syl zipping down from the roof to land on his shoulder.

'You don't have authority,' Gaz called. 'You're not some squadleader on the field. You're a storming *bridgeman*. You hear me? You can't have authority without a rank!'

Kaladin left the alleyway behind. 'He's wrong.'

Syl walked around to hang in front of his face, hovering there while he moved. She cocked her head at him.

'Authority doesn't come from a rank,' Kaladin said, fingering the spheres in his pocket.

'Where does it come from?'

'From the men who give it to you. That's the only way to get it.' He looked back the way he'd come. Gaz hadn't left the alleyway yet. 'Syl, you don't sleep, do you?'

'Sleep? A spren?' She seemed amused by the concept.

'Would you watch over me at night?' he said. 'Make sure Gaz doesn't sneak in and try something while I'm sleeping? He may try to have me killed.'

'You think he'd actually do that?'

Kaladin thought for a moment. 'No. No, probably not. I've known a dozen men like him – petty bullies with just enough power to be annoying. Gaz is a thug, but I don't think he's a murderer. Besides, in his opinion, he doesn't *have* to hurt me; he just has to wait until I get killed on a bridge run. Still, best to be safe. Watch over me, if you would. Wake me if he tries something.'

'Sure. But what if he just goes to more important men? Tells them to execute you?' Kaladin grimaced. 'Then there's nothing I can do. But I don't think he'd do that. It would make him look weak before his superiors.'

Besides, beheading was reserved for bridgemen who wouldn't run at the Parshendi. So long as he ran, he wouldn't be executed. In fact, the army leaders seemed hesitant to do much to punish bridgemen at all. One man had committed murder while Kaladin had been a bridgeman, and they'd strung the fool up in a highstorm. But other than that, all Kaladin had seen was a few men get their wages garnished for brawling, and a couple get whipped for being too slow during the early part of a bridge run.

Minimal punishments. The leaders of this army understood. The lives of bridgemen were as close to hopeless as possible; shove them down too much further, and the bridgemen might just stop caring and let themselves be killed.

Unfortunately, that also meant that there wouldn't be much Kaladin could do to punish his own crew, even if he'd had that authority. He had to motivate them in another way. He crossed the lumberyard to where the carpenters were constructing new bridges. After some searching, Kaladin found what he wanted – a thick plank waiting to be fitted into a new portable bridge. A handhold for a bridgeman had been affixed to one side.

'Can I borrow this?' Kaladin asked a passing carpenter.

The man raised a hand to scratch a sawdust-powdered head. 'Borrow it?'

'I'll stay right here in the lumberyard,' Kaladin explained, lifting the board and putting it on his shoulder. It was heavier than he'd expected, and he was thankful for the padded leather vest.

'We'll need it eventually . . .' the carpenter said, but didn't offer enough of an objection to stop Kaladin from walking away with the plank.

He chose a level stretch of stone directly in front of the barracks. Then he began to trot from one end of the lumberyard to the other, carrying the board on his shoulder, feeling the heat of the rising sun on his skin. He went back and forth, back and forth. He practiced running, walking, and jogging. He practiced carrying the plank on his shoulder, then carrying it up high, arms stretched out.

He worked himself ragged. In fact, he felt close to collapsing several times, but every time he did, he found a reserve of strength from somewhere. So he kept moving, teeth gritted against the pain and fatigue, counting his steps to focus. The apprentice carpenter he'd spoken to brought a supervisor over. That supervisor scratched his head beneath his cap, watching Kaladin. Finally, he shrugged, and the two of them withdrew.

Before long, he drew a small crowd. Workers in the lumberyard, some soldiers, and a large number of bridgemen. Some from the other bridge crews called gibes, but the members of Bridge Four were more withdrawn. Many ignored him. Others – grizzled Teft, youthful-faced Dunny, several more – stood watching in a line, as if they couldn't believe what he was doing.

Those stares – stunned and hostile though they were – were part of what kept Kaladin going. He also ran to work out his frustration, that boiling, churning pot of anger within. Anger at himself for failing Tien. Anger at the Almighty for creating a world where some dined in luxury while others died carrying bridges.

It felt surprisingly good to wear himself down in a way he chose. He felt as he had those first few months after Tien's death, training himself on the spear to forget. When the noon bells rang – calling the soldiers to lunch – Kaladin finally stopped and set the large plank down on the ground. He rolled his shoulder. He'd been running for hours. Where had he found the strength?

He jogged over to the carpenter's station, dripping sweat to the stones, and took a long drink from the water barrel. The carpenters usually chased off bridgemen who tried that, but none said a word as Kaladin slurped down two full ladles of metallic rainwater. He shook the ladle free and nodded to a pair of apprentices, then jogged back to where he'd left the plank.

Rock – the large, tan-skinned Horneater – was hefting it, frowning.

Teft noticed Kaladin, then nodded to Rock. 'He bet a few of us a chip each that you'd used a lightweight board to impress us.'

If they could have felt his exhaustion, they wouldn't have been so skeptical. He forced himself to take the plank from Rock. The large man let it go with a bewildered look, watching as Kaladin ran the plank back to where he'd found it. He waved his thanks to the apprentice, then trotted back to the small cluster of bridgemen. Rock was reluctantly paying out chips on his bet.

'You're dismissed for lunch,' Kaladin told them. 'We have afternoon bridge duty, so be back here in an hour. Assemble at the mess hall at last bell before sundown. Our camp chore today is cleaning up after supper. Last one to arrive has to do the pots.'

They gave him bemused expressions as he trotted away from the lumberyard. Two streets away, he ducked into an alleyway and leaned against the wall. Then, wheezing, he sank to the ground and stretched out.

He felt as if he'd strained every muscle in his body. His legs burned, and when he tried to make his hand into a fist, the fingers were too weak to fully comply. He breathed in and out in deep gasps, coughing. A passing soldier peeked in, but when he saw the bridgeman's outfit, he left without a word.

Eventually, Kaladin felt a light touch on his chest. He opened his eyes and found Syl lying prone in the air, face toward his. Her feet were toward the wall, but her posture – indeed, the way her dress hung – made it seem as if she were standing upright, not face toward the ground.

'Kaladin,' she said, 'I have something to tell you.'

He closed his eyes again.

'Kaladin, this is important!' He felt a slight *jolt* of energy on his eyelid. It was a very strange sensation. He grumbled, opening his eyes and forcing himself to sit. She walked in the air, as if circumnavigating an invisible sphere, until she was standing up in the right direction.

'I have decided,' Syl declared, 'that I'm glad you kept your word to Gaz, even if he is a disgusting person.'

It took Kaladin a moment to realize what she was talking about. 'The spheres?'

She nodded. 'I thought you might break your word, but I'm glad you didn't.'

'All right. Well, thank you for telling me, I guess.'

'Kaladin,' she said petulantly, making fists at her side. 'This is *important*.'

'I …' He trailed off, then rested his head back against the wall. 'Syl, I can barely breathe, let alone think. Please. Just tell me what's bothering you.'

'I know what a lie is,' she said, moving over and sitting on his knee. 'A few weeks ago, I didn't even understand the *concept* of lying. But now I'm happy that you didn't lie. Don't you see?'

'No.'

'I'm changing.' She shivered – it must have been an intentional action, for her entire figure fuzzed for a moment. 'I know things I didn't just a few days ago. It feels so strange.'

'Well, I guess that's a good thing. I mean, the more you understand, the better. Right?'

She looked down. 'When I found you near the chasm after the high-storm yesterday,' she whispered, 'you were going to kill yourself, weren't you?'

Kaladin didn't respond. Yesterday. That was an eternity ago.

'I gave you a leaf,' she said. 'A *poisonous* leaf. You could have used it to kill yourself or someone else. That's what you were probably planning to use it for in the first place, back in the wagons.' She looked back up into his eyes, and her tiny voice seemed terrified. 'Today, I know what death is. Why do I know what death is, Kaladin?'

Kaladin frowned. 'You've always been odd, for a spren. Even from the start.'

'From the very start?'

He hesitated, thinking back. No, the first few times she'd come, she'd acted like any other windspren. Playing pranks on him, sticking his shoe to the floor, then hiding. Even when she'd persisted with him during the months of his slavery, she'd acted mostly like any other spren. Losing interest in things quickly, flitting around.

'Yesterday, I didn't know what death was,' she said. 'Today I do. Months ago, I didn't know I was acting oddly for a spren, but I grew to realize that I was. How do I even know *how* a spren is supposed to act?' She shrank down, looking smaller. 'What's happening to me? What am I?'

'I don't know. Does it matter?'

'Shouldn't it?'

'I don't know what I am either. A bridgeman? A surgeon? A soldier? A slave? Those are all just labels. Inside, I'm me. A very different me than I was a year ago, but I can't worry about that, so I just keep moving and hope my feet take me where I need to go.'

'You aren't angry at me for bringing you that leaf?'

'Syl, if you hadn't interrupted me, I'd have stepped off into the chasm. That leaf was what I needed. It was the right thing, somehow.'

She smiled, and watched as Kaladin began to stretch. Once he finished, he stood and stepped out onto the street again, mostly recovered from his exhaustion. She zipped into the air and rested on his shoulder, sitting with her arms back and her feet hanging down in front, like a girl on the side of a cliff. 'I'm glad you're not angry. Though I *do* think that you're to blame for what's happening to me. Before I met you, I never had to think about death or lying.'

'That's how I am,' he said dryly. 'Bringing death and lies wherever I go. Me and the Nightwatcher.'

She frowned.

'That was—' he began.

'Yes,' she said. 'That was sarcasm.' She cocked her head. 'I know what sarcasm is.' Then she smiled deviously. 'I know what sarcasm is!'

Stormfather, Kaladin thought, looking into those gleeful little eyes. *That strikes me as ominous.*

'So, wait,' he said. 'This sort of thing has never happened to you before?'

'I don't know. I can't remember anything farther back than about a year ago, when I first saw you.'

'Really?'

'That's not odd,' Syl said, shrugging translucent shoulders. 'Most spren don't have long memories.' She hesitated. 'I don't know why I know that.'

'Well, maybe this is normal. You could have gone through this cycle before, but you've just forgotten it.'

'That's not very comforting. I don't like the idea of forgetting.'

'But don't death and lying make you uncomfortable?'

'They do. But, if I were to lose these memories ...' She glanced into the air, and Kaladin traced her movements, noting a pair of windspren darting through the sky on a gusting breeze, uncaring and free.

'Scared to go onward,' Kaladin said, 'but terrified to go back to what you were.'

She nodded.

'I know how you feel,' he said. 'Come on. I need to eat, and there are some things I want to pick up after lunch.'

You do not agree with my quest. I understand that, so much as it is possible to understand someone with whom I disagree so completely.

Four hours after the chasmfiend attack, Adolin was still overseeing the cleanup. In the struggle, the monster had destroyed the bridge leading back to the warcamps. Fortunately, some soldiers had been left on the other side, and they'd gone to fetch a bridge crew.

Adolin walked amid the soldiers, gathering reports as the late afternoon sun inched toward the horizon. The air had a musty, moldy scent. The smell of greatshell blood. The beast itself lay where it had fallen, chest cut open. Some soldiers were harvesting its carapace amid cremlings that had come out to feast on the carcass. To Adolin's left, long lines of men lay in rows, using cloaks or shirts as pillows on the ragged plateau surface. Surgeons from Dalinar's army tended them. Adolin blessed his father for always bringing the surgeons, even on a routine expedition like this one.

He continued on his way, still wearing his Shardplate. The troops could have made their way back to the warcamps by another route – there was still a bridge on the other side, leading farther out onto the Plains. They could have moved eastward, then wrapped back around. Dalinar, however, had made the call – much to Sadeas's dismay – that they would wait and tend the wounded, resting the few hours it would take to get a bridge crew.

Adolin glanced toward the pavilion, which tinkled with laughter. Several large rubies glowed brightly, set atop poles, with worked golden tines holding them in place. They were fabrials that gave off heat, though there was no fire involved. He didn't understand how fabrials worked, though the more spectacular ones needed large gemstones to function.

Once again, the other lighteyes enjoyed their leisure while he worked. This time he didn't mind. He would have found it difficult to enjoy himself after such a disaster. And it *had* been a disaster. A minor lighteyed officer approached, carrying a final list of casualties. The man's wife read it, then they left him with the sheet and retreated.

There were nearly fifty men dead, twice as many wounded. Many were men Adolin had known. When the king had been given the initial estimate, he had brushed aside the deaths, indicating that they'd be rewarded for their valor with positions in the Heraldic Forces above. He seemed to have conveniently forgotten that he'd have been one of the casualties himself, if not for Dalinar.

Adolin sought out his father with his eyes; Dalinar stood at the edge of the plateau, looking eastward again. What did he search for out there? This wasn't the first time Adolin had seen such extraordinary actions from his father, but they had seemed particularly dramatic. Standing beneath the massive chasmfiend, holding it back from killing his nephew, Plate glowing. That image was fixed in Adolin's memory.

The other lighteyes stepped more lightly around Dalinar now, and during the last few hours, Adolin hadn't heard a single mention of his weakness, not even from Sadeas's men. He feared it wouldn't last. Dalinar *was* heroic, but only infrequently. In the weeks that followed, the others would begin to talk again of how he rarely went on plateau assaults, about how he'd lost his edge.

Adolin found himself thirsting for more. Today when Dalinar had leaped to protect Elhokar, he'd acted like the stories said he had during his youth. Adolin wanted that man back. The kingdom needed him.

Adolin sighed, turning away. He needed to give the final casualty report to the king. Likely he'd be mocked for it, but perhaps – in waiting to deliver it – he might be able to listen in on Sadeas. Adolin still felt he was missing something about that man. Something his father saw, but he did not.

So, steeling himself for the barbs, he made his way toward the pavilion.

Dalinar faced eastward with gauntleted hands clasped behind his back. Somewhere out there, at the center of the Plains, the Parshendi made their base camp.

Alethkar had been at war for nearly six years, engaging in an extended siege. The siege strategy had been suggested by Dalinar himself – striking at the Parshendi base would have required camping on the Plains, weathering highstorms, and relying on a large number of fragile bridges. One failed battle, and the Alethi could have found themselves trapped and surrounded, without any way back to fortified positions.

But the Shattered Plains could also be a trap for the Parshendi. The eastern and southern edges were impassable – the plateaus there were weathered to the point that many were little more than spires, and the Parshendi could not jump the distance between them. The Plains were edged by mountains, and packs of chasmfiends prowled the land between, enormous and dangerous.

With the Alethi army boxing them in on the west and north – and with scouts placed south and east just in case – the Parshendi could not escape. Dalinar had argued that the Parshendi would run out of supplies. They'd either have to expose themselves and try to escape the Plains, or would have to attack the Alethi in their fortified warcamps.

It had been an excellent plan. Except, Dalinar hadn't anticipated the gemhearts.

He turned from the chasm, walking across the plateau. He itched to go see to his men, but he needed to show trust in Adolin. He was in command, and he would do well by it. In fact, it seemed he was already taking some final reports over to Elhokar.

Dalinar smiled, looking at his son. Adolin was shorter than Dalinar, and his hair was blond mixed with black. The blond was an inheritance from his mother, or so Dalinar had been told. Dalinar himself remembered nothing of the woman. She had been excised from his memory, leaving strange gaps and foggy areas. Sometimes he could remember an exact scene, with everyone else crisp and clear, but *she* was a blur. He couldn't even remember her name. When others spoke it, it slipped from his mind, like a pat of butter sliding off a too-hot knife.

He left Adolin to make his report and walked up to the chasmfiend's carcass. It lay slumped over on its side, eyes burned out, mouth lying open. There was no tongue, just the curious teeth of a greatshell, with a strange, complex network of jaws. Some flat platelike teeth for crushing and destroying shells and other, smaller mandibles for ripping off flesh or shoving it deeper into the throat. Rockbuds had opened nearby, their vines reaching out to lap up the beast's blood. There was a connection between a man and the beast he hunted, and Dalinar always felt a strange melancholy after killing a creature as majestic as a chasmfiend.

Most gemhearts were harvested quite differently than the one had been today. Sometime during the strange life cycle of the chasmfiends, they sought the western side of the Plains, where the plateaus were wider. They climbed up onto the tops and made a rocky chrysalis, waiting for the coming of a highstorm.

During that time, they were vulnerable. You just had to get to the plateau where it rested, break into its chrysalis with some mallets or a Shardblade, then cut out the gemheart. Easy work for a fortune. And the beasts came frequently, often several times a week, so long as the weather didn't get too cold.

Dalinar looked up at the hulking carcass. Tiny, near-invisible spren were floating out of the beast's body, vanishing into the air. They looked like the tongues of smoke that might come off a candle after being snuffed. Nobody knew what kind of spren they were; you only saw them around the freshly killed bodies of greatshells.

He shook his head. The gemhearts had changed everything for the war. The Parshendi wanted them too, wanted them badly enough to extend themselves. Fighting the Parshendi for the greatshells made sense, for the Parshendi could not replenish their troops from home as the Alethi could. So contests over the greatshells were both profitable and a tactically sound way of advancing the siege.

With the evening coming on, Dalinar could see lights twinkling across the Plains. Towers where men watched for chasmfiends coming up to pupate. They'd watch through the night, though chasmfiends rarely came in the evening or night. The scouts crossed chasms with jumping poles, moving very lightly from plateau to plateau without the need of bridges. Once a chasmfiend was spotted the scouts would sound warning, and it became a race—Alethi against Parshendi. Seize the plateau and hold it long enough to get out the gemheart, attack the enemy if they got there first.

Each highprince wanted those gemhearts. Paying and feeding thousands of troops was not cheap, but a single gemheart could cover a highprince's expenses for months. Beyond that, the larger a gemstone was when used by a Soulcaster, the less likely it was to shatter. Enormous gemheart stones offered near-limitless potential. And so, the highprinces raced. The first one to a chrysalis got to fight the Parshendi for the gemheart.

They could have taken turns, but that was not the Alethi way. Competition was doctrine to them. Vorinism taught that the finest warriors would have the holy privilege of joining the Heralds after death, fighting to reclaim the Tranquiline Halls from the Voidbringers. The highprinces were allies, but they were also rivals. To give up a gemheart to another ... well, it felt wrong. Better to have a contest. And so what had been a war had become sport instead. Deadly sport – but that was the best kind.

Dalinar left the fallen chasmfiend behind. He understood each step in the process of what had happened during these six years. He'd even hastened some of them. Only now did he worry. They *were* making headway in cutting down the Parshendi numbers, but the original goal of vengeance for Gavilar's murder had nearly been forgotten. The Alethi lounged, they played, and they idled.

Even though they'd killed plenty of Parshendi – as many as a quarter of their originally estimated forces were dead – this was just taking so long. The siege had lasted six years, and could easily take another six. That troubled him. Obviously the Parshendi had expected to be besieged here. They'd prepared supply dumps and had been ready to move their entire population to the Shattered Plains, where they could use these Heralds-forsaken chasms and plateaus like hundreds of moats and fortifications.

Elhokar had sent messengers, demanding to know why the Parshendi had killed his father. They had never given an answer. They'd taken credit for his murder, but had offered no explanation. Of late, it seemed that Dalinar was the only one who still wondered about that.

Dalinar turned to the side; Elhokar's attendants had retired to the pavilion, enjoying wine and refreshments. The large open-sided tent was dyed violet and yellow, and a light breeze ruffled the canvas. There was a small chance that another highstorm might arrive tonight, the storm-wardens said. Almighty send that the army was back to the camp if one did come.

Highstorms. Visions.

Unite them. . . .

Did he really believe in what he'd seen? Did he really think that the Almighty himself had spoken to him? Dalinar Kholin, the Blackthorn, a fearsome warlord?

Unite them.

At the pavilion, Sadeas walked out into the night. He had removed his helm, revealing a head of thick black hair that curled and tumbled around his shoulders. He cut an imposing figure in his Plate; he certainly looked much better in armor than he did wearing one of those ridiculous costumes of lace and silk that were popular these days.

Sadeas caught Dalinar's eyes, nodding slightly. *My part is done*, that nod said. Sadeas strolled for a moment, then reentered the pavilion.

So. Sadeas had remembered the reason for inviting Vamah on the hunt. Dalinar would have to seek out Vamah. He made his way toward the pavilion. Adolin and Renarin lurked near the king. Had the lad given his report yet? It seemed likely that Adolin was trying – yet again – to listen in on Sadeas's conversations with the king. Dalinar would have to do something about that; the boy's personal rivalry with Sadeas was understandable, perhaps, but counterproductive.

Sadeas was chatting with the king. Dalinar made to go find Vamah – the other highprince was near the back of the pavilion – but the king interrupted him.

'Dalinar,' the king said. 'Come here. Sadeas tells me he has won three gemhearts in the last few weeks alone!'

'He has indeed,' Dalinar said, approaching.

'How many have you won?'

'Including the one today?'

'No,' the king said. 'Before this.'

'None, Your Majesty,' Dalinar admitted.

'It's Sadeas's bridges,' Elhokar said. 'They're more efficient than yours.'

'I may not have won anything the last few weeks,' Dalinar said stiffly, 'but my army has won its share of skirmishes in the past.' *And the gemhearts can go to Damnation, for all I care.*

'Perhaps,' Elhokar said, 'but what have you done lately?'

'I have been busy with other important things.'

Sadeas raised an eyebrow. 'More important than the war? More important than vengeance? Is that possible? Or are you just making excuses?'

Dalinar gave the other highprince a pointed look. Sadeas just shrugged. They were allies, but they were *not* friends. Not any longer.

'You should switch to bridges like his,' Elhokar said.

'Your Majesty,' Dalinar said. 'Sadeas's bridges waste many lives.'

'But they are also fast,' Sadeas said smoothly. 'Relying on wheeled bridges is foolish, Dalinar. Getting them over this plateau terrain is slow and plodding.'

'The Codes state that a general may not ask a man to do anything he would not do himself. Tell me, Sadeas. Would *you* run at the front of those bridges you use?'

'I wouldn't eat gruel either,' Sadeas said dryly, 'or cut ditches.'

'But you might if you had to,' Dalinar said. 'The bridges are different. Stormfather, you don't even let them use armor or shields! Would you enter combat without your Plate?'

'The bridgemen serve a very important function,' Sadeas snapped. 'They distract the Parshendi from firing at my soldiers. I tried giving them shields at first. And you know what? The Parshendi ignored the bridgemen and fired volleys onto my soldiers and horses. I found that by doubling the number of bridges on a run, then making them extremely light – no armor, no shields to slow them – the bridgemen work far better.

'You see, Dalinar? The Parshendi are too tempted by the exposed bridgemen to fire at anyone else! Yes, we lose a few bridge crews in each assault, but rarely so many that it hinders us. The Parshendi just keep firing at them – I assume that, for whatever reason, they think killing the bridgemen hurts us. As if an unarmored man carrying a bridge was worth the same to the army as a mounted knight in Plate.' Sadeas shook his head in amusement at the thought.

Dalinar frowned. *Brother*, Gavilar had written. *You must find the most important words a man can say . . . .* A quote from the ancient text *The Way of Kings*. It would disagree strongly with the things Sadeas was implying.

'Regardless,' Sadeas continued. 'Surely you can't argue with how effective my method has been.'

'Sometimes,' Dalinar said, 'the prize is not worth the costs. The means by which we achieve victory are as important as the victory itself.'

Sadeas looked at Dalinar incredulously. Even Adolin and Renarin – who had come closer – seemed shocked by the statement. It was a very un-Alethi way of thinking.

With the visions and the words of that book spinning in his mind lately, Dalinar wasn't feeling particularly Alethi.

'The prize is worth *any* cost, Brightlord Dalinar,' Sadeas said. 'Winning the competition is worth any effort, any expense.'

'It is a war,' Dalinar said. '*Not* a contest.'

'Everything is a contest,' Sadeas said with a wave of his hand. 'All dealings among men are a contest in which some will succeed and others fail. And some are failing quite spectacularly.'

'My father is one of the most renowned warriors in Alethkar!' Adolin snapped, butting into the group. The king raised an eyebrow at him, but otherwise stayed out of the conversation. 'You saw what he did earlier, Sadeas, while you were hiding back by the pavilion with your bow. My father held off the beast. You're a cowa—'

'Adolin!' Dalinar said. That was going too far. 'Restrain yourself.'

Adolin clenched his jaw, hand to his side, as if itching to summon his Shardblade. Renarin stepped forward and gently placed a hand on Adolin's arm. Reluctantly, Adolin backed down.

Sadeas turned to Dalinar, smirking. 'One son can barely control himself, and the other is incompetent. This is your legacy, old friend?'

'I am proud of them both, Sadeas, whatever you think.'

'The firebrand I can understand,' Sadeas said. 'You were once impetuous just like him. But the other one? You saw how he ran out onto the field today. He even forgot to draw his sword or bow! He's useless!'

Renarin flushed, looking down. Adolin snapped his head up. He thrust his hand to the side again, stepping forward toward Sadeas.

'Adolin!' Dalinar said. 'I will handle this!'

Adolin looked at him, blue eyes alight with rage, but he did not summon his Blade.

Dalinar turned his attention to Sadeas, speaking very softly, very pointedly. 'Sadeas. Surely I did not just hear you openly – before the king – call my son *useless*. Surely you would not say that, as such an insult would *demand* that I summon my Blade and seek your blood. Shatter the Vengeance Pact. Cause the king's two greatest allies to kill one another. Surely you would not have been that foolish. Surely I misheard.'

Everything grew still. Sadeas hesitated. He didn't back down; he met Dalinar's gaze. But he did hesitate.

'Perhaps,' Sadeas said slowly, 'you did hear the wrong words. I would not insult your son. That would not have been . . . wise of me.'

An understanding passed between them, stares locked, and Dalinar nodded. Sadeas did as well – one curt nod of the head. They would not let their hatred of one another become a danger to the king. Barbs were one thing, but dueling offenses were another. They couldn't risk that.

'Well,' Elhokar said. He allowed his highprinces to jostle and contend for status and influence. He believed they were all stronger for it, and few faulted him; it was an established method of rule. More and more, Dalinar found himself disagreeing.

Unite them. . . .

'I guess we can be done with that,' Elhokar said.

To the side, Adolin looked unsatisfied, as if he'd really been hoping that Dalinar would summon his Blade and confront Sadeas. Dalinar's own blood felt hot, the Thrill tempting him, but he shoved it down. No. Not here. Not now. Not while Elhokar needed them.

'Perhaps we can be done, Your Majesty,' Sadeas said. 'Though I doubt this particular discussion between Dalinar and me will ever be done. At least until he relearns how to act as a man should.'

'I said that is quite enough, Sadeas,' Elhokar said.

'Quite enough, you say?' a new voice added. 'I believe that a single word from Sadeas is "quite enough" for anyone.' Wit picked his way through the groups of attendants, holding a cup of wine in one hand, silver sword belted at his side.

'Wit!' Elhokar exclaimed. 'When did you get here?'

'I caught up to your party just before the battle, Your Majesty,' Wit said, bowing. 'I was going to speak with you, but the chasmfiend beat me to you. I hear your conversation with it was rather energizing.'

'But, you arrived hours ago, then! What have you been doing? How could I have missed seeing you here?'

'I had . . . things to be about,' Wit said. 'But I couldn't stay away from the hunt. I wouldn't want you to lack for me.'

'I've done well so far.'

'And yet, you were still Witless,' Wit noted.

Dalinar studied the black-clad man. What to make of Wit? He *was* clever. And yet, he was too free with his thoughts, as he'd shown with Renarin earlier. This Wit had a strange air about him that Dalinar couldn't quite place.

'Brightlord Sadeas,' Wit said, taking a sip of wine. 'I'm terribly sorry to see you here.'

'I should think,' Sadeas said dryly, 'that you would be happy to see me. I seem always to provide you with such entertainment.'

'That is unfortunately true,' Wit said.

'Unfortunately?'

'Yes. You see, Sadeas, you make it too easy. An uneducated, half-brained serving boy with a hangover could make mock of you. I am left with no need to exert myself, and your very nature makes mockery of my mockery. And so it is that through sheer stupidity you make me look incompetent.'

'Really, Elhokar,' Sadeas said. 'Must we put up with this ... creature?'

'I like him,' Elhokar said, smiling. 'He makes me laugh.'

'At the expense of those who are loyal to you.'

'Expense?' Wit cut in. 'Sadeas, I don't believe you've ever paid me a sphere. Though no, please, don't offer. I can't take your money, as I know how many others you *must* pay to get what you wish of them.'

Sadeas flushed, but kept his temper. 'A whore joke, Wit? Is that the best you can manage?'

Wit shrugged. 'I point out truths when I see them, Brightlord Sadeas. Each man has his place. Mine is to make insults. Yours is to be in-sluts.'

Sadeas froze, then grew red-faced. 'You are a fool.'

'If the Wit is a fool, then it is a sorry state for men. I shall offer you this, Sadeas. If you can speak, yet say nothing ridiculous, I will leave you alone for the rest of the week.'

'Well, I think that shouldn't be too difficult.'

'And yet you failed,' Wit said, sighing. 'For you said "I think" and I can imagine nothing so ridiculous as the concept of *you* thinking. What of you, young Prince Renarin? Your father wishes me to leave you alone. Can you speak, yet say nothing ridiculous?'

Eyes turned toward Renarin, who stood just behind his brother. Renarin hesitated, eyes opening wide at the attention. Dalinar grew tense.

'Nothing ridiculous,' Renarin said slowly.

Wit laughed. 'Yes, I suppose that will satisfy me. Very clever. If Brightlord Sadeas should lose control of himself and finally kill me, perhaps you can be King's Wit in my stead. You seem to have the mind for it.'

Renarin perked up, which darkened Sadeas's mood further. Dalinar eyed the highprince; Sadeas's hand had gone to his sword. Not a Shardblade, for Sadeas didn't have one. But he did carry a lighteyes's side sword. Plenty deadly; Dalinar had fought beside Sadeas on many occasions, and the man was an expert swordsman.

Wit stepped forward. 'So what of it, Sadeas?' he asked softly. 'You going to do Alethkar a favor and rid it of us both?'

Killing the King's Wit was legal. But by so doing, Sadeas would forfeit his title and lands. Most men found it a poor enough trade not to do it in the open. Of course, if you could assassinate a Wit without anyone knowing it was you, that was something different.

Sadeas slowly removed his hand from the hilt of his sword, then nodded curtly to the king and strode away.

'Wit,' Elhokar said, 'Sadeas has my favor. There's no need to torment him so.'

'I disagree,' Wit said. 'The king's favor may be torment enough for most men, but not him.'

The king sighed and looked toward Dalinar. 'I should go placate Sadeas. I've been meaning to ask you, though. Have you looked into the issue I asked you about earlier?'

Dalinar shook his head. 'I have been busy with the needs of the army. But I will look into it now, Your Majesty.'

The king nodded, then hastened off after Sadeas.

'What was that, Father?' Adolin asked. 'Is it about the people he thinks were spying on him?'

'No,' Dalinar said. 'This is something new. I'll show you shortly.'

Dalinar looked toward Wit. The black-clad man was popping his knuckles one at a time, looking at Sadeas, seeming contemplative. He noticed Dalinar watching and winked, then walked away.

'I *like* him,' Adolin repeated.

'I might be persuaded to agree,' Dalinar said, rubbing his chin. 'Renarin,' Dalinar said, 'go and get a report on the wounded. Adolin, come with me. We need to check into the matter the king spoke of.'

Both young men looked confused, but they did as requested. Dalinar started across the plateau toward where the carcass of the chasmfiend lay.

Let us see what your worries have brought us this time, nephew, he thought.

◆◆

Adolin turned the long leather strap over in his hands. Almost a handspan wide and a finger's width thick, the strap ended in a ragged tear. It was the girth to the king's saddle, the strap that wrapped under the horse's barrel. It had broken suddenly during the fight, throwing the saddle – and the king – from horseback.

'What do you think?' Dalinar asked.

'I don't know,' Adolin said. 'It doesn't *look* that worn, but I guess it was, otherwise it wouldn't have snapped, right?'

Dalinar took the strap back, looking contemplative. The soldiers still hadn't returned with the bridge crew, though the sky was darkening.

'Father,' Adolin said. 'Why would Elhokar ask us to look into this? Does he expect us to discipline the grooms for not properly caring for his saddle? Is it . . .' Adolin trailed off, and he suddenly understood his father's hesitation. 'The king thinks the strap was cut, doesn't he?'

Dalinar nodded. He turned it over in his gauntleted fingers, and Adolin could see him thinking about it. A girth could get so worn that it would snap, particularly when strained by the weight of a man in Shardplate. This strap had broken off at the point where it had been affixed to the saddle, so it would have been easy for the grooms to miss it. That was the most rational explanation. But when looked at with slightly more irrational eyes, it could seem that something nefarious had happened.

'Father,' Adolin said, 'he's getting increasingly paranoid. You know he is.'

Dalinar didn't reply.

'He sees assassins in every shadow,' Adolin continued. 'Straps break. That doesn't mean someone tried to kill him.'

'If the king is worried,' Dalinar said, 'we should look into it. The break *is* smoother on one side, as if it were sliced so that it would rip when it was stressed.'

Adolin frowned. 'Maybe.' He hadn't noticed that. 'But think about it, Father. Why would someone cut his strap? A fall from horseback wouldn't

246

harm a Shardbearer. If it was an assassination attempt, then it was an incompetent one.'

'If it was an assassination attempt,' Dalinar said, 'even an incompetent one, then we have something to worry about. It happened on our watch, and his horse was cared for by our grooms. We will look into this.'

Adolin groaned, some of his frustration slipping out. 'The others already whisper that we've become bodyguards and pets of the king. What will they say if they hear that we're chasing down his every paranoid worry, no matter how irrational?'

'I have never cared what they say.'

'We spend all our time on bureaucracy while others win wealth and glory. We rarely go on plateau assaults because we're busy doing things like *this*! We need to be out there, fighting, if we're ever going to catch up to Sadeas!'

Dalinar looked at him, frown deepening, and Adolin bit off his next outburst.

'I see that we're no longer talking about this broken girth,' Dalinar said.

'I . . . I'm sorry. I spoke in haste.'

'Perhaps you did. But then again, perhaps I needed to hear it. I noticed that you didn't particularly like how I held you back from Sadeas earlier.'

'I know you hate him too, Father.'

'You do not know as much as you presume you do,' Dalinar said. 'We'll do something about that in a moment. For now, I swear . . . this strap *does* look like it was cut. Perhaps there is something we're not seeing. This could have been part of something larger that didn't work the way it had been anticipated.'

Adolin hesitated. It seemed overcomplicated, but if there was a group who liked their plots overly complicated, it was the Alethi lighteyes. 'Do you think one of the highprinces may have tried something?'

'Maybe,' Dalinar said. 'But I doubt any of them want him dead. So long as Elhokar rules, the highprinces get to fight in this war their way and fatten their purses. He doesn't make many demands of them. They like having him as their king.'

'Men can covet the throne for the distinction alone.'

'True. When we return, see if anyone has been bragging too much of late. Check to see if Roion is still bitter about Wit's insult at the feast last week and have Talata go over the contracts Highprince Bethab offered to the king for the use of his chulls. In previous contracts, he's tried to slip in language that would favor his claim in a succession. He's been bold ever since your aunt Navani left.'

Adolin nodded.

'See if you can backtrack the girth's history,' Dalinar said. 'Have a leatherworker look at it and tell you what he thinks of the rip. Ask the grooms if they noticed anything, and watch to see if any have received any suspicious windfalls of spheres lately.' He hesitated. 'And double the king's guard.'

Adolin turned, glancing at the pavilion. Sadeas was strolling out of it. Adolin narrowed his eyes. 'Do you think—'

'No,' Dalinar interrupted.

'Sadeas is an eel.'

'Son, you *have* to stop fixating on him. He likes Elhokar, which can't be said of most of the others. He's one of the few I'd trust the king's safety to.'

'I wouldn't do the same, Father, I can tell you that.'

Dalinar fell silent for a moment. 'Come with me.' He handed Adolin the saddle strap, then began to cross the plateau toward the pavilion. 'I want to show you something about Sadeas.'

Resigned, Adolin followed. They passed the lit pavilion. Inside, dark-eyed men served food and drink while women sat and scribed messages or wrote accounts of the battle. The lighteyes spoke with one another in verbose, excited tones, complimenting the king's bravery. The men wore dark, masculine colors: maroon, navy, forest green, deep burnt orange.

Dalinar approached Highprince Vamah, who stood outside the pavilion with a group of his own lighteyed attendants. He was dressed in a fashionable long brown coat that had slashes cut through it to expose the bright yellow silk lining. It was a subdued fashion, not as ostentatious as wearing silks on the outside. Adolin thought it looked nice.

Vamah himself was a round-faced, balding man. The short hair that remained stuck straight up, and he had light grey eyes. He had a habit of squinting – which he did as Dalinar and Adolin approached.

What is this about? Adolin wondered.

'Brightlord,' Dalinar said to Vamah. 'I have come to make certain your comfort has been seen to.'

'My comfort would be *best* seen to if we could be on our way back.' Vamah glared over at the setting sun, as if blaming it for some misdeed. He wasn't normally so foul-mooded.

'I'm certain that my men are moving as quickly as they can,' Dalinar said.

'It wouldn't be nearly as late if you hadn't slowed us so much on the way here,' Vamah said.

'I like to be careful,' Dalinar said. 'And, speaking of care, there is something I've been meaning to talk to you about. Might my son and I speak to you alone for a moment?'

Vamah scowled, but let Dalinar lead him away from his attendants. Adolin followed, more and more baffled.

'The beast was a large one,' Dalinar said to Vamah, nodding toward the fallen chasmfiend. 'The biggest I've seen.'

'I suppose.'

'I hear you've had success on your recent plateau assaults, killing a few cocooned chasmfiends of your own. You are to be congratulated.'

Vamah shrugged. 'The ones we won were small. Nothing like that gemheart that Elhokar took today.'

'A small gemheart is better than none,' Dalinar said politely. 'I hear that you have plans to augment the walls of your warcamp.'

'Hum? Yes. Fill in a few of the gaps, improve the fortification.'

'I'll be certain to tell His Majesty that you'll be wanting to purchase extra access to the Soulcasters.'

Vamah turned to him, frowning. 'Soulcasters?'

'For lumber,' Dalinar said evenly. 'Surely you don't intend to fill in the walls without using scaffolding? Out here, on these remote plains, it's fortunate that we have Soulcasters to provide things like wood, wouldn't you say?'

'Er, yes,' Vamah said, expression darkening further. Adolin looked from him to his father. There was a subtext to the conversation. Dalinar wasn't speaking only of wood for the walls – the Soulcasters were the means by which all of the highprinces fed their armies.

'The king is quite generous in allowing access to the Soulcasters,' Dalinar said. 'Wouldn't you agree, Vamah?'

'I take your point, Dalinar,' Vamah said dryly. 'No need to keep bashing the rock into my face.'

'I've never been known as a subtle man, Brightlord,' Dalinar said. 'Just an effective one.' He walked away, waving for Adolin to follow. Adolin did so, looking over his shoulder at the other highprince.

'He's been complaining vocally about the fees that Elhokar charges to use his Soulcasters,' Dalinar said softly. It was the primary form of taxation the king levied on the highprinces. Elhokar himself didn't fight for, or win, gemhearts except on the occasional hunt. He stood aloof from fighting personally in the war, as was appropriate.

'And so . . . ?' Adolin said.

'So I reminded Vamah of how much he relies on the king.'

'I suppose that's important. But what does it have to do with Sadeas?'

Dalinar didn't answer. He kept walking across the plateau, stepping up to the lip of the chasm. Adolin joined him, waiting. A few seconds later, someone approached from behind in clinking Shardplate, then Sadeas stepped up beside Dalinar at the lip of the chasm. Adolin narrowed his eyes at the man, and Sadeas raised an eyebrow, but said nothing about his presence.

'Dalinar,' Sadeas said, turning his eyes forward, looking out across the Plains.

'Sadeas.' Dalinar's voice was controlled and curt.

'You spoke with Vamah?'

'Yes. He saw through what I was doing.'

'Of course he did.' There was a hint of amusement in Sadeas's voice. 'I wouldn't have expected anything else.'

'You told him you were increasing what you charge him for wood?'

Sadeas controlled the only large forest in the region. 'Doubling it,' Sadeas said.

Adolin looked over his shoulder. Vamah was watching them stand there, and his expression was as thunderous as a highstorm, angerspren boiling up from the ground around him like small pools of bubbling blood. Dalinar and Sadeas together sent him a very sound message. *Why . . . this is probably why they invited him on the hunt*, Adolin realized. *So they could maneuver him.*

'Will it work?' Dalinar asked.

'I'm certain it will,' Sadeas said. 'Vamah's an agreeable enough fellow, when prodded – he'll see that it's better to use the Soulcasters than spend a fortune running a supply line back to Alethkar.'

'Perhaps we should tell the king about these sorts of things,' Dalinar said, glancing at the king, who stood in the pavilion, oblivious of what had been done.

Sadeas sighed. 'I've tried; he hasn't a mind for this sort of work. Leave the boy to his preoccupations, Dalinar. His are the grand ideals of justice, holding the sword high as he rides against his father's enemies.'

'Lately, he seems less preoccupied with the Parshendi, and more worried about assassins in the night,' Dalinar said. 'The boy's paranoia worries me. I don't know where he gets it.'

Sadeas laughed. 'Dalinar, are you *serious*?'

'I'm always serious.'

'I know, I know. But surely you can see where the boy comes by the paranoia!'

'From the way his father was killed?'

'From the way his uncle treats him! A thousand guards? Halts on each and every plateau to let soldiers "secure" the next one over? Really, Dalinar?'

'I like to be careful.'

'Others call that being paranoid.'

'The Codes—'

'The Codes are a bunch of idealized nonsense,' Sadeas said, 'devised by poets to describe the way they think things *should* have been.'

'Gavilar believed in them.'

'And look where it got him.'

'And where were you, Sadeas, when he was fighting for his life?'

Sadeas's eyes narrowed. 'So we're going to rehash that now? Like old lovers, crossing paths unexpectedly at a feast?'

Adolin's father didn't reply. Once again, Adolin found himself baffled by Dalinar's relationship with Sadeas. Their barbs were genuine; one needed only look in their eyes to see that the men could barely stand one another.

And yet, here they were, apparently planning and executing a joint manipulation of another highprince.

'I'll protect the boy my way,' Sadeas said. 'You do it your way. But don't complain to me about his paranoia when you insist on wearing your uniform to bed, just in case the Parshendi suddenly decide – against all reason and precedent – to attack the warcamps. "I don't know where he gets it" indeed!'

'Let's go, Adolin,' Dalinar said, turning to stride away. Adolin followed.

'Dalinar,' Sadeas called from behind.

Dalinar hesitated, looking back.

'Have you found it yet?' Sadeas asked. 'Why he wrote what he did?'

Dalinar shook his head.

'You're not going to find the answer,' Sadeas said. 'It's a foolish quest, old friend. One that's tearing you apart. I know what happens to you during storms. Your mind is unraveling because of all this stress you put upon yourself.'

Dalinar returned to walking away. Adolin hurried after him. What had that last part been about? Why 'he' wrote? Men didn't write. Adolin opened his mouth to ask, but he could sense his father's mood. This was not a time to prod him.

He walked with Dalinar up to a small rock hill on the plateau. They picked their way up it to the top, and from there looked out at the fallen chasmfiend. Dalinar's men continued harvesting its meat and carapace.

He and his father stood there for a time, Adolin brimming with questions, yet unable to find a way to phrase them.

Eventually, Dalinar spoke. 'Have I ever told you what Gavilar's final words to me were?'

'You haven't. I've always wondered about that night.'

'"Brother, follow the Codes tonight. There is something strange upon the winds." That's what he said to me, the last thing he told me just before we began the treaty-signing celebration.'

'I didn't realize that Uncle Gavilar followed the Codes.'

'He's the one who first showed them to me. He found them as a relic of old Alethkar, back when we'd first been united. He began following them shortly before he died.' Dalinar grew hesitant. 'Those were odd days, son. Jasnah and I weren't sure what to think of the changes in Gavilar. At the time, I thought the Codes foolishness, even the one that commanded an officer to avoid strong drink during times of war. Especially that one.' His voice grew even softer. 'I was unconscious on the ground when Gavilar was murdered. I can remember voices, trying to wake me up, but I was too addled by my wine. I should have been there for him.'

He looked to Adolin. 'I cannot live in the past. It is foolishness to do so. I blame myself for Gavilar's death, but there is nothing to be done for him now.'

Adolin nodded.

'Son, I keep hoping that if I make you follow the Codes long enough, you will see – as I have – their importance. Hopefully you will not need as dramatic an example of it as I did. Regardless, you need to understand. You speak of Sadeas, of beating him, of competing with him. Do you know of Sadeas's part in my brother's death?'

'He was the decoy,' Adolin said. Sadeas, Gavilar, and Dalinar had been good friends up until the king's death. Everyone knew it. They had conquered Alethkar together.

'Yes,' Dalinar said. 'He was with the king and heard the soldiers crying that a Shardbearer was attacking. The decoy idea was Sadeas's plan – he put on one of Gavilar's robes and fled in Gavilar's place. It was suicide, what he did. Wearing no Plate, making a Shardbearer assassin chase him. I honestly think it was one of the bravest things I've ever known a man to do.'

'But it failed.'

'Yes. And there's a part of me that can never forgive Sadeas for that failure. I know it's irrational, but he should have *been* there, with Gavilar. Just like I should have been. We both failed our king, and we cannot forgive one another. But the two of us are still united in one thing. We made a vow on that day. We'd protect Gavilar's son. No matter what the cost, no matter what other things came between us, *we would protect Elhokar.*

'And so that's why I'm here on these Plains. It isn't wealth or glory. I care nothing for those things, not any longer. I came for the brother I loved, and for the nephew I love in his own right. And, in a way, this is what divides Sadeas and me even as it unites us. Sadeas thinks that the best way to protect Elhokar is to kill the Parshendi. He drives himself, and his men, brutally, to get to those plateaus and fight. I believe a part of him thinks I'm breaking my vow by not doing the same.

'But that's not the way to protect Elhokar. He needs a stable throne, allies that support him, not highprinces that bicker. Making a strong Alethkar will protect him better than killing our enemies will. This was Gavilar's life's work, uniting the highprinces . . .'

He trailed off. Adolin waited for more, but it did not come.

'Sadeas,' Adolin finally said. 'I'm … surprised to hear you call him brave.'

'He *is* brave. And cunning. Sometimes, I make the mistake of letting his extravagant dress and mannerisms lead me to underestimate him. But there's a good man inside of him, son. He is not our enemy. We can be petty sometimes, the two of us. But he works to protect Elhokar, so I ask you to respect that.'

How did one respond to that? *You hate him, but you ask me not to?* 'All right,' Adolin said. 'I'll watch myself around him. But, Father, I still don't trust him. Please. At least consider the possibility that he's not as committed as you are, that he's playing you.'

'Very well,' Dalinar said. 'I'll consider it.'

Adolin nodded. It was something. 'What of what he said at the end? Something about writing?'

Dalinar hesitated. 'It is a secret he and I share. Other than us, only Jasnah and Elhokar know of it. I've contemplated for a time whether I should tell you, as you will take my place should I fall. I spoke to you of the last words my brother said to me.'

'Asking you to follow the Codes.'

'Yes. But there is more. Something else he said to me, but not with spoken words. Instead, these are words that … he wrote.'

'Gavilar could *write*?'

'When Sadeas discovered the king's body, he found words written on the fragment of a board, using Gavilar's own blood. "Brother," they said. "You must find the most important words a man can say." Sadeas hid the fragment away, and we later had Jasnah read the words. If it is true that he could write – and other possibilities seem implausible – it was a shameful secret he hid. As I said, his actions grew very odd near the end of his life.'

'And what does it mean? Those words?'

'It's a quote,' Dalinar said. 'From an ancient book called *The Way of Kings*. Gavilar favored readings from the volume near the end of his life – he spoke to me of it often. I didn't realize the quote was from it until recently; Jasnah discovered it for me. I've now had the text of the book read to me a few times, but so far, I find nothing to explain why he wrote what he did.' He paused. 'The book was used by the Radiants as a kind of guidebook, a book of counsel on how to live their lives.'

The Radiants? *Stormfather!* Adolin thought. The delusions his father had ... they often seemed to have something to do with the Radiants. This was further proof that the delusions were related to Dalinar's guilt over his brother's death.

But what could Adolin do to help?

Metal footsteps ground on the rock behind. Adolin turned, then nodded in respect as the king approached, still wearing his golden Shardplate, though he'd removed the helm. He was several years Adolin's senior, and had a bold face with a prominent nose. Some said they saw in him a kingly air and a regal bearing, and women Adolin trusted had confided that they found the king quite handsome.

Not as handsome as Adolin, of course. But still handsome.

The king was married, however; his wife the queen managed his affairs back in Alethkar. 'Uncle,' Elhokar said. 'Can we not be on our way? I'm certain that we Shardbearers could leap the chasm. You and I could be back at the warcamps shortly.'

'I will not leave my men, Your Majesty,' Dalinar said. 'And I doubt you want to be running across the plateaus for several hours alone, exposed, without proper guards.'

'I suppose,' the king said. 'Either way, I did want to thank you for your bravery today. It appears that I owe you my life yet again.'

'Keeping you alive is something else I try very hard to make a habit, Your Majesty.'

'I am glad for it. Have you looked into the item I asked you about?' He nodded to the girth, which Adolin realized he was still carrying in a gauntleted hand.

'I did,' Dalinar said.

'Well?'

'We couldn't decide, Your Majesty,' Dalinar said, taking the strap and handing it to the king. 'It *may* have been cut. The tear is smoother along one side. Like it was weakened so that it would rip.'

'I knew it!' Elhokar held the strap up and inspected it.

'We are not leatherworkers, Your Majesty,' Dalinar said. 'We need to give both sides of the strap to experts and get their opinions. I have instructed Adolin to look into the matter further.'

'It *was* cut,' Elhokar said. 'I can see it clearly, right here. I keep telling you, Uncle. Someone is trying to kill me. They want me, just like they wanted my father.'

'Surely you don't think the *Parshendi* did this,' Dalinar said, sounding shocked.

'I don't know *who* did it. Perhaps someone on this very hunt.'

Adolin frowned. What was Elhokar implying? The majority of the people on this hunt were Dalinar's men.

'Your Majesty,' Dalinar said frankly, 'we *will* look into the matter. But you have to be prepared to accept that this might have just been an accident.'

'You don't believe me,' Elhokar said flatly. 'You *never* believe me.'

Dalinar took a deep breath, and Adolin could see that his father had to struggle to keep his temper. 'I'm *not* saying that. Even a potential threat to your life worries me very much. But I *do* suggest that you avoid leaping to conclusions. Adolin has pointed out that this would be a terribly clumsy way to try to kill you. A fall from horseback isn't a serious threat to a man wearing Plate.'

'Yes, but during a hunt?' Elhokar said. 'Perhaps they wanted the chasmfiend to kill me.'

'We weren't supposed to be in danger from the hunt,' Dalinar said. 'We were *supposed* to pelt the greatshell from a distance, then ride up and butcher it.'

Elhokar narrowed his eyes, looking at Dalinar, then at Adolin. It was almost as if the king were suspicious of *them*. The look was gone in a second. Had Adolin imagined it? *Stormfather!* he thought.

From behind, Vamah began calling to the king. Elhokar glanced at him and nodded. 'This isn't over, Uncle,' he said to Dalinar. 'Look into that strap.'

'I will.'

The king handed the strap back, then left, armor clinking.

'Father,' Adolin said immediately, 'did you see—'

'I'll speak to him about it,' Dalinar said. 'Sometime when he isn't so worked up.'

'But—'

'I will speak to him, Adolin. You look into that strap. And go gather your men.' He nodded toward something in the distant west. 'I think I see that bridge crew coming.'

Finally, Adolin thought, following his gaze. A small group of figures was crossing the plateau in the distance, bearing Dalinar's banner and leading a bridge crew carrying one of Sadeas's mobile bridges. They'd sent for one of those, as they were faster than Dalinar's larger, chull-pulled bridges.

Adolin hurried off to give the orders, though he found himself distracted by his father's words, Gavilar's final message, and now the king's look of distrust. It seemed he would have plenty to preoccupy his mind on the long ride back to the camps.

❖

Dalinar watched Adolin rush away to do as ordered. The lad's breastplate still bore a web of cracks, though it had stopped leaking Stormlight. With time, the armor would repair itself. It could re-form even if it was completely shattered.

The lad liked to complain, but he was as good a son as a man could ask for. Fiercely loyal, with initiative and a strong sense of command. The soldiers liked him. Perhaps he was a little too friendly with them, but that could be forgiven. Even his hotheadedness could be forgiven, assuming he learned to channel it.

Dalinar left the young man to his work and went to check on Gallant. He found the Ryshadium with the grooms, who had set up a horse picket on the southern side of the plateau. They had bandaged the horse's scrapes, and he was no longer favoring his leg.

Dalinar patted the large stallion on the neck, looking into those deep black eyes. The horse seemed ashamed. 'It wasn't your fault you threw me, Gallant,' Dalinar said in a soothing voice. 'I'm just glad you weren't harmed too badly.' He turned to a nearby groom. 'Give him extra feed this evening, and two crispmelons.'

'Yes sir, Brightlord. But he won't eat extra food. He never does if we try to give it to him.'

'He'll eat it tonight,' Dalinar said, patting the Ryshadium's neck again. 'He only eats it when he feels he deserves it, son.'

The lad seemed confused. Like most of them, he thought of Ryshadium as just another breed of horse. A man couldn't really understand until he'd had one accept him as rider. It was like wearing Shardplate, an experience that was completely indescribable.

'You'll eat both of those crispmelons,' Dalinar said, pointing at the horse. 'You deserve them.'

Gallant blustered.

'You *do*,' Dalinar said. The horse nickered, seeming content. Dalinar checked the leg, then nodded to the groom. 'Take good care of him, son. I'll ride another horse back.'

'Yes, Brightlord.'

They got him a mount – a sturdy, dust-colored mare. He was extra careful when he swung into the saddle. Ordinary horses always seemed so fragile to him. The king rode out after the first squad of troops, Wit at his side. Sadeas, Dalinar noted, rode behind, where Wit couldn't get at him.

The bridge crew waited silently, resting as the king and his procession crossed. Like most of Sadeas's bridge crews, this one was constructed from a jumble of human refuse. Foreigners, deserters, thieves, murderers, and slaves. Many probably deserved their punishment, but the frightful way Sadeas chewed through them put Dalinar on edge. How long would it be before he could no longer fill the bridge crews with the suitably expendable? Did any man, even a murderer, deserve such a fate?

A passage from *The Way of Kings* came to Dalinar's head unbidden. He'd been listening to readings from the book more often than he'd represented to Adolin.

I once saw a spindly man carrying a stone larger than his head upon his back, the passage went. *He stumbled beneath the weight, shirtless under the sun, wearing only a loincloth. He tottered down a busy thoroughfare. People made way for him. Not because they sympathized with him, but because they feared the momentum of his steps. You dare not impede one such as this.*

The monarch is like this man, stumbling along, the weight of a kingdom on his shoulders. Many give way before him, but so few are willing to step in and help carry the stone. They do not wish to attach themselves to the work, lest they condemn themselves to a life full of extra burdens.

I left my carriage that day and took up the stone, lifting it for the man. I believe my guards were embarrassed. One can ignore a poor shirtless wretch doing such labor, but none ignore a king sharing the load. Perhaps we should switch places more often. If a king is seen to assume the burden of the poorest of men, perhaps there will be those who will help him with his own load, so invisible, yet so daunting.

Dalinar was shocked that he could remember the story word for word, though he probably shouldn't have been. In searching for the meaning behind Gavilar's last message, he'd listened to readings from the book almost every day of the last few months.

He'd been disappointed to find that there was no clear meaning behind the quote Gavilar had left. He'd continued to listen anyway, though he tried to keep his interest quiet. The book did not have a good reputation, and not just because it was associated with the Lost Radiants. Stories of a king doing the work of a menial laborer were the least of its discomforting passages. In other places, it outright said that lighteyes were *beneath* dark-eyes. That contradicted Vorin teachings.

Yes, best to keep this quiet. Dalinar had spoken truly when he'd told Adolin he didn't care what people said about him. But when the rumors impeded his ability to protect Elhokar, they could become dangerous. He had to be careful.

He turned his mount and clopped up onto the bridge, then nodded his thanks to the bridgemen. They were the lowest in the army, and yet they bore the weight of kings.

ALETHI CODES OF WAR

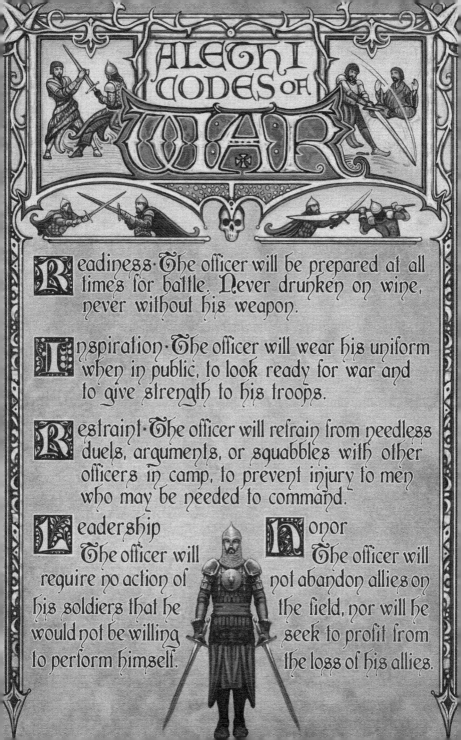

Readiness· The officer will be prepared at all times for battle. Never drunken on wine, never without his weapon.

Inspiration· The officer will wear his uniform when in public, to look ready for war and to give strength to his troops.

Restraint· The officer will refrain from needless duels, arguments, or squabbles with other officers in camp, to prevent injury to men who may be needed to command.

Leadership
The officer will require no action of his soldiers that he would not be willing to perform himself.

Honor
The officer will not abandon allies on the field, nor will he seek to profit from the loss of his allies.

16

COCOONS

He wants to send me to Kharbranth,' Kal said, perched atop his rock. 'To train to become a surgeon.'

'What, *really*?' Laral asked, as she walked across the edge of the rock just in front of him. She had golden streaks in her otherwise black hair. She wore it long, and it streamed out behind her in a gust of wind as she balanced, hands out to the sides.

The hair was distinctive. But, of course, her eyes were more so. Bright, pale green. So different from the browns and blacks of the townspeople. There really *was* something different about being a lighteyes.

'Yes, really,' Kal said with a grunt. 'He's been talking about it for a couple of years now.'

'And you didn't tell me?'

Kal shrugged. He and Laral were atop a low ridge of boulders to the east of Hearthstone. Tien, his younger brother, was picking through rocks at the base. To Kal's right, a grouping of shallow hillsides rolled to the west. They were sprinkled with lavis polyps, a planting halfway to being harvested.

He felt oddly sad as he looked over those hillsides, filled with working men. The dark brown polyps would grow like melons filled with grain. After being dried, that grain would feed the entire town and their high-prince's armies. The ardents who passed through town were careful to explain that the Calling of a farmer was a noble one, one of the highest save for the Calling of a soldier. Kal's father whispered under his breath that he saw far more honor in feeding the kingdom than he did in fighting and dying in useless wars.

'Kal?' Laral said, voice insistent. 'Why didn't you *tell* me?'

'Sorry,' he said. 'I wasn't sure if Father was serious or not. So I didn't say anything.'

That was a lie. He'd known his father was serious. Kal just hadn't wanted to mention leaving to become a surgeon, particularly not to Laral.

She placed her hands on her hips. 'I thought you were going to go become a soldier.'

Kal shrugged.

She rolled her eyes, hopping down off her ridge onto a stone beside him. 'Don't you want to become a lighteyes? Win a Shardblade?'

'Father says that doesn't happen very often.'

She knelt down before him. 'I'm sure *you* could do it.' Those eyes, so bright and alive, shimmering green, the color of life itself.

More and more, Kal found that he liked looking at Laral. Kal knew, logically, what was happening to him. His father had explained the process of growing with the precision of a surgeon. But there was so much *feeling* involved, emotions that his father's sterile descriptions hadn't explained. Some of those emotions were about Laral and the other girls of the town. Other emotions had to do with the strange blanket of melancholy that smothered him at times when he wasn't expecting.

'I . . .' Kal said.

'Look,' Laral said, standing up again and climbing atop her rock. Her fine yellow dress ruffled in the wind. One more year, and she'd start wearing a glove on her left hand, the mark that a girl had entered adolescence. 'Up, come on. Look.'

Kal hauled himself to his feet, looking eastward. There, snarlbrush grew in dense thickets around the bases of stout markel trees.

'What do you see?' Laral demanded.

'Brown snarlbrush. Looks like it's probably dead.'

'The Origin is out there,' she said, pointing. 'This is the stormlands. Father says we're here to be a windbreak for more timid lands to the west.' She turned to him. 'We've got a noble heritage, Kal, darkeyes and lighteyes alike. That's why the best warriors have always been from Alethkar.

Highprince Sadeas, General Amaram . . . King Gavilar himself.'

'I suppose.'

She sighed exaggeratedly. 'I *hate* talking to you when you're like this, you know.'

'Like what?'

'Like you are now. You know. Moping around, sighing.'

'*You're* the one who just sighed, Laral.'

'You know what I mean.'

She stepped down from the rock, walking over to go pout. She did that sometimes. Kal stayed where he was, looking eastward. He wasn't sure how he felt. His father really wanted him to be a surgeon, but he wavered. It wasn't just because of the stories, the excitement and wonder of them. He felt that by being a soldier, he could change things. Really change them. A part of him dreamed of going to war, of protecting Alethkar, of fighting alongside heroic lighteyes. Of doing good someplace other than a little town that nobody important ever visited.

He sat down. Sometimes he dreamed like that. Other times, he found it hard to care about anything. His dreary feelings were like a black eel, coiled inside of him. The snarlbrush out there survived the storms by growing together densely about the bases of the mighty markel trees. Their bark was coated with stone, their branches thick as a man's leg. But now the snarlbrush was dead. It hadn't survived. Pulling together hadn't been enough for it.

'Kaladin?' a voice asked from behind him.

He turned to find Tien. Tien was ten years old, two years Kal's junior, though he looked much younger. While other kids called him a runt, Lirin said that Tien just hadn't hit his height yet. But, well, with those round, flushed cheeks and that slight build, Tien *did* look like a boy half his age. 'Kaladin,' he said, eyes wide, hands cupped together. 'What are you looking at?'

'Dead weeds,' Kal said.

'Oh. Well, you *need* to see this.'

'What is it?'

Tien opened his hands to reveal a small stone, weathered on all sides but with a jagged break on the bottom. Kal picked it up, looking it over. He couldn't see anything distinctive about it at all. In fact, it was dull.

'It's just a rock,' Kal said.

'Not *just* a rock,' Tien said, taking out his canteen. He wetted his thumb, then rubbed it on the flat side of the stone. The wetness darkened the stone, and made visible an array of white patterns in the rock. 'See?' Tien asked, handing it back.

The strata of the rock alternated white, brown, black. The pattern was remarkable. Of course, it *was* still just a rock. But for some reason, Kal found himself smiling. 'That's nice, Tien.' He moved to hand the rock back.

Tien shook his head. 'I found it for you. To make you feel better.'

'I ...' It was just a stupid rock. Yet, inexplicably, Kal *did* feel better. 'Thanks. Hey, you know what? I'll bet there's a lurg or two hiding in these rocks somewhere. Want to see if we can find one?'

'Yes, yes, yes!' Tien said. He laughed and began moving down the rocks. Kal moved to follow, but paused, remembering something his father had said.

He poured some water on his hand from his own canteen and flung it at the brown snarlbrush. Wherever sprayed droplets fell, the brush grew instantly green, as if he were throwing paint. The brush wasn't dead; it just dried out, waiting for the storms to come. Kal watched the patches of green slowly fade back to tan as the water was absorbed.

'Kaladin!' Tien yelled. He often used Kal's full name, even though Kal had asked him not to. 'Is this one?'

Kal moved down across the boulders, pocketing the rock he'd been given. As he did so, he passed Laral. She was looking westward, toward her family's mansion. Her father was the citylord of Hearthstone. Kal found his eyes lingering on her again. That hair of hers was beautiful, with the two stark colors.

She turned to Kal and frowned.

'We're going to hunt some lurgs,' he explained, smiling and gesturing toward Tien. 'Come on.'

'You're cheerful suddenly.'

'I don't know. I feel better.'

'How does he do that? I wonder.'

'Who does what?'

'Your brother,' Laral said, looking toward Tien. 'He changes you.'

Tien's head popped up behind some stones and he waved eagerly, bouncing up and down with excitement.

'It's just hard to be gloomy when he's around,' Kal said. 'Come on. Do you want to watch the lurg or not?'

'I suppose,' Laral said with a sigh. She held out a hand toward him.

'What's that for?' Kal asked, looking at her hand.

'To help me down.'

'Laral, you're a better climber than me *or* Tien. You don't need help.'

'It's polite, stupid,' she said, proffering her hand more insistently. Kal sighed and took it, then she proceeded to hop down without even leaning on it or needing his help. *She*, he thought, *has been acting very strange lately.*

The two of them joined Tien, who jumped down into a hollow between some boulders. The younger boy pointed eagerly. A silky patch of white grew in a crevice on the rock. It was made of tiny threads spun together into a ball about the size of a boy's fist.

'I'm right, aren't I?' Tien asked. 'That is one?'

Kal lifted the flask and poured water down the side of the stone onto the patch of white. The threads dissolved in the simulated rainwater, the cocoon melting to reveal a small creature with slick brown and green skin. The lurg had six legs that it used to grip the stone, and its eyes were in the center of its back. It hopped off the stone, searching for insects. Tien laughed, watching it bounce from rock to rock, sticking to the stones. It left behind patches of mucus wherever it landed.

Kal leaned back against the stone, watching his brother, remembering days – not so long ago – when chasing lurgs had been more exciting.

'So,' Laral said, folding her arms. 'What are you going to do? If your father tries to send you to Kharbranth?'

'I don't know,' Kal said. 'The surgeons won't take anyone before their sixteenth Weeping, so I've got time to think.' The best surgeons and healers trained in Kharbranth. Everyone knew that. The city was said to have more hospitals than taverns.

'It sounds like your father is forcing you to do what he wants, not what you want,' Laral said.

'That's the way everyone does it,' Kal said, scratching his head. 'The other boys don't mind becoming farmers because their fathers were farmers, and Ral just became the new town carpenter. He didn't mind that it was what his father did. Why should I mind being a surgeon?'

'I just—' Laral looked angry. 'Kal, if you go to war and find a Shardblade, then you'd be a lighteyes .... I mean ... Oh, this is useless.' She settled back, folding her arms even more tightly.

Kal scratched his head. She really *was* acting oddly. 'I wouldn't mind going to war, winning honor and all that. Mostly, I'd like to travel. See what other lands are like.' He'd heard tales of exotic animals, like enormous crustaceans or eels that sang. Of Rall Elorim, City of Shadows, or Kurth, City of Lightning.

He'd spent a lot of time studying these last few years. Kal's mother said he should be allowed to have a childhood, rather than focusing so much on his future. Lirin argued that the tests to be admitted by the Kharbranthian surgeons were very rigorous. If Kal wanted a chance with them, he'd have to begin learning early.

And yet, to become a soldier ... The other boys dreamed of joining the army, of fighting with King Gavilar. There was talk of going to war with Jah Keved, once and for all. What would it be like, to finally see some of the heroes from stories? To fight with Highprince Sadeas, or Dalinar the Blackthorn?

Eventually, the lurg realized that it had been tricked. It settled down on a rock to spin its cocoon again. Kal grabbed a small, weathered stone off the ground, then laid a hand on Tien's shoulder, stopping the boy from prodding the tired amphibian. Kal moved forward and nudged the lurg with two fingers, making it hop off the boulder and onto his stone. He handed this to Tien, who watched with wide eyes as the lurg spun its cocoon, spitting out the wet silk and using tiny hands to shape it. That cocoon would be watertight from the inside, sealed by dried mucus, but rainwater outside would dissolve the sack.

Kal smiled, then lifted the flask and drank. This was cool, clean water, which had already had the crem settled out. Crem – the sludgy brown material that fell with rainwater – could make a man sick. Everybody knew that, not just surgeons. You always let water sit for a day, then poured off the fresh water on top and used the crem to make pottery.

The lurg eventually finished its cocoon. Tien immediately reached for the flask.

Kal held the flask high. 'It'll be tired, Tien. It won't jump around anymore.'

'Oh.'

Kal lowered the flask, patting his brother's shoulder. 'I put it on that stone so you could carry it around. You can get it out later.' He smiled. 'Or you could drop it in Father's bathwater through the window.'

Tien grinned at that prospect. Kal ruffled the boy's dark hair. 'Go see if you can find another cocoon. If we catch two, you'll have one to play with *and* one to slip into the bathwater.'

Tien carefully set the rock aside, then scampered up over the boulders. The hillside here had broken during a highstorm several months back. Shattered, as if it had been hit by the fist of some enormous creature. People said that it could have been a home that got destroyed. They burned prayers of thanks to the Almighty while at the same time whispering of dangerous things that moved in the darkness at full storm. Were the Voidbringers behind the destruction, or had it been the shades of the Lost Radiants?

Laral was looking toward the mansion again. She smoothed her dress nervously – lately she took far more care, not getting her clothes dirty as she once had.

'You still thinking about war?' Kal asked.

'Um. Yes. I am.'

'Makes sense,' he said. An army had come through recruiting just a few weeks back and had picked up a few of the older boys, though only after Citylord Wistiow had given permission. 'What do you think broke the rocks here, during the highstorm?'

'I couldn't say.'

Kal looked eastward. What sent the storms? His father said no ship had ever sailed for the Origin of Storms and returned safely. Few ships ever even left the coast. Being caught on the open seas during a storm meant death, so the stories said.

He took another sip from his flask, then capped it, saving the rest in case Tien found another lurg. Distant men worked the fields, wearing overalls, laced brown shirts, and sturdy boots. It was worming season. A single worm could ruin an entire polyp's worth of grain. It would incubate inside, slowly eating as the grain grew. When you finally opened up the polyp in the fall, all you'd find was a big fat slug the size of two men's hands. And so they searched in the spring, going over each polyp. Where they found a burrow, they'd stick in a reed tipped with sugar, which the worm would latch on to. You pulled it out and squished it under your heel, then patched the hole with crem.

It could take weeks to properly worm a field, and farmers usually went over their hills three or four times, fertilizing as they went. Kal had heard the process described a hundred times over. You didn't live in a town like Hearthstone without listening to men gripe about worms.

Oddly, he noticed a group of older boys gathering at the foot of one of the hills. He recognized all of them, of course. Jost and Jest, brothers. Mord, Tift, Naget, Khav, and others. They each had solid, Alethi darkeyes names. Not like Kaladin's own name. It was different.

'Why aren't they worming?' he asked.

'I don't know,' Laral said, shifting her attention to the boys. She got an odd look in her eyes. 'Let's go see.' She started down the hillside before Kal had a chance to object.

He scratched his head, looking toward Tien. 'We're going down to the hillside there.'

A youthful head popped up behind a boulder. Tien nodded energetically, then turned back to his searching. Kal slipped off the boulder and walked down the slope after Laral. She reached the boys, and they regarded her with uncomfortable expressions. She'd never spent much time with them, not like she had with Kal and Tien. Her father and his were pretty good friends, for all that one was lighteyed and the other dark.

Laral took a perch on a nearby rock, waiting and saying nothing. Kal walked up. Why had she wanted to come down here, if she wasn't going to talk to the other boys?

'Ho, Jost,' Kal said. Senior among the boys at fourteen, Jost was nearly a man – and he looked it too. His chest was broad beyond his years, his legs thick and stocky, like those of his father. He was holding a length of wood from a sapling that had been shaved into a rough approximation of a quarterstaff. 'Why aren't you worming?'

It was the wrong thing to say, and Kal knew it immediately. Several of the boys' expressions darkened. It was a sore point to them that Kal never had to work the hills. His protests – that he spent hours upon hours memorizing muscles, bones, and cures – fell on uncaring ears. All they saw was a boy who got to spend his days in the shade while they toiled in the burning sun.

'Old Tarn found a patch of polyps that ain't growing right,' Jost finally said, shooting a glance at Laral. 'Let us go for the day while they talked over whether to try another planting there, or just let them grow and see what comes of it.'

Kal nodded, feeling awkward as he stood before the nine boys. They were sweaty, the knees of their trousers stained with crem and patched from rubbing stone. But Kal was clean, wearing a fine pair of trousers his mother had purchased just a few weeks before. His father had sent him and Tien out for the day while he tended to something at the citylord's manor. Kal would pay for the break with late-night studying by Stormlight, but no use explaining that to the other boys.

'So, er,' Kal said, 'what were you all talking about?'

Rather than answering, Naget said, 'Kal, you know things.' Light haired and spindly, he was the tallest of the bunch. 'Don't you? About the world and the like?'

'Yeah,' Kal said, scratching his head. 'Sometimes.'

'You ever heard of a darkeyes becoming a lighteyes?' Naget asked.

'Sure,' Kal said. 'It can happen, Father says. Wealthy darkeyed merchants marry lowborn lighteyes and join their family. Then maybe have lighteyed children. That sort of thing.'

'No, not like that,' Khav said. He had low eyebrows and always seemed to have a perpetual scowl on his face. 'You know. Real darkeyes. Like us.'

Not like you, the tone seemed to imply. Kal's family were the only one of second nahn in the town. Everyone else was fourth or fifth, and Kal's rank made them uncomfortable around him. His father's strange profession didn't help either.

It all left Kal feeling distinctly out-of-place.

'You know how it can happen,' Kal said. 'Ask Laral. She was just talking about it. If a man wins a Shardblade on the battlefield, his eyes become light.'

'That's right,' Laral said. 'Everybody knows it. Even a *slave* could become a lighteyes if he won a Shardblade.'

The boys nodded; they all had brown, black, or other dark-colored eyes. Winning a Shardblade was one of the main reasons common men went to war. In Vorin kingdoms, everyone had a chance to rise. It was, as Kal's father would say, a fundamental tenet of their society.

'Yeah,' Naget said impatiently. 'But have you ever *heard* of it happening? Not just in stories, I mean. Does it happen for real?'

269

'Sure,' Kal said. 'It must. Otherwise, why would so many men go to war?'

'Because,' Jest said, 'we've gotta prepare men to fight for the Tranquiline Halls. We've gotta send soldiers to the Heralds. The ardents are always talking of it.'

'In the same breaths that they tell us it's all right to be a farmer too,' Khav said. 'Like, farming's some lonely second place or something.'

'Hey,' Tift said. 'My fah's a farmer, and he's right good at it. It's a noble Calling! All your fahs are farmers.'

'All right, fine,' Jost said. 'But we ain't talking of that. We're talking of Shardbearers. You go to war, you can win a Shardblade and become a light-eyes. My fah, see, he *should* have been given that Shardblade. But the man who was with him, he took it while my fah was knocked out. Told the officer that *he'd* been the one to kill the Shardbearer, so he got the Blade, and my fah—'

He was cut off by Laral's tinkling laughter. Kal frowned. That was a different kind of laughter than he normally heard from her, much more subdued and kind of annoying. 'Jost, you're claiming your father won a *Shardblade*?' she said.

'No. It was taken from him,' the larger boy said.

'Didn't your father fight in the wastescum skirmishes up north?' Laral said. 'Tell him, Kaladin.'

'She's right, Jost. There weren't any Shardbearers there – just Reshi raiders who thought they'd take advantage of the new king. They've never had any Shardblades. If your father saw one, he must be remembering incorrectly.'

'Remembering incorrectly?' Jost said.

'Er, sure,' Kal said quickly. 'I'm not saying he's lying, Jost. He just might have some trauma-induced hallucinations, or something like that.'

The boys grew silent, looking at Kal. One scratched his head.

Jost spat to the side. He seemed to be watching Laral from the corner of his eye. She pointedly looked at Kal and smiled at him.

'You always got to make a man feel like an idiot, don't you, Kal?' Jost said.

'What? No, I—'

'You want to make my fah sound like a fool,' Jost said, face red. 'And you want to make me sound stupid. Well, some of us ain't lucky enough to spend our days eating fruit and laying about. We've got to work.'

'I don't—'

Jost tossed the quarterstaff to Kal. He caught it awkwardly. Then Jost took the other staff from his brother. 'You insult my fah, you get a fight. That's honor. You have honor, lordling?'

'I'm no lordling,' Kal spat. 'Stormfather, Jost, I'm only a few nahn higher than you are.'

Jost's eyes grew angrier at the mention of nahn. He held up his quarterstaff. 'You going to fight me or not?' Angerspren began to appear in small pools at his feet, bright red.

Kal knew what Jost was doing. It wasn't uncommon for the boys to look for a way to make themselves look better than him. Kal's father said it had to do with their insecurity. He'd have told Kal to just drop the quarterstaff and walk away.

But Laral was sitting right there, smiling at him. And men didn't become heroes by walking away. 'All right. Sure.' Kal held up his quarterstaff.

Jost swung immediately, more quickly than Kal had anticipated. The other boys watched with a mixture of glee, shock, and amazement. Kal barely managed to get his staff up. The lengths of wood cracked together, sending a jolt up Kal's arms.

Kal was knocked off balance. Jost moved quickly, stepping to the side and swinging his staff down and hitting Kal in the foot. Kal cried out as a flash of agony lanced up his leg, and he released the staff with one hand and reached down.

Jost swung his staff around and hit Kal's side. Kal gasped, letting the staff clatter to the stones and grabbing his side as he fell to his knees. He breathed out in huffing breaths, straining against the pain. Small, spindly painspren – glowing pale orange hand shapes, like stretching sinew or muscles – crawled from the stone around him.

Kal dropped one hand to the stones, leaning forward as he held his side. *You'd better not have broken any of my ribs, you cremling*, he thought.

To the side, Laral pursed her lips. Kal felt a sudden, overpowering shame.

Jost lowered his staff, looking abashed. 'Well,' he said. 'You can see that my fah trained me right good. Maybe that will show you. The things he says are true, and—'

Kal growled in anger and pain, snatching his quarterstaff from the ground and leaping at Jost. The older boy cursed, stumbling backward as he raised his weapon. Kal bellowed, slamming his weapon forward.

Something changed in that moment. Kal felt an energy as he held the weapon, an excitement that washed away his pain. He spun, smashing the staff into one of Jost's hands.

Jost let go with that hand, screaming. Kal brought his weapon around and slammed it into the boy's side. Kal had never held a weapon before, never been in a fight any more dangerous than a wrestling match with Tien. But the length of wood felt *right* in his fingers. He was amazed by how wonderful the moment felt.

Jost grunted, stumbling again, and Kal brought his weapon back around, preparing to smash Jost's face. He raised his staff, but then froze. Jost was bleeding from the hand Kal had hit. Just a little, but it was blood.

He'd hurt someone.

Jost growled and lurched upright. Before Kal could protest, the larger boy swept Kal's legs from underneath him, sending him to the ground, knocking the breath from his lungs. That set afire the wound in his side, and the painspren scampered across the ground, latching on to Kal's side, looking like an orange scar as they fed on Kal's agony.

Jost stepped back. Kal lay on his back, breathing. He didn't know what to feel. Holding the staff in that moment had felt wonderful. Incredible. At the same time, he could see Laral to the side. She stood up and, instead of kneeling to help him, turned and walked away, toward her father's mansion.

Tears welled in Kal's eyes. With a shout, he rolled over and grabbed the quarterstaff again. He would *not* give in!

'None of that now,' Jost said from behind. Kal felt something hard on his back, a boot shoving him down to the stone. Jest took the staff from Kal's fingers.

I failed. I . . . lost. He hated the feeling, hated it far more than the pain.

'You did well,' Jost said grudgingly. 'But leave off. I don't want to have to hurt you for real.'

Kal bowed his head down, letting his forehead rest on the warm, sunlit rock. Jost removed his foot, and the boys withdrew, chatting, their boots scraping on rock. Kal forced himself to his hands and knees, then up onto his feet.

Jost turned back, wary, holding his quarterstaff in one hand.

'Teach me,' Kal said.

Jost blinked in surprise. He glanced at his brother.

'Teach me,' Kal pled, stepping forward. 'I'll worm for you, Jost. My father gives me two hours off each afternoon. I'll do your work then if you'll teach me, in the evenings, what your father is teaching you with that staff.'

He *had* to know. Had to feel the weapon in his hands again. Had to see if that moment he'd felt had been a fluke. Jost considered, then finally shook his head. 'Can't. Your fah would kill me. Get those surgeon's hands of yours all covered with calluses? Wouldn't be right.' He turned away. 'You go be what you are, Kal. I'll be what I am.'

Kal stood for a long while, watching them go. He sat down on the rock. Laral's figure was growing distant. There were some servants coming down the hillside to fetch her. Should he chase after her? His side still hurt, and he was annoyed at her for leading him down to the others in the first place. And, above all, he was *still* embarrassed.

He lay back down, emotions welling inside of him. He had trouble sorting through them.

'Kaladin?'

He turned, ashamed to find tears in his eyes, and saw Tien sitting on the ground behind him. 'How long have you been there?' Kal snapped.

Tien smiled, then set a rock on the ground. He climbed to his feet and hurried away, not stopping when Kal called after him. Grumbling, Kal forced himself to his feet and walked over to pick up the rock.

It was another dull, ordinary stone. Tien had a habit of finding those and thinking they were incredibly precious. He had an entire collection of them back in the house. He knew where he'd found each one, and could tell you what was special about it.

With a sigh, Kal began walking back toward the town.

You go be what you are. I'll be what I am.

His side smarted. Why hadn't he hit Jost when he'd had the chance? Could he train himself out of freezing in battle like that? He could learn to hurt. Couldn't he?

Did he want to?

You go be what you are.

What did a man do if he didn't *know* what he was? Or even what he wanted to be?

Eventually, he reached Hearthstone proper. The hundred or so buildings were set in rows, each one shaped like a wedge with the low side pointing stormward. The roofs were of thick wood, tarred to seal out the rain. The northern and southern sides of the buildings rarely had windows, but the fronts – facing west away from the storms – were nearly all window. Like the plants of the stormlands, the lives of men here were dominated by the highstorms.

Kal's home was near the outskirts. It was larger than most, built wide to accommodate the surgery room, which had its own entrance. The door was ajar, so Kal peeked in. He'd expected to see his mother cleaning, but instead found that his father had returned from Brightlord Wistiow's manor. Lirin sat on the edge of the operating table, hands in his lap, bald head bowed. He held his spectacles in his hand, and he looked exhausted.

'Father?' Kal asked. 'Why are you sitting in the dark?'

Lirin looked up. His face was somber, distant.

'Father?' Kal asked, growing more concerned.

'Brightlord Wistiow has been carried by the winds.'

'He's *dead*?' Kal was so shocked he forgot his side. Wistiow had *always* been there. He couldn't be gone. What of Laral? 'He was healthy just last week!'

'He has always been frail, Kal,' Lirin said. 'The Almighty calls all men back to the Spiritual Realm eventually.'

'You didn't do anything?' Kal blurted out; he regretted the words immediately.

'I did all I could,' his father said, rising. 'Perhaps a man with more training than I . . . Well, there is no use in regrets.' He walked to the side of the room, removing the black covering from the goblet lamp filled with diamond spheres. It lit the room immediately, blazing like a tiny sun.

'We have no citylord then,' Kal said, raising a hand to his head. 'He had no son. . . .'

'Those in Kholinar will appoint us a new citylord,' Lirin said. 'Almighty send them wisdom in the choice.' He looked at the goblet lamp. Those were the citylord's spheres. A small fortune.

Kal's father put the covering right back on the goblet, as if he hadn't just removed it. The motion plunged the room back into darkness, and Kal blinked as his eyes adjusted.

'He left these to us,' Kal's father said.

Kal started. '*What?*'

'You're to be sent to Kharbranth when you turn sixteen. These spheres will pay your way – Brightlord Wistiow requested it be done, a last act to care for his people. You will go and become a true master surgeon, then return to Hearthstone.'

In that moment, Kal knew his fate had been sealed. If Brightlord Wistiow had demanded it, Kal would go to Kharbranth. He turned and walked from the surgery room, passing out into the sunlight, not saying another word to his father.

He sat down on the steps. What *did* he want? He didn't know. That was the problem. Glory, honor, the things Laral had said . . . none of those really mattered to him. But there had been *something* there when he'd held the quarterstaff. And now, suddenly, the decision had been taken from him.

The rocks Tien had given him were still in his pocket. He pulled them out, then took his canteen off his belt and washed them with water. The first one he'd been given showed the white swirls and strata. It appeared the other one had a hidden design too.

It looked like a face, smiling at him, made of white bits in the rock. Kal smiled despite himself, though it quickly faded. A rock wasn't going to solve his problems.

Unfortunately, though he sat for a long while thinking, it didn't look like anything would solve his problems. He wasn't sure he wanted to be a surgeon, and he felt suddenly constricted by what life was forcing him to become.

But that one moment holding the quarterstaff sang to him. A single moment of clarity in an otherwise confusing world.

*Might I be quite frank? Before, you asked why I was so concerned.
It is for the following reason:*

He's *old*,' Syl said with awe, flitting around the apothecary. 'Really old. I didn't know men got this old. You sure he's not decayspren wearing a man's skin?'

Kaladin smiled as the apothecary shuffled forward with his cane, oblivious of the invisible windspren. His face was as full of chasms as the Shattered Plains themselves, weaving out in a pattern from his deeply recessed eyes. He wore a pair of thick spectacles on the tip of his nose, and was dressed in dark robes.

Kaladin's father had told him of apothecaries – men who walked the line between herbalists and surgeons. Common people regarded the healing arts with enough superstition that it was easy for an apothecary to cultivate an arcane air. The wooden walls were draped with cloth glyph-wards styled in cryptic patterns, and behind the counter were shelves with rows of jars. A full human skeleton hung in the far corner, held together by wires. The windowless room was lit with bundles of garnet spheres hanging from the corners.

Despite all that, the place was clean and tidy. It had the familiar scent of antiseptic Kaladin associated with his father's surgery.

'Ah, young bridgeman.' The short apothecary adjusted his spectacles.

He stooped forward, running his fingers through his wispy white beard. 'Come for a ward against danger, perhaps? Or maybe a young washwoman in the camp has caught your eye? I have a potion which, if slipped into her drink, will make her regard you with favor.'

Kaladin raised an eyebrow.

Syl, however, opened her mouth in an amazed expression. 'You should give that to Gaz, Kaladin. It would be nice if he liked you more.'

I doubt that's what it's intended for, Kaladin thought with a smile.

'Young bridgeman?' the apothecary asked. 'Is it a charm against evil you desire?'

Kaladin's father had spoken of these things. Many apothecaries purveyed supposed love charms or potions to cure all manner of ailments. They'd contain nothing more than some sugar and a few pinches of common herbs to give a spike of alertness or drowsiness, depending on the purported effect. It was all nonsense, though Kaladin's mother *had* put great stock in glyphwards. Kaladin's father had always expressed disappointment in her stubborn way of clinging to 'superstitions.'

'I need some bandages,' Kaladin said. 'And a flask of lister's oil or knobweed sap. Also, a needle and gut, if you have any.'

The apothecary's eyes opened wide in surprise.

'I'm the son of a surgeon,' Kaladin admitted. 'Trained by his hand. He was trained by a man who had studied in the Great Concourse of Kharbranth.'

'Ah,' the apothecary said. 'Well.' He stood up straighter, setting aside his cane and brushing his robes. 'Bandages, you said? And some antiseptic? Let me see . . . .' He moved back behind the counter.

Kaladin blinked. The man's age hadn't changed, but he didn't seem nearly as frail. His step was firmer, and his voice had lost its whispering raspiness. He searched through his bottles, mumbling to himself as he read off his labels. 'You could just go to the surgeon's hall. They would charge you far less.'

'Not for a bridgeman,' Kaladin said, grimacing. He'd been turned away. The supplies there were for real soldiers.

'I see,' the apothecary said, setting a jar on the counter, then bending down to poke in some drawers.

Syl flitted over to Kaladin. 'Every time he bends I think he'll snap like a twig.' She *was* growing able to understand abstract thought, and at a surprisingly rapid pace.

I know what death is . . . . He still wasn't certain whether to feel sorry for her or not.

Kaladin picked up the small bottle and undid the cork, smelling what was inside. 'Larmic mucus?' He grimaced at the foul smell. 'That's not nearly as effective as the two I asked for.'

'But it's far cheaper,' the old man said, coming up with a large box. He opened the lid, revealing sterile white bandages. 'And you, as has been noted, are a bridgeman.'

'How much for the mucus, then?' He'd been worried about this; his father had never mentioned how much his supplies cost.

'Two bloodmarks for the bottle.'

'That's what you consider *cheap*?'

'Lister's oil costs two sapphire marks.'

'And knobweed sap?' Kaladin said. 'I saw some reeds of it growing just outside of camp! It can't be *that* rare.'

'And do you know how much sap comes from a single plant?' the apothecary asked, pointing.

Kaladin hesitated. It wasn't true sap, but a milky substance that you could squeeze from the stalks. Or so his father had said. 'No,' Kaladin admitted.

'A single drop,' the man said. 'If you're lucky. It's cheaper than lister's oil, sure, but more expensive than the mucus. Even if the mucus *does* stink like the Nightwatcher's own backside.'

'I don't have that much,' Kaladin said. It was five diamond marks to a garnet. Ten days' pay to buy one small jar of antiseptic. Stormfather!

The apothecary sniffed. 'The needle and gut will cost two clearmarks. Can you afford that, at least?'

'Barely. How much for the bandages? Two full emeralds?'

'They're just old scraps that I bleached and boiled. Two clearchips an arm length.'

'I'll give a mark for the box.'

'Very well.' Kaladin reached into his pocket to get the spheres as the old apothecary continued, 'You surgeons, all the same. Never give a blink to consider where your supplies come from. You just use them like there will be no end.'

'You can't put a price on a person's life,' Kaladin said. One of his father's sayings. It was the main reason that Lirin had never charged for his services.

Kaladin brought out his four marks. He hesitated when he saw them, however. Only one was still glowing with its soft crystal light. The other three were dull, the bits of diamond barely visible at the center of the drops of glass.

'Here now,' the apothecary said, squinting. 'You trying to pass dun spheres off on me?' He snatched one before Kaladin could complain, then fished around under his counter. He brought up a jeweler's loupe, removing his spectacles and holding the sphere up toward the light. 'Ah. No, that's a real gemstone. You should get your spheres infused, bridgeman. Not everyone is as trusting as I am.'

'They were glowing this morning,' Kaladin protested. 'Gaz must have paid me with run-down spheres.'

The apothecary removed his loupe and replaced the spectacles. He selected three marks, including the glowing one.

'Could I have that one?' Kaladin asked.

The apothecary frowned.

'Always keep a glowing sphere in your pocket,' Kaladin said. 'It's good luck.'

'You certain you don't want a love potion?'

'If you get caught in the dark, you'll have light,' Kaladin said tersely. 'Besides, as you said, most people aren't as trusting as you.'

Reluctantly, the apothecary traded the infused sphere for the dead one – though he did check it with the loupe to be certain. A dun sphere was worth just as much as an infused one; all you had to do was leave it out in a high-storm, and it would recharge and give off light for a week or so.

Kaladin pocketed the infused sphere and picked up his purchase. He nodded farewell to the apothecary, and Syl joined him as he stepped out into the camp's street.

He'd spent some of the afternoon listening to soldiers at the mess hall, and he'd learned some things about the warcamps. Things he should have learned weeks ago, but had been too despondent to care about. He now understood more about the chrysalises on the plateaus, the gemhearts they contained, and the competition between the highprinces. He understood why Sadeas pushed his men so hard, and he was beginning to see why Sadeas turned around if they got to the plateau later than another army. That wasn't very common. More often, Sadeas arrived first, and the other Alethi armies that came up behind them had to turn back.

The warcamps were enormous. All told, there were over a hundred thousand troops in the various Alethi camps, many times the population of Hearthstone. And that wasn't counting the civilians. A mobile warcamp attracted a large array of camp followers; stationary warcamps like these on the Shattered Plains brought even more.

Each of the ten warcamps filled its own crater, and was filled with an incongruous mix of Soulcast buildings, shanties, and tents. Some merchants, like the apothecary, had the money to build a wooden structure. Those who lived in tents took them down for storms, then paid for shelter elsewhere. Even within the crater, the stormwinds were strong, particularly where the outer wall was low or broken. Some places – like the lumberyard – were completely exposed.

The street bustled with the usual crowd. Women in skirts and blouses – the wives, sisters, or daughters of the soldiers, merchants, or craftsmen. Workers in trousers or overalls. A large number of soldiers in leathers, carrying spear and shield. All were Sadeas's men. Soldiers of one camp didn't mix with those of another, and you stayed away from another brightlord's crater unless you had business there.

Kaladin shook his head in dismay.

'What?' Syl asked, settling on his shoulder.

'I hadn't expected there to be so much discord among the camps here. I thought it would all be one king's army, unified.'

'People are discord,' Syl said.

'What does that mean?'

'You all act differently and think differently. Nothing else is like that – animals act alike, and all spren are, in a sense, virtually the same individual. There's harmony in that. But not in you – it seems that no two of you can agree on anything. All the world does as it is supposed to, except for humans. Maybe that's why you so often want to kill each other.'

'But not *all* windspren act alike,' Kaladin said, opening the box and tucking some of the bandages into the pocket he'd sewn into the inside of his leather vest. 'You're proof of that.'

'I know,' she said softly. 'Maybe now you can see why it bothers me so.'

Kaladin didn't know how to respond to that. Eventually, he reached the lumberyard. A few members of Bridge Four lounged in the shade on the east side of their barrack. It would be interesting to see one of those barracks get made – they were Soulcast directly from air into stone. Unfortunately, Soulcastings happened at night, and under strict guard to keep the holy rite from being witnessed by anyone other than ardents or very high-ranking lighteyes.

The first afternoon bell sounded right as Kaladin reached the barrack, and he caught a glare from Gaz for nearly being late for bridge duty. Most of that 'duty' would be spent sitting around, waiting for the horns to blow. Well, Kaladin didn't intend to waste time. He couldn't risk tiring himself by carrying the plank, not when a bridge run could be imminent, but perhaps he could do some stretches or—

A horn sounded in the air, crisp and clean. It was like the mythical horn that was said to guide the souls of the brave to heaven's battlefield. Kaladin froze. As always, he waited for the second blast, an irrational part of him needing to hear confirmation. It came, sounding a pattern indicating the location of the pupating chasmfiend.

Soldiers began to scramble toward the staging area beside the lumberyard; others ran into camp to fetch their gear. 'Line up!' Kaladin shouted, dashing up to the bridgemen. 'Storm you! Every man in a line!'

They ignored him. Some of the men weren't wearing their vests, and they clogged the barrack doorway, all trying to get in. Those who had their vests ran for the bridge. Kaladin followed, frustrated. Once there, the men gathered around the bridge in a carefully prearranged manner. Each man got a chance to be in the best position: running in front up to the chasm, then moving to the relative safety of the back for the final approach.

There was a strict rotation, and errors were neither made nor tolerated. Bridge crews had a brutal system of self-management: If a man tried to cheat, the others forced him to run the final approach in front. That sort of thing was supposed to be forbidden, but Gaz turned a blind eye toward cheaters. He also refused bribes to let men change positions. Perhaps he knew that the only stability – the only hope – the bridgemen had was in their rotation. Life wasn't fair, being a bridgeman wasn't fair, but at least if you ran the deathline and survived, the next time you got to run at the back.

There was one exception. As bridgeleader, Kaladin got to run in the front most of the way, then move to the back for the assault. His was the safest position in the group, though no bridgeman was truly safe. Kaladin was like a moldy crust on a starving man's plate; not the first bite, but still doomed.

He got into position. Yake, Dunny, and Malop were the last stragglers. Once they'd taken their places, Kaladin commanded the men to lift. He was half surprised to be obeyed, but there was almost always a bridge-leader to give commands during a run. The voice changed, but the simple orders did not. Lift, run, lower.

Twenty bridges charged down from the lumberyard and toward the Shattered Plains. Kaladin noticed a group of bridgemen from Bridge Seven watching with relief. They'd been on duty until the first afternoon bell; they'd avoided this run by mere moments.

The bridgemen worked hard. It wasn't just because of threats of beatings – they ran so hard because they wanted to arrive at the target plateau before the Parshendi did. If they did so, there would be no arrows, no death. And so running their bridges was the one thing the bridgemen did without reservation or laziness. Though many hated their lives, they still clung to them with white-knuckled fervor.

They clomped across the first of the permanent bridges. Kaladin's muscles groaned in protest at being worked again so soon, but he tried not to dwell on his fatigue. The highstorm's rains from the night before meant that most plants were still open, rockbuds spewing out vines, flowering branzahs reaching clawlike branches out of crevices toward the sky. There were also occasional prickletacs: the needly, stone-limbed little shrubs Kaladin had noticed his first time through the area. Water pooled in the numerous crevices and depressions on the surface of the uneven plateau.

Gaz called out directions, telling them which pathway to take. Many of the nearby plateaus had three or four bridges, creating branching paths across the Plains. The running became rote. It was exhausting, but it was also familiar, and it was nice to be at the front, where he could see where he was going. Kaladin fell into his usual step-counting mantra, as he'd been advised to do by that nameless bridgeman whose sandals he still wore.

Eventually, they reached the last of the permanent bridges. They crossed a short plateau, passing the smoldering ruins of a bridge the

Parshendi had destroyed during the night. How had the Parshendi managed that, during a highstorm? Earlier, while listening to the soldiers, he'd learned that the soldiers regarded the Parshendi with hatred, anger, and not a little awe. These Parshendi weren't like the lazy, nearly mute parshmen who worked throughout Roshar. These Parshendi were warriors of no small skill. That still struck Kaladin as incongruous. Parshmen? Fighting? It was just so strange.

Bridge Four and the other crews got their bridges down, spanning a chasm where it was narrowest. His men collapsed to the ground around their bridge, relaxing while the army crossed. Kaladin nearly joined them – in fact, his knees nearly buckled in anticipation.

No, he thought, steadying himself. *No. I stand.*

It was a foolish gesture. The other bridgemen barely paid him any heed. One man, Moash, even swore at him. But now that Kaladin had made the decision, he stubbornly stuck to it, clasping his hands behind his back and falling into parade rest while watching the army cross.

'Ho, little bridgeman!' a soldier called from among those waiting their turn. 'Curious at what *real* soldiers look like?'

Kaladin turned toward the man, a solid, brown-eyed fellow with arms the size of many men's thighs. He was a squadleader, by the knots on the shoulder of his leather jerkin. Kaladin had borne those knots once.

'How do you treat your spear and shield, squadleader?' Kaladin called back.

The man frowned, but Kaladin knew what he was thinking. A soldier's gear was his life; you cared for your weapon as you'd care for your children, often seeing to its upkeep before you took food or rest.

Kaladin nodded to the bridge. 'This is *my* bridge,' he said in a loud voice. 'It is my weapon, the only one allowed me. Treat her well.'

'Or you'll do what?' called one of the other soldiers, prompting laughter among the ranks. The squadleader said nothing. He looked troubled.

Kaladin's words were bravado. In truth, he hated the bridge. Still, he remained standing.

A few moments later, Highprince Sadeas himself crossed on Kaladin's bridge. Brightlord Amaram had always seemed so heroic, so distinguished. A gentleman general. This Sadeas was a different creature entirely, with that round face, curly hair, and lofty expression. He rode as if he were in a parade, one hand lightly holding the reins before him, the other carrying his helm under his arm. His armor was painted red, and the helm bore frivolous tassels. There was so much pointless pomp that it nearly overshadowed the wonder of the ancient artifact.

Kaladin forgot his fatigue and formed his hands into fists. Here was a lighteyes he could hate even more than most, a man so callous that he threw away the lives of hundreds of bridgemen each month. A man who had expressly forbidden his bridgemen to have shields for reasons Kaladin still didn't understand.

Sadeas and his honor guard soon passed, and Kaladin realized that he probably should have bowed. Sadeas hadn't noticed, but it could have made trouble if he had. Shaking his head, Kaladin roused his bridge crew, though it took special prodding to get Rock – the large Horneater – up and moving. Once across the chasm, his men picked up their bridge and jogged toward the next chasm.

The process was repeated enough times that Kaladin lost count. At each crossing, he refused to lie down. He stood with hands behind his back, watching the army pass. More soldiers took note of him, jeering. Kaladin ignored them, and by the fifth or sixth crossing, the jeers faded. The one other time he saw Brightlord Sadeas, Kaladin gave a bow, though it made his stomach twist to do so. He did not serve this man. He did not give this man allegiance. But he *did* serve his men of Bridge Four. He would save them, and that meant he had to keep himself from being punished for insolence.

'Reverse runners!' Gaz called. 'Cross and reverse!'

Kaladin turned sharply. The next crossing would be the assault. He squinted, looking into the distance, and could just barely make out a line of dark figures gathering on another plateau. The Parshendi had arrived and were forming up. Behind them, a group worked on breaking open the chrysalis.

Kaladin felt a spike of frustration. Their speed hadn't been enough. And – tired though they were – Sadeas would want to attack quickly, before the Parshendi could get the gemheart out of its shell.

The bridgemen rose from their rest, silent, haunted. They knew what was coming. They crossed the chasm and pulled the bridge over, then rearranged themselves in reverse order. The soldiers formed ranks. It was all so silent, like men preparing to carry a bier to the pyre.

The bridgemen left a space for Kaladin at the back, sheltered and protected. Syl alighted on the bridge, looking at the spot. Kaladin walked up to it, so tired, mentally and physically. He'd pushed himself too hard in the morning, then again by standing instead of resting. What had possessed him to do such a thing? He could barely walk.

He looked over the bridgemen. His men were resigned, despondent, terrified. If they refused to run, they'd be executed. If they did run, they'd face the arrows. They didn't look toward the distant line of Parshendi archers. Instead, they looked down.

They are your men, Kaladin told himself. *They need you to lead them, even if they don't know it.*

How can you lead from the rear?

He stepped out of line and rounded the bridge; two of the men – Drehy and Teft – looked up in shock as he passed. The deathpoint – the spot in the very center of the front – was being held by Rock, the beefy, tan-skinned Horneater. Kaladin tapped him on the shoulder. 'You're in my spot, Rock.'

The man glanced at him, surprised. 'But—'

'To the back with you.'

Rock frowned. Nobody ever tried to jump *ahead* in the order. 'You're airsick, lowlander,' he said with his thick accent. 'You wish to die? Why do you not just go leap into the chasm? That would be easier.'

'I'm bridgeleader. It's my privilege to run at the front. Go.'

Rock shrugged, but did as ordered, taking Kaladin's position at the back. Nobody said a word. If Kaladin wanted to get himself killed, who were they to complain?

Kaladin looked over the bridgemen. 'The longer we take to get this bridge down, the more arrows they can loose at us. Stay firm, stay determined, and *be quick*. Raise bridge!'

The men lifted, inner rows moving underneath and situating themselves in rows of five across. Kaladin stood at the very front with a tall, stout man named Leyten to his left, a spindly man named Murk to his right. Adis and Corl were at the edges. Five men in front. The deathline.

Once all of the crews had their bridges up, Gaz gave the command. 'Assault!'

They ran, dashing alongside the standing ranks of the army, passing soldiers holding spears and shields. Some watched with curiosity, perhaps amused at the sight of the lowly bridgemen running so urgently to their deaths. Others looked away, perhaps ashamed of the lives it would cost to get them across that chasm.

Kaladin kept his eyes forward, squelching that incredulous voice in the back of his mind, one that screamed he was doing something very stupid. He barreled toward the final chasm, focused on the Parshendi line. Figures with black and crimson skin holding bows.

Syl flitted close to Kaladin's head, no longer in the form of a person, streaking like a ribbon of light. She zipped in front of him.

The bows came up. Kaladin hadn't been at the deathpoint during a charge this bad since his first day on the crew. They always put new men into rotation at the deathpoint. That way, if they died, you didn't have to worry about training them.

The Parshendi archers drew, aiming at five or six of the bridge crews. Bridge Four was obviously in their sights.

The bows loosed.

'Tien!' Kaladin screamed, nearly mad with fatigue and frustration. He bellowed the name aloud – uncertain why – as a wall of arrows zipped toward him. Kaladin felt a jolt of energy, a surge of sudden strength, unanticipated and unexplained.

The arrows landed.

Murk fell without a sound, four or five arrows striking him, spraying his blood across the stones. Leyten dropped as well, and with him both Adis and Corl. Shafts struck the ground at Kaladin's feet, shattering, and a good half dozen hit the wood around Kaladin's head and hands.

Kaladin didn't know if he'd been hit. He was too flush with energy and alarm. He continued running, screaming, holding the bridge on his shoulders. For some reason, a group of Parshendi archers ahead lowered their bows. He saw their marbled skin, strange reddish or orange helms, and simple brown clothing. They appeared confused.

Whatever the reason, it gained Bridge Four a few precious moments. By the time the Parshendi raised their bows again, Kaladin's team had reached the chasm. His men fell into line with the other bridge crews – there were only fifteen bridges now. Five had fallen. They closed the gaps as they arrived.

Kaladin screamed for the bridgemen to drop amid another spray of arrows. One sliced open the skin near his ribs, deflecting off the bone. He felt it hit, but didn't feel any pain. He scrambled around the side of the bridge, helping push. Kaladin's team slammed the bridge into place as a wave of Alethi arrows distracted the enemy archers.

A troop of cavalry charged across the bridges. The bridgemen were soon forgotten. Kaladin fell to his knees beside the bridge as the others of his crew stumbled away, bloodied and hurt, their part in the battle over.

Kaladin held his side, feeling the blood there. *Straight laceration, only about an inch long, not wide enough to be of danger.*

It was his father's voice.

Kaladin panted. He needed to get to safety. Arrows zipped over his head, fired by the Alethi archers.

Some people take lives. Other people save lives.

He wasn't done yet. Kaladin forced himself to his feet and staggered to where someone lay beside the bridge. It was a bridgeman named Hobber; he had an arrow through the leg. The man moaned, holding his thigh.

Kaladin grabbed him under the arms and pulled him away from the bridge. The man cursed at the pain, dazed, as Kaladin towed him to a cleft behind a small bulge in the rock where Rock and some of the other bridge-men had sought shelter.

After dropping off Hobber – the arrow hadn't hit any major arteries, and he would be fine for a time yet – Kaladin turned and tried to rush back out onto the battlefield proper. He slipped, however, stumbling in his fatigue. He hit the ground hard, grunting.

Some take lives. Some save lives.

He pushed himself to his feet, sweat dripping from his brow, and scrambled back toward the bridge, his father's voice in his ears. The next bridge-man he found, a man named Koorm, was dead. Kaladin left the body.

Gadol had a deep wound in the side where an arrow had passed completely through him. His face was covered with blood from a gash on his temple, and he'd managed to crawl a short distance from the bridge. He looked up with frenzied black eyes, orange painspren waving around him. Kaladin grabbed him under the arms and towed him away just before a thundering charge of cavalry trampled the place where he'd been lying.

Kaladin dragged Gadol over to the cleft, noting two more dead. He did a quick count. That made twenty-nine bridgemen, including the dead he'd seen. Five were missing. Kaladin stumbled back out onto the battlefield.

Soldiers had bunched up around the back of the bridge, archers forming at the sides and firing into the Parshendi lines as the heavy cavalry charge – led by Highprince Sadeas himself, virtually indestructible in his Shardplate – tried to push the enemy back.

Kaladin wavered, dizzy, dismayed at the sight of so many men running, shouting, firing arrows and throwing spears. Five bridgemen, probably dead, lost in all of that—

He spotted a figure huddled just beside the chasm lip with arrows flying back and forth over his head. It was Dabbid, one of the bridgemen. He curled up, arm twisted at an awkward angle.

Kaladin charged in. He threw himself to the ground and crawled beneath the zipping arrows, hoping that the Parshendi would ignore a couple of unarmed bridgemen. Dabbid didn't even notice when Kaladin reached him. He was in shock, lips moving soundlessly, eyes dazed. Kaladin grabbed him awkwardly, afraid to stand up too high lest an arrow hit him.

He dragged Dabbid away from the edge in a clumsy half crawl. He kept slipping on blood, falling, abrading his arms on the rock, hitting his face against the stone. He persisted, towing the younger man out from underneath the flying arrows. Finally, he got far enough away that he risked standing. He tried to pick up Dabbid. But his muscles were so weak. He strained and slipped, exhausted, falling to the stones.

He lay there, gasping, the pain of his side finally washing over him. *So tired. . . .*

He stood up shakily, then tried again to grab Dabbid. He blinked away tears of frustration, too weak to even pull the man.

'Airsick lowlander,' a voice growled.

Kaladin turned as Rock arrived. The massive Horneater grabbed Dabbid under the arms, pulling him. 'Crazy,' he grumbled to Kaladin, but easily lifted the wounded bridgeman and carried him back to the hollow.

Kaladin followed. He collapsed in the hollow, his back to the rock. The surviving bridgemen huddled around him, eyes haunted. Rock set Dabbid down.

'Four more,' Kaladin said between gasps. 'We have to find them. . . .'

'Murk and Leyten,' Teft said. The older bridgeman had been near the back this run, and hadn't taken any wounds. 'And Adis and Corl. They were in the front.'

That's right, Kaladin thought, exhausted. *How could I forget.* . . . 'Murk is dead,' he said. 'The others might live.' He tried to stumble to his feet.

'Idiot,' Rock said. 'Stay here. Is all right. I will do this thing.' He hesitated. 'Guess I'm an idiot too.' He scowled, but went back out onto the battlefield. Teft hesitated, then chased after him.

Kaladin breathed in and out, holding his side. He couldn't decide if the pain of the arrow impact hurt more than the cut.

Save lives. . . .

He crawled over to the three wounded. Hobber – with an arrow through the leg – would wait, and Dabbid had only a broken arm. Gadol was the worst off, with that hole in his side. Kaladin stared at the wound. He didn't have an operating table; he didn't even have antiseptic. How was he supposed to do anything?

He shoved despair aside. 'One of you go fetch me a knife,' he told the bridgemen. 'Take it off the body of a soldier who has fallen. Someone else build a fire!'

The bridgemen looked at each other.

'Dunny, you get the knife,' Kaladin said as he held his hand to Gadol's wound, trying to stanch the blood. 'Narm, can you make a fire?'

'With what?' the man asked. Kaladin pulled off his vest and shirt, then handed the shirt to Narm.

'Use this as tinder and gather some fallen arrows for wood. Does anyone have flint and steel?' Moash did, fortunately. You carried anything valuable you had with you on a bridge run; other bridgemen might steal it if you left it behind.

'Move quickly!' Kaladin said. 'Someone else, go rip open a rockbud and get me the watergourd inside.'

They stood for a few moments. Then, blessedly, they did as he demanded. Perhaps they were too stunned to object. Kaladin tore open Gadol's shirt, exposing the wound. It was bad, terribly bad. If it had cut the intestines or some of the other organs . . .

He ordered one of the bridgemen to hold a bandage to Gadol's forehead to stanch the smaller blood flow there – anything would help – and inspected the wounded side with the speed his father had taught him. Dunny returned quickly with a knife. Narm was having trouble with the fire, though. The man cursed, trying his flint and steel again.

Gadol was spasming. Kaladin pressed bandages to the wound, feeling helpless. There wasn't a place he could make a tourniquet for a wound like this. There wasn't anything he could do but—

Gadol spit up blood, coughing. 'They break the land itself!' he hissed, eyes wild. 'They want it, but in their rage they will destroy it. Like the jealous man burns his rich things rather than let them be taken by his enemies! They come!'

He gasped. And then he fell still, his dead eyes staring upward, bloody spittle running in a trail down his cheek. His final, haunting words hung over them. Not far away, soldiers fought and screamed, but the bridgemen were silent.

Kaladin sat back, stunned – as always – by the pain of losing someone. His father had always said that time would dull his sensitivity.

In this, Lirin had been wrong.

He felt so tired. Rock and Teft were hurrying back toward the cleft in the rock, bearing a body between them.

They wouldn't have brought anyone unless he was still alive, Kaladin told himself. *Think of the ones you can help.* 'Keep that fire going!' he said, pointing at Narm. 'Don't let it die! Someone heat the blade in it.'

Narm jumped, noticing as if for the first time that he'd actually managed to get a small flame started. Kaladin turned away from the dead Gadol and made room for Rock and Teft. They deposited a very bloody Leyten on the ground. He was breathing shallowly and had two arrows sticking from him, one from the shoulder, the other from the opposite arm. Another had grazed his stomach, and the cut there had been widened by movement. It looked like his left leg had been trampled by a horse; it was broken, and he had a large gash where the skin had split.

'The other three are dead,' Teft said. 'He nearly is too. Nothing much we can do. But you said to bring him, so—'

Kaladin knelt down immediately, working with careful, efficient speed. He pressed a bandage against the side, holding it in place with his knee, then tied a quick bandage on the leg, ordering one of the bridgemen to hold it firm and elevate the limb. 'Where's that knife!' Kaladin yelled, hurriedly tying a loose tourniquet around the arm. He needed to stop the blood right now; he'd worry about saving the arm later.

Youthful Dunny rushed over with the heated blade. Kaladin lifted the side bandage and quickly cauterized the wound there. Leyten was unconscious, his breathing growing more shallow.

'You will *not* die,' Kaladin muttered. 'You will not die!' His mind was numb, but his fingers knew the motions. For a moment, he was back in his father's surgery room, listening to careful instruction. He cut the arrow from Leyten's arm, but left the one in his shoulder, then sent the knife back to be reheated.

Peet finally returned with the watergourd. Kaladin snatched it, using it to clean the leg wound, which was the nastiest, as it had been caused by trampling. When the knife came back, Kaladin pulled the arrow free of the shoulder and cauterized the wound as best he could, then used another of his quickly disappearing bandages to tie the wound.

He splinted the leg with arrow shafts – the only thing they had. With a grimace, he cauterized the wound there too. He hated to cause so many scars, but he couldn't afford to let any more blood be lost. He was going to need antiseptic. How soon could he get some of that mucus?

'Don't you *dare* die!' Kaladin said, barely conscious that he was speaking. He quickly tied off the leg wound, then used his needle and thread to sew the arm wound. He bandaged it, then untied the tourniquet most of the way.

Finally, he settled back, looking at the wounded man, completely drained. Leyten was still breathing. How long would that last? The odds were against him.

The bridgemen stood or sat around Kaladin, looking strangely reverent. Kaladin tiredly moved over to Hobber and saw to the man's leg wound. It didn't need to be cauterized. Kaladin washed it out, cut away some splinters, then sewed it. There were painspren all around the man, tiny orange hands stretching up from the ground.

Kaladin sliced off the cleanest portion of bandage he'd used on Gadol and tied it around Hobber's wound. He hated the uncleanliness of it, but there was no other choice. Then he set Dabbid's arm with some arrows he had the other bridgemen fetch, using Dabbid's shirt to tie them in place. Then, finally, Kaladin sat back against the lip of stone, letting out a long, fatigued breath.

Bangs of metal on metal and shouts of soldiers rang from behind. He felt *so* tired. Too tired to even close his eyes. He just wanted to sit and stare at the ground forever.

Teft settled down beside him. The grizzled man had the watergourd, which still had some liquid in the bottom. 'Drink, lad. You need it.'

'We should clean the wounds of the other men,' Kaladin said numbly. 'They took scrapes – I saw some had cuts – and they should—'

'Drink,' Teft said, his crackly voice insistent.

Kaladin hesitated, then drank the water. It tasted strongly bitter, like the plant from which it had been taken.

'Where'd you learn to heal men like that?' Teft asked. Several of the nearby bridgemen turned toward him at the question.

'I wasn't always a slave,' Kaladin whispered.

'These things you did, they won't make a difference,' Rock said, walking up. The massive Horneater squatted down. 'Gaz makes us leave behind wounded who cannot walk. Is standing order from above.'

'I'll deal with Gaz,' Kaladin said, resting his head back against the stone. 'Go return that knife to the body you took it off. I don't want to be accused of thievery. Then, when the time comes to leave, I want two men in charge of Leyten and two men in charge of Hobber. We'll tie them to the top of the bridge and carry them. At the chasms, you'll have to move quickly and untie them before the army crosses, then retie them at the end. We'll also need someone to lead Dabbid, if his shock hasn't passed.'

'Gaz won't stand for this thing,' Rock said.

Kaladin closed his eyes, declining further argument.

The battle was a long one. As evening approached, the Parshendi finally retreated, jumping away across the chasms with their unnaturally powerful legs. There was a chorus of shouts from the Alethi soldiers, who had won the day. Kaladin forced himself to his feet and went looking for Gaz. It would be a while yet before they could get the chrysalis open – it was like pounding on stone – but he needed to deal with the bridge sergeant.

He found Gaz watching from well behind the battle lines. He glanced at Kaladin with his one eye. 'How much of that blood is yours?'

Kaladin looked down, realizing for the first time that he was crusted with dark, flaking blood, most belonging to the men he'd worked on. He didn't answer the question. 'We're taking our wounded with us.'

Gaz shook his head. 'If they can't walk, they stay behind. Standing orders. Not my choice.'

'We're taking them,' Kaladin said, no more firm, no more loud.

'Brightlord Lamaril won't stand for it.' Lamaril was Gaz's immediate superior.

'You'll send Bridge Four last, to lead the wounded soldiers back to camp. Lamaril won't go with that troop; he'll go on ahead with the main body, as he won't want to miss Sadeas's victory feast.'

Gaz opened his mouth.

'My men will move quickly and efficiently,' Kaladin said, interrupting him. 'They won't slow anyone.' He took the last sphere from his pocket and handed it over. 'You won't say anything.'

Gaz took the sphere, snorting. 'One clearmark? You think that will make me take a risk this big?'

'If you don't,' Kaladin said, voice calm, 'I will kill you and let them execute me.'

Gaz blinked in surprise. 'You'd never—'

Kaladin took a single step forward. He must have looked a dreadful sight, covered in blood. Gaz paled. Then he cursed, holding up the dark sphere. 'And a dun sphere at that.'

Kaladin frowned. He was sure it had still glowed before the bridge run. 'That's your fault. You gave it to me.'

'Those spheres were newly infused last night,' Gaz said. 'They came straight from Brightlord Sadeas's treasurer. What did you do with them?'

Kaladin shook his head, too exhausted to think. Syl landed on his shoulder as he turned to walk back to the bridgemen.

'What are they to you?' Gaz called after him. 'Why do you even care?'

'They're my men.'

He left Gaz behind. 'I don't trust him,' Syl said, looking over her shoulder. 'He could just say you threatened him and send men to arrest you.'

'Maybe he will,' Kaladin said. 'I guess I just have to count on him wanting more of my bribes.'

Kaladin continued on, listening to the shouts of the victors and the groans of their wounded. The plateaus were littered with corpses, bunched up along the edges of the chasm, where the bridges had made a focus for the battle. The Parshendi – as always – had left their dead behind. Even when they won, they reportedly left their dead. The humans sent back bridge crews and soldiers to burn their dead and send their spirits to the afterlife, where the best among them would fight in the Heralds' army.

'Spheres,' Syl said, still looking at Gaz. 'That doesn't seem like much to count on.'

'Maybe. Maybe not. I've seen the way he looks at them. He wants the money I give him. Perhaps badly enough to keep him in line.' Kaladin shook his head. 'What you said earlier is right; men are unreliable in many things. But if there's one thing you *can* count on, it's their greed.'

It was a bitter thought. But it had been a bitter day. A hopeful, bright beginning, and a bloody, red sunset.

Just like every day.

18

HIGHPRINCE OF WAR

Ati was once a kind and generous man, and you saw what became of him. Rayse, on the other hand, was among the most loathsome, crafty, and dangerous individuals I had ever met.

'Yeah, this was cut,' the portly leatherworker said, holding up the straps as Adolin watched. 'Wouldn't you agree, Yis?'

The other leatherworker nodded. Yis was a yellow-eyed Iriali, with stark golden hair. Not blond, golden. There was even a metallic sheen to it. He kept it short and wore a cap. Obviously, he didn't want to draw attention to it. Many considered a lock of Iriali hair to be a ward of good luck.

His companion, Avaran, was an Alethi darkeyes who wore an apron over his vest. If the two men worked in the traditional way, one would labor on the larger, more robust pieces – like saddles – while the other specialized in fine detail. A group of apprentices toiled in the background, cutting or sewing hogshide.

'Sliced,' Yis agreed, taking the straps from Avaran. 'I concur.'

'Well hie me to Damnation,' Adolin muttered. 'You mean Elhokar was actually *right*?'

'Adolin,' a feminine voice said from behind. 'You said we'd be going on a walk.'

'That's what we're doing,' he said, turning to smile. Janala stood with arms folded, wearing a sleek yellow dress of impeccable fashion, buttoning up the sides, cupping around the neck with a stiff collar embroidered with crimson thread.

'I had imagined,' she said, 'that a walk would involve more *walking*.'

'Hm,' he said. 'Yes. We'll be getting right to that soon. It'll be grand. Lots of prancing, sauntering, and, er . . .'

'Promenading?' Yis the leatherworker offered.

'Isn't that a type of drink?' Adolin asked.

'Er, no, Brightlord. I'm fairly certain it's another word for walking.'

'Well, then,' Adolin said. 'We'll do plenty of it too. Promenading. I always love a good promenading.' He rubbed his chin, taking the strap back. 'How certain are you about this strap?'

'There's really no room for question, Brightlord,' Avaran said. 'That's not a simple tear. You should be more careful.'

'Careful?'

'Yes,' Avaran said. 'Make sure that no loose buckles are scraping the leather, cutting into it. This looks like it came from a saddle. Sometimes, people let the girth straps hang down when setting the saddle for the night, and they get pinched underneath something. I'd guess that caused the slice.'

'Oh,' Adolin said. 'You mean it wasn't cut intentionally?'

'Well, it could have been that,' Avaran said. 'But why would someone cut a girth like this?'

Why indeed, Adolin thought. He bid farewell to the two leatherworkers, tucked the strap into his pocket, then held out his elbow to Janala. She took it with her freehand, obviously happy to finally be free of the leather-working shop. It had a faint odor about it, though not nearly as bad as a tannery. He'd seen her reaching for her handkerchief a few times, acting as if she wanted to hold it up to her nose.

They stepped out into the midday sunlight. Tibon and Marks – two lighteyed members of the Cobalt Guard – waited outside with Janala's handmaiden, Falksi, who was a young Azish darkeyes. The three fell into step behind Adolin and Janala as they walked out onto the street of the warcamp, Falksi muttering under her breath in an accented voice about the lack of a proper palanquin for her mistress.

Janala didn't seem to mind. She breathed deeply of the open air and clung to his arm. She was quite beautiful, even if she did like to talk about herself. Talkativeness was normally an attribute he was fond of in a woman, but today he had trouble paying attention as Janala began telling him about the latest court gossip.

The strap had been cut, but the leatherworkers had both assumed that it was the result of an accident. That implied they'd seen cuts like this before. A loose buckle or other mishap slicing the leather.

Except this time, that cut had thrown the king in the middle of a fight. Could there be something to it?

'. . . wouldn't you say, Adolin?' Janala asked.

'Undoubtedly,' he said, listening with half an ear.

'So you'll talk to him?'

'Hum?'

'Your father. You'll ask him about letting the men abandon that dreadfully unfashionable uniform once in a while?'

'Well, he's rather set on the idea,' Adolin said. 'Besides, it's really not *that* unfashionable.'

Janala gave him a flat stare.

'All right,' he admitted. 'It is a little drab.' Like every other high-ranked lighteyed officer in Dalinar's army, Adolin wore a simple blue outfit of militaristic cut. A long coat of solid blue – no embroidery – and stiff trousers in a time when vests, silk accents, and scarves were the fashion. His father's Kholin glyphpair was emblazoned quite obtrusively on the back and breast, and the front fastened with silver buttons up both sides. It was simple, distinctly recognizable, but awfully plain.

'Your father's men love him, Adolin,' Janala said. 'But his requirements *are* growing tiresome.'

'I know. Trust me. But I don't think I can change his mind.' How to explain? Despite six years at war, Dalinar wasn't weakening in his resolve to hold to the Codes. If anything, his dedication to them was strengthening.

At least now Adolin understood somewhat. Dalinar's beloved brother had made one last request: Follow the Codes. True, that request had been in reference to a single event, but Adolin's father was known to take things to extremes.

Adolin just wished he wouldn't make the same requirement of everyone else. Individually, the Codes were only minor inconveniences – always be in uniform when in public, never be drunken, avoid dueling. In aggregate, however, they were burdensome.

His response to Janala was cut off as a set of horns blared through the camp. Adolin perked up, spinning, looking eastward toward the Shattered Plains. He counted off the next series of horns. A chrysalis had been spotted on plateau one-forty-seven. That was within striking distance!

He held his breath, waiting for a third series of horns to blare, calling Dalinar's armies to battle. That would only happen if his father ordered it.

Part of him knew those horns wouldn't come. One-forty-seven was close enough to Sadeas's warcamp that the other highprince would certainly try for it.

Come on, Father, Adolin thought. *We can race him for it!*

No horns came.

Adolin glanced at Janala. She'd chosen music as her Calling and paid little attention to the war, though her father was one of Dalinar's cavalry officers. From her expression, Adolin could tell that even she understood what the lack of a third horn meant.

Once again, Dalinar Kholin had chosen not to fight.

'Come on,' Adolin said, turning and moving in another direction, practically towing Janala along by her elbow. 'There's something else I want to check into.'

⁂

Dalinar stood with hands clasped behind his back, looking out over the Shattered Plains. He was on one of the lower terraces outside Elhokar's elevated palace – the king didn't reside in one of the ten warcamps, but in a small compound elevated along a hillside nearby. Dalinar's climb to the palace had been interrupted by the horns.

He stood long enough see Sadeas's army gathering inside his camp. Dalinar could have sent a soldier to prepare his own men. He was close enough.

'Brightlord?' a voice asked from the side. 'Do you wish to continue?'

You protect him your way, Sadeas, Dalinar thought. *I'll protect him my way.*

'Yes, Teshav,' he said, turning to continue walking up the switchbacks.

Teshav joined him. She had streaks of blond in her otherwise black Alethi hair, which she wore up in an intricate crossing weave. She had violet eyes, and her pinched face bore a concerned expression. That was normal; she always seemed to need something to worry about.

Teshav and her attendant scribe were both wives of his officers. Dalinar trusted them. Mostly. It was hard to trust anyone completely. *Stop it*, he thought. *You're starting to sound as paranoid as the king.*

Regardless, he'd be very glad for Jasnah's return. If she ever decided to return. Some of his higher officers hinted to him that he should marry again, if only to have a woman who could be his primary scribe. They thought he rejected their suggestions because of love for his first wife. They didn't know that she was gone, vanished from his mind, a blank patch of fog in his memory. Though, in a way, his officers were right. He hesitated to remarry because he hated the idea of replacing her. He'd had everything of his wife taken from him. All that remained was the hole, and filling it to gain a scribe seemed callous.

Dalinar continued on his way. Other than the two women, he was attended by Renarin and three members of the Cobalt Guard. The latter wore deep blue felt caps and cloaks over silvery breastplates and deep blue trousers. They were lighteyes of low rank, able to carry swords for close fighting.

'Well, Brightlord,' Teshav said, 'Brightlord Adolin asked me to report the progress of the saddle girth investigation. He's speaking with leather-workers at this very moment, but so far, there is very little to say. Nobody witnessed anyone interfering with the saddle or His Majesty's horse. Our spies say there are no whispers of anyone in the other warcamps bragging, and nobody in our camp has suddenly received large sums of money, so far as we've discovered.'

'The grooms?'

'Say they checked over the saddle,' she said, 'but when pressed, they admit that they can't *specifically* remember checking the girth.' She shook her head. 'Carrying a Shardbearer places great strain on both horse and saddle. If there were only some way to tame more Ryshadium. . . .'

'I think you'll sooner tame the highstorms, Brightness. Well, this is good news, I suppose. Better for us all that this strap business turns out to be nothing. Now, there is another item I wish you to look into.'

'It is my pleasure to serve, Brightlord.'

'Highprince Aladar has begun to talk of taking a short vacation back to Alethkar. I want to know if he's serious.'

'Yes, Brightlord.' Teshav nodded. 'Would that be a problem?'

'I'm honestly not sure.' He didn't trust the highprinces, but at least with them all here, he could watch them. If one of them returned to Alethkar, the man could scheme unchecked. Of course, even brief visits might help stabilize their homeland.

Which was more important? Stability or the ability to watch over the others? *Blood of my fathers*, he thought. *I wasn't made for this politicking and scheming. I was made to wield a sword and ride down enemies.*

He'd do what needed to be done anyway. 'I believe you said you had information on the king's accounts, Teshav?'

'Indeed,' she said as they continued the short hike. 'You were correct to have me look into the ledgers, as it appears that three of the highprinces – Thanadal, Hatham, and Vamah – are well behind in their payments. Other than yourself, only Highprince Sadeas has actually paid ahead on what is owed, as the tenets of war require.'

Dalinar nodded. 'The longer this war stretches, the more comfortable the highprinces are getting. They're starting to question. Why pay high wartime rates for Soulcasting? Why not move farmers out here and start growing their own food?'

'Pardon, Brightlord,' Teshav said as they turned around a switchback. Her attendant scribe walked behind, several ledgers clipped to boards carried in a satchel. 'But do we really wish to discourage that? A second stream of supplies could be valuable as a redundancy.'

'The merchants already provide redundancy,' Dalinar said. 'Which is one of the reasons I haven't chased them off. I wouldn't mind another, but the Soulcasters are the only hold we have on the highprinces. They owed Gavilar loyalty, but they feel little of that for his son.' Dalinar narrowed his eyes. 'This is a vital point, Teshav. Have you read the histories I suggested?'

'Yes, Brightlord.'

'Then you know. The most fragile period in a kingdom's existence comes during the lifetime of its founder's heir. During the reign of a man like Gavilar, men stay loyal because of their respect for him. During subsequent generations, men begin to see themselves as part of a kingdom, a united force that holds together because of tradition.

'But the son's reign ... that's the dangerous point. Gavilar isn't here to hold everyone together, but there isn't yet a tradition of Alethkar being a kingdom. We've *got* to carry on long enough for the highprinces to begin seeing themselves as part of a greater whole.'

'Yes, Brightlord.'

She didn't question. Teshav was deeply loyal to him, as were most of his officers. They didn't question why it was so important to him that the ten princedoms regard themselves as one nation. Perhaps they assumed it was because of Gavilar. Indeed, his brother's dream of a united Alethkar was part of it. There was something else, though.

The Everstorm comes. The True Desolation. The Night of Sorrows.

He suppressed a shiver. The visions certainly didn't make it sound like he had a great deal of time to prepare.

'Draft a missive in the king's name,' Dalinar said, 'decreasing Soulcasting costs for those who have made their payments on time. That should wake up the others. Give it to Elhokar's scribes and have them explain it to him. Hopefully he will agree with the need.'

'Yes, Brightlord,' Teshav said. 'If I might note, I was quite surprised that you suggested I read those histories. In the past, such things haven't been particular to your interests.'

'I do a lot of things lately that aren't particular to my interests or my talents,' Dalinar said with a grimace. 'My lack of capacity doesn't change the kingdom's needs. Have you gathered reports of banditry in the area?'

'Yes, Brightlord.' She hesitated. 'The rates are quite alarming.'

'Tell your husband I give him command of the Fourth Battalion,' Dalinar said. 'I want the two of you to work out a better pattern of patrol in the Unclaimed Hills. So long as the Alethi monarchy has a presence here, I do *not* want it to be a land of lawlessness.'

'Yes, Brightlord,' Teshav said, sounding hesitant. 'You realize that means you've committed two entire battalions to patrolling?'

'Yes,' Dalinar said. He had asked for help from the other highprinces. Their reactions had ranged from shock to mirth. None had given him any soldiers.

'That is added to the battalion you assigned to peacekeeping in the areas between warcamps and the exterior merchant markets,' Teshav added. 'In total, that's over a quarter of your forces here, Brightlord.'

'The orders stand, Teshav.' he said. 'See to it. But first, I have more to discuss with you regarding the ledgers. Go on ahead to the ledger room and wait for us there.'

She nodded respect. 'Of course, Brightlord.' She withdrew with her attendant.

Renarin stepped up to Dalinar. 'She wasn't pleased about that, Father.'

'She wishes her husband to be fighting,' Dalinar said. 'They all hope that I'll win another Shardblade out there, then give it to them.' The Parshendi had Shards. Not many, but even a single one was surprising. Nobody had an explanation for where they'd gotten them. Dalinar had won a Parshendi Shardblade and Plate during his first year here. He'd given both to Elhokar to award to a warrior he felt would be the most useful to Alethkar and the war effort.

Dalinar turned and entered the palace proper. The guards at the doorway saluted him and Renarin. The young man kept his eyes forward, staring at nothing. Some people thought him emotionless, but Dalinar knew he was just preoccupied.

'I've been meaning to speak with you, son,' Dalinar said. 'About the hunt last week.'

Renarin's eyes flickered downward in shame, the edges of his mouth pulling back in a grimace. Yes, he *did* have emotions. He just didn't show them as often as others.

'You realize that you shouldn't have rushed into battle as you did,' Dalinar said sternly. 'That chasmfiend could have killed you.'

'What would you have done, Father, if it had been me in danger?'

'I don't fault your bravery; I fault your wisdom. What if you'd had one of your fits?'

'Then perhaps the monster would have swept me off the plateau,' Renarin said bitterly, 'and I would no longer be such a useless drain on everyone's time.'

'Don't say such things! Not even in jest.'

'Was it jest? Father, I can't fight.'

'Fighting is not the only thing of value a man can do.' The ardents were very specific about that. Yes, the highest Calling of men was to join the battle in the afterlife to reclaim the Tranquiline Halls, but the Almighty accepted the excellence of any man or woman, regardless of what they did.

You just did your best, picking a profession and an attribute of the Almighty to emulate. A Calling and a Glory, it was said. You worked hard at your profession, and you spent your life trying to live according

302

to a single ideal. The Almighty would accept that, particularly if you were lighteyed – the better your blood as a lighteyes, the more innate Glory you had already.

Dalinar's Calling was to be a leader, and his chosen Glory was determination. He'd chosen both in his youth, though he now viewed them very differently than he once had.

'You are right, of course, Father,' Renarin said. 'I am not the first hero's son to be born without any talent for warfare. The others all got along. So shall I. Likely I will end up as citylord of a small town. Assuming I don't tuck myself away in the devotaries.' The boy's eyes turned forward.

I still think of him as 'the boy,' Dalinar thought. *Even though he's now in his twentieth year.* Wit had been right. Dalinar underestimated Renarin. *How would I react, if I were forbidden to fight? Kept back with the women and the merchants?*

Dalinar would have been bitter, particularly against Adolin. In fact, Dalinar *had* often been envious of Gavilar during their boyhood. Renarin, however, was Adolin's greatest supporter. He all but worshipped his elder brother. And he was brave enough to dash heedless into the middle of a battlefield where a nightmare creature was smashing spearmen and tossing aside Shardbearers.

Dalinar cleared his throat. 'Perhaps it is time to again try training you in the sword.'

'My blood weakness—'

'Won't matter a bit if we get you into a set of Plate and give you a Blade,' Dalinar said. 'The armor makes any man strong, and a Shardblade is nearly as light as air itself.'

'Father,' Renarin said flatly, 'I'll never be a Shardbearer. You yourself have said that the Blades and Plate we win from the Parshendi must go to the most skilled warriors.'

'None of the other highprinces give up their spoils to the king,' Dalinar said. 'And who would fault me if, for once, I made a gift to my son?'

Renarin stopped in the hallway, displaying an unusual level of emotion, eyes opening wider, face eager. 'You are serious?'

'I give you my oath, son. If I can capture another Blade and Plate, they will go to you.' He smiled. 'To be honest, I'd do it simply for the joy of seeing Sadeas's face when you become a full Shardbearer. Beyond that, if your strength is made equal to others, I expect that your natural skill will make you shine.'

Renarin smiled. Shardplate wouldn't solve everything, but Renarin would have his chance. Dalinar would see to it. *I know what it's like to be a second son*, he thought as they continued walking toward the king's chambers, *overshadowed by an older brother you love yet envy at the same time. Stormfather, but I do.*

I still feel that way.

⁂

'Ah, good Brightlord Adolin,' the ardent said, walking forward with open arms. Kadash was a tall man in his later years, and wore the shaved head and square beard of his Calling. He also had a twisting scar that ran around the top of his head, a memento from his earlier days as an army officer.

It was uncommon to find a man such as him – a lighteyes who had once been a soldier – in the ardentia. In fact, it was odd for any man to change his Calling. But it wasn't forbidden, and Kadash had risen far in the ardentia considering his late start. Dalinar said it was a sign of either faith or perseverance. Perhaps both.

The warcamp's temple had started as a large Soulcast dome, then Dalinar had granted money and stonemasons to transform it into a more suitable house of worship. Carvings of the Heralds now lined the inside walls, and broad windows carved on the leeward side had been set with glass to let in the light. Diamond spheres blazed in bunches hung from the high ceiling, and stands had been set up for the instruction, practice, and testing of the various arts.

Many women were in at the moment, receiving instruction from the ardents. There were fewer men. Being at war, it was easy to practice the masculine arts in the field.

Janala folded her arms, scanning the temple with obvious dissatisfaction as she stood beside Adolin. 'First a stinky leatherworker's shop, now the temple? I had assumed we would walk someplace at least *faintly* romantic.'

'Religion's romantic,' Adolin said, scratching his head. 'Eternal love and all that, right?'

She eyed him. 'I'm going to go wait outside.' She turned and walked out with her handmaiden. 'And someone get me a storming palanquin.'

Adolin frowned, watching her go. 'I'll have to buy her something quite expensive to make up for this, I suspect.'

'I don't see what the problem is,' Kadash said. '*I* think religion is romantic.'

'You're an ardent,' Adolin said flatly. 'Besides, that scar makes you a little too unsightly for my tastes.' He sighed. 'It's not so much the temple that has set her off, but my lack of attention. I haven't been a very good companion today.'

'You have matters pressing upon your mind, bright one?' Kadash asked. 'Is this about your Calling? You haven't made much progress lately.'

Adolin grimaced. His chosen Calling was dueling. By working with the ardents to make personal goals and fulfill them, he could prove himself to the Almighty. Unfortunately, during war, the Codes said Adolin was supposed to limit his duels, as frivolous dueling could wound officers who might be needed in battle.

But Adolin's father avoided battle more and more. So what was the point of not dueling? 'Holy one,' Adolin said, 'we need to speak somewhere we can't be overheard.'

Kadash raised an eyebrow and led Adolin around the central apex. Vorin temples were always circular with a gently sloping mound at the center, by custom rising ten feet high. The building was dedicated to the Almighty, maintained by Dalinar and the ardents he owned. All devotaries were welcome to use it, though most would have their own chapter houses in one of the warcamps.

'What is it you wish to ask of me, bright one?' the ardent asked once they reached a more secluded section of the vast chamber. Kadash was deferential, though he had tutored and trained Adolin during his childhood.

'Is my father going mad?' Adolin asked. 'Or could he really be seeing visions sent by the Almighty, as I think he believes?'

'That's a rather blunt question.'

'You've known him longer than most, Kadash, and I know you to be loyal. I also know you to be one who keeps his ears open and notices things, so I'm sure you've heard the rumors.' Adolin shrugged. 'Seems like a time for bluntness if there ever was one.'

'I take it, then, the rumors are not unfounded.'

'Unfortunately, no. It happens during every highstorm. He raves and thrashes about, and afterward claims to have seen things.'

'What sorts of things?'

'I'm not certain, precisely.' Adolin grimaced. 'Things about the Radiants. And perhaps ... about what is to come.'

Kadash looked disturbed. 'This is dangerous territory, bright one. What you are asking me about risks tempting me to violate my oaths. I am an ardent, owned by and loyal to your father.'

'But he is not your religious superior.'

'No. But he *is* the Almighty's guardian of this people, set to watch me and make certain I don't rise above my station.' Kadash pursed his lips. 'It is a delicate balance we walk, bright one. Do you know much of the Hierocracy, the War of Loss?'

'The church tried to seize control,' Adolin said, shrugging. 'The priests tried to conquer the world – for its own good, they claimed.'

'That was part of it,' Kadash said. 'The part we speak of most often. But the problem goes much deeper. The church back then, it clung to knowledge. Men were not in command of their own religious paths; the priests controlled the doctrine, and few members of the Church were allowed to know theology. They were taught to follow the priests. Not the Almighty or the Heralds, but the priests.'

He began walking, leading Adolin around the back rim of the temple chamber. They passed statues of the Heralds, five male, five female. In truth, Adolin knew very little of what Kadash was saying. He'd never had much of a mind for history that didn't relate directly to the command of armies.

'The problem, bright one,' Kadash said, 'was mysticism. The priests claimed that common men could not understand religion or the Almighty. Where there should have been openness, there was smoke and whispers. The priests began to claim visions and prophecies, though such things had been denounced by the Heralds themselves. Voidbinding is a dark and evil thing, and the soul of it was to try to divine the future.'

Adolin froze. 'Wait, you're saying—'

'Don't get ahead of me please, bright one,' Kadash assured, turning back toward him. 'When the priests of the Hierocracy were cast down, the Sunmaker made a point of interrogating them and going through their correspondences with one another. It was discovered that there *had* been no prophecies. No mystical promises from the Almighty. That had all been an excuse, fabricated by the priests to placate and control the people.'

Adolin frowned. 'Where are you going with this, Kadash?'

'As close as I dare to the truth, bright one,' the ardent said. 'As I cannot be as blunt as you.'

'You think my father's visions are fabrications, then.'

'I would never accuse my highprince of lying,' Kadash said. 'Or even of feebleness. But neither can I condone mysticism or prophecy in any form. To do so would be to deny Vorinism. The days of the priests are gone. The days of lying to the people, of keeping them in darkness, are gone. Now, each man chooses his own path, and the ardents help him achieve closeness to the Almighty through it. Instead of shadowed prophecies and pretend powers held by a few, we have a population who understand their beliefs and their relationship with their God.'

He stepped closer, speaking very softly. 'Your father is not to be mocked or diminished. If his visions are true, then it is between him and the Almighty. All I can say is this: I know something of what it is to be haunted by the death and destruction of war. I see in your father's eyes much of what I have felt, but worse. My personal opinion is that the things he sees are likely more a reflection of his past than any mystical experience.'

'So he is going mad,' Adolin whispered.

'I did not say that.'

'You implied that the Almighty probably wouldn't send visions like these.'

'I did.'

'And that his visions are a product of his own mind.'

'*Likely* so,' the ardent said, raising his finger. 'A delicate balance, you see. One that is particularly difficult to keep when speaking to my high-prince's own son.' He reached out, taking Adolin's arm. 'If any are to help him, it must be you. It would not be the place of any other, even myself.'

Adolin nodded slowly. 'Thank you.'

'You should likely go see to that young woman now.'

'Yes,' Adolin said with a sigh. 'I fear that even with the right gift, she and I are not long for courting. Renarin will mock me again.'

Kadash smiled. 'Best not to give up so easily, bright one. Go now. But do return sometime so we can speak of your goals in regard to your Calling. It has been too long since you've Elevated.'

Adolin nodded and hurried from the chamber.

◆·◆

After hours going over the ledgers with Teshav, Dalinar and Renarin reached the hallway before the king's chambers. They walked in silence, the soles of their boots clapping the marble flooring, the sound echoing against stone walls.

The corridors of the king's war palace were growing richer by the week. Once, this hallway had been just another Soulcast stone tunnel. As Elhokar settled in, he had ordered improvements. Windows were cut into the leeward side. Marble tiling was set into the floor. The walls were carved with reliefs, with mosaic trim at the corners. Dalinar and Renarin passed a group of stonemasons carefully cutting a scene of Nalan'Elin, emitting sunlight, the sword of retribution held over his head.

They reached the king's antechamber, a large, open room guarded by ten members of the King's Guard, dressed in blue and gold. Dalinar recognized each face; he had personally organized the unit, handpicking its members.

Highprince Ruthar waited to see the king. He had brawny arms folded in front of him, and wore a short black beard that surrounded his mouth. His red silk coat was cut short and did not button; almost more of a sleeved vest, it was a mere token nod to traditional Alethi uniform. The shirt underneath was ruffled and white, and his blue trousers were loose, with wide cuffs.

Ruthar glanced Dalinar's way and nodded to him – a minor token of respect – then turned to chat with one of his attendants. He cut off, however, as the guards at the doorway stepped aside to let Dalinar enter. Ruthar sniffed in annoyance. Dalinar's easy access to the king galled the other highprinces.

The king wasn't in his wardroom, but the wide doors to his balcony were open. Dalinar's guardsmen waited behind as he stepped out onto the balcony, Renarin hesitantly following. The light outside was dimming as sunset neared. Setting the war palace up high like this was tactically sound, but it meant the place was mercilessly buffeted by storms. That was an old campaign conundrum. Did one choose the best position to weather storms, or did one seize the high ground?

Most would have chosen the former; their warcamps on the edge of the Shattered Plains were unlikely to be attacked, making the advantage of the high ground less important. But kings tended to prefer height. In this instance, Dalinar had encouraged Elhokar, just in case.

The balcony itself was a thick platform of rock cut onto the top of the small peak, edged with an iron railing. The king's rooms were a Soulcast dome sitting atop the natural formation, with covered ramps and stairways leading to tiers lower on the hillside. Those housed the king's various attendants: guards, stormwardens, ardents, and distant family members. Dalinar had his own bunker at his warcamp. He refused to call it a palace.

The king leaned against the railing, two guards watching from a distance. Dalinar motioned for Renarin to join them, so that he could speak with the king in private.

The air was cool – spring having come for a time – and it was sweet with the scents of evening: blooming rockbuds and wet stone. Below, the war-camps were starting to come alight, ten sparkling circles filled with watch-fires, cookfires, lamps, and the steady glow of infused gems. Elhokar stared over the camps and toward the Shattered Plains. They were utterly dark, save for the occasional twinkle of a watchpost.

'Do they watch us, from out there?' Elhokar asked as Dalinar joined him.

'We know their raiding bands move at night, Your Majesty,' Dalinar said, resting one hand on the iron railing. 'I can't help but think they watch us.'

The king's uniform had the traditional long coat with buttons up the sides, but it was loose and relaxed, and ruffled lace poked out of the collar and cuffs. His trousers were solid blue, and were cut in the same baggy fashion as Ruthar's. It all looked so informal to Dalinar. Increasingly, their soldiers were being led by a slack group who dressed in lace and spent their evenings at feasts.

This is what Gavilar foresaw, Dalinar thought. *This is why he grew so insistent that we follow the Codes.*

'You look thoughtful, Uncle,' Elhokar said.

'Just considering the past, Your Majesty.'

'The past is irrelevant. I only look forward.'

Dalinar was not certain he agreed with either statement.

'I sometimes think I should be able to see the Parshendi,' Elhokar said. 'I feel that if I stare long enough, I will find them, pin them down so I can challenge them. I wish they'd just fight me, like men of honor.'

'If they were men of honor,' Dalinar said, clasping his hands behind his back, 'then they would not have killed your father as they did.'

'Why did they do it, do you suppose?'

Dalinar shook his head. 'That question has churned in my head, over and over, like a boulder tumbling down a hill. Did we offend their honor? Was it some cultural misunderstanding?'

'A cultural misunderstanding would imply that they *have* a culture. Primitive brutes. Who knows why a horse kicks or an axehound bites? I shouldn't have asked.'

Dalinar didn't reply. He'd felt that same disdain, that same anger, in the months following Gavilar's assassination. He could understand Elhokar's desire to dismiss these strange, wildland parshmen as little more than animals.

But he'd *seen* them during those early days. Interacted with them. They were primitive, yes, but not brutes. Not stupid. *We never really understood them*, he thought. *I guess that's the crux of the problem.*

'Elhokar,' he said softly. 'It may be time to ask ourselves some difficult questions.'

'Such as?'

'Such as how long we will continue this war.'

Elhokar started. He turned, looking at Dalinar. 'We'll keep fighting until the Vengeance Pact is satisfied and my father is avenged!'

'Noble words,' Dalinar said. 'But we've been away from Alethkar for six years now. Maintaining two far-flung centers of government is not healthy for the kingdom.'

'Kings often go to war for extended periods, Uncle.'

'Rarely do they do it for so long,' Dalinar said, 'and rarely do they bring every Shardbearer and highprince in the kingdom with them. Our resources are strained, and word from home is that the Reshi border encroachments grow increasingly bold. We are still fragmented as a people, slow to trust one another, and the nature of this extended war – without a clear path to victory and with a focus on riches rather than capturing ground – is not helping at all.'

Elhokar sniffed, wind blowing at them atop the peaked rock. 'You say there's no clear path to victory? We've been winning! The Parshendi raids are coming less frequently, and aren't striking as far westward as they once did. We've killed thousands of them in battle.'

'Not enough,' Dalinar said. 'They still come in strength. The siege is straining us as much as, or more than, it is them.'

'Weren't *you* the one to suggest this tactic in the first place?'

'I was a different man, then, flush with grief and anger.'

'And you no longer feel those things?' Elhokar was incredulous. 'Uncle, I can't believe I'm hearing this! You aren't *seriously* suggesting that I abandon the war, are you? You'd have me slink home, like a scolded axehound?'

'I said they were difficult questions, Your Majesty,' Dalinar said, keeping his anger in check. It was taxing. 'But they *must* be considered.'

Elhokar breathed out, annoyed. 'It's true, what Sadeas and the others whisper. You're changing, Uncle. It has something to do with those episodes of yours, doesn't it?'

'They are unimportant, Elhokar. Listen to me! What are we willing to give, in order to get vengeance?'

'Anything.'

'And if that means everything your father worked for? Do we honor his memory by undermining his vision for Alethkar, all to get revenge in his name?'

The king hesitated.

'You pursue the Parshendi,' Dalinar said. 'That is laudable. But you can't let your passion for just retribution blind you to the needs of our kingdom. The Vengeance Pact has kept the highprinces channeled, but what will happen once we win? Will we shatter? I think we need to forge them together, to unite them. We fight this war as if we were ten different nations, fighting beside one another but not *with* one another.'

The king didn't respond immediately. The words, finally, seemed to be sinking in. He was a good man, and shared more with his father than others chose to admit.

He turned away from Dalinar, leaning against the railing. 'You think I'm a poor king, don't you, Uncle?'

'What? Of course not!'

'You always talk about what I *should* be doing, and where I am lacking.

311

Tell me truthfully, Uncle. When you look at me, do you wish you saw my father's face instead?'

'Of course I do,' Dalinar said.

Elhokar's expression darkened.

Dalinar laid a hand on his nephew's shoulder. 'I'd be a poor brother if I didn't wish that Gavilar had lived. I failed him – it was the greatest, most terrible failure of my life.' Elhokar turned to him, and Dalinar held his gaze, raising a finger. 'But just because I loved your father does *not* mean that I think you are a failure. Nor does it mean I do not love you in your own right. Alethkar itself could have collapsed upon Gavilar's death, but *you* organized and executed our counterattack. You are a fine king.'

The king nodded slowly. 'You've been listening to readings from that book again, haven't you?'

'I have.'

'You sound like him, you know,' Elhokar said, turning back to look eastward again. 'Near the end. When he began to act ... erratically.'

'Surely I'm not so bad as that.'

'Perhaps. But this is much like how he was. Talking about an end to war, fascinated by the Lost Radiants, insisting everyone follow the Codes ...'

Dalinar remembered those days – and his own arguments with Gavilar. *What honor can we find on a battlefield while our people starve?* the king had once asked him. *Is it honor when our lighteyes plot and scheme like eels in a bucket, slithering over one another and trying to bite each other's tails?*

Dalinar had reacted poorly to his words. Just as Elhokar was reacting to his words now. *Stormfather! I* am *starting to sound like him, aren't I?*

That was troubling, yet somehow encouraging at the same time. Either way, Dalinar realized something. Adolin was right. Elhokar – and the highprinces with him – would never respond to a suggestion that they retreat. Dalinar was approaching the conversation in the wrong way. *Almighty be blessed for sending me a son willing to speak his mind.*

'Perhaps you are right, Your Majesty,' Dalinar said. 'End the war? Leave a battlefield with an enemy still in control? That would shame us.'

Elhokar nodded in agreement. 'I'm glad you see sense.'

'But something *does* have to change. We need a better way to fight.'

'Sadeas has a better way already. I spoke of his bridges to you. They work so well, and he's captured so many gemhearts.'

'Gemhearts are meaningless,' Dalinar said. '*All* of this is meaningless if we don't find a way to get the vengeance we all want. You can't tell me you enjoy watching the highprinces squabble, practically ignoring our real purpose in being here.'

Elhokar fell silent, looking displeased.

Unite them. He remembered those words, booming in his head. 'Elhokar,' he said, an idea occurring to him. 'Do you remember what Sadeas and I spoke of to you when we first came here to war? The specialization of the highprinces?'

'Yes,' Elhokar said. In the distant past, each of the ten highprinces in Alethkar had been given a specific charge for the governing of the kingdom. One had been the ultimate law in regard to merchants, and his troops had patrolled the roadways of all ten princedoms. Another had administrated judges and magistrates.

Gavilar had been very taken by the idea. He claimed it was a clever device, meant to force the highprinces to work together. Once, this system had forced them to submit to one another's authority. Things hadn't been done that way in centuries, ever since the fragmenting of Alethkar into ten autonomous princedoms.

'Elhokar, what if you named me Highprince of War?' Dalinar asked.

Elhokar didn't laugh; that was a good sign. 'I thought you and Sadeas decided that the others would revolt if we tried something like that.'

'Perhaps I was wrong about that too.'

Elhokar appeared to consider it. Finally, the king shook his head. 'No. They barely accept my leadership. If I did something like this, they'd assassinate me.'

'I'd protect you.'

'Bah. You don't even take the *present* threats on my life seriously.'

Dalinar sighed. 'Your Majesty, I *do* take threats to your life seriously. My scribes and attendants are looking into the strap.'

'And what have they discovered?'

'Well, so far we have nothing conclusive. Nobody has taken credit for trying to kill you, even in rumor. Nobody saw anything suspicious. But Adolin is speaking with leatherworkers. Perhaps he'll bring something more substantial.'

'It *was* cut, Uncle.'

'We will see.'

'You don't believe me,' Elhokar said, face growing red. 'You should be trying to find out what the assassins' plan was, rather than pestering me with some arrogant quest to become overlord of the entire army!'

Dalinar gritted his teeth. 'I do this for you, Elhokar.'

Elhokar met his eyes for a moment, and his blue eyes flashed with suspicion again, as they had the week before.

Blood of my fathers! Dalinar thought. *He's getting worse.*

Elhokar's expression softened a moment later, and he seemed to relax. Whatever he'd seen in Dalinar's eyes had comforted him. 'I know you try for the best, Uncle,' Elhokar said. 'But you have to admit that you've been erratic lately. The way you react to storms, your infatuation with my father's last words—'

'I'm trying to understand him.'

'He grew weak at the end,' Elhokar said. 'Everyone knows it. I won't repeat his mistakes, and you should avoid them as well – rather than listening to a book that claims that lighteyes should be the slaves of the darkeyes.'

'That's *not* what it says,' Dalinar said. 'It has been misinterpreted. It's mostly just a collection of stories which teach that a leader should serve those he leads.'

'Bah. It was written by the Lost Radiants!'

'They didn't write it. It was their inspiration. Nohadon, an ordinary man, was its author.'

Elhokar glanced at him, raising an eyebrow. *See*, it seemed to say. *You defend it.* 'You are growing weak, Uncle. I will not exploit that weakness. But others will.'

'I am *not* getting weak.' Yet again, Dalinar forced himself to be calm. 'This conversation has gone off the path. The highprinces need a single leader to force them to work together. I vow that if you name me Highprince of War, I *will* see you protected.'

'As you saw my father protected?'

Dalinar's mouth snapped shut.

Elhokar turned away. 'I should not have said that. It was uncalled for.'

'No,' Dalinar said. 'No, it was one of the truest things you have said to me, Elhokar. Perhaps you are right to distrust my protection.'

Elhokar glanced at him, curious. 'Why do you react that way?'

'What way?'

'Once, if someone had said that to you, you'd have summoned your Blade and demanded a duel! Now you agree with them instead.'

'I—'

'My father started refusing duels, near the end.' Elhokar tapped on the railing. 'I see why you feel the need for a Highprince of War, and you may have a point. But the others very much like the present arrangement.'

'Because it is comfortable to them. If we are going to win, we will *need* to upset them.' Dalinar stepped forward. 'Elhokar, maybe it's been long enough. Six years ago, naming a Highprince of War might well have been a mistake. But now? We know one another better, and we've been working united against the Parshendi. Perhaps it is time to take the next step.'

'Perhaps,' the king said. 'You think they are ready? I'll let you prove it to me. If you can show me that they are willing to work with you, Uncle, then I'll consider naming you Highprince of War. Is that satisfactory?'

It was a solid compromise. 'Very well.'

'Good,' the king said, standing up. 'Then let us part for now. It is growing late, and I have yet to hear what Ruthar wishes of me.'

Dalinar nodded his farewell, walking back through the king's chambers, Renarin trailing him.

The more he considered, the more he felt that this was the right thing to do. Retreating would not work with the Alethi, particularly not with their current mind-set. But if he could shock them out of their complacency, force them to adopt a more aggressive strategy . . .

He was still lost in thought considering that as they left the king's palace and made their way down the ramps to where their horses waited. He climbed astride Gallant, nodding his thanks to the groom who had cared for the Ryshadium. The horse had recovered from his fall during the hunt, his leg solid and hale.

It was a short distance back to Dalinar's warcamp, and they rode in silence. *Which of the highprinces should I approach first?* Dalinar thought. *Sadeas?*

No. No, he and Sadeas were already seen working together too often. If the other highprinces began to smell a stronger alliance, it would drive them to turn against him. Best that he approach less powerful highprinces first and see if he could get them to work with him in some way. A joint plateau assault, perhaps?

He'd have to approach Sadeas eventually. He didn't relish the thought.

Things were always so much easier when the two of them could work at a safe distance from one another. He—

'Father,' Renarin said. He sounded dismayed.

Dalinar sat upright, looking around, hand going for his side sword even while he prepared to summon his Shardblade. Renarin pointed. Eastward. Stormward.

The horizon was growing dark.

'Was there supposed to be a highstorm today?' Dalinar asked, alarmed.

'Elthebar said it was unlikely,' Renarin said. 'But he's been wrong before.'

Everyone could be wrong about highstorms. They could be predicted, but it was never an exact science. Dalinar narrowed his eyes, heart thumping. Yes, he could sense the signs now. The dust picking up, the scents changing. It was evening, but there should still be more light left. Instead, it was rapidly growing darker and darker. The very air felt more frantic.

'Should we go to Aladar's camp?' Renarin said, pointing. They were nearest Highprince Aladar's warcamp, and perhaps only a quarter-hour ride from the rim of Dalinar's own.

Aladar's men would take him in. Nobody would forbid shelter to a highprince during a storm. But Dalinar shuddered, thinking of spending a highstorm trapped in an unfamiliar place, surrounded by another highprince's attendants. They would see him during an episode. Once that happened, the rumors would spread like arrows above a battlefield.

'We ride!' he called, kicking Gallant into motion. Renarin and the guardsmen fell in behind him, hooves a thunder to precurse the coming high-storm. Dalinar leaned low, tense. The grey sky grew clotted with dust and leaves blown ahead of the stormwall and the air grew dense with humid anticipation. The horizon burgeoned with thickening clouds. Dalinar and the others galloped past Aladar's perimeter guards, who bustled with activity, holding their coats or cloaks against the wind.

'Father?' Renarin called from behind. 'Are you—'

'We have time!' Dalinar shouted.

They eventually reached the jagged wall of the Kholin warcamp. Here, the remaining soldiers wore blue and white and saluted. Most had already retreated to their enclosures. He had to slow Gallant to get through the checkpoint. However, it would just be another short gallop to his quarters. He turned Gallant, preparing to go.

'Father!' Renarin said, pointing eastward.

The stormwall hung like a curtain in the air, speeding toward the camp. The massive sheet of rain was a silvery grey, the clouds above onyx black, lit from within by occasional flashes of lightning. The guards who had saluted him were hurrying to a nearby bunker.

'We can make it,' Dalinar said. 'We—'

'Father!' Renarin said, riding up beside him and catching his arm. 'I'm sorry.'

The wind whipped at them, and Dalinar gritted his teeth, looking at his son. Renarin's spectacled eyes were wide with concern.

Dalinar glanced at the stormwall again. It was only moments away.

He's right.

He handed Gallant's reins to an anxious soldier, who took the reins of Renarin's mount as well, and the two of them dismounted. The groom rushed away, towing the horses into a stone stable. Dalinar almost followed – there would be fewer people to watch him in a stable – but a nearby barrack had the door open, and those inside waved anxiously. That would be safer.

Resigned, Dalinar joined Renarin, dashing to the stone-walled barrack. The soldiers made room for them; there was a group of servants packed inside as well. In Dalinar's camp, no one was forced to weather the tempests in stormtents or flimsy wooden shacks, and nobody had to pay for protection inside stone structures.

The occupants seemed shocked to see their highprince and his son step in; several paled as the door thumped shut. Their only light was from a few garnets mounted on the walls. Someone coughed, and outside a scattering of windblown rock chips sprayed against the building. Dalinar tried to ignore the uncomfortable eyes around him. Wind howled outside. Perhaps nothing would happen. Perhaps this time—

The storm hit.

It began.

He holds the most frightening and terrible of all of the Shards. Ponder on that for a time, you old reptile, and tell me if your insistence on nonintervention holds firm. Because I assure you, Rayse will not be similarly inhibited.

Dalinar blinked. The stuffy, dimly lit barrack was gone. Instead, he stood in darkness. The air was thick with the scent of dried grain, and when he reached out with his left hand, he felt a wooden wall. He was in a barn of some sort.

The cool night was still and crisp; there was no sign of a storm. He felt carefully at his side. His side sword was gone, as was his uniform. Instead, he wore a homespun belted tunic and a pair of sandals. It was the type of clothing he'd seen depicted on ancient statues.

Stormwinds, where have you sent me this time? Each of the visions was different. This would be the twelfth one he'd seen. *Only twelve?* he thought. It seemed like so many more, but this had only begun happening to him a few months ago.

Something moved in the darkness. He flinched in surprise as something living pressed against him. He nearly struck it, but froze when he heard it whimper. He carefully lowered his arm, feeling the figure's back. Slight and small – a child. She was quivering.

'Father.' Her voice trembled. 'Father, what is happening?' As usual, he was being seen as someone of this place and time. The girl clutched him, obviously terrified. It was too dark to see the fearspren he suspected were climbing up through the ground.

Dalinar rested his hand on her back. 'Hush. It will be all right.' It seemed the right thing to say.

'Mother . . . '

'She will be fine.'

The girl huddled more closely against him in the black room. He remained still. Something felt wrong. The building creaked in the wind. It wasn't well built; the plank beneath Dalinar's hand was loose, and he was tempted to push it free so he could peek out. But the stillness, the terrified child . . . There was an oddly putrid scent in the air.

Something scratched, ever so softly, at the barn's far wall. Like a fingernail being drawn across a wooden tabletop.

The girl whimpered, and the scraping sound stopped. Dalinar held his breath, heart beating furiously. Instinctively, he held his hand out to summon his Shardblade, but nothing happened. It would never come during the visions.

The far wall of the building exploded inward.

Splintered wood flew through the darkness as a large shape burst in. Lit only by moonglow and starlight from outside, the black thing was bigger than an axehound. He couldn't make out details, but it seemed to have an unnatural wrongness to its form.

The girl screamed, and Dalinar cursed, grabbing her with one arm and rolling to the side as the black thing leaped for them. It nearly got the child, but Dalinar whipped her out of the creature's path. Breathless with terror, her scream cut off.

Dalinar spun, pushing the girl behind him. His side hit a stack of sacks filled with grain as he edged away. The barn fell silent. Salas's violet light shone in the sky outside, but the small moon wasn't bright enough to illuminate the barn's interior, and the creature had moved into a shadowed recess. He couldn't see much of it.

It seemed part of the shadows. Dalinar tensed, fists forward. It made a soft wheezing noise, eerie and faintly reminiscent of rhythmic whispering.

Breathing? Dalinar thought. *No. It's sniffing for us.*

The thing darted forward. Dalinar whipped a hand to the side and grabbed one of the grain sacks, pulling it in front of himself. The beast struck the sack, its teeth ripping into it, and Dalinar pulled, tearing the coarse fabric and flinging a fragrant cloud of dusty lavis grain into the air. Then he stepped to the side and kicked the beast as hard as he could.

The creature felt too soft under his foot, as if he'd kicked a waterskin. The blow knocked it to the ground, and it made a hissing sound. Dalinar flung the bag and its remaining contents upward, filling the air with more dried lavis and dust.

The beast scrambled to its feet and twisted around, smooth skin reflecting moonlight. It seemed disoriented. Whatever it was, it hunted by smell, and the dust in the air confused it. Dalinar grabbed the girl and threw her over his shoulder, then dashed past the confused creature, barreling through the hole in the broken wall.

He burst out into violet moonlight. He was in a small lait – a wide rift in the stone with good enough drainage to avoid flooding and a high stone outcropping to break the highstorms. In this case, the eastern rock formation was shaped like an enormous wave, creating shelter for a small village.

That explained the flimsiness of the barn. Lights flickered here and there across the hollow, indicating a settlement of several dozen homes. He was on the outskirts. There was a hogpen to Dalinar's right, distant homes to his left, and just ahead – nestled against the rock hill – was a midsized farmhouse. It was built in an archaic style, with crem bricks for walls.

His decision was easy. The thing had moved quickly, like a predator. Dalinar wouldn't outrun it, so he charged toward the farmhouse. The sound of the beast breaking out through the barn wall came from behind. Dalinar reached the home, but the front door was barred. Dalinar cursed loudly, pounding on it.

Claws scraped on stone from behind as the thing bounded toward them. Dalinar threw his shoulder against the door just as it opened.

He stumbled inside, dropping the girl to the floor as he found his balance. A middle-aged woman stood inside; violet moonlight revealed that she had thick curly hair and a wide-eyed terrified expression. She slammed the door closed behind him, then barred it.

'Praise the Heralds,' she exclaimed, scooping up the girl. 'You found her, Heb. Bless you.'

Dalinar sidled up to the glassless window, looking out. The shutter appeared to be broken loose, making the window impossible to latch closed.

He couldn't see the creature. He glanced back over his shoulder. The building's floor was simple stone and there was no second story. A fireless brick hearth was set on one side, with a rough-cast iron pot hanging above it. It all looked so primitive. What year was this?

It's just a vision, he thought. *A waking dream.*

Why did it feel so real, then?

He looked back out the window. It was silent outside. A twin row of rockbuds grew on the right side of the yard, probably curnips or some other kind of vegetable. Moonlight reflected off the smooth ground. Where was the creature? Had it—

Something slick-skinned and black leapt up from below and crashed against the window. It shattered the frame, and Dalinar cursed, falling as the thing landed on him. Something sharp slashed his face, cutting open his cheek, spilling blood across his skin.

The girl screamed again.

'Light!' Dalinar bellowed. 'Get me light!' He slammed his fist into the side of the creature's too-soft head, using his other arm to push back a clawed paw. His cheek burned with pain, and something raked his side, slashing his tunic and cutting his skin.

With a heave he threw the creature off him. It crashed against the wall, and he rolled to his feet, gasping. As the beast righted itself in the dark room, Dalinar scrambled away, old instincts kicking in, pain evaporating as the battle Thrill surged through him. He needed a weapon! A stool or a table leg. The room was so—

Light flickered on as the woman uncovered a lit pottery lamp. The primitive thing used oil, not Stormlight, but was more than enough to illuminate her terrified face and the girl clinging to her robelike dress. The room had a low table and a pair of stools, but his eyes were drawn to the small hearth.

There, gleaming like one of the Honorblades of ancient lore, was a simple iron fire poker. It leaned against the stone hearth, tip white with ash. Dalinar lunged forward, snatching it in one hand, twirling it to feel out its balance. He had been trained in classical Windstance, but he fell into Smokestance instead, as it was better with an imperfect weapon. One foot forward, one foot behind, sword – or, in this case, poker – held forward with the tip toward his opponent's heart.

Only years of training allowed him to maintain his stance as he saw what he was facing. The creature's smooth, dark-as-midnight skin reflected light like a pool of tar. It had no visible eyes and its black, knifelike teeth bristled in a head set on a sinuous, boneless neck. The six legs were slender and bent at the sides, appearing far too thin to bear the weight of the fluid, inklike body.

This isn't a vision, Dalinar thought. *It's a nightmare.*

The creature raised its head, clicking teeth together, and made a hissing sound. Tasting the air.

'Sweet wisdom of Battar,' the woman breathed, holding her child close. Her hands shook as she held up the lamp, as if to use it as a weapon.

A scraping came from outside, and was followed by another set of spindly legs slinking over the lip of the broken window. This new beast climbed into the room, joining its companion, which crouched anxiously, sniffing at Dalinar. It seemed wary, as if it could sense that it faced an armed – or at least determined – opponent.

Dalinar cursed himself for a fool, raising one hand to his side to stanch the blood. He knew, logically, that he was really back in the barrack with Renarin. This was all happening in his mind; there was no need for him to fight.

But every instinct, every shred of honor he had, drove him to step to the side, placing himself between the woman and the beasts. Vision, memory, or delusion, he could *not* stand aside.

'Heb,' the woman said, her voice nervous. Who did she see him as? Her husband? A farmhand? 'Don't be a fool! You don't know how—'

The beasts attacked. Dalinar leapt forward – remaining in motion was the essence of Smokestance – and spun between the creatures, striking to the side with his poker. He hit the one on the left, ripping a gash in its too-smooth skin.

The wound bled smoke.

Moving behind the creatures, Dalinar swung again, sweeping low at the feet of the unwounded beast, knocking it off balance. With the follow-through, he slammed the side of the poker into the face of the wounded beast as it turned and snapped at him.

The old Thrill, the sense of battle, consumed him. It did not enrage him, as it did some men, but everything seemed to become clearer, crisper.

His muscles moved easily; he breathed more deeply. He came *alive*.

He leaped backward as the creatures pressed at him. With a kick, he knocked over the table, tumbling it at one of the beasts. He drove the poker at the open maw of the other. As he had hoped, the inside of its mouth was sensitive. The creature let out a pained hiss and scrambled back.

Dalinar moved to the overturned table and kicked off one of the legs. He scooped it up, falling into Smokestance's sword-and-knife form. He used the wooden leg to fend off one creature while he thrust three times at the face of the other, ripping a gash in its cheek that bled smoke; it came out as a hiss.

There were distant screams outside. *Blood of my fathers*, he thought. *These aren't the only two.* He needed to be done, and quickly. If the fight dragged on, they'd wear him down faster than he wore them down. Who even knew if beasts like this got tired?

Bellowing, he jumped forward. Sweat streamed from his forehead, and the room seemed to grow just faintly darker. Or, no, more focused. Just him and the beasts. The only wind was that of his weapons spinning, the only sound that of his feet hitting the floor, the only vibration that of his heart thumping.

His sudden whirlwind of blows shocked the creatures. He smashed the table leg against one, forcing it back, then threw himself at the other one, earning a rake of the claws against his arm as he rammed the poker into the beast's chest. The skin resisted at first, but then broke, his poker moving through easily after that.

A powerful jet of smoke burst out around Dalinar's hand. He pulled his arm free, and the creature stumbled back, legs growing thinner, body deflating like a leaking wineskin.

He knew he'd exposed himself in attacking. There was nothing to do but throw his arm up as the other beast leapt on him, slashing his forehead and his arm, biting his shoulder. Dalinar screamed, slamming the table leg again and again at the beast's head. He tried forcing the creature back, but it was terribly strong.

So Dalinar let himself slip to the ground and kicked upward, tossing the beast over his head. The fangs ripped free of Dalinar's shoulder with a spray of blood. The beast hit the floor in a mess of black legs.

Dizzy, Dalinar forced himself to his feet and fell into his stance. *Always keep the stance.* The creature got to its feet at about the same time, and Dalinar ignored the pain, ignored the blood, letting the Thrill give him focus. He leveled the poker. The table leg had fallen from his blood-slick fingers.

The beast crouched, then charged. Dalinar let the fluid nature of Smoke-stance direct him, stepping to the side and smashing the poker into the beast's legs. It tripped as Dalinar turned around, wielding his poker with both hands and *slamming* it directly down into the creature's back.

The powerful blow broke the skin, passed through the creature's body, and hit the stone floor. The creature struggled, legs working ineffectively, as smoke hissed out the holes in its back and stomach. Dalinar stepped away, wiping blood from his forehead, leaving the weapon to fall to the side and clang to the ground, still impaling the beast.

'*Three Gods*, Heb,' the woman whispered.

He turned to find her looking completely shocked as she stared at the deflating carcasses. 'I should have helped,' she mumbled, 'should have grabbed something to hit them. But you were so fast. It – it was just a few heartbeats. Where— How—?' She focused on him. 'I've never seen anything like it, Heb. You fought like a ... like one of the Radiants themselves. Where did you learn that?'

Dalinar didn't answer. He pulled off his shirt, grimacing as the pain of his wounds returned. Only the shoulder was immediately dangerous, but it was bad; his left arm was growing numb. He ripped the shirt in half, tying one portion around his gashed right forearm, then wadded the rest and pressed it against his shoulder. He walked over and pulled the poker free of the deflated body, which now resembled a black silk sack. Then he moved to the window. The other homes showed signs of being attacked, fires burning, faint screams hanging on the wind.

'We need to get someplace safe,' he said. 'Is there a cellar nearby?'

'A what?'

'Cave in the rock, man-made or natural.'

'No caves,' the woman said, joining him at the window. 'How would men make a hole in the *rock*?'

With a Shardblade or a Soulcaster. Or even with basic mining – though that could be difficult, as the crem would seal up caverns and highstorm rains made for an extremely potent risk of flooding. Dalinar looked out the window again. Dark shapes moved in the moonlight; some were coming in their direction.

He wavered, dizzy. Blood loss. Gritting his teeth, he steadied himself against the frame of the window. How long was this vision going to last? 'We need a river. Something to wash away the trail of our scent. Is there one nearby?'

The woman nodded, growing pale faced as she noticed the dark forms in the night.

'Get the girl, woman.'

' "The girl"? Seeli, our *daughter*. And since when have you called me woman? Is Taffa so hard to say? Stormwinds, Heb, what has gotten into you?'

He shook his head, moving to the door and throwing it open, still carrying the poker. 'Bring the lamp. The light won't give us away; I don't think they can see.'

The woman obeyed, hurrying to collect Seeli – she looked to be about six or seven – then followed Dalinar out, the clay lamp's fragile flame quivering in the night. It looked a little like a slipper.

'The river?' Dalinar asked.

'You know where—'

'I hit my head, Taffa,' Dalinar said. 'I'm dizzy. It's hard to think.'

The woman looked worried at that, but seemed to accept this answer. She pointed away from the village.

'Let's go,' he said, moving out into the darkness. 'Are attacks by these beasts common?'

'During Desolations, perhaps, but not in my life! Stormwinds, Heb. We need to get you to—'

'No,' he said. 'We keep moving.'

They continued along a path, which ran up toward the back side of the wave formation. Dalinar kept glancing back at the village. How many people were dying below, murdered by those beasts from Damnation? Where were the landlord's soldiers?

Perhaps this village was too remote, too far from a citylord's direct protection. Or perhaps things didn't work that way in this era, this place. *I'll see the woman and child to the river, then I'll return to organize a resistance. If anyone is left.*

The thought seemed laughable. He had to use the poker to keep himself upright. How was *he* going to organize a resistance?

He slipped on a steep portion of the trail, and Taffa set down the lamp, grabbing his arm, concerned. The landscape was rough with boulders and rockbuds, their vines and leaves extended in the cool, wet night. Those rustled in the wind. Dalinar righted himself, then nodded to the woman, gesturing for her to continue.

A faint scraping sounded in the night; Dalinar turned, tense.

'Heb?' the woman asked, sounding afraid.

'Hold up the light.'

She raised the lamp, illuminating the hillside in flickering yellow. A good dozen midnight patches, skins too smooth, were creeping over rockbuds and boulders. Even their teeth and claws were black.

Seeli whimpered, pulling close to her mother.

'Run,' Dalinar said softly, raising his poker.

'Heb, they're—'

'Run!' he bellowed.

'They're in front of us too!'

He spun, picking out the dark patches ahead. He cursed, looking around. 'There,' he said, pointing to a nearby rock formation. It was tall and flat. He shoved Taffa forward, and she towed Seeli, their single-piece, blue dresses rippling in the wind.

They ran more quickly than he could in his state, and Taffa reached the rock wall first. She looked up, as if to climb to the top. It was too steep for that; Dalinar just wanted something solid to put at his back. He stepped onto a flat, open section of rock before the formation and raised his weapon. Black beasts crawled carefully over the stones. Could he distract them, somehow, and let the other two flee? He felt so dizzy.

What I'd give for my Shardplate . . .

Seeli whimpered. Her mother tried to comfort her, but the woman's voice was unnerved. She knew. Knew those bundles of blackness, like living night, would rip them and tear them. What was that word she'd used? Desolation. The book spoke of them. The Desolations had happened during the near-mythical shadowdays, before real history began. Before mankind had defeated the Voidbringers and taken the war to heaven.

The Voidbringers. Was that what these things were? Myths. Myths come to life to kill him.

Several of the creatures lunged forward, and he felt the Thrill surge within him again, strengthening him as he swung. They jumped back, cautious, testing for weakness. Others sniffed the air, pacing. They wanted to get at the woman and child.

Dalinar jumped at them, forcing them away, uncertain where he found the strength. One got close, and he swung at it, falling into Windstance, as it was most familiar. The sweeping strikes, the grace.

He struck at the beast, scoring it on its flank, but two others jumped at him from the side. Claws raked his back, and the weight threw him to the stones. He cursed, rolling, punching a creature and tossing it back. Another bit his wrist, causing him to drop the poker in a flash of pain. He bellowed and slammed his fist into the creature's jaw and it opened reflexively, freeing his hand.

The monsters pressed forward. Somehow he got to his feet and stumbled back against the rock wall. The woman threw the lamp at a creature that got too close, spraying oil across the stones and setting it alight. The fire didn't seem to bother the creatures.

The move exposed Seeli, as Taffa fell off balance in the throw. A monster knocked her down, and others scrambled for the child – but Dalinar leaped for her, wrapping his arms around her, huddling down and turning his back on the monsters. One leaped on his back. Claws sliced his skin.

Seeli whimpered in terror. Taffa was screaming as the monsters overwhelmed her.

'Why are you showing me this!' Dalinar bellowed into the night. 'Why must I live *this* vision? Curse you!' Claws raked his back; he clutched Seeli, back arching in pain. He cast his eyes upward, toward the sky.

And there, he saw a brilliant blue light falling through the air.

It was like a star rock, dropping at an incredible speed. Dalinar cried out as the light hit the ground a short distance away, cracking the stone, spraying rock chips in the air. The ground shook. The beasts froze.

Dalinar turned numbly to the side, then he watched in amazement as the light stood up, limbs unfolding. It wasn't a star at all. It was a man – a man in glowing blue Shardplate, bearing a Shardblade, trails of Storm-light rising from his body.

The creatures hissed furiously, suddenly throwing themselves at the figure, ignoring Dalinar and the other two. The Shardbearer raised his Blade and struck forward with skill, stepping into the attacks.

Dalinar lay stunned. This was unlike any Shardbearer he had ever seen. The Plate glowed with an even blue light, and glyphs – some familiar, others not – were etched into the metal. They trailed blue vapor.

Moving fluidly, Plate clinking, the man struck at the beasts. He effortlessly sheared a monster in half, flinging pieces into the night that trailed black smoke.

Dalinar pulled himself to Taffa. She was alive, though her side was torn and flayed. Seeli tugged at her, weeping. *Need to … do something …* Dalinar thought dully.

'Be at peace,' a voice said.

Dalinar lurched, turning to see a woman in delicate Shardplate kneeling beside him, holding something bright. It was a topaz entwined with a heliodor, both set into a fine metal framework, each stone as big as a man's hand. The woman had light tan eyes that almost seemed to glow in the night, and she wore no helm. Her hair was pulled back into a bun. She raised a hand and touched his forehead.

Ice washed across him. Suddenly, his pain was gone.

The woman reached out and touched Taffa. The flesh on her side regrew in an eyeblink; the torn muscle remained where it was, but other flesh just *grew* where the chunks had been torn out. The skin knitted up over it without flaw, and the female Shardbearer wiped away the blood and torn flesh with a white cloth.

Taffa looked up, awed. 'You came,' she whispered. 'Bless the Almighty.'

The female Shardbearer stood; her armor glowed with an even amber light. She smiled and turned to the side, a Shardblade forming from mist into her hand as she rushed to aid her companion.

A woman Shardbearer, Dalinar thought. He'd never seen such a thing.

He stood up, hesitant. He felt strong and healthy, as if he'd just awakened from a good night's sleep. He glanced down at his arm, pulling off his makeshift bandage. He had to wipe free blood and some torn skin, but underneath, the skin was perfectly healed. He took a few deep breaths. Then shrugged, picked up his poker, and joined the fight.

'Heb?' Taffa called from behind. 'Are you insane?'

He didn't respond. He couldn't very well just sit there while two strangers fought to protect him. There were dozens of the black creatures. As he watched, one landed a scraping hit on the Shardbearer in blue, and the claw scored the Shardplate, digging into and cracking it. The danger to these Shardbearers was real.

The female Shardbearer turned to Dalinar. She had her helm on now. When had she put it on? She seemed shocked as Dalinar threw himself at one of the black beasts, slashing it with his poker. He fell into Smokestance and fended against its counterattack. The female Shardbearer turned to her companion, then the two of them fell into stances forming a triangle with Dalinar, his position closest to the rock formation.

With two Shardbearers alongside him, the fighting went remarkably better than it had back at the house. He only managed to dispatch a single beast – they were quick and strong, and he fought defensively, trying to distract and keep pressure off the Shardbearers. The creatures did not retreat. They continued to attack until the last one was sliced in two by the female Shardbearer.

Dalinar stopped, puffing, lowering his poker. Other lights had fallen – and still were falling – from the sky in the direction of the village; presumably, some of these strange Shardbearers had landed there as well.

'Well,' a strong voice said, 'I must say that I've never before had the pleasure of fighting alongside a comrade with such ... unconventional means.'

Dalinar turned to find the male Shardbearer regarding him. Where had the man's helm gone? The Shardbearer stood with his Blade resting on his armored shoulder, and he inspected Dalinar with eyes of such bright blue, they were almost white. Were those eyes actually *glowing*, leaking Stormlight? His skin was dark brown, like a Makabaki, and he had short black curly hair. His armor no longer glowed, though one large symbol – emblazoned across the front of the breastplate – still gave off a faint blue light.

Dalinar recognized the symbol, the particular pattern of the stylized double eye, eight spheres connected with two at the center. It had been the symbol of the Lost Radiants, back when they'd been called the Knights Radiant.

The female Shardbearer watched the village.

'Who trained you in the sword?' the male knight asked Dalinar.

Dalinar met the eyes of the knight. He had no idea how to respond.

'This is my husband Heb, good knight,' Taffa said, rushing forward, leading her daughter by the hand. 'He's never seen a sword, far as I know.'

'Your stances are unfamiliar to me,' the knight said. 'But they were practiced and precise. This level of skill comes only with years of training. I have rarely seen a man – knight or soldier – fight as well as you did.'

Dalinar remained silent.

'No words for me, I see,' the knight said. 'Very well. But should you wish to put that mysterious training of yours to use, come to Urithiru.'

'Urithiru?' Dalinar said. He'd heard that name somewhere.

'Yes,' the knight said. 'I cannot promise you a position in one of the orders – that decision is not mine – but if your skill with the sword is similar to your skill with hearth-tending implements, then I am confident you will find a place with us.' He turned eastward, toward the village. 'Spread the word. Signs like this one are not without import. A Desolation is coming.' He turned to his companion. 'I will go. Guard these three and lead them to the village. We cannot leave them alone in the dangers of this night.'

His companion nodded. The blue knight's armor began to glow faintly, then he launched into the air, as if falling straight up. Dalinar stumbled back, shocked, watching the glowing blue figure rise, then arc downward toward the village.

'Come,' the woman said, voice ringing inside her helm. She began to hurry down the incline.

'Wait,' Dalinar said, hastening after her, Taffa scooping up her daughter and following. Behind them, the oil was burning out.

The female knight slowed to allow Dalinar and Taffa to keep pace with her.

'I must know,' Dalinar said, feeling foolish. 'What year is it?'

The knight turned to him. Her helm was gone. He blinked; when had that happened? Unlike her companion, she had light skin – not pale like someone from Shinovar, but a natural light tan, like an Alethi. 'It is Eighth Epoch, three thirty-seven.'

Eighth Epoch? Dalinar thought. *What does that mean?* This vision had been different from the others. They had been more brief, for one thing. And the voice that spoke to him. Where was it?

'Where am I?' Dalinar asked the knight. 'What kingdom?'

The knight frowned. 'Are you not healed?'

'I am well. I just ... I need to know. Which kingdom am I in?'

'This is Natanatan.'

Dalinar released an inhaled breath. *Natanatan*. The Shattered Plains lay in the land that had once been Natanatan. The kingdom had fallen centuries ago.

'And you fight for Natanatan's king?' he asked.

She laughed. 'The Knights Radiant fight for no king and for all of them.'

'Then where do you live?'

'Urithiru is where our orders are centered, but we live in cities all across Alethela.'

Dalinar froze in place. Alethela. It was the historical name for the place that had become Alethkar. 'You cross kingdom borders to fight?'

'Heb,' Taffa said. She seemed very concerned. 'You were the one who promised me that the Radiants would come protect us, just before you went out searching for Seeli. Is your mind still muddled? Lady knight, could you heal him again?'

'I should save Regrowth for others who might be wounded,' the woman said, glancing at the village. The fighting seemed to be dying down.

'I'm fine,' Dalinar said. 'Alethk ... Alethela. You live there?'

'It is our duty and our privilege,' the woman said, 'to stay vigilant for the Desolation. One kingdom to study the arts of war so that the others might have peace. We die so that you may live. It has ever been our place.'

Dalinar stood still, sorting through that.

'All who can fight are needed,' the woman said. 'And all who have a *desire* to fight should be compelled to come to Alethela. Fighting, even this fighting against the Ten Deaths, changes a person. We can teach you so that it will not destroy you. Come to us.'

Dalinar found himself nodding.

'Every pasture needs three things,' the woman said, voice changing, as if she were quoting from memory. 'Flocks to grow, herdsmen to tend, and watchers at the rim. We of Alethela are those watchers – the warriors who protect and fight. We maintain the terrible arts of killing, then pass them on to others when the Desolation comes.'

'The Desolation,' he said. 'That means the Voidbringers, right? Those are what we fought this night?'

The knight sniffed dismissively. 'Voidbringers? These? No, this was Midnight Essence, though who released it is still a mystery.' She looked to the side, expression growing distant. 'Harkaylain says the Desolation is close, and he is not often wrong. He—'

A sudden screaming sounded in the night. The knight cursed, looking toward it. 'Wait here. Call out if the Essence returns. I will hear.' She dashed off into the darkness.

Dalinar raised a hand, torn between following and staying to watch over Taffa and her daughter. *Stormfather!* he thought, realizing they'd been left in darkness, now that the knight's glowing armor was gone.

He turned back to Taffa. She stood on the trail beside him, eyes looking oddly distracted.

'Taffa?' he asked.

'I miss these times,' Taffa said.

Dalinar jumped. That voice wasn't hers. It was a man's voice, deep and powerful. It was the voice that spoke to him during every vision.

'Who are you?' Dalinar asked.

'They were one, once,' Taffa – or whatever it was – said. 'The orders. Men. Not without problems or strife, of course. But focused.'

Dalinar felt a chill. Something about that voice always seemed faintly familiar to him. It had even in the first vision. 'Please. You have to tell me what this is, why you are showing me these things. Who are you? Some servant of the Almighty?'

'I wish I could help you,' Taffa said, looking at Dalinar but ignoring his questions. 'You have to unite them.'

'As you've said before! But I need help. The things the knight said about Alethkar. Are they true? Can we really be that way again?'

'To speak of what might be is forbidden,' the voice said. 'To speak of what was depends on perspective. But I will try to help.'

'Then give me more than vague answers!'

Taffa regarded him, somber. Somehow, by starlight alone, he could make out her brown eyes. There was something deep, something daunting, hiding behind them.

'At least tell me this,' Dalinar said, grasping for a specific question to ask. 'I have trusted Highprince Sadeas, but my son – Adolin – thinks I am a fool to do so. Should I continue to trust Sadeas?'

'Yes,' the being said. 'This is important. Do not let strife consume you. Be strong. Act with honor, and honor will aid you.'

Finally, Dalinar thought. *Something concrete.*

He heard voices. The dark landscape around Dalinar grew vague. 'No!' He reached for the woman. 'Don't send me back yet. What should I do about Elhokar, and the war?'

'I will give you what I can.' The voice was growing indistinct. 'I am sorry for not giving more.'

'What kind of answer is that?' Dalinar bellowed. He shook himself, struggling. Hands held him. Where had they come from? He cursed, batting them away, twisting, trying to break free.

Then he froze. He was in the barrack at the Shattered Plains, soft rain rattling on the roof. The bulk of the storm had passed. A group of soldiers held Dalinar down while Renarin watched with concern.

Dalinar grew still, mouth open. He had been yelling. The soldiers looked uncomfortable, glancing at each other, not meeting his gaze. If it was like before, he'd have acted out his role in the vision, speaking in gibberish, flailing around.

'My mind is clear now,' Dalinar said. 'It's all right. You can all let me go.'

Renarin nodded to the others, and they hesitantly released him. Renarin tried to make some stuttering excuses, telling them that his father was simply eager for combat. It didn't sound very convincing.

Dalinar retreated to the back of the barrack, sitting down on the floor between two rolled up bedrolls, just breathing in and out and thinking. He trusted the visions, yet his life in the warcamps had been difficult enough lately without people presuming him mad.

Act with honor, and honor will aid you.

The vision had told him to trust Sadeas. But he'd never be able to explain that to Adolin – who not only hated Sadeas, but thought the visions were delusions from Dalinar's mind. The only thing to do was keep going as he had.

And find a way, somehow, to get the highprinces to work together.

20

SCARLET

SEVEN YEARS AGO

I can save her,' Kal said, pulling off his shirt.

The child was only five. She'd fallen far.

'I can save her.' He was mumbling. A crowd had gathered. It had been two months since Brightlord Wistiow's death; they still didn't have a replacement citylord. He had barely seen Laral at all in that time.

Kal was only thirteen, but he'd been trained well. The first danger was blood loss; the child's leg had broken, a compound fracture, and it was spurting red where bone had split the skin. Kal found his hands trembling as he pressed his fingers against the wound. The broken bone was slick, even the jagged end, wetted by blood. Which arteries had been torn?

'What are you doing to my daughter?' Thick-shouldered Harl pushed through the onlookers. 'You cremling, you storm's leavings! Don't touch Miasal! Don't—'

Harl broke off as several of the other men pulled him back. They knew that Kal – who had been passing by chance – was the girl's best hope. Alim had already been sent to fetch Kal's father.

'I can save her,' Kal said. Her face was pale, and she didn't move. That head wound, maybe it . . .

Can't think about that. One of the lower leg arteries was severed. He used his shirt to tie a tourniquet to stop the blood, but it kept slipping. Fingers still pressed against the cut, he called, 'Fire! I need fire! Hurry! And someone give me your shirt!'

Several men rushed off as Kal elevated the leg. One of the men hurriedly handed over his shirt. Kal knew where to pinch to cut off the artery; the tourniquet slipped, but his fingers did not. He held that artery closed, pressing the shirt on the rest of the wound until Valama came back with a candle's flame.

They'd already begun heating a knife. Good. Kal took the knife, burning it into the wound, releasing the sharply pungent smell of scorched flesh. A cool wind blew across them, carrying it away.

Kal's hands stopped shaking. He *knew* what to do. He moved with skill that surprised even him, perfectly cauterizing, as his training took control. He still needed to tie off the artery – a cauterization might not hold on an artery this large – but the two together should work.

When he was done, the bleeding had stopped. He sat back, smiling. And then he noticed that Miasal's head wound wasn't bleeding either. Her chest wasn't moving.

'No!' Harl fell to his knees. 'No! Do something!'

'I . . .' Kal said. He'd stopped the bleeding. He'd . . .

He'd lost her.

He didn't know what to say, how to respond. A deep, terrible, sickness washed over him. Harl shoved him aside, wailing, Kal fell backward. He found himself shaking again as Harl clutched the corpse.

Around them, the crowd was silent.

An hour later, Kal sat on the steps in front of the surgery room, crying. It was a soft thing, his grief. A shake here. A few persistent tears, slipping down his cheeks.

He sat with knees up, arms wrapped around his legs, trying to figure out how to stop hurting. Was there a salve to take away this pain? A bandage to stop the flow from his eyes? He should have been able to *save* her.

Footsteps approached, and a shadow fell on him. Lirin knelt down beside him. 'I inspected your work, son. You did well. I'm proud.'

'I failed,' Kal whispered. His clothing was stained red. Before he'd washed the blood free of his hands, it had been scarlet. But soaked into his clothing, it was a duller reddish brown.

'I've known men who practiced for hours and hours, yet still froze when confronted by a wounded person. It's harder when it takes you by surprise. *You* didn't freeze, you went to her, administered help. And you did it well.'

'I don't want to be a surgeon,' Kal said. 'I'm terrible at it.'

Lirin sighed, rounding the steps, sitting down beside his son. 'Kal, this happens. It's unfortunate, but you couldn't have done more. That little body lost blood too quickly.'

Kal didn't reply.

'You have to learn when to care, son,' Lirin said softly. 'And when to let go. You'll see. I had similar problems when I was younger. You'll grow calluses.'

And this is a good thing? Kal thought, another tear trickling down his cheek. *You have to learn when to care . . . and when to let go. . . .*

In the distance, Harl continued to wail.

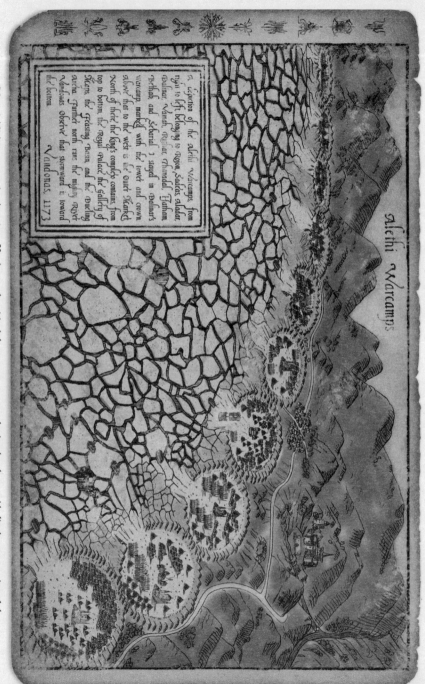

A description of the Alethi Warcamps, from right to left belonging to Nahan, Sadeas, Aladar, Dalinar, Vamah, Roion, Thanadal, Hatham, Bethab and Sebarial 3 stayed in Dalinar's warcamp, marked with the tower and crown above that to the west is the court Market. North of there the King's complex contains from top to bottom, the Royal palace, the Gallery of Maps, the Feasting Basin, and the Dueling arena. Further north runs the mighty River Vandonas. Observe that stormward is toward the bottom.

Vandonas, 1173

Alethi Warcamps

Map of Alethi warcamps by the painter Vandonas, who visited the warcamps once and painted perhaps an idealized representation of them.

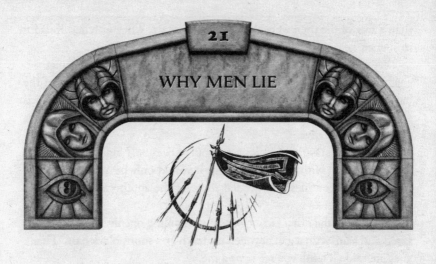

21

WHY MEN LIE

One need only look at the aftermath of his brief visit to Sel to see proof of what I say.

Kaladin didn't want to open his eyes. If he opened his eyes, he'd be awake. And if he were awake, that pain – the burning in his side, the aching of his legs, the dull throb in his arms and shoulders – wouldn't be just a nightmare. It would be real. And it would be his.

He stifled a groan, rolling onto his side. It all ached. Every length of muscle, every inch of skin. His head pounded. It seemed that his very *bones* were sore. He wanted to lie motionless and throbbing until Gaz was forced to come and tow him out by his ankles. That would be easy. Didn't he deserve to do what was easy, for once?

But he couldn't. To stop moving, to give up, would be the same as dying, and he could not let that happen. He'd made his decision already. He would help the bridgemen.

Curse you, Hav, he thought. *You can boot me out of my bunk even now.* Kaladin threw off his blanket, forcing himself to stand. The door to the barrack was cracked open to let in fresh air.

He felt worse standing up, but the life of a bridgeman wouldn't wait for him to recover. You either kept up or you got crushed. Kaladin steadied himself, hand against the unnaturally smooth, Soulcast rock of the barrack wall. Then he took a deep breath and crossed the room. Oddly, more than a few of the men were awake and sitting up. They watched Kaladin in silence.

They were waiting, Kaladin realized. *They wanted to see if I'd get up.*

He found the three wounded where he'd left them at the front of the barrack. He held his breath as he checked on Leyten. Amazingly, he was still alive. His breathing was still shallow, his pulse weak and his wounds dire, but he was alive.

He wouldn't stay that way long without antiseptic. None of the wounds looked infected with rotspren yet, but it would only be a matter of time in these dirty confines. He needed some of the apothecary's salves. But how?

He checked the other two. Hobber was smiling openly. He was round-faced and lean, with a gap between his teeth and short, black hair. 'Thank you,' he said. 'Thank you for saving me.'

Kaladin grunted, inspecting the man's leg. 'You'll be fine, but you won't be able to walk for a few weeks. I'll bring food from the mess hall for you.'

'Thank you,' Hobber whispered, taking Kaladin's hand, clutching it. He actually seemed to be tearing up.

That smile forced back the gloom, made the aches and soreness fade. Kaladin's father had described that kind of smile. Those smiles weren't why Lirin had become a surgeon, but they *were* why he'd remained one.

'Rest,' Kaladin said, 'and keep that wound clean. We don't want to attract any rotspren. Let me know if you see any. They are small and red, like tiny insects.'

Hobber nodded eagerly and Kaladin moved to Dabbid. The youthful bridgeman looked just as he had the day before, staring forward, eyes unfocused.

'He was sitting like that when I fell asleep too, sir,' Hobber said. 'It's like he hasn't moved all night. Gives me the chills, it does.'

Kaladin snapped his fingers in front of Dabbid's eyes. The man jumped at the sound, focusing on the fingers, following them as Kaladin moved his hand.

'He's been hit in the head, I think,' Hobber said.

'No,' Kaladin said. 'It's battle shock. It will wear off.' *I hope.*

'If you say so, sir,' Hobber said, scratching at the side of his head.

Kaladin stood and pushed the door open all the way, lighting the room.

It was a clear day, the sun just barely over the horizon. Already, sounds drifted from the warcamp, a blacksmith working early, hammer on metal. Chulls trumpeting in the stables. The air was cool, chilly, clinging to the vestiges of night. It smelled clean and fresh. Spring weather.

You got up, Kaladin told himself. *Might as well get on with it*. He forced himself to go out and do his stretches, body complaining at each motion. Then he checked his own wound. It wasn't too bad, though infection could make it worse.

Stormwinds take that apothecary! he thought, fetching a ladle full of water from the bridgeman barrel, using it to wash his wound.

He immediately regretted the bitter thought against the elderly apothecary. What was the man to do? Give Kaladin the antiseptic for free? It was Highprince Sadeas he should be cursing. Sadeas was responsible for the wound, and was also the one who had forbidden the surgeon's hall to give supplies to bridgemen, slaves, and servants of the lesser nahns.

By the time he finished stretching, a handful of bridgemen had risen to get something to drink. They stood around the barrel, regarding Kaladin.

There was only one thing to do. Setting his jaw, Kaladin crossed the lumber grounds and located the plank he'd carried the day before. The carpenters hadn't yet added it to their bridge, so Kaladin picked it up and walked back to the barracks. Then he began practicing the same way he had yesterday.

He couldn't go as fast. In fact, much of the time, he could only walk. But as he worked, his aches soothed. His headache faded. His feet and shoulders still hurt, and he had a deep, latent exhaustion. But he didn't embarrass himself by falling over.

In his practice, he passed the other bridgeman barracks. The men in front of them were barely distinguishable from those in Bridge Four. The same dark, sweat-stained leather vests over bare chests or loosely tied shirts. There was the occasional foreigner, Thaylens or Vedens most often. But they were unified in their scraggly appearances, unshaven faces, and haunted eyes. Several groups watched Kaladin with outright hostility. Were they worried that his practice would encourage their own bridge-leaders to work them?

He had hoped that some members of Bridge Four might join his workout. They'd obeyed him during the battle, after all, even going so far as to help him with the wounded. His hope was in vain. While some bridge-men watched, others ignored him. None took part.

Eventually, Syl flitted down and landed on the end of his plank, riding like a queen on her palanquin. 'They're talking about you,' she said as he passed the Bridge Four barrack again.

'Not surprising,' Kaladin said between puffs.

'Some think you've gone mad,' she said. 'Like that man who just sits and stares at the floor. They say the battle stress broke your mind.'

'Maybe they're right. I didn't consider that.'

'What *is* madness?' she asked, sitting with one leg up against her chest, vaporous skirt flickering around her calves and vanishing into mist.

'It's when men don't think right,' Kaladin said, glad for the conversation to distract him.

'Men *never* seem to think right.'

'Madness is worse than normal,' Kaladin said with a smile. 'It really just depends on the people around you. How different are you from them? The person that stands out is mad, I guess.'

'So you all just ... vote on it?' she asked, screwing up her face.

'Well, not so actively. But it's the right idea.'

She sat thoughtfully for a time longer. 'Kaladin,' she finally said. 'Why do men lie? I can see what lies are, but I don't know *why* people do it.'

'Lots of reasons,' Kaladin said, wiping the sweat from his brow with his free hand, then using it to steady the plank.

'Is it madness?'

'I don't know if I'd say that. Everyone does it.'

'So maybe you're all a little mad.'

He chuckled. 'Yes, perhaps.'

'But if everyone does it,' she said, leaning her head on her knee, 'then the one who *doesn't* would be the one who is mad, right? Isn't that what you said earlier?'

'Well, I guess. But I don't think there's a person out there who hasn't ever lied.'

'Dalinar.'

'Who?'

'The king's uncle,' Syl said. 'Everyone says he never lies. Your bridge-men even talk about it sometimes.'

That's right. The Blackthorn. Kaladin had heard of him, even in his youth. 'He's a lighteyes. That means he lies.'

'But—'

'They're all the same, Syl. The more noble they look, the more corrupt they are inside. It's all an act.' He fell quiet, surprised at the vehemence of his bitterness. *Storm you, Amaram. You did this to me.* He'd been burned too often to trust the flame.

'I don't think men were always this way,' she said absently, getting a far-off look in her face. 'I . . .'

Kaladin waited for her to continue, but she didn't. He passed Bridge Four again; many of the men relaxed, backs to the barrack wall, waiting for the afternoon shade to cover them. They rarely waited inside. Perhaps staying inside all day was too gloomy, even for bridgemen.

'Syl?' he finally prompted. 'Were you going to say something?'

'It seems I've heard men talk about times when there were no lies.'

'There are stories,' Kaladin said, 'about the times of the Heraldic Epochs, when men were bound by honor. But you'll always find people telling stories about supposedly better days. You watch. A man joins a new team of soldiers, and the first thing he'll do is talk about how wonderful his old team was. We remember the good times and the bad ones, forgetting that most times are neither good nor bad. They just are.'

He broke into a jog. The sun was growing warm overhead, but he wanted to move.

'The stories,' he continued between puffs, 'they prove it. What happened to the Heralds? They abandoned us. What happened to the Knights Radiant? They fell and became tarnished. What happened to the Epoch Kingdoms? They crashed when the church tried to seize power. You can't trust anyone with power, Syl.'

'What do you do, then? Have no leaders?'

'No. You give the power to the lighteyes and leave it to corrupt them. Then try to stay as far from them as possible.' His words felt hollow. How good a job had *he* done staying away from lighteyes? He always seemed to be in the thick of them, caught in the muddy mire they created with their plots, schemes, and greed.

Syl fell silent, and after that last jog, he decided to stop his practicing. He couldn't afford to strain himself again. He returned the plank. The carpenters scratched their heads, but didn't complain. He made his way back to the bridgemen, noticing that a small group of them – including Rock and Teft – were chatting and glancing at Kaladin.

'You know,' Kaladin said to Syl, 'talking to you probably doesn't do anything for my reputation of being insane.'

'I'll do my best to stop being so interesting,' Syl said, alighting on his shoulder. She put her hands on her hips, then plopped down to a sitting position, smiling, obviously pleased with her comment.

Before Kaladin could get back to the barrack, he noticed Gaz hustling across the lumberyard toward him. 'You!' Gaz said, pointing at Kaladin. 'Hold a season.'

Kaladin stopped, waiting with folded arms.

'I've news for you,' Gaz said, squinting with his good eye. 'Brightlord Lamaril heard what you did with the wounded.'

'How?'

'Storms, boy!' Gaz said. 'You think people wouldn't talk? What were you going to do? Hide three men in the middle of us all?'

Kaladin took a deep breath, but backed down. Gaz was right. 'All right. What does it matter? We didn't slow the army.'

'Yeah,' Gaz said, 'but Lamaril isn't too polished on the idea of paying and feeding bridgemen who can't work. He took the matter to Highprince Sadeas, intending to have you strung up.'

Kaladin felt a chill. Strung up would mean hung out during a highstorm for the Stormfather to judge. It was essentially a death sentence. 'And?'

'Brightlord Sadeas refused to let him do it,' Gaz said.

What? Had he misjudged Sadeas? But no. This was part of the act.

'Brightlord Sadeas,' Gaz said grimly, 'told Lamaril to let you keep the soldiers – but to forbid them food or pay while they're unable to work. Said it would show why he's forced to leave bridgemen behind.'

'That cremling,' Kaladin muttered.

Gaz paled. 'Hush. That's the highprince himself you're talking about, boy!' He glanced about to see if anyone had heard.

'He's trying to make an example of my men. He wants the other bridgemen to see the wounded suffer and starve. He wants it to seem like he's doing a *mercy* by leaving the wounded behind.'

'Well, maybe he's right.'

'It's heartless,' Kaladin said. 'He brings back wounded soldiers. He leaves the bridgemen because it's cheaper to find new slaves than it is to care for wounded ones.'

Gaz fell silent.

'Thank you for bringing me this news.'

'News?' Gaz snapped. 'I was *sent* to give you orders, lordling. Don't try to get extra food from the mess hall for your wounded; you'll be refused.' With that, he rushed away, muttering to himself.

Kaladin made his way back to the barrack. *Stormfather!* Where was he going to get food enough to feed three men? He could split his own meals with them, but while bridgemen were kept fed, they weren't given an excess. Even feeding one man beyond himself would be a stretch. Trying to split the meals four ways would leave the wounded too weak to recover and Kaladin too weak to run bridges. And he *still* needed antiseptic! Rotspren and disease killed far more men in war than the enemy did.

Kaladin stepped up to the men lounging by the barrack. Most were going about the usual bridgeman activities – sprawled on the ground and despondently staring into the air, sitting and despondently staring at the ground, standing and despondently staring into the distance. Bridge Four wasn't on bridge duty at all this day, and they didn't have work detail until third afternoon bell.

'Gaz says our wounded are to be refused food or pay until they are well,' Kaladin said to the collected men.

Some of them – Sigzil, Peet, Koolf – nodded, as if this was what they'd expected.

'Highprince Sadeas wants to make an example of us,' Kaladin said. 'He wants to *prove* that bridgemen aren't worth healing, and he's going to do it by making Hobber, Leyten, and Dabbid die slow, painful deaths.' He took a deep breath. 'I want to pool our resources to buy medicine and get food for the wounded. We can keep those three alive if a few of you will split your meals with them. We'll need about two dozen or so clear-marks to buy the right medicine and supplies. Who has something they can spare?'

The men stared at him, then Moash started laughing. Others joined him. They waved dismissive hands and broke up, walking away, leaving Kaladin with his hand out. 'Next time it could be you!' he called. 'What will you do if you're the one that needs healing?'

'I'll die,' Moash said, not even bothering to look back. 'Out on the field, quickly, rather than back here over a week's time.'

Kaladin lowered his hand. He sighed, turning, and almost ran into Rock. The beefy, towerlike Horneater stood with arms folded, like a tan-skinned statue. Kaladin looked up at him, hopeful.

'Don't have any spheres,' Rock said with a grunt. 'Is all spent already.'

Kaladin sighed. 'It wouldn't have mattered anyway. Two of us couldn't afford to buy the medicine. Not alone.'

'I will give some food,' Rock grumbled.

Kaladin glanced back at him, surprised.

'But *only* for this man with arrow in his leg,' Rock said, arms still folded. 'Hobber?'

'Whatever,' Rock said. 'He looks like he could get better. Other one, he will die. Is certain. And I have no pity for man who sits there, not doing anything. But for the other one, you may have my food. Some of it.'

Kaladin smiled, raising a hand and gripping the larger man's arm. 'Thank you.'

Rock shrugged. 'You took my place. Without this thing, I would be dead.'

Kaladin smirked at that logic. 'I'm not dead, Rock. You'd be fine.'

Rock shook his head. 'I'd be dead. Is something strange about you. All men can see it, even if they don't want to speak of this thing. I looked at bridge where you were. Arrows hit all around you – beside your head, next to your hands. But they weren't hitting you.'

'Luck.'

'Is no such thing.' Rock glanced at Kaladin's shoulder. 'Besides, there is *mafah'liki* who always follows you.' The large Horneater bowed his head reverently to Syl, then made a strange gesture with his hand touching his shoulders and then his forehead.

Kaladin started. 'You can *see* her?' He glanced at Syl. As a windspren, she could appear to those she wanted to – and that generally only meant Kaladin.

Syl seemed shocked. No, she hadn't appeared to Rock specifically.

'I am *alaii'iku*,' Rock said, shrugging.

'Which means . . .'

Rock scowled. 'Airsick lowlanders. Is there nothing proper you know? Anyway, you are special man. Bridge Four, it lost eight runners yesterday counting the three wounded.'

'I know,' Kaladin said. 'I broke my first promise. I said I wasn't going to lose a single one.'

Rock snorted. 'We are bridgemen. We die. Is how this thing works. You might as well promise to make the moons catch each other!' The large man turned, pointing toward one of the other barracks. 'Of the bridges that were fired upon, most lost many men. Five bridges fell. They lost over twenty men each and needed soldiers to help get bridges back. Bridge Two lost eleven men, and it wasn't even a focus of firing.'

He turned back to Kaladin. 'Bridge Four lost eight. Eight men, during one of the worst runs of the season. And, perhaps, you will save two of those. Bridge Four lost fewest men of any bridge that the Parshendi tried to drop. Bridge Four *never* loses fewest men. Everyone knows how it is.'

'Luck—'

Rock pointed a fat finger at him, cutting him off. 'Airsick lowlander.'

It *was* just luck. But, well, Kaladin would take it for the small blessing it was. No use arguing when someone had finally decided to start listening to him.

But one man wasn't enough. Even if both he and Rock went on half rations, one of the sick men would starve. He needed spheres. He needed them desperately. But he was a slave; it was illegal for him to earn money in most ways. If only he had something he could sell. But he owned nothing. He . . .

A thought occurred to him.

'Come on,' he said, striding away from the barrack. Rock followed curiously. Kaladin searched through the lumberyard until he found Gaz speaking with a bridgeleader in front of Bridge Three's barrack. As was growing more common, Gaz grew pale when Kaladin approached, and made as if to scurry away.

'Gaz, wait!' Kaladin said, holding out his hand. 'I have an offer for you.'

The bridge sergeant froze. Beside Gaz, Bridge Three's leader shot Kaladin a scowl. The way the other bridgemen had been treating him suddenly made sense. They were perturbed to see Bridge Four come out of a battle in such good shape. Bridge Four was supposed to be unlucky. Everyone needed someone else to look down on – and the other bridge crews could be consoled by the small mercy that they weren't in Bridge Four. Kaladin had upset that.

The dark-bearded bridgeleader retreated, leaving Kaladin and Rock alone with Gaz.

'What are you offering this time?' Gaz said. 'More dun spheres?'

'No,' Kaladin said, thinking quickly. This would have to be handled *very* carefully. 'I'm out of spheres. But we can't continue like this, you avoiding me, the other bridge crews hating me.'

'Don't see what we can do about it.'

'I tell you what,' Kaladin said, as if suddenly having a thought. 'Is anyone on stone-gathering detail today?'

'Yeah,' Gaz said, gesturing over his shoulder. 'Bridge Three. Bussik there was just trying to convince me that his team is too weak to go. Storms blast me, but I believe him. Lost two-thirds of his men yesterday, and *I'll* be the one who gets chewed out when they don't gather enough stones to meet quota.'

Kaladin nodded sympathetically. Stone gathering was one of the least desirable work details; it involved traveling outside of the camp and filling wagons with large rocks. Soulcasters fed the army by turning rocks into grain, and it was easier for them – for reasons only they knew – if they had distinct, separate stones. So men gathered rocks. It was menial, sweaty, tiring, mindless work. Perfect for bridgemen.

'Why don't you send a different bridge team?' Kaladin asked.

'Bah,' Gaz said. 'You know the kind of trouble that makes. If I'm seen playing favorites, I never hear an end of the complaining.'

'Nobody will complain if you make Bridge Four do it.'

Gaz glanced at him, single eye narrowed. 'I didn't think you'd react well to being treated differently.'

'I'll do it,' Kaladin said, grimacing. 'Just this once. Look, Gaz, I don't want to spend the rest of my time here fighting against you.'

Gaz hesitated. 'Your men are going to be angry. I won't let them think it was me who did this to them.'

'I'll tell them that it was my idea.'

'All right, then. Third bell, meet at the western checkpoint. Bridge Three can clean pots.' He walked away quickly, as if to escape before Kaladin changed his mind.

Rock stepped up beside Kaladin, watching Gaz. 'The little man is right, you know. The men will *hate* you for this thing. They were looking forward to easy day.'

'They'll get over it.'

'But why change for harder work? Is true – you are crazy, aren't you?'

'Maybe. But that craziness will get us outside of the warcamp.'

'What good is that?'

'It means everything,' Kaladin said, glancing back at the barrack. 'It means life and death. But we're going to need more help.'

'Another bridge crew?'

'No, I mean that we – you and I – will need help. One more man, at least.' He scanned the lumberyard, and noted someone sitting in the shadow of Bridge Four's barrack. Teft. The grizzled bridgeman hadn't been among the group that had laughed at Kaladin earlier, but he *had* been quick to help yesterday, going with Rock to carry Leyten.

Kaladin took a deep breath and strode out across the grounds, Rock trailing behind. Syl left his shoulder and zipped into the air, dancing on a sudden gust of wind. Teft looked up as Kaladin and Rock approached. The older man had fetched breakfast, and he was eating alone, a piece of flatbread peeking out beneath his bowl.

His beard was stained by the curry, and he regarded Kaladin with wary eyes before wiping his mouth on his sleeve. 'I like my food, son,' he said. 'Hardly think they feed me enough for one man. Let alone two.'

Kaladin squatted in front of him. Rock leaned up against the wall and folded his arms, watching quietly.

'I need you, Teft,' Kaladin said.

'I said—'

'Not your food. You. Your loyalty. Your allegiance.'

The older man continued to eat. He didn't have a slave brand, and neither did Rock. Kaladin didn't know their stories. All he knew was that these two had helped when others hadn't. They weren't completely beaten down.

'Teft—' Kaladin began.

'I've given my loyalty before,' the man said. 'Too many times now. Always works out the same.'

'Your trust gets betrayed?' Kaladin asked softly.

Teft snorted. 'Storms, no. I betray *it*. You can't depend on me, son. I belong here, as a bridgeman.'

'I depended on you yesterday, and you impressed me.'

'Fluke.'

'I'll judge that,' Kaladin said. 'Teft, we're *all* broken, in one way or another. Otherwise we wouldn't be bridgemen. I've failed. My own brother died because of me.'

'So why keep caring?'

'It's either that or give up and die.'

'And if death is better?'

It came back to this problem. This was why the bridgemen didn't care if he helped the wounded or not.

'Death isn't better,' Kaladin said, looking Teft in the eyes. 'Oh, it's easy to say that now. But when you stand on the ledge and look down into that dark, endless pit, you change your mind. Just like Hobber did. Just like I've done.' He hesitated, seeing something in the older man's eyes. 'I think you've seen it too.'

'Aye,' Teft said softly. 'Aye, I have.'

'So, are you with us in this thing?' Rock said, squatting down.

Us? Kaladin thought, smiling faintly.

Teft looked back and forth between the two of them. 'I get to keep my food?'

'Yes,' Kaladin said.

Teft shrugged. 'All right then, I guess. Can't be any harder than sitting here and having a staring contest with mortality.'

Kaladin held out a hand. Teft hesitated, then took it.

Rock held out a hand. 'Rock.'

Teft looked at him, finished shaking Kaladin's hand, then took Rock's. 'I'm Teft.'

Stormfather, Kaladin thought. *I'd forgotten that most of them don't even bother to learn each other's names.*

'What kind of name is Rock?' Teft asked, releasing the hand.

'Is a stupid one,' Rock said with an even face. 'But at least it has meaning. Does your name mean anything?'

'I guess not,' Teft said, rubbing his bearded chin.

'Rock, this is not my real name,' the Horneater admitted. 'Is just what lowlanders can pronounce.'

'What's your real name, then?' Teft asked.

'You won't be able to say it.'

Teft raised an eyebrow.

'Numuhukumakiaki'aialunamor,' Rock said.

Teft hesitated, then smiled. 'Well, I guess in that case, Rock will do just fine.'

Rock laughed, settling down. 'Our bridgeleader has a plan. Something glorious and daring. Has something to do with spending our afternoon moving stones in the heat.'

Kaladin smiled, leaning forward. 'We need to gather a certain kind of plant. A reed that grows in small patches outside the camp. . . .'

In case you have turned a blind eye to that disaster, know that Aona
and Skai are both dead, and that which they held has been Splintered.
Presumably to prevent anyone from rising up to challenge Rayse.

Two days after the incident with the highstorm, Dalinar walked
with his sons, crossing the rocky ground toward the king's feasting
basin.

Dalinar's stormwardens projected another few weeks of spring, followed
by a return to summer. Hopefully it wouldn't turn to winter instead.

'I've been to three more leatherworkers,' Adolin said softly. 'They have
different opinions. It seems that even before the strap was cut – if it was
cut – it was worn, so that's interfering with things. The best consensus
has been that the strap *was* sliced, but not necessarily by a knife. It could
have just been natural wear-and-tear.'

Dalinar nodded. 'That's the only evidence that even hints there might
be something odd about the girth breaking.'

'So we admit that this was just a result of the king's paranoia.'

'I'll talk to Elhokar,' Dalinar decided. 'Let him know we've run into a
wall and see if there are any other avenues he'd like us to pursue.'

'That'll do.' Adolin seemed to grow hesitant about something. 'Father.
Do you want to talk about what happened during the storm?'

'It was nothing that hasn't happened before.'

'But—'

'Enjoy the evening, Adolin,' Dalinar said firmly. 'I'm all right. Perhaps it's good for the men to see what is happening. Hiding it has only inspired rumors, some of them even worse than the truth.'

Adolin sighed, but nodded.

The king's feasts were always outdoors, at the foot of Elhokar's palace hill. If the stormwardens warned of a highstorm – or if more mundane weather turned bad – then the feast was canceled. Dalinar was glad for the outdoor location. Even with ornamentation, Soulcast buildings felt like caverns.

The feast basin had been flooded, turning it into a shallow artificial lake. Circular dining platforms rose like small stone islands in the water. The elaborate miniature landscape had been fabricated by the king's Soulcasters, who had diverted the water from a nearby stream. *It reminds me of Sela Tales*, Dalinar thought as he crossed the first bridge. He'd visited that western region of Roshar during his youth. *And the Purelake.*

There were five islands, and the railings of the bridges connecting them were done in scrollwork so fine that after each feast, the railings had to be stowed away lest a highstorm ruin them. Tonight, flowers floated in the slow current. Periodically, a miniature boat – only a handspan wide – sailed past, bearing an infused gemstone.

Dalinar, Renarin, and Adolin stepped onto the first dining platform. 'One cup of blue,' Dalinar said to his sons. 'After that, keep to the orange.'

Adolin sighed audibly. 'Couldn't we, just this once—'

'So long as you are of my house, you follow the Codes. My will is firm, Adolin.'

'Fine,' Adolin said. 'Come on, Renarin.' The two broke off from Dalinar to remain on the first platform, where the younger lighteyes congregated.

Dalinar crossed to the next island. This middle one was for the lesser lighteyes. To its left and right lay the segregated dining islands – men's island on the right, women's island on the left. On the three central ones, however, the genders mingled.

Around him, the favored invitees took advantage of their king's hospitality. Soulcast food was inherently bland, but the king's lavish feasts always served imported spices and exotic meats. Dalinar could smell roasting pork on the air, and even chickens. It had been a long time since he'd been served meat from one of the strange Shin flying creatures.

A darkeyed servant passed, wearing a gauzy red robe and carrying a tray of orange crab legs. Dalinar continued across the island, weaving around groups of revelers. Most drank violet wine, the most intoxicating and flavorful of the colors. Almost no one was in battle attire. A few men wore tight, waist-length jackets, but many had dropped all pretense, choosing instead loose silk shirts with ruffled cuffs worn with matching slippers. The rich material glistened in the lamplight.

These creatures of fashion shot glances at Dalinar, appraising him, weighing him. He could remember a time when he would have been swarmed by friends, acquaintances – and yes, even sycophants – at a feast like this. Now, none approached him, though they gave way before him. Elhokar might think his uncle was growing weak, but his reputation quelled most lesser lighteyes.

He soon approached the bridge to the final island – the king's island. Pole-mounted gem lamps ringed it, glowing with blue Stormlight, and a firepit dominated the center of the platform. Deep red coals simmered in its bowels, radiating warmth. Elhokar sat at his table just behind the firepit, and several highprinces ate with him. Tables along the sides of the platform were occupied by male or female diners – never both at the same.

Wit sat on a raised stool at the end of the bridge leading onto the island. Wit actually dressed as a lighteyes should – he wore a stiff black uniform, silver sword at his waist. Dalinar shook his head at the irony.

Wit was insulting each person as they stepped onto the island. 'Brightness Marakal! What a disaster that hairstyle is; how brave of you to show it to the world. Brightlord Marakal, I wish you'd warned us you were going to attend; I'd have forgone supper. I do so hate being sick after a full meal. Brightlord Cadilar! How good it is to see you. Your face reminds me of someone dear to me.'

'Really?' wizened Cadilar said, hesitating.

'Yes,' Wit said, waving him on, 'my horse. Ah, Brightlord Neteb, you smell unique today – did you attack a wet whitespine, or did one just sneeze on you? Lady Alami! No, please, don't speak – it's much easier to maintain my illusions regarding your intelligence that way. And Brightlord Dalinar.' Wit nodded to Dalinar as he passed. 'Ah, my dear Brightlord Taselin. Still engaged in your experiment to prove a maximum threshold of human idiocy? Good for you! Very empirical of you.'

Dalinar hesitated beside Wit's chair as Taselin waddled by with a huff. 'Wit,' Dalinar said, 'do you have to?'

'Two what, Dalinar?' Wit said, eyes twinkling. 'Eyes, hands, or spheres? I'd lend you one of the first, but – by definition – a man can only have one I, and if it is given away, who would be Wit then? I'd lend you one of the second, but I fear my simple hands have been digging in the muck far too often to suit one such as you. And if I gave you one of my spheres, what would I spend the remaining one on? I'm quite attached to both of my spheres, you see.' He hesitated. 'Or, well, you *can't* see. Would you like to?' He stood up off his chair and reached for his belt.

'Wit,' Dalinar said dryly.

Wit laughed, clapping Dalinar on the arm. 'I'm sorry. This lot brings out the basest humor in me. Perhaps it's that muck I spoke of earlier. I do try so hard to be elevated in my loathing of them, but they make it difficult.'

'Care for yourself, Wit,' Dalinar said. 'This lot won't suffer you forever. I wouldn't see you dead by their knives; I see a fine man within you.'

'Yes,' Wit said, scanning the platform. 'He tasted quite delicious. Dalinar, I fear I'm not the one who needs that warning. Speak your fears at a mirror a few times when you get home tonight. There are rumors about.'

'Rumors?'

'Yes. Terrible things. Grow on men like warts.'

'Tumors?'

'Both. Look, there is talk about you.'

'There is always talk about me.'

'This is worse than most,' Wit said, meeting his eyes. 'Did you really speak of abandoning the Vengeance Pact?'

Dalinar took a deep breath. 'That was between me and the king.'

'Well, he must have spoken of it to others. This lot are cowards – and no doubt that makes them feel like experts on the subject, for they've certainly been calling you that a great deal lately.'

'Stormfather!'

'No, I'm Wit. But I understand how easy a mistake that is to make.'

'Because you blow so much air,' Dalinar growled, 'or because you make so much noise?'

A wide smile split Wit's face. 'Why, Dalinar! I'm impressed! Maybe

I should make *you* Wit! Then I could be a highprince instead.' He stopped. 'No, that would be bad. I'd go mad after a mere second of listening to them, then would likely slaughter the lot. Perhaps appoint cremlings in their places. The kingdom would undoubtedly fare better.'

Dalinar turned to go. 'Thank you for the warning.'

Wit sat back down on his stool as Dalinar walked away. 'You're welcome. Ah, Brightlord Habatab! How thoughtful of you to wear a red shirt with a sunburn like that! If you continue to make my job this easy, I fear my mind shall become as dull as Brightlord Tumul's! Oh, Brightlord Tumul! How unexpected it is to see you standing there! I didn't mean to insult your stupidity. Really, it's quite spectacular and worthy of much praise. Lord Yonatan and Lady Meirav, I'll forgo an insult for you this once on account of your recent wedding, though I do find your hat quite impressive, Yonatan. I trust it is convenient to wear on your head something that doubles as a tent at night. Ah, and is that Lady *Navani* behind you? How long have you been back at the Plains and how did I not notice the smell?'

Dalinar froze. *What?*

'Obviously your own stench overpowered mine, Wit,' a warm feminine voice said. 'Has no one done my son a service and assassinated you yet?'

'No, no assassins yet,' Wit said, amused. 'I guess I've already got too much ass sass of my own.'

Dalinar turned with shock. Navani, the king's mother, was a stately woman with intricately woven black hair. And she was *not* supposed to be here.

'Oh really, Wit,' she said. 'I thought that kind of humor was beneath you.'

'So are you, technically,' Wit said, smiling, from atop his high-legged stool.

She rolled her eyes.

'Unfortunately, Brightness,' Wit replied with a sigh, 'I've taken to framing my insults in terms this lot will understand. If it will please you, I shall attempt to improve my diction to more elevated terms.' He paused. 'I say, do you know any words that rhyme with bescumber?'

Navani just turned her head and looked at Dalinar with a pair of light violet eyes. She wore an elegant dress, its shimmering red surface unbroken by embroidery. The gems in her hair – which was streaked with a few lines of grey – were red as well. The king's mother was known as one of the most beautiful women in Alethkar, though Dalinar had always found that description inadequate, for surely there wasn't a woman on all of Roshar to match her beauty.

Fool, he thought, tearing his eyes away from her. *Your brother's widow.* With Gavilar dead, Navani was now to be treated as Dalinar's sister. Besides, what of his own wife? Dead these ten years, wiped by his foolishness from his mind. Even if he couldn't remember her, he should honor her.

Why had Navani returned? As women called out greetings to her, Dalinar hurriedly made his way over to the king's table. He sat down; a servant arrived in moments with a plate for him – they knew his preferences.

It was steaming peppered chicken, cut in medallions and laid atop fried round slices of tenem, a soft, light orange vegetable. Dalinar grabbed a piece of flatbread and slipped his dining knife from the sheath on his right calf. So long as he was eating, it would be a breach of etiquette for Navani to approach him.

The food was good. It always was at these feasts of Elhokar's – in that, the son was like the father. Elhokar nodded to Dalinar from the end of the table, then continued his conversation with Sadeas. Highprince Roion sat a few seats down from him. Dalinar had an appointment with him in a few days, the first of the highprinces he'd approach and try to convince to work with him on a joint plateau assault.

No other highprinces came to sit near Dalinar. Only they – and people with specific invitations – could sit at the king's table. One man lucky enough to receive such an invitation sat on Elhokar's left, obviously uncertain if he should join in the conversation or not.

Water gurgled in the stream behind Dalinar. Before him, the festivities continued. It was a time for relaxation, but the Alethi were a reserved people, at least when compared with more passionate folk like the Horneaters or the Reshi. Still, his people seemed to have grown more opulent and self-indulgent since his childhood. Wine flowed freely and foods sizzled fragrantly. On the first island, several young men had stepped into a sparring ring for a friendly duel. Young men at a feast often found reason to remove their coats and show off their swordsmanship.

The women were more modest with their displays, but they engaged in them as well. On Dalinar's own island, several women had set up easels where they were sketching, painting, or doing calligraphy. As always, they kept their left hands shrouded in their sleeves, delicately creating art with the right. They sat on high stools, the kind that Wit had been using – in fact, Wit had probably stolen one for his little performance. A few of them attracted creationspren, the tiny shapes rolling across the tops of their easels or tables.

Navani had gathered a group of important lighteyed women to a table. A servant passed by in front of Dalinar, bringing the women some food. It appeared to also have been made with the exotic chicken, but had been mixed with steamed methi fruit and covered in a reddish-brown sauce. As a boy, Dalinar had secretly tried women's food out of curiosity. He'd found it distastefully sweet.

Navani placed something on her table, a device of polished brass about the size of a fist, with a large, infused ruby at its center. The red Stormlight lit the entire table, throwing shadows down the white tablecloth. Navani picked up the device, rotating it to show her dinner companions its leglike protrusions. Turned that way, it looked vaguely crustacean.

I've never seen a fabrial like that before. Dalinar looked up at her face, admiring the contours of her cheek. Navani was a renowned artifabrian. Perhaps this device was—

Navani glanced at him, and Dalinar froze. She flashed the briefest of smiles at him, covert and knowing, then turned away before he could react. *Storming woman!* he thought, pointedly turning his attention to his meal.

He was hungry, and got so involved in his food that he almost didn't notice Adolin approaching. The blond youth saluted Elhokar, then hurried to take one of the vacant seats beside Dalinar. 'Father,' Adolin said in a hushed tone, 'have you heard what they're saying?'

'About what?'

'About you! I've fought three duels so far against men who described you – and our house – as cowards. They're saying you asked the king to abandon the Vengeance Pact!'

Dalinar gripped the table and nearly rose to his feet. But he stopped himself. 'Let them speak if they wish,' he said, turning back to his meal, stabbing a chunk of peppered chicken with his knife and raising it to his lips.

'Did you really do it?' Adolin asked. 'Is that what you talked about at the meeting with the king two days back?'

'It is,' Dalinar admitted.

That elicited a groan from Adolin. 'I was worried already. When I—'

'Adolin,' Dalinar interjected. 'Do you trust me?'

Adolin looked at him, the youth's eyes wide, honest, but pained. 'I want to. Storms, Father. I really want to.'

'What I am doing is important. It *must be done*.'

Adolin leaned in, speaking softly. 'And what if they *are* delusions? What if you're just . . . getting old.'

It was the first time someone had confronted him with it so directly. 'I would be lying if I didn't admit that I'd considered it, but there was no sense in second-guessing myself. I believe they're real. I *feel* they're real.'

'But—'

'This is not the place for this discussion, son,' Dalinar said. 'We can talk of it later, and I will listen to – and consider – your objections. I promise.' Adolin drew his lips to a line. 'Very well.'

'You are right to be worried for our reputation,' Dalinar said, resting an elbow on the table. 'I had assumed that Elhokar would have the tact to keep our conversation quiet, but I should have asked him to do so directly. You were right about his reaction, by the way. I realized during the conversation he would never retreat, so I changed to another tactic.'

'Which is?'

'Winning the war,' Dalinar said firmly. 'No more scuffling over gem-hearts. No more patient, indefinite siege. We find a way to lure a large number of Parshendi onto the Plains, then execute an ambush. If we can kill a large enough number of them, we destroy their capacity to wage war. Failing that, we find a way to strike at their center and kill or capture their leaders. Even a chasmfiend stops fighting when it's been decapitated. The Vengeance Pact would be fulfilled, and we could go home.'

Adolin took a long moment considering, then he nodded sharply. 'All right.'

'No objections?' Dalinar asked. Normally, his elder son had plenty.

'You just asked me to trust you,' Adolin said. 'Besides, striking harder at the Parshendi? That's a tactic I can get behind. We'll need a good plan, though – a way to counter the very objections you yourself raised six years ago.'

Dalinar nodded, tapping the table with his finger. 'Back then, even I thought of us as separate princedoms. If we had attacked the center individually, each army alone, we'd have been surrounded and destroyed. But if all ten armies went together? With our Soulcasters to provide food, with the soldiers carrying portable shelters to set up for highstorms? Over a hundred and fifty thousand troops? Let the Parshendi try to surround us then. With the Soulcasters, we could even create wood for bridges if we had to.'

'That would take a lot of trust,' Adolin said hesitantly. He glanced down the high table, toward Sadeas. His expression darkened. 'We'd be stuck out there, together and isolated, for days. If the highprinces started squabbling midmarch, it could be disastrous.'

'We'll get them to work together first,' Dalinar said. 'We're close, closer than we've ever been. Six years, and not a single highprince has allowed his soldiers to skirmish against those of another.'

Except back in Alethkar. There, they still fought meaningless battles over land rights or old offenses. It was ridiculous, but stopping the Alethi from warring was like trying to stop the winds from blowing.

Adolin was nodding. 'It's a good plan, Father. Far better than talk of retreating. They won't like giving up the plateau skirmishes, though. They like the game of it.'

'I know. But if I can get one or two of them to start pooling soldiers and resources for plateau assaults, it might be a step toward what we'll need for the future. I'd still rather find a way to lure a large force of Parshendi out onto the Plains and meet them on one of the larger plateaus, but I haven't yet been able to figure out how to do that. Either way, our separate armies will need to learn to work together.'

'And what do we do about what people are saying about you?'

'I'll release an official refutation,' Dalinar said. 'I'll have to be careful not to make it sound like the king was in error, while also explaining the truth.'

Adolin sighed. 'An official refutation, Father?'

'Yes.'

'Why not fight a duel?' Adolin asked, leaning in, sounding eager. 'Some stuffy pronouncement may explain your ideas, but it won't make people *feel* them. Pick someone who is naming you coward, challenge them, and remind everyone what a mistake it is to insult the Blackthorn!'

'I cannot,' Dalinar said. 'The Codes forbid it for one of my stature.' Adolin probably shouldn't be dueling either, but Dalinar had not forced a complete prohibition on him. Dueling was his life. Well, that and the women he courted.

'Then charge me with the honor of our house,' Adolin said. 'I'll duel them! I'll face them with Plate and Blade and show them what your honor means.'

'That would be the same thing as me doing it, son.'

Adolin shook his head, staring at Dalinar. He seemed to be searching for something.

'What?' Dalinar asked.

'I'm trying to decide,' Adolin said. 'Which one has changed you most. The visions, the Codes, or that book. If there's any difference between them.'

'The Codes are separate from the other two,' Dalinar said. 'They are a tradition of old Alethkar.'

'No. They're related, Father. All three. They're tied together in you, somehow.'

Dalinar thought on that for a moment. Could the lad have a point? 'Have I told you the story of the king carrying the boulder?'

'Yes,' Adolin said.

'I have?'

'Twice. And you made me listen to the passage being read another time.'

'Oh. Well, in that same section, there's a passage about the nature of *forcing* people to follow you as opposed to *letting* them follow you. We do too much forcing in Alethkar. Dueling someone because they claim I'm a coward doesn't change their beliefs. It might stop them from making the claims, but it doesn't change hearts. I know I'm right about this. You'll just have to trust me on this as well.'

Adolin sighed, standing. 'Well, an official refutation is better than nothing, I guess. At least you haven't given up on defending our honor entirely.'

'I never will,' Dalinar said. 'I just need to be careful. I cannot afford to divide us any further.' He turned back to his meal, stabbing his last piece of chicken with his knife and shoving it in his mouth.

'I'll get back to the other island, then,' Adolin said. 'I . . . Wait, is that *Aunt Navani?*'

Dalinar looked up, surprised to see Navani walking toward them. Dalinar glanced at his plate. His food was gone; he'd eaten the last bit without realizing it.

He sighed, steeling himself, and rose to greet her. 'Mathana,' Dalinar said, bowing and using the formal term for an older sister. Navani was only three months his senior, but it was still applicable.

'Dalinar,' she said, a faint smile on her lips. 'And dear Adolin.'

Adolin smiled broadly; he rounded the table and hugged his aunt. She rested her clothed safehand on his shoulder, a gesture reserved only for family.

'When did you return?' Adolin asked, releasing her.

'Just this afternoon.'

'And *why* did you return?' Dalinar asked stiffly. 'I was under the impression that you were going to aid the queen in protecting the king's interests in Alethkar.'

'Oh, Dalinar,' Navani said, voice fond. 'So stiff, as always. Adolin, dear, how goes courtship?'

Dalinar snorted. 'He continues to change partners like he's in a dance that involves particularly quick music.'

'Father!' Adolin objected.

'Well, good for you, Adolin,' Navani said. 'You're too young to get tied down. The purpose of youth is to experience variety while it is still interesting.' She glanced at Dalinar. 'It isn't until we get older that we should be forced to be boring.'

'Thank you, Aunt,' Adolin said with a grin. 'Excuse me. I need to go tell Renarin that you've returned.' He hurried away, leaving Dalinar standing awkwardly across the table from Navani.

'Am I that much of a threat, Dalinar?' Navani asked, raising an eyebrow at him.

Dalinar glanced down, realizing that he was still gripping his dining knife – a wide, serrated blade that could double as a weapon in a pinch. He let it clatter to the table, then winced at the noise. All of the confidence he'd felt speaking with Adolin seemed gone in a heartbeat.

Compose yourself! he thought. *She's just family.* Every time he spoke with

Navani, he felt as if he were facing a predator of the most dangerous breed.

'Mathana,' Dalinar said, realizing they were still standing on opposite sides of the narrow table. 'Perhaps we should move to ...'

He trailed off as Navani waved to an attending girl who was barely old enough to wear a woman's sleeve. The child rushed forward, bearing a low stool. Navani pointed to the spot beside her, a spot only a few feet from the table. The child hesitated, but Navani pointed more insistently and the child set the stool down.

Navani sat gracefully, not sitting *at* the king's table – which was a masculine dining place – but certainly sitting near enough to be challenging protocol. The serving girl withdrew. At the end of the table, Elhokar noticed his mother's actions, but said nothing. One did not reprove Navani Kholin, not even if one were king.

'Oh, sit down, Dalinar,' she said, voice growing testy. 'We have matters of some moment to discuss.'

Dalinar sighed, but sat. The seats around them were still empty, and both the music and the hum of conversation on the island were loud enough to keep people from overhearing them. Some women had taken to playing flutes, musicspren spinning around them in the air.

'You ask why I returned,' Navani said, voice soft. 'Well, I have three reasons. First, I wanted to bring word that the Vedens have perfected their "half-shards" as they call them. They're claiming the shields can stop blows from a Shardblade.'

Dalinar folded his arms before him on the table. He'd heard rumors of this, though he'd discounted them. Men were always claiming to be close to creating new Shards, yet the promises were never fulfilled. 'Have you seen one?'

'No. But I have confirmation from someone I trust. She says they can only take the shape of a shield and don't lend any of Plate's other enhancements. But they *can* block a Shardblade.'

It was a step – a very small step – toward Shardplate. That was disturbing. He wouldn't believe it himself until he'd seen what these 'half-shards' could do. 'You could have sent this news via spanreed, Navani.'

'Well, I realized soon after reaching Kholinar that leaving here had been a political mistake. More and more, these warcamps are the true center of our kingdom.'

'Yes,' Dalinar said quietly. 'Our absence from our homeland is dangerous.' Hadn't that been the very argument that had convinced Navani to go home in the first place?

The stately woman waved a dismissive hand. 'I have determined that the queen is sufficiently endowed with the requisite skills needed to hold Alethkar. There are schemes and plots – there will always be schemes and plots – but the truly important players inevitably make their way here.'

'Your son continues to see assassins around every corner,' Dalinar said softly.

'And shouldn't he? After what happened to his father . . .'

'True, but I fear he carries it to extremes. He mistrusts even his allies.'

Navani folded her hands in her lap, freehand lying atop safehand. 'He's not very good at this, is he?'

Dalinar blinked in shock. 'What? Elhokar is a good man! He has more integrity than any other lighteyes in this army.'

'But his rule is weak,' Navani said. 'You must admit that.'

'He is king,' Dalinar said firmly, 'and my nephew. He has both my sword and my heart, Navani, and I will not hear ill spoken of him, even by his own mother.'

She eyed him. Was she testing his loyalty? Much like her daughter, Navani was a political creature. Intrigue made her blossom like a rockbud in calm wet air. However, unlike Jasnah, Navani was hard to trust. At least with Jasnah one knew where one stood – once again, Dalinar found himself wishing she'd put aside her projects and return to the Shattered Plains.

'I'm not speaking ill of my son, Dalinar,' Navani said. 'We both know I am as loyal to him as you are. But I like to know what I'm working with, and that requires a definition. He is seen as weak, and I intend to see him protected. Despite himself, if necessary.'

'Then we work for the same goals. But if protecting him was the second reason you returned, what was the third?'

She smiled a violet-eyed, red-lipped smile at him. A meaningful smile.

Blood of my ancestors . . . Dalinar thought. *Stormwinds, but she's beautiful. Beautiful and deadly.* It seemed a particular irony to him that his wife's face had been erased from his mind, and yet he could remember in complete and intricate detail the months this woman had spent toying with him and Gavilar. She'd played them off one another, fanning their desire before finally choosing the elder son.

They'd all known the entire time that she would choose Gavilar. It had hurt anyway.

'We need to talk sometime in private,' Navani said. 'I want to hear your opinion on some of the things being said in camp.'

That probably meant the rumors about him. 'I— I'm very busy.'

She rolled her eyes. 'I'm sure you are. We're meeting anyway, once I've had time to settle here and put out feelers. How about one week from today? I'll come read to you from that book of my husband's, and afterward we can chat. We'll do it in a public place. All right?'

He sighed. 'Very well. But—'

'Highprinces and lighteyes,' Elhokar suddenly proclaimed. Dalinar and Navani turned toward the end of the table, where the king stood wearing his uniform complete with royal cape and crown. He raised a hand toward the island. The people hushed, and soon the only sound was that of the water burbling through the streams.

'I'm sure many of you have heard the rumors regarding the attempt on my life during the hunt three days ago,' Elhokar announced. 'When my saddle girth was cut.'

Dalinar glanced at Navani. She raised her freehand toward him and rocked it back and forth, indicating that she didn't find the rumors to be persuasive. She knew about the rumors, of course. Give Navani five minutes in a city and she'd know anything and everything of significance being gossiped about.

'I assure you, I was never in real danger,' Elhokar said. 'Thanks, in part, to the protection of the King's Guard and the vigilance of my uncle. However, I believe it wise to treat all threats with due prudence and seriousness. Therefore, I am appointing Brightlord Torol Sadeas to be Highprince of Information, charging him to unearth the truth regarding this attempt on my life.'

Dalinar blinked in shock. Then he closed his eyes and let out a soft groan.

'Unearth the truth,' Navani said skeptically. 'Sadeas?'

'Blood of my … He thinks I'm ignoring the threats to him, so he's looking to Sadeas instead.'

'Well, I suppose that's all right,' she said. 'I *kind of* trust Sadeas.'

'Navani,' Dalinar said, opening his eyes. 'The incident happened on a hunt I planned, under the protection of my guard and my soldiers. The king's horse was prepared by my grooms. He publicly asked me to look into this strap business, and now he's just taken the investigation away from me.'

'Oh dear.' She understood. This was nearly the same thing as Elhokar proclaiming that he suspected Dalinar. Any information Sadeas unearthed regarding this 'assassination attempt' could only reflect unfavorably on Dalinar.

When Sadeas's hatred of Dalinar and his love of Gavilar conflicted, which would win? *But the vision. It said to trust him.*

Elhokar sat back down, and the buzz of conversation resumed across the island at a higher pitch. The king seemed oblivious of what he had just done. Sadeas was smiling broadly. He rose from his place, bidding farewell to the king, then began mingling.

'You still argue he isn't a bad king?' Navani whispered. 'My poor, distracted, oblivious boy.'

Dalinar stood up, then walked down the table to where the king continued to eat.

Elhokar looked up. 'Ah, Dalinar. I suspect you'll want to give Sadeas your aid.'

Dalinar sat down. Sadeas's half-eaten meal still sat on the table, brass plate scattered with chunks of meat and torn flatbread. 'Elhokar,' Dalinar forced out, 'I just spoke to you a few days ago. I asked to be Highprince of War, and you said it was too dangerous!'

'It is,' Elhokar said. 'I spoke to Sadeas about it, and he agreed. The highprinces will never stand for someone being put over them in war. Sadeas mentioned that if I started with something less threatening, like appointing someone to Highprince of Information, it might prepare the others for what you want to do.'

'Sadeas suggested this,' Dalinar said flatly.

'Of course,' Elhokar said. 'It is time we had a Highprince of Information, and he specifically noted the cut girth as something he wanted to look into. He knows you've always said you aren't suited to these sorts of things.'

Blood of my fathers, Dalinar thought, looking out at the center of the island, where a group of lighteyes gathered around Sadeas. *I've just been outmaneuvered. Brilliantly.*

The Highprince of Information had authority over criminal investigations, particularly those of interest to the Crown. In a way, it was nearly as threatening as a Highprince of War, but it wouldn't seem so to Elhokar. All he saw was that he would finally have someone willing to listen to his paranoid fears.

Sadeas was a clever, clever man.

'Don't look so morose, Uncle,' Elhokar said. 'I had no idea you'd want the position, and Sadeas just seemed so excited at the idea. Perhaps he'll find nothing at all, and the leather was simply worn out. You'll be vindicated in always telling me that I'm not in as much danger as I think I am.'

'Vindicated?' Dalinar asked softly, still watching Sadeas. *Somehow, I doubt that is likely.*

You have accused me of arrogance in my quest. You have accused me of perpetuating my grudge against Rayse and Bavadin. Both accusations are true.

Kaladin stood up in the wagon bed, scanning the landscape outside the camp as Rock and Teft put his plan – such as it was – into action.

Back home, the air had been drier. If you went about on the day before a highstorm, everything seemed desolate. After storms, plants soon pulled back into their shells, trunks, and hiding places to conserve water. But here in the moister climate, they lingered. Many rockbuds never quite pulled into their shells completely. Patches of grass were common. The trees Sadeas harvested were concentrated in a forest to the north of the war-camps, but a few strays grew on this plain. They were enormous, broad-trunked things that grew with a westward slant, their thick, finger-like roots clawing into the stone and – over the years – cracking and breaking the ground around them.

Kaladin hopped down from the cart. His job was to hoist up stones and place them on the bed of the vehicle. The other bridgemen brought them to him, laying them in heaps nearby.

Bridgemen worked across the broad plain, moving among rockbuds, patches of grass, and bunches of weeds that poked out from beneath boulders. Those grew most heavily on the west side, ready to pull back into their boulder's shadow if a highstorm approached. It was a curious effect, as if each boulder were the head of an aged man with tufts of green and brown hair growing out from behind his ears.

Those tufts were extremely important, for hidden among them were thin reeds known as knobweed. Their rigid stalks were topped with delicate fronds that could retract into the stem. The stems themselves were immobile, but they were fairly safe growing behind boulders. Some would be pulled free in each storm – perhaps to attach themselves in a new location once the winds abated.

Kaladin hoisted a rock, setting it on the bed of the wagon and rolling it beside some others. The rock's bottom was wet with lichen and crem.

Knobweed wasn't rare, but neither was it as common as other weeds. A quick description had been enough to send Rock and Teft searching with some success. The breakthrough, however, had happened when Syl had joined the hunt. Kaladin glanced to the side as he stepped down for another stone. She zipped around, a faint, nearly invisible form leading Rock from one stand of reeds to another. Teft didn't understand how the large Horneater could consistently find so many more than he did, but Kaladin didn't feel inclined to explain. He still didn't understand why Rock could see Syl in the first place. The Horneater said it was something he'd been born with.

A pair of bridgemen approached, youthful Dunny and Earless Jaks towing a wooden sled bearing a large stone. Sweat trickled down the sides of their faces. As they reached the wagon, Kaladin dusted off his hands and helped them lift the boulder. Earless Jaks scowled at him, muttering under his breath.

'That's a nice one,' Kaladin said, nodding to the stone. 'Good work.' Jaks glared at him and stalked off. Dunny gave Kaladin a shrug, then hurried after the older man. As Rock had guessed, getting the crew assigned to stone-gathering duty had not helped Kaladin's popularity. But it had to be done. It was the only way to help Leyten and the other wounded.

Once Jaks and Dunny left, Kaladin nonchalantly climbed into the wagon bed and knelt down, pushing aside a tarp and uncovering a large pile of knobweed stems. They were about as long as a man's forearm. He made as if he were moving stones around in the bed, but instead tied a large double handful of the reeds into a bundle using thin rockbud vines.

He dropped the bundle over the side of the wagon. The wagon driver had gone to chat with his counterpart on the other wagon. That left Kaladin alone, save for the chull that sat hunkered down in its rock shell, watching the sun with beady crustacean eyes.

Kaladin hopped down from the wagon and placed another rock in the bed. Then, he knelt as if to pull a large stone out from under the wagon. With deft hands, however, he tied the reeds into place underneath the bed right beside two other bundles. The wagon had a large open space to the side of the axle, and a wood dowel there provided an excellent place for mounting the bundles.

Jezerezeh send that nobody thinks to check the bottom as we roll back into camp.

The apothecary said one drop came per stem. How many reeds would Kaladin need? He felt he knew the answer to that question without even giving it much thought.

He'd need every drop he could get.

He climbed out and lifted another stone into the wagon. Rock was approaching; the large, tan-skinned Horneater carried an oblong stone that would have been too large for most of the bridgemen to handle alone. Rock shuffled forward slowly, Syl zipping around his head and occasionally landing on the rock to watch him.

Kaladin climbed down and trotted across the uneven ground to help. Rock nodded in thanks. Together they hauled the stone to the wagon and set it down on the bed. Rock wiped his brow, turning his back to Kaladin. Sprouting from his pocket was a handful of reeds. Kaladin swiped them and tucked them beneath the tarp.

'What do we do if someone notices this thing we are doing?' Rock asked casually.

'Explain that I'm a weaver,' Kaladin said, 'and that I thought I'd weave myself a hat to keep off the sun.'

Rock snorted.

'I might do just that,' Kaladin said. He wiped his brow. 'It would be nice in this heat. But best nobody sees. The mere fact that we want the reeds would probably be enough to make them deny them to us.'

'This thing is true,' Rock said, stretching and glancing upward as Syl zipped over in front of him. 'I miss the Peaks.'

Syl pointed, and Rock bowed his head in reverence before following after her. Once she had him going in the right direction, however, she flitted back to Kaladin, bobbing up into the air as a ribbon, then falling down to the side of the wagon and re-forming her womanly shape, her dress fluttering around her.

'I,' she declared, raising a finger, 'like him very much.'

'Who? Rock?'

'Yes,' she said, folding her arms. 'He is *respectful*. Unlike others.'

'Fine,' Kaladin said, lifting another stone into the wagon. 'You can follow him around instead of bothering me.' He tried not to show worry as he said it. He had grown accustomed to her company.

She sniffed. 'I can't follow him. He's too respectful.'

'You just said you *liked* that.'

'I do. Also, I detest it.' She said that with unaffected frankness, as if oblivious of the contradiction. She sighed, sitting down on the side of the wagon. 'I led him to a patch of chull dung as a prank. He didn't even yell at me! He just looked at it, as if trying to figure out some hidden meaning.' She grimaced. 'That's not normal.'

'I think the Horneaters must worship spren or something,' Kaladin said, wiping his brow.

'That's silly.'

'People believe much sillier things. In some ways, I guess it makes sense to revere the spren. You *are* kind of odd and magical.'

'I'm not odd!' she said, standing up. 'I'm beautiful and articulate.' She planted her hands on her hips, but he could see in her expression that she wasn't really mad. She seemed to be changing by the hour, growing more and more . . .

More and more what? Not exactly humanlike. More individual. Smarter.

Syl fell silent as another bridgeman – Natam – approached. The long-faced man was carrying a smaller stone, obviously trying not to strain himself.

'Ho, Natam,' Kaladin said, reaching down to take the stone. 'How goes the work?'

Natam shrugged.

'Didn't you say you were once a farmer?'

Natam rested beside the wagon, ignoring Kaladin.

Kaladin set down the rock, moving it into place. 'I'm sorry to make us work like this, but we need the good will of Gaz and the other bridge crews.'

Natam didn't respond.

'It will help keep us alive,' Kaladin said. 'Trust me.'

Natam just shrugged yet again, then wandered away.

Kaladin sighed. 'This would be a lot easier if I could pin the duty change on Gaz.'

'That wouldn't be very honest,' Syl said, affronted.

'Why do you care so much about honesty?'

'I just do.'

'Oh?' Kaladin said, grunting as he moved back to his work. 'And leading men to piles of dung? How honest is that?'

'That's different. It was a joke.'

'I fail to see how . . .'

He trailed off as another bridgeman approached. Kaladin doubted anyone else had Rock's strange ability to see Syl, and didn't want to be seen talking to himself.

The short, wiry bridgeman had said his name was Skar, though Kaladin couldn't see any obvious scars on his face. He had short dark hair and angular features. Kaladin tried to engage him in conversation too, but got no response. The man even went so far as to give Kaladin a rude gesture before tromping back out.

'I'm doing something wrong,' Kaladin said, shaking his head and hopping down from the sturdy wagon.

'Wrong?' Syl stepped up to the lip of the wagon, watching him.

'I thought that seeing me rescue those three might give them hope. But they're still indifferent.'

'Some watched you run earlier,' Syl said, 'when you were practicing with the plank.'

'They watched,' Kaladin said. 'But they don't care about helping the wounded. Nobody besides Rock, that is – and he's only doing it because he has a debt to me. Even Teft wasn't willing to share his food.'

'They're selfish.'

'No. I don't think that word can apply to them.' He lifted a stone, struggling to explain how he felt. 'When I was a slave . . . well, I'm still a slave. But during the worst parts, when my masters were trying to beat out of me the ability to resist, I was like these men. I didn't care enough to be selfish. I was like an animal. I just did what I did without thinking.'

Syl frowned. Little wonder – Kaladin himself didn't understand what he was saying. Yet, as he spoke, he began to work out what he meant. 'I've shown them that we can survive, but that doesn't mean anything. If those lives aren't *worth* living, then they aren't ever going to care. It's like I'm offering them piles of spheres, but not giving them anything to spend their wealth on.'

'I guess,' Syl said. 'But what can you do?'

He looked back across the plain of rock, toward the warcamp. The smoke of the army's many cookfires rose from the craters. 'I don't know. But I think we're going to need a *lot* more reeds.'

◆◆

That night, Kaladin, Teft, and Rock walked the makeshift streets of Sadeas's warcamp. Nomon – the middle moon – shone with his pale, blue-white light. Oil lanterns hung in front of buildings, indicating taverns or brothels. Spheres could provide more consistent, renewable light, but you could buy a bundle of candles or a pouch of oil for a single sphere. In the short run, it was often cheaper to do that, particularly if you were hanging your lights in a place they could be stolen.

Sadeas didn't enforce a curfew, but Kaladin had learned that a lone bridgeman had best remain in the lumberyard at night. Half-drunken soldiers in stained uniforms sauntered past, whispering in the ears of whores or boasting to their friends. They called insults at the bridgemen, laughing riotously. The streets felt dark, even with the lanterns and the moonlight, and the haphazard nature of the camp – some stone structures, some wooden shanties, some tents – made it feel disorganized and dangerous.

Kaladin and his two companions stepped aside for a large group of soldiers. Their coats were unbuttoned, and they were only mildly drunk. A soldier eyed the bridgemen, but the three of them together – one of them being a brawny Horneater – were enough to dissuade the soldier from doing more than laughing and shoving Kaladin as he passed.

The man smelled of sweat and cheap ale. Kaladin kept his temper. Fight back, and he'd be docked pay for brawling.

'I don't like this,' Teft said, glancing over his shoulder at the group of soldiers. 'I'm going back to the camp.'

'You will be staying,' Rock growled.

Teft rolled his eyes. 'You think I'm scared of a lumbering chull like you? I'll go if I want to, and—'

'Teft,' Kaladin said softly. 'We need you.'

Need. That word had strange effects on men. Some ran when you used it. Others grew nervous. Teft seemed to long for it. He nodded, muttering to himself, but stayed with them as they went on.

They soon reached the wagonyard. The fenced-off square of rock was near the western side of the camp. It was deserted for the night, the wagons sitting in long lines. Chulls lay slumbering in the nearby pen, looking like small hills. Kaladin crept forward, wary of sentries, but apparently nobody worried about something as large as a wagon being stolen from the middle of the army.

Rock nudged him, then pointed to the shadowy chull pens. A lone boy sat upon a pen post, staring up at the moon. Chulls were valuable enough to watch over. Poor lad. How often was he required to wait up nights guarding the sluggish beasts?

Kaladin crouched down beside a wagon, the other two mimicking him. He pointed down one row, and Rock moved off. Kaladin pointed the other direction, and Teft rolled his eyes, but did as asked.

Kaladin sneaked down the middle row. There were about thirty wagons, ten per row, but checking was quick. A brush of the fingers against the back plank, looking for the mark he'd made there. After just a few minutes, a shadowed figure entered Kaladin's row. Rock. The Horneater gestured to the side and held up five fingers. Fifth wagon from the top. Kaladin nodded and moved off.

Just as he reached the indicated wagon, he heard a soft yelp from the direction Teft had gone. Kaladin flinched, then peeked up toward the sentry. The boy was still watching the moon, kicking his toes absently against the post next to him.

A moment later, Rock and a sheepish Teft scurried up to Kaladin. 'Sorry,' Teft whispered. 'The walking mountain startled me.'

'If I am being a mountain,' Rock grumbled, 'then why weren't you hearing me coming? Eh?'

Kaladin snorted, feeling the back of the indicated wagon, fingers brushing the X mark in the wood. He took a breath, then climbed under the wagon on his back.

The reeds were still there, tied in twenty bundles, each about as thick as a handspan. 'Ishi, Herald of Luck be praised,' he whispered, untying the first bundle.

'All there, eh?' Teft said, leaning down, scratching at his beard in the moonlight. 'Can't believe we found so many. Must have pulled up every reed on the entire plain.'

Kaladin handed him the first bundle. Without Syl, they wouldn't have found a third this many. She had the speed of an insect in flight, and she seemed to have a sense of where to find things. Kaladin untied the next bundle, handing it out. Teft tied it to the other, making a larger bundle.

As Kaladin worked, a flurry of small white leaves blew under the wagon and formed into Syl's figure. She slid to a stop beside his head. 'No guards anywhere I could see. Just a boy in the chull pens.' Her white-blue translucent figure was nearly invisible in the darkness.

'I hope these reeds are still good,' Kaladin whispered. 'If they dried out too much . . . '

'They'll be fine. You worry like a worrier. I found you some bottles.'

'You did?' he asked, so eager that he nearly sat up. He caught himself before smacking his head.

Syl nodded. 'I'll show you. I couldn't carry them. Too solid.'

Kaladin quickly untied the rest of the bundles, handing them out to the nervous Teft. Kaladin scooted out, then took two of the larger, tied-together bundles of three. Teft took two of the others, and Rock managed three by tucking one under his arm. They'd need a place to work where they wouldn't be interrupted. Even if the knobweed seemed worthless, Gaz would find a way to ruin the work if he saw what was happening.

Bottle first, Kaladin thought. He nodded to Syl, who led them out of the wagonyard and to a tavern. It looked to have been hastily built from second-rate lumber, but that didn't stop the soldiers inside from enjoying themselves. Their rowdiness made Kaladin worry about the entire building collapsing.

Behind it, in a splintery half-crate, lay a pile of discarded liquor bottles. Glass was precious enough that whole bottles would be reused, but these had cracks or broken tops. Kaladin set down his bundles, then selected three nearly whole bottles. He washed them in a nearby water barrel before tucking them into a sack he'd brought for the purpose.

He picked up his bundles again, nodding to the others. 'Try to look like you're doing something monotonous,' he said. 'Bow your heads.' The other two nodded, and they walked out into a main road, carrying the bundles as if on some work detail. They drew far less attention than they had before.

They avoided the lumberyard proper, crossing the open field of rock used as the army's staging area before walking down the slope of rock leading to the Shattered Plains. A sentry saw them, and Kaladin held his breath, but he said nothing. He probably assumed from their postures that they had a reason to be doing what they were. If they tried to leave the warcamp, it would be a different story, but this section down near the first few chasms wasn't off limits.

Before long, they approached the place where Kaladin had nearly killed himself. What a difference a few days could make. He felt like a different person – a strange hybrid of the man he had once been, the slave he'd become, and the pitiful wretch he still had to fight off. He remembered standing on the edge of the chasm, looking down. That darkness still terrified him.

If I fail to save the bridgemen, that wretch will take control again. This time he'll get his way . . . . That gave Kaladin a shiver. He set his bundles down beside the chasm ledge, then sat. The other two followed more hesitantly.

'We're going to toss them into the chasm?' Teft asked, scratching his beard. 'After all that work?'

'Of course not,' Kaladin said. He hesitated; Nomon was bright, but it was still night. 'You don't have any spheres, do you?'

'Why?' Teft asked, suspicious.

'For light, Teft.'

Teft grumbled, pulling out a handful of garnet chips. 'Was going to spend these tonight . . . .' he said. They glowed in his palm.

'All right,' Kaladin said, slipping out a reed. What had his father said about these? Hesitantly, Kaladin broke off the furry top of the reed, exposing the hollow center. He took the reed by the other end and ran his fingers down its length, squeezing it tight. Two drops of milky white liquid dripped into the empty liquor bottle.

Kaladin smiled in satisfaction, then squeezed his fingers along the length again. Nothing came out this time, so he tossed the reed into the chasm. For all his talk of hats, he didn't want to leave evidence.

'I thought you said we aren't throwing them in!' Teft accused.

Kaladin held up the liquor bottle. 'Only after we have this out.'

'What is it?' Rock leaned closer, squinting.

'Knobweed sap. Or, rather, knobweed milk—I don't think it's really sap. Anyway, it's a powerful antiseptic.'

'Anti ... what?' Teft asked.

'It scares away rotspren,' Kaladin said. 'They cause infection. This milk is one of the best antiseptics there is. Spread it on a wound that's already infected, and it will still work.' That was good, because Leyten's wounds had begun to turn an angry red, rotspren crawling all over.

Teft grunted, then glanced at the bundles. 'There are a lot of reeds here.'

'I know,' Kaladin said, handing over the other two bottles. 'That's why I'm glad I don't have to milk them all on my own.'

Teft sighed, but sat down and untied a bundle. Rock did so without the complaining, sitting with his knees bent to the sides, feet pressed together to hold the bottle as he worked.

A faint breeze blew up, rattling some of the reeds. 'Why do you care about them?' Teft finally asked.

'They're my men.'

'That's not what being bridgeleader means.'

'It means whatever we decide,' Kaladin said, noting that Syl had come over to listen. 'You, me, the others.'

'You think they'll let you do that?' Teft asked. 'The lighteyes and the captains?'

'You think they'll pay enough attention to even notice?'

Teft hesitated, then grunted, milking another reed.

'Perhaps they will,' Rock said. There was a surprising level of delicacy to the large man's motions as he milked the reeds. Kaladin hadn't thought those thick fingers would be so careful, so precise. 'Lighteyes, they are often noticing those things that you wish they would not.'

Teft grunted again, agreeing.

'How did you come here, Rock?' Kaladin asked. 'How does a Horn-eater end up leaving his mountains and coming to the lowlands?'

'You shouldn't ask those kinds of things, son,' Teft said, wagging a finger at Kaladin. 'We don't talk about our pasts.'

'We don't talk about *anything*,' Kaladin said. 'You two didn't even know each other's names.'

'Names are one thing,' Teft grumbled. 'Backgrounds, they're different. I—'

'Is all right,' Rock said. 'I will speak of this thing.'

Teft muttered to himself, but he did lean forward to listen when Rock spoke.

'My people have no Shardblades,' Rock said in his low, rumbling voice.

'That's not unusual,' Kaladin said. 'Other than Alethkar and Jah Keved, few kingdoms have many Blades.' It was a matter of some pride among the armies.

'This thing is not true,' Rock said. 'Thaylenah has five Blades and three full suits of Plate, all held by the royal guards. The Selay have their share of both suits and Blades. Other kingdoms, such as Herdaz, have a single Blade and set of Plate – this is passed down through the royal line. But the Unkalaki, we have not a single Shard. Many of our *nuatoma* – this thing, it is the same as your lighteyes, only their eyes are not light—'

'How can you be a lighteyes without light eyes?' Teft said with a scowl.

'By having dark eyes,' Rock said, as if it were obvious. 'We do not pick our leaders this way. Is complicated. But do not interrupt story.' He milked another reed, tossing the husk into a pile beside him. 'The *nuatoma*, they see our lack of Shards as great shame. They want these weapons very badly. It is believed that the *nuatoma* who first obtains a Shardblade would become king, a thing we have not had for many years. No peak would fight another peak where a man held one of the blessed Blades.'

'So you came to *buy* one?' Kaladin asked. No Shardbearer would sell his weapon. Each was a distinctive relic, taken from one of the Lost Radiants after their betrayal.

Rock laughed. 'Ha! Buy? No, we are not so foolish as this. But my *nuatoma*, he knew of your tradition, eh? It says that if a man kills a Shardbearer, he may take the Blade and Plate as his own. And so my *nuatoma* and his house, we made a grand procession, coming down to find and kill one of your Shardbearers.'

Kaladin almost laughed. 'I assume it proved more difficult than that.'

'My *nuatoma* was not a fool,' Rock said, defensive. 'He knew this thing would be difficult, but your tradition, it gives us hope, you see? Occasionally, a brave *nuatoma* will come down to duel a Shardbearer. Someday, one will win, and we will have Shards.'

'Perhaps,' Kaladin said, tossing an empty reed into the chasm. 'Assuming they agree to duel you in a bout to the death.'

'Oh, they always duel,' Rock said, laughing. 'The *nuatoma* brings many riches and promises all of his possessions to the victor. Your lighteyes, they cannot pass by a pond so warm! To kill an Unkalaki with no Shardblade, they do not see this thing as difficult. Many *nuatoma* have died. But is all right. Eventually, we will win.'

'And have one set of Shards,' Kaladin said. 'Alethkar has dozens.'

'One is a beginning,' Rock said, shrugging. 'But my *nuatoma* lost, so I am bridgeman.'

'Wait,' Teft said. 'You came all of this way with your brightlord, and once he lost, you up and joined a bridge crew?'

'No, no, you do not see,' Rock said. 'My *nuatoma*, he challenged Highprince Sadeas. Is well known that there are many Shardbearers here on Shattered Plains. My *nuatoma* thought it easier to fight man with only Plate first, then win Blade next.'

'And?' Teft said.

'Once my *nuatoma* lost to Brightlord Sadeas, all of us became his.'

'So you're a slave?' Kaladin asked, reaching up and feeling the marks on his forehead.

'No, we do not have this thing,' Rock said. 'I was not a slave of my *nuatoma*. I was his family.'

'His *family*?' Teft said. 'Kelek! You're a lighteyes!'

Rock laughed again, loud and full-bellied. Kaladin smiled despite himself. It seemed like so long since he'd heard someone laugh like that. 'No, no. I was only *umarti'a*— his cousin, you would say.'

'Still, you were related to him.'

'On the Peaks,' Rock said, 'the relatives of a brightlord are his servants.'

'What kind of system is that?' Teft complained. 'You have to be a servant to your own relatives? Storm me! I'd rather die, I think I would.'

'It is not so bad,' Rock said.

'You don't know my relatives,' Teft said, shivering.

Rock laughed again. 'You would rather serve someone you do not know? Like this Sadeas? A man who is no relation to you?' He shook his head. 'Lowlanders. You have too much air here. Makes your minds sick.'

'Too much air?' Kaladin asked.

'Yes,' Rock said.

'How can you have too much air? It's all around.'

'This thing, it is difficult to explain.' Rock's Alethi was good, but he sometimes forgot to add in common words. Other times, he remembered them, speaking his sentences precisely. The faster he spoke, the more words he forgot to put in.

'You have too much air,' Rock said. 'Come to the Peaks. You will see.'

'I guess,' Kaladin said, shooting a glance at Teft, who just shrugged. 'But you're wrong about one thing. You said that we serve someone we don't know. Well, I *do* know Brightlord Sadeas. I know him well.'

Rock raised an eyebrow.

'Arrogant,' Kaladin said, 'vengeful, greedy, corrupt to the core.'

Rock smiled. 'Yes, I think you are right. This man is not among the finest of lighteyes.'

'There are no "finest" among them, Rock. They're all the same.'

'They have done much to you, then?'

Kaladin shrugged, the question uncovering wounds that weren't yet healed. 'Anyway, your master was lucky.'

'Lucky to be slain by a Shardbearer?'

'Lucky he didn't win,' Kaladin said, 'and discover how he'd been tricked. They wouldn't have let him walk away with Sadeas's Plate.'

'Nonsense,' Teft broke in. 'Tradition—'

'Tradition is the blind witness they use to condemn us, Teft,' Kaladin said. 'It's the pretty box they use to wrap up their lies. It makes us serve them.'

Teft set his jaw. 'I've lived a lot longer than you, son. I know things. If a common man killed an enemy Shardbearer, he'd become a lighteyes. That's the way of it.'

He let the argument lapse. If Teft's illusions made him feel better about his place in this mess of a war, then who was Kaladin to dissuade him? 'So you were a servant,' Kaladin said to Rock. 'In a brightlord's retinue? What kind of servant?' He struggled for the right word, remembering back to the times he'd interacted with Wistiow or Roshone. 'A footman? A butler?'

Rock laughed. 'I was cook. My *nuatoma* would not come down to the lowlands without his own cook! Your food here, it has so many spices that you cannot taste anything else. Might as well be eating stones powdered with pepper!'

'*You* should talk about food,' Teft said, scowling. 'A Horneater?'

Kaladin frowned. 'Why do they call your people that, anyway?'

'Because they eat the horns and shells of the things they catch,' Teft said. 'The outsides.'

Rock smiled, with a look of longing. 'Ah, but the taste is so good.'

'You actually eat the shells?' Kaladin asked.

'We have very strong teeth,' Rock said proudly. 'But there. You now know my story. Brightlord Sadeas, he wasn't certain what he should do with most of us. Some were made soldiers, others serve in his household. I fixed him one meal and he sent me to bridge crews.' Rock hesitated. 'I may have, uh, enhanced the soup.'

'Enhanced?' Kaladin asked, raising an eyebrow.

Rock seemed to grow embarrassed. 'You see, I was quite angry about my *nuatoma*'s death. And I thought, these lowlanders, their tongues are all scorched and burned by the food they eat. They have no taste, and ...'

'And what?' Kaladin asked.

'Chull dung,' Rock said. 'It apparently has stronger taste than I assumed.'

'Wait,' Teft said. 'You put *chull dung* in Highprince Sadeas's soup?'

'Er, yes,' Rock said. 'Actually, I put this thing in his bread too. And used it as a garnish on the pork steak. And made a chutney out of it for the buttered garams. Chull dung, it has many uses, I found.'

Teft laughed, his voice echoing. He fell on his side, so amused that Kaladin was afraid he'd roll right into the chasm. 'Horneater,' Teft finally said, 'I owe you a drink.'

Rock smiled. Kaladin shook his head to himself, amazed. It suddenly made sense.

'What?' Rock said, apparently noticing his expression.

'This is what we need,' Kaladin said. '*This!* It's the thing I've been missing.'

Rock hesitated. 'Chull dung? This is the thing you need?'

Teft burst into another round of laugher.

'No,' Kaladin said. 'It's ... well, I'll show you. But first we need this knobweed sap.' They'd barely made their way through one of the bundles, and already his fingers were aching from the milking.

'What of you, Kaladin?' Rock asked. 'I have been telling you my story.

You will tell me yours? How did you come to those marks on your forehead?'

'Yeah,' Teft said, wiping his eyes. 'Whose food did *you* trat in?'

'I thought you said it was taboo to ask about a bridgeman's past,' Kaladin said.

'You made Rock share, son,' Teft said. 'It's only fair.'

'So if I tell my story, that means you'll tell yours?'

Teft scowled immediately. 'Now look, I ain't going to—'

'I killed a man,' Kaladin said.

That quieted Teft. Rock perked up. Syl, Kaladin noticed, was still watching with interest. That was odd for her; normally, her attention wavered quickly.

'You killed a man?' Rock said. 'And after this thing, they made you a slave? Is not the punishment for murder usually death?'

'It wasn't murder,' Kaladin said softly, thinking of the scraggly bearded man in the slave wagon who had asked him these same questions. 'In fact, I was thanked for it by someone very important.'

He fell silent.

'And?' Teft finally asked.

'And . . .' Kaladin said, looking down at a reed. Nomon was setting in the west, and the small green disk of Mishim – the final moon – was rising in the east. 'And it turns out that lighteyes don't react very well when you turn down their gifts.'

The others waited for more, but Kaladin fell silent, working on his reeds. It shocked him, how painful it still was to remember those events back in Amaram's army.

Either the others sensed his mood, or they felt what he'd said was enough, for they each turned back to their work and prodded no further.

Neither point makes the things I have written to you here untrue.

The king's Gallery of Maps balanced beauty and function. The expansive domed structure of Soulcast stone had smooth sides that melded seamlessly with the rocky ground. It was shaped like a long loaf of Thaylen bread, and had large skylights in the ceiling, allowing the sun to shine down on handsome formations of shalebark.

Dalinar passed one of these, pinks and vibrant greens and blues growing in a gnarled pattern as high as his shoulders. The crusty, hard plants had no true stalks or leaves, just waving tendrils like colorful hair. Except for those, shalebark seemed more rock than vegetation. And yet, scholars said it must be a plant for the way it grew and reached toward the light.

Men did that too, he thought. *Once.*

Highprince Roion stood in front of one of the maps, hands clasped behind his back, his numerous attendants clogging the other side of the gallery. Roion was a tall, light-skinned man with a dark, well-trimmed beard. He was thinning on top. Like most of the others, he wore a short, open-fronted jacket, exposing the shirt underneath. Its red fabric poked out above the jacket's collar.

So sloppy, Dalinar thought, though it was very fashionable. Dalinar just wished that current fashion weren't so, well, sloppy.

'Brightlord Dalinar,' Roion said. 'I have difficulty seeing the point of this meeting.'

'Walk with me, Brightlord Roion,' Dalinar said, nodding to the side.

The other man sighed, but joined Dalinar and walked the pathway between the clusters of plants and the wall of maps. Roion's attendants followed; they included both a cupbearer and a shieldbearer.

Each map was illuminated by diamonds, their enclosures made of mirror-polished steel. The maps were inked, in detail, onto unnaturally large, seamless sheets of parchment. Such parchment was obviously Soulcast. Near the center of the chamber they came to the Prime Map, an enormous, detailed map fixed in a frame on the wall. It showed the entirety of the Shattered Plains that had been explored. Permanent bridges were drawn in red, and plateaus close to the Alethi side had blue glyphpairs on them, indicating which highprince controlled them. The eastern section of the map grew less detailed until the lines vanished.

In the middle was the contested area, the section of plateaus where the chasmfiends most often came to make their chrysalises. Few came to the near side, where the permanent bridges were. If they did come, it was to hunt, not to pupate.

Controlling the nearby plateaus was still important, as a highprince – by agreement – could not cross a plateau maintained by one of the others unless he had permission. That determined who had the best pathways to the central plateaus, and it also determined who had to maintain the watch-posts and permanent bridges on that plateau. Those plateaus were bought and sold among the highprinces.

A second sheet of parchment to the side of the Prime Map listed each highprince and the number of gemhearts he had won. It was a very Alethi thing to do – maintain motivation by making it very clear who was winning and who lagged behind.

Roion's eyes immediately went to his own name on the list. Of all the highprinces, Roion had won the fewest gemhearts.

Dalinar reached his hand up to the Prime Map, brushing the parchment. The middle plateaus were named or numbered for ease of reference. Foremost of them was a large plateau that stood defiantly near the Parshendi side. The Tower, it was called. An unusually massive and oddly shaped plateau that the chasmfiends seemed particularly fond of using as a spot for pupating.

Looking at it gave him pause. The size of a contested plateau determined the number of troops you could field on it. The Parshendi usually brought a large force to the Tower, and they had rebuffed the Alethi assaults there twenty-seven times now. No Alethi had ever won a skirmish upon it. Dalinar had been turned back there twice himself.

It was just too close to the Parshendi; they could always get there first and form up, using the slope to give them excellent high ground. *But if we could corner them there*, he thought, *with a large enough force of our own* ... It could mean trapping and killing a huge number of Parshendi troops. Maybe enough of them to break their ability to wage war on the Plains.

It was something to consider. Before that could happen, however, Dalinar would need alliances. He ran his fingers westward. 'Highprince Sadeas has been doing very well lately.' Dalinar tapped Sadeas's warcamp. 'He's been buying plateaus from other highprinces, making it easier and easier for him to get to the battlefields first.'

'Yes,' Roion said, frowning. 'One hardly needs to see a map to know that, Dalinar.'

'Look at the scope of it,' Dalinar said. 'Six years of continuous fighting, and nobody has even *seen* the center of the Shattered Plains.'

'That's never been the point. We hold them in, besiege them, starve them out, and force them to come to us. Wasn't that *your* plan?'

'Yes, but I never imagined it would take this long. I've been thinking that it might be time to change tactics.'

'Why? This one works. Hardly a week goes by without a couple of clashes with the Parshendi. Though, might I point out that *you* have hardly been a model of inspiration in battle lately.' He nodded to Dalinar's name on the smaller sheet.

There were a good number of scratches next to his name, noting gemhearts won. But very few of them were fresh.

'There are some who say the Blackthorn has lost his sting,' Roion said. He was careful not to insult Dalinar outright, but he went further than he once would have. News of Dalinar's actions while trapped in the barrack had spread.

Dalinar forced himself to be calm. 'Roion, we cannot continue to treat this war as a game.'

'All wars are games. The greatest kind, with the pieces lost real lives, the prizes captured making for real wealth! This is the life for which men exist. To fight, to kill, to win.' He was quoting the Sunmaker, the last Alethi king to unite the highprinces. Gavilar had once revered his name.

'Perhaps,' Dalinar said. 'Yet what is the point? We fight to get Shard-blades, then use those Shardblades to fight to get more Shardblades. It's a circle, round and round we go, chasing our tails so we can be better at chasing our tails.'

'We fight to prepare ourselves to reclaim heaven and take back what is ours.'

'Men can train without going to war, and men can fight without it being meaningless. It wasn't always this way. There were times when our wars *meant* something.'

Roion raised an eyebrow. 'You're almost making me believe the rumors, Dalinar. They say you've lost your taste for combat, that you no longer have the will to fight.' He eyed Dalinar again. 'Some are saying that it is time to abdicate in favor of your son.'

'The rumors are wrong,' Dalinar snapped.

'That is—'

'They are *wrong*,' Dalinar said firmly, 'if they claim that I no longer care.' He rested his fingers on the surface of the map again, running them across the smooth parchment. 'I care, Roion. I care deeply. About this people. About my nephew. About the future of this war. And that is why I suggest we pursue an aggressive course from now on.'

'Well, that is good to hear, I suppose.'

Unite them. . . .

'I want you to try a joint plateau assault with me,' Dalinar said.

'*What?*'

'I want the two of us to try coordinating our efforts and attack at the same time, working together.'

'Why would we want to do that?'

'We could increase our chances of winning gemhearts.'

'If more troops increased my chances of winning,' Roion said, 'then I'd just bring more of my own. The plateaus are too small for fielding large armies, and mobility is more important than sheer numbers.'

It was a valid point; on the Plains, more didn't necessarily mean better. Close confines and a requisite forced march to the battlefield changed warfare significantly. The exact number of troops used depended on the size of the plateau and the highprince's personal martial philosophy.

'Working together wouldn't just be about fielding more troops,' Dalinar said. 'Each highprince's army has different strengths. I'm known for my heavy infantry; you have the best archers. Sadeas's bridges are the fastest. Working together, we could try new tactics. We expend too much effort getting to the plateau in haste. If we weren't so rushed, competing against one another, maybe we could surround the plateau. We could try letting the Parshendi arrive first, then assault them on *our* terms, not theirs.'

Roion hesitated. Dalinar had spent days deliberating with his generals about the possibility of a joint assault. It seemed that there would be distinct advantages, but they wouldn't know for certain until someone tried it with him.

He actually seemed to be considering. 'Who would get the gemheart?'

'We split the wealth equally,' Dalinar said.

'And if we capture a Shardblade?'

'The man who won it would get it, obviously.'

'And that's most likely to be you,' Roion said, frowning. 'As you and your son already have Shards.'

It was the great problem of Shardblades and Shardplate – winning either was highly unlikely unless you already had Shards yourself. In fact, having only one or the other often wasn't enough. Sadeas had faced Parshendi Shardbearers on the field, and had always been forced to retreat, lest he be slain himself.

'I'm certain we could arrange something more equitable,' Dalinar finally said. If he won Shards, he'd been hoping to be able to give them to Renarin.

'I'm sure,' Roion said skeptically.

Dalinar drew in a breath. He needed to be bolder. 'What if I offer them to you?'

'Excuse me?'

'We try a joint attack. If I win a Shardblade or Plate, you get the first set. But I keep the second.'

Roion's eyes narrowed. 'You'd do that?'

'On my honor, Roion.'

'Well, nobody would doubt that. But can you blame a man for being wary?'

'Of what?'

'I am a highprince, Dalinar,' Roion said. 'My princedom is the smallest, true, but I am my own man. I would not see myself subordinated to someone greater.'

You've already become part of something greater, Dalinar thought with frustration. *That happened the moment you swore fealty to Gavilar.* Roion and the others refused to make good on their promises. 'Our kingdom can be so much more than it is, Roion.'

'Perhaps. But perhaps I'm satisfied with what I have. Either way, you make an interesting proposal. I shall have to think on it further.'

'Very well,' Dalinar said, but his instinct said that Roion would decline the offer. The man was too suspicious. The highprinces barely trusted one another enough to work together when there *weren't* Shardblades and gems at stake.

'Will I be seeing you at the feast this evening?' Roion asked.

'Why wouldn't you?' Dalinar asked with a sigh.

'Well, the stormwardens have been saying that there *could* be a high-storm tonight, you see—'

'I will be there,' Dalinar said flatly.

'Yes, of course,' Roion said, chuckling. 'No reason why you wouldn't be.' He smiled at Dalinar and withdrew, his attendants following.

Dalinar sighed, turning to study the Prime Map, thinking through the meeting and what it meant. He stood there for a long time. Looking down on the Plains, as if a god far above. The plateaus looked like close islands, or perhaps jagged pieces set in a massive stained-glass window. Not for the first time, he felt as if he should be able to make out a pattern to the plateaus. If he could see more of them, perhaps. What would it mean if there *was* an order to the chasms?

Everyone else was so concerned with looking strong, with proving themselves. Was he really the only one who saw how frivolous that was? Strength for strength's sake? What good was strength unless you did something with it?

Alethkar was a light, once, he thought. *That's what Gavilar's book claims, that's what the visions are showing me. Nohadon was king of Alethkar, so long ago. In the time before the Heralds left.*

Dalinar felt as if he could almost see it. The secret. The thing that had made Gavilar so excited in the months before his death. If Dalinar could just stretch a little farther, he'd make it out. See the pattern in the lives of men. And finally know.

But that was what he'd been doing for the last six years. Grasping, stretching, reaching just a little farther. The farther he reached, the more distant those answers seemed to become.

◆◆

Adolin stepped into the Gallery of Maps. His father was still there, standing alone. Two members of the Cobalt Guard watched over him from a distance. Roion was nowhere to be seen.

Adolin approached slowly. His father had that look in his eyes, the absent one he got so often lately. Even when he wasn't having an episode, he wasn't entirely here. Not in the way he once had been.

'Father?' Adolin said, stepping up to him.

'Hello, Adolin.'

'How was the meeting with Roion?' Adolin asked, trying to sound cheerful.

'Disappointing. I'm proving far worse at diplomacy than I once was at war-making.'

'There's no profit in peace.'

'That's what everyone says. But we had peace once, and seemed to do just fine. Better, even.'

'There hasn't been peace since the Tranquiline Halls,' Adolin said immediately. '"Man's life on Roshar is conflict."' It was a quotation from *The Arguments*.

Dalinar turned to Adolin, looking amused. 'Quoting scripture at me? You?'

Adolin shrugged, feeling foolish. 'Well, you see, Malasha is rather religious, and so earlier today I was listening to—'

'Wait,' Dalinar said. 'Malasha? Who's that?'

'Daughter of Brightlord Seveks.'

'And that other girl, Janala?'

Adolin grimaced, thinking back to the disastrous walk they'd gone on the other day. Several nice gifts had yet to repair that. She didn't seem half as excited about him now that he wasn't courting someone else. 'Things are rocky. Malasha seems like a better prospect.' He moved on quickly. 'I take it that Roion won't soon be going on any plateau assault with us.'

Dalinar shook his head. 'He's too afraid that I'm trying to maneuver him into a position where I can seize his lands. Perhaps it was wrong to approach the weakest highprince first. He'd rather hunker down and try to weather what comes at him, holding what he has, as opposed to making a risky play for something greater.'

Dalinar stared at the map, looking distant again. 'Gavilar dreamed of unifying Alethkar. Once I thought he'd achieved it, despite what he claimed. The longer I work with these men, the more I realize that Gavilar was right. We failed. We defeated these men, but we *never* unified them.'

'So you still intend to approach the others?'

'I do. I only need one to say yes in order to start. Who do you think we should go to next?'

'I'm not sure,' Adolin said. 'But for now, I think you should know something. Sadeas has sent to us, asking permission to enter our warcamp. He wants to interview the grooms who cared for His Majesty's horse during the hunt.'

'His new position gives him the right to make those kinds of demands.'

'Father,' Adolin said, stepping closer, speaking softly. 'I think he's going to move against us.'

Dalinar looked at him.

'I know you trust him,' Adolin said quickly. 'And I understand your reasons now. But *listen* to me. This move puts him in an ideal position to undermine us. The king has grown paranoid enough that he's suspicious even of you and me – I know you've seen it. All Sadeas needs to do is find imaginary "evidence" linking us to an attempt to kill the king, and he'll be able to turn Elhokar against us.'

'We may have to risk that.'

Adolin frowned. 'But—'

'I trust Sadeas, son,' Dalinar said. 'But even if I didn't, we couldn't forbid him entry or block his investigation. We'd not only look guilty in the king's eyes, but we'd be denying his authority as well.' He shook his head. 'If I ever want the other highprinces to accept me as their leader in war, I have to be willing to allow Sadeas his authority as Highprince of Information. I can't rely upon the old traditions for my authority yet deny Sadeas the same right.'

'I suppose,' Adolin admitted. 'But we could still prepare. You can't tell me you're not a little worried.'

Dalinar hesitated. 'Perhaps. This maneuver of Sadeas's is aggressive. But I've been told what to do. "Trust Sadeas. Be strong. Act with honor, and honor will aid you." That is the advice I've been given.'

'From where?'

Dalinar looked to him, and it became obvious to Adolin.

'So we're betting the future of our house on these visions now,' Adolin said flatly.

'I wouldn't say that,' Dalinar replied. 'If Sadeas did move against us, I wouldn't simply let him shove us over. But I'm also not going to make the first move against him.'

'Because of what you've seen,' Adolin said, growing frustrated. 'Father, you said you'd listen to what I had to say about the visions. Well, please listen now.'

'This isn't the proper place.'

'You always have an excuse,' Adolin said. 'I've tried to approach you about it five times now, and you always rebuff me!'

'Perhaps it's because I know what you'll say,' Dalinar said. 'And I know it won't do any good.'

'Or perhaps it's because you don't want to be confronted by the truth.'

'That's enough, Adolin.'

'No, no it's not! We're mocked in every one of the warcamps, our authority and reputation diminishes by the day, and *you* refuse to do anything substantial about it!'

'Adolin. I will *not* take this from my son.'

'But you'll take it from everyone else? Why is that, Father? When others say things about us, you let them. But when Renarin or I take the smallest step toward what *you* view as being inappropriate, we're immediately chastised! Everyone else can speak lies, but I can't speak the truth? Do your sons mean so little to you?'

Dalinar froze, looking as if he'd been slapped.

'You aren't *well*, Father,' Adolin continued. Part of him realized that he had gone too far, that he was speaking too loudly, but it boiled out anyway. 'We need to stop tiptoeing around it! *You* need to stop making up increasingly irrational explanations to reason away your lapses! I know it's hard to accept, but sometimes, people get old. Sometimes, the mind stops working right.

'I don't know what's wrong. Maybe it's your guilt over Gavilar's death. That book, the Codes, the visions – maybe they're all attempts to find escape, find redemption, something. What you see *is not* real. Your life now is a rationalization, a way of trying to pretend that what's happening isn't happening. But I'll go to *Damnation itself* before I'll let you drag the entire house down without speaking my mind on it!'

He practically shouted those last words. They echoed in the large chamber, and Adolin realized he was shaking. He had never, in all his years of life, spoken to his father in such a way.

'You think I haven't wondered these things?' Dalinar said, his voice cold, his eyes hard. 'I've gone through each point you've made a dozen times over.'

'Then maybe you should go over them a few more.'

'I *must* trust myself. The visions are trying to show me something important. I cannot prove it or explain how I know. But it's true.'

'Of course you think that,' Adolin said, exasperated. 'Don't you see? That's exactly what you *would* feel. Men are very good at seeing what they want to! Look at the king. He sees a killer in every shadow, and a worn strap becomes a convoluted plot to take his life.'

Dalinar fell silent again.

'Sometimes, the simple answers *are* the right ones, Father!' Adolin said. 'The king's strap just wore out. And you . . . you're seeing things that aren't there. I'm sorry.'

They locked expressions. Adolin didn't look away. He wouldn't look away.

Dalinar finally turned from him. 'Leave me, please.'

'All right. Fine. But I want you to think about this. I want you to—'

'Adolin. *Go.*'

Adolin gritted his teeth, but turned and stalked away. *It needed to be said*, he told himself as he left the gallery. That didn't make him feel any less sick about having to be the one who said it.

25

THE BUTCHER

SEVEN YEARS AGO

I t ain't right, what they do,' the woman's voice said. 'You ain't supposed to cut into folks, peering in to see what the Almighty placed hidden for good reason.'

Kal froze, standing in an alleyway between two houses in Hearthstone. The sky was wan overhead; winter had come for a time. The Weeping was near, and highstorms were infrequent. For now, it was too cold for plants to enjoy the respite; rockbuds spent winter weeks curled up inside their shells. Most creatures hibernated, waiting for warmth to return. Fortunately, seasons generally lasted only a few weeks. Unpredictability. That was the way of the world. Only after death was there stability. So the ardents taught, at least.

Kal wore a thick, padded coat of breachtree cotton. The material was scratchy but warm, and had been dyed a deep brown. He kept the hood up, his hands in his pockets. To his right sat the baker's place – the family slept in the triangular crawlspace in back, and the front was their store. To Kal's left was one of Hearthstone's taverns, where lavis ale and mudbeer flowed in abundance during winter weeks.

He could hear two women, unseen but chatting a short distance way.

'You know that he stole from the old citylord,' one woman's voice said, keeping her voice down. 'An entire goblet full of spheres. The surgeon says they were a gift, but he was the only one there when the citylord died.'

'There *is* a document, I hear,' the first voice said.

'A few glyphs. Not a proper will. And whose hand wrote those glyphs? The surgeon himself. It ain't right, the citylord not having a woman there to be scribe. I'm telling you. It ain't right what they do.'

Kal gritted his teeth, tempted to step out and let the women see that he'd heard them. His father wouldn't approve, though. Lirin wouldn't want to cause strife or embarrassment.

But that was his father. So Kal marched right out of the alleyway, passing Nanha Terith and Nanha Relina standing and gossiping in front of the bakery. Terith was the baker's wife, a fat woman with curly dark hair. She was in the middle of another calumny. Kal gave her a sharp look, and her brown eyes showed a satisfying moment of discomfiture.

Kal crossed the square carefully, wary of patches of ice. The door to the bakery slammed shut behind him, the two women fleeing inside.

His satisfaction didn't last long. Why did people always say such things about his father? They called him morbid and unnatural, but would scurry out to buy glyphwards and charms from a passing apothecary or luckmerch. The Almighty pity a man who actually did something *useful* to help!

Still stewing, Kal turned a few corners, walking to where his mother stood on a stepladder at the side of the town hall, carefully chipping at the eaves of the building. Hesina was a tall woman, and she usually kept her hair pulled back into a tail, then wrapped a kerchief around her head. Today, she wore a knit hat over that. She had a long brown coat that matched Kal's, and the blue hem of her skirt just barely peeked out at the bottom.

The objects of her attention were a set of icicle-like pendants of rock that had formed on the edges of the roof. Highstorms dropped stormwater, and stormwater carried crem. If left alone, crem eventually hardened into stone. Buildings grew stalactites, formed by stormwater slowly dripping from the eaves. You had to clean them off regularly, or risk weighing down the roof so much that it collapsed.

She noticed him and smiled, her cheeks flushed from the cold. With a narrow face, a bold chin, and full lips, she was a pretty woman. At least Kal thought so. Prettier than the baker's wife, for sure.

'Your father dismissed you from your lessons already?' she asked.

'Everyone hates Father,' Kal blurted out.

His mother turned back to her work. 'Kaladin, you're thirteen. You're old enough to know not to say foolish things like that.'

'It's true,' he said stubbornly. 'I heard some women talking, just now. They said that Father stole the spheres from Brightlord Wistiow. They say that Father enjoys slicing people open and doing things that ain't natural.'

'*Aren't* natural.'

'Why can't I speak like everyone else?'

'Because it isn't proper.'

'It's proper enough for Nanha Terith.'

'And what do you think of her?'

Kal hesitated. 'She's ignorant. And she likes to gossip about things she doesn't know anything about.'

'Well, then. If you wish to emulate her, I can obviously find no objection to the practice.'

Kal grimaced. You had to watch yourself when speaking with Hesina; she liked to twist words about. He leaned back against the wall of the town hall, watching his breath puff out in front of him. Perhaps a different tactic would work. 'Mother, *why* do people hate Father?'

'They don't hate him,' she said. However, his calmly asked question got her to continue. 'But he *does* make them uncomfortable.'

'Why?'

'Because some people are frightened of knowledge. Your father is a learned man; he knows things the others can't understand. So those things must be dark and mysterious.'

'They aren't afraid of luckmerches and glyphwards.'

'Those you can understand,' his mother said calmly. 'You burn a glyphward out in front of your house, and it will turn away evil. It's easy. Your father won't give someone a ward to heal them. He'll insist that they stay in bed, drinking water, taking some foul medicine, and washing their wound each day. It's hard. They'd rather leave it all to fate.'

Kal considered that. 'I think they hate him because he fails too often.'

'There is that. If a glyphward fails, you can blame it on the will of the Almighty. If your father fails, then it's his fault. Or such is the perception.' His mother continued working, flakes of stone falling to the ground around her. 'They'll never actually *hate* your father – he's too useful. But he'll never really be one of them. That's the price of being a surgeon. Having power over the lives of men is an uncomfortable responsibility.'

'And if I don't want that responsibility? What if I just want to be something normal, like a baker, or a farmer, or . . . ' *Or a soldier*, he added in his mind. He'd picked up a staff a few times in secret, and though he'd never been able to replicate that moment when he'd fought Jost, there *was* something invigorating about holding a weapon. Something that drew him and excited him.

'I think,' his mother said, 'that you'll find the lives of bakers and farmers are not so enviable.'

'At least they have friends.'

'And so do you. What of Tien?'

'Tien's not my friend, Mother. He's my brother.'

'Oh, and he can't be both at once?'

Kal rolled his eyes. 'You know what I mean.'

She climbed down from the stepladder, patting his shoulder. 'Yes, I do, and I'm sorry to make light of it. But you put yourself in a difficult position. You want friends, but do you really want to *act* like the other boys? Give up your studies so you can slave in the fields? Grow old before your time, weathered and furrowed by the sun?'

Kal didn't reply.

'The things that others have always seem better than what you have,' his mother said. 'Bring the stepladder.'

Kal followed dutifully, rounding the town hall to the other side, then putting down the ladder so his mother could climb up to begin work again.

'The others think Father stole those spheres.' Kal shoved his hands in his pockets. 'They think he wrote out that order from Brightlord Wistiow and had the old man sign it when he didn't know what he was doing.'

His mother was silent.

'I hate their lies and gossip,' Kal said. 'I hate them for making up things about us.'

'Don't hate them, Kal. They're good people. In this case, they're just repeating what they've heard.' She glanced at the citylord's manor, distant upon a hill above the town. Every time Kal saw it, he felt like he should go up and talk to Laral. But the last few times he'd tried, he hadn't been allowed to see her. Now that her father was dead, her nurse oversaw her time, and the woman didn't think mingling with boys from the town was appropriate.

The nurse's husband, Miliv, had been Brightlord Wistiow's head steward. If there was a source of bad rumors about Kal's family, it probably came from him. He never *had* liked Kal's father. Well, Miliv wouldn't matter soon. A new citylord was expected to arrive any day.

'Mother,' Kal said, 'those spheres are just sitting there doing nothing but glowing. Can't we spend some to keep you from having to come out here and work?'

'I like working,' she said, scraping away again. 'It clears the head.'

'Didn't you just tell me that I wouldn't like having to labor? My face furrowed before its time, or something poetic like that?'

She hesitated, then laughed. 'Clever boy.'

'Cold boy,' he grumbled, shivering.

'I work because I want to. We can't spend those spheres – they're for your education – and so my working is better than forcing your father to charge for his healings.'

'Maybe they'd respect us more if we did charge.'

'Oh, they respect us. No, I don't think that is the problem.' She looked down at Kal. 'You know that we're second nahn.'

'Sure,' Kal said, shrugging.

'An accomplished young surgeon of the right rank could draw the attention of a poorer noble family, one who wished money and acclaim. It happens in the larger cities.'

Kal glanced up at the mansion again. 'That's why you encouraged me to play with Laral so much. You wanted to marry me off to her, didn't you?'

'It was a possibility,' his mother said, returning to her work.

He honestly wasn't certain how he felt about that. The last few months had been strange for Kal. His father had forced him into his studies, but in secret he'd spent his time with the staff. Two possible paths. Both enticing. Kal *did* like learning, and he longed for the ability to help people, bind their wounds, make them better. He saw true nobility in what his father did.

But it seemed to Kal that if he could fight, he could do something even more noble. Protect their lands, like the great lighteyed heroes of the stories. And there was the way he felt when holding a weapon.

Two paths. Opposites, in many ways. He could only choose one.

His mother kept chipping away at the eaves, and – with a sigh – Kal fetched a second stepladder and set of tools from the workroom, then joined her. He was tall for his age, but he still had to stand high on the ladder. He caught his mother smiling as he worked, no doubt pleased at having raised such a helpful young man. In reality, Kal just wanted the chance to pound on something.

How would he feel, marrying someone like Laral? He'd never be her equal. Their children would have a chance of being lighteyed or darkeyed, so even his children might outrank him. He knew he'd feel terribly out of place. That was another aspect of becoming a surgeon. If he chose that path, he would be choosing the life of his father. Choosing to set himself apart, to be isolated.

If he went to war, however, he would have a place. Maybe he could even do the nearly unthinkable, win a Shardblade and become a true lighteyes. Then he could marry Laral and not have to be her inferior. Was that why she'd always encouraged him to become a soldier? Had she been thinking about these kinds of things, even back then? Back then, these kinds of decisions – marriage, his future – had seemed impossibly far-off to Kal.

He felt so young. Did he really have to consider these questions? It would still be another few years before the surgeons of Kharbranth would let him take their tests. But if he *were* going to become a soldier instead, he'd have to join the army before that happened. How would his father react if Kal just up and went with the recruiters? Kal wasn't certain he'd be able to face Lirin's disappointed eyes.

As if in response to his thoughts, Lirin's voice called from nearby. 'Hesina!'

Kal's mother turned, smiling and tucking a stray lock of dark hair back into her kerchief. Kal's father rushed down the street, his face anxious. Kal felt a sudden jolt of worry. Who was wounded? Why hadn't Lirin sent for him?

'What is it?' Kal's mother asked, climbing down.

'He's here, Hesina,' Kal's father said.

'About time.'

'Who?' Kal asked, jumping down from the stepladder. 'Who's here?'

'The new citylord, son,' Lirin said, his breath puffing in the cold air. 'His name is Brightlord Roshone. No time to change, I'm afraid. Not if we want to catch his first speech. Come on!'

The three of them hurried away, Kal's thoughts and worries banished in the face of the chance to meet a new lighteyes.

'He didn't send word ahead,' Lirin said under his breath.

'That could be a good sign,' Hesina replied. 'Maybe he doesn't feel he needs everyone to dote on him.'

'That, or he's inconsiderate. Stormfather, I hate getting a new Landed. Always makes me feel like I'm throwing a handful of stones into a game of breakneck. Will we throw the queen or the tower?'

'We shall see soon enough,' Hesina said, glancing at Kal. 'Don't let your father's words unnerve you. He always gets pessimistic at times like this.'

'I do *not*,' Lirin said.

She gave him a look.

'Name one other time.'

'Meeting my parents.'

Kal's father pulled up short, blinking. 'Stormwinds,' he muttered, 'let's hope this doesn't go *half* as poorly as that.'

Kal listened with curiosity. He'd never met his mother's parents; they weren't often spoken of. Soon, the three of them reached the south side of town. A crowd was gathered, and Tien was already there, waiting. He waved in his excitable way, jumping up and down.

'Wish I had half that boy's energy,' Lirin said.

'I've got a place for us picked out!' Tien called eagerly, pointing. 'By the rain barrels! Come on! We're going to miss it!'

Tien scurried over, climbing atop the barrels. Several of the town's other boys noticed him, and they nudged one another, one making some comment Kal couldn't hear. It set the others laughing at Tien, and that immediately made Kal furious. Tien didn't deserve mockery just because he was a little small for his age.

This wasn't a good time to confront the other boys, though, so Kal sullenly joined his parents beside the barrels. Tien smiled at him, standing atop his barrel. He'd piled a few of his favorite rocks near him, stones of different colors and shapes. There were rocks all around them, and yet Tien was the only person he knew who found wonder in them. After a moment's consideration, Kal climbed atop a barrel – careful not to disturb any of Tien's rocks – so he too could get a better view of the citylord's procession.

It was enormous. There must have been a dozen wagons in that line, following a fine black carriage pulled by four sleek black horses. Kal gawked despite himself. Wistiow had only owned one horse, and it had seemed as old as he was.

Could one man, even a lighteyes, own that much furniture? Where would he put it all? And there were people too. Dozens of them, riding in the wagons, walking in groups. There were also a dozen soldiers in gleaming breastplates and leather skirts. This lighteyes even had his own honor guard.

Eventually the procession reached the turn-off to Hearthstone. A man riding a horse led the carriage and its soldiers forward to the town while most of the wagons continued up to the manor. Kal grew increasingly excited as the carriage rolled slowly into place. Would he finally get to see a real, lighteyed hero? The word around town claimed it was likely that the new citylord would be someone King Gavilar or Highprince Sadeas had promoted because he'd distinguished himself in the wars to unite Alethkar.

The carriage turned sideways so that the door faced the crowd. The horses snorted and stomped the ground, and the carriage driver hopped down and quickly opened the door. A middle-aged man with a short, grey-streaked beard stepped out. He wore a ruffled violet coat, tailored so that it was short at the front – reaching only to his waist – but long at the back. Beneath it, he wore a golden takama, a long, straight skirt that went down to his calves.

A takama. Few wore them anymore, but old soldiers in town spoke of the days when they'd been popular as warrior's garb. Kal hadn't expected the takama to look so much like a woman's skirt, but still, it was a good sign. Roshone himself seemed a little too old, a little too flabby, to be a true soldier. But he wore a sword.

The lighteyed man scanned the crowd, a distasteful look on his face, as if he'd swallowed something bitter. Behind the man, two people peeked out. A younger man with a narrow face and an older woman with braided hair. Roshone studied the crowd, then shook his head and turned around to climb back in the carriage.

Kal frowned. Wasn't he going to say anything? The crowd seemed to share Kal's shock; a few of them began whispering in anxiety.

'Brightlord Roshone!' Kal's father called.

The crowd hushed. The lighteyed man glanced back. People shied away, and Kal found himself shrinking down beneath that harsh gaze. 'Who spoke?' Roshone demanded, his voice a low baritone.

Lirin stepped forward, raising a hand. 'Brightlord. Was your trip pleasant? Please, can we show you the town?'

'What is your name?'

'Lirin, Brightlord. Hearthstone's surgeon.'

'Ah,' Roshone said. 'You're the one who let old Wistiow die.' The brightlord's expression darkened. 'In a way, it's your fault I'm in this pitiful, miserable quarter of the kingdom.' He grunted, then climbed back in the carriage and slammed the door. Within seconds, the carriage driver had replaced the stairs, climbed into his place, and started turning the vehicle around.

Kal's father slowly let his arm fall to his side. The townspeople began to chatter immediately, gossiping about the soldiers, the carriage, the horses.

Kal sat down on his barrel. *Well*, he thought. *I guess we could expect a warrior to be curt, right?* The heroes from the legends weren't necessarily the polite types. Killing people and fancy talking didn't always go together, old Jarel had once told him.

Lirin walked back, his expression troubled.

'Well?' Hesina said, trying to sound cheerful. 'What do you think? Did we throw the queen or the tower?'

'Neither.'

'Oh? And what did we throw instead?'

'I'm not sure,' he said, glancing over his shoulder. 'A pair and a trio, maybe. Let's get back home.'

Tien scratched his head in confusion, but the words weighed on Kal. The tower was three pairs in a game of breakneck. The queen was two trios. The first was an outright loss, the other an outright win.

But a pair and a trio, that was called the butcher. Whether you won or not would depend on the other throws you made. ·

And, more importantly, on the throws of everyone else.

26

STILLNESS

I am being chased. Your friends of the Seventeenth Shard, I suspect. I believe they're still lost, following a false trail I left for them. They'll be happier that way. I doubt they have any inkling what to do with me should they actually catch me.

I stood in the darkened monastery chamber,"' Litima read, standing at the lectern with the tome open before her, "'its far reaches painted with pools of black where light did not wander. I sat on the floor, thinking of that dark, that Unseen. I could not know, for certain, what was hidden in that night. I suspected there were walls, sturdy and thick, but could I *know* without seeing? When all was hidden, what could a man rely upon as True?'"

Litima – one of Dalinar's scribes – was tall and plump and wore a violet silk gown with yellow trim. She read to Dalinar as he stood, regarding the maps on the wall of his sitting room. That room was fitted with handsome wood furnishings and fine woven rugs imported up from Marat. A crystal carafe of afternoon wine – orange, not intoxicating – sat on a high-legged serving table in the corner, sparkling with the light of the diamond spheres hanging in chandeliers above.

"'Candle flames,'" Litima continued. The selection was from *The Way of Kings*, read from the very copy that Gavilar had once owned. "'A dozen candles burned themselves to death on the shelf before me. Each of my breaths made them tremble. To them, I was a behemoth, to frighten and destroy. And yet, if I strayed too close, *they* could destroy *me*. My invisible breath, the pulses of life that flowed in and out, could end them freely, while my fingers could not do the same without being repaid in pain."'

Dalinar idly twisted his signet ring in thought; it was sapphire with his Kholin glyphpair on it. Renarin stood next to him, wearing a coat of blue and silver, golden knots on the shoulders marking him as a prince. Adolin wasn't there. Dalinar and he had been stepping gingerly around one another since their argument in the Gallery.

"'I understood in a moment of stillness,'" Litima read: "'Those candle flames were like the lives of men. So fragile. So deadly. Left alone, they lit and warmed. Let run rampant, they would destroy the very things they were meant to illuminate. Embryonic bonfires, each bearing a seed of destruction so potent it could tumble cities and dash kings to their knees. In later years, my mind would return to that calm, silent evening, when I had stared at rows of living lights. And I would understand. To be given loyalty is to be infused like a gemstone, to be granted the frightful license to destroy not only one's self, but all within one's care.'"

Litima fell still. It was the end of the sequence.

'Thank you, Brightness Litima,' Dalinar said. 'That will do.'

The woman bowed her head respectfully. She gathered her youthful ward from the side of the room and they withdrew, leaving the book on the lectern.

That sequence had become one of Dalinar's favorites. Listening to it often comforted him. Someone else had known, someone else had understood, how he felt. But today, it didn't bring the solace it usually did. It only reminded him of Adolin's arguments. None had been things Dalinar hadn't considered himself, but being confronted with them by someone he trusted had shaken everything. He found himself staring at his maps, smaller copies of those that hung in the Gallery. They had been re-created for him by the royal cartographer, Isasik Shulin.

What if Dalinar's visions really *were* just phantasms? He'd often longed for the glory days of Alethkar's past. Were the visions his mind's answer to that, a subconscious way of letting himself be a hero, of giving himself justification for doggedly seeking his goals?

A disturbing thought. Looked at another way, those phantom commands to 'unify' sounded a great deal like what the Hierocracy had said when it had tried to conquer the world five centuries before.

Dalinar turned from his maps and walked across the room, his booted feet falling on a soft rug. Too nice a rug. He'd spent the better part of his life in one warcamp or another; he'd slept in wagons, stone barracks, and tents pulled tight against the leeward side of stone formations. Compared with that, his present dwelling was practically a mansion. He felt as if he should cast out all of this finery. But what would that accomplish?

He stopped at the lectern and ran his fingers along the thick pages filled with lines in violet ink. He couldn't read the words, but he could almost *feel* them, emanating from the page like Stormlight from a sphere. Were the words of this book the cause of his problems? The visions had started several months after he'd first listened to readings from it.

He rested his hand on the cold, ink-filled pages. Their homeland was stressed nearly to breaking, the war was stalled, and suddenly he found himself captivated by the very ideals and myths that had led to his brother's downfall. This was a time the Alethi needed the Blackthorn, not an old, tired soldier who fancied himself a philosopher.

Blast it all, he thought. *I thought I'd figured this out!* He closed the leather-bound volume, the spine crackling. He carried it to the bookshelf and returned it to its place.

'Father?' Renarin asked. 'Is there something I can do for you?'

'I wish there were, son.' Dalinar tapped the spine of the book lightly. 'It's ironic. This book was once considered one of the great masterpieces of political philosophy. Did you know that? Jasnah told me that kings around the world used to study it daily. Now, it is considered borderline blasphemous.'

Renarin gave no reply.

'Regardless,' Dalinar said, walking back to the wall map. 'Highprince Aladar refused my offer of an alliance, just as Roion did. Do you have a thought on whom should I approach next?'

'Adolin says we should be far more worried about Sadeas's ploy to destroy us than we are.'

The room fell silent. Renarin had a habit of doing that, felling conversations like an enemy archer hunting officers on the battlefield.

'Your brother is right to worry,' Dalinar said. 'But moving against Sadeas would undermine Alethkar as a kingdom. For the same reason, Sadeas won't risk acting against us. He'll see.'

I hope.

Horns suddenly sounded outside, their deep, resounding calls echoing. Dalinar and Renarin froze. Parshendi spotted on the Plains. A second set came. Twenty-third plateau of the second quadrant. Dalinar's scouts thought the contested plateau close enough for their forces to reach first.

Dalinar dashed across the room, all other thoughts discarded for the moment, his booted feet thumping on the thick rug. He threw open the door and charged down the Stormlight-illuminated hallway.

The war room door was open, and Teleb – highofficer on duty – saluted as Dalinar entered. Teleb was a straight-backed man with light green eyes. He kept his long hair in a braid and had a blue tattoo on his cheek, marking him as an Oldblood. At the side of the room, his wife, Kalami, sat behind a long-legged desk on a high stool. She wore her dark hair with only two small side braids pinned up, the rest hanging down the back of her violet dress to brush the top of the stool. She was a historian of note, and had requested permission to record meetings like this one; she planned to scribe a history of the war.

'Sir,' Teleb said. 'A chasmfiend crawled atop the plateau here less than a quarter hour ago.' He pointed to the battle map, which had glyphs marking each plateau. Dalinar stepped up to it, a group of his officers gathering around him.

'How far would you say that is?' Dalinar asked, rubbing his chin.

'Perhaps two hours,' Teleb said, indicating a route one of his men had drawn on the map. 'Sir, I think we have a good chance at this one. Bright-lord Aladar will have to traverse six unclaimed plateaus to reach the contested area, while we have a nearly direct line. Brightlord Sadeas would have trouble, as he'd have to work his way around several large chasms too wide to cross with bridges. I'll bet he won't even try for it.'

Dalinar did, indeed, have the most direct line. He hesitated, though. It had been months since he'd last gone on a plateau run. His attention had been diverted, his troops needed for protecting roadways and patrol-ling the large markets that had grown up outside the warcamps. And now, Adolin's questions weighed upon him, pressing him down. It seemed like a terrible time to go out to battle.

No, he thought. *No, I need to do this.* Winning a plateau skirmish would do much for his troops' morale, and would help discredit the rumors in camp.

'We march!' Dalinar declared.

A few of the officers whooped in excitement, an extreme show of emotion for the normally reserved Alethi.

'And your son, Brightlord?' Teleb asked. He'd heard of the confrontation between them. Dalinar doubted there was a person in all ten war-camps who hadn't heard of it.

'Send for him,' Dalinar said firmly. Adolin probably needed this as much as, or more than, Dalinar did.

The officers scattered. Dalinar's armor bearers entered a moment later. It had only been a few minutes since the horns had sounded, but after six years of fighting, the machine of war ran smoothly when battle called. From outside, he heard the horns' third set begin, calling his forces to battle.

The armor bearers inspected his boots – checking to be certain the laces were tight – then brought a long padded vest to throw over his uniform. Next, they set the sabatons – armor for his boots – on the floor before him. They encased his boots entirely and had a rough surface on the bottoms that seemed to cling to rock. The interiors glowed with the light of the sapphires in their indented pockets.

Dalinar was reminded of his most recent vision. The Radiant, his armor glowing with glyphs. Modern Shardplate didn't glow like that. Could his mind have fabricated that detail? Would it have?

No time to consider that now, he thought. He discarded his uncertainties and worries, something he'd learned to do during his first battles as a youth. A warrior needed to be focused. Adolin's questions would still be waiting for him when he got back. For now, he couldn't afford self-doubt or uncertainty. It was time to be the Blackthorn.

He stepped into the sabatons, and the straps tightened of their own accord, fitting around his boots. The greaves came next, going over his legs and knees, locking on to the sabatons. Shardplate wasn't like ordinary armor; there was no mesh of steel mail and no leather straps at the joints. Shardplate seams were made of smaller plates, interlocking, overlapping, incredibly intricate, leaving no vulnerable gaps. There was very little rubbing or chafing; each piece fit together perfectly, as if it had been crafted specifically for Dalinar.

One always put the armor on from the feet upward. Shardplate was extremely heavy; without the enhanced strength it provided, no man would be able to fight in it. Dalinar stood still as the armor bearers affixed the cuisses over his thighs and locked them to the culet and faulds across his waist and lower back. A skirt made of small, interlocking plates came next, reaching down to just above the knees.

'Brightlord,' Teleb said, stepping up to him. 'Have you given thought to my suggestion about the bridges?'

'You know how I feel about man-carried bridges, Teleb,' Dalinar said as the armor bearers locked his breastplate into place, then worked on the rerebraces and vambraces for his arms. Already, he could feel the strength of the Plate surging through him.

'We wouldn't have to use the smaller bridges for the assault,' Teleb said. 'Just for getting to the contested plateau.'

'We'd still have to bring the chull-pulled bridges to get across that last chasm,' Dalinar said. 'I'm not convinced that bridge crews would move us any more quickly. Not when we have to wait for those animals.'

Teleb sighed.

Dalinar reconsidered. A good officer was one who accepted orders and fulfilled them, even when he disagreed. But the mark of a great officer was that he also tried to innovate and offer appropriate suggestions.

'You may recruit and train a single bridge crew,' Dalinar said. 'We shall see. In these races, even a few minutes can be meaningful.'

Teleb smiled. 'Thank you, sir.'

Dalinar waved with his left hand as the armor bearers locked the gauntlet onto his right. He made a fist, tiny plates curving perfectly. The left gauntlet followed. Then the gorget went over his head, covering his neck, the pauldrons on his shoulders, and the helm on his head. Finally, the armor bearers affixed his cape to the pauldrons.

Dalinar took a deep breath, feeling the Thrill build for the approaching battle. He strode from the war room, footfalls firm and *solid*. Attendants and servants scattered before him, making way. Wearing Shardplate again after a long period without was like waking up after a night of feeling groggy or disoriented. The spring of the step, the impetus the armor seemed to lend him, made him want to race down the hallway and—

And why not?

He broke into a sprint. Teleb and the others cried out in surprise, rushing to keep up. Dalinar outpaced them easily, reaching the front gates of the complex and leaping through, throwing himself off the long steps leading down from his enclave. He exulted, grinning as he hung in the air, then slammed to the ground. The force cracked the stone beneath him, and he crouched into the impact.

Before him, neat rows of barracks ran through his warcamp, formed in radials with a meeting ground and mess hall at the center of each battalion. His officers reached the top of the stairs, looking down with amazement. Renarin was with them, wearing his uniform that had never seen battle, his hand raised against the sunlight.

Dalinar felt foolish. Was he a youth just given his first taste of Shardplate? *Back to work. Stop playing.*

Perethom, his infantrylord, saluted as Dalinar strode up. 'Second and Third Battalions are on duty today, Brightlord. Forming ranks to march.'

'First Bridge Squad is gathered, Brightlord,' Havarah – the bridgelord – said, striding up. He was a short man, with some Herdazian blood in him as evidenced by his dark, crystalline fingernails, though he didn't wear a spark-flicker. 'I have word from Ashelem that the archery company is ready.'

'Cavalry?' Dalinar asked. 'And where is my son?'

'Here, Father,' called a familiar voice. Adolin – his Shardplate painted a deep Kholin blue – made his way through the gathering crowd. His visor was up, and he looked eager, though when he met Dalinar's eyes, he glanced away immediately.

Dalinar held up a hand, quieting several officers who were trying to give him reports. He strode to Adolin, and the youth looked up, meeting his gaze.

'You said what you felt you must,' Dalinar said.

'And I'm not sorry I did,' Adolin replied. 'But I *am* sorry for how, and where, I said it. That won't happen again.'

Dalinar nodded, and that was enough. Adolin seemed to relax, a weight coming off his shoulders, and Dalinar turned back to his officers. In moments, he and Adolin were leading a hurried group to the staging area. As they did, Dalinar did note Adolin waving to a young woman who stood beside the way, wearing a red dress, her hair up in a very nice braiding.

'Is that— er—'

'Malasha?' Adolin said. 'Yes.'

'She looks nice.'

'Most of the time she is, though she's somewhat annoyed that I wouldn't let her come with me today.'

'She wanted to come into *battle*?'

Adolin shrugged. 'Says she's curious.'

Dalinar said nothing. Battle was a masculine art. A woman wanting to come to the battlefield was like ... well, like a man wanting to read. Unnatural.

Ahead, in the staging area, the battalions were forming ranks, and a squat lighteyed officer hurried up to Dalinar. He had patches of red hair on his otherwise dark Alethi head and a long, red mustache. Ilamar, the cavalrylord.

'Brightlord,' he said, 'my apologies for the delay. Cavalry is mounted and ready.'

'We march, then,' Dalinar said. 'All ranks—'

'Brightlord!' a voice said.

Dalinar turned as one of his messengers approached. The darkeyed man wore leathers marked with blue bands on the arms. He saluted, saying, 'Highprince Sadeas has demanded admittance to the warcamp!'

Dalinar glanced at Adolin. His son's expression darkened.

'He claims the king's writ of investigation grants him the right,' the messenger said.

'Admit him,' Dalinar said.

'Yes, Brightlord,' the messenger said, turning back. One of the lesser officers, Moratel, went with him so that Sadeas could be welcomed and escorted by a lighteyes as befitted his station. Moratel was least among those in attendance; everyone understood he was the one Dalinar would send.

'What do you think Sadeas wants this time?' Dalinar said quietly to Adolin.

'Our blood. Preferably warm, perhaps sweetened with a shot of tallew brandy.'

Dalinar grimaced, and the two of them hurried past the ranks of soldiers. The men had an air of anticipation, spears held high, darkeyed citizen officers standing at the sides with axes on their shoulders. At the front of the force, a group of chulls snorted and rummaged at the rocks by their feet; harnessed to them were several enormous mobile bridges.

Gallant and Adolin's white stallion Sureblood were waiting, their reins held at the ready by grooms. Ryshadium hardly needed handlers. Once, Gallant had kicked open his stall and made his way to the staging grounds on his own when a groom had been too slow. Dalinar patted the midnight destrier on the neck, then swung into the saddle.

He scanned the staging field, then raised his arm to give the command to move. However, he noticed a group of mounted men riding up to the staging field, led by a figure in dark red Shardplate. Sadeas.

Dalinar stifled a sigh and gave the command to move out, though he himself waited for the Highprince of Information. Adolin came over on Sureblood, and he gave Dalinar a glance that seemed to say, 'Don't worry, I'll behave.'

As always, Sadeas was a model of fashion, his armor painted, his helm ornamented with a completely different metallic pattern than he had worn last time. This one was shaped like a stylized sunburst. It looked almost like a crown.

'Brightlord Sadeas,' Dalinar said. 'This is an inconvenient time for your investigation.'

'Unfortunately,' Sadeas said, reining in. 'His Majesty is very eager to have answers, and I cannot stop my investigation, even for a plateau assault. I need to interview some of your soldiers. I'll do it on the way out.'

'You want to come *with* us?'

'Why not? I won't delay you.' He glanced at the chulls, who lurched into motion, pulling the bulky bridges. 'I doubt that even were I to decide to *crawl*, I could slow you any further.'

'Our soldiers need to concentrate on the upcoming battle, Brightlord,' Adolin said. 'They should not be distracted.'

'The king's will must be done,' Sadeas said, shrugging, not even bothering to look at Adolin. 'Need I present the writ? Surely you don't intend to forbid me.'

Dalinar studied his former friend, looking into those eyes, trying to see into the man's soul. Sadeas lacked his characteristic smirk; he usually wore one of those when he was pleased with how a plot was going. Did he realize that Dalinar knew how to read his expressions, and so masked his emotions? 'No need to present anything, Sadeas. My men are at your disposal. If you have need of anything, simply ask. Adolin, with me.'

Dalinar turned Gallant and galloped down the line toward the front of the marching army. Adolin followed reluctantly, and Sadeas remained behind with his attendants.

The long ride began. The permanent bridges here were Dalinar's, maintained and guarded by his soldiers and scouts, connecting plateaus that he controlled. Sadeas spent the trip riding near the middle of the column of two thousand. He periodically sent an attendant to pull certain soldiers out of line.

Dalinar spent the ride mentally preparing himself for the battle ahead. He spoke with his officers about the layout of the plateau, got a report on where specifically the chasmfiend had chosen to make its chrysalis, and sent scouts ahead to watch for Parshendi. Those scouts carried their long poles to get them from plateau to plateau without bridges.

Dalinar's force eventually reached the end of the permanent bridges, and had to start waiting for the chull bridges to be lowered across the chasms. The big machines were built like siege towers, with enormous wheels and armored sections at the side where soldiers could push. At a chasm, they unhooked the chulls, pushed the machine forward by hand, and ratcheted a crank at the back to lower the bridge. Once the bridge was set down, the machinery was unlocked and pulled across. The bridge was built so they could lock the machine onto the other side, pull the bridge up, then turn and hook the chulls up again.

It was a slow process. Dalinar watched from horseback, fingers tapping the side of his hogshide saddle as the first chasm was spanned. Perhaps Teleb was right. Could they use lighter, more portable bridges to get across these early chasms, then resort to the siege bridges only for the final assault?

A clatter of hooves on rock announced someone riding up the side of the column. Dalinar turned, expecting Adolin, and instead found Sadeas.

Why *had* Sadeas asked to be Highprince of Information, and why was he so dogged in pursuing this matter of the broken girth? If he did decide to create some kind of false implication of Dalinar's guilt . . .

The visions told me to trust him, Dalinar told himself firmly. But he was growing less certain about them. How much dared he risk on what they'd said?

'Your soldiers are quite loyal to you,' Sadeas noted as he arrived.

'Loyalty is the first lesson of a soldier's life,' Dalinar said. 'I would be worried if these men *hadn't* yet mastered it.'

Sadeas sighed. 'Really, Dalinar. Must you always be so sanctimonious?'

Dalinar didn't reply.

'It's odd, how a leader's influence can affect his men,' Sadeas said. 'So many of these are like smaller versions of you. Bundles of emotion, wrapped up and tied until they become stiff from the pressure. They're so sure in some ways, yet so insecure in others.'

Dalinar kept his jaw clenched. *What is your game, Sadeas?*

Sadeas smiled, leaning in, speaking softly. 'You want so badly to snap at me, don't you? Even in the old days, you hated it when someone implied that you were insecure. Back then, your displeasure often ended with a head or two rolling across the stones.'

'I killed many who did not deserve death,' Dalinar said. 'A man should not fear losing his head because he took one too many sips of wine.'

'Perhaps,' Sadeas said lightly. 'But don't you ever want to let it out, as you used to? Doesn't it pound on you inside, like someone trapped within a large drum? Beating, banging, trying to claw free?'

'Yes,' Dalinar said.

The admission seemed to surprise Sadeas. 'And the Thrill, Dalinar. Do you still feel the Thrill?'

Men didn't often speak of the Thrill, the joy and lust for battle. It was a private thing. 'I feel each of the things you mention, Sadeas,' Dalinar said, eyes forward. 'But I don't always let them out. A man's emotions are what define him, and control is the hallmark of true strength. To lack feeling is to be dead, but to act on every feeling is to be a child.'

'That has the stink of a quote about it, Dalinar. From Gavilar's little book of virtues, I assume?'

'Yes.'

'Doesn't it bother you at all that the Radiants betrayed us?'

'Legends. The Recreance is an event so old, it might as well be in the shadowdays. What did the Radiants really do? Why did they do it? We don't know.'

'We know enough. They used elaborate tricks to imitate great powers and pretend a holy calling. When their deceptions were discovered, they fled.'

'Their powers were not lies. They were real.'

'Oh?' Sadeas said, amused. 'You know this? Didn't you just say the event was so old, it might as well have been in the shadowdays? If the

Radiants had such marvelous powers, why can nobody reproduce them? Where did those incredible skills go?'

'I don't know,' Dalinar said softly. 'Perhaps we're just not worthy of them any longer.'

Sadeas snorted, and Dalinar wished he'd bitten his tongue. His only evidence for what he said was his visions. And yet, if Sadeas belittled something, he instinctively wanted to stand up for it.

I can't afford this. I need to be focused on the battle ahead.

'Sadeas,' he said, determined to change the topic. 'We need to work harder to unify the warcamps. I want your help, now that you're Highprince of Information.'

'To do what?'

'To do what needs to be done. For the good of Alethkar.'

'That's exactly what I'm doing, old friend,' Sadeas said. 'Killing Parshendi. Winning glory and wealth for our kingdom. Seeking vengeance. It would be best for Alethkar if you'd stop wasting so much time in camp – and stop talking of fleeing like cowards. It would be *best* for Alethkar if you'd start acting like a man again.'

'Enough, Sadeas!' Dalinar said, more loudly than he'd intended. 'I gave you leave to come along for your investigation, not to taunt me!'

Sadeas sniffed. 'That book ruined Gavilar. Now it's doing the same to you. You've listened to those stories so much they've got your head full of false ideals. Nobody ever really lived the way the Codes claim.'

'Bah!' Dalinar said, waving a hand and turning Gallant. 'I don't have time for your snideness today, Sadeas.' He trotted his horse away, furious at Sadeas, then even more furious at himself for losing his temper.

He crossed the bridge, stewing, thinking of Sadeas's words. He found himself remembering a day when he stood with his brother beside the Impossible Falls of Kholinar.

Things are different now, Dalinar, Gavilar had said. *I see now, in ways I never did before. I wish I could show you what I mean.*

It had been three days before his death.

❖

Ten heartbeats.

Dalinar closed his eyes, breathing in and out – slowly, calmingly – as they prepared themselves behind the siege bridge. Forget Sadeas. Forget the visions. Forget his worries and fears. Just focus on the heartbeats.

Nearby, chulls scraped the rock with their hard, carapaced feet. The wind blew across his face, smelling wet. It always smelled wet out here, in these humid stormlands.

Soldiers clanked, leather creaked. Dalinar raised his head toward the sky, his heart thumping deep within him. The brilliant white sun stained his eyelids red.

Men shifted, called, cursed, loosened swords in their sheaths, tested bowstrings. He could *feel* their tension, their anxiety mixed with excitement. Among them, anticipationspren began to spring from the ground, streamers connected by one side to the stone, the others whipping in the air. Some fearspren boiled up among them.

'Are you ready?' Dalinar asked softly. The Thrill was rising within him.

'Yes.' Adolin's voice was eager.

'You never complain about the way we attack,' Dalinar said, eyes still closed. 'You never challenge me on this.'

'This is the best way. They're my men too. What is the point of being a Shardbearer if we cannot lead the charge?'

The tenth heartbeat sounded in Dalinar's chest; he could always hear the beats when he was summoning his Blade, no matter how loud the world around him was. The faster they passed, the sooner the sword arrived. So the more urgent you felt, the sooner you were armed. Was that intentional, or just some quirk of the Shardblade's nature?

Oathbringer's familiar weight settled into his hand.

'Go,' Dalinar said, snapping his eyes open. He slammed his visor down as Adolin did the same, Stormlight rising from the sides as the helms sealed shut and became translucent. The two of them burst out from behind the massive bridge – one Shardbearer on each side, a figure of blue and another of slate grey.

The energy of the armor pulsed through Dalinar as he dashed across the stone ground, arms pumping in rhythm with his steps. The wave of arrows came immediately, loosed from the Parshendi kneeling on the other side of the chasm. Dalinar flung his arm up in front of his eye slit as arrows sprayed across him, scraping metal, some shafts snapping. It felt like running against a hailstorm.

Adolin bellowed a war cry from the right, voice muffled by his helm. As they approached the chasm lip, Dalinar lowered his arm despite the arrows. He needed to be able to judge his approach. The gulf was mere feet away. His Plate gave him a surge of strength as he reached the edge of the chasm.

Then leaped.

For a moment, he soared above the inky chasm, cape flapping, arrows filling the air around him. He was reminded of the flying Radiant from his vision. But this was nothing so mystical, just a standard Shardplate-assisted jump. Dalinar cleared the chasm and crashed back to the ground on the other side, sweeping his Blade down and across to slay three Parshendi with a single blow.

Their eyes burned black and smoke rose as they collapsed. He swung again. Bits of armor and weapons sprayed into the air where arrows had once flown, sheared free by his Blade. As always, it sliced apart anything inanimate, but blurred when it touched flesh, as if turning to mist.

The way it reacted to flesh and cut steel so easily, it sometimes felt to Dalinar like he was swinging a weapon of pure smoke. As long as he kept the Blade in motion, it could not get caught in chinks or stopped by the weight of what it was cutting.

Dalinar spun, sweeping out with his Blade in a line of death. He sheared through souls themselves, leaving Parshendi to drop dead to the ground. Then he kicked, tossing a corpse into the faces of the Parshendi nearby. A few more kicks sent corpses flying – a Plate-driven kick could easily send a body tumbling thirty feet – clearing the ground around him for better footing.

Adolin hit the plateau not far away, spinning and falling into Windstance. Adolin shoved his shoulder into a group of archers, tossing them backward and throwing several into the chasm. Gripping his Shardblade with both hands, he did an initial sweep as Dalinar had, cutting down six enemies.

The Parshendi were singing, many of them wearing beards that glowed with small uncut gemstones. Parshendi always sang as they fought; that song changed as they abandoned their bows – pulling out axes, swords, or maces – and threw themselves at the two Shardbearers.

Dalinar put himself at the optimal distance from Adolin, allowing his son to protect his blind spots, but not getting too close. The two Shardbearers fought, still near the lip of the chasm, cutting down the Parshendi who tried desperately to push them backward by sheer force of numbers.

This was their best chance to defeat the Shardbearers. Dalinar and Adolin were alone, without their honor guard. A fall from this height would certainly kill even a man in Plate.

The Thrill rose within him, so sweet. Dalinar kicked away another corpse, though he didn't need the extra room. They'd noticed that the Parshendi grew enraged when you moved their dead. He kicked another body, taunting them, drawing them toward him to fight in pairs as they often did.

He cut down a group that came, singing in voices angry at what he'd done to their dead. Nearby, Adolin began to lay about him with punches as the Parshendi got too close; he was fond of the tactic, switching between using his sword in two hands or one. Parshendi corpses flew this way and that, bones and armor shattered by the blows, orange Parshendi blood spraying across the ground. Adolin moved back to his Blade a moment later, kicking away a corpse.

The Thrill consumed Dalinar, giving him strength, focus, and power. The glory of the battle grew grand. He'd stayed away from this too long. He saw with clarity now. They *did* need to push harder, assault more plateaus, win the gemhearts.

Dalinar was the Blackthorn. He was a natural force, never to be halted. He was death itself. He—

He felt a sudden stab of powerful revulsion, a sickness so strong that it made him gasp. He slipped, partially on a patch of blood, but partially because his knees grew suddenly weak.

The corpses before him suddenly seemed a horrifying sight. Eyes burned out like spent coals. Bodies limp and broken, bones shattered where Adolin had punched them. Heads cracked open, blood and brains and entrails spilled around them. Such butchery, such death. The Thrill vanished.

How could a man *enjoy* this?

The Parshendi surged toward him. Adolin was there in a heartbeat, attacking with more skill than any other man Dalinar had known. The lad was a genius with the Blade, an artist with paint of only one shade. He struck expertly, forcing the Parshendi back. Dalinar shook his head, recovering his stance.

He forced himself to resume fighting, and as the Thrill began to rise again, Dalinar hesitantly embraced it. The odd sickness faded, and his battle reflexes took control. He spun into the Parshendi advance, sweeping out with his Blade in broad, aggressive strokes.

He *needed* this victory. For himself, for Adolin, and for his men. Why had he been so horrified? The Parshendi had murdered Gavilar. It was right to kill them.

He was a soldier. Fighting was what he did. And he did it well.

The Parshendi advance unit broke before his assault, scattering back toward a larger mass of their troops, who were forming ranks in haste. Dalinar stepped back and found himself looking down at the corpses around him, with their blackened eyes. Smoke still curled from a few.

The sick feeling returned.

Life ended so quickly. The Shardbearer was destruction incarnate, the most powerful force on a battlefield. *Once these weapons meant protecting,* a voice inside of him whispered.

The three bridges crashed to the ground a few feet away, and the cavalry charged across a moment later, led by compact Ilamar. A few windspren danced past in the air, nearly invisible. Adolin called for his horse, but Dalinar just stood, looking down at the dead. Parshendi blood was orange, and it smelled like mold. Yet their faces – marbled black or white and red – looked so human. A parshman nurse had practically raised Dalinar.

Life before death.

What *was* that voice?

He glanced back across the chasm, toward where Sadeas – well outside of bow range – sat with his attendants. Dalinar could sense the disapproval in his ex-friend's posture. Dalinar and Adolin risked themselves, taking a dangerous leap across the chasm. An assault of the type Sadeas had pioneered would cost more lives. But how many lives would Dalinar's army lose if one of its Shardbearers was pushed into the chasm?

Gallant charged across the bridge alongside a line of soldiers, who cheered for the Ryshadium. He slowed near Dalinar, who grabbed the reins. Right now, he was needed. His men were fighting and dying, and this was not a time for regret or second-guessing.

A Plate-enhanced jump put him in the saddle. Then, Shardblade raised high, he charged into battle to kill for his men. That was not what the Radiants had fought for. But at least it was something.

❖

They won the battle.

Dalinar stepped back, feeling fatigued as Adolin did the honors of harvesting the gemheart. The chrysalis itself sat like an enormous, oblong rockbud, fifteen feet tall and attached to the uneven stone ground by something that looked like crem. There were bodies all around it, some human, others Parshendi. The Parshendi had tried to get into it quickly and flee, but they'd only managed to get a few cracks into the shell.

The fighting had been most furious here, around the chrysalis. Dalinar rested back against a shelf of rock and pulled his helm off, exposing a sweaty head to the cool breeze. The sun was high overhead; the battle had lasted two hours or so.

Adolin worked efficiently, using his Shardblade with care to shave off a section of the outside of the chrysalis. Then he expertly plunged it in, killing the pupating creature but avoiding the region with the gemheart.

Just like that, the creature was dead. Now the Shardblade could cut it, and Adolin carved away sections of flesh. Purple ichor spurted out as he reached in, questing for the gemheart. The soldiers cheered as he pulled it free, gloryspren hovering above the entire army like hundreds of spheres of light.

Dalinar found himself walking away, helm held in his left hand. He crossed the battlefield, passing surgeons tending the wounded and teams who were carrying his dead back to the bridges. There were sleds behind the chull carts for them, so they could be burned properly back at camp.

There were a lot of Parshendi corpses. Looking at them now, he was neither disgusted nor excited. Just exhausted.

He'd gone to battle dozens, perhaps hundreds of times. Never before had he felt as he had this day. That revulsion had distracted him, and that could have gotten him killed. Battle was no time for reflection; you had to keep your mind on what you were doing.

The Thrill had seemed subdued the entire battle, and he hadn't fought nearly as well as he once had. This battle should have brought him clarity. Instead, his troubles seemed magnified. *Blood of my fathers*, he thought, stepping up to the top of a small rock hill. *What is happening to me?*

His weakness today seemed the latest, and most potent, argument to fuel what Adolin – and, indeed, what many others – said about him. He stood atop the hill, looking eastward, toward the Origin. His eyes went that direction so often. Why? What was—

He froze, noticing a group of Parshendi on a nearby plateau. His scouts watched them warily; it was the army that Dalinar's people had driven off. Though they'd killed a lot of Parshendi today, the vast majority had still escaped, retreating when they realized the battle was lost to them. That was one of the reasons the war was lasting so long. The Parshendi understood strategic retreat.

This army stood in ranks, grouped in warpairs. A commanding figure stood at their head, a large Parshendi in glittering armor. Shardplate. Even at a distance, it was easy to tell the difference between it and something more mundane.

That Shardbearer hadn't been here during the battle itself. Why come now? Had he arrived too late?

The armored figure and the rest of the Parshendi turned and left, leaping across the chasm behind them and fleeing back toward their unseen haven at the center of the Plains.

If anything I have said makes a glimmer of sense to you, I trust that you'll call them off. Or maybe you could astound me and ask them to do something productive for once.

Kaladin pushed his way into the apothecary's shop, the door banging shut behind him. As before, the aged man pretended to be feeble, feeling his way with a cane until he recognized Kaladin. Then he stood up straighter. 'Oh. It's you.'

It had been two more long days. Daytime spent working and training – Teft and Rock now practiced with him – evenings spent at the first chasm, retrieving the reeds from their hiding place in a crevice and then milking for hours. Gaz had seen them go down last night, and the bridge sergeant was undoubtedly suspicious. There was no helping that.

Bridge Four had been called out on a bridge run today. Thankfully, they'd arrived before the Parshendi, and none of the bridge crews had lost any men. Things hadn't gone so well for the regular Alethi troops. The Alethi line had eventually buckled before the Parshendi assault, and the bridge crews had been forced to lead a tired, angry, and defeated troop of soldiers back to the camp.

Kaladin was bleary-eyed with fatigue from staying up late working on the reeds. His stomach growled perpetually from being given a fraction of the food it needed, as he shared his meals with two wounded. That all ended today. The apothecary walked back behind his counter, and Kaladin stepped up to it. Syl darted into the room, her small ribbon of light turning into a woman midtwist. She flipped like an acrobat, landing on the table in a smooth motion.

'What do you need?' the apothecary asked. 'More bandages? Well, I might just—'

He cut off as Kaladin slapped a medium-sized liquor bottle down on the table. It had a cracked top, but would still hold a cork. He pulled this free, revealing the milky white knobweed sap inside. He'd used the first of what they'd harvested to treat Leyten, Dabbid, and Hobber.

'What's this?' the elderly apothecary asked, adjusting his spectacles and leaning down. 'Offering me a drink? I don't take the stuff these days. Unsettles the stomach, you know.'

'It's not liquor. It's knobweed sap. You said it was expensive. Well, how much will you give me for this?'

The apothecary blinked, then leaned in closer, giving the contents a whiff. 'Where'd you get this?'

'I harvested it from the reeds growing outside of camp.'

The apothecary's expression darkened. He shrugged. 'Worthless, I'm afraid.'

'*What?*'

'The wild weeds aren't potent enough.' The apothecary replaced the cork. A strong wind buffeted the building, blowing under the door, stirring the scents of the many powders and tonics he sold. 'This is practically useless. I'll give you two clearmarks for it, which is being generous. I'll have to distill it, and will be lucky to get a couple of spoonfuls.'

Two marks! Kaladin thought with despair. *After three days of work, three of us pushing ourselves, getting only a few hours of sleep each night? All for something worth only a couple days' wage?*

But no. The sap had *worked* on Leyten's wound, making the rotspren flee and the infection retreat. Kaladin narrowed his eyes as the apothecary fished two marks out of his money pouch, setting them on the table. Like many spheres, these were flattened slightly on one side to keep them from rolling away.

'Actually,' the apothecary said, rubbing his chin. 'I'll give you three.' He took out one more mark. 'Hate to see all of your effort go to waste.'

'Kaladin,' Syl said, studying the apothecary. 'He's nervous about something. I think he's lying!'

'I know,' Kaladin said.

'What's that?' the apothecary said. 'Well, if you knew it was worthless, why did you spend so much effort on it?' He reached for the bottle.

Kaladin caught his hand. 'We got two or more drops from each reed, you know.'

The apothecary frowned.

'Last time,' Kaladin said, 'you told me I'd be lucky to get one drop per reed. You said that was why knobweed sap was so expensive. You said nothing about "wild" plants being weaker.'

'Well, I didn't think you'd go and try gathering them, and ... ' He trailed off as Kaladin locked eyes with him.

'The army doesn't know, do they?' Kaladin asked. 'They aren't aware how valuable those plants outside are. You harvest them, you sell the sap, and you make a killing, since the military needs a *lot* of antiseptic.'

The old apothecary cursed, pulling his hand back. 'I don't know what you're talking about.'

Kaladin took his jar. 'And if I go to the healing tent and tell them where I got this?'

'They'd take it from you!' the man said urgently. 'Don't be a fool. You've a slave brand, boy. They'll think you stole it.'

Kaladin moved to walk away.

'I'll give a skymark,' the apothecary said. 'That's half what I'd charge the military for this much.'

Kaladin turned. 'You charge them *two skymarks* for something that only takes a couple of days to gather?'

'It's not just me,' the apothecary said, scowling. 'Each of the apothecaries charges the same. We got together, decided on a fair price.'

'How is *that* a fair price?'

'We have to make a living here, in this Almighty-forsaken land! It costs us money to set up shop, to maintain ourselves, to hire guards.'

He fished in his pouch, pulling out a sphere that glowed deep blue. A sapphire sphere was worth about twenty-five times a diamond one. As Kaladin made one diamond mark a day, a skymark was worth as much as Kaladin made in half a month. Of course, a common darkeyed soldier earned five clearmarks a day, which would make this a week's wages to them.

Once, this wouldn't have seemed like much money to Kaladin. Now it was a fortune. Still, he hesitated. 'I should expose you. Men die because of you.'

'No they don't,' the apothecary said. 'The highprinces have more than enough to pay this, considering what they make on the plateaus. We supply them with bottles of sap as often as they need them. All you'd do by exposing us is let monsters like Sadeas keep a few more spheres in their pockets!'

The apothecary was sweating. Kaladin was threatening to topple his entire business on the Shattered Plains. And so much money was being earned on the sap that this could grow *very* dangerous. Men killed to keep such secrets.

'Line my pocket or line the brightlords',' Kaladin said. 'I guess I can't argue with that logic.' He set the bottle back on the counter. 'I'll take the deal, provided you throw in some more bandages.'

'Very well,' the apothecary said, relaxing. 'But stay away from those reeds. I'm surprised you found any nearby that hadn't already been harvested. My workers are having an increasingly difficult time.'

They don't have a windspren guiding them, Kaladin thought. 'Then why would you want to discourage me? I could get more of this for you.'

'Well, yes,' the apothecary said. 'But—'

'It's cheaper if you do it yourself,' Kaladin said, leaning down. 'But this way you have a clean trail. I provide the sap, charging one skymark. If the lighteyes ever discover what the apothecaries have been doing, you can claim ignorance – all you know is that some bridgeman was selling you sap, and you resold it to the army at a reasonable markup.'

That seemed to appeal to the old man. 'Well, perhaps I won't ask too many questions about how you harvested this. Your business, young man. Your business indeed. . . .' He shuffled to the back of his store, returning with a box of bandages. Kaladin accepted it and left the shop without a word.

'Aren't you worried?' Syl said, floating up beside his head as he entered the afternoon sunlight. 'If Gaz discovers what you're doing, you could get into trouble.'

'What more could they do to me?' Kaladin asked. 'I doubt they'd consider this a crime worth stringing me up for.'

Syl looked backward, forming into little more than a cloud with the faint suggestion of a female form. 'I can't decide if it's dishonest or not.'

'It's not dishonest; it's business.' He grimaced. 'Lavis grain is sold the same way. Grown by the farmers and sold at a pittance to merchants, who carry it to the cities and sell it to other merchants, who sell it to people for four or five times what it was originally bought for.'

'So why did it bother you?' Syl asked, frowning as they avoided a troop of soldiers, one of whom tossed the pit of a palafruit at Kaladin's head. The soldiers laughed.

Kaladin rubbed his temple. 'I've still got some strange scruples about charging for medical care because of my father.'

'He sounds like he's a very generous man.'

'For all the good it did him.'

Of course, in a way, Kaladin was just as bad. During his early days as a slave, he'd have done almost anything for a chance to walk around unsupervised like this. The army perimeter was guarded, but if he could sneak the knobweed in, he could probably find a way to sneak himself out.

With that sapphire mark, he even had money to aid him. Yes, he had the slave brand, but some quick if painful work with a knife could turn that into a 'battle scar' instead. He could talk and fight like a soldier, so it would be plausible. He'd be taken for a deserter, but he could live with that.

That had been his plan for most of the later months of his enslavement, but he'd never had the means. It took money to travel, to get far enough away from the area where his description would be in circulation. Money to buy lodging in a seedy section of town, a place where nobody asked questions, while he healed from his self-inflicted wound.

In addition, there had always been the others. So he'd stayed, trying to get as many out as he could. Failing every time. And he was doing it again.

'Kaladin?' Syl asked from his shoulder. 'You look very serious. What are you thinking?'

'I'm wondering if I should run. Escape this storm-cursed camp and find myself a new life.'

Syl fell silent. 'Life is hard here,' she finally said. 'I don't know if anyone would blame you.'

Rock would, he thought. *And Teft.* They'd worked for that knobweed sap. They didn't know what it was worth; they thought it was only for healing the sick. If he ran, he'd be betraying them. He'd be abandoning the bridgemen.

Shove over, you fool, Kaladin thought to himself. *You won't save these bridgemen. Just like you didn't save Tien. You should run.*

'And then what?' he whispered.

Syl turned to him. 'What?'

If he ran, what good would it do? A life working for chips in the underbelly of some rotting city? No.

He couldn't leave them. Just like he'd never been able to leave anyone who he'd thought needed him. He had to protect them. He *had* to.

For Tien. And for his own sanity.

⁂

'Chasm duty,' Gaz said, spitting to the side. The spittle was colored black from the yamma plant he chewed.

'What?' Kaladin had returned from selling the knobweed to discover that Gaz had changed Bridge Four's work detail. They weren't scheduled to be on duty for any bridge runs – their run the day before exempted them. Instead, they were supposed to be assigned to Sadeas's smithy to help lift ingots and other supplies.

That sounded like difficult work, but it was actually among the easiest jobs bridgemen got. The blacksmiths felt they didn't need the extra hands. That, or they presumed that clumsy bridgemen would just get in the way. On smithy duty, you usually only worked a few hours of the shift and could spend the rest lounging.

Gaz stood with Kaladin in the early afternoon sunlight. 'You see,' Gaz said, 'you got me thinking the other day. Nobody cares if Bridge Four is given unfair work details. Everyone hates chasm duty. I figured you wouldn't care.'

'How much did they pay you?' Kaladin asked, stepping forward.

'Storm off,' Gaz said, spitting again. 'The others resent you. It'll do your crew good to be seen paying for what you did.'

'Surviving?'

Gaz shrugged. 'Everyone knows you broke the rules in bringing back those men. If the others do what you did, we'd have each barrack filled with the dying before the leeward side of a month was over!'

'They're *people*, Gaz. If we don't "fill the barracks" with wounded, it's because we're leaving them out there to die.'

'They'll die here anyway.'

'We'll see.'

Gaz watched him, eyes narrow. It seemed like he suspected that Kaladin had somehow tricked him in taking the stone-gathering duty. Earlier, Gaz had apparently gone down to the chasm, probably trying to figure out what Kaladin and the other two had been doing.

Damnation, Kaladin thought. He'd thought he had Gaz cowed enough to stay in line. 'We'll go,' Kaladin snapped, turning away. 'But I'm not taking the blame among my men for this one. They'll know you did it.'

'Fine,' Gaz called after him. Then, to himself, he continued, 'Maybe I'll get lucky and a chasmfiend will eat the lot of you.'

❖

Chasm duty. Most bridgemen would rather spend all day hauling stones than get assigned to the chasms.

With an unlit oil-soaked torch tied to his back, Kaladin climbed down the precarious rope ladder. The chasm was shallow here, only about fifty feet down, but that was enough to take him into a different world. A world where the only natural light came from the rift high in the sky. A world that stayed damp on even the hottest days, a drowned landscape of moss, fungus, and hardy plants that survived in even dim light.

The chasms were wider at the bottom, perhaps a result of highstorms. They caused enormous floods to crash through the chasms; to be caught in a chasm during a highstorm was death. A sediment of hardened crem smoothed the pathway on the floor of the chasms, though it rose and fell with the varying erosion of the underlying rock. In some few places, the distance from the chasm floor to the edge of the plateau above was only about forty feet. In most places, however, it was closer to a hundred or more.

Kaladin jumped off the ladder, falling a few feet and landing with a splash in a puddle of rainwater. After lighting the torch, he held it high, peering along the caliginous rift. The sides were slick with a dark green moss, and several thin vines he didn't recognize trailed down from intermediate ledges above. Bits of bone, wood, and torn cloth lay strewn about or wedged into clefts.

Someone splashed to the ground beside him. Teft cursed, looking down at his soaked legs and trousers as he stepped out of the large puddle. 'Storms take that cremling Gaz,' the aging bridgeman muttered. 'Sending us down here when it isn't our turn. I'll have his beans for this.'

'I am certain that he is very scared of you,' Rock said, stepping down off the ladder onto a dry spot. 'Is probably back in camp crying in fear.'

'Storm off,' Teft said, shaking the water from his left leg. The two of them carried unlit torches. Kaladin had lit his with a flint and steel, but the others did not. They needed to ration the torches.

The other men of Bridge Four began to gather near the bottom of the ladder, staying in a clump. Every fourth man lit his torch, but the light didn't do much to dispel the gloom; it just allowed Kaladin to see more of the unnatural landscape. Strange, tube-shaped fungi grew in cracks. They were a wan yellow, like the skin of a child with jaundice. Scuttling cremlings moved away from the light. The tiny crustaceans were a translucent reddish color; as one scrambled past on the wall, he realized that he could see its internal organs through its shell.

The light also revealed a twisted, broken figure at the base of the chasm wall a short distance away. Kaladin raised his torch and stepped up to it. It was beginning to stink already. He raised a hand, unconsciously covering his nose and mouth as he knelt down.

It was a bridgeman, or had been, from one of the other crews. He was fresh. If he'd been here longer than a few days, the highstorm would have washed him away to some distant place. Bridge Four gathered behind Kaladin, looking silently at the one who had chosen to throw himself into the chasm.

'May you someday find a place of honor in the Tranquiline Halls, fallen brother,' Kaladin said, his voice echoing. 'And may we find a better end than you.' He stood, holding his torch high, and led the way past the dead sentry. His crew followed nervously.

Kaladin had quickly understood the basic tactics of fighting on the Shattered Plains. You wanted to advance forcefully, pressing your enemy to the plateau's edge. That was why the battles often turned bloody for the Alethi, who usually arrived after the Parshendi.

The Alethi had bridges, while these odd Eastern parshmen could leap most chasms, given a running start. But both had trouble when squeezed toward the cliffs, and that generally resulted in soldiers losing their footing and tumbling into the void. The numbers were significant enough for the Alethi to want to recover lost equipment. And so bridgemen were sent on chasm duty. It was like barrow robbing, only without the barrows.

They carried sacks, and would spend hours walking around, looking for the corpses of the fallen, searching for anything of value. Spheres, breast-plates, caps, weapons. Some days, when a plateau run was recent, they could try to make their way all the way out to where it had happened and scavenge from those bodies. But highstorms generally made that futile. Wait even a few days, and the bodies would be washed someplace else.

Beyond that, the chasms were a bewildering maze, and getting to a specific contested plateau and then returning in a reasonable time was near impossible. General wisdom was to wait for a highstorm to push the bodies toward the Alethi side of the Plains – highstorms always came east to west, after all – and then send bridgemen down to search them out.

That meant a lot of random wandering. But over the years, enough bodies had fallen that it wasn't too difficult to find places to harvest. The crew was required to bring up a specific amount of salvage or face docked pay for the week, but the quota wasn't onerous. Enough to keep the bridge-men working, but not enough to force them to fully exert themselves. Like most bridgeman work, this was meant to keep them occupied as much as anything else.

As they walked down the first chasm, some of his men got out their sacks and picked up pieces of salvage they passed. A helmet here, a shield there. They kept a keen watch for spheres. Finding a valuable fallen sphere would result in a small reward for the whole crew. They weren't allowed to bring their own spheres or possessions into the chasm, of course. And on their way out, they were searched thoroughly. The humiliation of that search – which included any place a sphere might be hidden – was part of the reason chasm duty was so loathed.

But only a part. As they walked, the chasm floor widened to about fifteen feet. Here, marks scarred the walls, gashes where the moss had been scraped away, the stone itself scored. The bridgemen tried not to look at those marks. Occasionally, chasmfiends stalked these pathways, searching for either carrion or a suitable plateau to pupate upon. Encoun-tering one of them was uncommon, but possible.

'Kelek, but I hate this place,' Teft said, walking beside Kaladin. 'I heard that once an entire bridge crew got eaten by a chasmfiend, one at a time, after it backed them into a dead end. It just sat there, picking them off as they tried to run past.'

Rock chuckled. 'If they were all eaten, then who was returning to tell this story?'

Teft rubbed his chin. 'I dunno. Maybe they just never returned.'

'Then perhaps they fled. Deserting.'

'No,' Teft said. 'You can't get out of these chasms without a ladder.' He glanced upward, toward the narrow rift of blue seventy feet above, following the curve of the plateau.

Kaladin glanced up as well. That blue sky seemed so distant. Unreachable. Like the light of the Halls themselves. And even if you could climb out at one of the shallower areas, you'd either be trapped on the Plains without a way to cross chasms, or you'd be close enough to the Alethi side that the scouts would spot you crossing the permanent bridges. You could try going eastward, toward where the plateaus were worn away to the point that they were just spires. But that would take weeks of walking, and would require surviving multiple highstorms.

'You ever been in a slot canyon when rains come, Rock?' Teft asked, perhaps thinking along the same lines.

'No,' Rock replied. 'On the Peaks, we have not these things. They only exist where foolish men choose to live.'

'*You* live here, Rock,' Kaladin noted.

'And I am foolish,' the large Horneater said, chuckling. 'Did you not notice this thing?' These last two days had changed him a great deal. He was more affable, returning in some measure to what Kaladin assumed was his normal personality.

'I was *talking*,' Teft said, 'about slot canyons. You want to guess what will happen if we get trapped down here in a highstorm?'

'Lots of water, I guess,' Rock said.

'Lots of water, looking to go any place it can,' Teft said. 'It gathers into enormous waves and goes crashing through these confined spaces with enough force to toss boulders. In fact, an *ordinary* rain will feel like a highstorm down here. A highstorm ... well, this would probably be the worst place in Roshar to be when one hits.'

Rock frowned at that, glancing upward. 'Best not to be caught in the storm, then.'

'Yeah,' Teft said.

'Though, Teft,' Rock added, 'it would give you bath, which you very much need.'

'Hey,' Teft grumbled. 'Is that a comment on how I smell?'

'No,' Rock said. 'Is comment on what *I* have to smell. Sometimes, I am thinking that a Parshendi arrow in the eye would be better than smelling entire bridge crew enclosed in barrack at night!'

Teft chuckled. 'I'd take offense at that if it weren't true.' He sniffed at the damp, moldy chasm air. 'This place ain't much better. It smells worse than a Horneater's boots in winter down here.' He hesitated. 'Er, no offense. I mean personally.'

Kaladin smiled, then glanced back. The thirty or so other bridgemen followed like ghosts. A few seemed to be edging close to Kaladin's group, as if trying to listen in without being obvious.

'Teft,' Kaladin said. '"Smells worse than a Horneater's boots"? How in the Halls isn't he supposed to take offense at *that* phrase?'

'It's just an expression,' Teft said, scowling. 'It was out of my mouth before I realized what I was saying.'

'Alas,' Rock said, pulling a tuft of moss off the wall, inspecting it as they walked. 'Your insult has offended me. If we were at the Peaks, we would have to duel in the traditional *alil'tiki'i* fashion.'

'Which is what?' Teft asked. 'With spears?'

Rock laughed. 'No, no. We upon the Peaks are not barbarians like you down here.'

'How then?' Kaladin asked, genuinely curious.

'Well,' Rock said, dropping the moss and dusting off his hands, 'is involving much mudbeer and singing.'

'How's *that* a duel?'

'He who can still sing after the most drinks is winner. Plus, soon, everyone is so drunk that they probably forget what argument was about.'

Teft laughed. 'Beats knives at dawn, I suppose.'

'I guess that depends,' Kaladin said.

'Upon what?' Teft asked.

'On whether or not you're a knife merchant. Eh, Dunny?'

The other two glanced to the side, where Dunny had moved up close to listen. The spindly youth jumped and blushed. 'Er— I—'

Rock chuckled at Kaladin's words. 'Dunny,' he said to the youth. 'Is odd name. What is meaning of it?'

'Meaning?' Dunny asked. 'I don't know. Names don't always have a meaning.'

Rock shook his head, displeased. 'Lowlanders. How are you to know who you are if your name has no meaning?'

'So your name means something?' Teft asked. 'Nu ... ma ... nu ...'

'Numuhukumakiaki'aialunamor,' Rock said, the native Horneater sounds flowing easily from his lips. 'Of course. Is description of very special rock my father discovered the day before my birth.'

'So your name is a whole sentence?' Dunny asked, uncertain – as if he wasn't sure he belonged.

'Is poem,' Rock said. 'On the Peaks, everyone's name is poem.'

'Is that so?' Teft said, scratching at his beard. 'Must make calling the family at mealtime a bit of a chore.'

Rock laughed. 'True, true. Is also making for some interesting arguments. Usually, the best insults on the Peaks are in the form of a poem, one which is similar in composition and rhyme to the person's name.'

'Kelek,' Teft muttered. 'Sounds like a lot of work.'

'Is why most arguments end in drinking, perhaps,' Rock said.

Dunny smiled hesitantly. 'Hey you big buffoon, you smell like a wet hog, so go out by the moon, and jump yourself in the bog.'

Rock laughed riotously, his booming voice echoing down the chasm. 'Is good, is good,' he said, wiping his eyes. 'Simple, but good.'

'That almost had the sound of a song to it, Dunny,' Kaladin said.

'Well, it was the first thing that came to mind. I put it to the tune of "Mari's Two Lovers" to get the beat right.'

'You can sing?' Rock asked. 'I must be hearing.'

'But—' Dunny said.

'Sing!' Rock commanded, pointing.

Dunny yelped, but obeyed, breaking into a song that wasn't familiar to Kaladin. It was an amusing tale involving a woman and twin brothers who she thought were the same person. Dunny's voice was a pure tenor, and he seemed to have more confidence when he sang than when he spoke.

He was good. Once he moved to the second verse, Rock began humming in a deep voice, providing a harmony. The Horneater was obviously very practiced at song. Kaladin glanced back at the other bridgemen, hoping to pull some more into the conversation or the song. He smiled at Skar, but got only a scowl in return. Moash and Sigzil – the dark-skinned Azish man – wouldn't even look at him. Peet looked only at his feet.

When the song was finished, Teft clapped appreciatively. 'That's a better performance than I've heard at many an inn.'

'Is good to meet a lowlander who can sing,' Rock said, stooping down to pick up a helm and stuff it in his bag. This particular chasm didn't seem to have much in the way of salvage this time. 'I had begun thinking you were all as tone deaf as my father's old axehound. Ha!'

Dunny blushed, but seemed to walk more confidently.

They continued, occasionally passing turns or rifts in the stone where the waters had deposited large clusters of salvage. Here, the work turned more gruesome, and they'd often have to pull out corpses or piles of bones to get what they wanted, gagging at the scent. Kaladin told them to leave the more sickening or rotted bodies for now. Rotspren tended to cluster around the dead. If they didn't find enough salvage later, they could get those on the way back.

At every intersection or branch, Kaladin made a white mark on the wall with a piece of chalk. That was the bridgeleader's duty, and he took it seriously. He wouldn't have his crew getting lost out in these rifts.

As they walked and worked, Kaladin kept the conversation going. He laughed – forced himself to laugh – with them. If that laughter felt hollow to him, the others didn't seem to notice. Perhaps they felt as he did, that even forced laughter was preferable to going back to the self-absorbed, mournful silence that cloaked most bridgemen.

Before long, Dunny was laughing and talking with Teft and Rock, his shyness faded. A few others hovered just behind – Yake, Maps, a couple of others – like wild creatures drawn to the light and warmth of a fire. Kaladin tried to draw them into the conversation, but it didn't work, so eventually he just let them be.

Eventually, they reached a place with a significant number of fresh corpses. Kaladin wasn't sure what combination of waterflow had made this section of chasm a good place for that – it looked the same as other stretches. A little narrower perhaps. Sometimes they could go to the same nooks and find good salvage there; other times, those were empty, but other places would have dozens of corpses.

These bodies looked like they'd floated in the wash of the highstorm flood, then been deposited as the water slowly receded. There were no

Parshendi among them, and they were broken and torn from either their fall or the crush of the flood. Many were missing limbs.

The stink of blood and viscera hung in the humid air. Kaladin held his torch aloft as his companions fell silent. The chill kept the bodies from rotting too quickly, though the dampness counteracted some of that. The cremlings had begun chewing the skin off hands and gnawing out the eyes. Soon the stomachs would bloat with gas. Some rotspren – tiny, red, translucent – scrambled across the corpses.

Syl floated down and landed on his shoulder, making disgusted noises. As usual, she offered no explanation for her absence.

The men knew what to do. Even with the rotspren, this was too rich a place to pass up. They went to work, pulling the corpses into a line so they could be inspected. Kaladin waved for Rock and Teft to join him as he picked up some stray bits of salvage that lay on the ground around the corpses. Dunny tagged along.

'Those bodies wear the highprince's colors,' Rock noted as Kaladin picked up a dented steel cap.

'I'll bet they're from that run a few days back,' Kaladin said. 'It went badly for Sadeas's forces.'

'*Brightlord* Sadeas,' Dunny said. Then he ducked his head in embarrassment. 'Sorry, I didn't mean to correct you. I used to forget to say the title. My master beat me when I did.'

'Master?' Teft asked, picking up a fallen spear and pulling some moss off its shaft.

'I was an apprentice. I mean, before . . .' Dunny trailed off, then looked away.

Teft had been right; bridgemen didn't like talking about their pasts. Anyway, Dunny was probably right to correct him. Kaladin would be punished if he were heard omitting a lighteyes's honorific.

Kaladin put the cap in his sack, then rammed his torch into a gap between two moss-covered boulders and started helping the others get the bodies into a line. He didn't prod the men toward conversation. The fallen deserved some reverence – if that was possible while robbing them.

Next, the bridgemen stripped the fallen of their armor. Leather vests from the archers, steel breastplates from the foot soldiers. This group included a lighteyes in fine clothing beneath even finer armor. Sometimes the bodies of fallen lighteyes would be recovered from the chasms by special teams so the corpse could be Soulcast into a statue. Darkeyes, unless they were very wealthy, were burned. And most soldiers who fell into the chasms were ignored; the men in camp spoke of the chasms being hallowed resting places, but the truth was that the effort to get the bodies out wasn't worth the cost or the danger.

Regardless, to find a lighteyes here meant that his family hadn't been wealthy enough, or concerned enough, to send men out to recover him. His face was crushed beyond recognition, but his rank insignia identified him as seventh dahn. Landless, attached to a more powerful officer's retinue.

Once they had his armor, they pulled daggers and boots off everyone in line – boots were *always* in demand. They left the fallen their clothing, though they took off the belts and cut free many shirt buttons. As they worked, Kaladin sent Teft and Rock around the bend to see if there were any other bodies nearby.

Once the armor, weapons, and boots had been separated, the most grisly task began: searching pockets and pouches for spheres and jewelry. This pile was the smallest of the lot, but valuable. They didn't find any broams, which meant no pitiful reward for the bridgemen.

As the men performed their morbid task, Kaladin noticed the end of a spear poking out of a nearby pool. It had gone unnoticed in their initial sweep.

Lost in thought, he fetched it, shaking off the water, carrying it over to the weapons pile. He hesitated there, holding the spear over the pile with one hand, cold water dripping from it. He rubbed his finger along the smooth wood. He could tell from the heft, balance, and sanding that it was a good weapon. Sturdy, well made, well kept.

He closed his eyes, remembering days as a boy holding a quarterstaff.

Words spoken by Tukks years ago returned to him, words spoken on that bright summer day when he'd first held a weapon in Amaram's army. *The first step is to care*, Tukks's voice seemed to whisper. *Some talk about being emotionless in battle. Well, I suppose it's important to keep your head. But I hate that feeling of killing while calm and cold. I've seen that those who care fight harder, longer, and better than those who don't. It's the difference between mercenaries and real soldiers. It's the difference between fighting to defend your homeland and fighting on foreign soil.*

It's good to care when you fight, so long as you don't let it consume you. Don't try to stop yourself from feeling. You'll hate who you become.

The spear quivered in Kaladin's fingers, as if begging him to swing it, spin it, dance with it.

'What are you planning to do, lordling?' a voice called. 'Going to ram that spear into your own gut?'

Kaladin glanced up at the speaker. Moash – still one of Kaladin's biggest detractors – stood near the line of corpses. How had he known to call Kaladin 'lordling'? Had he been talking to Gaz?

'He claims he's a deserter,' Moash said to Narm, the man working next to him. 'Says he was some important soldier, a squadleader or the like. But Gaz says that's all stupid boasting. They wouldn't send a man to the bridges if he actually knew how to fight.'

Kaladin lowered the spear.

Moash smirked, turning back to his work. Others, however, had now noticed Kaladin. 'Look at him,' Sigzil said. 'Ho, bridgeleader! You think that you're grand? That you are better than us? You think pretending that we're your own personal troop of soldiers will change anything?'

'Leave him alone,' Drehy said. He shoved Sigzil as he passed. 'At least he tries.'

Earless Jacks snorted, pulling a boot free from a dead foot. 'He cares about looking important. Even if he *was* in the army, I'll bet he spent his days cleaning out latrines.'

It appeared that there was something that would pull the bridgemen out of their silent stupors: loathing for Kaladin. Others began talking, calling gibes.

'. . . his fault we're down here . . .'

'. . . wants to run us ragged during our only free time, just so he can feel important . . .'

'. . . sent us to carry rocks to show us he could shove us around . . .'

'. . . bet he's never held a spear in his life.'

Kaladin closed his eyes, listening to their scorn, rubbing his fingers on the wood.

Never held a spear in his life. Maybe if he'd never picked up that first spear, none of this would have happened.

He felt the smooth wood, slick with rainwater, memories jumbling in his head. Training to forget, training to get vengeance, training to learn and make sense of what had happened.

Without thinking about it, he snapped the spear up under his arm into a guard position, point down. Water droplets from its length sprayed across his back.

Moash cut off in the middle of another gibe. The bridgemen sputtered to a stop. The chasm became quiet.

And Kaladin was in another place.

He was listening to Tukks chide him.

He was listening to Tien laugh.

He was hearing his mother tease him in her clever, witty way.

He was on the battlefield, surrounded by enemies but ringed by friends.

He was listening to his father tell him with a sneer in his voice that spears were only for killing. You could not kill to protect.

He was alone in a chasm deep beneath the earth, holding the spear of a fallen man, fingers gripping the wet wood, a faint dripping coming from somewhere distant.

Strength surged through him as he spun the spear up into an advanced kata. His body moved of its own accord, going through the forms he'd trained in so frequently. The spear danced in his fingers, comfortable, an extension of himself. He spun with it, swinging it around and around, across his neck, over his arm, in and out of jabs and swings. Though it had been months since he'd even held a weapon, his muscles knew what to do. It was as if the *spear itself* knew what to do.

Tension melted away, frustration melted away, and his body sighed in contentment even as he worked it furiously. This was familiar. This was welcome. This was what it had been created to do.

Men had always told Kaladin that he fought like nobody else. He'd felt it on the first day he'd picked up a quarterstaff, though Tukks's advice had helped him refine and channel what he could do. Kaladin had *cared* when he fought. He'd never fought empty or cold. He fought to keep his men alive.

Of all the recruits in his cohort, he had learned the quickest. How to hold the spear, how to stand to spar. He'd done it almost without instruction. That had shocked Tukks. But why should it have? You were not shocked when a child knew how to breathe. You were not shocked when a skyeel took flight for the first time. You should not be shocked when you hand Kaladin Stormblessed a spear and he knows how to use it.

Kaladin spun through the last motions of the kata, chasm forgotten, bridgemen forgotten, fatigue forgotten. For a moment, it was just him.

Him and the wind. He fought with her, and she laughed.

He snapped the spear back into place, holding the haft at the one-quarter position, spearhead down, bottom of the haft tucked underneath his arm, end rising back behind his head. He breathed in deeply, shivering.

Oh, how I've missed that.

He opened his eyes. Sputtering torchlight revealed a group of stunned bridgemen standing in a damp corridor of stone, the walls wet and reflecting the light. Moash dropped a handful of spheres in stunned silence, staring at Kaladin with mouth agape. Those spheres plopped into the puddle at his feet, causing it to glow, but none of the bridgemen noticed. They just stared at Kaladin, who was still in a battle stance, half crouched, trails of sweat running down the sides of his face.

He blinked, realizing what he'd done. If word got back to Gaz that he was playing around with spears . . . Kaladin stood up straight and dropped the spear into the pile of weapons. 'Sorry,' he whispered to it, though he didn't know why. Then, louder, he said, 'Back to work! I don't want to be caught down here when night falls.'

The bridgemen jumped into motion. Down the chasm corridor, he saw Rock and Teft. Had they seen the entire kata? Flushing, Kaladin hurried up to them. Syl landed on his shoulder, silent.

'Kaladin, lad,' Teft said reverently. 'That was—'

'It was meaningless,' Kaladin said. 'Just a kata. Meant to work the muscles and make you practice the basic jabs, thrusts, and sweeps. It's a lot showier than it is useful.'

'But—'

'No, really,' Kaladin said. 'Can you imagine a man swinging a spear around his neck like that in combat? He'd be gutted in a second.'

'Lad,' Teft said. 'I've *seen* katas before. But never one like that. The way you moved . . . The speed, the grace . . . And there was some sort of spren zipping around you, between your sweeps, glowing with a pale light. It was beautiful.'

Rock started. 'You could see that?'

'Sure,' Teft said. 'Never seen a spren like that. Ask the other men—I saw a few of them pointing.'

Kaladin glanced at his shoulder, frowning at Syl. She sat primly, legs crossed and hands folded atop her knee, pointedly not looking at him.

'It was nothing,' Kaladin repeated.

'No,' Rock said. 'That it certainly was not. Perhaps *you* should challenge Shardbearer. You could become brightlord!'

'I *don't* want to be a brightlord,' Kaladin snapped, perhaps more harshly than he should have. The other two jumped. 'Besides,' he added, looking away from them. 'I tried that once. Where's Dunny?'

'Wait,' Teft said, 'you—'

'Where is Dunny?' Kaladin said firmly, punctuating each word. *Storm-father. I need to keep my mouth shut.*

Teft and Rock shared a glance, then Teft pointed. 'We found some dead Parshendi around the bend. Thought you'd want to know.'

'Parshendi,' Kaladin said. 'Let's go look. Might have something valuable.' He'd never looted Parshendi bodies before; fewer of them fell into the chasms than Alethi.

'Is true,' Rock said, leading the way, carrying a lit torch. 'Those weapons they have, yes, very nice. And gemstones in their beards.'

'Not to mention the armor,' Kaladin said.

Rock shook his head. 'No armor.'

'Rock, I've *seen* their armor. They always wear it.'

'Well, yes, but we cannot use this thing.'

'I don't understand,' Kaladin said.

'Come,' Rock said, gesturing. 'Is easier than explaining.'

Kaladin shrugged, and they rounded the corner, Rock scratching at his red-bearded chin. 'Stupid hairs,' he muttered. 'Ah, to have it right again. A man is not proper man without proper beard.'

Kaladin rubbed his own beard. One of these days, he'd save up and buy a razor and be rid of the blasted thing. Or, well, probably not. His spheres would be needed elsewhere.

They rounded the corner and found Dunny pulling the Parshendi bodies into a line. There were four of them, and they looked like they'd been swept in from another direction. There were a few more Alethi bodies here too.

Kaladin strode forward, waving Rock to bring the light, and knelt to inspect one of the Parshendi dead. They were like parshmen, with skin in marbled patterns of black and crimson. Their only clothing was knee-length black skirts. Three wore beards, which was unusual for parshmen, and those were woven with uncut gemstones.

Just as Kaladin had expected, they wore armor of a pale red color.

Breastplates, helms on the heads, guards on the arms and legs. Extensive armor for regular foot soldiers. Some of it was cracked from the fall or the wash. It wasn't metal, then. Painted wood?

'I thought you said they weren't armored,' Kaladin said. 'What are you trying to tell me? That you don't dare take it off the dead?'

'Don't dare?' Rock said. 'Kaladin, Master Brightlord, brilliant bridge-leader, spinner of spear, perhaps *you* will get it off them.'

Kaladin shrugged. His father had instilled in him a familiarity with the dead and dying, and though it felt bad to rob the dead, he was not squeamish. He prodded the first Parshendi, noting the man's knife. He took it and looked for the strap that held the shoulder guard in place.

There was no strap. Kaladin frowned and peered underneath the guard, trying to pry it up. The skin lifted with it. 'Stormfather!' he said. He inspected the helm. It was grown into the head. Or grown *from* the head. 'What *is* this?'

'Do not know,' Rock said, shrugging. 'It is looking like they grow their own armor, eh?'

'That's ridiculous,' Kaladin said. 'They're just people. People – even parshmen – don't *grow* armor.'

'Parshendi do,' Teft said.

Kaladin and the other two turned to him.

'Don't look at me like that,' the older man said with a scowl. 'I worked in the camp for a few years before I ended up as a bridgeman – no, I'm not going to tell you how, so storm off. Anyway, the soldiers talk about it. The Parshendi grow carapaces.'

'I've *known* parshmen,' Kaladin said. 'There were a couple of them in my hometown, serving the citylord. None of them grew armor.'

'Well, these are a different kind of parshman,' Teft said with a scowl. 'Bigger, stronger. They can jump *chasms*, for Kelek's sake. And they grow armor. That's just how it is.'

There was no disputing it, so they just moved on to gathering what they could. Many Parshendi used heavy weapons – axes, hammers – and those hadn't been carried along with the bodies like many of the spears and bows Alethi soldiers had. But they did find several knives and one ornate sword, still in a sheath at the Parshendi's side.

The skirts didn't have pockets, but the corpses did have pouches tied to their waists. These just carried flint and tinder, whetstones, or other basic supplies. So, they knelt to begin pulling the gemstones from the beards. Those gemstones had holes drilled through them to facilitate weaving, and Stormlight infused them, though they didn't glow as brightly as they would have if they'd been properly cut.

As Rock pulled the gemstones out of the final Parshendi's beard, Kaladin held one of the knives up near Dunny's torch, inspecting the detailed carving. 'Those look like glyphs,' he said, showing it to Teft.

'I can't read glyphs, boy.'

Oh, right, Kaladin thought. Well, if they were glyphs, they weren't ones he was familiar with. Of course, you could draw most glyphs in complex ways that made it hard to read them, unless you knew exactly what to look for. There was a figure at the center of the hilt, nicely carved. It was a man in fine armor. Shardplate, certainly. A symbol was etched behind him, surrounding him, spreading out from his back like wings.

Kaladin showed it to Rock, who had walked up to see what he found so fascinating. 'The Parshendi out here are supposed to be barbarians,' Kaladin said. 'Without culture. Where did they get knives like these? I'd swear this is a picture of one of the Heralds. Jezerezeh or Nalan.'

Rock shrugged. Kaladin sighed and returned the knife to its sheath, then dropped it into his sack. Then they rounded the curve back to the others. The crew had gathered up sacks full of armor, belts, boots, and spheres. Each took up a spear to carry back to the ladder, holding them like walking sticks. They'd left one for Kaladin, but he tossed it to Rock. He didn't trust himself to hold one of them again, worried he'd be tempted to fall into another kata.

The walk back was uneventful, though with the darkening sky, the men began jumping at every sound. Kaladin engaged Rock, Teft, and Dunny in conversation again. He was able to get Drehy and Torfin to talk a little as well.

They safely reached the first chasm, much to the relief of his men. Kaladin sent the others up the ladder first, waiting to go up last. Rock waited with him, and as Dunny finally started up – leaving Rock and Kaladin alone – the tall Horneater put a hand on Kaladin's shoulder, speaking in a soft voice.

'You do good work here,' Rock said. 'I am thinking that in a few weeks, these men will be yours.'

Kaladin shook his head. 'We're bridgemen, Rock. We don't *have* a few weeks. If I take that long winning them over, half of us will be dead.'

Rock frowned. 'Is not a happy thought.'

'That's why we have to win over the other men *now*.'

'But how?'

Kaladin looked up at the dangling ladder, shaking as the men climbed up. Only four could go at a time, lest they overload it. 'Meet me after we're searched. We're going to the camp market.'

'Very well,' Rock said, swinging onto the ladder as Earless Jaks reached the top. 'What will be our purpose in this thing?'

'We're going to try out my secret weapon.'

Rock laughed as Kaladin held the ladder steady for him. 'And what weapon is this?'

Kaladin smiled. 'Actually, it's you.'

⁂

Two hours later, at Salas's first violet light, Rock and Kaladin walked back into the lumberyard. It was just past sunset, and many of the bridgemen would soon be going to sleep.

Not much time, Kaladin thought, gesturing for Rock to carry his burden to a place near the front of Bridge Four's barrack. The large Horneater set his burden down next to Teft and Dunny, who had done as Kaladin had ordered, building a small ring of stones and setting up some stumps of wood from the lumberyard scrap pile. That wood was free for anyone to take. Even bridgemen were allowed; some liked to take chunks to whittle.

Kaladin got out a sphere for light. The thing Rock had been carrying was an old iron cauldron. Even though it was secondhand, it had cost Kaladin a fair chunk of the knobweed sap money. The Horneater began to unpack supplies from inside the cauldron as Kaladin arranged some wood scraps inside the ring of stones.

'Dunny, water, if you please,' Kaladin said, getting out his flint. Dunny ran off to fetch a bucket from one of the rain barrels. Rock finished emptying the cauldron, laying out small packages that had cost another substantial portion of Kaladin's spheres. He had only a handful of clearchips left.

As they worked, Hobber limped out of the barrack. He was mending quickly, though the other two wounded that Kaladin had treated were still in bad shape.

'What are you up to, Kaladin?' Hobber asked just as Kaladin got a flame started.

Kaladin smiled, standing. 'Have a seat.'

Hobber did just that. He hadn't lost the near-devotion he'd shown Kaladin for saving his life. If anything, his loyalty had grown stronger.

Dunny returned with a bucket of water, which he poured into the cauldron. Then he and Teft ran off to get more. Kaladin built up the flames and Rock began to hum to himself as he diced tubers and unwrapped some seasonings. In under a half hour, they had a roaring flame and a simmering pot of stew.

Teft sat down on one of the stumps, warming his hands. 'This is your secret weapon?'

Kaladin sat down next to the older man. 'Have you known many soldiers in your life, Teft?'

'A few.'

'You ever known any who could turn down a warm fire and some stew at the end of a hard day?'

'Well, no. But bridgemen ain't soldiers.'

That was true. Kaladin turned to the barrack doorway. Rock and Dunny started up a song together and Teft began to clap along. Some of the men from other bridge crews were up late, and they gave Kaladin and the others nothing more than scowls.

Figures shifted inside the barrack, shadows moving. The door was open, and the scents of Rock's stew grew strong. Inviting.

Come on, Kaladin thought. *Remember why we live. Remember warmth, remember good food. Remember friends, and song, and evenings spent around the hearth.*

You aren't dead yet. Storm you! If you don't come out . . .

It all suddenly seemed so contrived to Kaladin. The singing was forced, the stew an act of desperation. It was all just an attempt to briefly distract from the pathetic life he had been forced into.

A figure moved in the doorway. Skar – short, square-bearded, and keen-eyed – stepped out into the firelight. Kaladin smiled at him. A forced smile. Sometimes that was all one could offer. *Let it be enough,* he prayed, standing up, dipping a wooden bowl into Rock's stew.

Kaladin held the bowl toward Skar. Steam curled from the surface of the brownish liquid. 'Will you join us?' Kaladin asked. 'Please.'

Skar looked at him, then back down at the stew. He laughed, taking the stew. 'I'd join the Nightwatcher herself around a fire if there was stew involved!'

'Be careful,' Teft said. 'That's Horneater stew. Might be snail shells or crab claws floating in it.'

'There is not!' Rock barked. 'Is unfortunate that you have unrefined lowlander tastes, but I prepare the food such as I am ordered by our dear bridgeleader.'

Kaladin smiled, letting out a deep breath as Skar sat down. Others trailed out after him, taking bowls, sitting. Some stared into the fire, not saying much, but others began to laugh and sing. At one point, Gaz walked past, eyeing them with his single eye, as if trying to decide if they were breaking any camp regulations. They weren't. Kaladin had checked.

Kaladin dipped out a bowl of stew and held it toward Gaz. The bridge sergeant snorted in derision and stalked away.

Can't expect too many miracles in one night, Kaladin thought with a sigh, settling back down and trying the stew. It was quite good. He smiled, joining in the next verse of Dunny's song.

The next morning, when Kaladin called for the bridgemen to rise, three-quarters of them piled out of the barrack – everyone but the loudest complainers: Moash, Sigzil, Narm, and a couple of others. The ones who came to his call looked surprisingly refreshed, despite the long evening spent singing and eating. When he ordered them to join him in practice carrying the bridge, almost all of those who had risen joined him.

Not everyone, but enough.

He had a feeling that Moash and the others would give in before too long. They'd eaten his stew. Nobody had turned that down. And now that he had so many, the others would feel foolish not joining in. Bridge Four was his.

Now he had to keep them alive long enough for that to mean something.

For I have never been dedicated to a more important purpose, and the very pillars of the sky will shake with the results of our war here. I ask again. Support me. Do not stand aside and let disaster consume more lives. I've never begged you for something before, old friend.
I do so now.

Adolin was frightened.

He stood beside his father on the staging ground. Dalinar looked ... weathered. Creases running back from his eyes, furrows in his skin. Black hair going white like bleached rock along the sides. How could a man standing in full Shardplate – a man who yet retained a warrior's frame despite his age – look fragile?

In front of them, two chulls followed their handler, stepping up onto the bridge. The wooden span linked two piles of cut stones, a mock chasm only a few feet deep. The chulls' whiplike antennae twitched, mandibles clacking, fist-size black eyes glancing about. They pulled a massive siege bridge, rolling on creaking wooden wheels.

'That's much wider than the bridges Sadeas uses,' Dalinar said to Teleb, who stood beside them.

'It's necessary to accommodate the siege bridge, Brightlord.'

Dalinar nodded absently. Adolin suspected that he was the only one who could see that his father was distressed. Dalinar maintained his usual confident front, his head high, his voice firm when he spoke.

Yet, those eyes. They were too red, too strained. And when Adolin's father felt strained, he grew cold and businesslike. When he spoke to Teleb, his tone was too controlled.

Dalinar Kholin was suddenly a man laboring beneath great weight. And Adolin had helped put him there.

The chulls advanced. Their boulderlike shells were painted blue and yellow, the colors and pattern indicating the island of their Reshi handlers. The bridge beneath them groaned ominously as the larger siege bridge rolled onto it. All around the staging area, soldiers turned to look. Even the workmen cutting a latrine into the stony ground on the eastern side stopped to watch.

The groans from the bridge grew louder. Then they became sharp cracks. The handlers halted the chulls, glancing toward Teleb.

'It's not going to hold, is it?' Adolin asked.

Teleb sighed. 'Storm it, I was hoping ... Bah, we made the smaller bridge too thin when we widened it. But if we make it thicker, it will get too heavy to carry.' He glanced at Dalinar. 'I apologize for wasting your time, Brightlord. You are correct; this is akin to the ten fools.'

'Adolin, what do you think?' Dalinar asked.

Adolin frowned. 'Well ... I think perhaps we should keep working with it. This is only the first attempt, Teleb. Perhaps there's still a way. Design the siege bridges to be narrower, maybe?'

'That could be very costly, Brightlord,' Teleb said.

'If it helps us win one extra gemheart, the effort would be paid for several times over.'

'Yes,' Teleb said, nodding. 'I will speak with Lady Kalana. Perhaps she can devise a new design.'

'Good,' Dalinar said. He stared at the bridge for an extended moment. Then, oddly, he turned to look toward the other side of the staging area, where the workers had been cutting the latrine ditch.

'Father?' Adolin asked.

'Why do you suppose,' Dalinar said, 'there are no Shardplate-like suits for workmen?'

'What?'

'Shardplate gives awesome strength, but we rarely use it for anything other than war and slaughter. Why did the Radiants fashion only weapons? Why didn't they make productive tools for use by ordinary men?'

'I don't know,' Adolin said. 'Perhaps because war was the most important thing around.'

'Perhaps,' Dalinar said, voice growing softer. 'And perhaps that's a final condemnation of them and their ideals. For all of their lofty claims, they never gave their Plate or its secrets to the common people.'

'I . . . I don't understand why that's important, Father.'

Dalinar shook himself slightly. 'We should get on with our inspections. Where's Ladent?'

'Here, Brightlord.' A short man stepped up to Dalinar. Bald and bearded, the ardent wore thick, blue-grey layered robes from which his hands barely extended. The effect was of a crab who was too small for his shell. It looked terribly hot, but he didn't seem to mind.

'Send a messenger to the Fifth Battalion,' Dalinar told him. 'We'll be visiting them next.'

'Yes, Brightlord.'

Adolin and Dalinar began to walk. They'd chosen to wear their Shardplate for this day's inspections. That wasn't uncommon; many Shardbearers found any excuse they could to wear Plate. Plus, it was good for the men to see their highprince and his heir in their strength.

They drew attention as they left the staging area and entered the warcamp proper. Like Adolin, Dalinar went about unhelmed, though the gorget of his armor was tall and thick, rising like a metal collar up to his chin. He nodded to soldiers who saluted.

'Adolin,' Dalinar said. 'In combat, do you feel the Thrill?'

Adolin started. He knew immediately what his father meant, but he was shocked to hear the words. This wasn't often discussed. 'I . . . Well, of course. Who doesn't?'

Dalinar didn't reply. He had been so reserved lately. Was that pain in his eyes? *The way he was before*, Adolin thought, *deluded but confident. That was actually better.*

Dalinar said nothing more, and the two of them continued through the camp. Six years had let the soldiers settle in thoroughly. Barracks were painted with company and squad symbols, and the space between them was outfitted with firepits, stools, and canvas-shaded dining areas. Adolin's father had forbidden none of this, though he had set guidelines to discourage sloppiness.

Dalinar had also approved most requests for families to be brought to the Shattered Plains. The officers already had their wives, of course – a good lighteyes officer was really a team, the man to command and fight, the woman to read, write, engineer, and manage camp. Adolin smiled, thinking of Malasha. Would she prove to be the one for him? She'd been a little cold to him lately. Of course, there was Danlan. He'd only just met her, but he was intrigued.

Regardless, Dalinar had also approved requests by darkeyed common soldiers to bring their families. He even paid half of the cost. When Adolin had asked why, Dalinar had replied that he didn't feel right forbidding them. The warcamps were never attacked anymore, so there was no danger. Adolin suspected his father felt that since he was living in a luxurious near-palace, his men might as well have the comfort of their families.

And so it was that children played and ran through the camp. Women hung wash and painted glyphwards as men sharpened spears and polished breastplates. Barrack interiors had been partitioned to create rooms.

'I think you were right,' Adolin said as they walked, trying to draw his father out of his contemplations. 'To let so many bring their families here, I mean.'

'Yes, but how many will leave when this is over?'

'Does it matter?'

'I'm not certain. The Shattered Plains are now a de facto Alethi province. How will this place appear in a hundred years? Will those rings of barracks become neighborhoods? The outer shops become markets? The hills to the west become fields for planting?' He shook his head. 'The gemhearts will always be here, it seems. And so long as they are, there will be people here as well.'

'That's a good thing, isn't it? So long as those people are Alethi.' Adolin chuckled.

'Perhaps. And what will happen to the value of gemstones if we continue to capture gemhearts at the rate we have?'

'I . . .' That was a good question.

'What happens, I wonder, when the scarcest, yet most desirable, substance in the land suddenly becomes commonplace? There's much going on here, son. Much we haven't considered. The gemhearts, the Parshendi, the death of Gavilar. You will have to be ready to consider these things.'

'Me?' Adolin said. 'What does that mean?'

Dalinar didn't answer, instead nodding as the commander of the Fifth Battalion hastened up to them and saluted. Adolin sighed and saluted back. The Twenty-first and Twenty-second Companies were doing close order drill here – an essential exercise whose true value few outside the military ever appreciated. The Twenty-third and Twenty-fourth Companies were doing extended order – or combat – drill, practicing the formations and movements used on the battlefield.

Fighting on the Shattered Plains was very different from conventional warfare, as the Alethi had learned from some embarrassing early losses. The Parshendi were squat, muscular, and had that strange, skin-grown armor of theirs. It didn't cover as fully as plate, but it was far more efficient than what most foot soldiers had. Each Parshendi was essentially an extremely mobile heavy infantryman.

The Parshendi always attacked in pairs, eschewing a regular line of battle. That should have made it easy for a disciplined line to defeat them. But each pair of Parshendi had such momentum – and was so well armored – that they could break right through a shield wall. Alternatively, their jumping prowess could suddenly deposit entire ranks of Parshendi behind Alethi lines.

Beyond all that, there was that distinctive way they moved as a group in combat. They maneuvered with an inexplicable coordination. What had seemed at first to be mere barbarian savagery turned out to disguise something more subtle and dangerous.

They'd found only two reliable ways to defeat the Parshendi. The first was to use a Shardblade. Effective, but of limited application. The Kholin army had only two Blades, and while Shards were incredibly powerful, they needed proper support. An isolated, outnumbered Shardbearer could be tripped and toppled by his adversaries. In fact, the one time Adolin had seen a full Shardbearer fall to a regular soldier, it had happened because he had been swarmed by spearmen who broke his breastplate. Then a light-eyed archer had slain him from fifty paces, winning the Shards for himself. Not exactly a heroic end.

The other reliable way to fight Parshendi depended on quick-moving formations. Flexibility mixed with discipline: flexibility to respond to the uncanny way Parshendi fought, discipline to maintain lines and make up for individual Parshendi strength.

Havrom, Fifth Battalionlord, waited for Adolin and Dalinar with his companylords in a line. They saluted, right fists to right shoulders, knuckles outward.

Dalinar nodded to them. 'Have my orders been seen to, Brightlord Havrom?'

'Yes, Highprince.' Havrom was built like a tower, and wore a beard with long sides after the Horneater fashion, chin clean-shaven. He had relatives among the Peakfolk. 'The men you wanted are waiting in the audience tent.'

'What's this?' Adolin asked.

'I'll show you in a moment,' Dalinar said. 'First, review the troops.'

Adolin frowned, but the soldiers were waiting. One company at a time, Havrom had the men fall in. Adolin walked before them, inspecting their lines and uniforms. They were neat and orderly, though Adolin knew that some of the soldiers in their army grumbled at the level of polish required of them. He happened to agree with them on that point.

At the end of the inspection, he questioned a few random men, asked their rank and if they had any specific concerns. None had any. Were they satisfied or just intimidated?

When he was done, Adolin returned to his father.

'You did that well,' Dalinar said.

'All I did was walk down a line.'

'Yes, but the presentation was good. The men know you care for their needs, and they respect you.' He nodded, as if to himself. 'You've learned well.'

'I think you're reading too much into a simple inspection, Father.'

Dalinar nodded to Havrom, and the battalionlord led the two of them to an audience tent near the side of the practice field. Adolin, puzzled, glanced at his father.

'I had Havrom gather the soldiers that Sadeas spoke to the other day,' Dalinar said. 'The ones he interviewed while we were on our way to the plateau assault.'

'Ah,' Adolin said. 'We'll want to know what he asked them.'

'Yes,' Dalinar said. He gestured for Adolin to enter before him, and they walked in – tailed by a few of Dalinar's ardents. Inside, a group of ten soldiers waited on benches. They rose and saluted.

'At ease,' Dalinar said, clasping plated hands behind his back. 'Adolin?' Dalinar nodded toward the men, indicating that Adolin should take the lead in the questioning.

Adolin stifled a sigh. Again? 'Men, we need to know what Sadeas asked you and how you responded.'

'Don't worry, Brightlord,' said one of the men, speaking with a rural northern Alethi accent. 'We didn't tell him nothing.'

The others nodded vigorously.

'He's an eel, and we know it,' another added.

'He is a highprince,' Dalinar said sternly. 'You will treat him with respect.'

The soldier paled, then nodded.

'What, *specifically*, did he ask you?' Adolin asked.

'He wanted to know our duties in the camp, Brightlord,' the man said. 'We're grooms, you see.'

Each soldier was trained in one or two additional skills beyond those of combat. Having a group of soldiers who could care for horses was useful, as it kept civilians from plateau assaults.

'He asked around,' said one of the men. 'Or, well, his people did. Found out we were in charge of the king's horse during the chasmfiend hunt.'

'But we didn't say nothing,' the first soldier repeated. 'Nothing to get you into trouble, sir. We're not going to give that ee – er, that highprince, Brightlord sir, the rope to hang you, sir.'

Adolin closed his eyes. If they had acted this way around Sadeas, it would have been more incriminating than the cut girth itself. He couldn't fault their loyalty, but they acted as if they assumed Dalinar *had* done something wrong, and needed to defend him.

He opened his eyes. 'I spoke to some of you before, I recall. But let me ask again. Did any of you see a cut strap on the king's saddle?'

The men looked at each other, shaking heads. 'No, Brightlord,' one of the men replied. 'If we'd seen it, we'd have changed it, right we would.'

'But, Brightlord,' one of the men added, 'there was a lot of confusion that day, and a lot of people. Wasn't a right regular plateau assault or nothing like that. And, well, to be honest, sir, who'd have thought that we'd need to protect the king's saddle, of all things under the Halls?'

Dalinar nodded to Adolin, and they stepped out of the tent. 'Well?'

'They probably didn't do much to help our cause,' Adolin said with a grimace. 'Despite their ardor. Or, rather, because of it.'

'Agreed, unfortunately.' Dalinar let out a sigh. He waved to Tadet; the short ardent was standing to the side of the tent. 'Interview them separately,' Dalinar told him softly. 'See if you can tease specifics from them. Try to find out the exact words Sadeas used, and what their exact responses were.'

'Yes, Brightlord.'

'Come, Adolin,' Dalinar said. 'We've still got a few inspections to do.'

'Father,' Adolin said, taking Dalinar's arm. Their armor clinked softly. Dalinar turned to him, frowning, and Adolin made a quick gesture toward the Cobalt Guard. A request for space to speak. The guards moved efficiently and quickly, clearing a private space around the two men.

'What is this about, Father?' Adolin demanded softly.

'What? We're doing inspections and seeing to camp business.'

'And in each case, you shove me out into the lead,' Adolin said. 'Awkwardly, in a few cases, I might add. What's wrong? What's going on inside that head of yours?'

'I thought you had a distinct problem with the things going on inside my head.'

Adolin winced. 'Father, I—'

'No, it's all right, Adolin. I'm just trying to make a difficult decision. It helps me to move about while I do it.' Dalinar grimaced. 'Another man might find a place to sit and brood, but that never seems to help me. I've got too much to do.'

'What is it you're trying to decide?' Adolin asked. 'Perhaps I can help.'

'You already have. I—' Dalinar cut off, frowning. A small force of soldiers was walking up to the Fifth Battalion's practice yards. They were escorting a man in red and brown. Those were Thanadal's colors.

'Don't you have a meeting with him this evening?' Adolin asked.

'Yes,' Dalinar said.

Niter – head of the Cobalt Guard – ran to intercept the newcomers. He could be overly suspicious at times, but that wasn't a terrible trait for a bodyguard to have. He returned to Dalinar and Adolin shortly. Tanfaced, Niter bore a black beard, cut short. He was a lighteyes of very low rank, and had been with the guard for years. 'He says that Highprince

Thanadal will be unable to meet with you today as planned.'

Dalinar's expression grew dark. 'I will speak to the runner myself.'

Reluctantly, Niter waved the spindly fellow forward. He approached and dropped to one knee before Dalinar. 'Brightlord.'

This time, Dalinar didn't ask for Adolin to take the lead. 'Deliver your message.'

'Brightlord Thanadal regrets that he is unable to attend you this day.'

'And did he offer another time to meet?'

'He regrets to say that he has grown too busy. But he would be happy to speak with you at the king's feast one evening.'

In public, Adolin thought, *where half the men nearby will be eavesdropping while the other half – likely including Thanadal himself – will probably be drunk.*

'I see,' Dalinar said. 'And did he give any indication of when he'd no longer be so busy?'

'Brightlord,' the messenger said, growing uncomfortable. 'He said that if you pressed, I should explain that he has spoken with several of the other highprinces, and feels he knows the nature of your inquiry. He said to tell you he does not wish to form an alliance, nor does he have any intention of going on a joint plateau assault with you.'

Dalinar's expression grew darker. He dismissed the messenger with a wave, then turned to Adolin. The Cobalt Guard still kept a space open around them so they could talk.

'Thanadal was the last of them,' Dalinar said. Each highprince had turned him down in his own way. Hatham with exceeding politeness, Bethab by letting his wife give the explanation, Thanadal with hostile civility. 'All of them but Sadeas, at least.'

'I doubt it would be wise to approach him with this, Father.'

'You're probably right.' Dalinar's voice was cold. He was angry. Furious, even. 'They're sending me a message. They've never liked the influence I have over the king, and they're eager to see me fall. They don't want to do something I ask them to, just in case it might help me regain my footing.'

'Father, I'm sorry.'

'Perhaps it's for the best. The important point is that I have failed. I *can't* get them to work together. Elhokar was right.' He looked to Adolin. 'I would like you to continue inspections for me, son. There's something I want to do.'

'What?'

'Just some work I see needs to be done.'

Adolin wanted to object, but he couldn't think of the words to say. Finally, he sighed and gave a nod. 'You'll tell me what this is about, though?'

'Soon,' Dalinar promised. 'Very soon.'

❖

Dalinar watched his son leave, striding purposefully away. He would make a good highprince. Dalinar's decision was a simple one.

Was it time to step aside, and let his son take his place?

If he took this step, Dalinar would be expected to stay out of politics, retiring to his lands and leaving Adolin to rule. It was a painful decision to contemplate, and he had to be careful not to make it hastily. But if he really was going mad, as everyone in the camp seemed to believe, then he *had* to step down. And soon, before his condition progressed to the point that he no longer had the presence of mind to let go.

A monarch is control, he thought, remembering a passage from *The Way of Kings*. *He provides stability. It is his service and his trade good. If he cannot control himself, then how can he control the lives of men? What merchant worth his Stormlight won't partake of the very fruit he sells?*

Odd, that those quotes still came to him, even as he was wondering if they had – in part – driven him to madness. 'Niter,' he said. 'Fetch my warhammer. Have it waiting for me at the staging field.'

Dalinar wanted to be moving, working, as he thought. His guards hastened to keep up as he strode down the pathway between the barracks of Battalions Six and Seven. Niter sent several men to fetch the weapon. His voice sounded strangely excited, as if he thought Dalinar was going to do something impressive.

Dalinar doubted he would think it so. He eventually strode out onto the staging field, cape fluttering behind him, plated boots clanking against the stones. He didn't have to wait long for the hammer; it came pulled by two men on a small cart. Sweating, the soldiers heaved it from the cart, the haft as thick as a man's wrist and the front of the head larger than an outspread palm. Two men together could barely lift it.

Dalinar grabbed the hammer with one gauntleted hand, swinging it up to rest on his shoulder. He ignored the soldiers performing exercises on the field, walking to where the group of dirty workers chipped at the latrine ditch. They looked up at him, horrified to see the highprince himself looming over them in full Shardplate.

'Who's in charge here?' Dalinar asked.

A scruffy civilian in brown trousers raised a nervous hand. 'Brightlord, how may we serve you?'

'By relaxing for a little while,' Dalinar said. 'Out with you.'

The worried workers scrambled out. Lighteyed officers gathered behind, confused by Dalinar's actions.

Dalinar gripped the haft of his warhammer in a gauntleted hand; the metal shaft was wrapped tightly with leather. Taking a deep breath, he leaped down into the half-finished ditch, lifted the hammer, then swung, slamming the weapon down against the rock.

A powerful *crack* rang across the practice field, and a wave of shock ran up Dalinar's arms. The Shardplate absorbed most of the recoil, and he left a large crack in the stones. He hefted and swung again, this time breaking free a large section of rock. Though it would have been difficult for two or three ordinary men to lift, Dalinar grabbed it with one hand and tossed it aside. It clattered across the stones.

Where *were* the Shards for ordinary men? Why hadn't the ancients, who were so wise, created anything to help them? As Dalinar continued to work, beats of his hammer throwing chips and dust into the air, he easily did the work of twenty men. Shardplate could be used for so many things to ease the lives of workers and darkeyes across Roshar.

It felt good to be working. To be doing something useful. Lately, he felt as if his efforts had been akin to running about in circles. The work helped him think.

He *was* losing his thirst for battle. That worried him, as the Thrill – the enjoyment and longing for war – was part of what drove the Alethi as a people. The grandest of masculine arts was to become a great warrior, and the most important Calling was to fight. The Almighty himself depended on the Alethi to train themselves in honorable battle so that when they died, they could join the Heralds' army and win back the Tranquiline Halls.

And yet, thinking about killing was starting to sicken him. It had grown worse since that last bridge assault. What would happen next time he went into battle? He could not lead this way. That was a major reason that abdicating in favor of Adolin looked right.

He continued to swing. Again and again, beating against the stones. Soldiers gathered above and – despite his orders – the workers did not leave to relax. They watched, dumbfounded, as a Shardbearer did their work. Occasionally, he summoned his Blade and used it to cut the rock, slicing out sections before returning to the hammer to break them apart.

He probably looked ridiculous. He couldn't do the work of all of the laborers in camp, and he had important tasks to fill his time. There was no reason for him to get down in a trench and toil. And yet it felt so *good*. So wonderful to pitch in directly with the needs of the camp. The results of what he did to protect Elhokar were often difficult to gauge; it was fulfilling to be able to do something where his progress was obvious.

But even in this, he was acting according to the ideals that had infected him. The book spoke of a king carrying the burdens of his people. It said that those who led were the lowest of men, for they were required to serve everyone. It all swirled around in him. The Codes, the teachings of the book, the things the visions – or delusions – showed.

Never fight other men except when forced to in war.

Bang!

Let your actions defend you, not your words.

Bang!

Expect honor from those you meet, and give them the chance to live up to it.

Bang!

Rule as you would be ruled.

Bang!

He stood waist-deep in what would eventually be a latrine, his ears filled with the groans of breaking stone. He was coming to believe those ideals. No, he'd already come to believe them. Now he was living them. What would the world be like if all men lived as the book proclaimed?

Someone had to start. Someone had to be the model. In this, he had a reason *not* to abdicate. Whether or not he was mad, the way he now did things was better than the way Sadeas or the others did them. One needed only look at the lives of his soldiers and his people to see that was true.

Bang!

Stone could not be changed without pounding. Was it the same with a man like him? Was that why everything was so hard for him suddenly? But why him? Dalinar wasn't a philosopher or idealist. He was a soldier. And – if he admitted the truth – in earlier years, he'd been a tyrant and a warmonger. Could twilight years spent pretending to follow the precepts of better men erase a lifetime of butchery?

He had begun to sweat. The swath he had cut through the ground was as wide as a man was tall, as deep as his chest, and some thirty yards long. The longer he worked, the more people gathered to watch and whisper.

Shardplate was sacred. Was the highprince really digging a *latrine* with it? Had the stress affected him that profoundly? Frightened of highstorms. Growing cowardly. Refusing to duel or defend himself from slurs. Afraid of fighting, wishing to give up the war.

Suspected of trying to kill the king.

Eventually, Teleb decided that letting all the people stare down at Dalinar wasn't respectful, and he ordered the men back to their separate duties. He cleared away the workers, taking Dalinar's order to heart and commanding them to sit in the shade and 'converse in a lighthearted manner.' From someone else, that command might have been said with a smile, but Teleb was as literal as the rocks themselves.

Still Dalinar worked. He knew where the latrine was supposed to end; he'd approved the work order. A long, sloping trough was to be cut, then covered with oiled and tarred boards to seal in the scent. A latrine house would be set at the high end, and the contents could be Soulcast to smoke once every few months.

The work felt even better once he was alone. One man, breaking rocks, pounding beat after beat. Like the drums the Parshendi had played on that day so long past. Dalinar could feel those beats still, could hear them in his mind, shaking him.

I'm sorry, brother.

He had spoken to the ardents about his visions. They felt that the visions were most likely a product of an overtaxed mind.

He had no reason to believe the truth of anything the visions showed him. In following them, he had done more than just ignore Sadeas's maneuvers; he'd depleted his resources precariously. His reputation was on the brink of ruin. He was in danger of dragging down the entire Kholin house.

And that was the most important point in favor of him abdicating. If he continued, his actions could very well lead to the deaths of Adolin, Renarin, and Elhokar. He would risk his own life for his ideals, but could he risk the lives of his sons?

Chips sprayed, bouncing off his Plate. He was beginning to feel worn and tired. The Plate didn't do the work for him – it enhanced his strength, so each strike of the hammer was his own. His fingers were growing numb from the repeated vibration of the hammer's haft. He was close to a decision. His mind was calm, clear.

He swung the hammer again.

'Wouldn't the Blade be more efficient?' asked a dry, feminine voice.

Dalinar froze, the hammer's head resting on broken stone. He turned to see Navani standing beside the trough, wearing a gown of blue and soft red, her grey-sprinkled hair reflecting light from a sun that was unexpectedly close to setting. She was attended by two young women – not her own wards, but ones she had 'borrowed' from other lighteyed women in the camp.

Navani stood with her arms folded, the sunlight behind her like a halo. Dalinar hesitantly raised an armored forearm to block the light. 'Mathana?'

'The rockwork,' Navani said, nodding to the trough. 'Now, I wouldn't *presume* to make judgments; hitting things is a masculine art. But are you not in the possession of a sword that can cut through stone as easily as – I once had it described to me – a highstorm blows over a Herdazian?'

Dalinar looked back at the rocks. Then he raised his hammer again and slammed it into the stones, making a satisfying crunch. 'Shardblades are too good at cutting.'

'Curious,' she said. 'I'll do my best to pretend there was sense in that. As an aside, has it ever struck you that most masculine arts deal with destroying, while feminine arts deal with creation?'

Dalinar swung again. *Bang!* Remarkable how much easier it was to have a conversation with Navani while not looking directly at her. 'I do use the Blade to cut down the sides and middle. But I still have to break up the rocks. Have you ever tried to lift out a chunk of stone that has been sliced by a Shardblade?'

'I can't say that I have.'

'It's not easy.' *Bang!* 'Blades make a very thin cut. The rocks still press against one another. It's hard to grasp or move them.' *Bang!* 'It's more complicated than it seems.' *Bang!* 'This is the best way.'

Navani dusted a few chips of stone from her dress. 'And more messy, I see.'

Bang!

'So, are you going to apologize?' she asked.

'For?'

'For missing our appointment.'

Dalinar froze in midswing. He'd completely forgotten that, at the feast when she'd first returned, he'd agreed to have Navani read for him today. He hadn't told his scribes of the appointment. He turned toward her, chagrined. He'd been angered because Thanadal had canceled their appointment, but at least *he* had thought to send a messenger.

Navani stood with arms folded, safehand tucked away, sleek dress seeming to burn with sunlight. She bore a hint of a smile on her lips. By standing her up, he'd put himself – by honor – in her power.

'I'm truly sorry,' he said. 'I've had some difficult things to consider lately, but that doesn't excuse forgetting you.'

'I know. I'll ponder a way to let you make up for the lapse. But for now, you should know that one of your spanreeds is flashing.'

'What? Which one?'

'Your scribes say it is the one bound to my daughter.'

Jasnah! It had been weeks since they'd last communicated; the messages he'd sent her had prompted only the tersest of answers. When Jasnah was deeply immersed in one of her projects, she often ignored all else. If she was sending to him now, either she'd discovered something or she was taking a break to renew her contacts.

Dalinar turned to look down the latrine. He'd nearly completed it; and he realized he'd been unconsciously planning to make his final decision once he reached the end. He itched to continue working.

But if Jasnah wanted to converse . . .

He needed to talk with her. Perhaps he could persuade her to return to the Shattered Plains. He would feel a lot more secure about abdicating if he knew that she would come watch over Elhokar and Adolin.

Dalinar tossed aside his hammer – his pounding had bent the haft a good thirty degrees and the head was a misshapen lump – and jumped out of the ditch. He'd have a new weapon forged; that was not unusual for Shardbearers.

'Your pardon, Mathana,' Dalinar said, 'but I fear I must beg your leave so soon after begging your forgiveness. I must receive this communication.'

He bowed to her and turned to hurry away.

'Actually,' Navani said from behind, 'I think *I'll* beg something of you. It has been months since I've spoken with my daughter. I'll join you, if you'll permit it.'

He hesitated, but he couldn't deny her so soon after giving her offense. 'Of course.' He waited as Navani walked to her palanquin and settled herself. The bearers lifted it, and Dalinar struck out again, the bearers and Navani's borrowed wards walking close.

'You are a kind man, Dalinar Kholin,' Navani said, that same sly smile on her lips as she sat back in the cushioned chair. 'I'm afraid that I'm compelled to find you fascinating.'

'My sense of honor makes me easy to manipulate,' Dalinar said, eyes forward. Dealing with her was *not* something he needed right now. 'I know it does. No need to toy with me, Navani.'

She laughed softly. 'I'm not trying to take advantage of you, Dalinar, I—' She paused. 'Well, perhaps I am taking advantage of you just a little. But I'm not "toying" with you. This last year in particular, you've begun to *be* the person the others all *claim* that they are. Can't you see how intriguing that makes you?'

'I don't do it to be intriguing.'

'If you did, it wouldn't work!' She leaned toward him. 'Do you know why I picked Gavilar instead of you all those years ago?'

Blast. Her comments – her presence – were like a goblet of dark wine poured into the middle of his crystal thoughts. The clarity he'd sought in hard labor was quickly vanishing. Did she have to be so forward? He didn't answer the question. Instead, he picked up his pace and hoped that she'd see he didn't want to discuss the topic.

It was no use. 'I didn't pick him because he would become king, Dalinar. Though that's what everyone says. I chose him because you *frightened* me. That intensity of yours ... it scared your brother too, you know.'

He said nothing.

'It's still in there,' she said. 'I can see it in your eyes. But you've wrapped armor around it, a glistening set of Shardplate to contain it. That is part of what I find fascinating.'

He stopped, looking at her. The palanquin bearers halted. 'This would not work, Navani,' he said softly.

'Wouldn't it?'

He shook his head. 'I will not dishonor my brother's memory.' He regarded her sternly, and she eventually nodded.

When he continued walking, she said nothing, though she did eye him slyly from time to time. Eventually, they reached his personal complex, marked by fluttering blue banners with the glyphpair *khokh* and *linil*, the former drawn in the shape of a tower, the second forming a crown. Dalinar's mother had drawn the original design, the same his signet ring bore, though Elhokar used a sword and crown instead.

The soldiers at the entrance to his complex saluted, and Dalinar waited for Navani to join him before entering. The cavernous interior was lit by infused sapphires. Once they reached his sitting chamber, he was again struck by just how lavish it had gotten over the months.

Three of his clerks waited with their attending girls. All six stood up when he entered. Adolin was also there.

Dalinar frowned at the youth. 'Shouldn't you be seeing to the inspections?'

Adolin started. 'Father, I finished those hours ago.'

'You did?' *Stormfather! How long did I spend pounding on those stones?*

'Father,' Adolin said, stepping up to him. 'Can we speak privately for a moment?' As usual, Adolin's black-peppered blond hair was an unruly mop. He'd changed from his Plate and bathed, and now he wore a fashionable – though battle-worthy – uniform with a long blue coat, buttoned at the sides, and straight, stiff brown trousers beneath.

'I'm not ready to discuss that as yet, son,' Dalinar said softly. 'I need a little more time.'

Adolin studied him, eyes concerned. *He will make a fine highprince,* Dalinar thought. *He's been reared to it in a way that I never was.*

'All right then,' Adolin said. 'But there's something else I want to ask you.' He pointed toward one of the clerks, a woman with auburn hair and only a few strands of black. She was lithe and long-necked, wearing a green dress, her hair arranged high on her head in a complex set of braids held together with four traditional steel hair-spikes.

'This is Danlan Morakotha,' Adolin said softly to Dalinar. 'She came into camp yesterday to spend a few months with her father, Brightlord Morakotha. She has been calling on me recently, and I took the liberty of offering her a position among your clerks while she is here.'

Dalinar blinked. 'What about . . .'

'Malasha?' Adolin sighed. 'Didn't work out.'

'And this one?' Dalinar asked, voice hushed, yet incredulous. 'How long did you say she's been in camp? Since yesterday? And you've already got her *calling* on you?'

Adolin shrugged. 'Well, I do have a reputation to maintain.'

Dalinar sighed, eyeing Navani, who stood close enough to hear. She pretended – for propriety – that she wasn't listening in. 'You know, it is customary to eventually choose just one woman to court.' *You're going to need a good wife, son. Perhaps very soon.*

'When I'm old and boring, perhaps,' Adolin said, smiling at the young woman. She *was* pretty. But only in camp one day? *Blood of my ancestors*, Dalinar thought. He'd spent three years courting the woman who'd eventually become his wife. Even if he couldn't remember her face, he *did* remember how persistently he'd pursued her.

Surely he'd loved her. All emotion regarding her was gone, wiped from his mind by forces he should never have tempted. Unfortunately, he *did* remember how much he'd desired Navani, years before meeting the woman who would become his wife.

Stop that, he told himself. Moments ago, he'd been on the brink of deciding to abdicate his seat as highprince. It was no time to let Navani distract him.

'Brightness Danlan Morakotha,' he said to the young woman. 'You are welcome among my clerks. I understand that I've received a communication?'

'Indeed, Brightlord,' the woman said, curtsying. She nodded to the line of five spanreeds sitting on his bookshelf, set upright in pen holders. The spanreeds looked like ordinary writing reeds, except that each had a small infused ruby affixed. The one on the far right pulsed slowly.

Litima was there, and though she had seniority, she nodded for Danlan to fetch the spanreed. The young woman hurried to the bookshelf and moved the still-blinking reed to the small writing desk beside the lectern. She carefully clipped a piece of paper onto the writing board and put the ink vial into its hole, twisting it snugly into place and then pulling the stopper. Lighteyed women were very proficient at working with just their freehand.

She sat down, looking up at him, seeming slightly nervous. Dalinar didn't trust her, of course – she could easily be a spy for one of the other highprinces. Unfortunately, there weren't *any* women in camp he trusted completely, not with Jasnah gone.

'I am ready, Brightlord,' Danlan said. She had a breathy, husky voice. Just the type that attracted Adolin. He hoped she wasn't as vapid as those he usually picked.

'Proceed,' Dalinar said, waving Navani toward one of the room's plush easy chairs. The other clerks sat back down on their bench.

Danlan turned the spanreed's gemstone one notch, indicating that the request had been acknowledged. Then she checked the levels on the sides of the writing board – small vials of oil with bubbles at the center, which allowed her to make the board perfectly flat. Finally, she inked the reed and placed it on the dot at the top left of the page. Holding it upright, she twisted the gemstone setting one more time with her thumb. Then she removed her hand.

The reed remained in place, tip against the paper, hovering as if held in a phantom hand. Then it began to write, mimicking the exact movements Jasnah made miles away, writing with a reed conjoined to this one.

Dalinar stood beside the writing table, armored arms folded. He could see that his proximity made Danlan nervous, but he was too anxious to sit.

Jasnah had elegant handwriting, of course – Jasnah rarely did anything without taking the time to perfect it. Dalinar leaned forward as the familiar – yet indecipherable – lines appeared on the page in stark violet. Faint wisps of reddish smoke floated up from the gemstone.

The pen stopped writing, freezing in place.

'"Uncle,"' Danlan read, '"I presume that you are well."'

'Indeed,' Dalinar replied. 'I am well cared for by those around me.' The words were code indicating that he didn't trust – or at least didn't know – everyone listening. Jasnah would be careful not to send anything too sensitive.

Danlan took the pen and twisted the gemstone, then wrote out the words, sending them across the ocean to Jasnah. Was she still in Tukar?

After Danlan finished writing, she returned it to the dot at the top left – the spot where the pens were both to be placed so Jasnah could continue the conversation – then turned the gemstone back to the previous setting.

'"As I expected, I have found my way to Kharbranth,' Danlan read. '"The secrets I seek are too obscure to be contained even in the Palanaeum, but I find hints. Tantalizing fragments. Is Elhokar well?"'

Hints? Fragments? Of what? She had a penchant for drama, Jasnah did, though she wasn't as flamboyant about it as the king.

'Your brother tried very hard to get himself killed by a chasmfiend a few weeks back,' Dalinar replied. Adolin smiled at that, leaning with his shoulder against the bookcase. 'But evidently the Heralds watch over him. He is well, though your presence here is sorely missed. I'm certain he could use your counsel. He is relying heavily on Brightness Lalai to act as clerk.'

Perhaps that would make Jasnah return. There was little love lost between herself and Sadeas's cousin, who was the king's head scribe in the queen's absence.

Danlan scratched away, writing the words. To the side, Navani cleared her throat.

'Oh,' Dalinar said, 'add this: Your mother is here in the warcamps again.'

A short time later, the pen wrote of its own volition. '"Send my mother my respect. Keep her at arm's length, Uncle. She bites."'

From the side, Navani sniffed, and Dalinar realized he hadn't signaled that Navani was actually listening. He blushed as Danlan continued speaking. '"I cannot speak of my work via spanreed, but I'm growing increasingly concerned. There *is* something here, hidden by the sheer number of accrued pages in the historical record."'

Jasnah was a Veristitalian. She'd explained it to him once; they were an order of scholars who tried to find the truth in the past. They wished to create unbiased, factual accounts of what had happened in order to extrapolate what to do in the future. He wasn't clear on why they thought themselves different from conventional historians.

'Will you be returning?' Dalinar asked.

'"I cannot say,"' Danlan read after the reply came. '"I do not dare stop my research. But a time may soon come when I dare not stay away either."'

What? Dalinar thought.

"'Regardless,'" Danlan continued, "'I have some questions for you. I need you to describe for me again what happened when you met that first Parshendi patrol seven years ago.'"

Dalinar frowned. Despite the Plate's augmentation, his digging had left him feeling tired. But he didn't dare sit on one of the room's chairs while wearing his Plate. He took off one of his gauntlets, though, and ran his hand through his hair. He wasn't fond of this topic, but part of him was glad of the distraction. A reason to hold off on making a decision that would change his life forever.

Danlan looked at him, prepared to dictate his words. Why did Jasnah want this story again? Hadn't she written an account of these very events in her biography of her father?

Well, she would eventually tell him why, and – if her past revelations were any indication – her current project would be of great worth. He wished Elhokar had received a measure of his sister's wisdom.

'These are painful memories, Jasnah. I wish I'd never convinced your father to go on that expedition. If we'd never discovered the Parshendi, then they couldn't have assassinated him. The first meeting happened when we were exploring a forest that wasn't on the maps. This was south of the Shattered Plains, in a valley about two weeks' march from the Drying Sea.'

During Gavilar's youth, only two things had thrilled him – conquest and hunting. When he hadn't been seeking one, it had been the other. Suggesting the hunt had seemed rational at the time. Gavilar had been acting oddly, losing his thirst for battle. Men had started to say that he was weak. Dalinar had wanted to remind his brother of the good times in their youth. Hence the hunt for a legendary chasmfiend.

'Your father wasn't with me when I ran across them,' Dalinar continued, thinking back. Camping on humid, forested hills. Interrogating Natan natives via translators. Looking for scat or broken trees. 'I was leading scouts up a tributary of the Deathbend River while your father scouted downstream. We found the Parshendi camped on the other side. I didn't believe it at first. Parshmen. *Camped*, free and organized. And they carried weapons. Not crude ones, either. Swords, spears with carved hafts . . .'

He trailed off. Gavilar hadn't believed either, when Dalinar told him.

There was no such thing as a free parshman tribe. They were servants, and always had been servants.

"'Did they have Shardblades then?'" Danlan said. Dalinar hadn't realized that Jasnah had made a response.

'No.'

A scratched reply eventually came. "'But they have them now. When did you first see a Parshendi Shardbearer?'"

'After Gavilar's death,' Dalinar said.

He made the connection. They'd always wondered why Gavilar had wanted a treaty with the Parshendi. They wouldn't have needed one just to harvest the greatshells on the Shattered Plains; the Parshendi hadn't lived on the Plains then.

Dalinar felt a chill. Could his brother have *known* that these Parshendi had access to Shardblades? Had he made the treaty hoping to get out of them where they'd found the weapons?

Is it his death? Dalinar wondered. *Is that the secret Jasnah's looking for?* She'd never shown Elhokar's dedication to vengeance, but she thought differently from her brother. Revenge wouldn't drive her. But *questions*. Yes, questions would.

"'One more thing, Uncle,'" Danlan read. "'Then I can go back to digging through this labyrinth of a library. At times, I feel like a cairn robber, sifting through the bones of those long dead. Regardless. The Parshendi, you once mentioned how quickly they seemed to learn our language.'"

'Yes,' Dalinar said. 'In a matter of days, we were speaking and communicating quite well. Remarkable.' Who would have thought that parshmen, of all people, had the wit for such a marvel? Most he'd known didn't do much speaking at all.

"'What were the first things they spoke to you about?'" Danlan said. "'The very *first* questions they asked? Can you remember?'"

Dalinar closed his eyes, remembering days with the Parshendi camped just across the river from them. Gavilar had become fascinated by them. 'They wanted to see our maps.'

'Did they mention the Voidbringers?'

Voidbringers? 'Not that I recall. Why?'

"'I'd rather not say right now. However, I want to show you something. Have your scribe get out a new sheet of paper.'"

Danlan affixed a new page to the writing board. She put the pen to the corner and let go. It rose and began to scratch back and forth in quick, bold strokes. It was a drawing. Dalinar stood up and stepped closer, and Adolin crowded near. Reed and ink wasn't the best medium, and drawing across spans wasn't precise. The pen leaked tiny globs of ink in places it wouldn't have on the other side, and though the inkwell was in the exact same place – allowing Jasnah to re-ink both her reed and Dalinar's at the same time – his reed sometimes ran out before the one on the other side.

Still, the picture was marvelous. *This isn't Jasnah*, Dalinar realized. Whoever was doing the drawing was far, far more talented than his niece.

The picture resolved into a depiction of a tall shadow looming over some buildings. Hints of carapace and claws showed in the thin ink lines, and shadows were made by drawing finer lines close together.

Danlan set it aside, getting out a third sheet of paper. Dalinar held the drawing up, Adolin at his side. The nightmarish beast in the lines and shadows was faintly familiar. Like . . .

'It's a chasmfiend,' Adolin said, pointing. 'It's distorted – far more menacing in the face and larger at the shoulders, and I don't see its second set of foreclaws – but someone was obviously trying to draw one of them.'

'Yes,' Dalinar said, rubbing his chin.

'"This is a depiction from one of the books here,"' Danlan read. '"My new ward is quite skilled at drawing, and so I had her reproduce it for you. Tell me. Does it remind you of anything?"'

A new ward? Dalinar thought. It had been years since Jasnah had taken one. She always said she didn't have the time. 'This picture's of a chasmfiend,' Dalinar said.

Danlan wrote the words. A moment later, the reply came. '"The book describes this as a picture of a Voidbringer."' Danlan frowned, cocking her head. '"The book is a copy of a text originally written in the years before the Recreance. However, the illustrations are copied from another text, even older. In fact, some think that picture was drawn only two or three generations after the Heralds departed."'

Adolin whistled softly. That would make it very old indeed. So far as Dalinar understood, they had few pieces of art or writing dating from the shadowdays, *The Way of Kings* being one of the oldest, and the only complete text. And even it had survived only in translation; they had no copies in the original tongue.

"'Before you jump to conclusions,'" Danlan read, "'I'm not implying that the Voidbringers were the same thing as chasmfiends. I believe that the ancient artist didn't *know* what a Voidbringer looked like, and so she drew the most horrific thing she knew of.'"

But how did the original artist know what a chasmfiend looked like? Dalinar thought. *We only just discovered the Shattered Plains—*

But of course. Though the Unclaimed Hills were now empty, they had once been an inhabited kingdom. Someone in the past had known about chasmfiends, known them well enough to draw one and label it a Voidbringer.

"'I must go now,'" Jasnah said via Danlan. "'Care for my brother in my absence, Uncle.'"

'Jasnah,' Dalinar sent, choosing his words very carefully. 'Things are difficult here. The storm begins to blow unchecked, and the building shakes and moans. You may soon hear news that shocks you. It would be very nice if you could return and lend your aid.'

He waited quietly for the reply, the spanreed scratching. "'I should like to promise a date when I will come.'" Dalinar could almost hear Jasnah's calm, cool voice. "'But I cannot estimate when my research will be completed.'"

'This is very important, Jasnah,' Dalinar said. 'Please reconsider.'

"'Be assured, Uncle, that I *am* coming. Eventually. I just can't say when.'"

Dalinar sighed.

"'Note,'" Jasnah wrote, "'that I am most eager to see a chasmfiend for myself.'"

'A dead one,' Dalinar said. 'I have no intention of letting you repeat your brother's experience of a few weeks ago.'

"'Ah,'" Jasnah sent back, "'dear, overprotective Dalinar. One of these years, you will *have* to admit that your favored niece and nephew have grown up.'"

'I'll treat you as adults so long as you act the part,' Dalinar said. 'Come speedily, and we'll get you a *dead* chasmfiend. Take care.'

They waited to see if a further response came, but the gem stopped blinking, Jasnah's transmission complete. Danlan put away the spanreed and the board, and Dalinar thanked the clerks for their aid. They withdrew; Adolin looked as if he wanted to linger, but Dalinar gestured for him to leave.

Dalinar looked down at the picture of the chasmfiend again, unsatisfied. What had he gained from the conversation? More vague hints? What could be so important about Jasnah's research that she would ignore threats to the kingdom?

He would have to compose a more forthright letter to her once he'd made his announcement, explaining why he had decided to step down. Perhaps that would bring her back.

And, in a moment of shock, Dalinar realized that he had made his decision. Sometime between leaving the trench and now, he'd stopped treating his abdication as an *if* and started thinking of it as a *when*. It was the right decision. He felt sick about it, but certain. A man sometimes needed to do things that were unpleasant.

It was the discussion with Jasnah, he realized. *The talk of her father.* He *was* acting like Gavilar at the end. That had nearly undermined the kingdom. Well, he needed to stop himself before he got that far. Perhaps whatever was happening to him was some kind of disease of the mind, inherited from their parents. It—

'You are quite fond of Jasnah,' Navani said.

Dalinar started, turning away from the picture of the chasmfiend. He'd assumed she'd followed Adolin out. But she still stood there, looking at him.

'Why is it,' Navani said, 'that you encourage her so strongly to return?' He turned to face Navani, and realized that she'd sent her two youthful attendants out with the clerks. They were now alone.

'Navani,' he said. 'This is inappropriate.'

'Bah. We're family, and I have questions.'

Dalinar hesitated, then walked to the center of the room. Navani stood near the door. Blessedly, her attendants had left open the door at the end of the antechamber, and beyond it were two guards in the hall outside. It wasn't an ideal situation, but so long as Dalinar could see the guards and they him, his conversation with Navani was just barely proper.

'Dalinar?' Navani asked. 'Are you going to answer me? Why is it you trust my daughter so much when others almost universally revile her?'

'I consider their disdain for her to be a recommendation,' he said.

'She is a heretic.'

'She refused to join any of the devotaries because she did not believe in their teachings. Rather than compromise for the sake of appearances, she has been honest and has refused to make professions she does not believe. I find that a sign of honor.'

Navani snorted. 'You two are a pair of nails in the same doorframe. Stern, hard, and storming annoying to pull free.'

'You should go now,' Dalinar said, nodding toward the hallway. He suddenly felt very exhausted. 'People will talk.'

'Let them. We need to plan, Dalinar. You are the most important high-prince in—'

'Navani,' he cut in. 'I'm going to abdicate in favor of Adolin.'

She blinked in surprise.

'I'm stepping down as soon as I can make the necessary arrangements. It will be a few days at most.' Speaking the words felt odd, as if saying them made his decision real.

Navani looked pained. 'Oh, Dalinar,' she whispered. 'This is a terrible mistake.'

'It is mine to make. And I must repeat my request. I have many things to think about, Navani, and I can't deal with you right now.' He pointed at the doorway.

Navani rolled her eyes, but left as requested. She shut the door behind her.

That's it, Dalinar thought, letting out a long exhalation. *I've made the decision.*

Too weary to remove his Plate unassisted, he sank down onto the floor, resting his head back against the wall. He would tell Adolin of his decision in the morning, then announce it at a feast within the week. From there, he would return to Alethkar and his lands.

It was over.

THE END OF

Part Two

İNTERLUDES

⬥⬥

RYSN • AXIES • SZETH

RYSN

Rysn hesitantly stepped down from the caravan's lead wagon. Her feet fell on soft, uneven ground that sank down a little beneath her. That made her shiver, particularly since the too-thick grass didn't move away as it should. Rysn tapped her foot a few times. The grass didn't so much as quiver.

'It's not going to move,' Vstim said. 'Grass here doesn't behave the way it does elsewhere. Surely you've heard that.' The older man sat beneath the bright yellow canopy of the lead wagon. He rested one arm on the side rail, holding a set of ledgers with the other hand. One of his long white eyebrows was tucked behind his ear and he let the other trail down beside his face. He preferred stiffly starched robes – blue and red – and a flat-topped conical hat. It was classic Thaylen merchant's clothing: several decades out of date, yet still distinguished.

'I've heard of the grass,' Rysn said to him. 'But it's just so *odd*.' She stepped again, walking in a circle around the lead wagon. Yes, she'd heard of the grass here in Shinovar, but she'd assumed that it would just be lethargic. That people said it didn't disappear because it moved too slowly.

But no, that wasn't it. It didn't move *at all*. How did it survive? Shouldn't it have all been eaten away by animals? She shook her head in wonder, looking up across the plain. The grass completely *covered* it. The blades were all crowded together, and you couldn't see the ground. What a mess it was.

'The ground is springy,' she said, rounding back to her original side of the wagon. 'Not just because of the grass.'

'Hmm,' Vstim said, still working on his ledgers. 'Yes. It's called soil.'

'It makes me feel like I'm going to sink down to my knees. How can the Shin stand living here?'

'They're an interesting people. Shouldn't you be setting up the device?'

Rysn sighed, but walked to the rear of the wagon. The other wagons in the caravan – six in all – were pulling up and forming a loose circle. She took down the tailgate of the lead wagon and heaved, pulling out a wooden tripod nearly as tall as she was. She carried it over one shoulder, marching to the center of the grassy circle.

She was more fashionable than her babsk; she wore the most modern of clothing for a young woman her age: a deep blue patterned silk vest over a light green long-sleeved shirt with stiff cuffs. Her ankle-length skirt – also green – was stiff and businesslike, utilitarian in cut but embroidered for fashion.

She wore a green glove on her left hand. Covering the safehand was a silly tradition, just a result of Vorin cultural dominance. But it was best to keep up appearances. Many of the more traditional Thaylen people – including, unfortunately, her babsk – still found it scandalous for a woman to go about with her safehand uncovered.

She set up the tripod. It had been five months since Vstim became her babsk and she his apprentice. He'd been good to her. Not all babsk were; by tradition, he was more than just her master. He was her father, legally, until he pronounced her ready to become a merchant on her own.

She did wish he wouldn't spend so much time traveling to such *odd* places. He was known as a great merchant, and she'd assumed that great merchants would be the ones visiting exotic cities and ports. Not ones who traveled to empty meadows in backward countries.

Tripod set up, she returned to the wagon to fetch the fabrial. The wagon back formed an enclosure with thick sides and top to offer protection against highstorms – even the weaker ones in the West could be dangerous, at least until one got through the passes and into Shinovar.

She hurried back to the tripod with the fabrial's box. She slid off the wooden top and removed the large heliodor inside. The pale yellow gemstone, at least two inches in diameter, was fixed inside a metal framework. It glowed gently, not as bright as one might expect of such a sizable gem.

She set it in the tripod, then spun a few of the dials underneath, setting the fabrial to the people in the caravan. Then she pulled a stool from the wagon and sat down to watch. She'd been astonished at what Vstim had paid for the device – one of the new, recently invented types that would give warning if people approached. Was it really so important?

She sat back, looking up at the gemstone, watching to see if it grew brighter. The odd grass of the Shin lands waved in the wind, stubbornly refusing to withdraw, even at the strongest of gusts. In the distance rose the white peaks of the Misted Mountains, sheltering Shinovar. Those mountains caused the highstorms to break and fade, making Shinovar one of the only places in all of Roshar where highstorms did not reign.

The plain around her was dotted with strange, straight-trunked trees with stiff, skeletal branches full of leaves that didn't withdraw in the wind. The entire landscape had an eerie feel to it, as if it were dead. Nothing moved. With a start, Rysn realized she couldn't see any spren. Not a one. No windspren, no lifespren, nothing.

It was as if the entire land were slow of wit. Like a man who was born without all his brains, one who didn't know when to protect himself, but instead just stared at the wall drooling. She dug into the ground with a finger, then brought it up to inspect the 'soil,' as Vstim had called it. It was dirty stuff. Why, a strong gust could uproot this entire field of grass and blow it away. Good thing the highstorms couldn't reach these lands.

Near the wagons, the servants and guards unloaded crates and set up camp. Suddenly, the heliodor began to pulse with a brighter yellow light. 'Master!' she called, standing. 'Someone's nearby.'

Vstim – who had been going through crates – looked up sharply. He waved to Kylrm, head of the guards, and his six men got out their bows.

'There,' one said, pointing.

In the distance, a group of horsemen was approaching. They didn't ride very quickly, and they led several large animals – like thick, squat horses – pulling wagons. The gemstone in the fabrial pulsed more brightly as the newcomers got closer.

'Yes,' Vstim said, looking at the fabrial. 'That is going to be *very* handy. Good range on it.'

'But we knew they were coming,' Rysn said, rising from her stool and walking over to him.

'This time,' he said. 'But if it warns us of bandits in the dark, it'll repay its cost a dozen times over. Kylrm, lower your bows. You know how they feel about those things.'

The guards did as they were told, and the group of Thaylens waited. Rysn found herself tucking her eyebrows back nervously, though she didn't know why she bothered. The newcomers were just Shin. Of course, Vstim insisted that she shouldn't think of them as savages. He seemed to have great respect for them.

As they approached, she was surprised by the variety in their appearance. Other Shin she'd seen had worn basic brown robes or other worker's clothing. At the front of this group, however, was a man in what must be Shin finery: a bright, multicolored cloak that completely enveloped him, tied closed at the front. It trailed down on either side of his horse, drooping almost to the ground. Only his head was exposed.

Four men rode on horses around him, and they wore more subdued clothing. Still bright, just not *as* bright. They wore shirts, trousers, and colorful capes.

At least three dozen other men walked alongside them, wearing brown tunics. More drove the three large wagons.

'Wow,' Rysn said. 'He brought a lot of servants.'

'Servants?' Vstim said.

'The fellows in brown.'

Her babsk smiled. 'Those are his guards, child.'

'What? They look so dull.'

'Shin are a curious folk,' he said. 'Here, warriors are the lowliest of men – kind of like slaves. Men trade and sell them between houses by way of little stones that signify ownership, and any man who picks up a weapon must join them and be treated the same. The fellow in the fancy robe? *He's* a farmer.'

'A landowner, you mean?'

'No. As far as I can tell, he goes out every day – well, the days when he's not overseeing a negotiation like this – and works the fields. They treat all farmers like that, lavish them with attention and respect.'

Rysn gaped. 'But most villages are *filled* with farmers!'

'Indeed,' Vstim said. 'Holy places, here. Foreigners aren't allowed near fields or farming villages.'

How strange, she thought. *Perhaps living in this place has affected their minds.*

Kylrm and his guards didn't look terribly pleased at being so heavily outnumbered, but Vstim didn't seem bothered. Once the Shin grew close, he walked out from his wagons without a hint of trepidation. Rysn hurried after him, her skirt brushing the grass below.

Bother, she thought. Another problem with its not retracting. If she had to buy a new hem because of this dull grass, it was going to make her very cross.

Vstim met up with the Shin, then bowed in a distinctive way, hands toward the ground. '*Tan balo ken tala*,' he said. She didn't know what it meant.

The man in the cloak – the *farmer* – nodded respectfully, and one of the other riders dismounted and walked forward. 'Winds of Fortune guide you, my friend.' He spoke Thaylen very well. 'He who adds is happy for your safe arrival.'

'Thank you, Thresh-son-Esan,' Vstim said. 'And my thanks to he who adds.'

'What have you brought for us from your strange lands, friend?' Thresh said. 'More metal, I hope?'

Vstim waved and some of the guards brought over a heavy crate. They set it down and pried off the top, revealing its peculiar contents. Pieces of scrap metal, mostly shaped like bits of shell, though some were formed like pieces of wood. It looked to Rysn like garbage that had – for some inexpli cable reason – been Soulcast into metal.

'Ah,' Thresh said, squatting down to inspect the box. 'Wonderful!'

'Not a bit of it was mined,' Vstim said. 'No rocks were broken or smelted to get this metal, Thresh. It was Soulcast from shells, bark, or branches. I have a document sealed by five separate Thaylen notaries attesting to it.'

'You needn't have done such a thing as this,' Thresh said. 'You have once earned our trust in this matter long ago.'

'I'd rather be proper about it,' Vstim said. 'A merchant who is careless with contracts is one who finds himself with enemies instead of friends.'

Thresh stood up, clapping three times. The men in brown with the downcast eyes lowered the back of a wagon, revealing crates.

'The others who visit us,' Thresh noted, walking to the wagon. 'All they seem to care about are horses. Everyone wishes to buy horses. But never you, my friend. Why is that?'

'Too hard to care for,' Vstim said, walking with Thresh. 'And there's too often a poor return on the investment, valuable as they are.'

'But not with these?' Thresh said, picking up one of the light crates. There was something alive inside.

'Not at all,' Vstim said. 'Chickens fetch a good price, and they're easy to care for, assuming you have feed.'

'We brought you plenty,' Thresh said. 'I cannot believe you buy these from us. They are not worth nearly so much as you outsiders think. And you give us metal for them! Metal that bears no stain of broken rock. A miracle.'

Vstim shrugged. 'Those scraps are practically worthless where I come from. They're made by ardents practicing with Soulcasters. They can't make food, because if you get it wrong, it's poisonous. So they turn garbage into metal and throw it away.'

'But it can be forged!'

'Why forge the metal,' Vstim said, 'when you can carve an object from wood in the precise shape you want, *then* Soulcast it?'

Thresh just shook his head, bemused. Rysn watched with her own share of confusion. This was the *craziest* trade exchange she'd ever seen. Normally, Vstim argued and haggled like a crushkiller. But here, he freely revealed that his wares were worthless!

In fact, as conversation proceeded, the two both took pains to explain how worthless their goods were. Eventually, they came to an agreement – though Rysn couldn't grasp how – and shook hands on the deal. Some of Thresh's soldiers began to unload their boxes of chickens, cloth, and exotic dried meats. Others began carting away boxes of scrap metal.

'You couldn't trade me a soldier, could you?' Vstim asked as they waited.

'They cannot be sold to an outsider, I am afraid.'

'But there was that one you traded me . . .'

'It's been nearly seven years!' Thresh said with a laugh. 'And still you ask!'

'You don't know what I got for him,' Vstim said. 'And you gave him to me for practically nothing!'

'He was Truthless,' Thresh said, shrugging. 'He wasn't worth anything at all. You *forced* me to take something in trade, though to confess, I had to throw your payment into a river. I could not take money for a Truthless.'

'Well, I suppose I can't take offense at that,' Vstim said, rubbing his chin. 'But if you ever have another, let me know. Best servant I ever had. I still regret that I traded him.'

'I will remember, friend,' Thresh said. 'But I do not think it likely we will have another like him.' He seemed to grow distracted. 'Indeed, I should hope that we never do. . . .'

Once the goods were exchanged, they shook hands again, then Vstim bowed to the farmer. Rysn tried to mimic what he did, and earned a smile from Thresh and several of his companions, who chattered in their whispering Shin language.

Such a long, boring ride for such a short exchange. But Vstim was right; those chickens would be worth good spheres in the East.

'What did you learn?' Vstim said to her as they walked back toward the lead wagon.

'That Shin are odd.'

'No,' Vstim said, though he wasn't stern. He never seemed to be stern. 'They are simply different, child. Odd people are those who act erratically. Thresh and his kind, they are anything but erratic. They may be a little *too* stable. The world is changing outside, but the Shin seem determined to remain the same. I've tried to offer them fabrials, but they find them worthless. Or unholy. Or too holy to use.'

'Those are rather different things, master.'

'Yes,' he said. 'But with the Shin, it's often hard to distinguish among them. Regardless, what did you *really* learn?'

'That they treat being humble like the Herdazians treat boasting,' she said. 'You both went out of your way to show how worthless your wares were. I found it strange, but I think it might just be how they haggle.'

He smiled widely. 'And already you are wiser than half the men I've brought here. Listen. Here is your lesson. *Never* try to cheat the Shin. Be forthright, tell them the truth, and – if anything – undervalue your goods. They will love you for it. And they'll pay you for it too.'

She nodded. They reached the wagon, and he got out a strange little pot. 'Here,' he said. 'Use a knife and go cut out some of that grass. Be sure to cut down far and get plenty of the soil. The plants can't live without it.'

'Why am I doing this?' she asked, wrinkling her nose and taking the pot.

'Because,' he said. 'You're going to learn to care for that plant. I want you to keep it with you until you stop thinking of it as odd.'

'But why?'

'Because it will make you a better merchant,' he said.

She frowned. Must he be so strange so much of the time? Perhaps that was why he was one of the only Thaylens who could get a good deal out of the Shin. He was as odd as they were.

She walked off to do as she was told. No use complaining. She did get out a rugged pair of gloves first, though, and roll up her sleeves. She was *not* going to ruin a good dress for a pot of drooling, wall-staring, imbecile grass. And that was that.

AXIES
THE COLLECTOR

Axies the Collector groaned, lying on his back, skull pounding with a headache. He opened his eyes and looked down the length of his body. He was naked.

Blight it all, he thought.

Well, best to check and see if he was hurt too badly. His toes pointed at the sky. The nails were a deep blue color, not uncommon for an Aimian man like himself. He tried to wiggle them and, pleasingly, they actually moved.

'Well, that's something,' he said, dropping his head back to the ground. It made a squishing sound as it touched something soft, likely a bit of rotting garbage.

Yes, that was what it was. He could smell it now, pungent and rank. He focused on his nose, sculpting his body so that he could no longer smell. *Ah*, he thought. *Much better*.

Now if he could only banish the pounding in his head. Really, did the sun *have* to be so garish overhead? He closed his eyes.

'You're still in my alley,' a gruff voice said from behind him. That voice had awakened him in the first place.

'I shall vacate it presently,' Axies promised.

'You owe me rent. One night's sleep.'

'In an alleyway?'

'Finest alleyway in Kasitor.'

'Ah. Is that where I am, then? Excellent.'

A few heartbeats of mental focus finally banished the headache. He opened his eyes, and this time found the sunlight quite pleasant. Brick walls rose toward the sky on either side of him, overgrown with a crusty red lichen. Small heaps of rotting tubers were scattered around him.

No. Not scattered. They looked to be arranged carefully. Odd, that. They were likely the source of the scents he'd noticed earlier. Best to leave his sense of smell inhibited.

He sat up, stretching, checking his muscles. All seemed to be in working order, though he had quite a few bruises. He'd deal with those in a bit. 'Now,' he said, turning, 'you wouldn't happen to have a spare pair of pants, would you?'

The owner of the voice turned out to be a scraggly-bearded man sitting on a box at the end of the alleyway. Axies didn't recognize him, nor did he recognize the location. That wasn't surprising, considering that he'd been beaten, robbed, and left for dead. Again.

The things I do in the name of scholarship, he thought with a sigh.

His memory was returning. Kasitor was a large Iriali city, second in size only to Rall Elorim. He'd come here by design. He'd also gotten himself drunk by design. Perhaps he should have picked his drinking companions more carefully.

'I'm going to guess that you don't have a spare pair of pants,' Axies said, standing and inspecting the tattoos on his arm. 'And if you did, I'd suggest that you wear them yourself. Is that a lavis sack you have on?'

'You owe me rent,' the man grumbled. 'And payment for destroying the temple of the northern god.'

'Odd,' Axies said, looking over his shoulder toward the alleyway's opening. There was a busy street beyond. The good people of Kasitor would likely not take well to his nudity. 'I don't *recall* destroying any temples. Normally I'm quite cognizant of that sort of thing.'

'You took out half of Hapron Street,' the beggar said. 'Number of homes as well. I'll let that slide.'

'Mighty kind of you.'

'They've been wicked lately.'

Axies frowned, looking back at the beggar. He followed the man's gaze, looking down at the ground. The heaps of rotting vegetables had been placed in a very particular arrangement. Like a city.

'Ah,' Axies said, moving his foot, which had been planted on a small square of vegetable.

'That was a bakery,' the beggar said.

'Terribly sorry.'

'The family was away.'

'That's a relief.'

'They were worshipping at the temple.'

'The one I ...'

'Smashed with your head? Yes.'

'I'm certain you'll be kind to their souls.'

The beggar narrowed his eyes at him. 'I'm still trying to decide how you fit into things. Are you a Voidbringer or a Herald?'

'Voidbringer, I'm afraid,' Axies said. 'I mean, I *did* destroy a temple.' The beggar's eyes grew more suspicious.

'Only the sacred cloth can banish me,' Axies continued. 'And since you don't ... I say, what is that you're holding?'

The beggar looked down at his hand, which was touching one of the ratty blankets draped over one of his equally ratty boxes. He perched atop them, like ... well, like a god looking down over his people.

Poor fool, Axies thought. It was really time to be moving on. Wouldn't want to bring any bad luck down upon the addled fellow.

The beggar held up the blanket. Axies shied back, raising his hands. That made the beggar smile a grin that could have used a few more teeth. He hopped off his box, holding the blanket up wardingly. Axies shied away.

The beggar cackled and threw the blanket at him. Axies snatched it from the air and shook a fist at the beggar. Then he retreated from the alleyway while wrapping the blanket around his waist.

'And lo,' the beggar said from behind, 'the foul beast was banished!'

'And lo,' Axies said, fixing the blanket in place, 'the foul beast avoided imprisonment for public indecency.' Iriali were very particular about their chastity laws. They were very particular about a lot of things. Of course, that could be said for most peoples – the only difference was the things they were particular about.

Axies the Collector drew his share of stares. Not because of his unconventional clothing – Iri was on the northwestern rim of Roshar, and its weather therefore tended to be much warmer than that of places like

Alethkar or even Azir. A fair number of the golden-haired Iriali men went about wearing only waist wraps, their skin painted various colors and patterns. Even Axies's tattoos weren't that noteworthy here.

Perhaps he drew stares because of his blue nails and crystalline deep blue eyes. Aimians – even Siah Aimians – were rare. Or perhaps it was because he cast a shadow the wrong way. Toward light, instead of away from it. It was a small thing, and the shadows weren't long, with the sun so high. But those who noticed muttered or jumped out of the way. Likely they'd heard of his kind. It hadn't been *that* long since the scouring of his homeland. Just long ago enough for stories and legends to have crept into the general knowledge of most peoples.

Perhaps someone important would take exception to him and have him brought before a local magistrate. Wouldn't be the first time. He'd learned long ago not to worry. When the Curse of Kind followed you, you learned to take what happened as it happened.

He began to whistle softly to himself, inspecting his tattoos and ignoring those observant enough to gawk. *I remember writing something somewhere . . .* he thought, looking over his wrist, then twisting his arm over and trying to see if there were any new tattoos on the back. Like all Aimians, he could change the color and markings of his skin at will. That was convenient, as when you were very regularly robbed of everything you owned, it was blighted difficult to keep a proper notebook. And so, he kept his notes on his skin, at least until he could return to a safe location and transcribe them.

Hopefully, he hadn't gotten so drunk that he'd written his observations someplace inconvenient. He'd done that once, and reading the mess had required two mirrors and a very confused bathing attendant.

Ah, he thought, discovering a new entry near the inside of his left elbow. He read it awkwardly, shuffling down the incline.

Test successful. Have noted spren who appear only when one is severely intoxicated. Appear as small brown bubbles clinging to objects nearby. Further testing may be needed to prove they were more than a drunken hallucination.

'Very nice,' he said out loud. 'Very nice indeed. I wonder what I should call them.' The stories he'd heard called them sudspren, but that seemed silly. Intoxicationspren? No, too unwieldy. Alespren? He felt a surge of excitement. He'd been hunting this particular type of spren for years. If they proved real, it would be quite a victory.

Why did they appear only in Iri? And why so infrequently? He'd gotten himself stupidly drunk a dozen times, and had only found them once. If, indeed, he had ever really found them.

Spren, however, could be very elusive. Sometimes, even the most common types – flamespren, for instance – would refuse to appear. That made it particularly frustrating for a man who had made it his life's work to observe, catalogue, and study every single type of spren in Roshar.

He continued whistling as he made his way through the town to the dockside. Around him flowed large numbers of the golden-haired Iriali. The hair bred true, like black Alethi hair – the purer your blood was, the more locks of gold you had. And it wasn't merely blond, it was truly gold, lustrous in the sun.

He had a fondness for the Iriali. They weren't *nearly* as prudish as the Vorin peoples to the east, and were rarely inclined to bickering or fighting. That made it easier to hunt spren. Of course, there were also spren you could find only during war.

A group of people had gathered at the docks. *Ah*, he thought, *excellent. I'm not too late.* Most were crowding onto a purpose-built viewing platform. Axies found himself a place to stand, adjusted his holy blanket, and leaned back against the railing to wait.

It wasn't long. At precisely seven forty-six in the morning – the locals could use it to set their timepieces – an enormous, sea-blue spren surged from the waters of the bay. It was translucent, and though it appeared to throw out waves as it rose, that was illusory. The actual surface of the bay wasn't disturbed.

It takes the shape of a large jet of water, Axies thought, creating a tattoo along an open portion of his leg, scribing the words. *The center is of the deepest blue, like the ocean depths, though the outer edges are a lighter shade. Judging by the masts of the nearby ships, I'd say that the spren has grown to a height of at least a hundred feet. One of the largest I've ever seen.*

The column sprouted four long arms that came down around the bay, forming fingers and thumbs. They landed on golden pedestals that had been placed there by the people of the city. The spren came at the same time every day, without fail.

They called it by name, Cusicesh, the Protector. Some worshipped it as a god. Most simply accepted it as part of the city. It was unique. One of the few types of spren he knew of that seemed to have only a single member.

But what kind *of spren is it?* Axies wrote, fascinated. *It has formed a face, looking eastward. Directly toward the Origin. That face is shifting, bewilderingly quick. Different human faces appear on the end of its stumplike neck, one after another in blurred succession.*

The display lasted a full ten minutes. Did any of the faces repeat? They changed so quickly, he couldn't tell. Some seemed male, others female. Once the display was finished, Cusicesh retreated down into the bay, sending up phantom waves again.

Axies felt drained, as if something had been leeched from him. That was reported to be a common reaction. Was he imagining it because it was expected? Or was it real?

As he considered, a street urchin scrambled past and grabbed his wrap, yanking it free and laughing to himself. He tossed it to some friends and they scrambled away.

Axies shook his head. 'What a bother,' he said as people around him began to gasp and mutter. 'There are guards nearby, I assume? Ah yes. Four of them. Wonderful.' The four were already stalking toward him, golden hair falling around their shoulders, expressions stern.

'Well,' he said to himself, making a final notation as one of the guards grabbed him on the shoulder. 'It appears I'll have another chance to search for captivityspren.' Odd, how those had eluded him all these years, despite his numerous incarcerations. He was beginning to consider them mythological.

The guards towed him off toward the city dungeons, but he didn't mind. Two new spren in as many days! At this rate, it might only take a few more centuries to complete his research.

Grand indeed. He resumed whistling to himself.

Szeth-son-son-Vallano, Truthless of Shinovar, crouched on a high stone ledge at the side of the gambling den. The ledge was meant for holding a lantern; both his legs and the shelf were hidden by his long, enveloping cloak, making him seem to be hanging from the wall.

There were few lights nearby. Makkek liked Szeth to remain cloaked in shadow. He wore a formfitting black costume beneath the cloak, the lower part of his face covered by a cloth mask; both were of Makkek's design. The cloak was too big and the clothing too tight. It was a terrible outfit for an assassin, but Makkek demanded drama, and Szeth did as his master commanded. Always.

Perhaps there was something useful to the drama. With only his eyes and bald head showing, he unnerved the people who passed by. Shin eyes, too round, slightly too large. The people here thought them similar to the eyes of a child. Why did that disturb them so?

Nearby, a group of men in brown cloaks sat chatting and rubbing their thumbs and forefingers together. Wisps of smoke rose between their fingers, accompanied by a faint crackling sound. Rubbing firemoss was said to make a man's mind more receptive to thoughts and ideas. The one time Szeth had tried it, it had given him a headache and two blistered fingers. But once you grew the calluses, it could apparently be euphoric.

The circular den had a bar at the center, serving a wide variety of drinks at a wider variety of prices. The barmaids were dressed in violet robes that had plunging necklines and were open at the sides. Their safehands were exposed, something that the Bavlanders – who were Vorin by descent – seemed to find extremely provocative. So odd. It was just a hand.

Around the perimeter of the den, various games were in progress. None of them were overt games of chance – no dice throws, no bets on card flips. There were games of breakneck, shallowcrab fights, and – oddly – guessing games. That was another oddity about Vorin peoples; they avoided overtly guessing the future. A game like breakneck would have throws and tosses, but they wouldn't bet on the outcome. Instead, they'd bet on the hand they held after the throws and the draws.

It seemed a meaningless distinction to Szeth, but it was deeply steeped in the culture. Even here, in one of the vilest pits in the city – where women walked with their hands exposed and men spoke openly of crimes – nobody risked offending the Heralds by seeking to know the future. Even predicting the highstorms made many uncomfortable. And yet they thought *nothing* of walking on stone or using Stormlight for everyday illumination. They ignored the spirits of things that lived around them, and they ate whatever they wanted on any day they wanted.

Strange. So strange. And yet this was his life. Recently, Szeth had begun to question some of the prohibitions he had once followed so strictly. How could these Easterners *not* walk on stone? There was no soil in their lands. How could they get about without treading on stone?

Dangerous thoughts. His way of life was all that remained to him. If he questioned Stone Shamanism, would he then question his nature as Truthless? Dangerous, dangerous. Though his murders and sins would damn him, at least his soul would be given to the stones upon his death. He would continue to exist. Punished, in agony, but not exiled to nothingness.

Better to exist in agony than to vanish entirely.

Makkek himself strode the floor of the gambling den, a woman on each arm. His scrawny leanness was gone, his face having slowly gained a juicy plumpness, like a fruit ripening after the drowning's waters. Also gone were his ragged footpad's garments, replaced with luxurious silks.

Makkek's companions – the ones with him when they'd killed Took – were all dead, murdered by Szeth at Makkek's orders. All to hide the secret of the Oathstone. Why were these Easterners always so ashamed of the way they controlled Szeth? Was it because they feared another would steal the Oathstone from them? Were they terrified that the weapon they employed so callously would be turned against them?

Perhaps he feared that if it were known how easily Szeth was controlled, it would spoil their reputation. Szeth had overheard more than one conversation centered around the mystery of Makkek's terribly effective bodyguard. If a creature like Szeth served Makkek, then the master himself must be even more dangerous.

Makkek passed the place where Szeth lurked, one of the women on his arms laughing with tinkling sound. Makkek glanced at Szeth, then gestured curtly. Szeth bowed his masked head in acknowledgment. He slid from his place, dropping to the ground, oversized cloak fluttering.

Games stilled. Men both drunken and sober turned to watch Szeth, and as he passed the three men with the firemoss, their fingers went limp. Most in the room knew what Szeth was about this night. A man had moved into Bornwater and opened his own gambling den to challenge Makkek. Likely this newcomer didn't believe the reputation of Makkek's phantom assassin. Well, he had reason to be skeptical. Szeth's reputation *was* inaccurate.

He was far, *far* more dangerous than it suggested.

He ducked out of the gambling den, passing up the steps through the darkened storefront and then out into the yard. He tossed the cloak and face mask into a wagon as he passed. The cloak would only make noise, and why cover his face? He was the only Shin in town. If someone saw his eyes, they'd know who he was. He retained the tight black clothing; changing would take too much time.

Bornwater was the largest town in the area; it hadn't taken Makkek long to outgrow Staplind. Now he was talking of moving up to Kneespike, the city where the local landlord had his mansion. If that happened, Szeth would spend months wading in blood as he systematically tracked down and killed each and every thief, cutthroat, and gambling master who refused Makkek's rule.

That was months off. For now, there was Bornwater's interloper, a man named Gavashaw. Szeth prowled through the streets, eschewing Stormlight or Shardblade, counting on his natural grace and care to keep him unseen. He enjoyed his brief freedom. These moments – when he wasn't trapped in one of Makkek's smoke-filled dens – were too few lately.

Slipping between buildings – moving swiftly in the darkness, with the wet, cold air on his skin – he could almost think himself back in Shinovar.

The buildings around him were not of blasphemous stone, but earthen ones, built with clay and soil. Those low sounds were not muffled cheers from within another of Makkek's gambling dens, but the thunder and whinnies of wild horses on the plains.

But no. In Shinovar he'd never smelled refuse like that – pungency compounded by weeks spent marinating. He was not home. There was no place for him in the Valley of Truth.

Szeth entered one of the richer sections of town, where buildings had more space between homes. Bornwater was in a lait, protected by a towering cliffside to the east. Gavashaw had arrogantly made his home in a large mansion on the eastern side of town. It belonged to the provincial landlord; Gavashaw had his favor. The landlord had heard of Makkek and his quick rise to prominence in the underground, and supporting a rival was a good way to create an early check on Makkek's power.

The citylord's local mansion was three stories tall, with a stone wall surrounding the compact, neatly gardened grounds. Szeth approached in a low crouch. Here on the outskirts of town, the ground was spotted with bulbous rockbuds. As he passed, the plants rustled, pulling back their vines and lethargically closing their shells.

He reached the wall and pressed himself against it. It was the time between the first two moons, the darkest period of night. The hateful hour, his people called it, for it was one of the only times when the gods did not watch men. Soldiers walked the wall above, feet scraping the stones. Gavashaw probably thought himself safe in this building, which was secure enough for a powerful lighteyes.

Szeth breathed in, infusing himself with Stormlight from the spheres in his pouch. He began to glow, luminescent vapors rising from his skin. In the darkness, it was quite noticeable. These powers had never been intended for assassination; Surgebinders had fought during the light of day, battling the night but not embracing it.

That was not Szeth's place. He would simply have to take extra care not to be seen.

Ten heartbeats after the passing of the guards, Szeth Lashed himself to the wall. That direction became down for him, and he was able to run up the side of the stone fortification. As he reached the top, he leaped forward, then briefly Lashed himself backward. He spun over the top of the wall in a tucked flip, then Lashed himself back to the wall again. He came down with feet planted on the stones, facing the ground. He ran and Lashed himself downward again, dropping the last few feet.

The grounds were laced with shalebark mounds, cultivated to form small terraces. Szeth ducked low, picking his way through the mazelike garden. There were guards at the building's doorways, watching by the light of spheres. How easy it would be to dash up, consume the Stormlight, and plunge the men into darkness before cutting them down.

But Makkek had not expressly commanded him to be so destructive. Gavashaw was to be assassinated, but the method was up to Szeth. He picked one that would not require killing the guards. That was what he always did, when given the chance. It was the only way to preserve what little humanity he had left.

He reached the western wall of the mansion and Lashed himself to it, then ran up it onto the roof. It was long and flat, sloped gently eastward – an unnecessary feature in a lait, but Easterners saw the world by the light of the highstorms. Szeth quickly crossed to the rear of the building, to where a small rock dome covered a lower portion of the mansion. He dropped down onto the dome, Stormlight streaming from his body. Translucent, luminescent, pristine. Like the ghost of a fire burning from him, consuming his soul.

He summoned his Shardblade in the stillness and dark, then used it to slice a hole in the dome, angling his Blade so that the chunk of rock did not fall down inside. He reached down with his free hand and infused the stone circle with Light, Lashing it toward the northwest section of the sky. Lashing something to a distant point like that was possible, but imprecise. It was like trying to shoot an arrow a great distance.

He stepped back as the stone circle lurched free and fell up into the air, streaming Stormlight as it soared toward the splattered paint drops of stars above. Szeth leapt into the hole, then immediately Lashed himself to the ceiling. He twisted in the air, landing with his feet planted on the underside of the dome beside the lip of the hole he'd cut. From his perspective, he was now standing at the bottom of a gigantic stone bowl, the hole cut in the very bottom, looking out on the stars beneath.

He walked up the side of the bowl, Lashing himself to the right. In seconds he was on the floor, reoriented so that the dome rose above him. Distantly, he heard a faint crashing: The chunk of stone, Stormlight exhausted, had fallen back to the ground. He had aimed it out of the town. Hopefully, it had not caused any accidental deaths.

The guards would now be distracted, searching for the source of the distant crash. Szeth breathed in deeply, draining his second pouch of gemstones. The light streaming from him became brighter, letting him see the room around him.

As he'd suspected, it was empty. This was a rarely used feasting hall, with cold firepits, tables, and benches. The air was still, silent, and musty. Like that of a tomb. Szeth hurried to the door, slid his Shardblade between it and the frame, and sliced through the deadbolt. He eased the door open. The Stormlight rising from his body illuminated the dark hallway outside.

Early during his time with Makkek, Szeth had been careful not to use the Shardblade. As his tasks had grown more difficult, however, he'd been forced to resort to it to avoid unnecessary killing. Now the rumors about him were populated with tales of holes cut through stone and dead men with burned eyes.

Makkek had begun to believe those rumors. He hadn't yet demanded that Szeth relinquish the Blade – if he did so, he would discover the second of Szeth's two forbidden actions. He was required to carry the Blade until his death, after which Shin Stone Shamans would recover it from whomever had killed him.

He moved through the hallways. He wasn't worried about Makkek taking the Blade, but he *was* worried about how bold the thief lord was growing. The more successful Szeth was, the more audacious Makkek became. How long before he stopped using Szeth to kill minor rivals, instead sending him to kill Shardbearers or powerful lighteyes? How long before someone made the connection? A Shin assassin with a Shardblade, capable of mysterious feats and extreme stealth? Could this be the now-infamous Assassin in White? Makkek could draw the Alethi king and highprinces away from their war on the Shattered Plains and bring them crashing down upon Jah Keved. Thousands would die. Blood would fall like the rain of a highstorm – thick, pervasive, destructive.

He continued down the hallway in a swift low run, Shardblade carried in a reverse grip, extending out behind him. Tonight, at least, he assassinated a man who deserved his fate. Were the hallways too quiet? Szeth hadn't seen a soul since leaving the rooftop. Could Gavashaw have been foolish enough to place all of his guards outside, leaving his bedchamber undefended?

Ahead, the doors into the master's rooms lay unwatched and dark at the end of a short hallway. Suspicious.

Szeth crept up to the doors, listening. Nothing. He hesitated, glancing to the side. A grand stairway led up to the second floor. He hustled over and used his Blade to shear free a wooden knob from the newel post. It was about the size of a small melon. A few hacks with the Blade cut a cloak-size section of drapery free from a window. Szeth hurried back to the doors and infused the wooden sphere with Stormlight, giving it a Basic Lashing that pointed it westward, directly ahead of him.

He cut through the latch between the doors and eased one open. The room beyond was dark. Was Gavashaw gone for the evening? Where would he go? This city was not safe for him yet.

Szeth placed the wooden ball in the middle of the drape, then held it up and dropped it. It fell forward, toward the far wall. Wrapped in the fabric, the ball looked vaguely like a person in a cloak running through the room in a crouch.

No concealed guards struck at it. The decoy bounced off a latched window, then came to rest hanging against the wall. It continued to leak Stormlight.

That light illuminated a small table with an object atop it. Szeth squinted, trying to make out what it was. He edged forward, slinking into the room, closer and closer to the table.

Yes. The object on the table was a head. One with Gavashaw's features. Shadows thrown by Stormlight gave the grisly face an even more haunted cast. Someone had beaten Szeth to the assassination.

'Szeth-son-Neturo,' a voice said.

Szeth turned, spinning his Shardblade around and falling into a defensive stance. A figure stood on the far side of the room, shrouded in the darkness. 'Who are you?' Szeth demanded, his Stormlight aura growing brighter once he stopped holding his breath.

'Are you satisfied with this, Szeth-son-Neturo?' the voice asked. It was male and deep. What was that accent? The man wasn't Veden. Alethi, perhaps? 'Are you satisfied with trivial crimes? Killing over meaningless turf in backwater mining villages?'

Szeth didn't reply. He scanned the room, looking for motion in the other shadows. None seemed to be hiding anyone.

'I've watched you,' the voice said. 'You've been sent to intimidate shopkeepers. You've killed footpads so unimportant even the authorities ignore them. You've been shown off to impress whores, as if they were high light-eyed ladies. What a waste.'

'I do as my master demands.'

'You are squandered,' the voice said. 'You are not meant for petty extortions and murders. Using you like this, it's like hitching a Ryshadium stallion to a run-down market wagon. It's like using a Shardblade to slice vegetables, or like using the finest parchment as kindling for a washwater fire. It is a *crime*. You are a work of art, Szeth-son-Neturo, a god. And each day Makkek throws dung at you.'

'Who are you?' Szeth repeated.

'An admirer of the arts.'

'Do not call me by my father's name,' Szeth said. 'He should not be sullied by association with me.'

The sphere on the wall finally ran out of Stormlight, dropping to the floor, the drapery muffling its fall. 'Very well,' the figure said. 'But do you not rebel against this frivolous use of your skills? Were you not meant for greatness?'

'There is no greatness in killing,' Szeth said. 'You speak like a *kukori*. Great men create food and clothing. He who adds is to be revered. I am he who takes away. At least in the killing of men such as these I can pretend to be doing a service.'

'This from the man who nearly toppled one of the greatest kingdoms in Roshar?'

'This from the man who committed one of the most heinous slaughters in Roshar,' Szeth corrected.

The figure snorted. 'What you did was a mere breeze compared to the storm of slaughter Shardbearers wreak on a battlefield each day. And *those* are breezes compared to the tempests you are capable of.'

Szeth began to walk away.

'Where are you going?' the figure asked.

'Gavashaw is dead. I must return to my master.'

Something hit the floor. Szeth spun, Shardblade down. The figure had dropped something round and heavy. It rolled across the floor toward Szeth.

Another head. It came to rest on its side. Szeth froze as he made out the features. The pudgy cheeks were stained with blood, the dead eyes wide with shock: Makkek.

'How?' Szeth demanded.

'We took him seconds after you left the gambling den.'

'We?'

'Servants of your new master.'

'My Oathstone?'

The figure opened his hand, revealing a gemstone suspended in his palm by a chain wrapped around his fingers. Sitting beside it, now illuminated, was Szeth's Oathstone. The figure's face was dark; he wore a mask.

Szeth dismissed his Shardblade and went down on one knee. 'What are your orders?'

'There is a list on the table,' the figure said, closing his hand and hiding the Oathstone. 'It details our master's wishes.'

Szeth rose and walked over. Beside the head, which rested on a plate to contain the blood, was a sheet of paper. He took it, and his Stormlight illuminated some two dozen names written in the warrior's script of his homeland. Some had a note beside them with instructions on how they were to be killed.

Glories within, Szeth thought. 'These are some of the most powerful people in the world! Six highprinces? A Selay gerontarch? The *king* of Jah Keved?'

'It is time you stopped wasting your talent,' the figure said, walking to the far wall, resting his hand upon it.

'This will cause chaos,' Szeth whispered. 'Infighting. War. Confusion and pain such as the world has rarely known.'

The chained gemstone on the man's palm flashed. The wall vanished, turned to smoke. A Soulcaster.

The dark figure glanced at Szeth. 'Indeed. Our master directs that you are to use tactics similar to those you employed so well in Alethkar years ago. When you are done, you will receive further instructions.'

He then exited through the opening, leaving Szeth horrified. This was his nightmare. To be in the hands of those who understood his capabilities and who had the ambition to use them properly. He stood for a time, silent, long past when his Stormlight ran out.

Then, reverently, he folded the list. He was surprised that his hands were so steady. He should be trembling.

For soon the world itself would shake.

THREE

Dying

KALADIN • SHALLAN

View of the City of Bells, from the Port to the Conclave, connected by the Kalissa

Khar-branth

'The ones of ash and fire, who killed like a swarm, relentless before the Heralds.'

—Noted in Masly, page 337. Corroborated by Coldwin and Hasavah.

I t sounds like you're getting into Jasnah's good graces quickly, the spanreed wrote out. *How long before you can make the switch?*

Shallan grimaced, turning the gemstone on the reed. *I don't know,* she wrote back. *Jasnah keeps a close watch on the Soulcaster, as you'd expect. She wears it all day. At night, she locks it away in her safe and wears the key around her neck.*

She turned the gemstone, then waited for a reply. She was in her chamber, a small, stone-carved room inside Jasnah's quarters. Her accommodations were austere: A small bed, a nightstand, and the writing table were her only furniture. Her clothing remained in the trunk she had brought. No rug adorned the floor, and there were no windows, as the rooms were in the Kharbranthian Conclave, which was underground.

That does make it troubling, the reed wrote. Eylita – Nan Balat's betrothed – was the one doing the writing, but all three of Shallan's surviving brothers would be in the room back in Jah Keved, contributing to the conversation.

I'm guessing she takes it off while bathing, Shallan wrote. *Once she trusts me more, she may begin using me as a bathing attendant. That may present an opportunity.*

That is a good plan, the spanreed wrote. *Nan Balat wants me to point out that we are very sorry to make you do this. It must be difficult for you to be away so long.*

Difficult? Shallan picked up the spanreed and hesitated.

Yes, it was difficult. Difficult not to fall in love with the freedom, difficult not to get too absorbed in her studies. It had been only two months since she'd convinced Jasnah to take her as a ward, but already she felt half as timid and twice as confident.

The most difficult thing of all was knowing that it would soon end. Coming to study in Kharbranth was, without doubt, the most wonderful thing that had ever happened to her.

I will manage, she wrote. *You are the ones living the difficult life, maintaining our family's interests at home. How are you doing?*

It took time for them to reply. *Poorly,* Eylita finally sent. *Your father's debts are coming due, and Wikim can barely keep the creditors distracted. The high-prince ails, and everyone wants to know where our house stands on the question of succession. The last of the quarries is running out. If it becomes known that we no longer have resources, it will go badly for us.*

Shallan grimaced. *How long do I have?*

A few more months, at best, Nan Balat sent back via his betrothed. *It depends on how long the highprince lasts and whether or not anyone realizes why Asha Jushu is selling our possessions.* Jushu was the youngest of the brothers, just older than Shallan. His old gambling habit was actually coming in handy. For years, he'd been stealing things from their father and selling them to cover his losses. He pretended he was still doing that, but he brought the money back to help. He was a good man, despite his habit. And, all things considered, he really couldn't be blamed for much of what he'd done. None of them could.

Wikim thinks that he can keep everyone at bay for a while longer. But we are getting desperate. The sooner you return with the Soulcaster, the better.

Shallan hesitated, then wrote, *Are we certain this is the best way? Perhaps we should simply ask Jasnah for help.*

You think she would respond to that? they wrote back. *She would help an unknown and disliked Veden house? She would keep our secrets?*

Probably not. Though Shallan was increasingly certain that Jasnah's reputation was exaggerated, the woman did have a ruthless side to her. She would not leave her important studies to go help Shallan's family.

She reached for the reed to reply, but it started scribbling again. *Shallan*, it said. *This is Nan Balat; I have sent the others away. It is only Eylita and me writing you now. There is something you need to know. Luesh is dead.*

Shallan blinked in surprise. Luesh, her father's steward, had been the one who had known how to use the Soulcaster. He was one of the few people she and her brothers had determined they could trust.

What happened? she wrote after switching to a new sheet of paper.

He died in his sleep, and there's no reason to suspect he was killed. But Shallan, a few weeks after his passing, some men visited here claiming to be friends of our father. In private with me, they implied they knew of Father's Soulcaster and suggested strongly *that I was to return it to them.*

Shallan frowned. She still carried her father's broken Soulcaster in the safepouch of her sleeve. *Return it?* she wrote.

We never did figure out where Father got it, Nan Balat sent. *Shallan, he was involved in something. Those maps, the things Luesh said, and now this. We continue to pretend that Father is alive, and occasionally he gets letters from other lighteyes that speak of vague 'plans.' I think he was going to make a play to become highprince. And he was supported by some very powerful forces.*

These men who came, they were dangerous, Shallan. The type of men you do not cross. And they want their Soulcaster back. Whoever they are, I suspect they gave it to Father so he could create wealth and make a bid for the succession. They know he's dead.

I believe that if we don't return a working Soulcaster to them, we could all be in serious danger. You need to bring Jasnah's fabrial to us. We'll quickly use it to create new quarries of valuable stone, and then we can give it up to these men. Shallan, you must succeed. I was hesitant about this plan when you suggested it, but other avenues are quickly vanishing.

Shallan felt a chill. She read over the paragraphs a few times, then wrote, *If Luesh is dead, then we don't know how to use the Soulcaster. That is problematic.*

I know, Nan Balat sent. *See if you can figure that out. This is dangerous, Shallan. I know it is. I'm sorry.*

She took a deep breath. *It must be done*, she wrote.

Here, Nan Balat sent. *I wanted to show you something. Have you ever seen this symbol?* The sketch that followed was crude. Eylita wasn't much of an artist. Fortunately, it was a simple picture – three diamond shapes in a curious pattern.

I've never seen it, Shallan wrote. *Why?*

Luesh wore a pendant with this symbol on it, Nan Balat sent. *We found it on his body. And one of the men who came searching for the Soulcaster had the same pattern tattooed on his hand, just below his thumb.*

Curious, Shallan wrote. *So Luesh . . .*

Yes, Nan Balat sent. *Despite what he said, I think he must have been the one who brought the Soulcaster to Father. Luesh was involved in this, perhaps as liaison between Father and the people backing him. I tried to suggest that they could back me instead, but the men just laughed. They did not stay long or give a specific time by which the Soulcaster must be returned. I doubt they'd be satisfied to receive a broken one.*

Shallan pursed her lips. *Balat, have you thought that we might be risking a war? If it becomes known that we've stolen an Alethi Soulcaster . . .*

No, there wouldn't be a war, Nan Balat wrote back. *King Hanavanar would just turn us over to the Alethi. They'd execute us for the theft.*

Wonderfully comforting, Balat, she wrote. *Thank you so much.*

You're welcome. We're going to have to hope that Jasnah doesn't realize that you took the Soulcaster. It seems likely she'll assume that hers broke for some reason.

Shallan sighed. *Perhaps*, she wrote.

Take care, Nan Balat sent her.

You too.

And that was it. She set the spanreed aside, then read over the entire conversation, memorizing it. Then she crumpled up the sheets and walked into the sitting room of Jasnah's quarters. She wasn't there – Jasnah rarely broke from her studies – so Shallan burned the conversation in the hearth.

She stood for a long moment, watching the fire. She was worried. Nan Balat was capable, but they all bore scars from the lives they'd led. Eylita was the only scribe they could trust, and she . . . well, she was incredibly nice but not very clever.

With a sigh, Shallan left the room to return to her studies. Not only would they help get her mind off her troubles, but Jasnah would grow testy if she dallied too long.

❖

Five hours later, Shallan wondered why it was she'd been so eager.

She *did* enjoy her chances at scholarship. But recently, Jasnah had set her to study the history of the Alethi monarchy. It wasn't the most interesting subject around. Her boredom was compounded by her being forced to read a number of books that expressed opinions she found ridiculous.

She sat in Jasnah's alcove at the Veil. The enormous wall of lights, alcoves, and mysterious researchers no longer awed her. The place was becoming comfortable and familiar. She was alone at the moment.

Shallan rubbed her eyes with her freehand, then slid her book closed. 'I,' she muttered, 'am really coming to hate the Alethi monarchy.'

'Is that so?' a calm voice said from behind. Jasnah walked past, wearing a sleek violet dress, followed by a parshman porter with a stack of books. 'I'll try not to take it personally.'

Shallan winced, then blushed furiously. 'I didn't mean *individually*, Brightness Jasnah. I meant categorically.'

Jasnah lithely took her seat in the alcove. She raised an eyebrow at Shallan, then gestured for the parshman to set down his burden.

Shallan still found Jasnah an enigma. At times, she seemed a stern scholar annoyed by Shallan's interruptions. At other times, there seemed to be a hint of wry humor hiding behind the stern facade. Either way, Shallan was finding that she felt remarkably comfortable around the woman. Jasnah encouraged her to speak her mind, something Shallan had taken to gladly.

'I assume from your outburst that this topic is wearing on you,' Jasnah said, sorting through her volumes as the parshman withdrew. 'You expressed interest in being a scholar. Well, you must learn that this *is* scholarship.'

'Reading argument after argument from people who refuse to see any other point of view?'

'They're confident.'

'I'm not an expert on confidence, Brightness,' Shallan said, holding up a book and inspecting it critically. 'But I'd like to think that I could recognize it if it were before me. I don't think that's the right word for books like this one from Mederia. They feel more arrogant than confident to me.' She sighed, setting the book aside. 'To be honest, "arrogant" doesn't feel like quite the right word. It's not specific enough.'

'And what *would* be the right word, then?'

'I don't know. "Errorgant," perhaps.'

Jasnah raised a skeptical eyebrow.

'It means to be twice as certain as someone who is merely arrogant,' Shallan said, 'while possessing only one-tenth the requisite facts.'

Her words drew a hint of a smile from Jasnah. 'What you are reacting against is known as the Assuredness Movement, Shallan. This *errorgance* is a literary device. The scholars are intentionally overstating their case.'

'The Assuredness Movement?' Shallan asked, holding up one of her books. 'I guess I could get behind that.'

'Oh?'

'Yes. Much easier to stab it in the back from that position.'

That got only an eyebrow raise. So, more seriously, Shallan continued. 'I suppose I can understand the device, Brightness, but these books you've given me on King Gavilar's death are more and more irrational in defending their points. What began as a rhetorical conceit seems to have descended into name-calling and squabbling.'

'They are trying to provoke discussion. Would you rather that the scholars hide from the truth, like so many? You would have men prefer ignorance?'

'When reading these books, scholarship and ignorance feel much alike to me,' Shallan said. 'Ignorance may reside in a man hiding from intelligence, but scholarship can seem ignorance hidden behind intelligence.'

'And what of intelligence without ignorance? Finding truth while not dismissing the possibility of being wrong?'

'A mythological treasure, Brightness, much like the Dawnshards or the Honorblades. Certainly worth seeking, but only with great caution.'

'Caution?' Jasnah said, frowning.

'It would make you famous, but actually *finding* it would destroy us all. Proof that one can be both intelligent *and* accept the intelligence of those who disagree with you? Why, I should think it would undermine the scholarly world in its entirety.'

Jasnah sniffed. 'You go too far, child. If you took half the energy you devote to being witty and channeled it into your work, I daresay you could be one of the greatest scholars of our age.'

'I'm sorry, Brightness,' Shallan said. 'I ... well, I'm confused. Considering the gaps in my education, I assumed you would have me studying things deeper in the past than a few years ago.'

Jasnah opened one of her books. 'I have found that youths like you have a relative lack of appreciation for the distant past. Therefore, I selected an area of study that is both more recent and sensational, to ease you into true scholarship. Is the murder of a king not of interest to you?'

'Yes, Brightness,' Shallan said. 'We children love things that are shiny and loud.'

'You have quite the mouth on you at times.'

'At times? You mean it's not there at others? I'll have to ...' Shallan trailed off, then bit her lip, realizing she'd gone too far. 'Sorry.'

'Never apologize for being clever, Shallan. It sets a bad precedent. However, one must apply one's wit with care. You often seem to say the first passably clever thing that enters your mind.'

'I know,' Shallan said. 'It's long been a foible of mine, Brightness. One my nurses and tutors tried very hard to discourage.'

'Likely through strict punishments.'

'Yes. Making me sit in the corner holding books over my head was the preferred method.'

'Which, in turn,' Jasnah said with a sigh, 'only trained you to make your quips *more* quickly, for you knew you had to get them out before you could reconsider and suppress them.'

Shallan cocked her head.

'The punishments were incompetent,' Jasnah said. 'Used upon one such as yourself, they were actually encouragement. A game. How much would you have to say to earn a punishment? Could you say something so clever that your tutors missed the joke? Sitting in the corner just gave you more time to compose retorts.'

'But it's unseemly for a young woman to speak as I so often do.'

'The only "unseemly" thing is to not channel your intelligence usefully. Consider. You have trained yourself to do something very similar to what annoys you in the scholars: cleverness without thought behind it – intelligence, one might say, without a foundation of proper consideration.' Jasnah turned a page. 'Errorgant, wouldn't you say?'

Shallan blushed.

'I prefer my wards to be clever,' Jasnah said. 'It gives me more to work with. I should bring you to court with me. I suspect that Wit, at least, would find you amusing – if only because your apparent natural timidity and your clever tongue make such an intriguing combination.'

'Yes, Brightness.'

'Please, just remember that a woman's mind is her most precious weapon. It must not be employed clumsily or prematurely. Much like the aforementioned knife to the back, a clever gibe is most effective when it is unanticipated.'

'I'm sorry, Brightness.'

'It wasn't an admonition,' Jasnah said, turning a page. 'Simply an observation. I make them on occasion: Those books are musty. The sky is blue today. My ward is a smart-lipped reprobate.'

Shallan smiled.

'Now, tell me what you've discovered.'

Shallan grimaced. 'Not much, Brightness. Or should I say too much? Each writer has her own theories on why the Parshendi killed your father. Some claim he must have insulted them at the feast that night. Others say that the entire treaty was a ruse, intended to get the Parshendi close to him. But that makes little sense, as they had much better opportunities earlier.'

'And the Assassin in White?' Jasnah asked.

'A true anomaly,' Shallan said. 'The undertexts are filled with commentary about him. Why would the Parshendi hire an outside assassin? Did they fear they could not accomplish the job themselves? Or perhaps they didn't hire him, and were framed. Many think that is unlikely, considering that the Parshendi took credit for the murder.'

'And your thoughts?'

'I feel inadequate to draw conclusions, Brightness.'

'What is the point of research if not to draw conclusions?'

'My tutors told me that supposition was only for the very experienced,' Shallan explained.

Jasnah sniffed. 'Your tutors were idiots. Youthful immaturity is one of the cosmere's great catalysts for change, Shallan. Do you realize that the Sunmaker was only seventeen when he began his conquest? Gavarah hadn't reached her twentieth Weeping when she proposed the theory of the three realms.'

'But for every Sunmaker or Gavarah, are there not a hundred Gregorhs?'

He had been a youthful king notorious for beginning a pointless war with kingdoms that had been his father's allies.

'There was only *one* Gregorh,' Jasnah said with a grimace, 'thankfully. Your point is a valid one. Hence the purpose of education. To be young is about action. To be a scholar is about *informed* action.'

'Or about sitting in an alcove reading about a six-year-old murder.'

'I would not have you studying this if there were no point to it,' Jasnah said, opening up another of her own books. 'Too many scholars think of research as purely a cerebral pursuit. If we *do* nothing with the knowledge we gain, then we have wasted our study. Books can store information better than we can – what we do that books cannot is *interpret*. So if one is not going to draw conclusions, then one might as well just leave the information in the texts.'

Shallan sat back, thoughtful. Presented that way, it somehow made her want to dig back into the studies. What was it that Jasnah wanted her to do with the information? Once again, she felt a stab of guilt. Jasnah was taking great pains to instruct her in scholarship, and she was going to reward the woman by stealing her most valuable possession and leaving a broken replacement. It made Shallan feel sick.

She had expected study beneath Jasnah to involve meaningless memorization and busywork, accompanied by chastisement for not being smart enough. That was how her tutors had approached her instruction. Jasnah was different. She gave Shallan a topic and the freedom to pursue it as she wished. Jasnah offered encouragement and speculation, but nearly all of their conversations turned to topics like the true nature of scholarship, the purpose of studying, the beauty of knowledge and its application.

Jasnah Kholin truly loved learning, and she wanted others to as well. Behind the stern gaze, intense eyes, and rarely smiling lips, Jasnah Kholin truly believed in what she was doing. Whatever that was.

Shallan raised one of her books, but covertly eyed the spines of Jasnah's latest stack of tomes. More histories about the Heraldic Epochs. Mythologies, commentaries, books by scholars known to be wild speculators. Jasnah's current volume was called *Shadows Remembered*. Shallan memorized the title. She would try to find a copy and look through it.

What was Jasnah pursuing? What secrets was she hoping to pry from these volumes, most of them centuries-old copies of copies? Though Shallan had discovered some secrets regarding the Soulcaster, the nature of Jasnah's quest – the reason the princess had come to Kharbranth – remained elusive. Maddeningly, yet tantalizingly, so. Jasnah liked to speak of the great women of the past, ones who had not just recorded history, but shaped it. Whatever it was she studied, she felt that it was important. World-changing.

You mustn't be drawn in, Shallan told herself, settling back with book and notes. *Your goal is not to change the world. Your goal is to protect your brothers and your house.*

Still, she needed to make a good show of her wardship. And that gave her a reason to immerse herself for two hours until footsteps in the hallway interrupted. Likely the servants bringing the midday meal. Jasnah and Shallan often ate on their balcony.

Shallan's stomach grumbled as she smelled the food, and she gleefully set aside her book. She usually sketched at lunch, an activity that Jasnah – despite her dislike of the visual arts – encouraged. She said that highborn men often thought drawing and painting to be 'enticing' in a woman, and so Shallan should maintain her skills, if only for the purpose of attracting suitors.

Shallan didn't know whether to find that insulting or not. And what did it say about Jasnah's own intentions for marriage that she herself never bothered with the more becoming feminine arts like music or drawing?

'Your Majesty,' Jasnah said, rising smoothly.

Shallan started and looked hastily over her shoulder. The elderly king of Kharbranth was standing in the doorway, wearing magnificent orange and white robes with detailed embroidery. Shallan scrambled to her feet.

'Brightness Jasnah,' the king said. 'Am I interrupting?'

'Your company is never an interruption, Your Majesty,' Jasnah said. She had to be as surprised as Shallan was, yet didn't display a moment of discomfort or anxiety. 'We were soon to take lunch, anyway.'

'I know, Brightness,' Taravangian said. 'I hope you don't mind if I join you.' A group of servants began bringing in food and a table.

'Not at all,' Jasnah said.

The servants hurried to set things up, putting two different tablecloths on the round table to separate the genders during dining. They secured the half-moons of cloth – red for the king, blue for the women – with weights at the center. Covered plates filled with food followed: a clear, cold stew with sweet vegetables for the women, a spicy-smelling broth for the king. Kharbranthians preferred soups for their lunches.

Shallan was surprised to see them set a place for her. Her father had never eaten at the same table as his children – even she, his favorite, had been relegated to her own table. Once Jasnah sat, Shallan did likewise. Her stomach growled again, and the king waved for them to begin. His motions seemed ungainly compared with Jasnah's elegance.

Shallan was soon eating contentedly – with grace, as a woman should, safehand in her lap, using her freehand and a skewer to spear chunks of vegetable or fruit. The king slurped, but he wasn't as noisy as many men. Why had he deigned to visit? Wouldn't a formal dinner invitation have been more proper? Of course, she'd learned that Taravangian wasn't known for his mastery of protocol. He was a popular king, beloved by the darkeyes as a builder of hospitals. However, the lighteyes considered him less than bright.

He was not an idiot. In lighteyed politics, unfortunately, being only average was a disadvantage. As they ate, the silence drew out, becoming awkward. Several times, the king looked as if he wanted to say something, but then turned back to his soup. He seemed intimidated by Jasnah.

'And how is your granddaughter, Your Majesty?' Jasnah eventually asked. 'She is recovering well?'

'Quite well, thank you,' Taravangian said, as if relieved to begin conversing. 'Though she now avoids the narrower corridors of the Conclave. I do want to thank you for your aid.'

'It is always fulfilling to be of service, Your Majesty.'

'If you will forgive my saying so, the ardents do not think much of your service,' Taravangian said. 'I realize it is likely a sensitive topic. Perhaps I shouldn't mention it, but–'

'No, feel free,' Jasnah said, eating a small green lurnip from the end of her skewer. 'I am not ashamed of my choices.'

'Then you'll forgive an old man's curiosity?'

'I always forgive curiosity, Your Majesty,' Jasnah said. 'It strikes me as one of the most genuine of emotions.'

'Then where did you find it?' Taravangian asked, nodding toward the Soulcaster, which Jasnah wore covered by a black glove. 'How did you keep it from the devotaries?'

'One might find those questions dangerous, Your Majesty.'

'I've already acquired some new enemies by welcoming you.'

'You will be forgiven,' Jasnah said. 'Depending on the devotary you have chosen.'

'Forgiven? Me?' The elderly man seemed to find that amusing, and for a moment, Shallan thought she saw deep regret in his expression. 'Unlikely. But that is something else entirely. Please. I stand by my questions.'

'And I stand by my evasiveness, Your Majesty. I'm sorry. I do forgive your curiosity, but I cannot reward it. These secrets are mine.'

'Of course, of course.' The king sat back, looking embarrassed. 'Now you probably assume I brought this meal simply to ambush you about the fabrial.'

'You had another purpose, then?'

'Well, you see, I've heard the most wonderful things about your ward's artistic skill. I thought that maybe . . .' He smiled at Shallan.

'Of course, Your Majesty,' Shallan said. 'I'd be happy to draw your likeness.'

He beamed as she stood, leaving her meal half eaten and gathering her things. She glanced at Jasnah, but the older woman's face was unreadable.

'Would you prefer a simple portrait against a white background?' Shallan asked. 'Or would you prefer a broader perspective, including surroundings?'

'Perhaps,' Jasnah said pointedly, 'you should wait until the meal is finished, Shallan?'

Shallan blushed, feeling a fool for her enthusiasm. 'Of course.'

'No, no,' the king said. 'I'm quite finished. A wider sketch would be perfect, child. How would you like me to sit?' He slid his chair back, posing and smiling in a grandfatherly way.

She blinked, fixing the image in her mind. 'That is perfect, Your Majesty. You can return to your meal.'

'Don't you need me to sit still? I've posed for portraits before.'

'It's all right,' Shallan assured him, sitting down.

'Very well,' he said, pulling back to the table. 'I do apologize for making you use me, of all people, as a subject for your art. This face of mine isn't the most impressive one you've depicted, I'm sure.'

'Nonsense,' Shallan said. 'A face like yours is just what an artist needs.'

'It is?'

'Yes, the—' She cut herself off. She'd been about to quip, *Yes, the skin is enough like parchment to make an ideal canvas.* '... that handsome nose of yours, and wise furrowed brow. It will be quite striking in the black charcoal.'

'Oh, well then. Proceed. Though I still can't see how you'll work without me holding a pose.'

'Brightness Shallan has some unique talents,' Jasnah said. Shallan began her sketch.

'I suppose that she must!' the king said. 'I've seen the drawing she did for Varas.'

'Varas?' Jasnah asked.

'The Palanaeum's assistant chief of collections,' the king said. 'A distant cousin of mine. He says the staff is quite taken with your young ward. How did you find her?'

'Unexpectedly,' Jasnah said, 'and in need of an education.'

The king cocked his head.

'The artistic skill, I cannot claim,' Jasnah said. 'It was a preexisting condition.'

'Ah, a blessing of the Almighty.'

'You might say that.'

'But you would not, I assume?' Taravangian chuckled awkwardly.

Shallan drew quickly, establishing the shape of his head. He shuffled uncomfortably. 'Is it hard for you, Jasnah? Painful, I mean?'

'Atheism is not a disease, Your Majesty,' Jasnah said dryly. 'It's not as if I've caught a foot rash.'

'Of course not, of course not. But ... er, isn't it difficult, having nothing in which to believe?'

Shallan leaned forward, still sketching, but keeping her attention on the conversation. Shallan had assumed that training under a heretic would be a little more exciting. She and Kabsal – the witty ardent whom she'd met on her first day in Kharbranth – had chatted several times now about Jasnah's faith. However, around Jasnah herself, the topic almost never came up. When it did, Jasnah usually changed it.

Today, however, she did not. Perhaps she sensed the sincerity in the king's question. 'I wouldn't say that I have nothing to believe in, Your Majesty. Actually, I have much to believe in. My brother and my uncle, my own abilities. The things I was taught by my parents.'

'But, what is right and wrong, you've ... Well, you've discarded that.'

'Just because I do not accept the teachings of the devotaries does not mean I've discarded a belief in right and wrong.'

'But the *Almighty* determines what is right!'

'Must someone, some unseen *thing*, declare what is right for it to *be* right? I believe that my own morality – which answers only to my heart – is more sure and true than the morality of those who do right only because they fear retribution.'

'But that is the soul of law,' the king said, sounding confused. 'If there is no punishment, there can be only chaos.'

'If there were no law, some men would do as they wish, yes,' Jasnah said. 'But isn't it remarkable that, given the chance for personal gain at the cost of others, so many people choose what is right?'

'Because they fear the Almighty.'

'No,' Jasnah said. 'I think something innate in us understands that seeking the good of society is usually best for the individual as well. Humankind is noble, when we give it the chance to be. That nobility is something that exists independent of any god's decree.'

'I just don't see how *anything* could be outside God's decrees.' The king shook his head, bemused. 'Brightness Jasnah, I don't mean to argue, but isn't the very definition of the Almighty that all things exist because of him?'

'If you add one and one, that makes two, does it not?'

'Well, yes.'

'No god needs declare it so for it to be true,' Jasnah said. 'So, could we not say that mathematics exists outside the Almighty, independent of him?'

'Perhaps.'

'Well,' Jasnah said, 'I simply claim that morality and human will are independent of him too.'

'If you say that,' the king said, chuckling, 'then you've removed all purpose for the Almighty's existence!'

'Indeed.'

The balcony fell silent. Jasnah's sphere lamps cast a cool, even white light across them. For an uncomfortable moment, the only sound was the scratching of Shallan's charcoal on her drawing pad. She worked with quick, scraping motions, disturbed by the things that Jasnah had said. They made her feel hollow inside. That was partly because the king, for all his affability, was not good at arguing. He was a dear man, but no match for Jasnah in a conversation.

'Well,' Taravangian said, 'I must say that you make your points quite effectively. I don't accept them, though.'

'My intention is not to convert, Your Majesty,' Jasnah said. 'I am content keeping my beliefs to myself, something most of my colleagues in the devotaries have difficulty doing. Shallan, have you finished yet?'

'Quite nearly, Brightness.'

'But it's been barely a few minutes!' the king said.

'She has remarkable skill, Your Majesty,' Jasnah said. 'As I believe I mentioned.'

Shallan sat back, inspecting her piece. She'd been so focused on the conversation, she'd just let her hands do the drawing, trusting in her instincts. The sketch depicted the king, sitting in his chair with a wise expression, the turretlike balcony walls behind him. The doorway into the balcony was to his right. Yes, it was a good likeness. Not her best work, but—

Shallan froze, her breath catching, her heart lurching in her chest. She had drawn *something* standing in the doorway behind the king. Two tall and willowy creatures with cloaks that split down the front and hung at the sides too stiffly, as if they were made of glass. Above the stiff, high collars, where the creatures' heads should be, each had a large, floating symbol of twisted design full of impossible angles and geometries.

Shallan sat, stunned. Why had she drawn those things? What had driven her to—

She snapped her head up. The hallway was empty. The creatures hadn't been part of the Memory she'd taken. Her hands had simply drawn them of their accord.

'Shallan?' Jasnah said.

By reflex, Shallan dropped her charcoal and grabbed the sheet in her freehand, crumpling it. 'I'm sorry, Brightness. I paid too much attention to the conversation. I let myself grow sloppy.'

'Well, certainly we can at least *see* it, child,' the king said, standing.

Shallan tightened her grip. 'Please, no!'

'She has an artist's temperament at times, Your Majesty.' Jasnah sighed. 'There will be no getting it out of her.'

'I'll do you another, Your Majesty,' Shallan said. 'I'm *so* sorry.'

He rubbed his wispy beard. 'Yes, well, it was going to be a gift for my granddaughter. . . .'

'By the end of the day,' Shallan promised.

'That would be wonderful. You're certain you don't need me to pose?'

'No, no, that won't be necessary, Your Majesty,' Shallan said. Her pulse was still racing and she couldn't shake the image of those two distorted figures from her mind, so she took another Memory of the king. She could use that to create a more suitable picture.

'Well then,' the king said. 'I suppose I should be going. I wish to visit one of the hospitals and the sick. You can send the drawing to my rooms, but take your time. Really, it is quite all right.'

Shallan curtsied, crushed paper still held to her breast. The king withdrew with his attendants, several parshmen entering to remove the table.

'I've never known you to make a mistake in drawing,' Jasnah said, sitting back down at the desk. 'At least not one so horrible that you destroyed the paper.'

Shallan blushed.

'Even the master of an art may err, I suppose. Go ahead and take the next hour to do His Majesty a proper portrait.'

Shallan looked down at the ruined sketch. The creatures were simply her fancy, the product of letting her mind wander. That was all. Just imagination. Perhaps there was something in her subconscious that she'd needed to express. But what could the figures mean, then?

'I noticed that at one point when you were speaking to the king, you hesitated,' Jasnah said. 'What didn't you say?'

'Something inappropriate.'

'But clever?'

'Cleverness never seems quite so impressive when regarded outside the moment, Brightness. It was just a silly thought.'

'And you replaced it with an empty compliment. I think you misunderstood what I was trying to explain, child. I do not wish for you to remain silent. It is good to be clever.'

'But if I'd spoken,' Shallan said, 'I'd have insulted the king, perhaps confused him as well, which would have caused him embarrassment. I am certain he knows what people say about his slowness of thought.'

Jasnah sniffed. 'Idle words. From foolish people. But perhaps it was wise not to speak, though keep in mind that *channeling* your capacities and *stifling* them are two separate things. I'd much prefer you to think of something both clever and appropriate.'

'Yes, Brightness.'

'Besides,' Jasnah said, 'I believe you might have made Taravangian laugh. He seems haunted by something lately.'

'You don't find him dull, then?' Shallan asked, curious. She herself didn't think the king dull or a fool, but she'd thought someone as intelligent and learned as Jasnah might not have patience for a man like him.

'Taravangian is a wonderful man,' Jasnah said, 'and worth a hundred self-proclaimed experts on courtly ways. He reminds me of my uncle Dalinar. Earnest, sincere, concerned.'

'The lighteyes here say he's weak,' Shallan said. 'Because he panders to so many other monarchs, because he fears war, because he doesn't have a Shardblade.'

Jasnah didn't reply, though she looked disturbed.

'Brightness?' Shallan prodded, walking to her own seat and arranging her charcoals.

'In ancient days,' Jasnah said, 'a man who brought peace to his kingdom was considered to be of great worth. Now that same man would be derided as a coward.' She shook her head. 'It has been centuries coming, this change. It should terrify us. We could do with more men like Taravangian, and I shall require you to never call him dull again, not even in passing.'

'Yes, Brightness,' Shallan said, bowing her head. 'Did you really believe the things you said? About the Almighty?'

Jasnah was quiet for a moment. 'I do. Though perhaps I overstated my conviction.'

'The Assuredness Movement of rhetorical theory?'

'Yes,' Jasnah said. 'I suppose that it was. I must be careful not to put my back toward you as I read today.'

Shallan smiled.

'A true scholar must not close her mind on any topic,' Jasnah said, 'no matter how certain she may feel. Just because I have not yet found a convincing reason to join one of the devotaries does not mean I never will. Though each time I have a discussion like the one today, my convictions grow firmer.'

Shallan bit her lip. Jasnah noticed the expression. 'You will need to learn to control that, Shallan. It makes your feelings obvious.'

'Yes, Brightness.'

'Well, out with it.'

'Just that your conversation with the king was not entirely fair.'

'Oh?'

'Because of his, well, you know. His limited capacity. He did quite remarkably, but didn't make the arguments that someone more versed in Vorin theology might have.'

'And what arguments might such a one have made?'

'Well, I'm not very well trained in that area myself. But I do think that you ignored, or at least minimized, one vital part of the discussion.'

'Which is?'

Shallan tapped at her breast. 'Our hearts, Brightness. I believe because I feel something, a closeness to the Almighty, a peace that comes when I live my faith.'

'The mind is capable of projecting expected emotional responses.'

'But didn't you yourself argue that the way we act – the way we feel about right and wrong – was a defining attribute of our humanity? You used our innate morality to prove your point. So how can you discard my feelings?'

'Discard them? No. Regard them with skepticism? Perhaps. Your feelings, Shallan – however powerful – are your own. Not mine. And what I feel is that spending my life trying to earn the favor of an unseen, unknown, and unknowable being who watches me from the sky is an exercise in sheer futility.' She pointed at Shallan with her pen. 'But your rhetorical method is improving. We'll make a scholar of you yet.'

Shallan smiled, feeling a surge of pleasure. Praise from Jasnah was more precious than an emerald broam.

But . . . I'm not going to be a scholar. I'm going to steal the Soulcaster and leave.

She didn't like to think about that. That was something else she'd have to get over; she tended to avoid thinking about things that made her uncomfortable.

'Now hurry and be about the king's sketch,' Jasnah said, lifting a book. 'You still have a great deal of real work to do once you are done drawing.'

'Yes, Brightness,' Shallan said.

For once, however, she found sketching difficult, her mind too troubled to focus.

'They were suddenly dangerous. Like a calm day that became a tempest.'

—This fragment is the origin of a Thaylen proverb that was eventually reworked into a more common derivation. I believe it may reference the Voidbringers. See Ixsix's *Emperor*, fourth chapter.

Kaladin walked from the cavernous barrack into the pure light of first morning. Bits of quartz in the ground sparkled before him, catching the light, as if the ground were sparking and burning, ready to burst from within.

A group of twenty-nine men followed him. Slaves. Thieves. Deserters. Foreigners. Even a few men whose only sin had been poverty. Those had joined the bridge crews out of desperation. The pay was good when compared with nothing, and they were promised that if they survived a hundred bridge runs, they would be promoted. Assignment to a watch post – which, in the mind of a poor man, sounded like a life of luxury. Being paid to stand and look at things all day? What kind of insanity was that? It was like being rich, almost.

They didn't understand. Nobody survived a hundred bridge runs. Kaladin had been on two dozen, and he was already one of the most experienced living bridgemen.

Bridge Four followed him. The last of the holdouts – a thin man named

Bisig – had given in yesterday. Kaladin preferred to think that the laughter, the food, and the humanity had finally gotten to him. But it had probably been a few glares or under-the-breath threats from Rock and Teft.

Kaladin turned a blind eye to those. He'd eventually need the men's loyalty, but for now, he'd settle for obedience.

He guided them through the morning exercises he'd learned his very first day in the military. Stretches followed by jumping motions. Carpenters in brown work overalls and tan or green caps passed on their way to the lumberyard, shaking their heads in amusement. Soldiers on the short ridge above, where the camp proper began, looked down and laughed. Gaz watched from beside a nearby barrack, arms folded, single eye dissatisfied.

Kaladin wiped his brow. He met Gaz's eye for a long moment, then turned back to the men. There was still time to practice hauling the bridge before breakfast.

◆◆

Gaz had never gotten used to having just one eye. *Could* a man get used to that? He'd rather have lost a hand or a leg than that eye. He couldn't stop feeling that *something* hid in that darkness he couldn't see, but others could. What lurked there? Spren that would drain his soul from his body? The way a rat could empty an entire wineskin by chewing the corner?

His companions called him lucky. 'That blow could have taken your life.' Well, at least then he wouldn't have had to live with that darkness. One of his eyes was always closed. Close the other, and the darkness swallowed him.

Gaz glanced left, and the darkness scuttled to the side. Lamaril stood leaning against a post, tall and slim. He was not a massive man, but he was not weak. He was all lines. Rectangular beard. Rectangular body. Sharp. Like a knife.

Lamaril waved Gaz over, so he reluctantly approached. Then he took a sphere out of his pouch and passed it over. A topaz mark. He hated losing it. He always hated losing money.

'You owe me twice as much as this,' Lamaril noted, raising the sphere up to look through it as it sparkled in the sunlight.

'Well, that's all you'll get for now. Be glad you get anything.'

'Be glad I've kept my mouth shut,' Lamaril said lazily, leaning back against his post. It was one that marked the edge of the lumberyard.

Gaz gritted his teeth. He hated to pay, but what else could he do? *Storms take him. Raging storms take him!*

'You have a problem, it seems,' Lamaril said.

At first, Gaz thought he meant the half payment. The lighteyed man nodded toward Bridge Four's barracks.

Gaz eyed the bridgemen, unsettled. The youthful bridgeleader barked an order, and the bridgemen raced the span of the lumberyard in a jog. He already had them running in time with one another. That one change meant so much. It sped them up, helped them think like a team.

Could this boy actually have military training, as he'd once claimed? Why would he be wasted as a bridgeman? Of course, there was that *shash* brand on his forehead. . . .

'I don't see a problem,' Gaz said with a grunt. 'They're fast. That's good.'

'They're insubordinate.'

'They follow orders.'

'*His* orders, perhaps.' Lamaril shook his head. 'Bridgemen exist for one purpose, Gaz. To protect the lives of more valuable men.'

'Really? And here I thought their purpose was to carry bridges.'

Lamaril gave him a sharp look. He leaned forward. 'Don't try me, Gaz. And don't forget your place. Would you like to join them?'

Gaz felt a spike of fear. Lamaril was a very lowly lighteyes, one of the landless. But he *was* Gaz's immediate superior, a liaison between bridge crews and the higher-ranked lighteyes who oversaw the lumberyard.

Gaz looked down at the ground. 'I'm sorry, Brightlord.'

'Highprince Sadeas holds an edge,' Lamaril said, leaning back against his post. 'He maintains it by pushing us all. Hard. Each man in his place.' He nodded toward the members of Bridge Four. 'Speed is not a bad thing. Initiative is not a bad thing. But men with initiative like that boy's are not often happy in their position. The bridge crews function as they are, without need for modification. Change can be unsettling.'

Gaz doubted that any of the bridgemen really understood their place in Sadeas's plans. If they knew why they were worked as pitilessly as they were – and why they were forbidden shields or armor – they likely would just cast themselves into the chasm. Bait. They were bait. Draw the Parshendi attention, let the savages think they were doing some good by felling a few bridges' worth of bridgemen every assault. So long as you took plenty of men, that didn't matter. Except to those who were slaughtered.

Stormfather, Gaz thought, *I hate myself for being a part of this*. But he'd hated himself for a long time now. It wasn't anything new to him. 'I'll do something,' he promised Lamaril. 'A knife in the night. Poison in the food.' That twisted his insides. The boy's bribes were small, but they were all that let him keep ahead of his payments to Lamaril.

'No!' Lamaril hissed. 'You want it seen that he was really a threat? The real soldiers are already talking about him.' Lamaril grimaced. 'The last thing we need is a martyr inspiring rebellion among the bridgemen. I don't want any *hint* of it; nothing our highprince's enemies could take advantage of.' Lamaril glanced at Kaladin, jogging past again with his men. 'That one has to fall on the field, as he deserves. Make certain it happens. And get me the rest of the money you owe, or you'll soon find yourself carrying one of those bridges.'

He swept away, forest-green cloak fluttering. In his time as a soldier, Gaz had learned to fear the minor lighteyes the most. They were galled by their closeness in rank to the darkeyes, yet those darkeyes were the only ones they had any authority over. That made them dangerous. Being around a man like Lamaril was like handling a hot coal with bare fingers. There was no way to avoid burning yourself. You just hoped to be quick enough to keep the burns to a minimum.

Bridge Four ran by. A month ago, Gaz wouldn't have believed this possible. A group of bridgemen, *practicing*? And all it seemed to have cost Kaladin was a few bribes of food and some empty promises that he would protect them.

That shouldn't have been enough. Life as a bridgeman was hopeless. Gaz *couldn't* join them. He just couldn't. Kaladin the lordling had to fall. But if Kaladin's spheres vanished, Gaz could just as easily end up as a bridgeman for failing to pay Lamaril. *Storming Damnation!* he thought. It was like trying to choose which claw of the chasmfiend would crush you.

Gaz continued to watch Kaladin's crew. And *still* that darkness waited for him. Like an itch that couldn't be scratched. Like a scream that couldn't be silenced. A tingling numbness that he could never be rid of.

It would probably follow him even into death.

❖

'Bridge up!' Kaladin bellowed, running with Bridge Four. They raised the bridge over their heads while still moving. It was harder to run this way, holding the bridge up, rather than resting it on the shoulders. He felt its enormous weight on his arms.

'Down!' he ordered.

Those at the front let go of the bridge and ran out to the sides. The others lowered the bridge in a quick motion. It hit the ground awkwardly, scraping the stone. They got into position, pretending to move it across a chasm. Kaladin helped at the side.

We'll need to practice on a real chasm, he thought as the men finished. *I wonder what kind of bribe it would take for Gaz to let me do that.*

The bridgemen, finished with their mock bridge run, looked toward Kaladin, exhausted but excited. He smiled at them. As a squadleader those months in Amaram's army, he'd learned that praise should be honest, but it should never be withheld.

'We need to work on that set-down,' Kaladin said. 'But overall, I'm impressed. Two weeks and you're already working together as well as some teams I trained for months. I'm pleased. And proud. Go get something to drink and take a break. We'll do one or two more runs before work detail.'

It was stone-gathering duty again, but that was nothing to complain about. He'd convinced the men that lifting the stones would improve their strength, and had enlisted the few he trusted the most to help gather the knobweed, the means by which he continued to – just barely – keep the men supplied with extra food and build his stock of medical supplies.

Two weeks. An easy two weeks, as the lives of bridgemen went. Only two bridge runs, and on one they'd gotten to the plateau too late. The Parshendi had escaped with the gemheart before they'd even arrived. That was good for bridgemen.

The other assault hadn't been too bad, by bridgeman numbers. Two more dead: Amark and Koolf. Two more wounded: Narm and Peet. A fraction of what the other crews had lost, but still too many. Kaladin tried to keep his expression optimistic as he walked to the water barrel and took a ladle from one of the men, drinking it down.

Bridge Four would drown in its own wounded. They were only thirty strong, with five wounded who drew no pay and had to be fed out of the knobweed income. Counting those who'd died, they'd taken nearly thirty percent casualties in the weeks he'd begun trying to protect them. In

Amaram's army, that rate of casualties would have been catastrophic.

Back then, Kaladin's life had been one of training and marching, punctuated by occasional frenzied bursts of battle. Here, the fighting was relentless. Every few days. That kind of thing could – *would* – wear an army down.

There has to be a better way, Kaladin thought, swishing the lukewarm water in his mouth, then pouring another ladle on his head. He couldn't continue to lose two men a week to death and wounds. But how could they survive when their own officers didn't care if they lived or died?

He barely kept himself from throwing the ladle into the barrel in frustration. Instead, he handed it to Skar and gave him an encouraging smile. A lie. But an important one.

Gaz watched from the shadow of one of the other bridgeman barracks. Syl's translucent figure – shaped now like floating knobweed fluff – flitted around the bridge sergeant. Eventually, she made her way over to Kaladin, landing on his shoulder, taking her female form.

'He's planning something,' she said.

'He hasn't interfered,' Kaladin said. 'He hasn't even tried to stop us from having the nightly stew.'

'He was talking to that lighteyes.'

'Lamaril?'

She nodded.

'Lamaril's his superior,' Kaladin said as he walked into the shade of Bridge Four's barrack. He leaned against the wall, looking over at his men by the water barrel. They talked to one another now. Joked. Laughed. They went out drinking together in the evenings. Stormfather, but he never thought he'd be *glad* that the men under his command went drinking.

'I didn't like their expressions,' Syl said, sitting down on Kaladin's shoulder. 'Dark. Like thunderclouds. I didn't hear what they were saying. I noticed them too late. But I don't like it, particularly that Lamaril.'

Kaladin nodded slowly.

'You don't trust him either?' Syl asked.

'He's a lighteyes.' That was enough.

'So we—'

'So we do nothing,' Kaladin said. 'I can't respond unless they try something. And if I spend all of my energy worrying about what they *might* do, I won't be able to solve the problems we're facing right now.'

What he didn't add was his real worry. If Gaz or Lamaril decided to have Kaladin killed, there was little he could to do to stop them. True, bridgemen were rarely executed for anything other than failing to run their bridge. But even in an 'honest' force like Amaram's, there had been rumors of trumped-up charges and fake evidence. In Sadeas's undisciplined, barely regulated camp, nobody would blink if Kaladin – a *shash*-branded slave – were strung up on some nebulous charge. They could leave him for the highstorm, washing their hands of his death, claiming that the Stormfather had chosen his fate.

Kaladin stood up straight and walked toward the carpentry section of the lumberyard. The craftsmen and their apprentices were hard at work cutting lengths of wood for spear hafts, bridges, posts, or furniture.

The craftsmen nodded to Kaladin as he passed. They were familiar with him now, used to his odd requests, like pieces of lumber long enough for four men to hold and run with to practice keeping cadence with one another. He found a half-finished bridge. It had eventually grown out of that one plank that Kaladin had used.

Kaladin knelt down, inspecting the wood. A group of men worked with a large saw just to his right, slicing thin rounds off a log. Those would probably become chair seats.

He ran his fingers along the smooth hardwood. All mobile bridges were made of a kind of wood called makam. It had a deep brown color, the grain almost hidden, and was both strong and light. The craftsmen had sanded this length smooth, and it smelled of sawdust and musky sap.

'Kaladin?' Syl asked, walking through the air then stepping onto the wood. 'You look distant.'

'It's ironic how well they craft these bridges,' he said. 'This army's carpenters are far more professional than its soldiers.'

'That makes sense,' she said. 'The craftsmen want to make bridges that last. The soldiers I listen to, they just want to get to the plateau, grab the gemheart, and get away. It's like a game to them.'

'That's astute. You're getting better and better at observing us.'

She grimaced. 'I feel more like I'm remembering things I once knew.'

'Soon you'll hardly be a spren at all. You'll be a little translucent philosopher. We'll have to send you off to a monastery to spend your time in deep, important thoughts.'

'Yes,' she said, 'like how to best get the ardents there to accidentally drink a mixture that will turn their mouths blue.' She smiled mischievously.

Kaladin smiled back, but kept running his finger across the wood. He still didn't understand why they wouldn't let bridgemen carry shields. Nobody would give him a straight answer on the question. 'They use makam because it's strong enough for its weight to support a heavy cavalry charge,' he said. 'We should be able to use this. They deny us shields, but we already carry one on our shoulders.'

'But how would they react if you try that?'

Kaladin stood. 'I don't know, but I also don't have any other choice.'

Trying this would be a risk. A huge risk. But he'd run out of nonrisky ideas days ago.

✦ ✦

'We can hold it here,' Kaladin said, pointing for Rock, Teft, Skar, and Moash. They stood beside a bridge turned up on its side, its underbelly exposed. The bottom was a complicated construction, with eight rows of three positions accommodating up to twenty-four men directly underneath, then sixteen sets of handles – eight on each side – for sixteen more men on the outside. Forty men, running shoulder to shoulder, if they had a full complement.

Each position underneath the bridge had an indentation for the bridgeman's head, two curved blocks of wood to rest on his shoulders, and two rods for handholds. The bridgemen wore shoulder pads, and those who were shorter wore extras to compensate. Gaz generally tried to assign new bridgemen to crews based on their height.

That didn't hold for Bridge Four, of course. Bridge Four just got the leftovers.

Kaladin pointed to several rods and struts. 'We could grab here, then run straight forward, carrying the bridge on its side to our right at a slant. We put our taller men on the outside and our shorter men on the inside.'

'What good would that do?' Rock asked, frowning.

Kaladin glanced at Gaz, who was watching from nearby. Uncomfortably close. Best not to speak of why he really wanted to carry the bridge on its side. Besides, he didn't want to get the men's hopes up until he knew if it would work.

'I just want to experiment,' he said. 'If we can shift positions occasionally, it might be easier. Work different muscles.' Syl frowned as she stood on the top of the bridge. She always frowned when Kaladin obscured the truth.

'Gather the men,' Kaladin said, waving to Rock, Teft, Skar, and Moash. He'd named the four as his subsquad commanders, something that bridgemen didn't normally have. But soldiers worked best in smaller groups of six or eight.

Soldiers, Kaladin thought. *Is that how I think of them?*

They didn't fight. But yes, they were soldiers. It was too easy to underestimate men when you considered them to be 'just' bridgemen. Charging straight at enemy archers without shields took courage. Even when you were compelled to do it.

He glanced to the side, noticing that Moash hadn't left with the other three. The narrow-faced man had dark green eyes and brown hair flecked with black.

'Something wrong, soldier?' Kaladin asked.

Moash blinked in surprise at the use of the word, but he and the others had grown to expect all kinds of unorthodoxy from Kaladin. 'Why did you make me leader of a subsquad?'

'Because you resisted my leadership longer than almost any of the others. And you were flat-out more vocal about it than *any* of them.'

'You made me a squad leader because I refused to obey you?'

'I made you squad leader because you struck me as capable and intelligent. But beyond that, you weren't swayed too easily. You're strong-willed. I can use that.'

Moash scratched his chin, with its short beard. 'All right then. But unlike Teft and that Horneater, I don't think you're a gift straight from the Almighty. I don't trust you.'

'Then why obey me?'

Moash met his eyes, then shrugged. 'Guess I'm curious.' He moved off to gather his squad.

❖

What in the raging winds ... Gaz thought, dumbfounded as he watched Bridge Four charge past. What had possessed them to try carrying the bridge to the *side*?

It required them to clump up in an odd way, forming three rows instead of five, awkwardly clutching the underside of the bridge and holding it off to their right. It was one of the strangest things he'd ever seen. They could barely all fit, and the handholds weren't made for carrying the bridge that way.

Gaz scratched his head as he watched them pass, then held out a hand, stopping Kaladin as he jogged by. The lordling let go of the bridge and hurried up to Gaz, wiping his brow as the others continued running. 'Yes?'

'What is that?' Gaz said, pointing.

'Bridge crew. Carrying what I believe is . . . yes, it's a *bridge*.'

'I didn't ask for lip,' Gaz snarled. 'I want an explanation.'

'Carrying the bridge over our heads gets tiring,' Kaladin said. He was a tall man, tall enough to tower over Gaz. *Storm it, I will not be intimidated!* 'This is a way to use different muscles. Like shifting a pack from one shoulder to the other.'

Gaz glanced to the side. Had something moved in the darkness?

'Gaz?' Kaladin asked.

'Look, lordling,' Gaz said, looking back to him. 'Carrying it overhead may be tiring, but carrying it like *that* is just plain stupid. You look like you're about to stumble over one another, and the handholds are terrible. You can barely fit the men.'

'Yes,' Kaladin said more softly. 'But a lot of the time, only half of a bridge crew will survive a bridge run. We can carry it back this way when there are fewer of us. It will let us shift positions, at least.'

Gaz hesitated. *Only half a bridge crew . . .*

If they carried the bridge like that on an actual assault, they'd go slowly, expose themselves. It could be a *disaster*, for Bridge Four at least.

Gaz smiled. 'I like it.'

Kaladin looked shocked. '*What?*'

'Initiative. Creativity. Yes, keep practicing. I'd very much like to see you make a plateau approach carrying the bridge that way.'

Kaladin narrowed his eyes. 'Is that so?'

'Yes,' Gaz said.

'Well then. Perhaps we will.'

Gaz smiled, watching Kaladin retreat. A disaster was exactly what he needed. Now he just had to find some other way to pay Lamaril's blackmail.

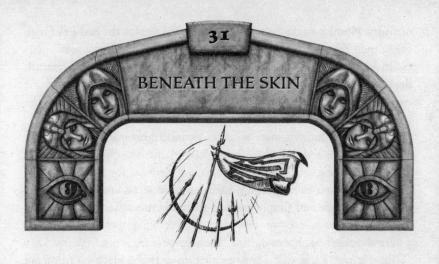

31

BENEATH THE SKIN

SIX YEARS AGO

Don't make the same mistake I did, son.'

Kal looked up from his folio. His father sat on the other side of the operating room, one hand to his head, half-empty cup of wine in his other. Violet wine, among the strongest of liquors.

Lirin set the cup down, and the deep purple liquid – the color of cremling blood – shivered and trembled. It refracted Stormlight from a couple of spheres sitting on the counter.

'Father?'

'When you get to Kharbranth, stay there.' His voice was slurred. 'Don't get sucked back to this tiny, backward, *foolish* town. Don't force your beautiful wife to live away from everyone else she's ever known or loved.'

Kal's father didn't often get drunk; this was a rare night of indulgence. Perhaps because Mother had gone to sleep early, exhausted from her work.

'You've always said I should come back,' Kal said softly.

'I'm an idiot.' His back to Kal, he stared at the wall splashed with white light from the spheres. 'They don't want me here. They never wanted me here.'

Kal looked down at his folio. It contained drawings of dissected bodies, the muscles splayed and pulled out. The drawings were so detailed. Each had glyphpairs to designate every part, and he'd committed those to memory. Now he studied the procedures, delving into the bodies of men long dead.

Once, Laral had told him that men weren't supposed to see beneath the skin. These folios, with their pictures, were part of what made everyone so mistrustful of Lirin. Seeing beneath was like seeing beneath the clothing, only worse.

Lirin poured himself more wine. How much the world could change in a short time. Kal pulled his coat close against the chill. A season of winter had come, but they couldn't afford charcoal for the brazier, for patients no longer gave offerings. Lirin hadn't stopped healing or surgery. The townspeople had simply stopped their donations, all at a word from Roshone.

'He shouldn't be able to do this,' Kal whispered.

'But he can,' Lirin said. He wore a white shirt and black vest atop tan trousers. The vest was unbuttoned, the front flaps hanging down by his sides, like the skin pulled back from the torsos of the men in Kal's drawings.

'We could spend the spheres,' Kal said hesitantly.

'Those are for your education,' Lirin snapped. 'If I could send you now, I would.'

Kal's father and mother had sent a letter to the surgeons in Kharbranth, asking them to let Kal take the entry tests early. They'd responded in the negative.

'He wants us to spend them,' Lirin said, words slurred. 'That's why he said what he did. He's trying to bully us into needing those spheres.'

Roshone's words to the townspeople hadn't *exactly* been a command. He'd just implied that if Kal's father was too foolish to charge, then he shouldn't be paid. The next day, people had stopped donating.

The townsfolk regarded Roshone with a confusing mixture of adoration and fear. In Kal's opinion, he didn't deserve either. Obviously, the man had been banished to Hearthstone because he was so bitter and flawed. He clearly didn't deserve to be among the *real* lighteyes, who fought for vengeance on the Shattered Plains.

'Why do the people try so hard to please him?' Kal asked of his father's back. 'They never reacted this way around Brightlord Wistiow.'

'They do it because Roshone is unappeasable.'

Kal frowned. Was that the wine talking?

Kal's father turned, his eyes reflecting pure Stormlight. In those eyes, Kal saw a surprising lucidity. He wasn't so drunk after all. 'Brightlord Wistiow let men do as they wished. And so they ignored him. Roshone lets them know he finds them contemptible. And so they scramble to please him.'

'That makes no sense,' Kal said.

'It is the way of things,' Lirin said, playing with one of the spheres on the table, rolling it beneath his finger. 'You'll have to learn this, Kal. When men perceive the world as being right, we are content. But if we see a hole – a deficiency – we scramble to fill it.'

'You make it sound noble, what they do.'

'It is in a way,' Lirin said. He sighed. 'I shouldn't be so hard on our neighbors. They're petty, yes, but it's the pettiness of the ignorant. I'm not disgusted by them. I'm disgusted by the one who manipulates them. A man like Roshone can take what is honest and true in men and twist it into a mess of sludge to walk on.' He took a sip, finishing the wine.

'We should just spend the spheres,' Kal said. 'Or send them somewhere, to a moneylender or something. If they were gone, he'd leave us alone.'

'No,' Lirin said softly. 'Roshone is not the kind to spare a man once he is beaten. He's the type who keeps kicking. I don't know what political mistake landed him in this place, but he obviously can't get revenge on his rivals. So we're all he has.' Lirin paused. 'Poor fool.'

Poor fool? Kal thought. *He's trying to destroy our lives, and that's all Father can say?*

What of the stories men sang at the hearths? Tales of clever herdsmen outwitting and overthrowing a foolish lighteyed man. There were dozens of variations, and Kal had heard them all. Shouldn't Lirin fight back somehow? Do something other than sit and wait?

But he didn't say anything; he knew exactly what Lirin would say. *Let me worry about it. Get back to your studies.*

Sighing, Kal settled back in his chair, opening his folio again. The surgery room was dim, lit by the four spheres on the table and a single one Kal used for reading. Lirin kept most of the spheres closed up in their cupboard, hidden away. Kal held up his own sphere, lighting the page. There were longer explanations of procedures in the back that his mother could read to him. She was the only woman in the town who could read, though Lirin said it wasn't uncommon among wellborn darkeyed women in the cities.

As he studied, Kal idly pulled something from his pocket. A rock that had been sitting on his chair for him when he'd come in to study. He recognized it as a favorite one that Tien had been carrying around recently. Now he'd left it for Kaladin; he often did that, hoping that his older brother would be able to see the beauty in it too, though they all just looked like ordinary rocks. He'd have to ask Tien what he found so special about this particular one. There was always something.

Tien spent his days now learning carpentry from Ral, one of the men in the town. Lirin had set him to it reluctantly; he'd been hoping for another surgery assistant, but Tien couldn't stand the sight of blood. He froze every time, and hadn't gotten used to it. That was troubling. Kal had hoped that his father would have Tien as an assistant when he left. And Kal *was* leaving, one way or another. He hadn't decided between the army or Kharbranth, though in recent months, he'd begun leaning toward becoming a spearman.

If he took that route, he'd have to do it stealthily, once he was old enough that the recruiters would take him over his parents' objections. Fifteen would probably be old enough. Five more months. For now, he figured that knowing the muscles – and vital parts of a body – would be pretty useful for either a surgeon or a spearman.

A thump came at the door. Kal jumped. It hadn't been a knock, but a *thump*. It came again. It sounded like something heavy pushing or slamming against the wood.

'What in the stormwinds?' Lirin said, rising from his stool. He crossed the small room; his undone vest brushed the operating table, button scraping the wood.

Another thump. Kal scrambled out of his chair, closing the folio. At fourteen and a half, he was nearly as tall as his father now. A scraping came at the door, like nails or claws. Kal raised a hand toward his father, suddenly terrified. It was late at night, dark in the room, and the town was silent.

There was *something* outside. It sounded like a beast. Inhuman. A den of whitespines were said to be making trouble nearby, striking at travelers on the roadway. Kal had an image in his head of the reptilian creatures, as big as horses but with carapace across their backs. Was one of them sniffing at the door? Brushing it, trying to force its way in?

'Father!' Kal yelped.

Lirin pulled open the door. The dim light of the spheres revealed not a monster, but a man wearing black clothing. He had a long metal bar in his hands, and he wore a black wool mask with holes cut for the eyes. Kal felt his heart race in panic as the would-be intruder leapt backward.

'Didn't expect to find anyone inside, did you?' Kal's father said. 'It's been years since there was a theft in the town. I'm ashamed of you.'

'Give us the spheres!' a voice called out of the darkness. Another figure moved in the shadows, and then another.

Stormfather! Kal clutched the folio to his chest with trembling hands. *How many are there?* Highwaymen, come to rob the town! Such things happened. More and more frequently these days, Kal's father said.

How could Lirin be so calm?

'Those spheres ain't yours,' another voice called.

'Is that so?' Kal's father said. 'Does that make them yours? You think he'd let you keep them?' Kal's father spoke as if they weren't bandits from outside the town. Kal crept forward to stand just behind his father, frightened – but at the same time ashamed of that fear. The men in the darkness were shadowy, nightmarish things, moving back and forth, faces of black.

'We'll give them to him,' one voice said.

'No need for this to get violent, Lirin,' another added. 'You ain't going to spend them anyway.'

Kal's father snorted. He ducked into the room. Kal cried out, moving back as Lirin threw open the cabinet where he kept the spheres. He grabbed the large glass goblet that he stored them in; it was covered with a black cloth.

'You want them?' Lirin called, walking to the doorway, passing Kal.

'Father?' Kal said, panicked.

'You want the light for yourself?' Lirin's voice grew louder. 'Here!'

He pulled the cloth free. The goblet exploded with fiery radiance, the brightness nearly blinding. Kal raised his arm. His father was a shadowed silhouette that seemed to hold the sun itself in its fingers.

The large goblet shone with a calm light. Almost a *cold* light. Kal blinked away tears, his eyes adjusting. He could see the men outside clearly now. Where dangerous shadows had once loomed, cringing men now raised hands. They didn't seem so intimidating; in fact, the cloths over their faces looked ridiculous.

Where Kal had been afraid, he now felt strangely confident. For a moment, it wasn't light his father held, but understanding itself. *That's Luten*, Kal thought, noticing a man who limped. It was easy to distinguish him, despite the mask. Kal's father had operated on that leg; it was because of him that Luten could still walk. He recognized others too. Harl was the one with the wide shoulders, Balsas the man wearing the nice new coat.

Lirin didn't say anything to them at first. He stood with that light blazing, illuminating the entire stone square outside. The men seemed to shrink down, as if they knew he recognized them.

'Well?' Lirin said. 'You've threatened violence against me. Come. Hit me. Rob me. Do it knowing I've lived among you almost my entire life. Do it knowing that I've healed your children. Come in. Bleed one of your own!'

The men faded into the night without a word.

32

SIDE CARRY

'They lived high atop a place no man could reach, but all could visit. The tower city itself, crafted by the hands of no man.'

—Though *The Song of the Last Summer* is a fanciful tale of romance from the third century after the Recreance, it is likely a valid reference in this case. See page 27 of Varala's translation, and note the undertext.

They got better at carrying the bridge on its side. But not much better.

Kaladin watched Bridge Four pass, moving awkwardly, maneuvering the bridge at their sides. Fortunately, there were plenty of handles on the bridge's underside, and they'd found how to grip them in the right way. They had to carry it at less steep an angle than he'd wanted. That would expose their legs, but maybe he could train them to adjust to it as the arrows flew.

As it was, their carry was slow, and the bridgemen were so bunched up that if the Parshendi managed to drop a man, the others would stumble over him. Lose just a few men, and the balance would be upset so they'd drop it for certain.

This will have to be handled very carefully, Kaladin thought.

Syl fluttered along behind the bridge crew as a flurry of nearly translucent leaves. Beyond her, something caught Kaladin's eye: a uniformed soldier leading a ragged group of men in a despondent clump. *Finally*, Kaladin thought. He'd been waiting for another group of recruits. He waved curtly to Rock. The Horneater nodded; he'd take over training. It was time for a break anyway.

Kaladin jogged up the short incline at the rim of the lumberyard, arriving just as Gaz intercepted the newcomers.

'What a sorry batch,' Gaz said. 'I thought we'd been sent the dregs last time, but this lot ...'

Lamaril shrugged. 'They're yours now, Gaz. Split them up how you like.' He and his soldiers departed, leaving the unfortunate conscripts. Some wore decent clothing; they'd be recently caught criminals. The rest had slave brands on their foreheads. Seeing them brought back feelings that Kaladin had to force down. He still stood on the very top of a steep slope; one wrong step could send him tumbling back down into that despair.

'In a line, you cremlings,' Gaz snapped at the new recruits, pulling free his cudgel and waving it. He eyed Kaladin, but said nothing.

The group of men hastily lined up.

Gaz counted down the line, picking out the taller members. 'You five men, you're in Bridge Six. Remember that. Forget it, and I'll see you get a whipping.' He counted off another group. 'You six men, you're in Bridge Fourteen. You four at the end, Bridge Three. You, you, and you, Bridge One. Bridge Two doesn't need any ... You four, Bridge Seven.'

That was all of them.

'Gaz,' Kaladin said, folding his arms. Syl landed on his shoulder, her small tempest of leaves forming into a young woman.

Gaz turned to him.

'Bridge Four is down to thirty fighting members.'

'Bridge Six and Bridge Fourteen have fewer than that.'

'They each had twenty-nine and you just gave them both a big helping of new members. And Bridge One is at thirty-seven, and you sent *them* three new men.'

'You barely lost anyone on the last run, and—'

Kaladin caught Gaz's arm as the sergeant tried to walk away. Gaz flinched, lifting his cudgel.

Try it, Kaladin thought, meeting Gaz's eye. He almost wished that the sergeant would.

Gaz gritted his teeth. 'Fine. One man.'

'I pick him,' Kaladin said.

'Whatever. They're all worthless anyway.'

Kaladin turned to the group of new bridgemen. They'd gathered into clusters by which bridge crew Gaz had put them in. Kaladin immediately turned his attention to the taller men. By slave standards, they appeared well fed. Two of them looked like they'd—

'Hey, gancho!' a voice said from another group. 'Hey! You want me, I think.'

Kaladin turned. A short, spindly man was waving to him. The man had only one arm. Who would assign him to be a bridgeman?

He'd stop an arrow, Kaladin thought. *That's all some bridgemen are good for, in the eyes of the uppers.*

The man had brown hair and deep tan skin just a shade too dark to be Alethi. The fingernails on his hand were slate-colored and crystalline – he was a Herdazian, then. Most of the newcomers shared the same defeated look of apathy but this man was *smiling*, though he wore a slave's mark on his head.

That mark is old, Kaladin thought. *Either he had a kind master before this, or he has somehow resisted being beaten down.* The man obviously didn't understand what awaited him as a bridgeman. No person would smile if they understood that.

'You can use me,' the man said. 'We Herdazians are great fighters, gon.' He pronounced that last word like 'gone' and it appeared to refer to Kaladin. 'You see, this one time, I was with, sure, three men and they were drunk and all but I still beat them.' He spoke at a very quick pace, his thick accent slurring the words together.

He'd make a terrible bridgeman. He *might* be able to run with the bridge on his shoulders, but not maneuver it. He even looked a little flabby around the waist. Whatever bridge crew got him would put him right in the front and let him take an arrow, then be rid of him.

Gotta do what you can to stay alive, a voice from his past seemed to whisper. *Turn a liability into an advantage. . . .*

Tien.

'Very well,' Kaladin said, pointing. 'I'll take the Herdazian at the back.'

'*What?*' Gaz said.

The short man sauntered up to Kaladin. 'Thanks, gancho! You'll be glad you picked me.'

Kaladin turned to walk back, passing Gaz. The bridge sergeant scratched his head. 'You pushed me that hard so you could pick the one-armed runt?'

Kaladin walked on without a word for Gaz. Instead, he turned to the one-armed Herdazian. 'Why did you want to come with me? You don't know anything about the different bridge crews.'

'You were only picking one,' the man said. 'That means one man gets to be special, the others don't. I've got a good feeling about you. It's in your eyes, gancho.' He paused. 'What's a bridge crew?'

Kaladin found himself smiling at the man's nonchalant attitude. 'You'll see. What's your name?'

'Lopen,' the man said. 'Some of my cousins, they call me *the* Lopen because they haven't ever heard anyone else named that. I've asked around a lot, maybe one hundred . . . or two hundred . . . lots of people, sure. And nobody has heard of that name.'

Kaladin blinked at the torrent of words. Did the man ever stop to breathe?

Bridge Four was taking their break, their massive bridge resting on one side and giving shade. The five wounded had joined them and were chatting; even Leyten was up, which was encouraging. He'd been having a lot of trouble walking, what with that crushed leg. Kaladin had done what he could, but the man would always have a limp.

The only one who didn't talk to the others was Dabbid, the man who had been so profoundly shocked by battle. He followed the others, but he didn't talk. Kaladin was starting to fear that the man would never recover from his mind fatigue.

Hobber – the round-faced, gap-toothed man who had taken an arrow to the leg – was walking without a crutch. It wouldn't be long before he could start running bridges again, and a good thing, too. They needed every pair of hands they could get.

'Head to the barrack there,' Kaladin said to Lopen. 'There's a blanket, sandals, and vest for you in the pile at the very back.'

'Sure,' Lopen said, sauntering off. He waved at a few of the men as he passed.

Rock walked up to Kaladin, folding his arms. 'Is new member?'

'Yes,' Kaladin said.

'The only kind Gaz would give us, I assume.' Rock sighed. 'This thing, we should have expected it. He will give us only the very most useless of bridgemen from now on.'

Kaladin was tempted to say something in the way of agreement, but hesitated. Syl would probably see it as a lie, and that would annoy her.

'This new way of carrying the bridge,' Rock said. 'Is not very useful, I think. Is—'

He cut off as a horn call blared over the camp, echoing against stone buildings like the bleat of a distant greatshell. Kaladin grew tense. His men were on duty. He waited, tense, until the third set of horns blew.

'Line up!' Kaladin yelled. 'Let's move!'

Unlike the other nineteen crews on duty, Kaladin's men didn't scramble about in confusion, but assembled in an orderly fashion. Lopen dashed out, wearing a vest, then hesitated, looking at the four squads, not knowing where to go. He'd be cut to ribbons if Kaladin put him in front, but he'd probably just slow them down anywhere else.

'Lopen!' Kaladin shouted.

The one-armed man saluted. *Does he think he's actually in the military?* 'You see that rain barrel? Go get some waterskins from the carpenter's assistants. They told me we could borrow some. Fill as many as you can, then catch up down below.'

'Sure, gancho,' Lopen said.

'Bridge up!' Kaladin shouted, moving into position at the front. 'Shoulder carry!'

Bridge Four moved. While some of the other bridge crews were crowded around their barracks, Kaladin's team charged across the lumber-yard. They were first down the incline, and reached the first permanent bridge before the army even formed up. There, Kaladin ordered them to put their bridge down and wait.

Shortly thereafter, Lopen trotted down the hillside – and, surprisingly, Dabbid and Hobber were with him. They couldn't move fast, not with Hobber's limp, but they had constructed a sort of litter with a tarp and two lengths of wood. Piled into the middle of it were a good twenty waterskins. They trotted up to the bridge team.

'What's this?' Kaladin said.

'You told me to bring whatever I could carry, gon,' Lopen said. 'Well, we got this thing from the carpenters. They use it to carry pieces of wood, they said, and they weren't using it so we took it and now we're here. Ain't that right, moolie?' He said that last to Dabbid, who just nodded.

'Moolie?' Kaladin asked.

'Means mute,' Lopen said, shrugging. ''Cuz he doesn't seem to talk much, you see.'

'I see. Well, good job. Bridge Four, back in position. Here comes the rest of the army.'

The next few hours were what they had grown to expect from bridge runs. Grueling conditions, carrying the heavy bridge across plateaus. The water proved a huge help. The army occasionally watered the bridgemen during runs, but never as often as the men needed it. Being able to take a drink after crossing each plateau was as good as having a half-dozen more men.

But the real difference came from the practice. Bridge Four's men no longer fell exhausted each time they set a bridge down. The work was still difficult, but their bodies were ready for it. Kaladin caught more than a few glances of surprise or envy from the other bridge crews as his men laughed and joked instead of collapsing. Running a bridge once a week or so – as the other men did – just wasn't enough. An extra meal each night combined with training had built up his men's muscles and prepared them to work.

The march was a long one, as long as Kaladin had ever made. They traveled eastward for hours. That was a bad sign. When they aimed for closer plateaus, they often got there before the Parshendi. But this far out they were racing just to prevent the Parshendi from escaping with the gemheart; there was no chance they'd arrive before the enemy.

That meant it would probably be a difficult approach. *We're not ready for the side carry,* Kaladin thought nervously, as they finally drew close to an enormous plateau rising in an unusual shape. He'd heard of it – the Tower, it was called. No Alethi force had ever won a gemheart here.

They set their bridge down before the penultimate chasm, positioning it, and Kaladin felt a foreboding as the scouts crossed. The Tower was wedge-shaped, uneven, with the eastern point rising far into the air, creating a steep hillside. Sadeas had brought a large number of soldiers; this plateau was enormous, allowing the deployment of a larger force. Kaladin waited, anxious. Maybe they'd be lucky, and the Parshendi would already be gone with the gemheart. It was possible, this far out.

The scouts came charging back. 'Enemy lines on the opposing rim! They haven't gotten the chrysalis open yet!'

Kaladin groaned softly. The army began to cross on his bridge, and Bridge Four regarded him, solemn, expressions grim. They knew what would come next. Some of them, perhaps many of them, would not survive.

It was going to be very bad this time. On previous runs, they'd had a buffer. When they'd lost four or five men, they'd still been able to keep going. Now they were running with just thirty members. Every man they lost would slow them measurably, and the loss of just four or five more would cause them to wobble, or even topple. When that happened, the Parshendi would focus everything on them. He'd seen it happen before. If a bridge crew started to teeter, the Parshendi pounced.

Besides, when a bridge crew was visibly low on numbers, it always got targeted by the Parshendi to be taken down. Bridge Four was in trouble. This run could easily end with fifteen or twenty deaths. Something had to be done.

This was it.

'Gather close,' Kaladin said.

The men frowned, stepping up to him.

'We're going to carry the bridge in side position,' Kaladin said softly. 'I'll go first. I'm going to steer; be ready to go in the direction I do.'

'Kaladin,' Teft said, 'side position is slow. It was an interesting idea, but—'

'Do you trust me, Teft?' Kaladin asked.

'Well, I guess.' The grizzled man glanced at the others. Kaladin could see that many of them did not, at least not fully.

'This will work,' Kaladin said intently. 'We're going to use the bridge as a shield to block arrows. We need to hurry out in front, faster than the other bridges. It'll be hard to outrun them with the side carry, but it's the only thing I can think of. If it doesn't work, I'll be in front, so I'll be the first to drop. If I die, move the bridge to shoulder-carry. We've practiced doing that. Then you'll be rid of me.'

The bridgemen were silent.

'What if we don't want to be rid of you?' long-faced Natam asked.

Kaladin smiled. 'Then run swiftly and follow my lead. I'm going to turn us unexpectedly during the run; be ready to change directions.'

He went back to the bridge. The common soldiers were across, and the lighteyes – including Sadeas in his ornate Shardplate – were riding over the span. Kaladin and Bridge Four followed, then pulled the bridge behind them. They shoulder-carried it to the front of the army and put it down, waiting for the other bridges to get in place. Lopen and the other two water-carriers hung back with Gaz; it looked like they wouldn't get into trouble for not running. That was a small blessing.

Kaladin felt sweat bead on his forehead. He could just barely make out the Parshendi ranks ahead, on the other side of the chasm. Men of black and crimson, shortbows held at the ready, arrows nocked. The enormous slope of the Tower rose behind them.

Kaladin's heart beat faster. Anticipationspren sprung up around members of the army, but not his team. To their credit, there weren't any fearspren either – not that they didn't feel fear, they just weren't as panicked as the other bridge crews, so the fearspren went there instead.

Care, Tukks seemed to whisper at him from the past. *The key to fighting isn't lack of passion, it's controlled passion. Care about winning. Care about those you defend. You* have *to care about something.*

I care, Kaladin thought. *Storm me as a fool, but I do.*

'Bridges up!' Gaz's voice echoed across the front lines, repeating the order given him by Lamaril.

Bridge Four moved, quickly turning the bridge on its side and hoisting it up. The shorter men made a line, holding the bridge up to their right, with the taller men forming a bunched-up line behind them, reaching through and lifting or reaching high and steadying the bridge. Lamaril gave them a harsh look, and Kaladin's breath caught in his throat.

Gaz stepped up and whispered something to Lamaril. The lighteyes nodded slowly, and said nothing. The assault call sounded.

Bridge Four charged.

From behind them, arrows flew in a wave over the bridge crews' heads, arcing down toward the Parshendi. Kaladin ran, jaw clenched. He had trouble keeping himself from stumbling over the rockbuds and shale-bark growths. Fortunately, though his team was slower than normal, their practice and endurance meant they were still faster than the other crews. With Kaladin at their lead, Bridge Four managed to get out ahead of the others.

That was important, because Kaladin angled his team slightly to the right, as if his crew were just a tad off-course with the heavy bridge at the side. The Parshendi knelt down and began to chant together. Alethi arrows fell among them, distracting some, but the others raised bows.

Get ready ... Kaladin thought. He pushed harder, and felt a sudden surge of strength. His legs stopped straining, his breath stopped wheezing. Perhaps it was the anxiety of battle, perhaps it was numbness setting in, but the unexpected strength gave him a slight sense of euphoria. He felt as if something were buzzing within him, mixing with his blood.

In that moment it felt like he was *pulling* the bridge behind him all alone, like a sail towing the ship beneath it. He turned farther to the right, running at a deeper angle, putting himself and his men in full sight of the Parshendi archers.

The Parshendi continued to chant, somehow knowing – without orders – when to draw their bows. They pulled arrows to marbled cheeks, sighting on the bridgemen. As expected, many aimed at his men.

Almost close enough!

Just a few heartbeats more ...

Now!

Kaladin turned sharply to the left just as the Parshendi loosed. The bridge moved with him, now charging with the face of the bridge pointed toward the archers. Arrows flew, snapping against the wood, digging into it. Some arrows rattled against the stone beneath their feet. The bridge resounded with the impacts.

Kaladin heard desperate screams of pain from the other bridge crews. Men fell, some of them probably on their first run. In Bridge Four, nobody cried out. Nobody fell.

Kaladin turned the bridge again, running angled in the other direction, the bridgemen exposed again. The surprised Parshendi nocked arrows. Normally, they fired in waves. That gave Kaladin an opportunity, for as soon as the Parshendi got the arrows drawn, he turned, using the bulky bridge as a shield.

Again, arrows snapped into the wood. Again, other bridge crews screamed. Again, Kaladin's zigzagging run protected his men.

One more, Kaladin thought. This would be the tough one. The Parshendi would know what he was doing. They'd be ready to fire once he turned back.

He turned.

Nobody fired.

Amazed, he realized that the Parshendi archers had turned all of their attention to the other bridge crews, seeking easier targets. The space in front of Bridge Four was virtually empty.

The chasm was near, and – despite his angling – Kaladin brought his team in on-mark to place their bridge in the right spot. They all had to be aligned close together for the cavalry charge to work. Kaladin quickly gave the order to drop. Some of the Parshendi archers turned their attention back, but most ignored them, firing their arrows at the other crews.

A crash from behind announced a bridge falling. Kaladin and his men pushed, the Alethi archers behind pelting the Parshendi to distract them and keep them from shoving the bridge back. Still pushing, Kaladin risked a glance over his shoulder.

The next bridge in line was close. It was Bridge Seven, but they were floundering, arrow after arrow striking them, cutting them down in rows. They fell as he watched, bridge crashing to the stones. Now Bridge Twenty-seven was wavering. Two other bridges were already down. Bridge Six had reached the chasm, but just barely, over half its members down. Where were the other bridge crews? He couldn't tell from his quick glance, and had to turn back to his work.

Kaladin's men placed their bridge with a thump, and Kaladin gave the call to pull back. He and his men dashed away to let the cavalry charge across. But no cavalry came. Sweat dripping from his brow, Kaladin spun.

Five other bridge crews had set their bridges, but others were still struggling to reach the chasm. Unexpectedly, they'd tried tilting their bridges to block the arrows, emulating Kaladin and his team. Many stumbled, some men attempting to lower the bridge for protection while others still ran forward.

It was chaos. These men hadn't practiced the side carry. As one straggling crew tried to hold their bridge up in the new position, they dropped it. Two more bridge crews were cut down completely by the Parshendi, who continued to fire.

Heavy cavalry charged, crossing the six bridges that had been set. Normally, two riders abreast on each bridge added up to a mass of a hundred horsemen, thirty to forty across and three ranks deep. That depended on many bridges aligned in a row, allowing an effective charge against the hundreds of Parshendi archers.

But the bridges had been set too erratically. Some cavalry got across, but they were scattered, and couldn't ride down the Parshendi without fear of being surrounded.

Foot soldiers had started to help push Bridge Six into place. *We should go help*, Kaladin realized. *Get those other bridges across.*

But it was too late. Though Kaladin stood near the battlefield, his men – as was their practice – had fallen back to the nearest rock outcropping for shelter. The one they'd chosen was close enough to see the battle, but was well protected from arrows. The Parshendi always ignored bridgemen after the initial assault, though the Alethi were careful to leave rear guards to protect the landing point and watch for Parshendi trying to cut off their retreat.

The soldiers finally maneuvered Bridge Six into place, and two more bridge crews got theirs down, but half of the bridges hadn't made it. The army had to reorganize on the run, dashing forward to support the cavalry, splitting to cross where the bridges had been set.

Teft left the outcropping and grabbed Kaladin by the arm, tugging him back to relative safety. Kaladin allowed himself to be pulled along, but he still looked at the battlefield, a horrible realization coming to him.

Rock stepped up beside Kaladin, clapping him on the shoulder. The large Horneater's hair was plastered to his head with sweat, but he was smiling broadly. 'Is miracle! Not a single man wounded!'

Moash stepped up beside them. 'Stormfather! I can't believe what we just did. Kaladin, you've changed bridge runs forever!'

'No,' Kaladin said softly. 'I've completely undermined our assault.'

'I— What?'

Stormfather! Kaladin thought. The heavy cavalry had been cut off. A cavalry charge needed an unbroken line; it was the intimidation as much as anything that made it work.

But here, the Parshendi could dodge out of the way, then come at the horsemen from the flanks. And the foot soldiers hadn't gotten in quickly enough to help. Several groups of horsemen fought completely sur-rounded. Soldiers bunched up around the bridges that had been set, trying to get across, but the Parshendi had a solid foothold and were repelling them. Spearmen fell from the bridges, and the Parshendi then managed to topple one entire bridge into the chasm. The Alethi forces were soon on the defensive, the soldiers focused on holding the bridgeheads to secure an avenue of retreat for the cavalry.

Kaladin watched, really *watched*. He'd never studied the tactics and needs of the entire army in these assaults. He'd considered only the needs of his own crew. It was a foolish mistake, and he should have known better. He *would* have known better, if he'd still thought of himself as a real soldier. He hated Sadeas; he hated the way the man used bridge crews. But he shouldn't have changed Bridge Four's basic tactics without considering the larger scheme of the battle.

I deflected attention to the other bridge crews, Kaladin thought. *That got us to the chasm too soon, and slowed some of the others.*

And, since he'd run out in front, many other bridgemen had gotten a good view of how he'd used the bridge as a shield. That had led them to emulate Bridge Four. Each of the crews had ended up running at a different speed, and the Alethi archers hadn't known where to focus their volleys to soften the Parshendi for the bridge landings.

Stormfather! I've just cost Sadeas this battle.

There would be repercussions. The bridgemen had been forgotten while the generals and captains scrambled to revise their battle plans. But once this was over, they would come for him.

Or maybe it would happen sooner. Gaz and Lamaril, with a group of reserve spearmen, were marching toward Bridge Four.

Rock stepped up beside Kaladin on one side, a nervous Teft on the other, holding a stone in his hands. The bridgemen behind Kaladin began to mutter.

'Stand down,' Kaladin said softly to Rock and Teft.

'But, Kaladin!' Teft said. 'They—'

'Stand down. Gather the bridgemen. Get them back to the lumberyard safely, if you can.' *If any of us escape this disaster.*

When Rock and Teft didn't back away, Kaladin stepped forward. The battle still raged on the Tower; Sadeas's group – led by the Shardbearer himself – had managed to claim a small section of ground and were holding it doggedly. Corpses piled up on both sides. It wouldn't be enough.

Rock and Teft moved up beside Kaladin again, but he stared them down, forcing them back. Then he turned to Gaz and Lamaril. *I'll point out that Gaz told me to do this*, he thought. *He suggested I use a side carry on a bridge assault.*

But no. There were no witnesses. It would be his word against Gaz's. That wouldn't work – plus, that argument would leave Gaz and Lamaril with good reason to see Kaladin dead immediately, before he could speak to their superiors.

Kaladin needed to do something else.

'Do you have any idea what you've done?' Gaz sputtered as he grew near.

'I've upended the army's strategy,' Kaladin said, 'throwing the entire assault force into chaos. You've come to punish me so that when your superiors come screaming to you for what happened, you can at least show that you acted quickly to deal with the one responsible.'

Gaz paused, Lamaril and the spearmen stopping around him. The bridge sergeant looked surprised.

'If it's worth anything,' Kaladin said grimly, 'I didn't know this would happen. I was just trying to survive.'

'Bridgemen aren't *supposed* to survive,' Lamaril said curtly. He waved to a pair of his soldiers, then pointed at Kaladin.

'If you leave me alive,' Kaladin said, 'I promise I will tell your superiors that you had nothing to do with this. If you kill me, it will look like you were trying to hide something.'

'Hide something?' Gaz said, glancing at the battle on the Tower. A stray arrow clattered across the rocks a short distance from him, shaft breaking. 'What would we have to hide?'

'Depends. This very well *could* look like it was your idea from the start. Brightlord Lamaril, you didn't stop me. You could have, but you didn't, and soldiers saw Gaz and you speaking when you saw what I did. If I can't vouch for your ignorance of what I was going to do, then you'll look very, very bad.'

Lamaril's soldiers looked to their leader. The lighteyed man scowled. 'Beat him,' he said, 'but don't kill him.' He turned and marched back toward the Alethi reserve lines.

The beefy spearmen walked up to Kaladin. They were darkeyed, but they might as well have been Parshendi for all the sympathy they would show him. Kaladin closed his eyes and steeled himself. He couldn't fight them all off. Not and remain with Bridge Four.

A spear butt to the gut knocked him to the ground, and he gasped as the soldiers began to kick. One booted foot tore open his belt pouch. His spheres – too precious to leave in the barrack – scattered across the stones. They had somehow lost their Stormlight, and were now dun, their life run out.

The soldiers kept kicking.

Analysis of four world cities and their underlying forms based on city plans found in the archives of the Palanaeum, Kharbranth.

Akinah

When one removes the current streets and main byways of Akinah, Thaylen City, Vedenar, and Kholinar and combines the street blocks into larger shapes, leaving behind the natural rock formations upon which these cities were originally built, the underlying pattern of the stone becomes more clear.

Thaylen City

The divine ten-part symmetry of Akinah is accentuated when the shape of the city is viewed from above. Amidst the lines of Thaylen City a star pattern emerges. Twisting streets of Vedenar become an organized pattern of arrows and circles.

Vedenar

In the case of Kholinar, even the city walls follow the contour of the subcartographal rock formations known as the Windblades. The walls incorporate the formations, using them to augment the defensive strength of the city.

Kholinar

I am left wondering if this is a strange coincidence. And if not, then what does it all mean?

The Scholar, Kabsal

*'They changed, even as we fought them. Like shadows they were, that
can transform as the ame dances. Never underestimate them because
of what you first see.'*

—Purports to be a scrap collected from Talatin, a Radiant of the Order of
Stonewards. The source – Guvlow's *Incarnate* – is generally held as
reliable, though this is from a copied fragment of 'The Poem of the
Seventh Morning,' which has been lost.

Sometimes, when Shallan walked into the Palanaeum proper – the
grand storehouse of books, manuscripts, and scrolls beyond the
study areas of the Veil – she grew so distracted by the beauty and
scope of it that she forgot everything else.

The Palanaeum was shaped like an inverted pyramid carved down into
the rock. It had balcony walkways suspended around its perimeter. Slanted
gently downward, they ran around all four walls to form a majestic square
spiral, a giant staircase pointing toward the center of Roshar. A series of
lifts provided a quicker method of descending.

Standing at the top level's railing, Shallan could see only halfway to the
bottom. This place seemed too large, too grand, to have been shaped by
the hands of men. How had the terraced levels been aligned so perfectly?

Had Soulcasters been used to create the open spaces? How many gemstones would that have taken?

The lighting was dim; there was no general illumination, only small emerald lamps focused to illuminate the walkway floors. Ardents from the Devotary of Insight periodically moved through the levels, changing the spheres. There had to be hundreds upon hundreds of the emeralds here; apparently, they made up the Kharbranthian royal treasury. What better place for them than the extremely secure Palanaeum? Here they could both be protected and serve to illuminate the enormous library.

Shallan continued on her way. Her parshman servant carried a sphere lantern containing a trio of sapphire marks. The soft blue light reflected against the stone walls, portions of which had been Soulcast into quartz purely for ornamentation. The railings had been carved from wood, then transformed to marble. When she ran her fingers across one, she could feel the original wood's grain. At the same time, it had the cold smoothness of stone. An oddity that seemed designed to confuse the senses.

Her parshman carried a small basket of books full of drawings by famous natural scientists. Jasnah had begun allowing Shallan to spend some of her study time on topics of her own choosing. Just a single hour a day, but it was remarkable how precious that hour had become. Recently, she'd been digging through Myalmr's *Western Voyages*.

The world was a wondrous place. She hungered to learn more, wished to observe each and every one of its creatures, to have sketches of them in her books. To organize Roshar by capturing it in images. The books she read, though wonderful, all felt incomplete. Each author would be good with words or with drawings, but rarely both. And if the author *was* good with both, then her grasp of science would be poor.

There were so many holes in their understanding. Holes that Shallan could fill.

No, she told herself firmly as she walked. *That's not what I'm here to do.*

It was getting harder and harder to stay focused on the theft, though Jasnah – as Shallan had hoped – had begun using her as a bathing attendant. That might soon present the opportunity she needed. And yet, the more she studied, the more she hungered for knowledge.

She led her parshman to one of the lifts. There, two other parshmen began lowering her. Shallan eyed the basket of books. She could spend her time on the lift reading, maybe finish that section of *Western Voyages* . . .

She turned away from the basket. *Stay focused*. On the fifth level down, she stepped out into the smaller walkway that connected the lift to the sloping ramps set into the walls. Upon reaching the wall, she turned right and continued down a little farther. The wall was lined with doorways and, finding the one she wanted, she entered a large stone chamber filled with tall bookshelves. 'Wait here,' she said to her parshman as she dug her drawing folio out of the basket. She tucked it under her arm, took the lantern, and hurried into the stacks.

One could disappear for hours in the Palanaeum and never see another soul. Shallan rarely saw anyone while searching out an obscure book for Jasnah. There were ardents and servants to fetch volumes, of course, but Jasnah thought it important for Shallan to practice doing it herself. Apparently the Kharbranthian filing system was now standard for many of Roshar's libraries and archives.

At the back of the room, she found a small desk of cobwood. She set her lantern on one side and sat on the stool, getting out her portfolio. The room was silent and dark, her lantern light revealing the ends of bookshelves to her right and a smooth stone wall to her left. The air smelled of old paper and dust. Not wet. It was never damp in the Palanaeum. Perhaps the dryness had something to do with the long troughs of white powder at the ends of each room.

She undid her portfolio's leather ties. Inside, the top sheets were blank, and the next few contained drawings she'd done of people in the Palanaeum. More faces for her collection. Hidden in the middle was a far more important set of drawings: sketches of Jasnah performing Soulcastings.

The princess used her Soulcaster infrequently; perhaps she hesitated to use it when Shallan was around. But Shallan had caught a handful of occasions, mostly when Jasnah had been distracted, and had apparently forgotten she wasn't alone.

Shallan held up one picture. Jasnah, sitting in the alcove, hand to the side and touching a crumpled piece of notepaper, a gem on her Soulcaster glowing. Shallan held up the next picture. It depicted the same scene just seconds later. The paper had become a ball of flames. It hadn't burned. No, it had *become fire*. Tongues of flame coiling, a flash of heat in the air. What had been on it that Jasnah wished to hide?

Another picture showed Jasnah Soulcasting the wine in her cup into a chunk of crystal to use as a paperweight, the goblet itself holding down another stack, on one of the rare occasions when they'd dined – and studied – on a patio outside the Conclave. There was also the one of Jasnah burning words after running out of ink. When Shallan had seen her burning letters into a page, she'd been amazed at the Soulcaster's precision.

It seemed that this Soulcaster was attuned to three Essences in particular: Vapor, Spark, and Lucentia. But it should be able to create any of the Ten Essences, from Zephyr to Talus. That last one was the most important to Shallan, as Talus included stone and earth. She *could* create new mineral deposits for her family to exploit. It would work; Soulcasters were very rare in Jah Keved, and her family's marble, jade, and opal would sell at a premium. They couldn't create actual gemstones with a Soulcaster – that was said to be impossible – but they could create other deposits of near equal value.

Once those new deposits ran out, they'd have to move to less lucrative trades. That would be all right, though. By then, they'd have paid off their debts and compensated those to whom promises had been broken. House Davar would become unimportant again, but would not collapse.

Shallan studied the pictures again. The Alethi princess seemed remarkably casual about Soulcasting. She held one of the most powerful artifacts in all of Roshar, and she used it to create *paperweights*? What else did she use the Soulcaster for, when Shallan wasn't watching? Jasnah seemed to use it less frequently in her presence now than she had at first.

Shallan fished in the safepouch inside her sleeve, bringing out her father's broken Soulcaster. It had been sheared in two places: across one of the chains and through the setting that held one of the stones. She inspected it in the light, looking – not for the first time – for signs of that damage. The link in the chain had been replaced perfectly and the setting reforged equally well. Even knowing exactly where the cuts had been, she couldn't find any flaw. Unfortunately, repairing only the outward defects hadn't made it functional.

She hefted the heavy construction of metal and chains. Then she put it on, looping chains around her thumb, small finger, and middle finger. There were no gemstones in the device at present. She compared the broken Soulcaster to the drawings, inspecting it from all sides. Yes, it looked identical. She'd worried about that.

Shallan felt her heart flutter as she regarded the broken Soulcaster. Stealing from Jasnah had seemed acceptable when the princess had been a distant, unknown figure. A heretic, presumably ill-tempered and demanding. But what of the real Jasnah? A careful scholar, stern but fair, with a surprising level of wisdom and insight? Could Shallan really steal from her?

She tried to still her heart. Even as a little child, she'd been this way. She could remember her tears at fights between her parents. She was not good with confrontation.

But she'd do it. For Nan Balat, Tet Wikim, and Asha Jushu. Her brothers depended on her. She pressed her hands against her thighs to keep them from shaking, breathing in and out. After a few minutes, nerves under control, she took off the damaged Soulcaster and returned it to her safepouch. She gathered up her papers. They might be important in discovering how to use the Soulcaster. What was she going to do about that? Was there a way to ask Jasnah about using a Soulcaster without arousing suspicion?

A light flickering through nearby bookcases startled her, and she tucked away her folio. It turned out to be just an old, berobed female ardent, shuffling with a lantern and followed by a parshman servant. She didn't look in Shallan's direction as she turned between two rows of shelves, her lantern's light shining out through the spaces between the books. Lit that way – with her figure hidden but the light streaming between the shelves – it looked as if one of the Heralds themselves were walking through the stacks.

Her heart racing again, Shallan raised her safehand to her breast. *I make a terrible thief*, she thought with a grimace. She finished gathering her things and moved through the stacks, lantern held before her. The head of each row was carved with symbols, indicating the date the books had entered the Palanaeum. That was how they were organized. There were enormous cabinets filled with indexes on the top level.

Jasnah had sent Shallan to fetch – and then read – a copy of *Dialogues*, a famous historical work on political theory. However, this was also the room that contained *Shadows Remembered* – the book Jasnah was reading when the king had visited. Shallan had later looked it up in the index. It might have been reshelved by now.

Suddenly curious, Shallan counted off the rows. She stepped in and counted shelves inward. Near the middle and at the bottom, she found a thin red volume with a red hogshide cover. *Shadows Remembered*. Shallan set her lantern on the ground and slipped the book free, feeling furtive as she flipped through the pages.

She was confused by what she discovered. She hadn't realized this was a book of children's stories. There was no undertext commentary, just a collection of tales. Shallan sat down on the floor, reading through the first one. It was the story of a child who wandered away from his home at night and was chased by Voidbringers until he hid in a cavern beside a lake. He whittled a piece of wood into a roughly human shape and sent it floating across the lake, fooling the creatures into attacking and eating it instead.

Shallan didn't have much time – Jasnah would grow suspicious if she remained down here too long – but she skimmed the rest of the stories. They were all of a similar style, ghost stories about spirits or Voidbringers. The only commentary was at the back, explaining that the author had been curious about the folktales told by common darkeyes. She had spent years collecting and recording them.

Shadows Remembered, Shallan thought, *would have been better off forgotten.*

This was what Jasnah had been reading? Shallan had expected *Shadows Remembered* to be some kind of deep philosophical discussion of a hidden historical murder. Jasnah was a Veristitalian. She constructed the truth of what happened in the past. What kind of truth could she find in stories told to frighten disobedient darkeyed children?

Shallan slid the volume back in place and hurried on her way.

❖

A short time later, Shallan returned to the alcove to discover that her haste had been unnecessary. Jasnah wasn't there. Kabsal, however, was.

The youthful ardent sat at the long desk, flipping through one of Shallan's books on art. Shallan noticed him before he saw her, and she found herself smiling despite her troubles. She folded her arms and adopted a dubious expression. 'Again?' she asked.

Kabsal leaped up, slapping the book closed. 'Shallan,' he said, his bald head reflecting the blue light of her parshman's lantern. 'I came looking for—'

'For Jasnah,' Shallan said. 'As always. And yet, she's never here when you come.'

'An unfortunate coincidence,' he said, raising a hand to his forehead. 'I am a poor judge of timing, am I not?'

'And is that a basket of bread at your feet?'

'A gift for Brightness Jasnah,' he said. 'From the Devotary of Insight.'

'I doubt a bread basket is going to persuade her to renounce her heresy,' Shallan said. 'Perhaps if you'd included jam.'

The ardent smiled, picking up the basket and pulling out a small jar of red simberry jam.

'Of course, I've told you that Jasnah doesn't like jam,' Shallan said. 'And yet you bring it anyway, knowing jam to be among my favorite foods. And you've done this oh . . . a dozen times in the last few months?'

'I'm growing a bit transparent, aren't I?'

'Just a tad,' she said, smiling. 'It's about my soul, isn't it? You're worried about me because I'm apprenticed to a heretic.'

'Er . . . well, yes, I'm afraid.'

'I'd be insulted,' Shallan said. 'But you *did* bring jam.' She smiled, waving for her parshman to deposit her books and then wait beside the doorway. Was it true that there were parshmen on the Shattered Plains who were *fighting*? That seemed hard to credit. She'd never known any parshman to as much as raise their voice. They didn't seem bright enough for disobedience.

Of course, some reports she'd heard – including those Jasnah had made her read when studying King Gavilar's murder – indicated that the Parshendi weren't like other parshmen. They were bigger, had odd armor that grew from their skin itself, and spoke far more frequently. Perhaps they weren't parshmen at all, but some kind of distant cousin, a different race entirely.

She sat down at the desk as Kabsal got out the bread, her parshman waiting at the doorway. A parshman wasn't much of a chaperone, but Kabsal *was* an ardent, which meant technically she didn't need one.

The bread had been purchased from a Thaylen bakery, which meant it was fluffy and brown. And, since he was an ardent, it didn't matter that jam was a feminine food – they could enjoy it together. She eyed him as he cut the bread. The ardents in her father's employ had all been crusty men or women in their later years, stern-eyed and impatient with children.

She'd never even *considered* that the devotaries would attract young men like Kabsal.

During these last few weeks, she'd found herself thinking of him in ways that would better have been avoided.

'Have you considered,' he noted, 'what kind of person you declare yourself to be by preferring simberry jam?'

'I wasn't aware that my taste in jams could be that significant.'

'There are those who have studied it,' Kabsal said, slathering on the thick red jam and handing her the slice. 'You run across some very odd books, working in the Palanaeum. It's not hard to conclude that perhaps *everything* has been studied at one time or another.'

'Hum,' Shallan said. 'And simberry jam?'

'According to *Palates of Personality* – and before you object, *yes* it is a real book, and that is its title – a fondness for simberries indicates a spontaneous, impulsive personality. And also a preference for—' He cut off as a wadded-up piece of paper bounced off his forehead. He blinked.

'Sorry,' Shallan said. 'It just kind of happened. Must be all that impulsiveness and spontaneity I have.'

He smiled. 'You disagree with the conclusions?'

'I don't know,' she said with a shrug. 'I've had people tell me they could determine my personality based on the day I was born, or the position of Taln's Scar on my seventh birthday, or by numerological extrapolations of the tenth glyphic paradigm. But I think we're more complicated than that.'

'People are more complicated than the numerological extrapolations of the tenth glyphic paradigm?' Kabsal said, spreading jam on a piece of bread for himself. 'No wonder I have such difficulty understanding women.'

'Very funny. I *mean* that we're more complex than mere bundles of personality traits. Am I spontaneous? Sometimes. You might describe my chasing Jasnah here to become her ward that way. But before that, I spent seventeen years being about as *un*spontaneous as someone could be. In many situations – if I'm encouraged – my tongue can be quite spontaneous, but my actions rarely are. We're *all* spontaneous sometimes, and we're *all* conservative sometimes.'

'So you're saying that the book is right then. It says you're spontaneous; you're spontaneous sometimes. Ergo, it's correct.'

'By that argument, it's right about *everybody*.'

'One hundred percent accurate!'

'Well, not one hundred percent,' Shallan said, swallowing another bite of the sweet, fluffy bread. 'As has been noted, Jasnah hates jam of all kinds.'

'Ah yes,' Kabsal said. 'She's a *jam heretic* too. Her soul is in more danger than I had realized.' He grinned and took a bite of his bread.

'Indeed,' Shallan said. 'So what else does that book of yours say about me – and half the world's population – because of our enjoyment of foods with far too much sugar in them?'

'Well, a fondness for simberry is also supposed to indicate a love of the outdoors.'

'Ah, the outdoors,' Shallan said. 'I visited that mythical place once. It was so very long ago, I've nearly forgotten it. Tell me, does the sun still shine, or is that just my dreamy recollection?'

'Surely your studies aren't *that* bad.'

'Jasnah is inordinately fond of dust,' Shallan said. 'I believe she thrives on it, feeding off the particles like a chull crunching rockbuds.'

'And you, Shallan? On what do *you* thrive?'

'Charcoal.'

He looked confused at first, then glanced at her folio. 'Ah yes. I was surprised at how quickly your name, and pictures, spread through the Conclave.'

Shallan ate the last of her bread, then wiped her hands on a damp rag Kabsal had brought. 'You make me sound like a disease.' She ran a finger through her red hair, grimacing. 'I guess I do have the coloring of a rash, don't I?'

'Nonsense,' he said sternly. 'You shouldn't say such things, Brightness. It's disrespectful.'

'Of myself?'

'No. Of the Almighty, who made you.'

'He made cremlings too. Not to mentions rashes and diseases. So being compared to one is actually an honor.'

'I fail to follow that logic, Brightness. As he created all things, comparisons are meaningless.'

'Like the claims of your *Palates* book, eh?'

'A point.'

'There are worse things to be than a disease,' she said, idly thoughtful.

'When you have one, it reminds you that you're alive. Makes you fight for what you have. When the disease has run its course, normal healthy life seems wonderful by comparison.'

'And would you not rather be a sense of euphoria? Bringing pleasant feelings and joy to those you infect?'

'Euphoria passes. It is usually brief, so we spend more time longing for it than enjoying it.' She sighed. 'Look what we've done. Now I'm depressed. At least turning back to my studies will seem exciting by comparison.'

He frowned at the books. 'I was under the impression that you enjoyed your studies.'

'As was I. Then Jasnah Kholin stomped into my life and proved that even something pleasant could become boring.'

'I see. So she's a harsh mistress?'

'Actually, no,' Shallan said. 'I'm just fond of hyperbole.'

'I'm not,' he said. 'It's a real bastard to spell.'

'Kabsal!'

'Sorry,' he said. Then he glanced upward. 'Sorry.'

'I'm sure the ceiling forgives you. To get the Almighty's attention, you might want to burn a prayer instead.'

'I owe him a few anyway,' Kabsal said. 'You were saying?'

'Well, Brightness Jasnah *isn't* a harsh mistress. She's actually everything she's said to be. Brilliant, beautiful, mysterious. I'm fortunate to be her ward.'

Kabsal nodded. 'She is said to be a sterling woman, save for one thing.'

'You mean the heresy?'

He nodded.

'It's not as bad for me as you think,' she said. 'She's rarely vocal about her beliefs unless provoked.'

'She's ashamed, then.'

'I doubt that. Merely considerate.'

He eyed her.

'You needn't worry about me,' Shallan said. 'Jasnah doesn't try to persuade me to abandon the devotaries.'

Kabsal leaned forward, growing more somber. He was older than she – a man in his mid-twenties, confident, self-assured, and earnest. He was practically the only man near her age that she'd ever talked to outside of her father's careful supervision.

But he was also an ardent. So, of course, nothing could come of it. Could it?

'Shallan,' Kabsal said gently, 'can you not see how we – how I – would be concerned? Brightness Jasnah is a very powerful and intriguing woman. We would expect her ideas to be infectious.'

'Infectious? I thought you said *I* was the disease.'

'I never said that!'

'Yes, but I pretended you did. Which is virtually the same thing.'

He frowned. 'Brightness Shallan, the ardents *are* worried about you. The souls of the Almighty's children are our responsibility. Jasnah has a history of corrupting those with whom she comes in contact.'

'Really?' Shallan asked, genuinely interested. 'Other wards?'

'It is not my place to say.'

'We can move to another place.'

'I'm firm on this point, Brightness. I will not speak of it.'

'Write it, then.'

'Brightness . . .' he said, voice taking on a suffering tone.

'Oh, all right,' she said, sighing. 'Well, I can assure you, my soul is quite well and thoroughly *un*infected.'

He sat back, then cut another piece of bread. She found herself studying him again, but grew annoyed at her own girlish foolishness. She would soon be returning to her family, and he was only visiting her for reasons relating to his Calling. But she truly *was* fond of his company. He was the only one here in Kharbranth that she felt she could really talk to. And he was handsome; the simple clothing and shaved head only highlighted his strong features. Like many young ardents, he kept his beard short and neatly trimmed. He spoke with a refined voice, and he was so well-read.

'Well, if you're certain about your soul,' he said, turning back to her. 'Then perhaps I could interest you in our devotary.'

'I have a devotary. The Devotary of Purity.'

'But the Devotary of Purity isn't the place for a scholar. The Glory it advocates has nothing to do with your studies or your art.'

'A person doesn't need a devotary that focuses directly on their Calling.'

'It is nice when the two coincide, though.'

Shallan stifled a grimace. The Devotary of Purity focused on – as one might imagine – teaching one to emulate the Almighty's honesty and wholesomeness. The ardents at the devotary hall hadn't known what to make of her fascination with art. They'd always wanted her to do sketches of things they found 'pure.' Statues of the Heralds, depictions of the Double Eye.

Her father had chosen the devotary for her, of course.

'I just wonder if you made an informed choice,' Kabsal said. 'Switching devotaries is allowed, after all.'

'Yes, but isn't recruitment frowned upon? Ardents competing for members?'

'It is indeed frowned upon. A deplorable habit.'

'But you do it anyway?'

'I curse occasionally too.'

'I hadn't noticed. You're a very curious ardent, Kabsal.'

'You'd be surprised. We're not nearly as stuffy a bunch as we seem. Well, except Brother Habsant; he spends so much time staring at the rest of us.' He hesitated. 'Actually, now I think about it, he might actually *be* stuffed. I don't know that I've ever seen him move. ...'

'We're getting distracted. Weren't you trying to recruit me to your devotary?'

'Yes. And it's not so uncommon as you think. All of the devotaries engage in it. We do a lot of frowning at one another for our profound lack of ethics.' He leaned forward again, growing more serious. 'My devotary has relatively few members, as we don't have as much exposure as others. So whenever someone seeking knowledge comes to the Palanaeum, we take it upon ourselves to inform them.'

'Recruit them.'

'Let them see what it is they are missing.' He took a bite of his bread and jam. 'In the Devotary of Purity, did they teach you about the nature of the Almighty? The divine prism, with the ten facets representing the Heralds?'

'They touched on it,' she said. 'Mostly we talked about achieving my goals of ... well, purity. Somewhat boring, I'll admit, since there wasn't much chance for *im*purity on my part.'

Kabsal shook his head. 'The Almighty gives everyone talents – and when we pick a Calling that capitalizes on them, we are worshipping him in the most fundamental way. A devotary – and its ardents – should help nurture that, encouraging you to set and achieve goals of excellence.' He waved to the books stacked on the desk. 'This is what your devotary should be helping you with, Shallan. History, logic, science, art. Being honest and good is important, but we should be working harder to encourage the natural talents of people, rather than forcing them to adapt to the Glories and Callings we feel are most important.'

'That is a reasonable argument, I guess.'

Kabsal nodded, looking thoughtful. 'Is it any wonder a woman like Jasnah Kholin turned away from that? Many devotaries encourage women to leave difficult studies of theology to the ardents. If only Jasnah had been able to see the true beauty of our doctrine.' He smiled, digging a thick book out of his bread basket. 'I really had hoped, originally, to be able to show her what I mean.'

'I doubt she'd react well to that.'

'Perhaps,' he said idly, hefting the tome. 'But to be the one who finally convinced her!'

'Brother Kabsal, that sounds almost like you're seeking distinction.'

He blushed, and she realized she'd said something that genuinely embarrassed him. She winced, cursing her tongue.

'Yes,' he said. 'I do seek distinction. I *shouldn't* wish so badly to be the one who converts her. But I do. If she would just listen to my proof.'

'Proof?'

'I have real evidence that the Almighty exists.'

'I'd like to see it.' Then she raised a finger, cutting him off. 'Not because I doubt his existence, Kabsal. I'm just curious.'

He smiled. 'It will be my pleasure to explain. But first, would you like another slice of bread?'

'I should say no,' she said, 'and avoid excess, as my tutors trained me. But instead I'll say yes.'

'Because of the jam?'

'Of course,' she said, taking the bread. 'How did your book of oracular preserves describe me? Impulsive and spontaneous? I can do that. If it means jam.'

He slathered a piece for her, then wiped his fingers on his cloth and opened his book, flipping through the pages until he reached one that had a drawing on it. Shallan slid closer for a better look. The picture wasn't of a person; it depicted a pattern of some kind. A triangular shape, with three outlying wings and a peaked center.

'Do you recognize this?' Kabsal asked.

It seemed familiar. 'I feel that I should.'

'It's Kholinar,' he said. 'The Alethi capital, drawn as it would appear from above. See the peaks here, the ridges there? It was built around the rock formation that was already there.' He flipped the page. 'Here's Vedenar, capital of Jah Keved.' This one was a hexagonal pattern. 'Akinah.' A circular pattern. 'Thaylen City.' A four-pointed star pattern.

'What does it mean?'

'It is proof that the Almighty is in all things. You can see him here, in these cities. Do you see how symmetrical they are?'

'The cities were built by men, Kabsal. They wanted symmetry because it is holy.'

'Yes, but in each case they built around existing rock formations.'

'That doesn't mean anything,' Shallan said. 'I do believe, but I don't know if *this* is proof. Wind and water can create symmetry; you see it in nature all the time. The men picked areas that were roughly symmetrical, then designed their cities to make up for any flaws.'

He turned to his basket again, rummaging. He came out with – of all things – a metal plate. As she opened her mouth to ask a question, he held up his finger again and set the plate down on a small wooden stand that raised it a few inches above the tabletop.

Kabsal sprinkled white, powdery sand on the sheet of metal, coating it. Then he got out a bow, the kind drawn across strings to make music.

'You came prepared for this demonstration, I see,' Shallan noted. 'You really *did* want to make your case to Jasnah.'

He smiled, then drew the bow across the edge of the metal plate, making it vibrate. The sand hopped and bounced, like tiny insects dropped onto something hot.

'This,' he said, 'is called cymatics. The study of the patterns that sounds make when interacting with a physical medium.'

As he drew the bow again, the plate made a sound, almost a pure note. It was actually enough to draw a single musicspren, which spun for a moment in the air above him, then vanished. Kabsal finished, then gestured to the plate with a flourish.

'So . . . ?' Shallan asked.

'Kholinar,' he said, holding up his book for comparison.

Shallan cocked her head. The pattern in the sand looked *exactly* like Kholinar.

He dropped more sand on the plate and then drew the bow across it at another point and the sand rearranged itself.

'Vedenar,' he said.

She compared again. It was an exact match.

'Thaylen City,' he said, repeating the process at another spot. He carefully chose another point on the plate's edge and bowed it one final time. 'Akinah. Shallan, proof of the Almighty's existence is in the very cities we live in. Look at the perfect symmetry!'

She had to admit, there was something compelling about the patterns. 'It could be a false correlation. Both caused by the same thing.'

'Yes. The Almighty,' he said, sitting. 'Our very language is symmetrical. Look at the glyphs – each one can be folded in half perfectly. And the alphabet too. Fold any line of text down across itself, and you'll find symmetry. Surely you know the story, that both glyphs and letters came from the Dawnsingers?'

'Yes.'

'Even our names. Yours is nearly perfect. Shallan. One letter off, an ideal name for a lighteyed woman. Not *too* holy, but ever so close. The original names for the ten Silver Kingdoms. Alethela, Valhav, Shin Kak Nish. Perfect, symmetrical.'

He reached forward, taking her hand. 'It's here, around us. Don't forget that, Shallan, no matter what she says.'

'I won't,' she said, realizing how he'd guided the conversation. He'd said he believed her, but still he'd gone through his proofs. It was touching and annoying at the same time. She did not like condescension. But, then, could one really blame an ardent for preaching?

Kabsal looked up suddenly, releasing her hand. 'I hear footsteps.' He stood, and Shallan turned as Jasnah walked into the alcove, followed by a parshman carrying a basket of books. Jasnah showed no surprise at the presence of the ardent.

'I'm sorry, Brightness Jasnah,' Shallan said, standing. 'He—'

'You are not a captive, child,' Jasnah interrupted brusquely. 'You are allowed visitors. Just be careful to check your skin for tooth marks. These types have a habit of dragging their prey out to sea with them.'

Kabsal flushed. He moved to gather up his things.

Jasnah waved for the parshman to place her books on the table. 'Can that plate reproduce a cymatic pattern corresponding to Urithiru, priest?

Or do you only have patterns for the standard four cities?'

Kabsal looked at her, obviously shocked to realize that she knew exactly what the plate was for. He picked up his book. 'Urithiru is just a fable.'

'Odd. One would think that your type would be used to believing in fables.'

His face grew redder. He finished packing his things, then nodded curtly to Shallan and walked hastily from the room.

'If I may say so, Brightness,' Shallan said, 'that was *exceptionally* rude of you.'

'I'm prone to such bouts of incivility,' Jasnah said. 'I'm certain he has heard what I'm like. I simply wanted to make sure he got what he expected.'

'You haven't acted that way toward other ardents in the Palanaeum.'

'The other ardents in the Palanaeum haven't been working to turn my ward against me.'

'He wasn't . . .' Shallan trailed off. 'He was simply worried about my soul.'

'Has he asked you to try to steal my Soulcaster yet?'

Shallan felt a sudden spike of shock. Her hand went to the pouch at her waist. Did Jasnah know? *No*, Shallan told herself. *No, listen to the question*. 'He didn't.'

'Watch,' Jasnah said, opening a book. 'He will eventually. I've experience with his type.' She looked at Shallan, and her expression softened. 'He's not interested in you. Not in any of the ways you think. In particular, this isn't about your soul. It's about me.'

'That is somewhat arrogant of you,' Shallan said, 'don't you think?'

'Only if I'm wrong, child,' Jasnah said, turning back to her book. 'And I rarely am.'

STORMWALL

'I walked from Abamabar to Urithiru.'

—This quote from the Eighth Parable of *The Way of Kings* seems to contradict Varala and Sinbian, who both claim the city was inaccessible by foot. Perhaps there was a way constructed, or perhaps Nohadon was being metaphorical.

B ridgemen aren't supposed to survive . . . .
    Kaladin's mind felt fuzzy. He knew that he *hurt*, but other than that, he floated. As if his head were detached from his body and bouncing off the walls and ceilings.

'Kaladin!' a concerned voice whispered. 'Kaladin, please. Please don't be hurt anymore.'

Bridgemen aren't supposed to survive. Why did those words bother him so much? He remembered what had happened, using the bridge as a shield, throwing the army off, dooming the assault. *Stormfather,* he thought, *I'm an idiot!*

'Kaladin?'

It was Syl's voice. He risked opening his eyes and looked out on an upside-down world, sky extending below him, familiar lumberyard in the air above him.

No. *He* was upside down. Hanging against the side of Bridge Four's barrack. The Soulcast building was fifteen feet tall at its peak, with a shallowly slanted roof. Kaladin was tied by his ankles to a rope, which would – in turn – be affixed to a ring set into the slanted roof. He'd seen it happen to other bridgemen. One who had committed a murder in camp, another who had been caught stealing for the fifth time.

His back was to the wall so that he faced eastward. His arms were free, hanging down at his sides, and they almost touched the ground. He groaned again, hurting everywhere.

As his father had trained him, he began to prod his side to check for broken ribs. He winced as he found several that were tender, at least cracked. Probably broken. He felt at his shoulder too, where he feared that his collarbone was broken. One of his eyes was swollen. Time would show if he'd sustained any serious internal damage.

He rubbed his face, and flakes of dried blood cracked free and fluttered toward the ground. Gash on his head, bloodied nose, split lip. Syl landed on his chest, feet planted on his sternum, hands clasped before her. 'Kaladin?'

'I'm alive,' he mumbled, words slurred by his swollen lip. 'What happened?'

'You were beaten by those soldiers,' she said, seeming to grow smaller. 'I've gotten back at them. I made one of them trip three times today.' She looked concerned.

He found himself smiling. How long could a man hang like this, blood going to his head?

'There was a lot of yelling,' Syl said softly. 'I think several men were demoted. The soldier, Lamaril, he . . .'

'What?'

'He was executed,' Syl said, even more quietly. 'Highprince Sadeas did it himself, the hour the army got back from the plateau. He said something about the ultimate responsibility falling on the lighteyes. Lamaril kept screaming that you had promised to absolve him, and that Gaz should be punished instead.'

Kaladin smirked ruefully. 'He shouldn't have had me beaten senseless. Gaz?'

'They left him in his position. I don't know why.'

'Right of responsibility. In a disaster like this, the lighteyes are supposed to take most of the blame. They like to make a show of obeying old precepts like that, when it suits them. Why am I still alive?'

'Something about an example,' Syl said, wrapping her translucent arms around herself. 'Kaladin, I feel cold.'

'You can feel temperature?' Kaladin said, coughing.

'Not usually. I can now. I don't understand it. I . . . I don't like it.'

'It'll be all right.'

'You shouldn't lie.'

'Sometimes it's all right to lie, Syl.'

'And this is one of those times?'

He blinked, trying to ignore his wounds, the pressure in his head, trying to clear his mind. He failed on all counts. 'Yes,' he whispered.

'I think I understand.'

'So,' Kaladin said, resting his head back, the parietal knob of his skull resting against the wall, 'I'm to be judged by the highstorm. They'll let the storm kill me.'

Hanging here, Kaladin would be exposed directly to the winds and everything they would throw at him. If you were prudent and took appropriate action, it *was* possible to survive outside in a highstorm, though it was a miserable experience. Kaladin had done it on several occasions, hunkered down, taking shelter in the lee of a rock formation. But hanging on a wall facing directly stormward? He'd be cut to ribbons and crushed by stones.

'I'll be right back,' Syl said, dropping off his chest, taking the form of a falling stone, then changing into windblown leaves near the ground and fluttering away, curving to the right. The lumberyard was empty. Kaladin could smell the crisp, chill air, the land bracing for a highstorm. The lull, it was called, when the wind fell still, the air cold, the pressure dropping, the humidity rising right before a storm.

A few seconds later, Rock poked his head around the wall, Syl on his shoulder. He crept up to Kaladin, a nervous Teft following. They were joined by Moash; despite the latter's protests that he didn't trust Kaladin, he looked almost as concerned as the other two.

'Lordling?' Moash said. 'You awake?'

'I'm conscious,' Kaladin croaked. 'Everyone get back from the battle all right?'

'All of our men, sure enough,' Teft said, scratching at his beard. 'But we lost the battle. It was a disaster. Over two hundred bridgemen dead.

Those who survived were only enough to carry eleven bridges.'

Two hundred men, Kaladin thought. *That's my fault. I protected my own at the cost of others. I was too hasty.*

Bridgemen aren't supposed to survive. There's something about that. He wouldn't be able to ask Lamaril. That man had gotten what he deserved, though. If Kaladin had the ability to choose, such would be the end of all lighteyes, the king included.

'We wanted to say something,' Rock said. 'Is from all of the men. Most wouldn't come out. Highstorm coming, and—'

'It's all right,' Kaladin whispered.

Teft nudged Rock to continue.

'Well, is this. We will remember you. Bridge Four, we won't go back to how we were. Maybe all of us will die, but we'll show the new ones. Fires at night. Laughter. Living. We'll make a tradition out of it. For you.' Rock and Teft knew about the knobweed. They could keep earning extra money to pay for things.

'You did this for us,' Moash put in. 'We'd have died on that field. Perhaps as many as died in the other bridge crews. This way, we're only going to lose one.'

'I say it isn't right, what they're doing,' Teft said with a scowl. 'We talked about cutting you down. . . .'

'No,' Kaladin said. 'That would only earn you a similar punishment.'

The three men shared glances. It seemed they'd come to the same conclusion.

'What did Sadeas say?' Kaladin asked. 'About me.'

'That he understood how a bridgeman would want to save his life,' Teft said, 'even at others' expense. He called you a selfish coward, but acted like that was all that could be expected.'

'He says he's letting the Stormfather judge you,' Moash added. 'Jezerezeh, king of Heralds. He says that if you deserve to live, you will. . . .' He trailed off. He knew as well as the others that unprotected men didn't survive highstorms, not like this.

'I want you three to do something for me,' Kaladin said, closing his eyes against the blood trickling down his face from his lip, which he'd cracked open by speaking.

'Anything, Kaladin,' Rock said.

'I want you to go back into the barrack and tell the men to come out after the storm. Tell them to look up at me tied here. Tell them I'll open my eyes and look back at them, and they'll know that I survived.'

The three bridgemen fell silent.

'Yes, of course, Kaladin,' Teft said. 'We'll do it.'

'Tell them,' Kaladin continued, voice firmer, 'that it won't end here. Tell them I *chose* not to take my own life, and so there's no way in *Damnation* I'm going to give it up to Sadeas.'

Rock smiled one of those broad smiles of his. 'By the *uli'tekanaki*, Kaladin. I almost believe you'll do it.'

'Here,' Teft said, handing him something. 'For luck.'

Kaladin took the object in a weak, bloodstained hand. It was a sphere, a full skymark. It was dun, the Stormlight gone from it. *Carry a sphere with you into the storm*, the old saying said, *and at least you'll have light by which to see.*

'It's all we were able to save from your pouch,' Teft said. 'Gaz and Lamaril got the rest. We complained, but what were we to do?'

'Thank you,' Kaladin said.

Moash and Rock retreated to the safety of the barrack, Syl leaving Rock's shoulder to stay with Kaladin. Teft lingered too, as if thinking to spend the storm with Kaladin. He eventually shook his head, muttering, and joined the others. Kaladin thought he heard the man calling himself a coward.

The door to the barrack shut. Kaladin fingered the smooth glass sphere. The sky was darkening, and not just because the sun was setting. Blackness gathered. The highstorm.

Syl walked up the side of the wall, then sat down on it, looking at him, tiny face somber. 'You told them you'd survive. What happens if you don't?'

Kaladin's head was pounding with his pulse. 'My mother would cringe if she knew how quickly the other soldiers taught me to gamble. First night in Amaram's army, and they had me playing for spheres.'

'Kaladin?' Syl said.

'Sorry,' Kaladin said, rocking his head from side to side. 'What you said, it reminded me of that night. There's a term in gambling, you see. "In for all," they say. It's when you put all of your money on one bet.'

'I don't understand.'

'I'm putting it all on the long bet,' Kaladin whispered. 'If I die, then they'll come out, shake their heads, and tell themselves they knew it would happen. But if I live, they'll remember it. And it will give them hope. They might see it as a miracle.'

Syl was silent for a moment. 'Do you want to be a miracle?'

'No,' Kaladin whispered. 'But for them, I will be.'

It was a desperate, foolish hope. The eastern horizon, inverted in his sight, was growing darker. From this perspective, the storm was like the shadow of some enormous beast lumbering across the ground. He felt the disturbing fuzziness of a person who had been hit too hard on the head. Concussion. That was what it was called. He was having trouble thinking, but he didn't want to fall unconscious. He wanted to stare at the highstorm straight on, though it terrified him. He felt the same panic he'd felt looking down into the black chasm, back when he'd nearly killed himself. It was the fear of what he could not see, what he could not know.

The stormwall approached, the visible curtain of rain and wind at the advent of a highstorm. It was a massive wave of water, dirt, and rocks, hundreds of feet high, thousands upon thousands of windspren zipping before it.

In battle, he'd been able to fight his way to safety with the skill of his spear. When he'd stepped to the edge of the chasm, there had been a line of retreat. This time, there was nothing. No way to fight or avoid that black beast, that shadow spanning the entirety of the horizon, plunging the world into an early night. The eastern edge of the crater that made the war-camp had been worn away, and Bridge Four's barrack was first in its row. There was nothing between him and the Plains. Nothing between him and the storm.

Staring at that raging, blustering, churning wave of wind-pushed water and debris, Kaladin felt as if he were watching the end of the world descend upon him.

He took a deep breath, the pain of his ribs forgotten, as the stormwall crossed the lumberyard in a flash and slammed into him.

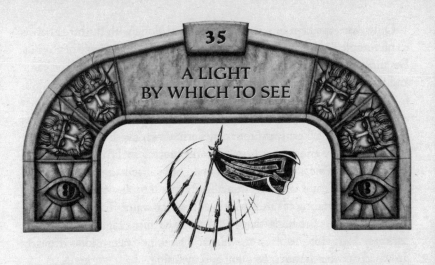

35

A LIGHT BY WHICH TO SEE

'Though many wished Urithiru to be built in Alethela, it was obvious that it could not be. And so it was that we asked for it to be placed westward, in the place nearest to Honor.'

—Perhaps the oldest surviving original source mentioning the city, requoted in *The Vavibrar*, line 1804. What I wouldn't give for a way to translate the Dawnchant.

The force of the stormwall nearly knocked him unconscious, but the sudden chill of it shocked him lucid.

For a moment, Kaladin couldn't feel anything but that coldness. He was pressed against the side of the barrack by the extended blast of water. Rocks and bits of branch crashed against the stone around him; he was already too numb to tell how many slashed or beat against his skin.

He bore it, dazed, eyes pressed shut and breath held. Then the storm-wall passed, crashing onward. The next blast of wind came in from the side – the air was swirling and gusting from all directions now. The wind flung him sideways – his back scraping against stone – and up into the air. The wind stabilized, blowing out of the east again. Kaladin hung in darkness, and his feet yanked against the rope. In a panic, he realized that he was now flapping in the wind like a kite, tied to the ring in the barrack's slanted roof.

Only that rope kept him from being blown along with the other debris to be tumbled and tossed before the storm across the entirety of Roshar. For those few heartbeats, he could not think. He could only feel the panic and the cold – one boiling out of his chest, the other trying to freeze him from the skin inward. He screamed, clutching his single sphere as if it were a lifeline. The scream was a mistake, as it let that coldness course into his mouth. Like a spirit forcing its arm down his throat.

The wind was like a maelstrom, chaotic, moving in different directions. One buffet ripped at him, then passed, and he fell to the roof of the barrack with a thud. Almost immediately, the terrible winds tried to lift him again, pounding his skin with waves of icy water. Thunder crashed, the heartbeat of the beast that had swallowed him. Lightning split the darkness like white teeth in the night. The wind was so loud it nearly drowned out the thunder; howling and moaning.

'Grab the roof, Kaladin!'

Syl's voice. So soft, so small. How could he hear it at all?

Numbly, he realized he was lying facedown on the sloped roof. It wasn't so steeply peaked that he was immediately pitched off, and the wind was generally blowing him backward. He did as Syl said, grabbing the lip of the roof with cold, slick fingers. Then he lay facedown, head tucked between his arms. He still had the sphere in his hand, pressed against the stone rooftop. His fingers started to slip. The wind was blowing so hard, trying to push him to the west. If he let go, he'd end up dangling in the air again. His rope tether was not long enough for him to get to the other side of the shallow-peaked rooftop, where he'd be sheltered.

A boulder hit the roof beside him – he couldn't hear its impact or see it in the tempest's darkness, but he could *feel* the building vibrate. The boulder rolled forward and crashed down to the ground. The entire storm didn't have such force, but occasional gusts could pick up and toss large objects, hurling them hundreds of feet.

His fingers slipped further.

'The ring,' Syl whispered.

The ring. The rope tied his legs to a steel ring on the side of the roof behind him. Kaladin let go, then snatched the ring as he was blown backward. He clutched to it. The rope continued down to his ankles, about the length of his body. He thought for a moment of untying the ropes, but he didn't dare let go of the ring. He clung there, like a pennant flapping in the wind, holding the ring in both hands, sphere cupped inside one of them and pressed against the steel.

Each moment was a struggle. The wind yanked him left, then hurled him right. He couldn't know how long it lasted; time had no meaning in this place of fury and tumult. His numbed, battered mind started to think he was in a nightmare. A terrible dream inside his head, full of black, living winds. Screams in the air, bright and white, the flash of lightning revealing a terrible, twisted world of chaos and terror. The very buildings seemed blown sideways, the entire world askew, warped by the storm's terrible power.

In those brief moments of light when he dared to look, he thought he saw Syl standing in front of him, her face to the wind, tiny hands forward. As if she were trying to hold back the storm and split the winds as a stone divided the waters of a swift stream.

The cold of the rainwater numbed the scrapes and bruises. But it also numbed his fingers. He didn't feel them slipping. The next he knew, he was whipping in the air again, tossed to the side, being slammed down against the roof of the barrack.

He hit hard. His vision flashed with sparkling lights that melded together and were followed by blackness.

Not unconsciousness, blackness.

Kaladin blinked. All was still. The storm was quiet, and everything was purely dark. *I'm dead*, he thought immediately. But why could he feel the wet stone roof beneath him? He shook his head, dripping rainwater down his face. There was no lightning, no wind, no rain. The silence was unnatural.

He stumbled to his feet, managing to stand on the gently sloped roof. The stone was slick beneath his toes. He couldn't feel his wounds. The pain just wasn't there.

He opened his mouth to call out into the darkness, but hesitated. That silence was not to be broken. The air itself seemed to weigh less, as did he. He almost felt as if he could float away.

In that darkness, an enormous face appeared just in front of his. A face of blackness, yet faintly traced in the dark. It was wide, the breadth of a massive thunderhead, and extended far to either side, yet it was somehow still visible to Kaladin. Inhuman. Smiling.

Kaladin felt a deep chill – a rolling prickle of ice – scurry down his spine and through his entire body. The sphere suddenly burst to life in his hand, flaring with a sapphire glow. It illuminated the stone roof beneath him, making his fist blaze with blue fire. His shirt was in tatters, his skin lacerated. He looked down at himself, shocked, then looked up at the face.

It was gone. There was only the darkness.

Lightning flashed, and Kaladin's pains returned. He gasped, falling to his knees before the rain and the wind. He slipped down, face hitting the rooftop.

What had that been? A vision? A delusion? His strength was fleeing him, his thoughts growing muddled again. The winds weren't as strong now, but the rain was still so cold. Lethargic, confused, nearly overwhelmed by his pain, he brought his hand up to the side and looked at the sphere. It was glowing. Smeared with his blood and glowing.

He hurt so much, and his strength had faded. Closing his eyes, he felt himself enveloped by a second blackness. The blackness of unconsciousness.

Rock was the first to the door when the highstorm subsided. Teft followed more slowly, groaning to himself. His knees hurt. His knees *always* hurt near a storm. His grandfather had complained about that in his later years, and Teft had called him daft. Now he felt it too.

Storming Damnation, he thought, wearily stepping outside. It was still raining, of course. These were the after-flurries of drizzle that trailed a highstorm, the riddens. A few rainspren sat in puddles, like blue candles, and a few windspren danced in the stormwinds. The rain was cold, and he splashed through puddles that soaked his sandaled feet, chilling them straight through the skin and muscle. He hated being wet. But, then, he hated a lot of things.

For a while, life had been looking up. Not now.

How did everything go so wrong so quickly? he thought, holding his arms close, walking slowly and watching his feet. Some soldiers had left their barracks and stood nearby, wearing raincloaks, watching. Probably to make certain nobody had snuck out to cut Kaladin down early. They didn't try to stop Rock, though. The storm had passed.

Rock charged around the side of the building. Other bridgemen left the barrack behind as Teft followed Rock. Storming Horneater. Like a big lumbering chull. He actually believed. He thought they'd find that foolish young bridgeleader alive. Probably figured they'd discover him having a nice cup of tea, relaxing in the shade with the Stormfather himself.

And you don't believe? Teft asked himself, still looking down. *If you don't, why are you following? But if you did believe, you'd look. You wouldn't stare at your feet. You'd look up and see.*

Could a man both believe, and not believe, at the same time? Teft stopped beside Rock and – steeling himself – looked up at the wall of the barrack.

There he saw what he'd expected and what he'd feared. The corpse looked like a hunk of slaughterhouse meat, skinned and bled. Was that a person? Kaladin's skin was sliced in a hundred places, dribbles of blood mixing with rainwater running down the side of the building. The lad's body still hung by the ankles. His shirt had been ripped off; his bridgeman trousers were ragged. Ironically, his face was cleaner now than when they'd left him, washed by the storm.

Teft had seen enough dead men on the battlefield to know what he was looking at. *Poor lad*, he thought, shaking his head as the rest of Bridge Four gathered around him and Rock, quiet, horrified. *You almost made me believe in you.*

Kaladin's eyes snapped open.

The gathered bridgemen gasped, several cursing and falling to the ground, splashing in the pools of rainwater. Kaladin drew in a ragged breath, wheezing, eyes staring forward, intense and unseeing. He exhaled, blowing flecks of bloody spittle out over his lips. His hand, hanging below him, slipped open.

Something dropped to the stones. The sphere Teft had given him. It splashed into a puddle and stopped there. It was dun, no Stormlight in it.

What in the name of Kelek? Teft thought, kneeling. You left a sphere out in the storm, and it gathered Stormlight. Held in Kaladin's hand, this one should have been fully infused. What had gone wrong?

'*Umalakai'ki!*' Rock bellowed, pointing. '*Kama mohoray namavau*—' He stopped, realizing he was speaking the wrong language. 'Somebody be helping me get him down! Is still alive! We need ladder and knife! Hurry!'

The bridgemen scrambled. The soldiers approached, muttering, but they didn't stop the bridgemen. Sadeas himself had declared that the Stormfather would choose Kaladin's fate. Everyone knew that meant death.

Except ... Teft stood up straight, holding the dun sphere. *An empty sphere after a storm*, he thought. *And a man who's still alive when he should be dead. Two impossibilities.*

Together they bespoke something that should be even *more* impossible.

'Where's that ladder!' Teft found himself yelling. 'Curse you all, hurry, hurry! We need to get him bandaged. Somebody go fetch that salve he always puts on wounds!'

He glanced back at Kaladin, then spoke much more softly. 'And you'd *better* survive, son. Because I want some answers.'

"Taking the Dawnshard, known to bind any creature voidish or mortal, he crawled up the steps crafted for Heralds, ten strides tall apiece, toward the grand temple above."

—From *The Poem of Ista*. I have found no modern explanation of what these 'Dawnshards' are. They seem ignored by scholars, though talk of them was obviously prevalent among those recording the early mythologies.

I t was not uncommon for us to meet native peoples while traveling through *the Unclaimed Hills,* Shallan read. *These ancient lands were once one of the Silver Kingdoms, after all. One must wonder if the great-shelled beasts lived among them back then, or if the creatures have come to inhabit the wilderness left by humankind's passing.*

She settled back in her chair, the humid air warm around her. To her left, Jasnah Kholin floated quietly in the pool inset in the floor of the bathing chamber. Jasnah liked to soak in the bath, and Shallan couldn't blame her. During most of Shallan's life, bathing had been an ordeal involving dozens of parshmen carting heated buckets of water, followed by a quick scrub in the brass tub before the water cooled.

Kharbranth's palace offered far more luxury. The stone pool in the ground resembled a small personal lake, luxuriously warmed by clever fabrials that produced heat. Shallan didn't know much about fabrials yet, though part of her was very intrigued. This type was becoming increasingly common. Just the other day, the Conclave staff had sent Jasnah one to heat her chambers.

The water didn't have to be carried in but came out of pipes. At the turn of a lever, water flowed in. It was warm when it entered, and was kept heated by the fabrials set into the sides of the pool. Shallan had bathed in the chamber herself, and it was absolutely marvelous.

The practical decor was of rock decorated with small colorful stones set in mortar up the sides of the walls. Shallan sat beside the pool, fully dressed, reading as she waited on Jasnah's needs. The book was Gavilar's account – as spoken to Jasnah herself years ago – after his first meeting with the strange parshmen later known as the Parshendi.

Occasionally, during our explorations, we'd meet with natives, she read. *Not parshmen. Natan people, with their pale bluish skin, wide noses, and woollike white hair. In exchange for gifts of food, they would point us to the hunting grounds of greatshells.*

Then we met the parshmen. I'd been on a half-dozen expeditions to Natanatan, but never had I seen anything like this! Parshmen, living on their own? All logic, experience, and science declared that to be an impossibility. Parshmen need the hand of civilized peoples to guide them. This has been proven time and time again. Leave one out in the wilderness, and it will just sit there, doing nothing, until someone comes along to give it orders.

Yet here was a group who could hunt, make weapons, build buildings, and – indeed – create their own civilization. We soon realized that this single discovery could expand, perhaps overthrow, all we understood about our gentle servants.

Shallan moved her eyes down to the bottom of the page where – separated by a line – the undertext was written in a small, cramped script. Most books dictated by men had an undertext, notes added by the woman or ardent who scribed the book. By unspoken agreement, the undertext was never shared out loud. Here, a wife would sometimes clarify – or even contradict – the account of her husband. The only way to preserve such honesty for future scholars was to maintain the sanctity and secrecy of the writing.

It should be noted, Jasnah had written in the undertext to this passage, *that I have adapted my father's words – by his own instruction – to make them more appropriate for recording.* That meant she made his dictation sound more scholarly and impressive. *In addition, by most accounts, King Gavilar originally ignored these strange, self-sufficient parshmen. It was only after explanation by his scholars and scribes that he understood the import of what he'd discovered. This inclusion is not meant to highlight my father's ignorance; he was, and is, a warrior. His attention was not on the anthropological import of our expedition, but upon the hunt that was to be its culmination.*

Shallan closed the cover, thoughtful. The volume was from Jasnah's own collection – the Palanaeum had several copies, but Shallan wasn't allowed to bring the Palanaeum's books into a bathing chamber.

Jasnah's clothing lay on a bench at the side of the room. Atop the folded garments, a small golden pouch held the Soulcaster. Shallan glanced at Jasnah. The princess floated face-up in the pool, black hair fanning out behind her in the water, her eyes closed. Her daily bath was the one time she seemed to relax completely. She looked much younger now, stripped of both clothing and intensity, floating like a child resting after a day of active swimming.

Thirty-four years old. That seemed ancient in some regards – some women Jasnah's age had children as old as Shallan. And yet it was also young. Young enough that Jasnah was praised for her beauty, young enough that men declared it a shame she wasn't yet married.

Shallan glanced at the pile of clothing. She carried the broken fabrial in her safepouch. She could swap them here and now. It was the opportunity she'd been waiting for. Jasnah now trusted her enough to relax, soaking in the bathing chamber without worrying about her fabrial.

Could Shallan really do it? Could she betray this woman who had taken her in?

Considering what I've done before, she thought, *this is nothing*. It wouldn't be the first time she betrayed someone who trusted her.

She stood up. To the side, Jasnah cracked an eye.

Blast, Shallan thought, tucking the book under her arm, pacing, trying to look thoughtful. Jasnah watched her. Not suspiciously. Curiously.

'Why did your father want to make a treaty with the Parshendi?' Shallan found herself asking as she walked.

'Why wouldn't he want to?'

'That's not an answer.'

'Of course it is. It's just not one that tells you anything.'

'It would help, Brightness, if you would give me a *useful* answer.'

'Then ask a useful question.'

Shallan set her jaw. 'What did the Parshendi have that King Gavilar wanted?'

Jasnah smiled, closing her eyes again. 'Closer. But you can probably guess the answer to that.'

'Shards.'

Jasnah nodded, still relaxed in the water.

'The text doesn't mention them,' Shallan said.

'My father didn't speak of them,' Jasnah said. 'But from things he said . . . well, I now suspect that they motivated the treaty.'

'Can you be sure he knew, though? Maybe he just wanted the gemhearts.'

'Perhaps,' Jasnah said. 'The Parshendi seemed amused at our interest in the gemstones woven into their beards.' She smiled. 'You should have seen our shock when we discovered where they'd gotten them. When the lanceryn died off during the scouring of Aimia, we thought we'd seen the last gemhearts of large size. And yet here was another great-shelled beast with them, living in a land not too distant from Kholinar itself.

'Anyway, the Parshendi were willing to share them with us, so long as they could still hunt them too. To them, if you took the trouble to hunt the chasmfiends, their gemhearts were yours. I doubt a treaty would have been needed for that. And yet, just before leaving to return to Alethkar, my father suddenly began talking fervently of the need for an agreement.'

'So what happened? What changed?'

'I can't be certain. However, he once described the strange actions of a Parshendi warrior during a chasmfiend hunt. Instead of reaching for his spear when the greatshell appeared, this man held his hand to the side in a very suspicious way. Only my father saw it; I suspected he believed the man planned to summon a Blade. The Parshendi realized what he was doing, and stopped himself. My father didn't speak of it further, and I assume he didn't want the world's eyes on the Shattered Plains any more than they already were.'

Shallan tapped her book. 'It seems tenuous. If he was sure about the Blades, he must have seen more.'

'I suspect so as well. But I studied the treaty carefully, after his death. The clauses for favored trade status and mutual border crossing could very well have been a step toward folding the Parshendi into Alethkar as a nation. It certainly would have prevented the Parshendi from trading their Shards to other kingdoms without coming to us first. Perhaps that was all he wanted to do.'

'But why kill him?' Shallan said, arms crossed, strolling in the direction of Jasnah's folded clothing. 'Did the Parshendi realize that he intended to have their Shardblades, and so struck at him preemptively?'

'Uncertain,' Jasnah said. She sounded skeptical. Why did *she* think the Parshendi killed Gavilar? Shallan nearly asked, but she had a feeling she wouldn't get any more out of Jasnah. The woman expected Shallan to think, discover, and draw conclusions on her own.

Shallan stopped beside the bench. The pouch holding the Soulcaster was open, the drawstrings loose. She could see the precious artifact curled up inside. The swap would be easy. She had used a large chunk of her money to buy gemstones that matched Jasnah's, and had put them into the broken Soulcaster. The two were now exactly identical.

She still hadn't learned anything about using the fabrial; she'd tried to find a way to ask, but Jasnah avoided speaking of the Soulcaster. Pushing harder would be suspicious. Shallan would have to get information elsewhere. Perhaps from Kabsal, or maybe from a book in the Palanaeum.

Regardless, the time was upon her. Shallan found her hand going to her safepouch, and she felt inside of it, running her fingers along the chains of her broken fabrial. Her heart beat faster. She glanced at Jasnah, but the woman was just lying there, floating, eyes closed. What if she opened her eyes?

Don't think of that! Shallan told herself. *Just do it. Make the swap. It's so close. . . .*

'You are progressing more quickly than I had assumed you would,' Jasnah said suddenly.

Shallan spun, but Jasnah's eyes were still closed. 'I was wrong to judge you so harshly because of your prior education. I myself have often said that passion outperforms upbringing. You have the determination and the capacity to become a respected scholar, Shallan. I realize that the answers seem slow in coming, but continue your research. You will have them eventually.'

Shallan stood for a moment, hand in her pouch, heart thumping uncontrollably. She felt sick. *I can't do it*, she realized. *Stormfather, but I'm a fool. I came all of this way . . . and now I can't do it!*

She pulled her hand from her pouch and stalked back across the bathing chamber to her chair. What was she going to tell her brothers? Had she just doomed her family? She sat down, setting her book aside and sighing, prompting Jasnah to open her eyes. Jasnah watched her, then righted herself in the water and gestured for the hairsoap.

Gritting her teeth, Shallan stood up and fetched the soap tray for Jasnah, bringing it over and squatting down to proffer it. Jasnah took the powdery hairsoap and mashed it in her hand, lathering it before putting it into her sleek black hair with both hands. Even naked, Jasnah Kholin was composed and in control.

'Perhaps we have spent too much time indoors of late,' the princess said. 'You look penned up, Shallan. Anxious.'

'I'm fine,' Shallan said brusquely.

'Hum, yes. As evidenced by your perfectly reasonable, relaxed tone. Perhaps we need to shift some of your training from history to something more hands-on, more visceral.'

'Like natural science?' Shallan asked, perking up.

Jasnah tilted her head back. Shallan knelt down on a towel beside the pool, then reached down with her freehand, massaging the soap into her mistress's lush tresses.

'I was thinking philosophy,' Jasnah said.

Shallan blinked. 'Philosophy? What good is that?' *Isn't it the art of saying nothing with as many words as possible?*

'Philosophy is an important field of study,' Jasnah said sternly. 'Particularly if you're going to be involved in court politics. The nature of morality must be considered, and preferably before one is exposed to situations where a moral decision is required.'

'Yes, Brightness. Though I fail to see how philosophy is more "hands-on" than history.'

'History, by definition, cannot be experienced directly. As it is happening, it is the present, and that is philosophy's realm.'

'That's just a matter of definition.'

'Yes,' Jasnah said, 'all words have a tendency to be subject to how they are defined.'

'I suppose,' Shallan said, leaning back, letting Jasnah dunk her hair to clean off the soap.

The princess began scrubbing her skin with mildly abrasive soap. 'That was a particularly bland response, Shallan. What happened to your wit?'

Shallan glanced at the bench and its precious fabrial. After all this time, she had proven too weak to do what needed to be done. 'My wit is on temporary hiatus, Brightness,' she said. 'Pending review by its colleagues, sincerity and temerity.'

Jasnah raised an eyebrow at her.

Shallan sat back on her heels, still kneeling on the towel. 'How *do* you know what is right, Jasnah? If you don't listen to the devotaries, how do you decide?'

'That depends upon one's philosophy. What is most important to you?'

'I don't know. Can't you tell me?'

'No,' Jasnah replied. 'If I gave you the answers, I'd be no better than the devotaries, prescribing beliefs.'

'They aren't evil, Jasnah.'

'Except when they try to rule the world.'

Shallan drew her lips into a thin line. The War of Loss had destroyed the Hierocracy, shattering Vorinism into the devotaries. That was the inevitable result of a religion trying to rule. The devotaries were to teach morals, not enforce them. Enforcement was for the lighteyes.

'You say you can't give me answers,' Shallan said. 'But can't I ask for the advice of someone wise? Someone who's gone before? Why write our philosophies, draw our conclusions, if not to influence others? You yourself told me that information is worthless unless we use it to make judgments.'

Jasnah smiled, dunking her arms and washing off the soap. Shallan caught a victorious glimmer in her eye. She wasn't necessarily advocating ideas because she believed them; she just wanted to push Shallan. It was infuriating. How was Shallan to know what Jasnah really thought if she adopted conflicting points of view like this?

'You act as if there were one answer,' Jasnah said, gesturing to Shallan to fetch a towel and climbing from the pool. 'A single, eternally perfect response.'

Shallan hastily complied, bearing a large, fluffy towel. 'Isn't that what philosophy is about? Finding the answers? Seeking the truth, the real meaning of things?'

Toweling off, Jasnah raised an eyebrow at her.

'What?' Shallan asked, suddenly self-conscious.

'I believe it is time for a field exercise,' Jasnah said. 'Outside of the Palanaeum.'

'Now?' Shallan asked. 'It's so late!'

'I told you philosophy was a hands-on art,' Jasnah said, wrapping the towel around herself, then reaching down and taking the Soulcaster out of its pouch. She slipped the chains around her fingers, securing the gemstones to the back of her hand. 'I'll prove it to you. Come, help me dress.'

As a child, Shallan had relished those evenings when she'd been able to slip away into the gardens. When the blanket of darkness rested atop the grounds, they had seemed a different place entirely. In those shadows, she'd been able to imagine that the rockbuds, shalebark, and trees were some foreign fauna. The scrapings of cremlings climbing out of cracks had become the footsteps of mysterious people from far-off lands. Large-eyed traders from Shinovar, a greatshell rider from Kadrix, or a narrowboat sailor from the Purelake.

She didn't have those same imaginings when walking Kharbranth at night. Imagining dark wanderers in the night had once been an intriguing game – but here, dark wanderers were likely to be real. Instead of becoming a mysterious, intriguing place at night, Kharbranth seemed much the same to her – just more dangerous.

Jasnah ignored the calls of rickshaw pullers and palanquin porters. She walked slowly in a beautiful dress of violet and gold, Shallan following in blue silk. Jasnah hadn't taken time to have her hair done following her bath, and she wore it loose, cascading across her shoulders, almost scandalous in its freedom.

They walked the Ralinsa – the main thoroughfare that led down the hillside in switchbacks, connecting Conclave and port. Despite the late hour, the roadway was crowded, and many of the men who walked here seemed to bear the night inside of them. They were gruffer, more shadowed of face. Shouts still rang through the city, but those carried the night in them too, measured by the roughness of their words and the sharpness of their tones. The steep, slanted hillside that formed the city was no less crowded with buildings than always, yet these too seemed to draw in the night. Blackened, like stones burned by a fire. Hollow remains.

The bells still rang. In the darkness, each ring was a tiny scream. They made the wind more present, a living thing that caused a chiming cacophony each time it passed. A breeze rose, and an avalanche of sound came tumbling across the Ralinsa. Shallan nearly found herself ducking before it.

'Brightness,' Shallan said. 'Shouldn't we call for a palanquin?'

'A palanquin might inhibit the lesson.'

'I'll be all right learning that lesson during the day, if you wouldn't mind.'

Jasnah stopped, looking off the Ralinsa and toward a darker side street. 'What do you think of that roadway, Shallan?'

'It doesn't look particularly appealing to me.'

'And yet,' Jasnah said, 'it is the most direct route from the Ralinsa to the theater district.'

'Is that where we're going?'

'We aren't "going" anywhere,' Jasnah said, taking off down the side street. 'We are acting, pondering, and learning.'

Shallan followed nervously. The night swallowed them; only the occasional light from late-night taverns and shops offered illumination. Jasnah wore her black, fingerless glove over her Soulcaster, hiding the light of its gemstones.

Shallan found herself creeping. Her slippered feet could feel every change in the ground underfoot, each pebble and crack. She looked about nervously as they passed a group of workers gathered around a tavern doorway. They were darkeyes, of course. In the night, that distinction seemed more profound.

'Brightness?' Shallan asked in a hushed tone.

'When we are young,' Jasnah said, 'we want simple answers. There is no greater indication of youth, perhaps, than the desire for everything to be *as it should*. As it has ever been.'

Shallan frowned, still watching the men by the tavern over her shoulder.

'The older we grow,' Jasnah said, 'the more we question. We begin to ask why. And yet, we still want the answers to be simple. We assume that the people around us – adults, leaders – will have those answers. Whatever they give often satisfies us.'

'I was never satisfied,' Shallan said softly. 'I wanted more.'

'You were mature,' Jasnah said. 'What you describe happens to most of us, as we age. Indeed, it seems to me that aging, wisdom, and *wondering* are synonymous. The older we grow, the more likely we are to reject the simple answers. Unless someone gets in our way and demands they be accepted regardless.' Jasnah's eyes narrowed. 'You wonder why I reject the devotaries.'

'I do.'

'Most of them seek to stop the questions.' Jasnah halted. Then she briefly pulled back her glove, using the light beneath to reveal the street around her. The gemstones on her hand – larger than broams – blazed like torches, red, white, and grey.

'Is it wise to be showing your wealth like that, Brightness?' Shallan said, speaking very softly and glancing about her.

'No,' Jasnah said. 'It is most certainly not. Particularly not here. You see, this street has gained a particular reputation lately. On three separate occasions during the last two months, theatergoers who chose this route to the main road were accosted by footpads. In each case, the people were murdered.'

Shallan felt herself grow pale.

'The city watch,' Jasnah said, 'has done nothing. Taravangian has sent them several pointed reprimands, but the captain of the watch is cousin to a very influential lighteyes in the city, and Taravangian is not a terribly powerful king. Some suspect that there is more going on, that the footpads might be bribing the watch. The politics of it are irrelevant at the moment for, as you can see, no members of the watch are guarding the place, despite its reputation.'

Jasnah pulled her glove back on, plunging the roadway back into darkness. Shallan blinked, her eyes adjusting.

'How foolish,' Jasnah said, 'would you say it is for us to come here, two undefended women wearing costly clothing and bearing riches?'

'*Very* foolish. Jasnah, can we go? Please. Whatever lesson you have in mind isn't worth this.'

Jasnah drew her lips into a line, then looked toward a narrow, darker alleyway off the road they were on. It was almost completely black now that Jasnah had replaced her glove.

'You're at an interesting place in your life, Shallan,' Jasnah said, flexing her hand. 'You are old enough to wonder, to ask, to reject what is presented to you simply *because* it was presented to you. But you also cling to the idealism of youth. You feel there must be some single, all-defining Truth – and you think that once you find it, all that once confused you will suddenly make sense.'

'I . . .' Shallan wanted to argue, but Jasnah's words were tellingly accurate. The terrible things Shallan had done, the terrible thing she had planned to do, haunted her. Was it possible to do something horrible in the name of accomplishing something wonderful?

Jasnah walked into the narrow alleyway.

'Jasnah!' Shallan said. 'What are you doing?'

'This is philosophy in action, child,' Jasnah said. 'Come with me.'

Shallan hesitated at the mouth of the alleyway, her heart thumping, her thoughts muddled. The wind blew and bells rang, like frozen raindrops shattering against the stones. In a moment of decision, she rushed after Jasnah, preferring company, even in the dark, to being alone. The shrouded glimmer of the Soulcaster was barely enough to light their way, and Shallan followed in Jasnah's shadow.

Noise from behind. Shallan turned with a start to see several dark forms crowding into the alley. 'Oh, Stormfather,' she whispered. Why? Why was Jasnah doing this?

Shaking, Shallan grabbed at Jasnah's dress with her freehand. Other shadows were moving in front of them, from the far side of the alley. They grew closer, grunting, splashing through foul, stagnant puddles. Chill water had already soaked Shallan's slippers.

Jasnah stopped moving. The frail light of her cloaked Soulcaster reflected off metal in the hands of their stalkers. Swords or knives.

These men meant murder. You didn't rob women like Shallan and Jasnah, women with powerful connections, then leave them alive as witnesses. Men like these were not the gentlemen bandits of romantic stories. They lived each day knowing that if they were caught, they would be hanged.

Paralyzed by fear, Shallan couldn't even scream.

Stormfather, Stormfather, Stormfather!

'And now,' Jasnah said, voice hard and grim, 'the lesson.' She whipped off her glove.

The sudden light was nearly blinding. Shallan raised a hand against it, stumbling back against the alley wall. There were four men around them. Not the men from the tavern entrance, but others. Men she hadn't noticed watching them. She could see the knives now, and she could also see the murder in their eyes.

Her scream finally broke free.

The men grunted at the glare, but shoved their way forward. A thick-chested man with a dark beard came up to Jasnah, weapon raised. She calmly reached her hand out – fingers splayed – and pressed it against his chest as he swung a knife. Shallan's breath caught in her throat.

Jasnah's hand sank into the man's skin, and he froze. A second later he burned.

No, he *became fire*. Transformed into flames in an eyeblink. Rising around Jasnah's hand, they formed the outline of a man with head thrown back and mouth open. For just a moment, the blaze of the man's death outshone Jasnah's gemstones.

Shallan's scream trailed off. The figure of flames was strangely beautiful. It was gone in a moment, the fire dissipating into the night air, leaving an orange afterimage in Shallan's eyes.

The other three men began to curse, scrambling away, tripping over one another in their panic. One fell. Jasnah turned casually, brushing his shoulder with her fingers as he struggled to his knees. He became crystal, a figure of pure, flawless quartz – his clothing transformed along with him. The diamond in Jasnah's Soulcaster faded, but there was still plenty of Stormlight left to send rainbow sparkles through the transformed corpse.

The other two men fled in opposite directions. Jasnah took a deep breath, closing her eyes, lifting her hand above her head. Shallan held her safehand to her breast, stunned, confused. Terrified.

Stormlight shot from Jasnah's hand like twin bolts of lightning, sym-metrical. One struck each of the footpads and they popped, puffing into smoke. Their empty clothing dropped to the ground. With a sharp snap, the smokestone crystal on Jasnah's Soulcaster cracked, its light vanishing, leaving her with just the diamond and the ruby.

The remains of the two footpads rose into the air, small billows of greasy vapor. Jasnah opened her eyes, looking eerily calm. She tugged her glove back on – using her safehand to hold it against her stomach and sliding her freehand fingers in. Then she calmly walked back the way they had come. She left the crystal corpse kneeling with hand upraised. Frozen forever.

Shallan pried herself off the wall and hastened after Jasnah, sickened and amazed. Ardents were forbidden to use their Soulcasters on people. They rarely even used them in front of others. And how had Jasnah struck down two men at a distance? From everything Shallan had read – what little there was to find – Soulcasting required physical contact.

Too overwhelmed to demand answers, she stood silent – freehand held to the side of her head, trying to control her trembling and her gasping breaths – as Jasnah called for a palanquin. One came eventually, and the two women climbed in.

The bearers carried them toward the Ralinsa, their steps jostling Shallan and Jasnah, who sat across from one another in the palanquin. Jasnah idly popped the broken smokestone from her Soulcaster, then tucked it into a pocket. It could be sold to a gemsmith, who could cut smaller gemstones from the salvaged pieces.

'That was horrible,' Shallan finally said, hand still held to her breast. 'It was one of the most awful things I've ever experienced. You *killed* four men.'

'Four men who were planning to beat, rob, kill, and possibly rape us.'

'You tempted them into coming for us!'

'Did I force them to commit any crimes?'

'You showed off your gemstones.'

'Can a woman not walk with her possessions down the street of a city?'

'At night?' Shallan asked. 'Through a rough area? Displaying wealth? You all but asked for what happened!'

'Does that make it right?' Jasnah said, leaning forward. 'Do you condone what the men were planning to do?'

'Of course not. But that doesn't make what you did right either!'

'And yet, those men are off the street. The people of this city are that much safer. The issue that Taravangian has been so worried about has been solved, and no more theatergoers will fall to those thugs. How many lives did I just save?'

'I know how many you just took,' Shallan said. 'And through the power of something that should be holy!'

'Philosophy in action. An important lesson for you.'

'You did all this just to prove a point,' Shallan said softly. 'You did this to *prove* to me that you could. Damnation, Jasnah, how could you *do* something like that?'

Jasnah didn't reply. Shallan stared at the woman, searching for emotion in those expressionless eyes. *Stormfather. Did I ever really know this woman? Who is she, really?*

Jasnah leaned back, watching the city pass. 'I did *not* do this just to prove a point, child. I have been feeling for some time that I took advantage of His Majesty's hospitality. He doesn't realize how much trouble he could face for allying himself with me. Besides, men like those ...' There was something in her voice, an edge Shallan had never heard before.

What was done to you? Shallan wondered with horror. *And who did it?* 'Regardless,' Jasnah continued, 'tonight's actions came about because I chose this path, not because of anything I felt you needed to see. However, the opportunity also presented a chance for instruction, for questions. Am I a monster or am I a hero? Did I just slaughter four men, or did I stop four murderers from walking the streets? Does one *deserve* to have evil done to her by consequence of putting herself where evil can reach her? Did I have a right to defend myself? Or was I just looking for an excuse to end lives?'

'I don't know,' Shallan whispered.

'You will spend the next week researching it and thinking on it. If you wish to be a scholar – a *true* scholar who changes the world – then you will need to face questions like this. There will be times when you must make decisions that churn your stomach, Shallan Davar. I'll have you ready to make those decisions.'

Jasnah fell silent, looking out the side as the palanquin bearers marched them up to the Conclave. Too troubled to say more, Shallan suffered the rest of the trip in silence. She followed Jasnah through the hushed hallways to their rooms, passing scholars on their way to the Palanaeum for some midnight study.

Inside their rooms, Shallan helped Jasnah undress, though she hated touching the woman. She shouldn't have felt that way. The men Jasnah had killed were terrible creatures, and she had little doubt that they would have killed her. But it wasn't the act itself so much as the cold callousness of it that bothered her.

Still feeling numb, Shallan fetched Jasnah a sleeping robe as the woman removed her jewelry and set it on the dressing table. 'You could have let the other three get away,' Shallan said, walking back toward

Jasnah, who had sat down to brush her hair. 'You only needed to kill one of them.'

'No, I didn't,' Jasnah said.

'Why? They would have been too frightened to do something like that again.'

'You don't know that. I sincerely wanted those men *gone*. A careless barmaid walking home the wrong way cannot protect herself, but I can. And I will.'

'You have no authority to do so, not in someone else's city.'

'True,' Jasnah said. 'Another point to consider, I suppose.' She raised the brush to her hair, pointedly turning away from Shallan. She closed her eyes, as if to shut Shallan out.

The Soulcaster sat on the dressing table beside Jasnah's earrings. Shallan gritted her teeth, holding the soft, silken robe. Jasnah sat in her white underdress, brushing her hair.

There will be times when you must make decisions that churn your stomach, Shallan Davar. . . .

I've faced them already.

I'm facing one now.

How *dare* Jasnah do this? How *dare* she make Shallan a part of it? How *dare* she use something beautiful and holy as a device for destruction?

Jasnah didn't deserve to own the Soulcaster.

With a swift move of her hand, Shallan tucked the folded robe under her safearm, then shoved her hand into her safepouch and popped out the intact smokestone from her father's Soulcaster. She stepped up to the dressing table, and – using the motion of placing the robe onto the table as a cover – made the exchange. She slid the working Soulcaster into her safehand within its sleeve, stepping back as Jasnah opened her eyes and glanced at the robe, which now sat innocently beside the nonfunctional Soulcaster.

Shallan's breath caught in her throat.

Jasnah closed her eyes again, handing the brush toward Shallan. 'Fifty strokes tonight, Shallan. It has been a fatiguing day.'

Shallan moved by rote, brushing her mistress's hair while clutching the stolen Soulcaster in her hidden safehand, panicked that Jasnah would notice the swap at any moment.

She didn't. Not when she put on her robe. Not when she tucked the broken Soulcaster away in her jewelry case and locked it with a key she wore around her neck as she slept.

Shallan walked from the room stunned, in turmoil. Exhausted, sickened, confused.

But undiscovered.

BRANDON SANDERSON

The Way of Kings has been a long time in the making. It's been some twenty years that I've worked on this book now, in one form or another. The original draft was completed in 2002, though I decided it was not yet good enough for publication. It took me another seven years to get the characters, world, and plot to the level I wanted.

During all those years, I waited eagerly for the chance to finally do a grand epic on the scale I'd dreamed of achieving. One of the difficulties over the last few years has been knowing that the first book – in order to set the stage appropriately, yet include a complete story of its own – was going to have to be long. The longest book in the series, most likely. I knew this size would make it difficult to print the book in a single volume.

I debated this for a great long time. I toyed with cutting sequences completely to make the book shorter, toyed with removing characters. In the end, I decided that couldn't be done. At least, not while creating the story I wanted. And so, when I wrote the book in 2009 (and did so from scratch, throwing away previous drafts) I wrote it at the length I knew it needed to be. I also gave publishers the option to split the book if they absolutely had to.

I chose the breaking point myself. While it would have been easiest to break at the end of one of the five 'Parts' within the book, this didn't feel right. Those breaks were chosen to signify the end of a sequence and the beginning of a new one, but were not intended to be satisfying ends unto themselves. Instead, I broke the novel in the middle of one of the parts. I strongly feel that, if we are going to end one half and begin another, this is the best place.

The break point was chosen for its fulfillment of several plot cycles while beginning the whispers of the true challenges ahead. I want you to understand, however, that this is a single story with a single arc, not meant to be taken as two divided parts. I encourage readers to view them as a single whole.

I apologize for the need to do this, but it was what the story demanded.

As always, you have my sincere thanks for reading and for supporting me in my writing. I look forward to seeing you back for Part 2 of this Gollancz edition of *The Way of Kings*.